全新！NEW GEPT 全民英檢

中高級 聽力&閱讀 題庫解析

新制修訂版

全書MP3一次下載

9789864541737.zip

此為 ZIP 壓縮檔，iOS 系統請升級至 iOS 13 以上再行下載，
其他系統請先安裝解壓縮程式或 APP。
此為大型檔案（約 240MB），建議使用 WIFI 連線下載，
以免占用流量，並確認連線狀況，以利下載順暢。

PRELUDE

全民英語能力分級檢定測驗的問與答

Q 教育部為何補助LTTC中心研發「全民英語能力分級檢定測驗」(以下簡稱「全民英檢」)？

近年來在國際化的趨勢下，推展全民英語學習運動已成為教育界及民間普遍的共識，而LTTC多年來辦理「外語能力測驗」(FLPT)及「大專學生英語能力測驗」(CSEPT)的經驗也顯示國內需要一套完整並具公信力之英語能力分級檢定系統，以適應各級教育及社會各階層的需求。因此，在86年度LTTC邀集國內相關領域之學者專家成立研究及諮詢委員會，開始著手研發這項測驗系統，希望能藉此提供國內各階段英語學習者公平、可靠、具效度的英語能力評量工具。為落實「終身學習」的教育理念，及推動全民學外語的方案，本項「全民英檢」的研發計畫已獲教育部重視，並自88年3月起每年由教育部撥款補助。

Q 本項測驗研發的進度如何? 各個級數於何時推出？

本項測驗研發預計91年3月完成。初期的研發工作已於87年度完成，確立這項測驗的整體方向、分級指標及各級初步的題型設計。中級測驗初試已於89年1月22日首度推出，第二次測驗亦已於89年

7月22日舉行。90年則推出初級與中高級，91年推出高級與優級，各個級數除高級與優級外，每年舉辦兩次。

Q 本項測驗在目的及性質方面有何特色？

整體而言，有四項特色：

(1)本測驗的對象包含在校學生及一般社會人士，測驗目的在評量一般英語能力（general English proficiency），命題不侷限於特定領域或教材；

(2)整套系統共分五級--初級(Elementary)、中級(Intermediate)、中高級(High-Intermediate)、高級(Advanced)、優級(Superior)一根據各階段英語學習者的特質及需求，分別設計題型及命題內容，考生可依能力選擇適當等級報考；

(3)各級測驗均重視聽、說、讀、寫四種能力的評量；

(4)本測驗係「標準參照測驗」(criterion-referenced test)，每級訂有明確的能力指標，考生只要通過所報考級數即可取得該級的合格證書。

Q 「全民英檢」與美國的「托福測驗」(TOEFL)、英國的測驗(如FCE或IELTS)有何不同？

IELTS的性質與TOEFL類似，對象均是擬赴英語系國家留學的留學生，內容均與校園生活與學習情境有關，因此並不一定適合國內各階段英語學習者。FCE則是英國劍橋大學研發的英語檢定測驗中的一級，在內容方面未必符合國內英語教學目標及考生生活經驗。

PRELUDE

其實近年來，日本及中國大陸均已研發自己的英語能力分級測驗，日本有STEP測驗，中國大陸則有PET及CET等測驗。由此可見，發展本土性的英語能力分級測驗實為時勢所趨。

Q 本測驗既包含聽、說、讀、寫四項，各項測驗方式為何？

聽力及閱讀測驗採選擇題方式，口說及寫作測驗則採非選擇題方式，每級依能力指標設計題型。以中高級為例，聽力部分含40題，作答時間約35分鐘；閱讀部分含40題，作答時間50分鐘；寫作部分含中翻英、引導寫作，作答時間50分鐘；口說測驗採錄音方式進行，作答時間約15分鐘。

Q 這項測驗各級命題方向為何？考生應如何準備？

全民英檢在設計各級的命題方向時，均曾參考目前各級英語教育之課程大綱，同時也廣泛搜集相關教材進行內容分析，以求命題內容能符合國內各級英語教育的需求。同時，為了這項測驗的內容能反應本土的生活經驗與特色，因此命題內容力求生活化，並包含流行話題及時事。

由於這項測驗並未針對特定領域或教材命題，考生應無需特別準備。但因各級測驗均包含聽、說、讀、寫四部分，而目前國內英語教育仍偏重讀與寫，因此考生必須平日加強聽、說訓練，同時多接觸英語媒體(如報章雜誌、廣播、電視、電影等)，以求在測驗時有較好的表現。

Q 口說及寫作測驗既採非選擇題方式，評分方式為何？

口說及寫作測驗的評分工作將由受過訓練的專業人士擔任，每位考生的表現都會經過至少兩人的評分。每級口說及寫作測驗均訂有評分指標，評分人員在確切掌握評分指標後，依據考生的整體表現評分。

Q 通過「全民英檢」合格標準者是否取得合格證書？又合格證書有何用途或效力？

是的，通過「全民英檢」合格標準者將頒給證書。全民英檢測驗之合格證明書能成為民眾求學或就業的重要依據，同時各級學校也可利用本測驗做為學習成果檢定及教學改進的參考。

Q 全民英檢測驗的分數如何計算？

初試各項成績採標準計分方式，60分為平均數，每一標準差加減20分，滿分120分。初試兩項測驗成績總和達160分，且其中任一項成績不低於72分者，始可參加複試。如以傳統粗分計分概念來說，聽力測驗每題3分，閱讀測驗每題3分，各項得分為答對題數乘上每題分數，可以大概計算是否通過本項測驗。實際計分方式會視當次考生程度與試題難易作調整，因此每題分數及最高分與粗分計分方式略有差異。複試各項成績採整體式評分，使用級分制，分為0~5級分，再轉換成百分制。複試各項成績均達八十分以上，視為通過。

Q採標準計分方式有何優點？

考生不會受不同次測驗中考生程度與試題難易之影響。

Q 國中、高中學生若無國民身分證，如何報考？

國中生未請領身分證者，可使用印有相片之健保IC卡替代；高中生以上中華民國國民請使用國民身份證正面影本。外籍人士需備有效期限內之台灣居留證。

Q 初試與複試一定在同一考場嗎？

不一定，因聽讀、說寫測驗所需試場設備不同，故所安排的考場不盡相同，恕無法指定考場。但參加一日考者，聽說讀寫四項測驗將安排於同一試場應試。

Q 請問合格證書的有效期限只有兩年嗎？

合格證書並無有效期限，而是成績紀錄保存兩年，意即兩年內的成績單，如因故遺失，可申請補發。成績單及合格證書可透過紙本或網路申請，收件及款項確認後，以掛號方式寄發。

Q 什麼是一日考？與現行兩階段考試有什麼不同？

一日考是在一日內考完聽說讀寫四項測驗，考後 6-7 週即可得知四項成績，大幅縮短約2個月時間。若僅通過聽讀測驗或說寫測驗，可於 2 年內報名未通過之項目。

Q 報考全民英檢是否有年齡、學歷的限制？

一般社會人士及各級學校學生均可報考本測驗。

Q 合格之標準為何？

初試兩項測驗成績總和達160分，且其中任一項成績不低於72分者，複試成績除初級寫作為70分，其餘級數的寫作、口說測驗都80分以上才算通過，可獲核發合格證書。

Q 初試通過，複試未通過，下一次是否還需要再考一次初試？

初試通過者，可於二年內單獨報考複試未通過項目。

★關於「全民英語能力分級檢定測驗」之內容及相關問題請洽：

財團法人語言訓練測驗中心

中心地址：106台北市辛亥路二段170號（台灣大學校總區內）

全民英檢專線：(02)2369-7127

全民英檢傳真：(02)2364-6367

辦公日：週一至週五(週六、日及政府機構放假日不上班)

辦公時間：上午八點至十二點、下午一點至五點

CONTENTS

目錄

NEW GEPT
全新全民英檢中高級 聽力&閱讀題庫解析

測驗成績記錄表

（自己的姓名）＿＿＿＿＿＿＿＿＿ 這次英檢初試一定會過！

填表日期：＿＿＿＿年＿＿＿＿月＿＿＿＿日

達成日期：＿＿＿＿年＿＿＿＿月＿＿＿＿日

	示範	第一回	第二回	第三回	第四回	第五回	第六回	
120								滿分！
110								
100								
90								
80								過關了
70								
60								
50								
40								
30	●閱讀							
20	●聽力							
10	我一定要過英檢！							
0								

完成每次測驗後，請將所得到的成績用黑點●標示在表格上，就能感受到自己分數的進步。

全民英語能力分級檢定測驗

GENERAL ENGLISH PROFICIENCY TEST

中高級聽力測驗　第一回

HIGH-INTERMEDIATE LISTENING COMPREHENSION TEST

This listening comprehension test will test your ability to understand spoken English. In this test, each conversation, short talk and question will be spoken JUST ONE TIME. They will not be written out for you. There are three parts to this test. Special instructions will be given to you at the beginning of each part.

Part I: Answering Questions

In Part I, you will hear ten questions. After you hear a question, read the four choices in your test booklet and decide which one is the best answer to the question you have heard.

Example:

You will hear: Why did you slam the door?

You will read:
A. I just can't open it.
B. I didn't. I guess it's the wind.
C. Because someone is at the door.
D. Because the door knob is missing.

The best answer to the question "Why did you slam the door?" is B: "I didn't. I guess it's the wind." Therefore, you should choose answer B.

1. A. I thought you already knew.
   B. You shouldn't make calls during the meeting.
   C. I was supposed to inform everyone, and I did.
   D. I was in the meeting when you called.

2. A. I'm sure we will have perfect weather.
   B. I don't think I'll be available tomorrow.
   C. Gosh. I haven't even started on it.
   D. Let's not worry about the future.

3. A. I would rather not gossip.
   B. I can't accept your proposal.
   C. I can't believe he has a daughter.
   D. I am too young to talk about marriage.

4. A. There is no purpose in doing that.
   B. Everything will be fine.
   C. You can't wait for a minute, can you?
   D. Sorry. It's hard to cope all by myself.

5. A. She is a professional critic.
   B. She knows you have tried hard enough.
   C. She may be expecting highly of you.
   D. She really adores you.

6. A. Cut it out. We're just friends.
   B. Yeah. That's what friends are for.
   C. I think you are made for each other.
   D. Go for it. She's my girlfriend.

7. A. Remove the price label on the present.
   B. Try adding a ribbon on the gift.
   C. Speak slower and look at your audience.
   D. Prove that you are not guilty.

8. A. Maybe we should do it ourselves.
   B. Maybe we should plant some trees.
   C. Maybe we should buy a new house.
   D. Maybe we should buy it later.

9. A. To help me with my wedding arrangements.
   B. To keep them away from the sun.
   C. To grow some vegetables in the yard.
   D. To decorate the dish I prepared.

10. A. He didn't arrive at the place in time.
    B. Perhaps we should assist him.
    C. We have to keep our word anyway.
    D. At least we came in second.

Please turn to the next page. ⇨

Part II: Conversation

In part II, you will hear several conversations between a man and a woman. After each conversation, you will hear a question about the conversation. After you hear the question, read the four choices in your test booklet and choose the best answer to the question you have heard.

Example:

You will hear:	(Man)	Did you happen to see my earphones? I remember leaving them in the drawer. Someone must have taken it.
	(Woman)	It's more likely that you misplaced them. Did you search your briefcase?
	(Man)	I did, but they are not there. Wait a second. Oh. They are right here in my pocket.
	Question:	Who took the man's earphones?

You will read:
A. The woman.
B. Someone else.
C. No one.
D. Another man.

The best answer to the question "Who took the man's earphones?" is C: "No one." Therefore, you should choose answer C.

11. A. She is under the weather.
    B. She needs some change.
    C. She can't stand the low temperature.
    D. She has a headache.

12. A. She got an autograph from a Hollywood star.
    B. She met a politician in an elevator.
    C. She talked to Brad Pitt in private.
    D. She saw a movie star in person.

13. A. Put up the notice.
    B. Support the table.
    C. Fill out the form.
    D. Purchase some stationery.

14. A. How to review a biography.
    B. When to watch a movie.
    C. Where to go for lunch.
    D. What they learned from a book.

15. A. In a consulting room.
    B. In a convention center.
    C. In a health club.
    D. In a chemistry laboratory.

16. A. The man and woman are already late for work.
    B. There was a fatal car accident.
    C. The police blocked off the roads.
    D. Traffic was temporarily disrupted.

17. A. He will propose to the woman, too.
    B. He will borrow Henry's idea.
    C. He will hire twenty thousand people.
    D. He will watch a soccer match live.

18. A. They should be taught certain things.
    B. They should be wise about money.
    C. They should not be held responsible.
    D. They should not be lazy.

19. A. She was talking with her mouth full.
    B. She was staring at others.
    C. She was doing something unproductive.
    D. She was too worried about her future.

Please turn to the next page.

20. A. To invite him for a drink.
    B. To cancel a plan with her family.
    C. To complain about her job.
    D. To show that she is an independent woman.

21. A. A bartender.
    B. A salesperson.
    C. A high school teacher.
    D. A consultant.

22. A. A talk show.
    B. A cooking show.
    C. A variety show.
    D. An educational show.

23. A. A food critic.
    B. A travel writer.
    C. A public relations specialist.
    D. A YouTuber.

24.

Weekly Planner	
Monday	Call Andrea
Tuesday	Claudia's piano class
Wednesday	Visit amusement park with friends Call Andrea
Thursday	Claudia's piano class
Friday	Take a boat ride with friends

A. Monday.
B. Tuesday.
C. Wednesday.
D. Thursday.

25.

Second Foreign Language Courses		
Course	Percentage of Students	Student Rating
Spanish	15%	8.67
French	36%	7.85
Japanese	41%	8.21
Korean	8%	9.10

A. Spanish.
B. French.
C. Japanese.
D. Korean.

Part III: Short Talks

In part III, you will hear several short talks. After each talk, you will hear two to three questions about the talk. After you hear each question, read the four choices in your test booklet and choose the best answer to the question you have heard.

Example:

You will hear: Hello, thank you everyone for coming together to share this special day with Chris and I. We have been waiting for this moment forever, and after five years of dating, I can happily say that I am ready. Chris is caring and charming, and I appreciate my good fortune in marrying such a warm-hearted man. When he proposed to me, I realized that he had already become a part of my life. Even though I'm not a perfect cook or housekeeper, I know for sure that I will be a wonderful partner for Chris.

Question number 1: On what occasion is this talk most probably being given?

You will read: A. A funeral.
B. A wedding.
C. A housewarming.
D. A farewell party.

The best answer to the question "On what occasion is this talk most probably being given?" is B: "A wedding." Therefore, you should choose answer B.

Now listen to another question based on the same talk.

Please turn to the next page.

You will hear:	Question number 2: According to this talk, what does the woman like about Chris?
You will read:	A. His perseverance. B. His abundant wealth. C. His cooking skill. D. His amiable personality.

The best answer to the question "According to this talk, what does the woman like about Chris?" is D: "His amiable personality." Therefore, you should choose answer D.

Please turn to the next page. Now let us begin Part III with question number 26.

26. A. Exactly one o'clock.
    B. A quarter after six.
    C. A quarter to six.
    D. Half past six.

27. A. Safety of the crew.
    B. Behavior of the passengers.
    C. Availability of beverage.
    D. Visibility of the city.

28. A. He felt out of place.
    B. He was expelled.
    C. He hated detention class.
    D. He couldn't keep up with the rest.

29. A. He transferred his emotions to the school.
    B. He stood out as an individual.
    C. He made fun of the punishment he received.
    D. He sounded more confident than he actually was.

30. A. He is skeptical about the school system.
    B. He is concerned about school bullying.
    C. He is confident that he will be transferred soon.
    D. He is grateful that he has become a better person.

31. A. It is governed by Rome, Italy.
    B. It is a sovereign state.
    C. It is home to mostly women.
    D. It is the largest city in Europe.

32. A. It is a financial center.
    B. It is a cultural hub.
    C. It is a military stronghold.
    D. It is an industrial region.

33. A. Separating different racial groups into areas.
    B. Putting students of different ethnic backgrounds into different schools.
    C. Deciding a common language among different races.
    D. Allowing a certain level of racial discrimination.

34. A. Social policies to reduce racial conflicts.
    B. The school system in Singapore.
    C. How history repeats itself.
    D. The absence of human rights.

Please turn to the next page.

35-37.

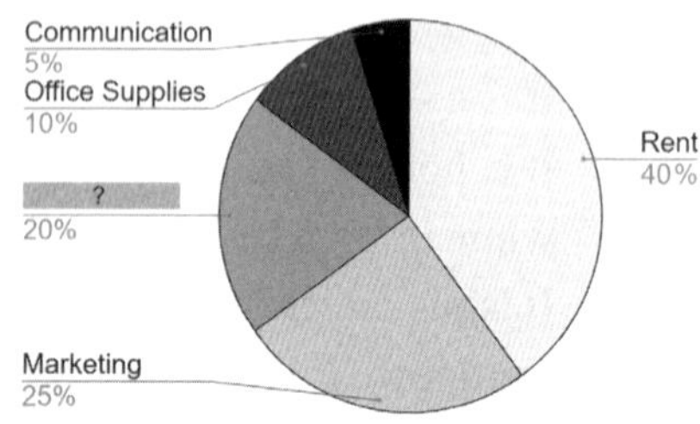

35. A. Increasing sales volume.
    B. Being more eco-friendly.
    C. Evaluating employees' performance.
    D. Saving money on business operations.

36. A. Communication.
    B. Office supplies.
    C. Marketing.
    D. Rent.

37. A. Utilities.
    B. Insurance.
    C. Maintenance.
    D. Accounting.

38-40.

University	Acceptance Rate	Popular Majors
Harvard	4.9%	?, business
Yale	6.5%	Social sciences, biological sciences
Princeton	5.5%	Social sciences, engineering
Columbia	6.3%	Business, law, engineering

38. A. He is preparing to apply.
    B. He has sent his applications.
    C. He is going to be interviewed.
    D. He is waiting for the results.

39. A. Harvard.
    B. Yale.
    C. Princeton.
    D. Columbia.

40. A. Education.
    B. Literature.
    C. Chemistry.
    D. Medicine.

READING COMPREHESION TEST

This is a three-part test with forty multiple-choice questions. Each question has four choices. Special instructions will be provided for each part. You will have fifty minutes to complete this test.

Part I: Sentence Completion

In this part of the test, there are ten incomplete sentences. Beneath each sentence you will see four words or phrases, marked A, B, C and D. You are to choose the word or phrase that best completes the sentence. Then on your answer sheet, find the number of the question and mark your answer.

1. The company allocates a significant amount of resources to Research and Development to gain a ________ edge.
   A. excessive B. competitive
   C. quantitative D. impulsive

2. Because of the ________ of information online, many people choose to read headlines instead of reading articles thoroughly.
   A. abundance B. correspondence
   C. eloquence D. indifference

3. Salespeople who exceed their ________ are entitled to bonuses based on their performance.
   A. genres B. quotas
   C. realms D. slumps

4. ________ the disastrous last ten minutes, the home team has been doing just fine during the game.
   A. Except for B. In addition to
   C. Together with D. In case of

5. The man waited for what seemed like an ________ before he laid his eyes on his newborn child.
   A. anticipation B. eternity
   C. illusion D. obsession

6. In the Dark Ages, men accused women of being witches who ________ on misfortunes in the society.
   A. brought B. passed
   C. gave up D. turned

7. I merely turned the handle with a little more force than usual, and it ________ .
   A. came out B. came off
   C. came around D. came down

8. The company ________ updates its software programs to keep up with ever-changing needs of customers.
   A. coherently B. distinctively
   C. exclusively D. periodically

9. Whatever the mind of man can ________ and believe, he certainly can achieve.
   A. deceive B. conceive
   C. perceive D. receive

10. According to company regulations, any truck driver caught drunk-driving will have their contract ________ .
   A. suspended B. canceled
   C. terminated D. revoked

Part Two: Cloze

In this part of the test, you will read two passages. Each passage contains five missing words or phrases. Beneath each passage, you will see five items, each with four choices, marked A, B, C and D. You are to choose the best answer for each missing word or phrase in the two passages. Then, on your answer sheet, find the number of the question and mark your answer.

Questions 11-15

As a foreigner residing in Taipei city, I would like to ___(11)___ the city's effort in launching eco-friendly initiatives, especially the bicycle sharing system called "YouBike". The system enables everyone to rent a bike anytime, anywhere. What is more, ___(12)___, so you do not need to keep your rented bike after riding to work.

You can rent a bike for as long as you wish ___(13)___, and the renting process is a breeze. First of all, you need to register your EasyCard. While registering, you need to provide your EasyCard's ___(14)___ number, which can be found on the lower right corner of the card. Next, just go to the bicycle rental station and tap your card on the sensor on the rack to get a bike. When you return the bike, remember to tap your card again to have the fee ___(15)___ from the card.

11. A. sustain
    B. commend
    C. disclose
    D. provoke

12. A. renting YouBikes is totally free of charge
    B. YouBikes are designed to be disposed after use
    C. you can rent a YouBike from one station and return at another
    D. there is a discount when transferring between YouBike and the MRT

Please turn to the next page.

13. A. every half hour
    B. based on half hours
    C. on a half-hourly basis
    D. basically half-hourly

15. A. deduct
    B. to deduct
    C. deducting
    D. deducted

14. A. series
    B. serial
    C. sequence
    D. sequel

Questions 16-20

Intelligence Quotient (IQ) and Emotional Quotient (EQ) reflect different aspects of human mind. The former is a measure of cognitive intelligence, whereas the latter is a measure of emotional intelligence. ___(16)___ it is generally accepted that an individual's IQ ___(17)___ , the same individual's EQ, on the other hand, can develop over time and through training.

The idea of EQ was first introduced by Dr. Reuven Bar-On. He ___(18)___ emotional intelligence as being concerned with effectively understanding oneself and others and adapting to one's immediate surroundings. Emotional intelligence helps individuals to cope with their situations and to deal with environmental demands. Individuals with a higher than average EQ are generally more competent ___(19)___ their pressures. A ___(20)___ in emotional intelligence can mean a lack of mental toughness and impulse control.

16. A. However
    B. While
    C. Since
    D. Provided

17. A. can improve very quickly
    B. can be tested and measured
    C. is more or less determined at birth
    D. decides how successful he or she is

18. A. defined
    B. presumed
    C. implied
    D. advocated

19. A. to handle
    B. by handling
    C. handled by
    D. in order to handle

20. A. proficiency
    B. deficiency
    C. efficiency
    D. sufficiency

Please turn to the next page.

Part III: Reading Comprehension

In this part of the test, you will find several tasks. Each task contains one or two passages or charts, which are followed by two to six questions. You are to choose the best answer, A, B, C, or D, to each question on the basis of the information provided or implied in the passage or chart. Then, on your answer sheet, find the number of the question and mark your answer.

Questions 21-22 are based on the information provided in the following chart.

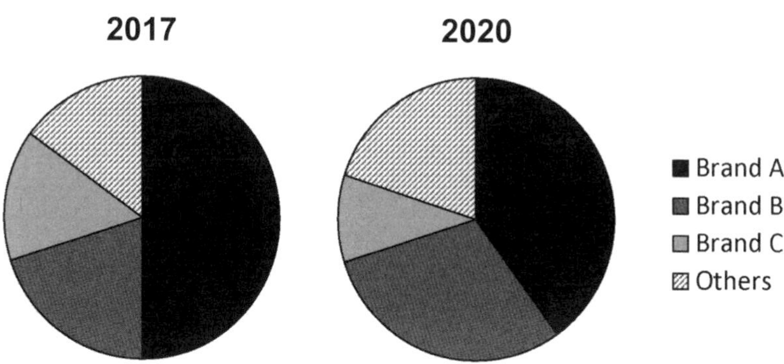

21. Based on the chart, which of the following statements is true?
    A. Brand A has lost a significant amount of market share, but it remains the market leader.
    B. Brand B has not managed to increase its market share.
    C. Brand C has exceeded Brand B in terms of market share.
    D. Growth for the brands other than brand A was stagnant for the past three years.
22. What might you read about Brand C in a business magazine?
    A. The company's prospects are bright and promising.
    B. The company is likely to overtake the market leader in the near future.
    C. The company needs to reinvent itself or be eliminated by its competitors.
    D. The company has lived up to shareholders' expectations.

Please turn to the next page.

Questions 23-25

Ancient Egypt is a distinct civilization, which can be dated back 5,000 years ago. No ancient civilization has so captured the Western mind as that of Egypt. Its impressive architectural remains and the close connection with Greece and Rome, in addition to its historical events described in the Holy Bible, probably explain this fascination. Another factor surely is the Egyptian obsession with the afterlife, which left a lot of archaeological evidence, including mummies. The origins of ancient Egypt are still clouded in mystery. What we know is that it has a mysterious religion with inspiring monumental architecture, including temples, pyramids, and the Sphinx.

Usually seen on the walls of ancient temples and tombs, hieroglyphics were the pictographic writing of the ancient Egyptians. They form a complicated system, which is the basis of a developing alphabet, using both pictures and sounds to convey ideas. Even in ancient Egypt, few could read hieroglyphics. This knowledge was reserved primarily to the priests and nobility. For centuries, the meaning of hieroglyphics was a mystery, until French scholar Jean-François Champollion deciphered it.

When it comes to the religion itself, the sun was ancient Egypt's principal god. The sun's passage daily across the sky from sunrise to sunset represented the eternal cycle of birth, death, and rebirth. As in many Asian cultures, the kings or pharaohs were seen as gods by the common people. Therefore, obedience to the king is akin to following the instructions of the gods.

23. What is **NOT** a reason that Westerners are attracted by Egyptian culture?
    A. The architectural wonders of ancient Egypt
    B. The abundant fuel hidden under Egyptian deserts
    C. What happened there as described in the Bible
    D. The preservation of dead bodies

24. According to this article, what is true about Egyptian hieroglyphics?
    A. They were purely drawings that bear no meaning.
    B. They were closely related to Greek and Roman alphabets.
    C. They were only accessible by a privileged group.
    D. They were translated using modern technology.

25. How did the pharaohs strengthen their rule over the people with the help of religion?
    A. By emphasizing the eternal cycle of birth, death, and rebirth
    B. By keeping their burial sites a mystery to all
    C. By promoting literacy among the general public through schools
    D. By portraying kings as legitimate heirs appointed by the gods

Please turn to the next page.

Questions 26-29

Cases of random murders have enraged the public, especially when the latest victim was an innocent four-year-old girl, who was slaughtered right in front of her mother in broad daylight, for no apparent reason. It is outrageous for such an inhuman act to take place in Taiwan, a society well-known for its friendly and helpful people. This tragic incident, the third in three years with the victim being a child, raised a highly controversial issue: should the death penalty be abolished? With regard to this question, public opinion is divided, though recent polls suggested that the majority of Taiwanese are in favor of executing child murderers so they can do no more harm to other children.

Supporters of the death penalty believe that only such a drastic measure will prevent similar crimes from happening, and they take the fact that previous murderers were not given a death sentence as a reason why the number of murders keeps growing. Many also argued that there is no justice to the family of murder victims unless evildoers pay with their lives. Furthermore, life imprisonment instead of a death sentence is a heavy burden for the government since the criminals are to be taken care of for as long as they live. On the other hand, those who urge the government to abolish the death penalty claim that harsh laws do not act as a deterrent of crime, let alone solve the causes of crime. Actually, a death penalty may even be an easy way out for murderers who do not care about human life, including their own. Since many murderers have a few problems deeply rooted in their upbringing, it is possible that improving home and school education can better prevent such crimes. Besides, there were cases in which innocent people were convicted and executed. There is always the danger of a mistaken execution, especially when there is strong pressure of public opinion but no sufficient evidence.

26. What is the cause of the latest murder case mentioned in this article?
   A. A dispute in the family
   B. A personal financial crisis
   C. A lack of death penalty laws
   D. The cause is unknown.

27. What is the main reason that the recent incident made a lot of people angry?
   A. It was carried out during the daytime.
   B. It happened to a very young girl.
   C. It caused controversy.
   D. It happened in Taiwan.

28. According to the result of the opinion survey, what kind of opinion is dominant?
   A. All murderers ought to be given the death penalty.
   B. Murderers of children must not be forgiven.
   C. Human rights of both criminals and victims should be respected.
   D. Death penalty should be abolished.

29. Which of the following is a reason that some people are against the death penalty?
   A. The judicial system is not without flaws.
   B. Our education system is good enough to prevent crimes.
   C. There are more terrifying punishments for criminals.
   D. The public opinion is usually wrong.

Please turn to the next page.

Questions 30-34 are based on the information provided in the following advertisement and email.

Gyrotonix
Job Opening

Gyrotonix is a multinational corporation based in India with businesses in Taiwan and Peru. We focus on selling real estate to the affluent population. We are currently seeking to hire a project manager for our team.

The project manager will be required to lead a team of 20 people. They will coordinate the team to work on the branding and promotion of real estate projects. This position will be trained in Taiwan and then relocate to Lima, Peru.

Desired qualifications:

- Master's degree in real estate management
- Five years of experience in the real estate industry
- English fluency with basic knowledge of Chinese or Spanish
- Being a team player
- Excellent analytical and communication skills

If you meet the required qualifications, please send your résumé to hr@gyrotonix.com along with a cover letter.

From: Marie Flores <Marie.flores@rmail.com>
To: <hr@gyrotnixs.com>
Subject: Project Manager Applicant

Dear representative,

My name is Marie Flores. I am responding to the ad posted on your company website about an opening for a project manager at Gyrotonix. My multicultural background and educational experiences make me an ideal candidate.

I have four years of experience in the real estate field. I was raised in both Taiwan and Honduras. I also completed my bachelor's degree in real estate in the United States before coming back to Taiwan. As a result, I am fluent in Chinese, Spanish, and English. My strong communication skills have allowed me to work with teams all over the world. My multicultural experience leads me to be able to manage a multicultural team.

It is my goal to combine my range of experience with my ability to be a passionate and energetic leader who will make a positive contribution to your community. Please find my résumé attached. I would welcome an interview and hope to hear from you at your earliest convenience. Please do not hesitate to contact me at 1234-567-8900 or Marie.flores@rmail.com.

Thank you for your consideration.

Sincerely,
Marie Flores

30. What is true about Gyrotonix?
    A. It has offices in three continents.
    B. Its customers are mostly rich people.
    C. It deals with the construction of buildings.
    D. It encourages an independent working style.

31. Where will the project manager work?
    A. In india
    B. In Taiwan
    C. In Peru
    D. All of the above

32. What is the purpose of the email?
    A. To ask for more information about the company
    B. To share the sender's multicultural experience
    C. To seek employment
    D. To seek a higher education

33. According to the articles, which requirement does Marie meet?
    A. Educational background
    B. Experience in the industry
    C. Language proficiency
    D. Analytical skills

34. What can be inferred about Marie?
    A. She lives in Taiwan now.
    B. She was born in Honduras.
    C. She could not speak English before living in the US.
    D. She has experience in managing a multicultural team.

Questions 35-40

Insomnia is a symptom rather than a stand-alone disease. By definition, insomnia is "difficulty initiating or maintaining sleep, or both." It may therefore negatively affect the quality or quantity of sleep. Insomnia is not defined by a specific number of hours of sleep that one gets since everyone is different in terms of the length of sleep needed, and it is how we feel that matters. Most of us have experienced the feeling of not getting enough sleep, but only a few have consulted doctors, while others don't even know there are methods that can treat the problem.

Insomnia affects all age groups. Among adults, insomnia affects women more often than men. The likelihood of this problem occurring tends to increase with age. It is typically more common in people in lower socioeconomic (income) groups, chronic alcoholics, and mental health patients. Stress most commonly triggers short-term or acute insomnia. If you do not address your insomnia, however, it may develop into chronic insomnia. Some surveys have shown that 30% to 35% of subjects interviewed reported difficulty falling asleep during the previous year, and about 10% reported problems with long-standing insomnia. There also seems to be an association between depression, anxiety, and insomnia. Although the nature of this correlation is unknown, people with depression or anxiety were significantly more likely to develop insomnia. Some common causes of insomnia are stimulants including caffeine and nicotine. Alcohol is also associated with sleep disruption and creates a sense of drowsiness in the morning. Another factor could be a bed partner with loud snoring that makes it difficult to fall asleep.

Long-term insomnia can cause serious health consequences because human body needs to repair itself during sleep. It seems that the body is not at work while sleeping, but the brain is actually still active, maintaining the normal functioning of all the systems. Most importantly, the immune system produces more of certain substances that help fight diseases while we sleep. Therefore, getting adequate sleep is the first step toward good health.

Please turn to the next page.

35. What is the definition of insomnia based on the article?
    A. A specific disease of the brain
    B. Not being able to get enough sleep
    C. Less than eight hours of sleep a day
    D. A sleep full of dreams or nightmares

36. According to this article, how come very few people with sleeping disorders ask a doctor for help?
    A. They are too embarrassed to talk about the problem.
    B. They remain unaware that they suffer from insomnia.
    C. They do not know that insomnia can be treated.
    D. They think that treatment for insomnia is too expensive.

37. What kind of people have high risks of suffering from insomnia?
    A. Children who do sports
    B. People who come from wealthy families
    C. Men in their early twenties
    D. Heavy drinkers

38. Which of the following statements is **NOT** consistent with this article?
    A. Emotional states have a lot to do with insomnia.
    B. Causes of insomnia can be both internal and external.
    C. Caffeine and alcohol may affect one's ability to sleep.
    D. Sleep is a passive state in which the brain shuts down to rest.

39. According to this article, what is true about sleep?
    A. Too much sleep can result in mental health problems.
    B. Our brain stops working during sleep to remain healthy.
    C. Sleep helps maintain the body's self-healing ability.
    D. One can hear one's own snoring while asleep.

40. Which of the following is a suitable title for this article?
    A. Difference between Rest and Sleep
    B. Factors Related to Insomnia and the Role of Sleep
    C. The Causes, Consequences, and Cures of Insomnia
    D. Overcoming Insomnia and Achieving Sound Sleep.

第一回 初試 聽力測驗解析

第一部分 回答問題

Q1

You could have told me that they called off the meeting, couldn't you? Why didn't you do it?
你當時可以告訴我他們取消了會議的，不是嗎？你為什麼沒告訴我？

A. I thought you already knew.
B. You shouldn't make calls during the meeting.
C. I was supposed to inform everyone, and I did.
D. I was in the meeting when you called.

A. 我以為你已經知道了。
B. 你不應該在開會的時候打電話。
C. 我必須通知所有人，而且我有這麼做。
D. 你打來的時候我在開會。

詳解 **答案：A**

動詞片語 called off 意為取消，但是和打電話沒關係，所以 B 和 D 是錯誤的。說話者的問題 Why didn't you do it? 表示對方沒有通知他，所以 C 不合理，最適合的回應為 A。

|單字片語| **call off** 取消 / **supposed** [sə`pozd] adj. 應當的 / **inform** [ɪn`fɔrm] v. 通知

Q2

Isn't your chemistry paper due tomorrow? You will fail the course if you miss the deadline. 你的化學報告不是明天到期嗎？你如果沒趕上期限，這門課就會不及格。

A. I'm sure we will have perfect weather. A. 我很確定我們會有完美的天氣。
B. I don't think I'll be available tomorrow. B. 我想我明天不會有空。
C. Gosh. I haven't even started on it. C. 天啊。我根本還沒開始做。
D. Let's not worry about the future. D. 我們不要擔心未來的事情。

詳解 答案：C

A 顯然是答非所問，B 也沒有針對化學報告做出回答。D 說起來很輕鬆，但在回答重要問題時不太可能會用這樣的口吻。最佳的答案是 C。

|單字片語| **due** [dju] adj. 到期的 / **fail** [fel] v. 沒有通過…，…不及格 / **deadline** [ˋdɛdˏlaɪn] n. 最後期限

Q3

Have you heard the rumor that our manager is marrying a woman young enough to be his daughter?
你有聽到關於我們經理要娶一個年輕到可以當他女兒的女人當妻子的傳聞嗎？

A. I would rather not gossip. A. 我選擇不要說長道短。
B. I can't accept your proposal. B. 我不能接受你的求婚。
C. I can't believe he has a daughter. C. 我無法相信他有個女兒。
D. I am too young to talk about marriage. D. 我太年輕不能談論婚姻。

詳解 答案：A

如果只注意到 marrying、daughter 等單字，或許會以為答案是 B、C 或 D。但是，題目的重點其實在「Have you heard the rumor」（你有沒有聽到傳聞），而且是談論某人要結婚的消息，所以答案是 A，回答者用 gossip（說長道短）來呼應題目裡的 rumor（傳聞）。

|單字片語| **rumor** [ˋrumɚ] n. 傳聞，謠言 / **gossip** [ˋgɑsəp] n. 流言，八卦消息 v. 說長道短 / **proposal** [prəˋpozl] n. 提案；求婚

Q4

How could you mix up the customers' orders? Our restaurant will get bad reviews.
你怎麼可以把客人點的餐搞混？我們的餐廳會得到不好的評價。

A. There is no purpose in doing that.　A. 那麼做是沒有意義的。
B. Everything will be fine.　B. 一切都會沒事的。
C. You can't wait for a minute, can you?　C. 你連一分鐘都不能等，對嗎？
D. Sorry. It's hard to cope all by myself.　D. 抱歉。我自己一個人很難應付。

詳解

答案：D

說話者可能是餐廳經理或老闆，說話對象可能是服務生。A、C 和問題無關，而考慮到犯錯可能造成的後果，B 顯得太過樂觀而不負責任，也不是適當的回答。D 先表示歉意，再解釋自己犯錯的理由，是合理的回答。

|單字片語| **mix up** 把…搞混 / **review** [rɪˋvju] n. 評論 / **cope** [kop] v. 應對，應付

Q5

Why does my teacher criticize and pick on me no matter how hard I try?
為什麼不管我多麼努力，我的老師還是批評我和找我麻煩？

A. She is a professional critic.　A. 她是一個專業的評論家。
B. She knows you have tried hard enough.　B. 她知道你已經夠努力了。
C. She may be expecting highly of you.　C. 她可能對你的期望很高。
D. She really adores you.　D. 她真的很寵愛你。

詳解

答案：C

一個喜歡 criticize（批評）別人的人不一定是 critic（評論家），所以 A 是錯誤的。B 也不合理，因為從批評的行為中無法直接推斷是否了解對方的努力。C 用推測的口氣（may be expecting），表示老師的批評可能是因為期待更好的表現，是比較合理的答案。

|單字片語| **pick on** 找某人的麻煩 / **critic** [ˋkrɪtɪk] n. 評論家 / **adore** [əˋdor] v. 愛慕，寵愛

Q6

Are you hinting that I should propose to Adeline? What if she turns me down?
你在暗示我應該向 Adeline 求婚嗎？假如她拒絕我該怎麼辦？

A. Cut it out. We're just friends.	A. 別鬧了。我們只是朋友。
B. Yeah. That's what friends are for.	B. 是的。當朋友就應該這樣。
C. I think you are made for each other.	C. 我認為你們兩個是天生一對。
D. Go for it. She's my girlfriend.	D. 去爭取吧。她是我的女朋友。

詳解 答案：C

A 聽起來和題目相關，但問題在於，這句話要和題目連在一起說才合理。因為這裡要選擇對方適當的回答，所以答案不會是「自己不求婚的理由」，而是「之所以建議求婚的理由」。C 表示自己建議對方求婚的理由是「你們是天生一對」，是最合理的答案。「... are made for each other」表示兩個人好像是專為彼此而打造的一樣，意思和中文的「天造地設的一對」類似。

|單字片語| **hint** [hɪnt] n. 提示，暗示 v. 暗示 / **propose to** 向…求婚 / **turn down** 拒絕 / **Cut it out.** 別再說了。 / **go for it** 努力爭取

Q7

How can I improve on the presentation I'll be giving at the convention?
我要如何改進我在大會上做簡報的方式？

A. Remove the price label on the present.	A. 把禮物上的價格標籤拿掉。
B. Try adding a ribbon on the gift.	B. 試試看在禮物上加個蝴蝶結。
C. Speak slower and look at your audience.	C. 說慢一點並看著你的觀眾。
D. Prove that you are not guilty.	D. 證明你是無罪的。

詳解 答案：C

若把 presentation 聽成 present（禮物），就有可能被誤導而選擇 A 或 B。如果能正確聽到關鍵字 presentation（簡報）和 convention（大會），就知道討論的主題是會議上要進行的報告，所以 C 關於說話姿態的建議是正確答案。

|單字片語| **improve on** 改進… / **presentation** [ˌprizɛnˋteʃən] n. 簡報 / **convention** [kənˋvɛnʃən] n. 大會，會議 / **guilty** [ˋgɪltɪ] adj. 有罪的

Q8

Shouldn't we get someone to mow the lawn? It looks terrible with weeds all over.
我們是不是應該找人來割草皮了？到處都是雜草，看起來很糟糕。

A. Maybe we should do it ourselves.	A. 或許我們應該自己來。
B. Maybe we should plant some trees.	B. 或許我們應該種些樹。
C. Maybe we should buy a new house.	C. 或許我們應該買棟新房子。
D. Maybe we should buy it later.	D. 或許我們應該晚一點再買。

詳解

答案：A

「Shouldn't we...?」表示提出建議，字面上是「我們不是應該…嗎？」，可以理解為「我們是不是應該…？」的意思。get someone to mow the lawn 表示「請人割草皮」，也可以用 have the lawn mowed (by someone) 來表達同樣的意思。只有 A 回答了上述問題。B 說的種樹跟割草沒有關係，不會因為種了樹就不用割草。一般人不會因為草太長就買新的房子，所以 C 不對。D 也沒有回答問題，問題是說找人來割草，沒有提到要買東西，從上下文也無法判斷 it 指的是什麼。

Q9

What do you need these onions for? I always cry when I cut them.
你需要這些洋蔥做什麼？我每次切洋蔥都會哭。

A. To help me with my wedding arrangements.	A. 為了幫忙我的婚禮籌備事宜。
B. To keep them away from the sun.	B. 為了讓它們不要曬到太陽。
C. To grow some vegetables in the yard.	C. 為了在院子裡種一些蔬菜。
D. To decorate the dish I prepared.	D. 為了點綴我準備的菜餚。

詳解

答案：D

應該選擇準備洋蔥的原因，最合理的用途是拿來做菜，所以 D 是正確答案。B 應該是對於「為什麼把洋蔥放在某個地方」之類問題的答案。

Q10

We should never have agreed to help him in the first place, should we?
我們當初就不應該答應幫助他，對嗎？

A. He didn't arrive at the place in time. A. 他沒有及時到達那個地方。
B. Perhaps we should assist him. B. 或許我們應該協助他。
C. We have to keep our word anyway. C. 無論如何我們必須遵守諾言。
D. At least we came in second. D. 至少我們得了第二名。

詳解

答案：C

這裡談論的是「答應幫助他」（agreed to help him）這件事。C 的 keep our word（遵守諾言）呼應 agreed（同意）這個字，表示雖然對方覺得當初不應該答應，但既然已經答應就要做到，是正確答案。B 雖然也提到 assist（協助），但 Perhaps we should assist him（或許我們應該協助他）表示一個新的提議，不適合用在之前已經答應過要幫忙的情況。

補充說明

做出了承諾，就必須 keep our word（遵守承諾），不能 go back on one's word（食言反悔）。要表示一個人遵守自己的承諾，可以這樣說：

He is a man of his word. 他是個遵守承諾的人。

His word is his bond. 他講話有信用。

|單字片語| **in the first place** 起初，一開始

Q11

M: Look at you. You are shivering. Here. You can have my coat.
你看看你。你在發抖耶。拿去，你可以用我的大衣。

W: I should have checked the weather forecast before I selected what to wear. It was a bright sunny day when I left home this morning.
我在選要穿的衣服之前應該查看氣象預報的。我今天早上出門的時候，天氣很晴朗。

M: With such wild fluctuations between day and night temperatures, it can be quite a headache. I make it a habit to keep an extra coat in my car. 現在日夜溫度波動這麼大，真的會讓人很頭痛。我習慣在車裡多放一件大衣。

W: Thanks. You are such a gentleman. 謝謝。你真是個紳士。

M: It's my pleasure. 不客氣。

Q: What is the woman's problem?
女子的問題是什麼？

A. She is under the weather. A. 她身體不適。
B. She needs some change. B. 她需要一點改變。
C. She can't stand the low temperature. C. 她受不了低溫。
D. She has a headache. D. 她頭痛。

詳解 **答案：C**

從 shivering（顫抖）和 coat（大衣）這兩個關鍵字，可以馬上得知男子是看到女子很冷的樣子，要借她大衣，所以 C 是正確答案。雖然 A 感覺也是合理的答案，但從對話中我們無法判斷女子是否生病了，她所說的 it can be quite a headache 並不是指真正的頭痛，而是說溫度變化讓人很傷腦筋，所以不能選擇 A。

|單字片語| **shiver** [ˋʃɪvɚ] v. 顫抖 / **fluctuation** [ˏflʌktʃʊˋeʃən] n. 波動

Q12

W: Guess what. I saw Brad Pitt. He had shades on, but I recognized him on the spot.
你猜怎麼了。我看到布萊德・彼特。他戴著墨鏡，但我當場認出他。

M: Brad Pitt? Are you serious? I just saw his latest movie.
布萊德・彼特？你是認真的嗎？我才剛看過他最新的電影。

W: He was with his children, and apparently, he didn't want any attention. 他跟他的孩子在一起，顯然他不希望別人注意他們。

M: Tell me. Did you manage to get his autograph?
告訴我。你有設法要到他的簽名嗎？

W: No. I think celebrities deserve their own privacy. I don't want to disturb him. 沒有。我認為名人應該要有自己的隱私。我不想打擾他。

Q: What happened to the woman?
女子發生了什麼事？

A. She got an autograph from a Hollywood star.	A. 她得到好萊塢明星的簽名。
B. She met a politician in an elevator.	B. 她在電梯裡遇到一位政治人物。
C. She talked to Brad Pitt in private.	C. 她跟布萊德・彼特私底下交談。
D. She saw a movie star in person.	D. 她親眼看到一位電影明星。

詳解 **答案：D**

女子開頭就說 I saw Brad Pitt（我看到布萊德・彼特），男子接著又說 I just saw his latest movie.（我才剛看過他最新的電影），所以 D 是正確答案。女子最後說自己沒有要簽名，從對話中也無法得知她有沒有和布萊德・彼特交談，所以 A、C 都不對。

|單字片語| **shades** [ʃedz] n. 墨鏡 / **on the spot** 當場，立即 / **manage to do** 設法做到… / **autograph** [ˋɔtəˏgræf] n. 親筆簽名 / **celebrity** [sɪˋlɛbrətɪ] n. 名人 / **privacy** [ˋpraɪvəsɪ] n. 隱私 / **politician** [ˏpɑləˋtɪʃən] n. 政治人物 / **in private** 私底下

Q13

M: Excuse me. How do I apply for a scholarship? I mean, how do I make sure that I even qualify for it? 不好意思。我要怎麼申請獎學金呢？我是說，我要怎麼確認自己是不是有資格呢？

W: Please read through this notice to see if you are eligible.
請閱讀這份通知，看看你是否有資格。

M: Well. I guess I am. What is the next step? 嗯，大概有吧。下一步呢？

W: Here's the form. The supporting documents required are all stated at the bottom. There's a table over there you can use. Do you need a pen? 這是（申請）表格。需要的證明文件都列在最下面。那邊有張桌子可以用。你需要筆嗎？

M: I have one in my pocket. Thank you so much.
我口袋裡有一枝。非常謝謝你。

Q: What will the man probably do next?
男子接下來可能會做什麼？

A. Put up the notice. A. 張貼通知。
B. Support the table. B. 支撐桌子。
C. Fill out the form. C. 填寫表格。
D. Purchase some stationery. D. 購買文具。

詳解 答案：C

男子詢問獎學金如何申請，並且拿到了申請表格。最後，女子問男子是否需要筆，男子回答自己已經有了，可以推測他將會填寫表格，所以 C 是正確答案。

|單字片語| **scholarship** [ˋskɑlɚ͵ʃɪp] n. 獎學金 / **qualify for** 對於…有資格 / **eligible** [ˋɛlɪdʒəbḷ] adj. 有資格的 / **support** [səˋport] v. 證實；支撐

Q14

W: I just finished reading Steve Job's biography. 我剛讀完賈伯斯的傳記。

M: What are your thoughts after reading about the founder of Apple Computer? 你讀了這位蘋果電腦創辦人的經歷，有什麼感想呢？

W: I am impressed. No wonder they made it into a movie. I'm grateful that you insisted I read it.
我印象很深刻。難怪他們拍成了電影。我很感謝你堅持要我讀這本書。

M: A quote from the great man: The journey's the reward.
這個偉大的人有句名言：過程就是收穫。

W: And your reward is a free lunch. My treat.
所以你的收穫（回報）就是免費午餐。我請客。

M: Where shall we go? 我們去哪裡好呢？

W: Any restaurant within my budget. 在我預算以內的任何餐廳都可以。

Q: What are the man and woman mainly discussing?
男子和女子主要在討論什麼？

A. How to review a biography. A. 如何評論傳記。
B. When to watch a movie. B. 什麼時候看電影。
C. Where to go for lunch. C. 去哪裡吃午餐。
D. What they learned from a book. D. 他們從一本書裡學到的事情。

詳解 **答案：D**

題目問的是說話者主要在談論什麼（What are... mainly discussing）。雖然最後三句提到了午餐和餐廳，不過他們談論的主要內容是他們從一本傳記中得到的心得，所以答案是 D。

單字片語 **biography** [baɪˋɑgrəfɪ] n. 傳記 / **founder** [ˋfaʊndɚ] n. 創立者 / **grateful** [ˋgretfəl] adj. 感謝的 / **quote** [kwot] n. 引用的文句 / **review** [rɪˋvju] v. 評論

Q15

M: The blood test results are back. 驗血的結果回來了。

W: Good or bad news? 是好消息還是壞消息？

M: I'm afraid it is not very encouraging. 恐怕不是很令人振奮。

W: How bad is it? 那有多糟糕呢？

M: Not terrible, but... 不是很糟，但…

W: Are you trying to say that I have cancer or something?
你是想說我有癌症還是什麼嗎？

M: No. I'm referring to your cholesterol level. It's on the high side, and it is a cause for concern.
不是。我是指你的膽固醇高低。指數偏高，這是讓人擔心的原因。

W: What can I do about it? 我可以怎麼處理呢？

M: Same old advice. A balanced diet and regular exercise.
還是老建議。均衡飲食和定期運動。

Q: Where is this conversation probably taking place?
這段對話可能發生在哪裡？

A. In a consulting room. A. 在診療室。
B. In a convention center. B. 在會議中心。
C. In a health club. C. 在健身俱樂部。
D. In a chemistry laboratory. D. 在化學實驗室。

詳解 **答案：A**

從 blood test（驗血）、cholesterol level（膽固醇水平）等關鍵字，還有男子最後給的建議 A balanced diet and regular exercise.（均衡飲食和定期運動），可以推測這是醫師或營養師和患者的對話，所以 A 是正確答案。consulting room 雖然字面上是「諮詢的房間」，但實際上都是指提供診療服務的地方，如果不了解這個詞的話，可能就無法選出正確答案。C 似乎和對話內容相關，但 health club 主要是讓人做運動的地方，一般而言並不會有醫學檢查的諮詢處，如果誤以為 health club 是「健檢中心」就有可能選錯。雖然這是問場景的問題，但選項卻有測試詞彙能力的感覺。

|單字片語| **cholesterol** [kə`lɛstə,rol] n. 膽固醇

Q16

W: Looks like there is an accident somewhere in front of us.
看樣子我們前面好像有哪裡發生車禍。

M: We have been driving at a snail's pace for more than ten minutes.
我們已經用蝸牛的速度開了十幾分鐘了。

W: I was wrong. The outer lanes are blocked due to maintenance work.
我錯了。外側車道因為維修工程封閉了。

M: So that means traffic should be smooth again after we pass it.
意思就是我們通過（維修地點）以後，交通應該又會順暢了。

W: I'm sure we will make it to the office just in time.
我確定我們會及時到達辦公室。

M: Well, keep your fingers crossed. 嗯，但願如此。

Q: What is true based on the conversation?
根據這段對話，何者正確？

A. The man and woman are already late for work. A. 這對男女已經上班遲到了。
B. There was a fatal car accident. B. 發生了死亡車禍。
C. The police blocked off the roads. C. 警察封閉了道路。
D. Traffic was temporarily disrupted. D. 交通暫時受到堵塞。

詳解 **答案：D**

女子一開始說可能有 accident（事故），後來又說 I was wrong（我錯了），是 outer lanes are blocked due to maintenance work（外側車道因為維修工程封閉了），所以 D 是正確答案，要知道 disrupt（使中斷，擾亂）的意思才能選對。女子最後說她確定會及時（in time）到達辦公室，表示現在還沒遲到，所以 A 不對。B 和 C 感覺上有可能是對的，但女子已經否定了有車禍的猜測，也沒提到現場是否有 police（警察），所以不對。

|單字片語| **maintenance** [`mentənəns] n. 維護，養護 / **make it to** 及時趕到⋯ / **keep one's fingers crossed** 祈求好運 / **fatal** [`fetl] adj. 致命的 / **disrupt** [dɪs`rʌpt] v. 使中斷，擾亂

Q17

M: You seem to be in a good mood. You're smiling from ear to ear. 你看起來心情很好。你嘴角都上揚了。

W: Henry finally proposed to me. Henry 終於跟我求婚了。

M: Oh my! 天啊！

W: And he did it in front of at least twenty thousand people. 而且是在至少兩萬人面前。

M: What? That's unbelievable! 什麼？真不敢相信！

W: It was a big surprise. 真的是個大驚喜。

M: How did he manage to do that? 他怎麼做到的？

W: He made a public announcement before the soccer match kicked off. 他在足球比賽開始之前廣播的。

M: Wow! Maybe I should learn a trick or two from him. 哇！或許我應該跟他學一兩招。

W: You should. It's about time. 是啊。差不多是時候了。

Q: What does the man imply?
男子暗示什麼？

A. He will propose to the woman, too. A. 他也會跟這位女子求婚。
B. He will borrow Henry's idea. B. 他會借用 Henry 的點子。
C. He will hire twenty thousand people. C. 他會雇用兩萬人。
D. He will watch a soccer match live. D. 他會看足球比賽的直播。

詳解 **答案：B**

兩人在討論 Henry 向女子求婚（proposed）的事，而男子最後說 I should learn a trick or two from him（我應該跟他學一兩招），表示可能會模仿 Henry 的求婚方法，B 是合理的答案。模仿 Henry 的作法，並不是指和同一個人求婚，所以 A 不對。Henry 是跟看足球的觀眾宣告自己的求婚，並不是雇用了那兩萬人，所以 C 不對。

|單字片語| **smile from ear to ear** 笑得嘴角上揚，好像可以碰到耳朵一樣 / **kick off** （足球比賽）開球

Q18

W: You've got to read this. Three young adults committed suicide together. 你一定要讀這個。有三名青少年集體自殺。

M: That's horrible. How could they do such a thing!
真恐怖。他們怎麼可以這樣做呢！

W: It's always the same old story. It's either out of love, work, or money.
老是一樣的，不是因為愛情的話，就是因為工作或金錢。

M: No matter what problems they faced, that is something really irresponsible to do. 不管他們面對的是什問題，這樣真的很不負責任。

W: We should educate young people on the value of life and strengthen their will to overcome obstacles in life. 我們應該教育年輕人生命的價值，並且增強他們克服生命中的阻礙的意志力。

Q: What is the woman's view on young people?
女子對於年輕人的看法是什麼？

A. They should be taught certain things.	A. 他們應該被教育某些事情。
B. They should be wise about money.	B. 他們應該對於金錢有智慧。
C. They should not be held responsible.	C. 他們不應該被認為負有責任。
D. They should not be lazy.	D. 他們不應該懶惰。

詳解 **答案：A**

女子最後說應該 educate（教育）年輕人 the value of life（生命的價值），所以 A. They should be taught...（他們應該被教導…）是正確答案。其他選項無法對應對話中的內容。

|單字片語| **commit suicide** 自殺 / **irresponsible** [ˌɪrɪˋspɑnsəbḷ] 不負責任的 / **will** [wɪl] n. 意志 / **obstacle** [ˋɑbstəkḷ] n. 障礙 / **hold someone responsible** 認為某人負有責任

Q19

M: Can you turn that thing off during meal time?
你吃飯的時候可以把那東西關掉嗎？

W: I'm just trying to kill time. 我只是想要殺時間。

M: That's not the point. You are wasting time on those mindless and useless games. 那不是重點。你是在浪費時間玩沒腦又沒用的遊戲。

W: What do you expect me to do when I wait for the food to be served? Stare blankly at other people's food?
你希望我等上菜的時候幹嘛呢？呆呆盯著別人的食物看嗎？

M: You could have done something meaningful. Like discussing your future with me.
你可以做點有意義的事啊。例如跟我討論你的未來之類的。

Q: Why is the man upset with the woman?
男子為什麼對女子生氣？

A. She was talking with her mouth full. A. 她嘴裡邊吃東西邊講話。
B. She was staring at others. B. 她盯著別人看。
C. She was doing something unproductive. C. 她在做沒有生產力的事情。
D. She was too worried about her future. D. 她太擔心自己的未來。

詳解

答案：C

男子一開始對女子說 Can you turn that thing off（你可以把那東西關掉嗎），又說 You are wasting time on those mindless and useless games（你在浪費時間玩不動腦又沒用的遊戲），可能是要制止她玩手機或平板電腦遊戲，所以 C 是正確答案，unproductive（沒有生產力的）呼應對話中的 useless（沒有用的）。

|單字片語| **mindless** [ˋmaɪndlɪs] adj. 不需要動腦筋的 / **stare** [stɛr] v. 盯，凝視 / **blankly** [ˋblæŋklɪ] adv. 茫然地 / **unproductive** [ˌʌnprəˋdʌktɪv] 非生產性的，徒勞的

Questions 20-21

Questions number 20 and 21 are based on the following conversation.

W: Hi Dad, are you free to speak right now? 嗨，爸，你現在有空講話嗎？

M: Yes, what's wrong, honey? Where are you?
嗯，親愛的，怎麼了？你在哪裡？

W: I'm at a bar. I'm so upset. Everything went wrong today.
我在酒吧。我很生氣。今天一切都很糟糕。

M: Are you still going to the mall then? Aren't Tom and the kids waiting for you? 那你還要去購物中心嗎？湯姆和孩子們不是在等你嗎？

W: No, I canceled the plan. I had such a difficult day. Teaching teenagers is so hard. They're so noisy.
沒有，我取消了計畫。我今天過得很辛苦。教青少年好困難。他們好吵。

M: Can you speak up? I cannot hear you well.
你可以大聲一點嗎？我聽不太清楚。

W: Teenagers are noisy, I said. I know everyone is waiting for me, but I really want to be by myself right now. 我說青少年很吵。我知道每個人都在等我，但我現在真的想要自己一個人。

M: What about consulting Andrea? She's well-experienced.
請教安潔雅怎麼樣？她很有經驗。

W: Oh, yeah, I'll call her after we hang up.
噢，對耶，掛電話之後我會打給她。

|單字片語| **consult** [kən`sʌlt] v. 諮詢，和…商量 / **experienced** [ɪk`spɪrɪənst] adj. 有經驗的

Q20

Why does the woman call the man?
女子為什麼打電話給男子？

A. To invite him for a drink.
B. To cancel a plan with her family.
C. To complain about her job.
D. To show that she is an independent woman.

A. 為了邀請他喝一杯。
B. 為了取消和家人的計畫。
C. 為了抱怨她的工作。
D. 為了表現自己是獨立的女性。

詳解

答案：C

女子打電話給男子，說自己因為過了糟糕的一天而待在酒吧，之後提到是因為教很吵鬧的青少年所以很辛苦，所以她打這通電話主要是為了抱怨自己的工作，C 是正確答案。

Q21

Who might the woman be?
女子可能是什麼人？

A. A bartender.
B. A salesperson.
C. A high school teacher.
D. A consultant.

A. 調酒師。
B. 售貨員。
C. 中學老師。
D. 顧問。

詳解

答案：C

女子在對話中間說 Teaching teenagers is so hard.（教青少年好困難），可知她的工作應該是教青少年的老師，所以 C 是正確答案。A 和 D 是試圖利用對話中出現的 bar、consult 造成混淆的錯誤選項。

|單字片語| **bartender** [`bɑr͵tɛndɚ] n. 調酒師 / **salesperson** [`selz͵pɝsən] n. 銷售員，店員 / **consultant** [kən`sʌltənt] n. 顧問

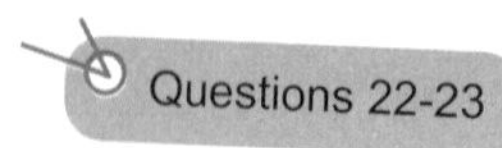

Questions 22-23

Questions number 22 and 23 are based on the following conversation.

W: Welcome to *The Helen Show*, I'm your host Helen DeAngelo, and today's guest is David Kovacs. Hello, David.
歡迎來到《海倫秀》，我是你的主持人海倫．迪安傑羅，今天的來賓是大衛．科瓦克斯。哈囉，大衛。

M: Hi, I'm David Kovacs. I'm from Hungary, and I like to write about the amazing food I've tasted during my journeys. It is my passion.
嗨，我是大衛．科瓦克斯。我來自匈牙利，我喜歡寫自己在旅程中品嚐過的驚人美食。那是我的愛好。

W: You're famous for being a food critic. Is that your main source of income? 你因為美食評論家的身分而知名。那是你的主要收入來源嗎？

M: Actually, I'm employed by a public relations company, but I hope to one day work for the *Michelin Guide*. 事實上，我受雇於一間公關公司，但我希望有一天能為米其林指南工作。

W: I know that you also make YouTube videos. How's that going?
我知道你也製作 YouTube 影片。進展得怎麼樣？

M: It's going extremely well, and I have a lot of followers. Even though the income is not enough to cover my rent, I'm still happy that I can help more people learn about food. 非常順利，我也有很多追蹤者。儘管收入不夠支付我的房租，我還是很高興能幫助更多人了解食物。

|單字片語| **food critic** 美食評論家 / **public relations** 公共關係，公關

Q22

What kind of program is *The Helen Show*?
《海倫秀》是什麼樣的節目？

A. A talk show.	A. 談話性節目。
B. A cooking show.	B. 烹飪節目。
C. A variety show.	C. 綜藝節目。
D. An educational show.	D. 教育性節目。

詳解

答案：A

我們聽到的內容主要是關於男子工作與嗜好方面的訪談，所以 A 是最恰當的答案。對話中並沒有出現關於其他三個選項的具體內容。

Q23

What most likely does the man work full-time as?
男子最有可能以什麼作為正職工作？

A. A food critic. A. 美食評論家。
B. A travel writer. B. 旅遊作家。
C. A public relations specialist. C. 公關專家。
D. A YouTuber. D. YouTuber。

詳解 **答案：C**

雖然男子一直在談自己對於食物方面的興趣，但對於主持人的問題 Is that your main source of income?（那是你主要的收入來源嗎？），他回答 I'm employed by a public relations company（我受雇於一間公關公司），間接表示美食評論並不是他的正職，C 才是正確答案。

|單字片語| **specialist** [ˋspɛʃəlɪst] n. 專家

For question number 24, please look at the schedule.

M: Hey, Sandy! Looks like you didn't sleep well last night. What's the matter? 嘿，珊蒂！你看起來昨晚沒睡好。怎麼回事？

W: Yesterday I had a call with Andrea. We spoke for four hours. 昨天我和安潔雅打了電話。我們講了四小時。

M: That's crazy! You must've had a great time talking with her. By the way, is your daughter alright? 真瘋狂！你和她聊天一定很愉快。對了，你的女兒還好嗎？

W: Yeah, but Claudia says she's exhausted today, so I'm considering cancelling her piano class tonight. How have you been? 還好，但克勞蒂亞說她今天筋疲力盡了，所以我在考慮取消她今晚的鋼琴課。你過得怎樣？

M: Great! What's your schedule like tomorrow? Let's have lunch! 很好！你明天的行程怎樣？我們吃午餐吧！

W: Tomorrow Claudia and I will meet up with some of my friends and their kids. We'll ride some rides there. 明天克勞蒂亞和我會和一些朋友以及他們的小孩見面。我們會在那裡搭乘遊樂設施。

M: You mean the newly opened Lala Adventure Island? Can my family join you? 你是說新開的拉拉冒險島嗎？我們一家可以加入你們嗎？

W: Of course! I believe you'll also enjoy the dance show there. 當然！我相信你們也會很喜歡那裡的舞蹈表演。

Weekly Planner 週計畫表	
Monday 星期一	Call Andrea 打電話給安潔雅
Tuesday 星期二	Claudia's piano class 克勞蒂亞的鋼琴課
Wednesday 星期三	Visit amusement park with friends 和朋友一起拜訪遊樂園 Call Andrea 打電話給安潔雅
Thursday 星期四	Claudia's piano class 克勞蒂亞的鋼琴課
Friday 星期五	Take a boat ride with friends 和朋友搭船

|單字片語| **ride** [raɪd] n. 遊樂園中可搭乘的設施 / **amusement park** 遊樂園

Q: Look at the schedule. What day is today?
請看行程表。今天是星期幾？

A. Monday. A. 星期一。
B. Tuesday. B. 星期二。
C. Wednesday. C. 星期三。
D. Thursday. D. 星期四。

詳解

答案：B

女子提到 Yesterday I had a call with Andrea（昨天我和安潔雅打了電話）、her piano class tonight（她〔女子的女兒〕今晚的鋼琴課），對照表格內容，可知今天可能是星期二或星期四。之後女子又提到 Tomorrow Claudia and I will meet up with some of my friends and their kids（明天克勞蒂亞和我會和一些朋友以及他們的小孩見面），以及那裡的 rides（遊樂設施）、dance show（舞蹈表演），可知她明天要去的地方是遊樂園，所以 B 是正確答案。

Q25

For question number 25, please look at the table.

W: Hey, Ben. Which second foreign language course are you going to take? You know it's required for all students.
嘿，班。你要修哪一門第二外語課？你知道所有學生都必須要修的。

M: I haven't decided yet. Maybe I'll go for one of the more popular languages. I want to make new friends, so it'll be better if there are more classmates with me. 我還沒決定。或許我會選比較受歡迎的語言。我想要交新朋友，所以如果有比較多同學跟我一起會比較好。

W: But the popular ones have lower ratings, which means the students don't like the courses very much. I think I won't follow the crowd.
但受歡迎的課評價比較低，意味著學生不是很喜歡那些課。我想我不會從眾。

M: You have a point there. So which one will you pick?
你說的有道理。所以你會選哪個？

W: Well, I guess I'll choose that Asian language. I'm fond of the pop music there, and I want to know what the lyrics mean. Besides, the course has a very high rating. 嗯，我猜我會選那個亞洲語言。我很喜歡那裡的流行音樂，也想要知道歌詞是什麼意思。而且，那門課的評價很高。

|單字片語| **go for** 選擇 / **rating** [ˋretɪŋ] n. 評價，評分 / **follow the crowd** 從眾（跟大部分的人做同樣的事） / **lyrics** [ˋlɪrɪks] n. 歌詞

Second Foreign Language Courses 第二外語課程		
Course 課程	Percentage of Students 學生百分比	Student Rating 學生評價
Spanish 西班牙語	15%	8.67
French 法語	36%	7.85
Japanese 日語	41%	8.21
Korean 韓語	8%	9.10

Q: According to the conversation, which course will the woman most likely choose?
根據這段對話，女子最有可能選哪個課程？

A. Spanish.
B. French.
C. Japanese.
D. Korean.

A. 西班牙語。
B. 法語。
C. 日語
D. 韓語。

詳解

答案：D

在聽題目的時候，要注意詢問的是誰想選的課。關於女子的意見，她先是提到 the popular ones have lower ratings（受歡迎的課評價比較低），而且 I won't follow the crowd（我不會從眾），所以她應該會選擇學生百分比較低的課程。然後她又說 I'll choose that Asian language（我會選那個亞洲語言），以及 the course has a very high rating（那門課的評價很高），所以她想選擇的是屬於亞洲語言而且評價最高的 Korean（韓語），D 是正確答案。

第三部分 / 短篇獨白

Questions 26-27

Questions number 26 to 27 are based on the following announcement.

Good afternoon passengers. This is your captain speaking. Welcome on board Rightwing Flight 86A. We are currently flying at an altitude of 33,000 feet at an airspeed of 400 miles per hour. The time is exactly 1:00 pm. The weather looks good, and we are expecting to land in London approximately fifteen minutes ahead of the scheduled time originally set at half past six. The weather in London is clear and sunny, with a high of 25 degrees today. If the weather cooperates, we should get a great view of the city as we descend. The cabin crew will be coming around in about twenty minutes' time to offer you a light snack and beverage. I'll talk to you again before we reach our destination. Until then, sit back, relax, and enjoy the rest of the flight.

各位乘客午安。我是機長。歡迎搭乘 Rightwing 航空 86A 班機。我們目前正以 33,000 英尺的高度、每小時 400 英里的空速飛行。現在時間是下午 1 點整。天氣看起來很好，我們預計比原定的 6 點半大約提早 15 分鐘降落倫敦。倫敦天氣晴朗，今天高溫 25 度。如果天氣配合的話，我們應該可以在下降時把倫敦市區看得很清楚。空服組員大約 20 分鐘後會提供簡單的食物和飲料。我會在抵達目的地之前再次廣播。在那之前，請坐好、放鬆，並且享受接下來的旅程。

|單字片語| **captain** [ˋkæptɪn] n. 飛機機長 / **on board** 在船上，在飛機上 / **altitude** [ˋæltəˏtjud] n. 海拔高度 / **airspeed** [ˋɛrspid] n. 空速 / **cooperate** [koˋɑpəˏret] v. 合作，配合 / **descend** [dɪˋsɛnd] v. 下降 / **cabin crew** 機艙全體服務人員 / **beverage** [ˋbɛvərɪdʒ] n. 飲料 / **destination** [ˏdɛstəˋneʃən] n. 目的地

Q26

When will the plane touch down in England?
飛機什麼時候會降落英格蘭？

A. Exactly one o'clock.	A. 1 點整。
B. A quarter after six.	B. 6 點 15 分。
C. A quarter to six.	C. 5 點 45 分。
D. Half past six.	D. 6 點半。

第1回 第2回 第3回 第4回 第5回 第6回

詳解

答案：B

從選項可以得知，要注意關於時間的敘述，並且記錄說話者提到的重要時間。現在時間是一點整，預計可以比原本預定的 6 點半早 15 分鐘（fifteen minutes ahead of the scheduled time originally set at half past six）在倫敦降落。題目中的 touch down in England（在英格蘭降落）對應說話者所說的 land in London（在倫敦降落），所以答案是 6 點半的 15 分鐘之前，也就是 B. 6 點 15 分。

|單字片語| **touch down** 著陸，降落

Q27

What is dependent on the weather condition?
什麼事情取決於天氣狀況？

A. Safety of the crew.
B. Behavior of the passengers.
C. Availability of beverage.
D. Visibility of the city.

A. 機組人員的安全。
B. 乘客的行為。
C. 是否有飲料。
D. 城市的可見度。

詳解

答案：D

提到 weather 的部分是 If the weather cooperates, we should get a great view of the city（如果天氣配合的話，我們應該可以在下降時把倫敦市區看得很清楚），答案是 D. Visibility of the city（城市的可見度）。visibility（可見度）對應說話者所說的 a great view（很好的眺望景色）。

|單字片語| **dependent** [dɪˋpɛndənt] adj. 依靠的，依賴的，取決於什麼的 / **behavior** [bɪˋhevjɚ] n. 行為 / **availability** [əˌveləˋbɪlətɪ] n. 可得性 / **visibility** [ˌvɪzəˋbɪlətɪ] n. 可見度

Questions 28-30

Questions number 28 to 30 are based on the following speech.

Today I feel nervous again, pretty much the same emotions I felt when I first transferred here three years ago. If my classmates remember, I used to stand out like a sore thumb. After all, I joined school in the middle of the academic year. I thought it would take much longer for me to be accepted, but thanks to my gracious classmates, who made life so simple for me, I was able to adapt and blend in after a month or two. Of course, detention class from Ms. Collins helped. Spending time rearranging books in the library is a great way to make friends. Try it out sometime. But jokes apart, today I leave this school a much more confident person than I previously was.

今天我再次感到緊張，就跟我三年前剛轉學到這裡的心情差不多。如果我的同學記得的話，我以前顯得很突兀。畢竟我是在學年中間進入學校的。我以為需要花更長的時間讓別人接受我，但多虧了我親切的同學們，他們讓我的生活簡單容易，我才能在一兩個月之後適應並且融入。當然，Collins 老師的放學後留校輔導也很有幫助。花時間在圖書館整理書，是交朋友的好方法。改天你也試試看吧。不開玩笑了，今天離開這所學校的我，比以前的我有自信得多。

|單字片語| **transfer** [træns`fɝ] v. 轉移；轉學 / **stand/stick out like a sore thumb** 「像很痛的姆指一樣突出」→和其他人明顯不同 / **academic year** 學年 / **gracious** [`greʃəs] adj. 親切的，仁慈的 / **blend in** 融入 / **detention** [dɪ`tɛnʃən] n. 拘留；課後留校 / **rearrange** [ˌriə`rendʒ] v. 重新排列，重新整理

Q28

What was the speaker's problem in school initially?
說話者一開始在學校的問題是什麼？

A. He felt out of place.	A. 他覺得格格不入。
B. He was expelled.	B. 他被退學了。
C. He hated detention class.	C. 他討厭放學後的留校輔導。
D. He couldn't keep up with the rest.	D. 他跟不上其他人。

詳解 **答案：A**

題目的關鍵字是 initially（一開始），對應說話者在開頭說到的 when I first transferred here...（當我一開始轉學到這裡的時候），而接下來的句子就提到 I used to stand out like a sore thumb（我當時顯得很突兀）。和 stand out like a sore thumb 相近的說法是 out of place（不適合環境的，格格不入的），所以 A 是正確答案。這是需要知道慣用語才能解答的題目，不過也有可能從 out 這個字猜到兩種表達方式之間的關聯。

|單字片語| **out of place** 不在正確的位置，不適合周遭情況的 / **expel** [ɪk`spɛl] 驅逐，開除 / **keep up with** 跟上…

Q29

In what way was the speaker being humorous?
說話者用什麼方式表現幽默？

A. He transferred his emotions to the school. A. 他把情緒轉移到學校。
B. He stood out as an individual. B. 他表現獨立。
C. He made fun of the punishment he received. C. 他自嘲他受到的處罰。
D. He sounded more confident than he actually was. D. 他聽起來比實際上更有自信。

詳解

答案：C

接近結尾的部分說 jokes apart（不開玩笑了，認真說），表示前面所說的話是想表現幽默。前面的部分說 detention class... helped. Spending time rearranging books in the library is a great way to make friends.（留校…很有幫助。花時間在圖書館整理書，是交朋友的好方法）。detention 是課後把學生留在學校的處罰，但說話者卻說這樣可以交朋友，所以 C. He made fun of the punishment he received（他自嘲他受到的處罰）是正確答案。

|單字片語| **humorous** [ˋhjumərəs] adj. 幽默的 / **individual** [ˏɪndəˋvɪdʒʊəl] n. （獨立的）個人 / **make fun of** 嘲笑… / **punishment** [ˋpʌnɪʃmənt] n. 處罰

Q30

According to the speech, what can we tell about the speaker?
根據這段演說，關於說話者我們可以知道什麼？

A. He is skeptical about the school system. A. 他懷疑學校體系。
B. He is concerned about school bullying. B. 他擔心校園霸淩。
C. He is confident that he will be transferred soon. C. 他相信自己很快會被轉學。
D. He is grateful that he has become a better person. D. 他感謝自己成為了更好的人。

詳解

答案：D

說話者提到了一開始不適應、親切的同學、被留校的經驗，最後說 today I leave this school a much more confident person than I previously was（今天離開這所學校的我，比以前的我有自信得多），暗示這些經歷提升了自己，所以 D 是正確答案。說話者並沒有批評學校，所以 A 不對。B 在談話中沒有提到。today I leave this school 表示今天要離開學校，所以他可能是在畢業典禮上發表演說；就算他真的是因為轉學而離校，離開學校也是已經確定的事情，所以 C. He is confident that he will...（他相信自己將會…）這種表示推測的說法不是適當的答案。

|單字片語| **skeptical** [ˋskɛptɪkl̩] adj. 懷疑的，懷疑論的 / **concerned** [kənˋsɝnd] adj. 擔心的 / **bullying** [ˋbʊlɪŋ] n. 霸凌行為 / **grateful** [ˋgretfəl] adj. 感謝的

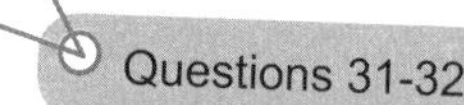

Questions number 31 to 32 are based on the following introduction.

Vatican City is an inland sovereign surrounded by Rome and Italy. It is the smallest independent state in the world in terms of land size and population. The Vatican City is itself of great cultural significance. Buildings such as St. Peter's Basilica and the Sistine Chapel are known to house some of the most beautiful art in the world. The Vatican Library and the collections of the Vatican Museums are of the highest historical, scientific, and cultural importance. The permanent population of the Vatican City is mainly male, although two orders of nuns live in the Vatican. Many workers in the Vatican City live outside its walls, including the Swiss Guard and embassy personnel. Millions of tourists flock to this tiny city every year, making it the most visited European city.

梵蒂岡是被羅馬城和義大利圍繞的內陸主權國家。以土地面積和人口數而言，它是世界上最小的獨立國家。梵蒂岡本身有很重要的文化意義。諸如聖彼得大教堂及西斯廷禮拜堂等建築物，以擁有世界上最美的藝術作品而聞名。梵蒂岡圖書館和梵蒂岡博物館的收藏，具有最高的歷史、科學及文化重要性。梵蒂岡的固定人口主要為男性，雖然也有兩個修女團住在梵蒂岡。許多梵蒂岡的工作者住在它的圍牆外，包括瑞士近衛隊和大使館人員。每年都有數百萬名觀光客蜂湧前往這座小城市，使它成為最多人拜訪的歐洲城市。

|單字片語| **inland** [ˋɪnlənd] adj. 內陸的 / **sovereign** [ˋsɑvrɪn] n. 主權國家 / **state** [stet] n. 國家；（美國）州 / **in terms of** 就…方面來說 / **population** [ˌpɑpjəˋleʃən] n. 人口 / **significance** [sɪgˋnɪfəkəns] n. 重要性，意義 / **house** [haʊs] v. （建築物）收藏 / **permanent** [ˋpɝmənənt] adj. 永久的，固定性的 / **order** [ˋɔrdɚ] n. 教團 / **nun** [nʌn] n. 修女 / **embassy** [ˋɛmbəsɪ] n. 大使館 / **personnel** [ˌpɝsn̩ˋɛl] n. 人員，員工 / **flock** [flɑk] v. 群聚，簇擁

Q31

What is true about the Vatican City?
關於梵蒂岡，何者正確？

A. It is governed by Rome, Italy.
B. It is a sovereign state.
C. It is home to mostly women.
D. It is the largest city in Europe.

A. 它由義大利的羅馬城管轄。
B. 它是主權國家。
C. 它的居民大部分是女人。
D. 它是歐洲最大的城市。

詳解

答案：B

要對照每個選項是否正確的題目並不容易，但對於這一題來說，只要聽到第一句話 Vatican City is an inland sovereign（梵蒂岡是一個內陸主權國家），就可以選出正確答案 B。sovereign 在談話中是當名詞使用，但在選項中是形容詞，表示「有獨立主權的」。從 Vatican City is an inland sovereign 這句話也可以知道 A 是錯的。說話者提到 The permanent population of the Vatican City is mainly male（梵蒂岡的固定人口主要為男性），所以 C 是錯的。D 在談話中沒有提到，但最後一句話的 this tiny city（這個小城市）顯示它應該不會是歐洲最大的城市。

|單字片語| **govern** [ˋgʌvɚn] v. 統治，治理 / **sovereign** [ˋsɑvrɪn] adj. 有獨立主權的

Q32

Why is the Vatican City of great significance?
為什麼梵蒂岡很重要？

A. It is a financial center.
B. It is a cultural hub.
C. It is a military stronghold.
D. It is an industrial region.

A. 它是金融中心。
B. 它是文化中樞。
C. 它是軍事強權。
D. 它是工業地區。

詳解

答案：B

The Vatican City is itself of great cultural significance（梵蒂岡本身有很重要的文化意義）已經提到它的文化意義，後面的 The Vatican Library and the collections of the Vatican Museums are of the highest historical, scientific, and cultural importance（梵蒂岡圖書館和梵蒂岡博物館的收藏，具有最高的歷史、科學及文化重要性）也提到文化方面的重要性，所以 B 是正確答案。其他選項完全沒有提到。

|單字片語| **stronghold** [ˋstrɔŋˏhold] 堡壘；勢力強大的地方

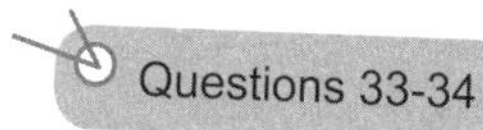

Questions number 33 to 34 are based on the following talk.

Singapore is a multiracial society, which is predominantly Chinese. As a result of racial conflicts between the Chinese and the Malays back in the 1950s, the government took several drastic measures to ensure that such a tragedy would not repeat itself. First, English was made the first language in order to eliminate the linguistic barrier, which is a principle cause of division among the population. Second, the government implemented a multi-racial housing program, allowing people of different ethnic groups to mix together within a certain community. Third, with the exception of a few Chinese schools, the majority of schools are multi-racial. This encourages students to interact with one another from a young age so that they learn to tolerate differences and live in harmony.

新加坡是多種族的社會，其中主要是華人。由於 1950 年代華人與馬來人之間的種族衝突，政府採取了幾個極端的手段，確保這樣的悲劇不再發生。首先，政府將英語定為第一語言，以減少語言障礙，而語言障礙是居民分裂的主要原因。第二，政府實施了多種族住宅計畫，使不同種族的人能夠在單一社區裡混居。第三，除了一些華人學校以外，大部分的學校都是多種族的。這樣能鼓勵學生從年輕時就開始和彼此互動，讓他們學習包容差異，並且和諧地生活。

|單字片語| **multiracial** [`mʌltɪ`reʃəl] adj. 多種族的 / **predominantly** [prɪ`dɑmɪnəntlɪ] adv. 佔主導地位地 / **conflict** [`kɑnflɪkt] n. 衝突 / **drastic** [`dræstɪk] adj. 激烈的 / **measure** [`mɛʒɚ] n. 措施 / **tragedy** [`trædʒədɪ] n. 悲劇 / **repeat** [rɪ`pit] v. 重複 / **eliminate** [ɪ`lɪmə͵net] v. 排除，消除 / **linguistic** [lɪŋ`gwɪstɪk] adj. 語言的 / **barrier** [`bærɪr] n. 障礙，阻礙 / **division** [də`vɪʒən] n. 分開，分裂 / **population** [͵pɑpjə`leʃən] n. 人口 / **implement** [`ɪmplə͵mɛnt] v. 實施 / **housing** [`haʊzɪŋ] n. 住房供給 / **ethnic** [`ɛθnɪk] adj. 種族上的 / **community** [kə`mjunətɪ] n. 社區，社會 / **with the exception of** 除了…以外 / **majority** [mə`dʒɔrətɪ] n. 多數，大多數 / **interact** [͵ɪntə`rækt] v. 互動 / **tolerate** [`tɑlə͵ret] v. 容忍 / **harmony** [`hɑrmənɪ] n. 和諧

Q33

Which of the following is a measure taken in Singapore? 以下何者是新加坡採取的措施？

A. Separating different racial groups into areas. A. 將不同種族族群分到不同的區域。
B. Putting students of different ethnic backgrounds into different schools. B. 將不同種族背景的學生分到不同的學校。
C. Deciding a common language among different races. C. 決定不同種族之間的共通語言。
D. Allowing a certain level of racial discrimination. D. 允許一定程度的種族歧視。

詳解 答案：C

這一題要對照談話內容，看哪個選項正確。... allowing people of different ethnic groups to mix together within a certain community（…使不同種族的人能夠在單一社區裡混居）提到前述的政策讓不同種族的人能夠混合，與 A 的敘述不符。the majority of schools are multi-racial（大部分的學校是多種族的）顯示 B 是錯的。English was made the first language in order to eliminate the linguistic barrier（英語被定為第一語言，以減少語言障礙）顯示政府決定讓不同的種族用英語溝通，所以 C 是正確答案。D 在談話中沒有提到。

|單字片語| **discrimination** [dɪˌskrɪməˋneʃən] n. 差別待遇，歧視

Q34

What is the main subject of this talk? 這段談話的主題是什麼？

A. Social policies to reduce racial conflicts. A. 減少種族衝突的社會政策。
B. The school system in Singapore. B. 新加坡的學校系統。
C. How history repeats itself. C. 歷史如何重覆。
D. The absence of human rights. D. 人權的缺乏。

詳解 答案：A

第二句話提到，As a result of racial conflicts... the government took several drastic measures to ensure that such a tragedy will not repeat itself（由於種族衝突，政府採取了幾個極端的手段，確保這樣的悲劇不再發生），接下來描述了其中三項政策，所以 A 是最適當的答案。

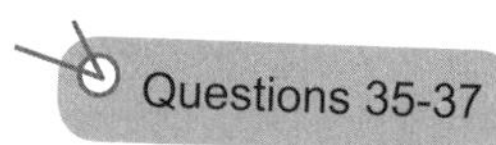

For questions number 35 to 37, please look at the chart.

Good morning, everyone. Recently, I noticed that our company's overhead expenses are rising, and we need to cut them in order to increase our profits. As you can see in the chart, over half of the expenses are related to rent and marketing. Unfortunately, our rent is fixed, and we need a lot of marketing to attract customers, so there is no way they can be cut. You may think that making less calls or using less paper can be helpful, but they only make up a fraction of our expenses. In fact, about one fifth is spent on electricity and tap water, and once in a while I find that the air conditioner is left on over the weekend. I hope you'll help save on energy and not let such a thing happen again.

大家早安。最近，我注意到我們公司的經常開支費用正在上升，而我們需要減少它們來增加利潤。大家在圖表中可以看到，超過一半的費用與房租和行銷相關。遺憾的是，我們的房租是固定的，而我們需要許多行銷來吸引顧客，所以它們不可能被減少。你們可能認為少打電話或少用紙張可能有幫助，但它們只佔我們支出的一小部分。事實上，大約五分之一是花在電和自來水上，而且我偶爾會發現空調在週末被開著沒關掉。我希望你們會幫忙節約用電，並且不要讓這樣的事情再度發生。

|單字片語| **overhead expense** 經常開支費用（並非直接和公司產品、服務、人力相關的經常性支出）/ **marketing** [`mɑrkɪtɪŋ] n. 行銷 / **fraction** [`frækʃən] n. 微小的部分 / **tap water** 自來水

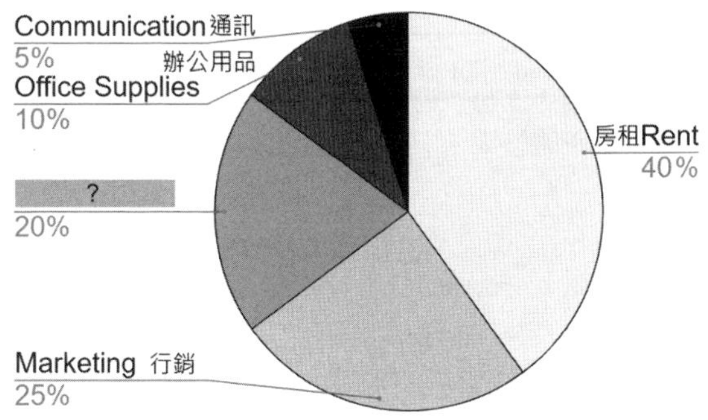

Q35

What is the main subject of this talk?
這段談話的主題是什麼？

A. Increasing sales volume. A. 增加銷售量。
B. Being more eco-friendly. B. 變得更環保。
C. Evaluating employees' performance. C. 評價員工的表現。
D. Saving money on business operations. D. 在企業營運方面省錢。

詳解

答案：D

說話者一開始說，他注意到公司的 overhead expenses（經常開支費用）在上升，並且說 we need to cut them（我們需要減少它們），之後都在討論可以節省費用的方法，所以 D 是正確答案。

Q36

What kind of expense is related to the company's sales performance?
哪一種費用和這家公司的銷售業績有關？

A. Communication. A. 通訊。
B. Office supplies. B. 辦公用品。
C. Marketing. C. 行銷。
D. Rent. D. 房租。

詳解

答案：C

說話者提到 we need a lot of marketing to attract customers（我們需要許多行銷來吸引顧客），表示多投入行銷費用，顧客就會增加，而顧客增加也會使業績增加，所以 C 是正確答案。

Q37

Based on the talk, what should be written in the shaded area?
根據這段談話，灰底部分應該填入什麼？

A. Utilities. A. 公用事業。
B. Insurance. B. 保險。
C. Maintenance. C. 維護保養。
D. Accounting. D. 會計。

詳解 答案：A

說話者提到 about one fifth is spent on electricity and tap water（大約五分之一是花在電和自來水上），圖表中沒有名稱的項目正好就佔 20%，所以 A 是正確答案。utilities 是指公用事業服務，也就是水、電、天然氣等等的總稱。

Questions 38-40

For questions number 38 to 40, please look at the table.

I'm worried about my son. He's trying to apply to universities, and he wants to go to an ivy league school, but his scores aren't very high. The universities are famous for their low acceptance rates, so I don't expect he will succeed. That said, he may have a better chance of being admitted if he applies to Yale or Columbia. He's interested in sociology, so I think he should choose the university which is more famous for it. Even though Harvard is the most prestigious, especially its medical school, I don't think he even stands a chance. Besides, he's not good at biology.

我很擔心我的兒子。他正在試著申請大學，而他想要上常春藤聯盟的學校，但他的分數不是很高。那些大學以很低的接受入學率聞名，所以我不期望他會成功。話雖如此，如果他申請耶魯或哥倫比亞大學的話，他可能會有比較高的機率被錄取。他對社會學有興趣，所以我認為他應該選擇這方面比較有名的大學。儘管哈佛大學是最有名望的，尤其是醫學院，但我認為他根本沒有機會。而且，他的生物學不好。

|單字片語| **ivy league** 常春藤聯盟（美國東北部八所大學的聯盟）/ **sociology** [ˌsoʃɪˋɑlədʒɪ] **n.** 社會學 / **prestigious** [prɛsˋtɪdʒɪəs] **adj.** 有名望的 / **medical school** 醫學院

University 大學	Acceptance Rate 接受入學率	Popular Majors 熱門主修
Harvard 哈佛	4.9%	?, business ?、商業
Yale 耶魯	6.5%	Social sciences, biological sciences 社會科學、生物科學
Princeton 普林斯頓	5.5%	Social sciences, engineering 社會科學、工程
Columbia 哥倫比亞	6.3%	Business, law, engineering 商業、法律、工程

Q38

What stage of the application process is the speaker's son in?
說話者的兒子在申請過程的哪個階段？

A. He is preparing to apply. A. 他正在準備申請。
B. He has sent his applications. B. 他已經寄出申請書。
C. He is going to be interviewed. C. 他將要接受面試。
D. He is waiting for the results. D. 他正在等候結果。

詳解 **答案：A**

說話者說 He's trying to apply to universities（他正在試著申請大學），然後討論兒子可以申請的大學，所以 A 是正確答案。

Q39

Which of the universities will the speaker most likely suggest his son to apply to?
說話者最有可能建議他的兒子申請哪一所大學？

A. Harvard.	A. 哈佛。
B. Yale.	B. 耶魯。
C. Princeton.	C. 普林斯頓。
D. Columbia.	D. 哥倫比亞。

詳解

答案：B

說話者先是提到接受入學率，並且說 he may have a better chance... if he applies to Yale or Columbia（如果他申請耶魯或哥倫比亞大學的話，他可能會有比較高的機率），然後又說 He's interested in sociology（他對社會學有興趣）。在兩所學校之中，「熱門主修」欄目有 social sciences（社會科學）的是耶魯大學，所以 B 是正確答案。

補充說明

social sciences 的範圍可大可小，狹義的範圍包括 politics（政治學）、economics（經濟學）、sociology（社會學），比較廣義的範圍則可包括 psychology（心理學）、anthropology（人類學）、archaeology（考古學）、geography（地理學）等等。

Q40

Based on the talk, what should be written in the shaded area?
根據這段談話，灰底部分應該填入什麼？

A. Education.	A. 教育。
B. Literature.	B. 文學。
C. Chemistry.	C. 化學。
D. Medicine.	D. 醫學。

詳解

答案：D

關於哈佛大學，說話者提到 Harvard is the most prestigious, especially its medical school（哈佛大學是最有名望的，尤其是醫學院），所以 D 是正確答案。

第一部分 句子填空

Q1

The company allocates a significant amount of resources to research and development to gain a _______ edge.

這家公司分配相當多的資源到研究和開發方面，以獲得競爭優勢。

A. excessive　B. competitive　C. quantitative　D. impulsive

詳解　答案：B

edge 的基本意義是「邊緣」，但在關於企業經營的文章中使用這個字時，經常表示「優勢」的意思。這家公司分配資源到研究和開發方面，能增進自己的實力，所以能修飾 edge，表示「競爭優勢」的 B 是正確答案。

補充說明

edge 也有「刀鋒」的意思，a double-edged sword 是「雙刃劍」。competitive 是從動詞 compete（競爭）衍生的字，competition 表示「競賽」或「比賽」。

|單字片語| **allocate** [ˋæləˏket] v. 分配 / **significant** [sɪgˋnɪfəkənt] adj. 相當大的，相當多的 / **resources** [rɪˋsorsɪz] n. 資源 / **research and development** 研究與開發，研發 / **excessive** [ɪkˋsɛsɪv] adj. 過度的 / **competitive** [kəmˋpɛtətɪv] adj. 競爭的，競爭性的，有競爭力的 / **quantitative** [ˋkwɑntəˏtetɪv] adj. 量的，量化的 / **impulsive** [ɪmˋpʌlsɪv] adj. 衝動的

Q2

Because of the _______ of information online, many people choose to read headlines instead of reading articles thoroughly.

因為網路上有大量的資訊，所以許多人選擇閱讀標題而不是徹底讀完報導文章。

A. abundance　B. correspondence　C. eloquence　D. indifference

詳解 答案：A

句子前半用 Because of 開頭，表示理由，而句子後半表示結果是「許多人讀標題而不讀完文章」，所以能表示資訊量很多，讓人很難讀完全部內容的 A 是最適當的答案。

|單字片語| **headline** [`hɛd͵laɪn] n.（新聞的）標題 / **thoroughly** [`θɝolɪ] adv. 徹底地 / **abundance** [ə`bʌndəns] n. 豐富，大量 / **correspondence** [͵kɔrə`spɑndəns] n. 對應；通信 / **eloquence** [`ɛləkwəns] n. 口才 / **indifference** [ɪn`dɪfərəns] n. 漠不關心

Q3

Salespeople who exceed their ________ are entitled to bonuses based on their performance.

超過（業績）配額的銷售員有資格得到根據業績而定的獎金。

A. genres　B. quotas　C. realms　D. slumps

詳解 答案：B

從 Salespeople 到空格的部分是主詞，動詞部分是 are entitled。這個題目的重點在於看懂 are entitled to something（有資格得到…）這個用法，既然有資格得到獎金，那麼超過的應該就是業績目標了，所以能表示「分配的業績額度」的 B 是正確答案。

|單字片語| **exceed** [ɪk`sid] v. 超過 / **be entitled to** 有資格得到… / **bonus** [`bonəs] n. 獎金 / **genre** [`ʒɑnrə] n. 作品的類型 / **quota** [`kwotə] n. 配額 / **realm** [rɛlm] n. 領域 / **slump** [slʌmp] n. 低潮期

Q4

________ the disastrous last ten minutes, the home team has been doing just fine during the game.

除了災難性的最後十分鐘以外，主隊在比賽中表現得還不錯。

A. Except for　B. In addition to　C. Together with　D. In case of

詳解 答案：A

前半提到 disastrous last ten minutes（災難性的最後十分鐘），後面卻說 has been doing just fine during the game（在比賽中表現得還不錯），前後表示相反的意思，所以空格應該填入表示語意轉折的詞。A 和 B 在中文都翻譯成「除了…」，但 except for 表示「除了…以外，其他的都不是」，in addition to 則表示「除了…以外，還有其他哪些也是一樣」，符合這一題的答案是 A. Except for。together with 表示「和…一起」，in case of 表示「萬一發生…」。

|單字片語| **disastrous** [dɪz`æstrəs] adj. 災難性的，悲慘的 / **home team** 本地的隊伍，主隊

Q5

The man waited for what seemed like an ________ before he laid his eyes on his newborn child.
那個男人在親眼看到他的新生寶寶之前，等了像是一輩子（永遠）似的。

A. anticipation　B. eternity　C. illusion　D. obsession

詳解　答案：B

for 的受詞是 what seemed like a ________，表示對這個男人而言「似乎像是…的事物」。雖然 wait for 經常表示「等待（某個對象）」的意思，但在選項中並沒有適合當成等待對象的答案。所以，應該把 for 當成表示期間長度的介系詞，選項中表示「永遠」的 B 是正確答案。

|單字片語| **lay eyes on** 看到… / **newborn** [`nju͵bɔrn] adj. 剛出生的，新生的 / **anticipation** [æn͵tɪsə`peʃən] n. 預期，期待 / **eternity** [ɪ`tɝnətɪ] n. 永遠，永恆 / **illusion** [ɪ`ljuʒən] n. 幻覺 / **obsession** [əb`sɛʃən] n. 著迷

Q6

In the Dark Ages, men accused women of being witches who ________ on misfortunes in the society.
在黑暗時期，男人指控女人是在社會上造成不幸的巫婆。

A. brought　B. passed　C. gave up　D. turned

詳解　答案：A

選項中，能和後面的介系詞 on 搭配，形成 brought on（導致…，造成…，引起…）的 A 是正確答案。pass on 表示「傳遞…」，give up on 表示「不再對某人有信心」，turn on 表示「打開…」。

|單字片語| **Dark Ages** 黑暗時期（古羅馬帝國滅亡後，公元五世紀到十三世紀的時期） / **accuse** [ə`kjuz] v. 指控 / **misfortune** [mɪs`fɔrtʃən] n. 不幸

Q7

I merely turned the handle with a little more force than usual, and it ________.

我只是比平常多用了一點力轉動把手，它就脫落了。

A. came out　　B. came off　　C. came around　　D. came down

詳解

答案：B

with a little more force than usual（用比平常多一點的力）顯示這是和平常不同的情況，這時候把手有可能發生的現象是 B. came off（脫落）。

補充說明

動詞＋介系詞的組合，有時候不太能從字面上直接看出意義，或者使用的介系詞並不是那麼直覺，這時候就要當成獨立的詞彙來背。

The results came out this morning. 今天早上成績出來了。

The handle came off. 把手脫落了。

The patient finally came around. 病人終於甦醒了。

|單字片語| **merely** [`mɪrlɪ] adv. 僅僅，只是 / **handle** [`hændl] n. 把手 / **force** [fors] n. 力量 / **than usual** 和平常比起來

Q8

The company ________ updates its software programs to keep up with ever-changing needs of customers.

這家公司定期更新它的軟體程式，好跟上顧客一直在改變的需求。

A. coherently　　B. distinctively　　C. exclusively　　D. periodically

詳解

答案：D

句子後面有表示目的的 to 不定詞片語 to keep up with...，可知更新軟體程式是為了跟上顧客的需求。這裡要注意的是 ever-changing 這個詞彙，意思是「不斷改變的」，所以應該隨時更新程式才能趕上需求，因此選項中表示「定期」的 D 是正確答案。

|單字片語| **keep up with** 跟上 / **ever-changing** 不斷改變的 / **coherently** [ko`hɪrəntlɪ] adv. 連貫一致地 / **distinctively** [dɪ`stɪŋktɪvlɪ] adv. 特殊地 / **exclusively** [ɪk`sklusɪvlɪ] adv. 獨佔地 / **periodically** [pɪrɪ`ɑdɪklɪ] adv. 定期地

Whatever the mind of man can ________ and believe, he certainly can achieve.

不管人的頭腦能想到什麼，只要他相信，他就能達成。

A. deceive　B. conceive　C. perceive　D. receive

詳解　**答案：B**

這是一句廣泛流傳的名言。雖然四個選項在意義上都有可能是主詞 the mind of man（人的心智／頭腦）的動詞，但因為受詞 Whatever（任何東西）同時也是人 believe（相信）、achieve（達成）的東西，所以這個「Whatever」指的應該是想像、計畫、目標等等還沒有實現的東西，意義最適當的答案是 B。whatever 是複合關係代名詞，文法上具有先行詞和關係代名詞的雙重地位，所以前面不需要先行詞。

|單字片語| **deceive** [dɪˋsiv] v. 欺騙 / **conceive** [kənˋsiv] v. 構想出，想像 / **perceive** [pɚˋsiv] v. 察覺，感知

Q10

According to company regulations, any truck driver caught drunk-driving will have their contract ________.

根據公司的規定，任何被逮到酒駕的卡車司機，合約將會被終止。

A. suspended　B. canceled　C. terminated　D. revoked

詳解　**答案：C**

have something p.p. 表示「（自己的）某事物被…」的意思。這題考的不僅僅是單字，還有單字的運用和搭配。contract（合約）被結束時，動詞要用 terminate（終止），其他答案和英語的使用習慣不符。其他選項的用法舉例如下：suspend one's license（吊銷某人的執照）、cancel the plan（取消計畫）。revoke（撤銷）也可以接 license 當受詞，但和 suspend 有所差別：suspend 之後是可以恢復的，revoke 則是完全撤銷，經過重新申請、重新接受測試等等才有可能再度取得。

|單字片語| **regulation** [ˌrɛgjəˋleʃən] n. 規定，規章 / **contract** [ˋkɑntrækt] n. 合約 / **suspend** [səˋspɛnd] v. 暫停，吊銷 / **terminate** [ˋtɝməˌnet] v. 使終止 / **revoke** [rɪˋvok] v. 撤銷

第二部分 / 段落填空

Questions 11-15

As a foreigner residing in Taipei city, I would like to (11) commend the city's effort in launching eco-friendly initiatives, especially the bicycle sharing system called "YouBike". The system enables everyone to rent a bike anytime, anywhere. What is more, (12) you can rent a YouBike from one station and return at another, so you do not need to keep your rented bike after riding to work.

You can rent a bike for as long as you wish (13) on a half-hourly basis, and the renting process is a breeze. First of all, you need to register your EasyCard. While registering, you need to provide your EasyCard's (14) serial number, which can be found on the lower right corner of the card. Next, just go to the bicycle rental station and tap your card on the sensor on the rack to get a bike. When you return the bike, remember to tap your card again to have the fee (15) deducted from the card.

身為居住在台北市的外國人，我想要稱讚這個城市發起環保行動的努力，尤其是叫做「YouBike」的共享單車系統。這個系統讓每個人都能隨時隨地租用腳踏車。而且，你可以從一個站點租 YouBike，並且在另一個站點歸還，所以在騎車上班之後，你不必把租來的單車留在身邊。

你可以用每半小時的計費方式租借腳踏車，想租多久就租多久，而且租借過程非常簡單。首先，你需要註冊你的悠遊卡。在註冊時，你需要提供悠遊卡的序號，它可以在卡片的右下角找到。接下來，只要去單車租借站，並且在車架上的感應器碰一下（感應）卡片來取車。還單車的時候，記得再碰一下卡片，讓費用從卡片中被扣除。

|單字片語| **reside** [rɪˋzaɪd] v. 居住 / **commend** [kəˋmɛnd] v. 稱讚 / **launch** [lɔntʃ] v. 發動，開辦，發起 / **eco-friendly** [ˋikoˏfrɛndlɪ] adj. 對環境友善的，環保的 / **initiative** [ɪˋnɪʃətɪv] n. 主動的行動 / **breeze** [briz] n. 輕而易舉的事 / **serial number** 序號 / **sensor** [ˋsɛnsɚ] n. 感應器 / **rack** [ræk] 架子（在這裡指 **bicycle rack** 腳踏車架） / **deduct** [dɪˋdʌkt] v. 扣除

Q11

A. sustain　B. commend　C. disclose　D. provoke

詳解

答案：B

這個句子的主詞是作者本人（I），空格的受詞是 the city's effort in...（城市在…方面的努力），是正面的敘述，所以表示「稱讚」的 B 是最適當的答案。

|單字片語| **sustain** [sə`sten] v. 維持 / **disclose** [dɪs`kloz] v. 透露 / **provoke** [prə`vok] v. 激怒，激起

Q12

A. renting YouBikes is totally free of charge
租借 YouBike 是完全免費的
B. YouBikes are designed to be disposed after use
YouBike 是設計成使用後就被丟棄的
C. you can rent a YouBike from one station and return at another
你可以從一個站點租 YouBike，並且在另一個站點歸還
D. there is a discount when transferring between YouBike and the MRT
在 YouBike 和捷運之間轉乘時有折扣

詳解

答案：C

空格後面接 so 開頭的子句，所以空格是後面子句的原因。後面的子句說「在騎車上班後不必把車留在身邊」，所以意味著在騎車之後可以在目的地歸還（而不是回到一開始出發的地方歸還）的 C 是正確答案。另外，因為第二段提到要從悠遊卡扣款，所以租借 YouBike 不是免費的，選項 A 是錯誤答案。選項 B 的 be disposed after use 是指「用完以後就被當成垃圾處理掉」，和 YouBike 系統「租借」的性質不符合。

|單字片語| **dispose of** 處理掉

Q13

A. every half hour　B. based on half hours
C. on a half-hourly basis　D. basically half-hourly

詳解

答案：C

第二段介紹 YouBike 的租借方法，所以空格要填入和租借制度有關的內容。on a ... basis（以…的基礎）是一個固定的用法，例如 on a daily basis 可以表示「每天」做某事，或者「以天為計算單位」。所以，也有 on a monthly basis、on a weekly basis、on an hourly basis 等等說法。這裡是表示 YouBike 以每半小時計費，所以 C. on a half-hourly basis 是正確答案。A 表示「每半個小時一

次」的意思，和空格前面 as long as you wish（你想要多久都可以）的意義不符。B 的 based on 是「根據…」的意思，以這一句而言，可以說 based on the length of time（根據時間長度），但不會使用 based on half hours（根據半小時的時間）這種奇怪的說法。D 表示「基本上每半小時」，意思也很奇怪。

補充說明

on a first-come-first-serve basis 以先到先服務的原則；先到者先得
on a regular basis 定期地
on a pay-as-you-go basis 以預付方式，付多少就用多少

|單字片語| **half-hourly** adj. 每半小時的 adv. 每半小時

Q14

A. series　　B. serial　　C. sequence　　D. sequel

詳解　　　　答案：B

產品之類的「序號」，固定的說法是 serial number（serial：連續的，一連串的），所以答案是 B。

補充說明

arrange ... in sequence 按照順序排放…
a series of ... 一系列的…

|單字片語| **series** [`siriz] n. 系列 / **sequence** [`sikwəns] n. 連續；次序，順序 / **sequel** [`sikwəl] n. 續集，續篇

A. deduct　　B. to deduct　　C. deducting　　D. deducted

詳解　　　　答案：D

空格前面的 have 是使役動詞，句型有可能是 have O do ...（使受詞做某事），或者是 have O V-ing/p.p.（使受詞成為什麼狀態）。在這裡，受詞 fee（費用）是「被」扣除的東西，所以表示被動的過去分詞 D. deducted 是正確答案。

Questions 16-20

Intelligence Quotient (IQ) and Emotional Quotient (EQ) reflect different aspects of human mind. The former is a measure of cognitive intelligence, whereas the latter is a measure of emotional intelligence. (16) While it is generally accepted that an individual's IQ (17) is more or less determined at birth, the same individual's EQ, on the other hand, can develop over time and through training.

The idea of EQ was first introduced by Dr. Reuven Bar-On. He (18) defined emotional intelligence as being concerned with effectively understanding oneself and others and adapting to one's immediate surroundings. Emotional intelligence helps individuals to cope with their situations and to deal with environmental demands. Individuals with a higher than average EQ are generally more competent (19) to handle their pressures. A (20) deficiency in emotional intelligence can mean a lack of mental toughness and impulse control.

智力商數（IQ）和情緒商數（EQ）反映人類心智的不同面向。前者是認知智能的衡量標準，而後者是情緒智能的衡量標準。雖然人們大致同意一個人的 IQ 多少是在出生時決定的，但另一方面，同一個人的 EQ 則可以隨著時間、透過訓練而發展。

EQ 的概念是由 Reuven Bar-On 博士首先提出的。他把情緒智能定義為和有效了解自我和他人、適應週遭環境有關。情緒智能幫助個人應付自己的處境，並且處理環境的要求。EQ 高於平均的人，大致上比較有能力處理自己的壓力。情緒智能的缺乏可能意味著缺少心理韌性和衝動控制能力。

|單字片語| **intelligence** [ɪn`tɛlədʒəns] n. 智能 / **quotient** [`kwoʃənt] n. （數學）商數 / **emotional** [ɪ`moʃənl] adj. 情緒的 / **measure** [`mɛʒɚ] n. 度量單位，基準，尺度 / **cognitive** [`kɑgnətɪv] adj. 認知的 / **determine** [dɪ`tɝmɪn] v. 決定 / **introduce**[ˌɪntrə`djus] v. 介紹，引進，提出 / **define** [dɪ`faɪn] v. 定義 / **be concerned with** 和…相關 / **effectively** [ɪ`fɛktɪvlɪ] adv. 有效地 / **adapt to** 適應… / **immediate** [ɪ`midɪɪt] adj. 立即的，最接近的 / **surroundings** [sə`raʊndɪŋz] n. 環境，周圍 / **cope with** 處理…，應付…，承受… / **environmental** [ɪnˌvaɪrən`mɛntl] adj. 環境的 / **demand** [dɪ`mænd] n. 要求，需求 v. 要求 / **average** [`ævərɪdʒ] n. 平均，平均數 adj. 平均的 / **generally** [`dʒɛnərəlɪ] adv. 通常，一般，大致上 / **competent** [`kɑmpətənt] adj. 有能力的 / **deficiency** [dɪ`fɪʃənsɪ] n. 不足，缺乏 / **mental toughness** 心理韌性 / **impulse** [`ɪmpʌls] n. 衝動

Q16

A. However　B. While　C. Since　D. Provided

詳解

答案：B

空格後面有兩個完整的子句，中間用逗號分隔，可知空格應該填入連接詞，B、C、D 是可能的答案；A. However 是連接副詞，不能用來連接同一個句子裡的兩個子句。從意義來看，因為前後分別說明 IQ 和 EQ，而且 EQ 的後面插入了 on the other hand（另一方面），表示兩者之間有對比的關係，所以表示對比的 B. While（雖然，儘管，然而）是正確答案。除了表示對比以外，連接詞 while 也可以表示「當…的時候」的意思。C. Since（因為；自從）表示理由或時間，D. Provided（假如）表示條件。

補充說明

While 也可以使用在句子的中間。
Some people prefer coffee while others prefer tea.
While some prefer coffee, others prefer tea.
（有些人比較喜歡咖啡，而其他人比較喜歡茶。）

Q17

A. can improve very quickly
可以改善得非常快
B. can be tested and measured
可以被測試並且衡量
C. is more or less determined at birth
多少是在出生時決定的
D. decides how successful he or she is
決定他或她有多成功

詳解

答案：C

因為前後兩個子句之間是對比的關係（參照上一題的說明），所以相對於後面說的「EQ 可以隨著時間、透過訓練而發展」，前面的內容應該表示 IQ 比較固定，所以 C 是正確答案。

Q18

A. defined　B. presumed　C. implied　D. advocated

詳解

答案：A

空格後面接受詞 emotional intelligence，而從 as 一直到句尾的部分都是受詞補語，是對於受詞 emotional intelligence 的說明。所以，能和介系詞 as 連用，表示「將…定義為…」的 A. defined 是正確答案（define A as B：將 A 定義為 B）。presume（假定）、imply（暗示）通常接 that 子句當受詞，advocate（提倡）常接名詞或動名詞當受詞。

|單字片語| **presume** [prɪ`zum] v. 假定 / **imply** [ɪm`plaɪ] v. 暗示 / **advocate** [`ædvə͵ket] v. 提倡，主張

A. to handle
B. by handling
C. handled by
D. in order to handle

詳解 **答案：A**

空格前後的部分是表達「有能力處理壓力」的意思，而形容詞 competent（有能力的）後面可以接 to 不定詞表示「有能力做…」，所以 A 是正確答案。B 表示方法，C 是可以表示條件的分詞構句，D 表示目的。

A. proficiency
B. deficiency
C. efficiency
D. sufficiency

詳解 **答案：B**

句意是 A ______ in emotional intelligence（情緒智能的______）可能意味著 a lack of mental toughness（心理韌性的缺乏）。前面的句子提到 emotional intelligence 可以幫助人們應付他們的處境和環境的要求，所以這裡顯示的應該是缺乏 emotional intelligence 的相反情況，B. deficiency（缺乏，不足）是正確答案，意思和 lack 相近。

|單字片語| **proficiency** [prə`fɪʃənsɪ] n. 精通，熟練 / **efficiency** [ɪ`fɪʃənsɪ] n. 效率 / **sufficiency** [sə`fɪʃənsɪ] n. 充分，足夠的量

第三部分 / 閱讀理解

Questions 21-22

Questions 21 and 22 are based on the information provided in the following chart.

Market Share of Major Smartphone Manufacturers

主要智慧型手機製造商市占率

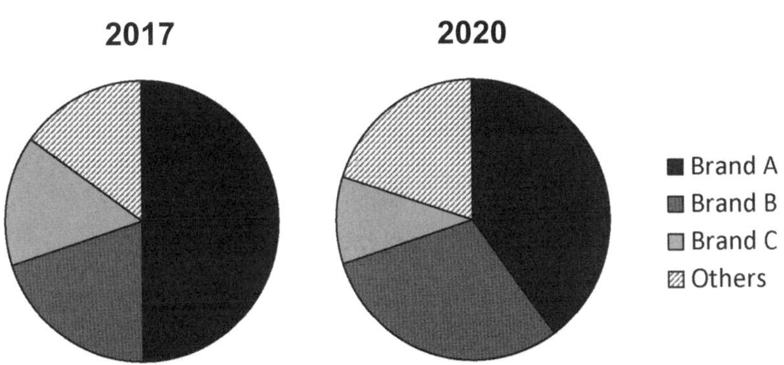

|單字片語| **market share** 市占率 / **smartphone** [\`smartfon] n. 智慧型手機 / **manufacturer** [ˌmænjə\`fæktʃərə] n. 製造業者，製造商

Q21

Based on the chart, which of the following statements is true?　根據圖表，以下哪個敘述正確？

A. Brand A has lost a significant amount of market share, but it remains the market leader.
品牌 A 失去了相當多的市占率，但它仍然是市場上的領先者。

B. Brand B has not managed to increase its market share.
品牌 B 沒有成功增加市占率。

C. Brand C has exceeded Brand B in terms of market share.
品牌 C 在市占率方面超越了品牌 B。

D. Growth for the brands other than brand A was stagnant for the past three years.　品牌 A 以外的品牌，在過去三年是停滯的。

詳解

答案：A

根據圖表內容，一一對照各選項是否正確。A. 從 2017 年到 2020 年，品牌 A 的市占率從大約一半下降到四成左右，但在圖中仍然占據最大的一份，符合選項敘述，所以 A 是正確答案。B. 代表品牌 B 的部分，從 2017 年到 2020 年變大了，不符合選項敘述。C. 從 2017 年到 2020 年，品牌 C 不但沒有超越品牌 B，市占率還變少了，不符合選項敘述。D. 品牌 B 和其他廠商的市占率增加了，不符合選項敘述。

|單字片語| **market leader** 市場上的領先者，市場龍頭 / **manage to do...** 設法做到…，成功做到… / **stagnant** [`stægnənt] adj. 停滯的

What might you read about Brand C in a business magazine?

關於品牌 C，你在商業雜誌裡可能會讀到什麼？

A. The company's prospects are bright and promising.
這家公司的前景既光明又有希望。

B. The company is likely to overtake the market leader in the near future.
這家公司很有可能在不久的將來超越市場領先者。

C. The company needs to reinvent itself or be eliminated by its competitors.
這家公司需要重新發明（重新創造）自己，不然就會被競爭者淘汰。

D. The company has lived up to shareholders' expectation.
這家公司實現了股東的期望。

詳解

答案：C

在三年之間，品牌 C 的市占率變得相當小，所以對於它的敘述應該是比較負面的。選項 C 使用了「動詞片語 or 動詞片語」的句型：reinvent itself or be eliminated，表示如果不重新發明自己（重新創造自己→改革），就會被淘汰，符合表格中呈現的情況，是正確答案。

|單字片語| **prospect** [`prɑspɛkt] n. 前景，前途 / **promising** [`prɑmɪsɪŋ] adj. 有希望的，有前途的 / **overtake** [ˌovɚ`tek] v. 追過 / **reinvent** [ˌriɪn`vɛnt] v. 重新發明，重新創造 / **eliminate**[ɪ`lɪməˌnet] v. 消除，淘汰 / **competitor** [kəm`pɛtətɚ] n. 競爭對手 / **live up to someone's expectations** 實現某人的期望，不辜負某人的期望

Questions 23-25

Ancient Egypt is a distinct civilization, which can be dated back 5,000 years ago. No ancient civilization has so captured the Western mind as that of Egypt. Its impressive architectural remains and the close connection with Greece and Rome, in addition to its historical events described in the Holy Bible, probably explain this fascination. Another factor surely is the Egyptian obsession with the afterlife, which left a lot of archaeological evidence, including mummies. The origins of ancient Egypt are still clouded in mystery. What we know is that it has a mysterious religion with inspiring monumental architecture, including temples, pyramids, and the Sphinx.

Usually seen on the walls of ancient temples and tombs, hieroglyphics were the pictographic writing of the ancient Egyptians. They form a complicated system, which is the basis of a developing alphabet, using both pictures and sounds to convey ideas. Even in ancient Egypt, few could read hieroglyphics. This knowledge was reserved primarily to the priests and nobility. For centuries, the meaning of hieroglyphics was a mystery, until French scholar Jean-François Champollion deciphered it.

When it comes to the religion itself, the sun was ancient Egypt's principal god. The sun's passage daily across the sky from sunrise to sunset represented the eternal cycle of birth, death, and rebirth. As in many Asian cultures, the kings or pharaohs were seen as gods by the common people. Therefore, obedience to the king is akin to following the instructions of the gods.

古埃及是一個獨特的文明，可以追溯到 5,000 年前。沒有什麼古文明像埃及的文明這麼讓西方人的心著迷。它令人印象深刻的建築遺跡、與希臘和羅馬的緊密關聯，還有聖經中敘述它的歷史事件，或許能解釋這種迷戀。另一個因素當然是埃及對於來世的著迷，留下了許多考古證據，包括木乃伊。古埃及的起源仍然在迷霧之中。我們知道的，是它有個神祕的宗教，有激發人心的紀念建築，其中包括廟宇、金字塔和人面獅身像。

通常在古代廟宇和墳墓的牆上會看到，象形文字是古埃及人的圖象書寫系統。它們形成複雜的系統，這是發展中的字母系統的基礎，使用圖畫和聲音來傳達想法。即使是在古埃及，也很少人能讀懂象形文字。這個知識主要保留給神職人員和貴族。有許多世紀的時間，象形文字的意義都是個謎，直到法國學者 Jean-François Champollion 破解了為止。

說到宗教本身，太陽是埃及主要的神。太陽每天從日出到日落通過天空的過程，代表出生、死亡和重生的永恆循環。就像在許多亞洲文化一樣，國王，或者說法老，被一般人視為神。所以，對國王的服從就類似遵守神的指示。

|單字片語|

（第一段）

ancient [ˋenʃənt] adj. 古代的，古老的 / **distinct** [dɪˋstɪŋkt] adj. 與其他不同的 / **civilization** [ˌsɪvḷəˋzeʃən] n. 文明 / **capture** [ˋkæptʃɚ] v. 捕獲，抓到 / **impressive** [ɪmˋprɛsɪv] adj. 令人印象深刻的 / **architectural** [ˌɑrkəˋtɛktʃərəl] adj. 建築的 / **remains** [rɪˋmenz] n. 遺跡 / **fascination** [ˌfæsnˋeʃən] n. 魅力，迷戀 / **obsession** [əbˋsɛʃən] n. 著迷 / **afterlife** [ˋæftɚˌlaɪf] n. 來世 / **archaeological** [ˌɑrkɪəˋlɑdʒɪkḷ] adj. 考古學的 / **mummy** [ˋmʌmɪ] n. 木乃伊 / **cloud** [klaʊd] v. 使模糊 / **mystery** [ˋmɪstərɪ] n. 神祕的事物 / **mysterious** [mɪsˋtɪrɪəs] adj. 神祕的 / **inspiring** [ɪnˋspaɪrɪŋ] adj. 激發人心的 / **monumental** [ˌmɑnjəˋmɛntḷ] adj. 紀念碑式的，紀念的 / **pyramid** [ˋpɪrəmɪd] n. 金字塔

（第二段）

hieroglyphics [haɪərəˋglɪfɪks] n. 象形文字 / **pictographic** [ˌpɪktəˋgræfɪk] adj. 繪畫文字的 / **alphabet** [ˋælfəˌbɛt] n. 字母系統，全套字母 / **priest** [prist] n. 神職人員，祭司 / **nobility** [noˋbɪlətɪ] n. 貴族 / **decipher** [dɪˋsaɪfɚ] v. 破解（密碼等）

（第三段）

principal [ˋprɪnsəpḷ] adj. 主要的 / **passage** [ˋpæsɪdʒ] n. 通行，通過 / **eternal** [ɪˋtɝnḷ] adj. 永恆的 / **pharaoh** [ˋfɛro] 法老（古埃及國王）/ **obedience** [əˋbidjəns] n. 服從 / **be akin to** 類似於⋯ / **instruction** [ɪnˋstrʌkʃən] n. 指示

Q23

What is NOT a reason that Westerners are attracted by Egyptian culture? 何者不是西方人受到埃及文化吸引的理由？

A. The architectural wonders of ancient Egypt 古埃及的建築奇觀
B. The abundant fuel hidden under Egyptian deserts 藏在埃及沙漠的大量燃料
C. What happened there as described in the Bible 聖經中描述以前在那裡發生的事
D. The preservation of dead bodies 對屍體的保存

詳解 **答案：B**

題目問被吸引（are attracted）的理由，文章中相關的部分在第一段。第二句先說 No ancient civilization has so captured the Western mind as that of Egypt.（沒有什麼古文明像埃及的文明這麼讓西方人的心著迷），接下來就提到 Its impressive architectural remains... in addition to its historical events described in the

Holy Bible, probably explain this fascination.（它令人印象深刻的建築遺跡…還有聖經中敘述它的歷史事件，或許能解釋這種迷戀），對應選項 A 和選項 C。後面又說 Another factor surely is the Egyptian obsession with the afterlife, which left... mummies.（另一個因素當然是埃及對於來世的著迷，留下了…木乃伊），對應選項 D（木乃伊是被保存的屍體）。選項 B 沒有提到，所以是正確答案。

|單字片語| **wonder** [ˋwʌndɚ] n. 奇觀 / **abundant** [əˋbʌndənt] adj. 大量的，充足的 / **fuel** [ˋfjʊəl] n. 燃料 / **preservation** [ˌprɛzɚˋveʃən] n. 保護，保存

Q24

According to this article, what is true about Egyptian hieroglyphics?

根據這篇文章，關於埃及的象形文字，何者正確？

A. They were purely drawings that bear no meaning.
它們純粹是沒有意義的圖畫。

B. They were closely related to Greek and Roman alphabets.
它們和希臘羅馬字母有密切關係。

C. They were only accessible by a privileged group.
它們只有一群有特權的人能夠使用。

D. They were translated using modern technology.
它們是用現代技術被翻譯的。

詳解　　答案：C

提到 hieroglyphics（象形文字）的部分是第二段。第二句話提到象形文字系統是 the basis of a developing alphabet（發展中的字母系統的基礎），但並沒有說是發展成希臘羅馬字母，所以 B 不對；using both pictures and sounds to convey ideas（用圖畫和聲音傳達想法）表示象形文字是有意義的，所以 A 不對。接下來的內容提到... few could read hieroglyphics. This knowledge was reserved primarily to the priests and nobility.（…很少人能讀懂象形文字。這個知識主要保留給神職人員和貴族），所以符合這部分敘述的 C 是正確答案。最後一句話提到 French scholar... deciphered it（法國學者破解了它），但並沒有說是用現代技術／科技破解的，所以 D 不對。

|單字片語| **accessible** [ækˋsɛsəbl̩] adj. 可接近的，可利用的 / **privileged** [ˋprɪvɪlɪdʒd] adj. 有特權的

Q25

How did the pharaohs strengthen their rule over the people with the help of religion?

法老如何藉著宗教的幫助來強化對人民的統治？

A. By emphasizing the eternal cycle of birth, death, and rebirth
藉由強調生、死與重生的永恆循環
B. By keeping their burial sites a mystery to all
藉由將他們的埋葬地點對所有人保持祕密
C. By promoting literacy among the general public through schools
藉由透過學校提升一般大眾的讀寫能力
D. By portraying kings as legitimate heirs appointed by the gods
藉由將國王描繪成由神指定的合法繼承人

詳解

答案：D

提到 pharaoh 的部分是第三段。... the kings or pharaohs were seen as gods by the common people. Therefore, obedience to the king is akin to following the instructions of the gods.（國王，或者說法老，被一般人視為神。所以，對國王的服從就類似遵守神的指示）的部分顯示，因為法老被當成神，使得人民服從他們，符合這段敘述的 D 是正確答案。

|單字片語| **strengthen** [ˋstrɛŋθən] v. 加強 / **rule** [rul] n. 規則；統治 / **emphasize** [ˋɛmfəˏsaɪz] v. 強調 / **burial** [ˋbɛrɪəl] n. 埋葬，葬禮 / **literacy** [ˋlɪtərəsɪ] n. 讀寫能力 / **portray** [porˋtre] v. 描繪 / **legitimate** [lɪˋdʒɪtəmɪt] adj. 合法的，合理的 / **heir** [ɛr] n. 繼承人 / **appoint** [əˋpɔɪnt] v. 任命

Questions 26-29

Cases of random murders have enraged the public, especially when the latest victim was an innocent four-year-old girl, who was slaughtered right in front of her mother in broad daylight, for no apparent reason. It is outrageous for such an inhuman act to take place in Taiwan, a society well-known for its friendly and helpful people. This tragic incident, the third in three years with the victim being a child, raised a highly controversial issue: should the death penalty be abolished? With regard to this question, public opinion is divided, though recent polls suggested that the majority of Taiwanese are in favor of executing child murderers so they can do no more harm to other children.

Supporters of the death penalty believe that only such a drastic measure will prevent similar crimes from happening, and they take the fact that previous murderers were not given a death sentence as a reason why the number of murders keeps growing. Many also argued that there is no justice to the family of murder victims unless evildoers pay with their lives. Furthermore, life imprisonment instead of a death sentence is a heavy burden for the government since the criminals are to be taken care of for as long as they live. On the other hand, those who urge the government to abolish the death penalty claim that harsh laws do not act as a deterrent of crime, let alone solve the causes of crime. Actually, a death penalty may even be an easy way out for murderers who do not care about human life, including their own. Since many murderers have a few problems deeply rooted in their upbringing, it is possible that improving home and school education can better prevent such crimes. Besides, there were cases in which innocent people were convicted and executed. There is always the danger of a mistaken execution, especially when there is strong pressure of public opinion but no sufficient evidence.

隨機殺人的案件使大眾很憤怒，尤其是因為最近的受害者是個無辜的四歲女孩，她就在光天化日之下在她母親面前被屠殺，沒有明顯的理由。在台灣這個以友善而且樂於助人的人們聞名的社會，發生這種沒有人性的行為是很無法無天的。這個悲劇事件是三年來小孩受害的第三件，它引起了非常具爭議性的議題：死刑應該被廢除嗎？關於這個問題，大眾的意見分歧，但最近的民意調查顯示，多數台灣人支持處決殺小孩的人，讓他們不能再傷害其他小孩。

死刑的支持者相信只有這麼激烈的手段能防止類似的犯罪發生，而他們認為之前的殺人犯沒有被判死刑的事實，是殺人案件數持續成長的原因。很多人也主張，除非做壞事的人付出生命作為代價，不然對殺人受害者的家屬是不公平的。而且，用無期徒刑取代死刑，對於政府而言是沉重的負擔，因為罪犯需要終生受到照顧。另一方面，力勸政府廢除死刑的人主張嚴厲的法律並沒有遏阻犯罪的效果，更別說解決犯罪的原因了。事實上，對於不在乎人的性命，包括自己的生命的殺人犯而言，死刑可能是個容易的出路。因為很多殺人犯都有一些深植於養育（成長）過程的問題，所以改善家庭與學校教育有可能對於預防這種犯罪更有效。而且，以前曾經有過無辜的人被判有罪而且處決的案例。總是會有錯誤處決的危險性，尤其是在輿論壓力很強但沒有足夠證據的時候。

|單字片語|

（第一段）

random [`rændəm] adj. 隨機的 / **murder** [`mɝdɚ] n. 謀殺 v. 謀殺 / **enrage** [ɪn`redʒ] v. 激怒，使憤怒 / **victim** [`vɪktɪm] n. 受害者 / **slaughter** [`slɔtɚ] v. 屠宰，屠殺 / **in broad daylight** 在光天化日下 / **outrageous** [aʊt`redʒəs] adj. 粗暴的，無法無天的 / **inhuman** [ɪn`hjumən] adj. 沒有人性的 / **tragic** [`trædʒɪk] adj. 悲劇的 / **incident** [`ɪnsədənt] n. 事件 / **controversial** [ˌkɑntrə`vɝʃəl] adj. 有爭議的 / **penalty** [`pɛnḷtɪ] n. 處罰，刑罰 / **abolish** [ə`bɑlɪʃ] v. 廢除，廢止 / **with regard to** 關於… / **public opinion** 輿論 / **poll** [pol] n. 民意調查 / **majority** [mə`dʒɔrətɪ] n. 多數，大多數 / **execute** [`ɛksɪˌkjut] v. 執行；將…處決 / **murderer** [`mɝdərɚ] n. 殺人犯

（第二段）

drastic [`dræstɪk] adj. 激烈的 / **death sentence** 死刑判決 / **justice** [`dʒʌstɪs] n. 正義，公平 / **evildoer** [`ivḷ`duɚ] n. 做壞事的人 / **life imprisonment** 無期徒刑 / **deterrent** [dɪ`tɝənt] n. 遏止物 / **let alone** 更不用說… / **easy way out** 簡單的解決方法 / **upbringing** [`ʌp͵brɪŋɪŋ] n. 養育，教養（過程、環境） / **convict** [kən`vɪkt] v. 判…有罪

Q26

What is the cause of the latest murder case mentioned in this article?

這篇文章提到最近的殺人案件，起因是什麼？

A. A dispute in the family　家庭裡的爭吵
B. A personal financial crisis　個人財務危機
C. A lack of death penalty laws　死刑法律的缺乏
D. The cause is unknown.　起因還不知道。

詳解

答案：D

第一段的第一句話的前面提到 Cases of random murders（隨機殺人的案件），後面就說 the latest victim... was slaughtered... for no apparent reason（最近的〔隨機殺人〕受害者沒有明顯的理由就被屠殺）。for no apparent reason 表示沒有明顯的理由，也就是不知道為什麼，所以答案是 D。第二段雖然提到有些人認為之前的殺人犯沒有被判死刑是殺人案件數持續成長的原因（they take the fact that previous murderers were not given a death sentence as a reason why the number of murders keeps growing），但並不表示沒有死刑的法律，所以 C 不對。

|單字片語| **dispute** [dɪ`spjut] v. 爭論，爭執 n. 爭論，爭執 / **financial** [faɪ`nænʃəl] adj. 財務的 / **crisis** [`kraɪsɪs] n. 危機

What is the main reason that the recent incident made a lot of people angry?

最近的事件使很多人憤怒的原因是什麼？

A. It was carried out during the daytime.　是在白天犯案的。
B. It happened to a very young girl.　它發生在很年輕的女孩身上。
C. It caused controversy.　它造成了爭議。
D. It happened in Taiwan.　它發生在台灣。

詳解

答案：B

題目的關鍵語 made a lot of people angry，對應文章第一句話裡的 Cases of random murders have enraged the public（隨機殺人的案件使大眾很憤怒），隨後馬上就提到 especially when the latest victim was an innocent four-year-old girl（尤其是因為最近的受害者是個無辜的四歲女孩），所以答案是 B。雖然也提到 in broad daylight（在光天化日下），但在這裡只是對於犯案情況的補充敘述，而不是引起憤怒的主要原因，所以 A 不對。第二句話提到 It is outrageous for such an inhuman act to take place in Taiwan（在台灣發生這種沒有人性的行為是很無法無天的），是表示這個犯行對台灣社會而言很離譜，但也不是引起憤怒的主因，所以 D 不對。第三句話提到 This tragic incident... raised a highly controversial issue（這個悲劇事件引起了非常具爭議性的議題），但這是事件引起的結果之一，並不是令人憤怒的原因，所以 C 不對。

|單字片語| **daytime** [ˋdeˏtaɪm] n. 白天 / **controversy** [ˋkɑntrəˏvɝsɪ] n. 爭論，爭議

Q28

According to the result of the opinion survey, what kind of opinion is dominant?

根據意見調查的結果，哪一種意見佔優勢？

A. All murderers ought to be given the death penalty.
所有殺人犯都應該被判死刑。

B. Murderers of children must not be forgiven.
殺小孩的人絕對不能被原諒。

C. Human rights of both criminals and victims should be respected.
罪犯和受害者的人權都應該受到尊重。

D. Death penalty should be abolished.
死刑應該被廢除。

詳解

答案：B

題目裡的關鍵詞 opinion survey（意見調查），對應第一段最後一句裡的 poll（民意調查）；recent polls suggested that the majority of Taiwanese are in favor of executing child murderers so they can do no more harm to other children（最近的民意調查顯示，多數台灣人支持處決殺小孩的人，讓他們不能再傷害其他小孩）顯示比較多的人認為應該判殺小孩的人死刑，所以 B 是正確答案。因為這句話說的是 child murderers，我們並不知道這些人對於其他的殺人犯是否也有相同的意見，所以 A 並不是最適當的答案。

|單字片語| **dominant** [ˋdɑmənənt] adj. 佔優勢的

Which of the following is a reason that some people are against the death penalty?

以下何者是有些人反對死刑的理由？

A. The judicial system is not without flaws.
司法體系並不是沒有瑕疵。

B. Our education system is good enough to prevent crimes.
我們的教育體系夠好了，可以預防犯罪。

C. There are more terrifying punishments for criminals.
對罪犯而言還有更可怕的處罰。

D. The public opinion is usually wrong.
輿論通常是錯的。

詳解

答案：A

第二段的 On the other hand 之後列舉反對死刑的理由。there were cases in which innocent people were convicted and executed. There is always the danger of a mistaken execution（以前曾經有過無辜的人被判有罪而且處決的案例。總是會有錯誤處決的危險性）顯示司法體系有時候會有瑕疵，所以 A 是正確答案。選項 B 對應 improving home and school education can better prevent such crimes（改善家庭與學校教育對於預防這種犯罪更有效），但需要 improve 表示現在的教育還不夠好，所以 B 不對。選項 C 對應 a death penalty may even be an easy way out for murderers（死刑對於殺人犯而言可能是個容易的出路），但並沒有說應該用更可怕的方法對付他們，所以 C 不對。選項 D 對應 There is always the danger of a mistaken execution, especially when there is strong pressure of public opinion（總是會有錯誤處決的危險性，尤其是在輿論壓力很強的時候），但並沒有說輿論通常是錯的，所以 D 不對。

|單字片語| **judicial** [dʒuˋdɪʃəl] adj. 司法的 / **flaw** [flɔ] n. 瑕疵 / **terrifying** [ˋtɛrəˏfaɪɪŋ] adj. 可怕的

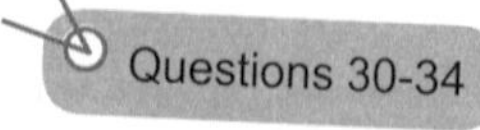

Questions 30-34 are based on the information provided in the following advertisement and email.

Gyrotonix
Job Opening

Gyrotonix is a multinational corporation based in India with businesses in Taiwan and Peru. We focus on selling real estate to the affluent population. We are currently seeking to hire a project manager for our team.

The project manager will be required to lead a team of 20 people. They will coordinate the team to work on the branding and promotion of real estate projects. This position will be trained in Taiwan and then relocate to Lima, Peru.

Desired qualifications:

- Master's degree in real estate management
- Five years of experience in the real estate industry
- English fluency with basic knowledge of Chinese or Spanish
- Being a team player
- Excellent analytical and communication skills

If you meet the required qualifications, please send your résumé to hr@gyrotonix.com along with a cover letter.

Gyrotonix 公司
職缺

Gyrotonix 公司是總部位於印度、在台灣和秘魯有業務的跨國公司。我們專注於向富裕層販售不動產。我們現在希望為我們的團隊雇用專案經理。

專案經理將必須領導 20 人的團隊，協調團隊進行不動產專案的品牌打造與宣傳。本職位將在台灣受訓，然後搬遷到秘魯的利瑪。

希望的資格條件：

- 不動產管理碩士
- 不動產業界五年經驗
- 英語流利，有華語或西班牙語的基本知識
- 善於團隊合作
- 優秀的分析與溝通能力

如果您符合要求的資格條件，請將履歷連同求職信寄至 hr@gyrotonix.com。

|單字片語|

multinational [`mʌltɪ`næʃənḷ] adj. 跨國的 / **real estate** 不動產 / **affluent** [`æflʊənt] adj. 富裕的 / **project manager** 專案經理 / **coordinate** [ko`ɔrdnet] v. 協調 / **relocate** [ri`loket] v. 搬遷 / **fluency** [`fluənsɪ] n. 流暢 / **team player** 善於團隊合作的人 / **analytical** [ˌænḷ`ɪtɪkḷ] adj. 分析的

From: Marie Flores <Marie.flores@rmail.com>
To: <hr@gyrotnixs.com>
Subject: Project Manager Applicant

Dear representative,

My name is Marie Flores. I am responding to the ad posted on your company website about an opening for a project manager at Gyrotonix. My multicultural background and educational experiences make me an ideal candidate.

I have four years of experience in the real estate field. I was raised in both Taiwan and Honduras. I also completed my bachelor's degree in real estate in the United States before coming back to Taiwan. As a result, I am fluent in Chinese, Spanish, and English. My strong communication skills have allowed me to work with teams all over the world. My multicultural experience leads me to be able to manage a multicultural team.

It is my goal to combine my range of experience with my ability to be a passionate and energetic leader who will make a positive contribution to your community. Please find my résumé attached. I would welcome an interview and hope to hear from you at your earliest convenience. Please do not hesitate to contact me at 1234-567-8900 or Marie.flores@rmail.com.

Thank you for your consideration.

Sincerely,
Marie Flores

寄件者：瑪麗・佛羅里斯 <Marie.flores@rmail.com>
收件者：<hr@gyrotnixs.com>
主旨：專案經理應徵者

親愛的代表人：

我的名字是瑪麗・佛羅里斯。我寫信是要回應張貼在貴公司網站上的 Gyrotonix 專案經理職缺廣告。我的多文化背景和教育經驗讓我成為理想的人選。

我在不動產領域有四年經驗。我在台灣和宏都拉斯長大。我也在回到台灣之前在美國完成了不動產學士學位。所以，我的華語、西班牙語、英語都很流利。我優良的溝通能力讓我能和全世界的團隊合作。我的多文化經驗讓我能管理多文化的團隊。

我的目標是將我的經驗與能力結合，成為對你們的社群做出正面貢獻、既熱情又有活力的領導者。請看我所附的履歷。我很歡迎你們面試，也希望儘早收到你們的回覆。請隨時撥打 1234-567-8900 或寄至 Marie.flores@rmail.com 聯絡我。

謝謝你們的考慮。

誠摯地
瑪麗・佛羅里斯

|單字片語|
multicultural [ˌmʌltɪˋkʌltʃərəl] adj. 多種文化的

Q30

What is true about Gyrotonix?
關於 Gyrotonix 公司，何者正確？

A. It has offices in three continents. 在三個大陸有辦事處。
B. Its customers are mostly rich people. 顧客大多是富有的人。
C. It deals with the construction of buildings. 處理建築物的建設工作。
D. It encourages an independent working style. 鼓勵獨立的工作型態。

詳解 答案：B

關於 Gyrotonix 公司的資訊，要從他們的徵才廣告（第一篇文章）尋找。We focus on selling real estate to the affluent population（我們專注於向富裕層販售不動產）的部分顯示，他們主要把不動產賣給富有的人，所以 B 是正確答案。A. 徵才廣告中提到這家公司 based in India with businesses in Taiwan and Peru，雖然的確在三個地方有辦事處，但台灣和印度都屬於亞洲，所以並不是跨足三個大陸。C. D. 文章中沒有提到。

Q31

Where will the project manager work?
專案經理會在哪裡工作？

A. In india 印度
B. In Taiwan 台灣
C. In Peru 秘魯
D. All of the above 以上皆是

詳解

關於工作地點，徵才廣告（第一篇文章）提到 This position will be trained in Taiwan and then relocate to Lima, Peru（本職位將在台灣受訓，然後搬遷到秘魯的利瑪），所以受訓以後要搬過去的秘魯才是工作的地點，C 是正確答案。

Q32

What is the purpose of the email?
電子郵件的目的是什麼？

A. To ask for more information about the company
要求關於公司的更多資訊
B. To share the sender's multicultural experience
分享寄件者的多文化經驗
C. To seek employment 求職
D. To seek a higher education 尋求高等教育

詳解

答案：C

電子郵件（第二篇文章）的開頭就說 I am responding to the ad posted on your company website about an opening（我寫信是要回應張貼在貴公司網站上的職缺廣告），之後說明自己適合這份工作的理由，並且說自己附上了履歷，所以 C 是正確答案。

Q33

According to the articles, which requirement does Marie meet?
根據這兩篇文章，瑪麗符合哪一項要求條件？

A. Educational background 教育背景
B. Experience in the industry 業界經驗
C. Language proficiency 語言能力
D. Analytical skills 分析能力

詳解

答案：C

這一題必須對照徵才廣告（第一篇文章）列出的條件和電子郵件（第二篇文章）的自我介紹來解題。電子郵件中提到 I am fluent in Chinese, Spanish, and English（我的華語、西班牙語、英語都很流利），符合徵才廣告中的條件 English fluency with basic knowledge of Chinese or Spanish（英語流利，有華語或西班牙語的基本知識），所以 C 是正確答案。A. 徵才廣告要求 master's degree（碩士學位），但瑪麗只有 bachelor's degree（學士學位）。B. 徵才廣告要求

five years of experience（五年經驗），但瑪麗只有 four years of experience（四年經驗）。D. 在電子郵件中沒有提到這一點。

What can be inferred about Marie?
關於瑪麗，可以推知什麼？

A. She lives in Taiwan now. 她現在住在台灣。
B. She was born in Honduras. 她在宏都拉斯出生。
C. She could not speak English before living in the US.
在美國生活之前，她不會說英語。
D. She has experience in managing a multicultural team.
他有管理多文化團隊的經驗。

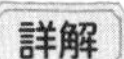

在電子郵件中，瑪麗提到自己 completed my bachelor's degree... in the United States before coming back to Taiwan（在回到台灣之前，在美國完成了學士學位），也就是說她大學畢業後回到了台灣，由此可知 A 是正確答案。B. 雖然提到了 I was raised in both Taiwan and Honduras（我在台灣和宏都拉斯長大），但沒辦法確定她在哪裡出生。C. D. 在文章中沒有提到。

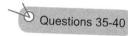

Insomnia is a symptom rather than a stand-alone disease. By definition, insomnia is "difficulty initiating or maintaining sleep, or both." It may therefore negatively affect the quality or quantity of sleep. Insomnia is not defined by a specific number of hours of sleep that one gets since everyone is different in terms of the length of sleep needed, and it is how we feel that matters. Most of us have experienced the feeling of not getting enough sleep, but only a few have consulted doctors, while others don't even know there are methods that can treat the problem.

Insomnia affects all age groups. Among adults, insomnia affects women more often than men. The likelihood of this problem occurring tends to increase with age. It is typically more common in people in lower socioeconomic (income) groups, chronic alcoholics, and mental health patients. Stress most commonly triggers short-term or acute insomnia. If you do not address your insomnia, however, it may develop into chronic insomnia. Some surveys have shown that 30% to 35% of subjects interviewed reported difficulty falling asleep during the previous year, and about 10% reported problems with long-standing insomnia. There also seems to be an association between depression, anxiety, and insomnia. Although the nature of this correlation is unknown, people with depression or anxiety were significantly more likely to develop insomnia. Some common causes of insomnia are stimulants including caffeine and nicotine. Alcohol is also associated with sleep disruption and creates a sense of drowsiness in the morning. Another factor could be a bed partner with loud snoring that makes it difficult to fall asleep.

Long-term insomnia can cause serious health consequences because human body needs to repair itself during sleep. It seems that the body is not at work while sleeping, but the brain is actually still active, maintaining the normal functioning of all the systems. Most importantly, the immune system produces more of certain substances that help fight diseases while we sleep. Therefore, getting adequate sleep is the first step toward good health.

失眠是一種症狀，而不是一種獨立的疾病。就定義而言，失眠是「開始或維持睡眠的困難，或者兩者皆有」。所以，失眠有可能對睡眠的品質或量造成負面影響。失眠不是以特定的睡眠時數定義的，因為每個人在需要的睡眠長度方面是不一樣的，重要的是我們感覺如何。我們大部分的人都經歷過沒有睡夠的感覺，但只有一些人看過醫生，而其他人根本不知道有方法可以治療這個問題。

失眠會影響所有年齡層。在成人之中，失眠對女人的影響比男人常見。這個問題發生的可能性傾向於隨著年齡增加。它通常比較常見於社會經濟地位（收入）低的族群、慢性酗酒者，還有心理健康問題的患者。壓力最常引起短期或急性的失眠。不過，如果你不處理你的失眠，就有可能發展成慢性失眠。有些調查顯示，有 30% 到 35% 的受訪者表示在過去一年有入睡困難，而大約有 10% 的人表示有長期持續的失眠。憂鬱症、焦慮和失眠之間似乎也有關聯。雖然這個關聯的本質並不清楚，但有憂鬱或焦慮症的人得到失眠的可能性顯著較高。有些常見的失眠原因是包括咖啡因和尼古丁在內的興奮劑。酒精也和睡眠中斷有關，而且會產生早上想睡覺的感覺。另一個因素可能是打鼾很大聲的床伴，使得伴侶很難睡著。

長期的失眠可能會造成嚴重的健康後果，因為人體需要在睡覺時修復自己。身體在睡覺時似乎沒在運作，但大腦其實還是活躍的，維持著所有系統的正常運作。最重要的是，免疫系統會在我們睡覺的時候產生更多能幫助對抗疾病的物質。所以，得到充足的睡眠是通往健康的第一步。

|單字片語|

（第一段）

insomnia [ɪn`sɑmnɪə] n. 失眠症 / **symptom** [`sɪmptəm] n. 症狀 / **disease** [dɪ`ziz] n. 疾病 / **initiate** [ɪ`nɪʃɪˏet] v. 開始… / **consult** [kən`sʌlt] v. 諮詢，看（醫生）

（第二段）

likelihood [`laɪklɪˏhʊd] n. 可能性 / **socioeconomic** [ˏsosɪoikə`nɑmɪk] adj. 社會經濟的 / **chronic** [`krɑnɪk] adj. 慢性的 / **alcoholic** [ˏælkə`hɔlɪk] adj. 酒精的，嗜酒成癮的 n. 嗜酒成癮的人 / **mental health** 心理健康 / **trigger** [`trɪgɚ] v. 觸發，引起 / **acute** [ə`kjut] adj. 劇烈的，急性的 / **long-standing** [`lɔŋ`stændɪŋ] adj. 長期存在的 / **association** [əˏsosɪ`eʃən] n. 聯合，關聯 / **depression** [dɪ`prɛʃən] n. 沮喪，憂鬱症 / **anxiety** [æŋ`zaɪətɪ] n. 焦慮 / **correlation** [ˏkɔrə`leʃən] n. 相互關係，關聯 / **stimulant** [`stɪmjələnt] n. 刺激物，興奮劑 / **caffeine** [`kæfiɪn] n. 咖啡因 / **nicotine** [`nɪkəˏtin] n. 尼古丁 / **disruption** [dɪs`rʌpʃən] n. 中斷，擾亂 / **drowsiness** [`draʊzɪnɪs] n. 睡意，昏昏欲睡 / **snore** [snor] v. 打鼾

（第三段）

consequence [`kɑnsəˏkwɛns] n. 結果，後果 / **immune system** 免疫系統 / **substance** [`sʌbstəns] n. 物質 / **adequate** [`ædəkwɪt] adj. 適當的，足夠的

Q35

What is the definition of insomnia based on the article?

根據這篇文章，失眠的定義是什麼？

A. A specific disease of the brain　一種特定的腦部疾病
B. Not being able to get enough sleep　沒辦法得到充足的睡眠
C. Less than eight hours of sleep a day　一天睡眠時間少於八小時
D. A sleep full of dreams or nightmares　充滿夢或者惡夢的睡眠

詳解　　**答案：B**

題目的關鍵字 definition（定義）出現在第一段第二句話 By definition, insomnia is "difficulty initiating or maintaining sleep, or both."（就定義而言，失眠是「開始或維持睡眠的困難，或者兩者皆有」），所以 B 是正確答案。

Q36

According to this article, how come very few people with sleeping disorders ask a doctor for help?

根據這篇文章，為什麼有睡眠障礙的人很少向醫生尋求協助？

A. They are too embarrassed to talk about the problem.
他們太羞於談論這個問題。
B. They remain unaware that they suffer from insomnia.
他們還不知道他們有失眠症。
C. They do not know that insomnia can be treated.
他們不知道失眠症可以治療。
D. They think that treatment for insomnia is too expensive.
他們覺得失眠症的治療太貴了。

詳解

答案：C

問題的關鍵語 very few people... ask a doctor for help（很少人向醫生尋求協助）對應第一段最後一句的 only a few have consulted doctors（只有很少人看過醫生），接下來就提到 others don't even know there are methods that can treat the problem（其他人根本不知道有方法可以治療這個問題），所以他們是因為不知道可以治療而沒有看醫生，C 是正確答案。

|單字片語| **disorder** [dɪs`ɔrdɚ] n. 失調 / **suffer from** 受…之苦，患有（疾病）

What kind of people have high risks of suffering from insomnia?

什麼樣的人得到失眠症的風險很高？

A. Children who do sports　做運動的小孩
B. People who come from wealthy families　來自富有家庭的人
C. Men in their early twenties　二十歲出頭的男人
D. Heavy drinkers　嚴重酗酒者

詳解

答案：D

第二段列舉出容易得到失眠症的條件，將選項和內文逐一比對，看看是否正確。A. 在文中沒有提到。B. 文中的 It is typically more common in people in lower socioeconomic (income) groups（它通常比較常見於社會經濟地位（收入）低的族群），選項的敘述正好相反，所以不對。C. 文中的 insomnia affects women more often than men. The likelihood of this problem occurring tends to increase with age.（失眠對女人的影響多過男人。這個問題發生的可能性傾向於隨著年齡增加。）顯示年紀大的女性風險較高，和選項的敘述相反，所以不對。D. 文中的 It is typically more common in... chronic alcoholics（它通常比較常見於慢性酗酒者），符合選項敘述，所以 D 是正確答案。

Q38

Which of the following statements is NOT consistent with this article?

以下哪個敘述不符合這篇文章？

A. Emotional states have a lot to do with insomnia.
情緒狀態和失眠很有關係。

B. Causes of insomnia can be both internal and external.
失眠的原因可以是內在和外在的。

C. Caffeine and alcohol may affect one's ability to sleep.
咖啡因和酒精可能影響一個人睡眠的能力。

D. Sleep is a passive state in which the brain shuts down to rest.
睡眠是一種大腦關機休息的被動狀態。

詳解 **答案：D**

一一對照每個選項是否符合文章內容。A. 對應第二段的 people with depression or anxiety were significantly more likely to develop insomnia（有憂鬱或焦慮症的人得到失眠的可能性顯著較高）。B. 第二段提到的 age（年齡）、mental health（心理健康）等等是內在因素，socioeconomic group（社會經濟族群）、bed partner（床伴）等等是外在因素，符合選項敘述。C. 對應第二段的 Some common causes of insomnia are stimulants including caffeine and nicotine（有些常見的失眠原因是包括咖啡因和尼古丁在內的興奮劑）。D. 和第三段提到的 It seems that the body is not at work while sleeping, but the brain is actually still active（身體在睡覺時似乎沒在運作，但大腦其實還是活躍的）不符合，所以 D 是正確答案。

|單字片語| **consistent** [kən`sɪstənt] adj. 一致的，符合的

According to this article, what is true about sleep?

根據這篇文章，關於睡眠何者正確？

A. Too much sleep can result in mental health problems.
睡得太多可能導致心理健康問題。

B. Our brain stops working during sleep to remain healthy.
我們的大腦在睡眠時停止運作以維持健康。

C. Sleep helps maintain the body's self-healing ability.
睡眠能幫助維持身體的自癒能力。

D. One can hear one's own snoring while asleep.
一個人可以在睡覺的時候聽到自己打鼾。

詳解

答案：C

在文章各處找到相關的內容，判斷各選項是否正確。A. 在文章中沒有提到。B. 第三段第二句話的 while sleeping... the brain is actually still active（睡覺時大腦其實還是活躍的），和選項的敘述不一致。C. 第三段第一句話的 human body needs to repair itself during sleep（人體需要在睡覺時修復自己）和選項敘述相符，所以 C 是正確答案。D. 第二段最後一句話的 a bed partner with loud snoring that makes it difficult to fall asleep（打鼾很大聲，使伴侶很難睡著的床伴）是指一個人的打鼾聲導致另一個人難以入睡，而不是人會聽到自己打鼾的意思，和選項的敘述不一致。

Q40

Which of the following is a suitable title for this article?

以下哪個是這篇文章適合的標題？

A. Difference between Rest and Sleep
休息和睡眠的差別

B. Factors Related to Insomnia and the Role of Sleep
與失眠相關的因素，以及睡眠的角色

C. The Causes, Consequences, and Cures of Insomnia
失眠的原因、後果與治療方式

D. Overcoming Insomnia and Achieving Sound Sleep
克服失眠並達成安穩的睡眠

詳解

答案：B

文章的第一段到第三段，分別敘述失眠的定義、與失眠相關的因素，以及睡眠對人體的重要性。所以，最適當的答案是 B。選項 C 和 D 分別提到 cures（治療法）和 achieving sound sleep（達成安穩的睡眠），但文章中並沒有深入解說治療失眠、安穩入睡的方法，所以不對。

全民英語能力分級檢定測驗
GENERAL ENGLISH PROFICIENCY TEST

中高級聽力測驗　第二回
HIGH-INTERMEDIATE LISTENING COMPREHENSION TEST

This listening comprehension test will test your ability to understand spoken English. In this test, each conversation, short talk and question will be spoken JUST ONE TIME. They will not be written out for you. There are three parts to this test. Special instructions will be given to you at the beginning of each part.

Part I: Answering Questions

In Part I, you will hear ten questions. After you hear a question, read the four choices in your test booklet and decide which one is the best answer to the question you have heard.

Example:

You will hear: Why did you slam the door?

You will read:
A. I just can't open it.
B. I didn't. I guess it's the wind.
C. Because someone is at the door.
D. Because the door knob is missing.

The best answer to the question "Why did you slam the door?" is B: "I didn't. I guess it's the wind." Therefore, you should choose answer B.

1. A. You like it, don't you?
   B. It's time to rock and roll.
   C. I'm already used to it.
   D. Let's dance to the beat.

2. A. I can't seem to make up my mind.
   B. I haven't arrived at my destination.
   C. I couldn't accept that present.
   D. I usually write the summary in the end.

3. A. He always feels rushed.
   B. In fact, it is quite simple.
   C. All vital signs are stable.
   D. It's been seriously cold.

4. A. Why don't you find it out yourself?
   B. How could you do that to me?
   C. Are you pulling my leg, or are you serious?
   D. No, I don't know my sales quota.

5. A. It's always hard the first time.
   B. No, you can wear your suit.
   C. Wear something suitable for dancing.
   D. You can't go wrong with that.

6. A. There is no other way.
   B. I'll return it to you as soon as I can.
   C. I failed the final exam.
   D. I heard that it's very demanding.

7. A. Maybe hiring an accountant will help.
   B. Why don't you leave them blank?
   C. Maybe you can do it next time.
   D. Perhaps you should consult a physician.

8. A. You must have skipped breakfast.
   B. OK, you go first.
   C. No, I have a bite on my back.
   D. Are you on a diet now?

9. A. No way. I won't settle for second best.
   B. Relax. I have a valid driver's license.
   C. Sure. I got myself a good bargain.
   D. You're right. I'm being too impulsive.

10. A. It's better late than never.
    B. Take it or leave it.
    C. How low can you go?
    D. Why don't you go for it?

Part II: Conversation

In part II, you will hear several conversations between a man and a woman. After each conversation, you will hear a question about the conversation. After you hear the question, read the four choices in your test booklet and choose the best answer to the question you have heard.

Example:

You will hear:

(Man) Did you happen to see my earphones? I remember leaving them in the drawer. Someone must have taken it.

(Woman) It's more likely that you misplaced them. Did you search your briefcase?

(Man) I did, but they are not there. Wait a second. Oh. They are right here in my pocket.

Question: Who took the man's earphones?

You will read:

A. The woman.
B. Someone else.
C. No one.
D. Another man.

The best answer to the question "Who took the man's earphones?" is C: "No one." Therefore, you should choose answer C.

Please turn to the next page.

11. A. He's jealous of the woman's handwriting skills.
    B. He's embarrassed about his poor handwriting.
    C. He's confused about Professor Wang's teaching.
    D. He's arrogant about having taken the course before.

12. A. In Zurich.
    B. In America.
    C. In Syria.
    D. In Greece.

13. A. She doesn't have a good appetite.
    B. She doesn't like children.
    C. She is allergic to seafood.
    D. She is worried about her weight.

14. A. A brain surgeon.
    B. A psychiatrist.
    C. A physical therapist.
    D. A veterinarian.

15. A. Get a notebook computer.
    B. Get a computer desk.
    C. Get a tablet computer.
    D. Get a new software program.

16. A. In a forest.
    B. In a clinic.
    C. In a temple.
    D. In a library.

17. A. The coach is good-looking and friendly.
    B. The man offered her a special price.
    C. The weight control program is interesting.
    D. The gym provides a unique service.

18. A. The man's concerns are unfounded.
    B. Food labels are not reliable.
    C. Organic and non-organic foods are alike.
    D. The authorities are short of manpower.

19. A. He is jealous about the woman's new position.
    B. He is not advancing in his career.
    C. He is good at predicting.
    D. He is going to retire soon.

20. A. He hit another man's car.
    B. His car was hit by another car.
    C. His car slipped off the road.
    D. He hit a deer.

21. A. It was snowing.
    B. The car behind was too close.
    C. Bruce didn't turn on his headlights.
    D. Bruce hit the brakes suddenly.

22. A. She will pay for a medium latte.
    B. She will pay for a large latte.
    C. She will just buy a sandwich.
    D. She will cancel her order.

23. A. It offers discounts for every purchase.
    B. It charges for extra sugar.
    C. It's the only café in the area.
    D. It's the least expensive café in the area.

24.

Flight No.	Destination	Airline	Departure	Arrival
GL 310	JFK	Gamma	06:45 AM	03:35 PM
JB 616	JFK	JetBlack	07:30 AM	04:09 PM
AA 2304	Newark	Associated	08:45 AM	05:12 PM
AA 2603	Newark	Associated	10:40 AM	07:19 PM

A. GL 310.
B. JB 616.
C. AA 2304.
D. AA 2603.

25.

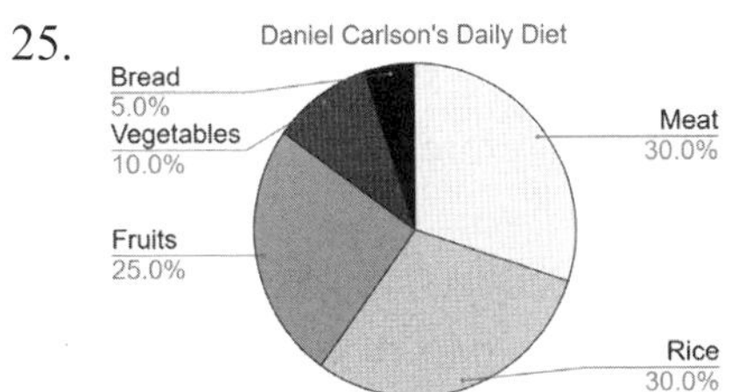

A. Bread.
B. Vegetables.
C. Fruits.
D. Rice.

Please turn to the next page.

Part III: Short Talks

In part III, you will hear several short talks. After each talk, you will hear two to three questions about the talk. After you hear each question, read the four choices in your test booklet and choose the best answer to the question you have heard.

Example:

You will hear: Hello, thank you everyone for coming together to share this special day with Chris and I. We have been waiting for this moment forever, and after five years of dating, I can happily say that I am ready. Chris is caring and charming, and I appreciate my good fortune in marrying such a warm-hearted man. When he proposed to me, I realized that he had already become a part of my life. Even though I'm not a perfect cook or housekeeper, I know for sure that I will be a wonderful partner for Chris.

Question number 1: On what occasion is this talk most probably being given?

You will read:
A. A funeral.
B. A wedding.
C. A housewarming.
D. A farewell party.

The best answer to the question "On what occasion is this talk most probably being given?" is B: "A wedding." Therefore, you should choose answer B.

Now listen to another question based on the same talk.

You will hear: Question number 2: According to this talk, what does the woman like about Chris?

You will read: A. His perseverance.
B. His abundant wealth.
C. His cooking skill.
D. His amiable personality.

The best answer to the question "According to this talk, what does the woman like about Chris?" is D: "His amiable personality." Therefore, you should choose answer D.

Please turn to the next page. Now let us begin Part III with question number 26.

26. A. Two people were attacked by wild animals.
    B. Bears are not used to the presence of mankind.
    C. Wild animals may enter the campsite in search of food.
    D. A bear was brought into the campsite as part of the training program.

27. A. To ensure that wild animals are not hunted.
    B. To ensure that bears are not in danger.
    C. To ensure that campers do not get hurt.
    D. To ensure that campers do not feed the bears.

28. A. Our parents.
    B. Our schools.
    C. Our age.
    D. Our gender.

29. A. We swallow our pride.
    B. We learn from our mistakes.
    C. We deny that we have weaknesses.
    D. We admit our faults immediately.

30. A. Arrogance hinders learning.
    B. Negativity produces resistance.
    C. Prejudice leads to maturity.
    D. Pride creates self-confidence.

31. A. He has no access to his password.
    B. He has no authority to use the computer.
    C. The system is infected with a virus.
    D. The system failed to recognize his password.

32. A. He entered the wrong password for the third time.
    B. He has trouble communicating with the customers.
    C. He is desperate for help because he has a deadline to meet.
    D. He is on leave and doesn't have his computer with him.

33. A. Country club membership.
    B. An apartment building.
    C. A day-care service.
    D. A consumer loan.

34. A. Peaceful surroundings.
    B. Low cash requirement.
    C. High rental income.
    D. Reasonable interest rates.

35-37.

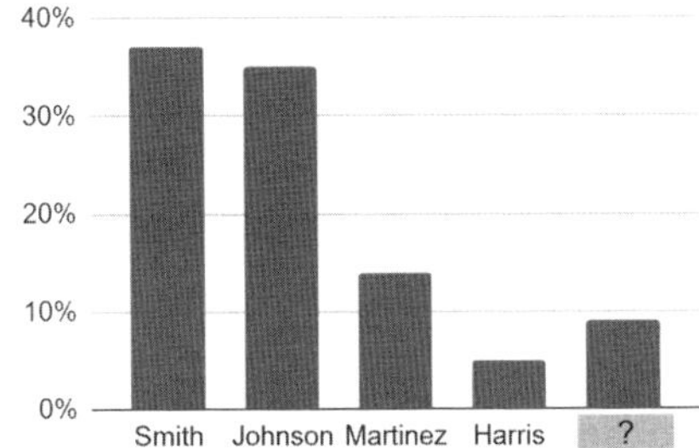

35. A. The result of the election.
    B. The popularity of policies.
    C. The survey results on how people will vote.
    D. The evaluation of the candidates' performance.

36. A. Undecided.
    B. Will not vote.
    C. Other candidates.
    D. Not a registered voter.

37. A. Smith.
    B. Johnson.
    C. Martinez.
    D. Harris.

38-40.

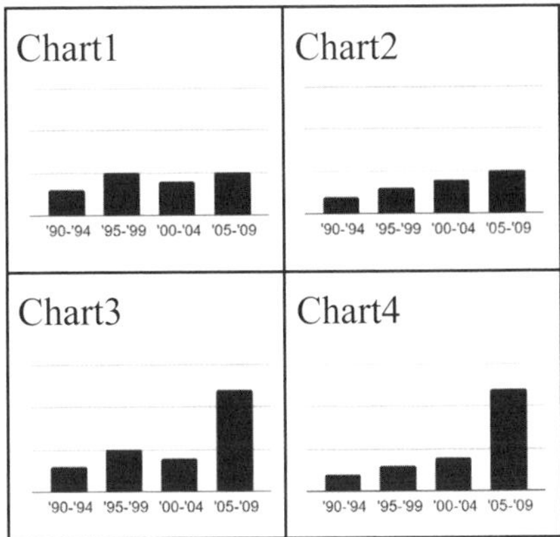

38. A. Chart 1.
    B. Chart 2.
    C. Chart 3.
    D. Chart 4.

39. A. Its investments went down.
    B. The economic situation was bad.
    C. It gave the money to local students.
    D. There were too many international students.

40. A. It is a financial burden for the government.
    B. It has nothing to do with the economy.
    C. It helps to improve the country's image.
    D. It is a way to bring in foreign professionals.

Please turn to the next page.

READING COMPREHESION TEST

This is a three-part test with forty multiple-choice questions. Each question has four choices. Special instructions will be provided for each part. You will have fifty minutes to complete this test.

Part I: Sentence Completion

In this part of the test, there are ten incomplete sentences. Beneath each sentence you will see four words or phrases, marked A, B, C and D. You are to choose the word or phrase that best completes the sentence. Then on your answer sheet, find the number of the question and mark your answer.

1. In view of the latest education reform and initiatives, schools will require a more ________ curriculum to cater to the needs of students with different interests.

   A. various　　B. advantageous
   C. extensive　　D. compulsory

2. The power outage did not cause much damage as it has been ________ and prepared for.

   A. prevented　　B. prospected
   C. anticipated　　D. overlooked

3. Making inappropriate comments about a woman's figure can be considered a form of sexual ________.

   A. interference　　B. harassment
   C. prosecution　　D. manipulation

4. ________ any of the information provided by candidates be found false, legal actions will be taken.

   A. Though　　B. Should
   C. Notwithstanding　　D. Whether

5. Physical characteristics are transmitted from parents to their ________ through genes.
   A. aftermath B. downturn
   C. offspring D. subordinate

6. One of my colleagues kept finding fault with my proposal in the previous meeting. I will ________ him one of these days.
   A. get along with B. get around with
   C. get even with D. get away with

7. The ballet dancers appeared on stage as the background music began to ________.
   A. wear out B. reach out
   C. fade out D. go out

8. As more and more confirmed cases are recorded, the city is on the ________ of becoming the epicenter of the pandemic.
   A. agony B. doom
   C. peril D. verge

9. The argument between the group members was so heated that the professor had no choice but to ________ and act as a mediator.
   A. interrupt B. interact
   C. interfere D. intervene

10. Cosmetics companies made a fortune in anti-aging skin care products by promising a fairer and wrinkle-free ________.
   A. modification B. complexion
   C. operation D. transformation

Please turn to the next page.

Part Two: Cloze

In this part of the test, you will read two passages. Each passage contains five missing words or phrases. Beneath each passage, you will see five items, each with four choices, marked A, B, C and D. You are to choose the best answer for each missing word or phrase in the two passages. Then, on your answer sheet, find the number of the question and mark your answer.

Questions 11-15

Parents of the 21st century are faced with a dilemma: is home learning more effective and efficient than traditional schools? ___(11)___, homeschooling is beneficial for children as long as parents play an active role in coaching and monitoring. In fact, virtually all the available data show that ___(12)___. In addition, studies found that the academic performance of homeschoolers is ___(13)___ that of children in prestigious private schools. On the other hand, one major concern is whether homeschooling helps or hampers a child's social development. Children ___(14)___ homeschooling spend less time with same-aged children and miss out on social interaction in school settings. In spite of this "flaw" in home learning, many parents are still willing to give it a try as they can counter this problem by taking their children to church, ___(15)___ they can develop friendship with other children of similar age.

11. A. Generally speaking
    B. On speaking terms
    C. Speaking of
    D. So to speak

12. A. homeschooling helps children develop their social skills
    B. the performance of homeschooled children is above average
    C. homeschooling can have negative effects on children's performance
    D. homeschooled children report high levels of satisfaction with their lives

13. A. on par with
    B. no way near
    C. inferior to
    D. unlike

14. A. compelled to
    B. engaged in
    C. refrained from
    D. paralyzed by

15. A. yet
    B. where
    C. because
    D. as if

Questions 16-20

Steven Paul Jobs, the co-founder, two-time CEO, and chairman of Apple Inc., passed away on October 5, 2011 after a courageous yet unsuccessful battle with cancer. He was only 56, and Apple fanatics around the world ___(16)___ the loss of such a genius. The achievement in Jobs' career is phenomenal. He literally saved the music industry from collapsing by launching the iTunes Store. ___(17)___, the genius himself has once been shown the door as a result of office politics. Undaunted, he ___(18)___ his endless energy into driving the then pretty much unknown Pixar Animation Studios from obscurity to prominence. *Toy Story* was a global success ___(19)___ Steve Jobs' charisma, drive, and extraordinary vision. With his multiple inventions that shaped the future, the great man will surely go down in history ___(20)___ the likes of Thomas Edison, Isaac Newton, and even Albert Einstein.

16. A. lamented
    B. coveted
    C. relieved
    D. oppressed

17. A. As a consequence
    B. On a personal level
    C. Despite his accomplishment
    D. Being committed to his vision

18. A. compensated
    B. diverted
    C. salvaged
    D. evacuated

19. A. owing to
    B. resulting in
    C. based on
    D. deprived of

20. A. prior to
    B. along with
    C. in place of
    D. as well as

Part III: Reading Comprehension

In this part of the test, you will find several tasks. Each task contains one or two passages or charts, which are followed by two to six questions. You are to choose the best answer, A, B, C, or D, to each question on the basis of the information provided or implied in the passage or chart. Then, on your answer sheet, find the number of the question and mark your answer.

Please turn to the next page.

Questions 21-22 are based on the information provided in the following chart.

Product Profitability Analysis

Product	Revenue	Production Cost	Net Profit/ Loss	% of Total Profit
A	$852,000	$720,000	$132,000	32
B	$647,000	$550,000	$97,000	22
C	$439,000	$250,000	$189,000	46
D	$245,000	$250,000	-$5,000	N/A

26. Based on the chart, which of the following statements is true?
    A. All products are in the black.
    B. Product A is the most profitable.
    C. Product B generates the highest turnover in sales.
    D. About 80 percent of the total profits come from two products.

27. What action should be taken according to the information provided in this chart?
    A. The company should scrap product A.
    B. The company should invest the most marketing resources on product B.
    C. The company should focus more on product C.
    D. The company should produce more of product D.

Questions 23-25

There is no doubt that global warming is responsible for radical weather conditions experienced in the past decade. The polar bear's home – the Arctic – is experiencing the effects of global warming more than any other place. Temperatures in the Arctic are rising at almost twice the rate of the rest of the world, placing not only the polar bears but the entire Arctic ecosystem in jeopardy. Based on data provided by *National Geographic*, the amount of summer ice has declined by about 30 percent since 1979. The amount of sea ice is significant because apart from providing a hunting ground for polar bears, it is also a shelter for seals, walruses, arctic foxes, and the Inuit people.

Arctic sea ice also has a cooling effect on climate by reflecting light away from Earth's surface. With less sea ice than before, global warming advances even more quickly, and it in turn triggers a chain reaction which could negatively impact the environment around the world. Viewed from this perspective, saving polar bears' home is equivalent to saving ourselves from extinction.

Please turn to the next page.

23. What is true about conditions in the Arctic according to the article?
    A. Temperatures are within normal range.
    B. The population of polar bears has doubled.
    C. Ice area has shrunk by close to one-third.
    D. Polar bears can threaten the life of the Inuit people.

24. How does global warming affect animals and people in the Arctic?
    A. It takes away their natural habitat.
    B. It allows them to migrate.
    C. It provides more food for the local.
    D. It forces animals to rise up against humans.

25. Why would saving the polar bears be the same as saving the human race?
    A. Polar bears are at the top of the Arctic food chain.
    B. The Arctic provides oxygen that cools down the Earth.
    C. Lack of rain and water in the Arctic can cut down food supply.
    D. A further reduction in ice mass in the Arctic could lead to global destruction.

Questions 26-29

Drunk driving is among the top causes of automobile accidents. Each year, drunk drivers cause tragedy and grief in thousands of car accidents. Drinkers will never admit that drinking affects their ability to drive, but the fact remains that the consumption of alcohol can temporarily impair vision and hearing and thus result in decreased muscle coordination and slower reaction. Ironically, after drunk-driving accidents, sometimes those who drive under the influence (DUI) of alcohol survive, while those who follow the rules are killed. This **paradox** can only be solved by stricter laws, better enforcement, and random checkpoints. The goal is to arrest more people who drive drunk to get them off the road. Without getting caught, drunk drivers might take their chances, thinking that a drink or two will not affect their judgment. Some US states even require repeated DUI offenders to install a key-ignition lock on their car that has an attached breathalyzer.

In all fifty states in America, the legal limit for driving under the influence of alcohol is a blood alcohol concentration (BAC) level of .08 or higher. BAC level is the percentage of alcohol in a person's blood, and it is related to one's drunkenness and sobriety. While a high BAC level makes it illegal to drive, a BAC level lower than .08 can still impair a person's senses somewhat, causing a higher risk than driving sober. As a precaution, all drivers should refrain from alcohol intake, no matter how small the amount is.

Although the enforcement of the laws can reduce drinking and driving to a certain extent, the easiest way is to educate people to make better decisions. For instance, something as simple as a designated driver can save people from car accidents. By putting a sober person behind the wheel, everyone can feel free to have a good time at the bar without putting anyone's life at risk on the road.

Please turn to the next page. ⇨

26. What is the main subject for this article?
    A. New technology that deters drunk drivers from driving
    B. Different methods to test alcohol levels of drivers
    C. The importance of prohibiting drinking during social events
    D. Consequences of drunk driving and corrective measures

27. Which word has the closest meaning to the word **paradox**?
    A. Joke
    B. Irony
    C. Symptom
    D. Metaphor

28. Why is it important to catch drunk-drivers in the act?
    A. Otherwise they might turn themselves in.
    B. Otherwise they might commit suicide.
    C. Otherwise they might be tempted to do it again.
    D. Otherwise they might be judged innocent.

29. According to this article, what is true about accidents involving drunk drivers?
    A. They can sometimes escape death.
    B. They often hurt their loved ones.
    C. They are usually killed on the spot.
    D. They are often caught red-handed.

Questions 30-34 are based on the information provided in the following advertisement and email.

Fantastic Asia Tours
Discover different faces of Japan!

Japan is a country of incredible contrast. You can experience the most modern and the most traditional in this one country. From the dazzling neon lights of its futuristic cities, to ancient temples in the mountains, this country makes you feel like traveling through time in the cultural sense. It's truly like nowhere else on earth! Please consider our tour packages and let our guides help you discover the past and future of Japan.

Our Popular Tours

Best of Tokyo Tour Perfect for those who want to visit the most popular sites in Tokyo	Tokyo	5 days	NT$ 30,000 per person
Anime Flavor Tour Visit some of the popular anime spots while learning about Japan's subculture	Tokyo	5 days	NT$ 40,000 per person
Essence of Japan Tour In-depth travel with focus on traditional culture	Tokyo & Osaka	10 days	NT$ 60,000 per person
Luxury Japan Tour Travel luxuriously while enjoying top tier accommodations	Tokyo & Osaka	8 days	NT$ 80,000 per person

**Discounts available for groups of 10 or above*

All prices include flights, accommodations, breakfasts, entrance fees, and local transportation.

For more detail, please contact service@fantasticasiatours.com.

From: Weimin Zhang <weimin88@lownet.net>
To: Tom Smith <tsmith@yabaimail.com>
Subject: Plan of visiting Japan
Attachment: FantasticAsia_Japan.pdf

Dear Tom,

After the pandemic years, we can finally travel to Japan without quarantine! I guess you must be as eager as me to revisit the places we've been to, so I'm planning to book a tour for us and our families.

I have attached a file, in which you can see some packages provided by Fantastic Asia Tours. I've heard that their cheaper tours are not bad, and the Anime Flavor Tour is popular among anime and comic fans because it includes attending subculture events in Akihabara. However, even though we both like Japan's animations, it seems to me that we should increase our budget and go for a better package. We're already familiar with Tokyo with our many travel experiences, but we rarely went to Osaka, so I think it will be great to explore the city this time. I'd like to stay in Japan as long as possible, and I also want to know more about the past of Japan, which we don't know much about yet.

Please let me know what you think. By the way, my parents, my wife and two sons are going with me, so if you bring your family with you, we'll be eligible for the discount.

Sincerely,
Weimin

30. How does the advertisement make customers interested in Japan?
    A. By introducing its history
    B. By emphasizing its peacefulness
    C. By demonstrating its economic development
    D. By focusing on its contrast of different aspects

31. What is true about Weimin and Tom?
    A. They frequently attend subculture events.
    B. They know Japan's history well.
    C. They have been to Tokyo many times.
    D. They have never been to Osaka.

32. Which feature of the tours is **NOT** indicated in the advertisement?
    A. The date of each tour
    B. The cost of each tour
    C. The destination of each tour
    D. The duration of each tour

33. Which tour does Weimin prefer to book?
    A. Best of Tokyo Tour
    B. Anime Flavor Tour
    C. Essence of Japan Tour
    D. Luxury Japan Tour

34. At least how many people are there in Tom's family?
    A. Two people
    B. Three people
    C. Four people
    D. Five people

Please turn to the next page.

Questions 35-40

"Whatever the mind of man can conceive and believe, it can achieve." These are the famous words of a revolutionary thinker, Napoleon Hill. As a human race, we are inferior to most animals in terms of physical prowess. Yet incredibly, we can fly in airplanes faster than the speed of sound without wings on our backs. We conquered the moon and, more recently, sent a spacecraft into the orbit of Jupiter, the largest planet in the solar system. According to Napoleon Hill's Law of Attraction, intense desire combined with faith and strong emotions triggers an invincible mechanism within our subconscious mind. Once activated, a thought continues to gather strength until it manifests into physical being.

Since our brain cells communicate with each other by electrical impulses, thoughts are actually energy. The more committed we are to our cause, the stronger our beliefs, the faster our thoughts, ideas, and inspirations will materialize. Many of the world's most successful individuals remember the "Aha" moment that defined their breakthroughs. With your heart full of desire and your mind open to suggestions, a plan will gradually form. Once it takes shape, your path will become crystal-clear. Having said that, it doesn't necessarily mean a bed of roses ahead of you. Obstacles are thrown into the way to test your resolve and make you stronger. Oftentimes, you cannot see beyond the next step, and that's when you take a leap of faith, in the literal sense. Once you conquer your fears, be ready to witness miraculous events taking place before your eyes. Your success will exceed your wildest imagination.

Alas! Achieving is not so much a challenge as the believing part, where most people failed. Imagine an elephant that has been tied with a rope to a tree since it was young. Even though it grows up to possess the strength to uproot the tree, it will still believe that it cannot break free. Such is the power of negative thinking. People who are pessimistic tend to lack self-esteem and self-confidence. They often make excuses for themselves and drag their feet when confronted with problems. Their motto in life is "I won't fail as long as I put things off." In essence, this is a loser's mentality. In rare circumstances where they did try and failed, they simply shrug their shoulders rather than find out the reasons that lead to their failure.

35. Which of the following statements is in line with Napoleon Hill's saying?
    A. The sky is the limit.
    B. Laughter is the best medicine.
    C. Time and tide wait for no man.
    D. Never bite off more than what you can chew.

36. What does the article imply about humans and animals?
    A. Humans have superior physical strength.
    B. Animals are conscious about their weaknesses.
    C. Humans and animals are similar in many areas.
    D. Animals have better physical attributes compared to humans.

37. What can be assumed about the Law of Attraction?
    A. It was discovered by a prominent physicist.
    B. It involves the development of a single idea.
    C. It makes patients with mental disorder violent.
    D. It only works on rare occasions.

38. How can we put the Law of Attraction into motion?
    A. By studying and passing an exam
    B. By undergoing a brain surgery
    C. By committing ourselves to our goals
    D. By venting our frustrations on others

39. What is likely to happen once you formulate a plan?
    A. Everything will be smooth sailing.
    B. Rewards will come very soon.
    C. Barriers will start to show up.
    D. People will pledge their support to you.

40. What is **NOT** true about people who have a negative mindset?
    A. They often find reasons for not trying.
    B. They are accustomed to self-denial.
    C. They hold on to their faith in the face of failure.
    D. They lack the initiative to look for solutions.

第二回 初試 聽力測驗解析

第一部分 回答問題

Q1

Don't you think the music is a distraction? How can you possibly study in such an environment?
你不覺得音樂讓人分心嗎？你怎麼能在這種環境讀書呢？

A. You like it, don't you? A. 你喜歡，不是嗎？
B. It's time to rock and roll. B. 搖滾的時間到了。
C. I'm already used to it. C. 我已經習慣了。
D. Let's dance to the beat. D. 我們跟著節拍舞動吧。

詳解 答案：C

說話者說 music is a distraction（音樂是讓人分心的事情），並且問 How can you... study in such an environment（你怎麼能在這種環境讀書），所以應該回答有音樂也能讀書的理由，C 是最恰當的答案。

|單字片語| **distraction** [dɪˋstrækʃən] n. 令人分心的事物

Q2

Based on the data given to you last week, have you reached a conclusion?
根據上禮拜給你的資料，你得到結論了嗎？

A. I can't seem to make up my mind. A. 我好像沒辦法拿定主意。
B. I haven't arrived at my destination. B. 我還沒到達我的目的地。
C. I couldn't accept that present. C. 我不能接受那份禮物。
D. I usually write the summary in the end. D. 我通常在最後寫摘要。

詳解

答案：A

說話者提到 data given to you（給你的資料），問 have you reached a conclusion（你有沒有得到結論）。reach 雖然是「抵達」的意思，但這裡的 reach a conclusion 是表示「推導」出一個結論，所以不要誤選 B。選項 A 用 can't... make up my mind（沒辦法拿定主意）表示還不知道要怎麼總結，是正確答案。選項 D 的 summary 表示「摘要」，通常在報告或論文的前面，用簡短的方式概述整體的內容，和 conclusion（結論）有些不同。

|單字片語| **make up one's mind** 下定決心，拿定主意

Q3

How's the patient's condition so far? I hope there are no complications.

患者目前為止的情況怎麼樣？我希望沒有併發症。

A. He always feels rushed.
B. In fact, it is quite simple.
C. All vital signs are stable.
D. It's been seriously cold.

A. 他總是感到匆忙。
B. 其實還蠻簡單的。
C. 所有生命徵象都是穩定的。
D. 這陣子非常冷。

詳解

答案：C

說話者問 patient's condition（患者的狀況）如何，又說希望沒有 complications（併發症），所以可以得知這是與醫療相關的場景。complication 基本的意思是「變得複雜的情況」，也可以指疾病的「併發症」。選項中，表示「生命徵象（呼吸、心跳等等）穩定」的 C 是最適當的答案。選項 B 和 D 的主詞 it 不能代表「患者」，描述的內容也和問題不相關；D 如果改成 It's a serious cold（那是很嚴重的感冒）或者 He caught a serious cold（他得了嚴重的感冒）就會是適合的答案。

|單字片語| **complication** [ˌkɑmplə`keʃən] n. 變得複雜的情況，併發症 / **rushed** [rʌʃt] adj. 匆忙的 / **vital sign** 生命徵象

Q4

Are you aware that you will be promoted to senior sales executive with effect from today?

你知道你會被升上資深業務主管，而且今天開始生效嗎？

A. Why don't you find it out yourself?
B. How could you do that to me?
C. Are you pulling my leg, or are you serious?
D. No, I don't know my sales quota.

A. 你何不自己查明真相呢？
B. 你怎麼能那樣對我？
C. 你是在開我玩笑還是認真的？
D. 不，我不知道我的銷售配額。

詳解

答案：C

說話者問 Are you aware（你知不知道），後面詳細說出對方會升上的職位、時間等等細節，所以應該是自己已經知道了，要問當事人知不知道。選項 C 的 pull one's leg 表示「開某人玩笑」，但即使不知道這個特殊的慣用語，聽到 are you serious?（你是認真的嗎？）也可以知道是表示不敢置信、向對方再次確認的意思，間接表示自己不知道這件事，是正確答案。A 雖然感覺像是正確答案，但說話者問的是「你知不知道」，而不是「那件事情是不是真的」，所以這不是適當的回答。選項 D 雖然用 No 回答了 Yes/No 問句，但後面的 sales quota（銷售配額）和問題無關，所以不對。

|單字片語| **with effect from** 自…起生效 / **pull one's leg** 開某人的玩笑 / **quota** [ˋkwotə] n. 配額

Q5

This is the first time I go to a symphony concert. Is formal attire required?

這是我第一次去交響音樂會。正式穿著是必要的嗎？

A. It's always hard the first time.
B. No, you can wear your suit.
C. Wear something suitable for dancing.
D. You can't go wrong with that.

A. 第一次總是很難。
B. 不，你可以穿你的西裝。
C. 穿適合跳舞的衣服。
D. 那樣絕對不會出錯。

詳解

答案：D

說話者要去 symphony concert（交響音樂會），問 Is formal attire required（正式服裝是不是必要的）。A 沒有回答說話者的問題，所以不對；B 回答了

No，表示「不需要穿得正式」，但後面接「你可以穿西裝」，前後矛盾；C 說要穿適合跳舞的衣服，但交響音樂會通常不能跳舞。D 的 You can't go wrong with that 表示「你選擇那個就不可能出錯」，在這裡指穿得正式是最安全的作法，是正確答案。

|單字片語| **symphony** [ˋsɪmfənɪ] n. 交響樂 / **attire** [əˋtaɪr] n. 服裝 / **required** [rɪˋkwaɪrd] adj. 必須的，必要的

Q6

Will you be taking the new course in biochemistry next semester? It's optional, though.
你會修下個學期新的生物化學課嗎？不過那是選修的。

A. There is no other way. A. 沒有別的辦法了。
B. I'll return it to you as soon as I can. B. 我會盡快還你。
C. I failed the final exam. C. 我期末考不及格。
D. I heard that it's very demanding. D. 我聽說那門課很吃力。

詳解

答案：D

說話者問 Will you be taking the new course（你會不會修新的課程），後面補充說那是 optional（選修的）。D 提到這門課很吃力，表示自己對這門課抱著觀望的態度，是最適當的答案。

|單字片語| **biochemistry** [ˋbaɪoˋkɛmɪstrɪ] n. 生物化學 / **optional** [ˋɑpʃənl̩] adj. 選擇性的；選修的 / **demanding** [dɪˋmændɪŋ] adj. 苛求的，吃力的

Q7

I get a headache whenever I have to fill out the tax return forms. They are so confusing.
每次要填納稅申報單我就頭痛。真的很讓人困惑。

A. Maybe hiring an accountant will help. A. 或許雇用會計師會有幫助。
B. Why don't you leave them blank? B. 何不留白呢？
C. Maybe you can do it next time. C. 或許你可以下次再做。
D. Perhaps you should consult a physician. D. 或許你應該諮詢醫生。

詳解

答案：A

tax return forms 是「納稅申報單」，說話者說的 headache、confusing 顯示他覺得處理起來很困難。A 建議雇用會計師，是正確答案。

Q8

It's not even noontime, but I am starving. Would you like to go and grab a bite?

都還沒到中午我就餓了。你想去吃點東西嗎？

A. You must have skipped breakfast.	A. 你一定沒吃早餐。
B. OK, you go first.	B. OK，你先。
C. No, I have a bite on my back.	C. 不，我的背上被（蚊蟲等）咬了一口。
D. Are you on a diet now?	D. 你現在在節食嗎？

詳解

答案：A

說話者說 I am starving（我很餓），邀請對方去 grab a bite（吃點東西）。A 並沒有回答要不要去，而是說出自己推測對方之所以很餓的理由 you... have skipped breakfast（你沒吃早餐），是適當的答案。B 的 OK 表示要一起去，後面卻說你先去，前後矛盾；C 的 bite 是「蚊蟲咬傷」的意思；D 應該是看到別人少吃或不吃東西才會有的反應。

|單字片語| **starving** [ˋstɑrvɪŋ] adj. 很餓的 / **grab a bite** 簡單吃點東西

補充說明

grab a bite 表示吃點簡單、方便吃的東西，像是 burger（漢堡）等等，如果是吃火鍋（eat a hot pot）的話就不會用 grab a bite 來表達。

Q9

Purchasing a car right now isn't a wise move. Why don't you give it a second thought?

現在買車不是明智的舉動。你何不重新考慮呢？

A. No way. I won't settle for second best.	A. 當然不行。我不會退而求其次。
B. Relax. I have a valid driver's license.	B. 放輕鬆。我有有效的駕照。
C. Sure. I got myself a good bargain.	C. 當然。我用很划算的價錢買到了。
D. You're right. I'm being too impulsive.	D. 你說得對。我太衝動了。

詳解

答案：D

說話者說現在買車子不是一個 wise move（明智的行動），要對方 give it a second thought（再次考慮）。A 看起來像是正確答案，但 settle for second best 表示「勉強接受第二好的東西」，以買車的情況而言，是指「買沒有那麼好的車」，而不是「不買車」的意思，所以不對。B、C 和題目不相關。D 先說 You're right 肯定對方的意見，並且說自己太 impulsive（衝動的），暗示會重新考慮，是正確答案。

|單字片語| **settle for** 勉強接受…，滿足於… / **good bargain** 划算的交易 / **impulsive** [ɪm`pʌlsɪv] adj. 衝動的

Q10

Is the camera on display the only one left? If that's the case, I deserve a better price. **展示中的相機是剩下的唯一一台嗎？這樣的話，我應該得到更好的價格。**

A. It's better late than never.	A. 遲做總比不做好。
B. Take it or leave it.	B. 要不要隨你。
C. How low can you go?	C. 你可以給到多低的價錢？
D. Why don't you go for it?	D. 你何不全力以赴呢？

詳解

答案：B

說話者要求得到 a better price（更好的價格），希望對方能算便宜一點，可以推測對方應該是店家。A 是用在有一件事情應該要做，雖然晚了但總比沒做來得好的情況。B 表示要就 take（接受→買），不要就放棄它，暗示不願意降價的意思，是正確答案。C 是顧客殺價時會說的話，是詢問對方可以降價的底限。D 的 go for it 表示為了某件事全力以赴的意思。

|單字片語| **on display** 展示中

補充說明

take it or leave it 表現的態度比較強硬，以店家的立場而言，應該只會在拒絕交涉的情況丟下這句話。

Q11

M: I didn't know you can write Chinese characters so well. Your handwriting is beautiful.
我不知道你能把中文字寫得這麼好看。你的字跡很美。

W: I'm taking a course in Chinese calligraphy by Professor Wang.
我正在上王教授的中文書法課。

M: Really? I took it last year, but my Chinese handwriting hasn't improved by a bit. 真的嗎？我去年修過，但我的中文字跡一點也沒進步。

W: Well, you know what they say. "Practice makes perfect."
嗯，你知道大家是這樣說的：「熟能生巧」。

M: You're right. I should be ashamed of myself.
你說得對。我應該為自己感到丟臉。

W: I can give you a tip or two if you don't mind.
如果你不介意的話，我可以給你一兩個建議。

M: It's probably too late. 可能太晚了。

Q: How does the man feel?
男子覺得怎麼樣？

A. He's jealous of the woman's handwriting skills. A. 他嫉妒女子的手寫技巧。
B. He's embarrassed about his poor handwriting. B. 他對自己不好看的字跡感到不好意思。
C. He's confused about Professor Wang's teaching. C. 他對王教授的教導感到困惑。
D. He's arrogant about having taken the course before. D. 他對於以前上過那門課感到自負。

詳解 **答案：B**

從選項的開頭都是 He's 來看，可以推測題目會問男子的想法，所以要特別注意男子的說話內容。他先說 Your handwriting is beautiful.（你的字跡很美），又說 my Chinese handwriting hasn't improved（我的中文字跡沒有進步）、I should be ashamed of myself（我應該為自己感到丟臉），所以 B 是正確答案；對話中的 hasn't improved、ashamed 對應選項中的 poor、embarrassed。選項 A 的 jealous（嫉妒的）是有點負面的字，表示心裡見不得人家好，但男子在對話中比較像是單純稱讚女子。

|單字片語| **handwriting** [ˋhænd͵raɪtɪŋ] n. 手寫筆跡 / **calligraphy** [kəˋlɪgrəfɪ] n. 書法 / **jealous** [ˋdʒɛləs] adj. 嫉妒的 / **arrogant** [ˋærəgənt] adj. 傲慢的，自大的

Q12

W: Feel free to take a look. This is the largest flea market in Zurich. It's like a garage sale in America. Most of the vendors, like me, are doing business just for fun.
請隨意看看。這是蘇黎世最大的跳蚤市場。就像美國的車庫拍賣一樣。大部分的攤販，像我一樣，是為了好玩而做生意。

M: Wow. There are so many exotic items. Is this lamp from the Middle East? 哇。有好多異國風格的東西。這盞燈是從中東來的嗎？

W: It's a replica of a Syrian oil lamp, but I actually bought it in Greece.
這是敘利亞油燈的複製品，但我其實是在希臘買的。

M: How much does it cost? 這要多少錢？

W: Ten Swiss Francs and it's yours. 付十法郎，這就是你的。

Q: Where did the woman purchase the lamp?
女子是在哪裡買到這盞燈的？

A. In Zurich. A. 在蘇黎世。
B. In America. B. 在美國。
C. In Syria. C. 在敘利亞。
D. In Greece. D. 在希臘。

詳解 **答案：D**

選項出現了四個地名，可以預期對話中會出現這些地名，而且會問某個細節的正確地點，所以要特別注意這些字。這些地名出現在 This is the largest flea market in Zurich. It's like a garage sale in America.（這是蘇黎世最大的跳蚤市場。就像美國的車庫拍賣一樣。）、It's a replica of a Syrian oil lamp, but I actually bought it in Greece.（這是敘利亞油燈的複製品，但我其實是在希臘買的。）等句中。題目問燈是在哪裡買的，只要正確掌握了細節，就能選出答案 D。

|單字片語| **flea market** 跳蚤市場 / **garage sale** 車庫拍賣（在自家車庫前或者庭院進行的舊物拍賣）/ **vendor** [ˋvɛndɚ] n. 小販 / **exotic** [ɛgˋzɑtɪk] adj. 異國風情的

Q13

M: Let's have Japanese sushi for lunch. 我們吃日式壽司當午餐吧。

W: Thanks but no, thanks. I don't want to spoil the fun.
謝謝，但我不要。我不想破壞樂趣。

M: Don't tell me you are on a diet. Pardon me for saying this, but you seem to put on a little weight lately.
別告訴我你在節食。抱歉我這樣說，但你最近似乎胖了一點。

W: It's not what you think. I get sick at the smell of food.
不是你想的那樣。我聞到食物的氣味就覺得噁心。

M: Oh my gosh! You are pregnant? 噢我的天啊！你懷孕了？

W: I know I should eat more because I am feeding two instead of one, but I don't find anything delicious. 我知道我應該吃更多，因為我吃東西要養兩個人而不是一個，但我不覺得有任何東西好吃。

M: It happens sometimes during the first three months.
前三個月有時候會發生。

W: Really? Is this normal? 真的嗎？這是正常的嗎？

M: My wife went through the same thing. 我老婆也經歷過一樣的事。

Q: What's wrong with the woman?
女子有什麼問題？

A. She doesn't have a good appetite.	A. 她的胃口不好。
B. She doesn't like children.	B. 她不喜歡小孩。
C. She is allergic to seafood.	C. 她對海鮮過敏。
D. She is worried about her weight.	D. 她擔心她的體重。

詳解 **答案：A**

選項都是以 She 開頭，所以要注意對話中提到女子的狀況的部分。她一開始先是拒絕了男子的午餐邀約，接著又提到 I get sick at the smell of food.（我聞到食物的氣味就覺得噁心）、I don't find anything delicious.（我不覺得有任何東西好吃），所以選項 A 是正確答案。

|單字片語| **put on weight** 體重變重 / **pregnant** [`prɛgnənt] adj. 懷孕的 / **appetite** [`æpə͵taɪt] n. 食慾 / **allergic** [ə`lɝdʒɪk] adj. 過敏的

Q14

W: My left leg looks much thinner than my right leg.
我的左腿看起來比右腿細多了。

M: Don't worry. Let's do a little workout and in a month or two, both your legs will look the same again. Does it hurt? 別擔心。我們做點運動，這樣過了一兩個月，你的兩條腿看起來又會一樣了。會痛嗎？

W: A little. But it sure feels better than having to carry a cast around. How soon can I start running again? 有點。但比起必須拖著石膏移動真的感覺好多了。我多快可以重新開始跑步？

M: You will need crutches for at least a month. Don't push yourself too hard. 你需要用拐杖至少一個月。不要太勉強自己。

W: Ouch! It's all right. I can take it. 噢！沒關係。我受得了。

M: Good. That's it. Slow and easy. 很好。就是這樣。慢慢來，放輕鬆。

Q: What is the man's profession?
男子的職業是什麼？

A. A brain surgeon.	A. 腦科醫師。
B. A psychiatrist.	B. 精神科醫師。
C. A physical therapist.	C. 物理治療師。
D. A veterinarian.	D. 獸醫。

詳解 **答案：C**

選項出現了四種和醫學相關的職業，所以要特別注意對話中提示情境的關鍵字。從男子說的 Let's do a little workout... both your legs will look the same again（我們做點運動，你的兩條腿看起來又會一樣了）和女子說的 it sure feels better than having to carry a cast around.（比起必須拖著石膏移動真的感覺好多了），可以判斷女子的腿受過傷，而男子在幫她做恢復的運動。physical therapy（物理治療）包括身體的復健工作，所以 C 是正確答案。

|單字片語| **cast** [kæst] n. 固定受傷部位的石膏 / **crutch** [krʌtʃ] n. 夾在腋下，通常是病患用的拐杖 / **push oneself too hard** 太過勉強自己 / **surgeon** [ˋsɝdʒən] n. 外科醫師 / **psychiatrist** [saɪˋkaɪətrɪst] n. 精神科醫師 / **physical therapist** 物理治療師 / **veterinarian** [ˌvɛtərəˋnɛrɪən] n. 獸醫

Q15

M: Do you think I should get a notebook computer or a tablet?
你覺得我應該買筆記型電腦還是平板電腦？

W: That depends. What's your main usage? 看情況。主要用途是什麼？

M: I am a freelance graphic designer. I use a software program which takes up quite a lot of memory.
我是自由接案的平面設計師。我用會佔很多記憶空間的軟體。

W: In that case, I suggest you get a notebook or a desktop computer. They will serve your needs better.
那樣的話，我建議你買筆記型或桌上型電腦。它們比較能滿足你的需求。

M: But everybody I know has a tablet. 但我認識的每個人都有平板。

W: Most tablet users use it for gaming or as a digital photo album.
大部分的平板使用者用它玩遊戲或者當成數位相簿。

Q: What does the woman recommend the man do?
女子建議男子做什麼？

A. Get a notebook computer. A. 買筆記型電腦。
B. Get a computer desk. B. 買電腦桌。
C. Get a tablet computer. C. 買平板電腦。
D. Get a new software program. D. 買新的軟體。

詳解 答案：A

在對話的開頭，男子就先說出了主題：Do you think I should get a notebook computer or a tablet?（你覺得我應該買筆記型電腦還是平板電腦？）女子詢問男子的 usage（用途）之後，回答 I suggest you get a notebook or a desktop computer.（我建議你買筆記型或桌上型電腦），對於平板電腦則說 Most tablet users use it for gaming or as a digital photo album.（大部分的平板使用者用它玩遊戲或者當成數位相簿）。題目問女子的建議，所以 A 是正確答案。

|單字片語| **notebook computer** 筆記型電腦 / **tablet** [ˋtæblɪt] n. 平板電腦 / **freelance** [ˋfriˋlæns] adj. 自由接案工作的 / **graphic designer** 平面設計師 / **desktop computer** 桌上型電腦

Q16

W: The Buddha statue is made entirely of jade. It is the biggest in Asia.
這座佛像完全以玉製成。它是全亞洲最大的。

M: It's magnificent. Can I take a picture of it? 真是壯觀。我可以拍照嗎？

W: Yes. But don't use the flash, and please keep your volume down because this is a sacred place for worship. Can you see the monks meditating over there? 可以。但不要使用閃光燈，也請壓低說話音量，因為這是神聖的崇拜之地。你看到那邊在靜坐的和尚嗎？

M: I can hear someone reciting something. By the way, what are these boxes for? 我可以聽到有人在唸著什麼。對了，這些箱子是做什麼用的？

W: If you wish to make a donation, just drop it into the box.
如果你想要捐獻的話，就投進箱子。

Q: Where are the speakers?
說話者在哪裡？

A. In a forest.	A. 在森林。
B. In a clinic.	B. 在診所。
C. In a temple.	C. 在寺廟。
D. In a library.	D. 在圖書館。

詳解 **答案：C**

選項出現了四個地點，可以判斷這可能是詢問對話地點的題目，需要從對話中的關鍵詞判斷地點。從 Buddha statue（佛像）其實就能得知答案是 C，但如果不知道這個詞的話，還有 sacred place for worship（神聖的崇拜之地）、monks meditating（靜坐的和尚）可以幫助判斷。

|單字片語| **Buddha** [`bʊdə] n. 佛陀 / **jade** [dʒed] n. 玉 / **magnificent** [mæg`nɪfəsənt] adj. 壯麗的 / **volume** [`vɑljəm] n. 音量 / **sacred** [`sekrɪd] adj. 神聖的 / **worship** [`wɝʃɪp] n. 崇拜，敬神 / **monk** [mʌŋk] n. 僧侶 / **meditate** [`mɛdə͵tet] 沉思；冥想，靜心 / **recite** [ri`saɪt] v. 背誦，朗誦

Q17

M: As you can see, we have the best equipment. You will be assigned a personal coach, and we are more interested in your health and well-being than just weight control.
您可以看到，我們有最好的設備。您會被分配一位個人教練，而且比起單純的體重控制，我們更在意您的健康和幸福。

W: Will the gym be packed on the weekends? 健身房週末會很擠嗎？

M: We have many members, but you can reserve the equipment you wish to use in advance.
我們有很多會員，但您可以先預約您想要使用的設備。

W: Really? That's something unheard of. I think you just helped me make up my mind.

真的嗎？我沒聽過這種服務。我想你剛剛幫我下定決心了。

M: Let me tell you more about our special programs.
讓我告訴您更多關於我們特別課程的資訊。

Q: Why did the woman agree to become a member of the gym?
為什麼女子同意成為健身房的會員？

A. The coach is good-looking and friendly. A. 教練很好看而且友善。
B. The man offered her a special price. B. 男子給她特別的價格。
C. The weight control program is interesting. C. 體重控制課程很有趣。
D. The gym provides a unique service. D. 健身房提供獨特的服務。

詳解 **答案：D**

選項提到健身房的一些特色，所以要注意對話中關於這方面的敘述。對話中提到了 best equipment、personal coach、you can reserve the equipment 等等，但並沒有和選項直接相關的內容。最後才會聽到題目問的是女子同意加入會員的理由，她在對話中表示做出決定的部分是 That's something unheard of. I think you just helped me make up my mind.（我沒聽過這種服務。我想你剛剛幫我下定決心了），意指前面男子提到的 you can reserve the equipment（你可以預約設備）對她而言很特別，所以願意加入。正確答案是 D。

|單字片語| **assign** [ə`saɪn] v. 分配 / **coach** [kotʃ] n. 教練 / **well-being** [`wɛl`biɪŋ] n. 健康與幸福 / **packed** [pækt] adj. 擁擠的 / **in advance** 事先 / **unheard of** 沒聽說過的 / **make one's mind** 下定決心

Q18

W: Let's buy some organic vegetables. What about these? 我們買些有機蔬菜吧。這些怎麼樣？

M: Know what? Some farms that claim to produce organic foodstuffs actually use insecticide.
你知道嗎？有些宣稱生產有機食物的農場，其實使用農藥。

W: Are you sure the news is reliable? These vegetables come with organic certification marks.
你確定這個消息可靠嗎？這些蔬菜有有機認證標誌。

M: Do you think government officials actually visit the farms regularly?
你覺得政府官員真的有定期拜訪農場嗎？

W: I think you are just concerned about the money you have to pay.
我覺得你只是在擔心你要付的錢。

M: Fine. It's your money, and you can do whatever you like with it.
沒差。那是你的錢，你想怎樣都可以。

W: I think I still have some faith in the government.
我想我還是對政府有點信心。

Q: What is the woman's opinion?
女子的意見是什麼？

A. The man's concerns are unfounded.
B. Food labels are not reliable.
C. Organic and non-organic foods are alike.
D. The authorities are short of manpower.

A. 男子的擔心是沒有根據的。
B. 食物的標籤不可靠。
C. 有機和非有機的食物是一樣的。
D. 政府當局人力不足。

詳解 **答案：A**

女子首先說出對話的主題 Let's buy some organic vegetables（我們買些有機蔬菜吧），男子在對話中則是說 Some farms... actually use insecticide（有些農場其實使用農藥）、Do you think government officials actually visit the farms regularly?（你覺得政府官員真的有定期拜訪農場嗎），對有機蔬菜表現懷疑的態度；女子反駁 I think you are just concerned about the money you have to pay.（我覺得你只是在擔心你要付的錢），並且說 I still have some faith in the government（我還是對政府有點信心）。題目問女子的意見，所以 A 是正確答案。

|單字片語| **organic** [ɔr`gænɪk] adj. 有機的，採用有機農法的 / **foodstuffs** [`fud͵stʌfs] n. 食品，糧食 / **insecticide** [ɪn`sɛktə͵saɪd] n. 殺蟲藥 / **certification** [͵sɝtɪfə`keʃən] n. 證明，認證 / **official** [ə`fɪʃəl] n. 官員，公務員 / **faith** [feθ] n. 信心，信任 / **unfounded** [ʌn`faʊndɪd] adj. 沒有事實根據的 / **authorities** [ə`θɔrətɪz] n. 官方，當局 / **manpower** [`mæn͵paʊɚ] n. 人力

Q19

M: Our immediate supervisor will retire soon.
我們的直屬上司很快要退休了。

W: He is tough. Sometimes I dread going into his office.
他很嚴厲。有時候我很害怕走進他的辦公室。

M: He's actually pretty easy to get along with. Why are you smiling?
他其實很好相處。你為什麼在微笑？

W: Try to read my mind. 猜猜看我在想什麼。

M: Well, oh my gosh. Don't tell me... 呃，噢我的天啊。別跟我說…

W: Go on. You are on the right track. 繼續說啊。你的方向對了。

M: You will take over his place? That's a huge step up the corporate ladder! 你要接他的位子嗎？你在公司往上爬了很大一步！

W: It is. I am already taking over some of the responsibilities. 是啊。我已經接下一些職責了。

M: Poor me. I am still stuck at the bottom. 我真可憐，還卡在底層。

Q: What does the man imply?
男子暗示什麼？

A. He is jealous about the woman's new position. A. 他嫉妒女子的新職位。
B. He is not advancing in his career. B. 他在職場上沒有往前進。
C. He is good at predicting. C. 他擅長預測。
D. He is going to retire soon. D. 他很快會退休。

詳解 **答案：B**

選項都是以 He 開頭，可能是問關於男子的事情，所以要特別注意男子說了什麼。他先提到 Our immediate supervisor will retire soon.（我們的直屬上司很快要退休了），中間問女子 You will take over his place?（你要接他的位子嗎？），而且得到了證實，最後則說 Poor me. I am still stuck at the bottom.（我真可憐，還卡在底層）。選項中最符合男子說法的是 B，not advancing（沒有往前進）和對話中的 stuck at the bottom（卡在底層）對應。

|單字片語| **immediate supervisor** 直屬上司 / **retire** [rɪ`taɪr] v. 退休 / **dread** [drɛd] v. 害怕 / **get along with** 和…和睦相處 / **read one's mind** 猜某人的心思 / **on the right track** 想法或做法是對的 / **take over** 接管 / **ladder** [`lædɚ] n. 梯子

Questions 20-21

Questions number 20 and 21 are based on the following conversation.

M: Officer, my name is Bruce Wilson. This man rear-ended me with his car. 警官，我的名字是布魯斯．威爾森。這個男的開車追撞我。

W: Can you tell me what happened? 你可以告訴我發生了什麼事嗎？

M: The road was slippery, probably because it snowed last week. There was a deer that ran across the road at lightning speed. I hit the brakes to avoid him. It was also very dark.
路很滑，可能是因為上禮拜下了雪。有一頭鹿用閃電的速度穿越道路。我踩煞車來避開鹿。天色也很暗。

W: Alright, where was the second car? Did you have your lights on when you were driving? 好，那第二輛車在哪裡？你們開車時有開燈嗎？

M: Well, the car behind me didn't have its lights on, so I didn't see that it was behind me. I didn't mean to hurt him. 嗯，我後面的車沒有開燈，所以我沒看到它在我後面。我不是有意讓他受傷的。

W: We'll first get you an ambulance to make sure you're both OK, and then we'll call your insurance companies. 我們會先為你們叫救護車，確保你們兩個都沒事，然後我們會打電話給你們的保險公司。

|單字片語| **rear-end** v. 撞到…的後面 / **hit the brakes** 踩煞車

Q20

What happened to Bruce?

布魯斯發生了什麼事？

A. He hit another man's car. A. 他撞上另一名男子的車。
B. His car was hit by another car. B. 他的車被另一輛車撞上。
C. His car slipped off the road. C. 他的車滑出道路外。
D. He hit a deer. D. 他撞上一頭鹿。

詳解 **答案：B**

首先要聽到男子一開始說自己是 Bruce，然後他馬上就說在場的另一名男子 rear-ended me（追撞我），從這裡就能判斷答案是 B。就算不知道 rear-end 這個說法，從對話中的 I hit the brakes（我踩了煞車）、I didn't see that it was behind me（我沒看到它〔另一輛車〕在我後面）也可以推測答案是 B。

Q21

What is the main cause of the accident?
這場意外的主要原因是什麼？

A. It was snowing.
B. The car behind was too close.
C. Bruce didn't turn on his headlights.
D. Bruce hit the brakes suddenly.

A. 當時正在下雪。
B. 後面的車靠得太近了。
C. 布魯斯沒有打開他的車頭燈。
D. 布魯斯突然煞車。

詳解

答案：D

在對話的開頭，Bruce 說自己被追撞，中間則說明自己因為鹿突然出現而踩煞車，所以 D 是他被追撞的主要原因。對話中說上禮拜下了雪，而不是事故當時在下雪，所以 A 不正確。B 和 C 在對話中沒有提到，也無法判斷是否為事實。

Questions 22-23

Questions number 22 and 23 are based on the following conversation.

M: Hello, Ma'am. How may I help you?
哈囉，女士。有什麼我能幫您的嗎？

W: Yes, I'd like to order a medium latte with oat milk.
是的，我想要點中杯燕麥奶拿鐵。

M: Would you like to add sugar? We also have a special today. With every purchase of a large latte, you get a free ham sandwich. Would you like to do that? It will only be $1 more.
您想要加糖嗎？我們今天也有特餐。只要買大杯拿鐵，就會得到一個免費的火腿三明治。您想要買大杯的嗎？只要多 1 美元。

W: Alright, let's go with that. One cream, two sugars.
好，那就點那個吧。加一份鮮奶油，兩份糖。

M: OK, that'll be $7.50. 好的，價錢是 7.50 美元。

W: That's way too expensive. Cancel my order. I'll go somewhere else.
那太貴了。取消我的訂單。我要去別的地方。

M: This is the cheapest café in the area unless you want to walk another 30 minutes. I suggest you buy the set. It's a fair price for California.
這是這個區域最便宜的咖啡店，除非您想要再走 30 分鐘。我建議您買套餐。這對於加州而言是合理的價錢。

W: I guess I have no choice then. Here's the money.
那我猜我沒有選擇了，錢在這裡。

|單字片語| **oat milk** 燕麥奶（用燕麥代替牛奶的飲料）

Q22

What will the woman do next?

女子接下來會做什麼？

A. She will pay for a medium latte. A. 她會付中杯拿鐵的錢。
B. She will pay for a large latte. B. 她會付大杯拿鐵的錢。
C. She will just buy a sandwich. C. 她只會買三明治。
D. She will cancel her order. D. 她會取消訂單。

詳解 **答案：B**

女子一開始點中杯拿鐵，但店員建議點大杯的，可以獲得免費的三明治，於是女子說 let's go with that（就點那個吧），接受了店員的建議。雖然中途女子抱怨太貴而想要取消訂單，但得知這家店是區域內最便宜之後，還是付錢給店員，所以 B 是正確答案。

Q23

What is true about the café?

關於這間咖啡店，何者正確？

A. It offers discounts for every purchase. A. 它為每一筆消費提供折扣。
B. It charges for extra sugar. B. 它會收取額外加糖的費用。
C. It's the only café in the area. C. 它是區域中唯一的咖啡店。
D. It's the least expensive café in the area. D. 它是區域中最不貴的咖啡店。

詳解 **答案：D**

店員說 This is the cheapest café in the area（這是這個區域最便宜的咖啡店），所以 D 是正確答案，同時也間接表達區域中還有其他比較貴的咖啡店，所以 C 不正確。雖然買大杯拿鐵送三明治，但並不是買什麼都有折扣，所以 A 不正確。B 的正確性無法從對話內容判斷。

For question number 24, please look at the flight schedule.

M: Good afternoon. Welcome to Sunshine Travels. My name is Henry. How may I help you?
下午好。歡迎來到陽光旅行社。我的名字是亨利。有什麼我能幫您的？

W: I'd like to book a flight from San Francisco to New York tomorrow. What's the earliest you have?
我想要預訂明天從舊金山到紐約的航班。你們最早的是什麼？

M: Let me look it up for you. You can see on the monitor that the earliest flight will depart at 6:45 A.M. Would you like to book that flight? 讓我為您查詢。您可以在螢幕上看到，最早的一班會在上午 6:45 出發。您想要訂這班飛機嗎？

W: I'm afraid I won't be able to get up that early. Hmm, maybe the other flight to JFK is more suitable, but I prefer not to fly with JetBlack. 恐怕我沒辦法那麼早起。嗯，或許另一班往 JFK 機場的比較適合，但我比較希望不要搭 JetBlack 航空的飛機。

M: How about the flights to Newark? If you're going to the west of New York, It'll be more convenient to fly there.
往紐瓦克的航班怎麼樣？如果您要到紐約西部，飛到那邊會比較便利。

W: Actually, I'm meeting my friend in Jersey, so it's indeed more convenient. We'll meet at 6:30 in the evening. 事實上，我要在澤西市和朋友見面，所以那的確比較便利。我們會在傍晚 6:30 見面。

M: OK, I'll book the earlier one for you. 好的，我會為您預訂比較早的那一班。

Flight No. 航班號碼	Destination 目的地	Airline 航空公司	Departure 出發	Arrival 抵達
GL 310	JFK	Gamma	06:45 AM	03:35 PM
JB 616	JFK	JetBlack	07:30 AM	04:09 PM
AA 2304	Newark	Associated	08:45 AM	05:12 PM
AA 2603	Newark	Associated	10:40 AM	07:19 PM

Q: Look at the flight schedule. Which flight will the woman take tomorrow?
請看航班時間表。女子明天會搭哪個航班？

A. GL 310.
B. JB 616.
C. AA 2304.
D. AA 2603.

詳解　答案：C

女子一開始雖然詢問最早的航班，但得知出發時間之後，她回答 I won't be able to get up that early（我沒辦法那麼早起）；對於另一個往 JFK 機場的航班，她則是說 I prefer not to fly with JetBlack（我比較希望不要搭 JetBlack 航空的飛機），所以往 JFK 機場的航班都不是她想要的。之後男子建議飛往紐瓦克，女子回答 it's indeed more convenient（那的確比較便利），又說當天傍晚 6:30 要和朋友見面，於是男子幫他預訂 the earlier one，也就是往紐瓦克的兩個航班中比較早的，所以 C 是正確答案。

Q25

For question number 25, please look at the pie chart.

W: Mr. Carlson, I think your cholesterol level is too high, and the reason might be you're eating way too many carbohydrates. You can see that in your diet chart.
卡爾森先生，我認為您的膽固醇水平太高了，原因可能是您吃太多碳水化合物。您可以在您的飲食圖表中看到這一點。

M: I thought it's because I eat a lot of meat. What should I do?
我還以為是因為我吃很多肉。我該怎麼做？

W: Well, both rice and bread are rich in carbs, so my suggestion is to eliminate them to about a quarter of your daily diet.
嗯，米飯和麵包都含有豐富的碳水化合物，所以我的建議是把它們減少到您每天飲食的大約四分之一。

M: Hmm, so I should eat more fruits and vegetables instead, right?
嗯，所以我應該改吃更多水果和蔬菜，對嗎？

W: I would say not both of them. Look at this sector. It takes up only one tenth of your diet, so I recommend that you increase it to about 20%. 我會說不是兩個都吃更多。請看這個部分。它只佔您飲食的十分之一，所以我建議您把它增加到大約 20%。

|單字片語| **cholesterol** [kə`lɛstə,rol] n. 膽固醇 / **carbohydrate** [,kɑrbə`haɪdret] n. 碳水化合物（口語稱為 **carb**）/ **take up** 佔據

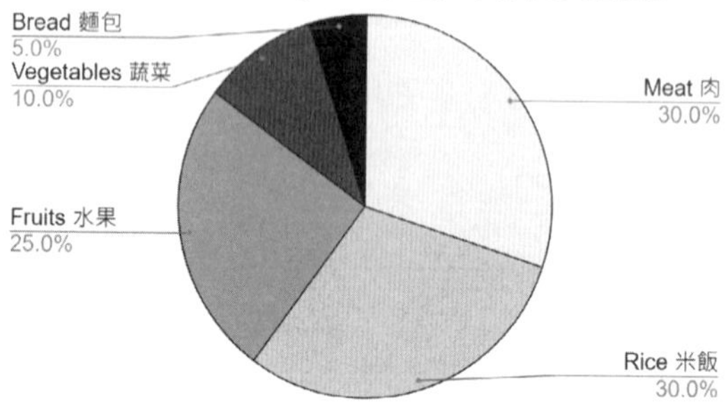

Q: Look at the pie chart. What does the woman suggest that the man eat more?
請看圓餅圖。女子建議男子吃更多的什麼？

A. Bread.	A. 麵包。
B. Vegetables.	B. 蔬菜。
C. Fruits.	C. 水果。
D. Rice.	D. 米飯。

詳解

答案：B

關於男子的飲食，女子的第一個建議是少吃米飯和麵包，於是男子問是否應該多吃水果和蔬菜。女子回答 not both of them（不是兩個都吃更多），並且特別指出其中一個只佔 one tenth（十分之一）的部分，建議男子 increase it to about 20%（把它增加到大約 20%）。從圓餅圖中可以看到蔬菜目前佔 10%，也就是十分之一，所以 B 是正確答案。

第三部分 / 短篇獨白

Questions number 26 to 27 are based on the following announcement.

Attention all campers. There was a case of an unexpected “bear-visit” yesterday. While these bears in the natural reserve are accustomed to human activity, please bear in mind that they are powerful animals which may cause fatal injuries if provoked. To ensure the safety of all personnel in the campsite, please refrain from any form of physical contact with these creatures. One more thing, remember not to leave any food or leftovers in your tents as these bears have an extraordinary sense of smell. That said, you may take pictures of them from a safe distance.

所有露營者請注意。昨天發生了「不速之熊」出沒的事件。雖然自然保護區的熊已經習慣人類活動，但請記住牠們是強壯的動物，如果被激怒的話可能會造成致命的傷害。為了確保營區所有人員的安全，請避免與這些動物的任何身體接觸。還有一件事，請記住不要將任何食物或吃剩的飯菜留在帳篷裡，因為這些熊有非常好的嗅覺。話雖如此，你還是可以從安全的距離拍牠們的照片。

|單字片語| **camper** [ˋkæmpɚ] n. 露營者 / **reserve** [rɪˋzɝv] n. 保護區 / **accustomed** [əˋkʌstəmd] adj. 習慣的 / **bear in mind** 記在心上 / **provoke** [prəˋvok] v. 激怒 / **personnel** [ˌpɝsṇˋɛl] n.（總稱）人員 / **campsite** [ˋkæmpˌsaɪt] n. 露營地 / **refrain from** 忍住…，避免… / **physical** [ˋfɪzɪkḷ] adj. 身體的；物質的 / **leftovers** [ˋlɛftovɚz] n. 剩飯剩菜

Q26

What is true about the announcement?

關於這段公告，何者正確？

A. Two people were attacked by wild animals.
A. 有兩個人遭到野生動物攻擊。

B. Bears are not used to the presence of mankind.
B. 熊不習慣人類的存在。

C. Wild animals may enter the campsite in search of food.
C. 野生動物可能會進入營區尋找食物。

D. A bear was brought into the campsite as part of the training program.
D. 有一隻熊被帶進營區，作為訓練的一部分。

詳解

答案：C

公告提到 "bear-visit"「有熊到訪」，並警告這些熊 may cause fatal injuries if they are provoked（如果被激怒的話可能會造成致命的傷害），但沒有提到有人被攻擊，所以 A 不對。公告中的 these bears... are accustomed to human activity（這些熊習慣人類活動），are accustomed to 相當於 are used to，所以 B 不對。remember not to leave any food or leftovers in your tents as these bears have an extraordinary sense of smell（記住不要將任何食物或吃剩的飯菜留在帳篷裡，因為這些熊有非常好的嗅覺）暗示如果留下食物的話，熊會聞到並且接近，所以 C 是正確答案。

|單字片語| **presence** [`prɛzn̩s] n. 在場，存在 / **mankind** [`mæn͵kaɪnd] n. 人類

Q27

What is the main purpose of this announcement?
這段公告的主要目的是什麼？

A. To ensure that wild animals are not hunted.
B. To ensure that bears are not in danger.
C. To ensure that campers do not get hurt.
D. To ensure that campers do not feed the bears.

A. 為了確保野生動物不被獵殺。
B. 為了確保熊不會有危險。
C. 為了確保露營者不會受傷。
D. 為了確保露營者不會餵食熊。

詳解

答案：C

在這段公告之中，提到 To ensure the safety of all personnel in the campsite, please refrain from...（為了確保營區所有人員的安全，請避免…），所以是為了保護人員安全而公告，C 是正確答案。

Questions 28-30

Questions number 28 to 30 are based on the following lecture.

One sign of maturity is the ability to view things from an objective point of view. However, there is no denying that all of us are prejudiced and biased in many ways. Our family background, education, and even the movies we watch play an important role in shaping our perspectives.

Our opinions also change as we mature. Take criticism for example, how many of us can feel neutral when a negative comment is targeted at us? More often than not, we adopt a defensive stance and refuse to acknowledge our shortcomings. When we offer a suggestion, we tend to identify ourselves with that idea. Anything said against that idea is seen as a personal attack. To be truly objective, we have to put aside our ego and pride. That is the only way we can learn from our mistakes.

成熟的一個跡象是夠從客觀的觀點去看事情。但不可否認，我們所有人都在很多方面有成見和偏見。我們的家庭背景、教育甚至我們所看的電影，都在形塑我們的觀點方面扮演重要角色。我們的意見也會隨著我們的成熟而改變。以批評為例，我們有多少人能夠在有負面意見針對我們的時候感覺中立呢？我們通常會採取防禦的立場，並且拒絕承認我們的缺點。當我們提供建議的時候，我們傾向於將自己和那個（建議的）想法認同。任何反對那個想法的意見，都被視為人身攻擊。要達到真正的客觀，我們必須將自我和自尊心放在一邊。這是我們能夠從自己的錯誤中學習的唯一方法。

|單字片語| **maturity** [mə`tjʊrətɪ] n. 成熟 / **objective** [əb`dʒɛktɪv] adj. 客觀的 / **there is no denying that...** 不可否認… / **prejudiced** [`prɛdʒədɪst] adj. 有成見的 / **biased** [`baɪəst] adj. 有偏見的 / **shape** [ʃep] n. 形狀 v. 使成形，形塑 / **perspective** [pɚ`spɛktɪv] n. 觀點 / **mature** [mə`tjʊr] v. 成熟 / **criticism** [`krɪtəˌsɪzəm] n. 批評 / **neutral** [`njutrəl] adj. 中立的 / **target something at** 把某物對準… / **defensive** [dɪ`fɛnsɪv] adj. 防禦的 / **stance** [stæns] n. 立場 / **shortcoming** [`ʃɔrtˌkʌmɪŋ] n. 缺點 / **identify oneself with** 和…認同

Q28

What is not mentioned as a reason for our biased views?

這段話沒有提到哪個造成我們偏見的理由？

A. Our parents. A. 我們的父母。
B. Our schools. B. 我們的學校。
C. Our age. C. 我們的年齡。
D. Our gender. D. 我們的性別。

詳解

談話中提到 Our family background, education... play an important role in shaping our perspectives（我們的家庭背景、教育在形塑我們的觀點方面扮演重要角色）、Our opinions also change as we mature（我們的意見也會隨著我們的成熟而改變），所以 A、B、C 都是提到的理由，沒有提到的 D 是正確答案。

Q29

What do we tend to do when we are criticized?

當我們被批評的時候，我們傾向於做什麼？

A. We swallow our pride.
B. We learn from our mistakes.
C. We deny that we have weaknesses.
D. We admit our faults immediately.

A. 我們吞下（壓抑）我們的自尊。
B. 我們從錯誤中學習。
C. 我們拒絕承認自己有缺點。
D. 我們立刻承認自己的錯誤。

詳解

答案：C

題目中的關鍵語 when we are criticized 對應談話中的 when a negative comment is targeted at us（在有負面意見針對我們的時候），在這之後提到 we... refuse to acknowledge our shortcomings（我們拒絕承認我們的缺點），對應選項 C 的 deny that we have weaknesses，所以 C 是正確答案。

|單字片語| **weakness** [ˋwiknɪs] n. 弱點，缺點

Q30

What is a suitable title for the lecture?

這段演說適當的標題是什麼？

A. Arrogance hinders learning.
B. Negativity produces resistance.
C. Prejudice leads to maturity.
D. Pride creates self-confidence.

A. 傲慢會阻礙學習。
B. 消極性會產生抗拒。
C. 偏見會導向成熟。
D. 自尊會創造自信。

詳解

答案：A

談話中提到我們通常拒絕承認缺點，最後則指出 we have to put aside our ego and pride. That is the only way we can learn from our mistakes（我們必須將自我和自尊心放在一邊。這是我們能夠從自己的錯誤中學習的唯一方法），所以 A 是比較適當的標題。

|單字片語| **arrogance** [ˋærəgəns] n. 傲慢 / **hinder** [ˋhɪndɚ] v. 妨礙，阻礙 / **negativity** [ˏnɛgəˋtɪvətɪ] n. 消極性 / **resistance** [rɪˋzɪstəns] n. 抵抗，反抗 / **prejudice** [ˋprɛdʒədɪs] n. 偏見，成見

第1回 第2回 第3回 第4回 第5回 第6回

Questions 31-32

Questions number 31 to 32 are based on the following telephone message.

John, this is Christopher. I have been trying to contact you the whole morning. I understand that you are on leave, but this is an urgent matter. Did you reset the password for the system? I can't log in with the code assigned to me. It kept saying that my password is incorrect. I tried using uppercase letters, but it didn't help. The system will lock itself up if I enter the wrong password three times in a row. I'm supposed to access the database and categorize the clients according to their spending habits. You have probably noticed my tense relationship with our immediate supervisor. He will not let me off the hook if I don't manage to get the job done today. Please return my call as soon as possible. Thank you.

John，我是 Christopher。我整個早上都在想辦法聯絡你。我知道你在休假，但這件事很急。你重設了系統的密碼嗎？我沒辦法用分配到的密碼登入。系統一直說我的密碼不正確。我試過用大寫字母，但沒有幫助。如果我連續三次輸入錯誤的密碼，系統就會鎖住。我必須進入資料庫，並且依照消費習慣將客戶分類。你可能注意到我和直屬上司的緊張關係了。如果我今天不設法把工作完成，他就不會放過我。請盡快回我電話。謝謝。

|單字片語| **on leave** 休假中的 / **urgent** [ˋɝdʒənt] adj. 緊急的 / **uppercase** [ˋʌpɚˏkes] adj. 大寫字母的 / **in a row** 連續 / **categorize** [ˋkætəgəˏraɪz] v. 分類 / **let someone off the hook** 讓某人脫身 / **manage to do** 設法做到…

Q31

What is Christopher's problem?

Christopher 的問題是什麼？

A. He has no access to his password.	A. 他沒有辦法得到自己的密碼。
B. He has no authority to use the computer.	B. 他沒有使用電腦的權力。
C. The system is infected with a virus.	C. 系統被病毒感染了。
D. The system failed to recognize his password.	D. 系統無法辨認他的密碼。

詳解

答案：D

this is Christopher 表示說話者就是 Christopher。他說 Did you reset the password for the system? I can't log in with the code assigned to me.（你重設了系統的密碼嗎？我沒辦法用分配到的密碼登入），表示他有密碼，只是不知道為什麼無法登入。所以 A 是錯的，最合理的答案是 D。

|單字片語| **authority** [ə`θɔrətɪ] n. 權力 / **infect** [ɪn`fɛkt] v. 感染

Q32

What is true about Christopher?

關於 Christopher，何者正確？

A. He entered the wrong password for the third time. A. 他輸入了錯誤的密碼三次。

B. He has trouble communicating with the customers. B. 他和顧客溝通有問題。

C. He is desperate for help because he has a deadline to meet. C. 他因為需要趕上期限而急需幫助。

D. He is on leave and doesn't have his computer with him. D. 他正在休假，而且身邊沒有電腦。

詳解

答案：C

說話者說 The system will lock itself up if I enter the wrong password three times in a row（如果我連續三次輸入錯誤的密碼，系統就會鎖住），表示他還沒輸入第三次，所以 A 是錯的。He (our immediate supervisor) will not let me off the hook if I don't manage to get the job done today. Please return my call as soon as possible.（如果我今天不設法把工作完成，他就不會放過我。請盡快回我電話）顯示他為了在今天完成工作，而希望對方趕快回電話，所以 C 是正確答案。

|單字片語| **have trouble doing** 做…有困難 / **be desperate for** 極度渴望得到…

Questions 33-34

Questions number 33 to 34 are based on the following commercial.

Finally, it's time to have a place that you can call your own. Instead of paying rent that goes into your landlord's pockets, why not be your own landlord? At Green Mansion, you can wake up every morning with the harmonious sounds of nature and the rejuvenating smell of fresh air. Our site is located right next to the 60-hectare Sunshine Park, an ideal place for both your children and your pets. Advance booking is now available at very attractive prices. Only a 5% down payment is required. Our partnering bank is offering an incredible fixed interest rate of 1.5% for the first three years, provided that you meet the basic requirements. Call now and make an appointment with our friendly customer officers who are more than willing to answer your inquiries.

終於，現在是你擁有可以稱為自己家的時候了。與其付租金進房東的口袋，何不當自己的房東呢？在格林大廈，你可以每天早上都在和諧的自然聲響和讓人恢復精神的清新空氣中醒來。我們的地點就位於 60 公頃的陽光公園旁，對於你的孩子和寵物是理想的地方。現在開放以非常吸引人的價格預訂。只需要付 5% 的頭期款。我們的合作銀行現在提供難以置信的前三年固定利率 1.5%，只要你符合基本必要條件即可。現在就打電話給我們友善的客服預約面談，他們非常樂意回答你的問題。

|單字片語| **landlord** [`lænd͵lɔrd] n. 房東 / **harmonious** [hɑr`monɪəs] adj. 和諧的 / **rejuvenating** [rɪ`dʒuvənetɪŋ] v. 使變得年輕，使恢復精神 / **hectare** [`hɛktɛr] n. 公頃 / **down payment** （分期付款的）頭期款 / **partner** [`pɑrtnɚ] v. 合夥，合作 / **requirement** [rɪ`kwaɪrmənt] n. 必要條件 / **more than willing to do** 非常願意做…

Q33

What type of product or service is being advertised?
廣告宣傳的是哪一種產品或服務？

A. Country club membership.	A. 鄉村俱樂部會員。
B. An apartment building.	B. 公寓大樓。
C. A day-care service.	C. 日間托兒服務。
D. A consumer loan.	D. 消費者貸款。

詳解 答案：B

廣告中說的 be your own landlord（當你自己的房東），意思是買自己的房子，而不用租的。後面也提到 down payment（頭期款），說明貸款購屋的方案，所以 B 是正確答案。雖然 D 也是廣告提到的部分內容，但那是因為宣傳房子而附帶提到的，所以不是正確答案。

|單字片語| **country club** 鄉村俱樂部（位於郊區或鄉野地區，可以進行高爾夫球等休閒運動的私人俱樂部）

Q34

Which is NOT an attraction mentioned in the commercial?

廣告沒有提到什麼吸引人的地方？

A. Peaceful surroundings.
B. Low cash requirement.
C. High rental income.
D. Reasonable interest rates.

A. 寧靜的環境。
B. 低現金需求。
C. 高租金收入。
D. 合理的利率。

詳解

答案：C

harmonious sounds of nature and the rejuvenating smell of fresh air（和諧的自然聲響和讓人恢復精神的清新空氣）對應選項 A，Only a 5% down payment is required（只需要 5% 的頭期款）對應選項 B，an incredible fixed interest rate（難以置信的固定利率）對應選項 D。雖然廣告提到 be your own landlord，但沒有提到租金行情，所以 C 是正確答案。

Questions 35-37

For questions number 35-37, please look at the chart.

It seems the presidential election will be a tight race. According to the poll, most respondents, about 70% of them, say they will vote for Smith or Johnson. Smith has a 2-point lead over Johnson, but with nearly 10% of the respondents who haven't yet made up their mind, it's still possible that Johnson will overtake. The other candidates don't seem to stand a chance. The least popular one, who gets only 5 points, proposes a *laissez-faire* policy, which means not doing anything to regulate the economy. Well, it seems that only a few people can accept such an idea.

總統選舉似乎會是一場勢均力敵的競爭。根據民意調查，大部分的回答者，大約 70%，說他們會投票給史密斯或強森。史密斯領先強森 2 個百分點，但因為有將近 10% 還沒有下定決心的回答者，所以強森還是有可能超前。其他候選人似乎沒有機會。最不受歡迎、只得到 5 個百分點的候選人，提出自由放任的政策，意思是不做任何事來管制經濟。嗯，似乎只有少數人能接受這樣的想法。

|單字片語| **tight race** 勢均力敵的比賽 / **respondent** [rɪˋspɑndənt] n. 回答者 / **stand a chance** 有成功的希望 / **laissez-faire** [ˏleseˋfɛr] n. 自由放任

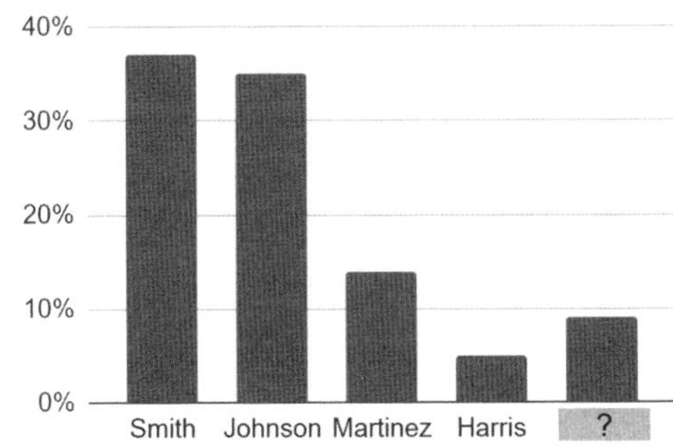

Q35

What is the chart about?

這張圖表是關於什麼？

A. The result of the election.
B. The popularity of policies.
C. The survey results on how people will vote.
D. The evaluation of the candidates' performance.

A. 選舉的結果。
B. 政策受歡迎的程度。
C. 關於人們會怎麼投票的調查結果。
D. 候選人表現的評價。

詳解

答案：C

從一開始提到的 poll（民意調查）、most respondents... say they will vote for...（大部分回答者說他們會投票給…），就可以確定 C 是正確答案。因為是未來才會投票，還沒進行選舉，所以 A 是錯的。

Q36

Based on the report, what should be written in the shaded area?
根據報導，灰底部分應該填入什麼？

A. Undecided. A. 未決定的。
B. Will not vote. B. 不會投票。
C. Other candidates. C. 其他候選人。
D. Not a registered voter. D. 不是已登記的選民。

詳解 答案：A

關於圖中將近 10% 的部分，說話者提到 nearly 10% of the respondents who haven't yet made up their mind（將近 10% 還沒有下定決心的回答者），haven't made up their mind 就是 are undecided（還沒有決定）的意思，所以 A 是正確答案。

Q37

Which candidate believes that the government should never intervene in the economy?
哪一位候選人認為政府絕對不應該干預經濟？

A. Smith. A. 史密斯。
B. Johnson. B. 強森。
C. Martinez. C. 馬丁尼茲。
D. Harris. D. 哈里斯。

詳解 答案：D

關於候選人提出的政策，說話者提到 The least popular one, who gets only 5 points, proposes a *laissez-faire* policy, which means not doing anything to regulate the economy（最不受歡迎、只得到 5 個百分點的候選人，提出自由放任的政策，意思是不做任何事來管制經濟），也就是指圖表中的 Harris，所以 D 是正確答案。

|單字片語| **intervene** [ˌɪntɚˋvin] **v.** 介入，干預

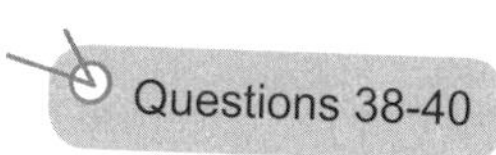

For questions number 38-40, please look at the charts.

Every year, the government awards scholarships to international students. In the 1990s, there was a steady increase in the number of scholarships that were awarded. However, in the early 2000s, the number dropped a little bit. This could be due to the financial hardships that the government was facing at the time as did the rest of the world. Because of the tech market crash in 2000, international trade significantly decreased, forcing the government to cut expenses. However, in order to stay competitive in the increasingly globalized world, the government invested again in the scholarships in later years, and the number multiplied from 2005 to 2009. The result is that there are more and more international students in our universities, and some of them stay here after they graduate and become an important part of the workforce.

每一年，政府都頒發獎學金給國際學生。在 1990 年代，頒發獎學金的人數有穩定的增加。不過，在 2000 年代的初期，數字稍微下降了。這可能是因為政府在當時和世界其他國家一樣面臨的財務困難。因為 2000 年的科技市場崩盤，國際貿易顯著減少，迫使政府減少支出。不過，為了在逐漸全球化的世界中保持競爭力，政府在之後的年度再度投資於獎學金，而數字在 2005 至 2009 年間倍數增加。結果是我們的大學有越來越多國際學生，其中一些人在畢業後留在這裡，並且成為勞動力之中重要的一部分。

|單字片語| **international trade** 國際貿易 / **workforce** [ˋwɝkfors] 勞動力

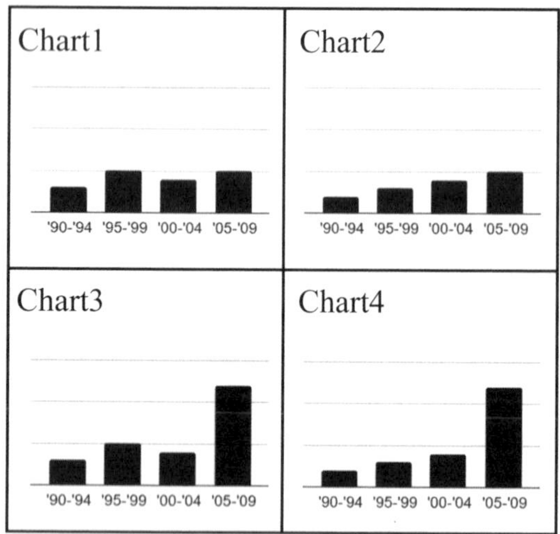

Q38

Which chart best represents the number of scholarships awarded to international students every year?

哪張圖表最能表示每年頒發獎學金給國際學生的數量？

A. Chart 1.
B. Chart 2.
C. Chart 3.
D. Chart 4.

A. 圖表 1。
B. 圖表 2。
C. 圖表 3。
D. 圖表 4。

詳解

關於頒發獎學金的數字，說話者提到 In the 1990s, there was a steady increase（在 1990 年代有穩定的增加）、in the early 2000s, the number dropped a little bit（在 2000 年代的初期，數字稍微下降了）、the number multiplied from 2005 to 2009（數字在 2005 至 2009 年間倍數增加），所以數量一開始上升、2000-2004 年下降、2005-2009 年大幅上升的 C 是正確答案。

Q39

What is the reason that the government cut the expenses on the scholarships?
政府過去減少獎學金支出的原因是什麼？

A. Its investments went down. A. 投資虧損。
B. The economic situation was bad. B. 經濟情況不佳。
C. It gave the money to local students. C. 把這筆錢給本國學生了。
D. There were too many international students. D. 當時國際學生太多了。

詳解

關於減少獎學金時面臨的情況，說話者提到 international trade significantly decreased, forcing the government to cut expenses（國際貿易顯著減少，迫使政府減少支出），所以最符合這段敘述的 B 是正確答案。

Q40

What is the speaker's thought about the policy of awarding scholarships to international students?
說話者對於頒發獎學金給國際學生的政策有什麼想法？

A. It is a financial burden for the government. A. 對於政府是財政上的負擔。
B. It has nothing to do with the economy. B. 和經濟無關。
C. It helps to improve the country's image. C. 幫助提升國家的形象。
D. It is a way to bring in foreign professionals. D. 是帶來國外專業人才的方法。

詳解

答案：D

關於國際學生，說話者最後提到 some of them stay here after they graduate and become an important part of the workforce（其中一些人在畢業後留在這裡，並且成為勞動力之中重要的一部分），表示留在國內的外籍學生成為了重要的人才，所以 D 是正確答案。

第一部分 句子填空

Q1

In view of the latest education reform and initiatives, schools will require a more ________ curriculum to cater to the needs of students with different interests.

有鑑於最近的教育改革與倡議，學校將需要更廣泛的課程內容，以符合不同興趣的學生需求。

A. various　　B. advantageous　　C. extensive　　D. compulsory

詳解　　答案：C

空格是修飾 curriculum（學校提供的全部課程）的形容詞，而且這樣的 curriculum 可以 cater to the needs of students with different interests（符合有各種不同興趣的學生的需求），所以表示「範圍很廣」的 C. extensive 是正確答案。various 通常修飾名詞複數形，表示「各種各樣的」（彼此之間各有不同）。compulsory 可以修飾 subject、course，表示「必修的」。

|單字片語| **in view of** 考慮到，有鑑於 / **reform** [ˌrɪˋfɔrm] v. 改革 n. 改革 / **initiative** [ɪˋnɪʃətɪv] n. 主動的行動，倡議 / **cater to** 滿足（需求等） / **advantageous** [ˌædvənˋtedʒəs] adj. 有利的 / **extensive** [ɪkˋstɛnsɪv] adj. 範圍廣的 / **compulsory** [kəmˋpʌlsərɪ] adj. 必須做的，必修的

Q2

The power outage did not cause much damage as it has been ________ and prepared for.

停電並沒有造成很大的損害，因為它已經被預料到，並且做好準備了。

A. prevented　　B. prospected　　C. anticipated　　D. overlooked

詳解　　答案：C

句子後半用連接詞 as 開頭，表示原因。在選項中，C 表示已經預料到會發

生停電，也和為停電做準備的行為有關，所以是正確答案。要注意的是選項 A，prevent 表示預防某事發生→事情沒有發生，但句子前半描述的情況是停電已經發生了，所以這個選項會讓前後語意矛盾。

|單字片語| **power outage** 停電 / **prospect** [prəˋspɛkt] v. 勘探（礦藏） / **anticipate** [ænˋtɪsəˏpet] v. 預期 / **overlook** [ˏovɚˋlʊk] v. 忽略

Q3

Making inappropriate comments about a woman's figure can be considered a form of sexual _______.

對女人的體型做出不適當的評論，可能被認為是一種性騷擾。

A. interference B. harassment C. prosecution D. manipulation

詳解

答案：B

對女人體型的不當評論，有時被認為是性騷擾；性騷擾的英文是 sexual harassment，所以答案是 B. harassement。雖然「騷擾、打擾」有其他的單字可以表達，但這是一個固定的說法，所以用其他單字都不正確。

補充說明

請分辨和 harass（騷擾）相似的動詞 harness（控制，駕馭）。
sexual discrimination：性別歧視

|單字片語| **inappropriate** [ˏɪnəˋpropriɪt] adj. 不適當的 / **figure** [ˋfɪgjɚ] n. 體型 / **interference** [ˏɪntɚˋfɪrəns] n. 干涉，干擾 / **harassment** [ˋhærəsmənt] n. 騷擾 / **prosecution** [ˏprɑsɪˋkjuʃən] n. 起訴，控訴 / **manipulation** [məˏnɪpjʊˋleʃən] n. 操縱

Q4

_______ any of the information provided by candidates be found false, legal actions will be taken.

若發現應徵者所提供之任何資訊不實，將採取法律行動。

A. Though B. Should C. Notwithstanding D. Whether

詳解

答案：B

逗號前後都是完整子句，但正確答案 B 並不是連接詞，這是因為本題使用了「省略 if 的假設語氣」。原本的句型是「If + 主詞1 + should + 動詞, 主詞2 + will + 動詞」，但 if 子句可以把 should 移到句首，同時省略連接詞 if，就形成了本題的句型。though 表示「雖然」，notwithstanding 表示「儘管」，而 whether 當連接詞時通常會接「... or...」的句型，表示「不管是否…」。

補充說明

試以其他選項的連接詞，改寫本題的句子如下：

Though the information provided by the candidate was false, the company decided not to take legal actions.
雖然應徵者所提供的資訊不實，但公司決定不採取法律行動。
Notwithstanding the false information provided by the candidate, the company decided not to take legal actions.
儘管應徵者提供不實的資訊，但公司決定不採取法律行動。
Whether the information is true or false, the company will not take legal actions.
無論資訊真實與否，公司將不採取法律行動。

Q5

Physical characteristics are transmitted from parents to their ________ through genes.
身體特徵透過基因從父母遺傳給後代。

A. aftermath　B. downturn　C. offspring　D. subordinate

詳解

答案：C

這個句子是說明遺傳的現象，所以 from parents to their ______ 的部分當然要填入表示後代子孫的單字，C 是正確答案。另外，請注意 offspring 的複數和單數同形，不需要加 -s。

|單字片語| **physical** [ˋfɪzɪkḷ] adj. 身體的 / **characteristic** [ˏkærəktəˋrɪstɪk] n. 特徵，特性 / **transmit** [trænsˋmɪt] v. 傳送，遺傳 / **aftermath** [ˋæftɚˏmæθ] n. 後果，餘波 / **downturn** [ˋdaʊntɝn] n. 衰退 / **offspring** [ˋɔfˏsprɪŋ] n. 子女，後代 / **subordinate** [səˋbɔrdnɪt] n. 部下，下屬

Q6

One of my colleagues kept finding fault with my proposal in the previous meeting. I will ________ him one of these days.
我的一位同事在上次會議一直挑剔我的提案。我有一天要報復他。

A. get along with　B. get around with
C. get even with　D. get away with

詳解

答案：C

同事 kept finding fault with my proposal（一直挑剔我的提案），要從選項選

出「我」的回應。選項 C 的 get even with (someone) 表示「報復」，是合理的答案。get along with someone 表示「與某人和睦相處」，get around something 表示「避開某事」（注意不能加 with），get away with something 表示「做了某事而僥倖逃過懲罰」。

Q7

The ballet dancers appeared on stage as the background music began to ________.
背景音樂開始淡出時，芭蕾舞者出現了。

A. wear out B. reach out C. fade out D. go out

詳解 **答案：C**

空格所在子句的主詞是 background music（背景音樂），所以能表示音樂逐漸淡出的 C. fade out 是正確答案。wear out 表示「（鞋子、衣服等）磨壞」，reach out 表示「伸出手」，go out 表示「外出」。

Q8

As more and more confirmed cases are recorded, the city is on the ________ of becoming the epicenter of the pandemic.
隨著越來越多確診病例被記錄，這個城市幾乎將要成為疫情的爆發點。

A. agony B. doom C. peril D. verge

詳解 **答案：D**

比起語意，這個題目更重要的是知道固定的片語用法。在選項中，只有 D 能用在 on the ______ of doing 的句型中，表示「瀕臨…邊緣」的意思。

補充說明

doom 除了當名詞表示「厄運，劫數」以外，也有動詞的用法，通常會以被動形式 be doomed to do 表示「註定（遭遇不好的結果）」。

|單字片語| **epicenter** [ˋɛpɪˏsɛntɚ] n. 震央（在這裡是比喻疫情爆發的地點） / **pandemic** [pænˋdɛmɪk] n. 疾病的大規模流行 / **agony** [ˋægənɪ] n. 極度痛苦 / **doom** [dum] n. 厄運，劫數 / **peril** [ˋpɛrəl] n. （嚴重的）危險 / **verge** [vɝdʒ] n. 邊緣

The argument between the group members was so heated that the professor had no choice but to ________ and act as a mediator.

小組成員之間的爭論很激烈，所以教授不得不介入並且扮演調停者。

A. interrupt　　B. interact　　C. interfere　　D. intervene

詳解　　　　答案：D

因為發生了 argument（爭論），所以 professor 要做某事，並且扮演 mediator（調停者）。選項 A、C、D 的意思非常接近，都有介入或打斷的意思，但相較於 interrupt（打斷）和 interfere（妨礙），intervene 包含了「介入」和「調停」的意思，更符合本句調停爭端的情況，所以 D. intervene 是最適當的答案。

|單字片語| **heated** [`hitɪd] adj. 激烈的 / **interrupt** [ˌɪntə`rʌpt] v. 打斷（別人說話）/ **interact** [ˌɪntə`rækt] v. 互動 / **interfere** [ˌɪntɚ`fɪr] v. 妨礙，插手 / **intervene** [ˌɪntɚ`vin] v. 介入，調停

Q10

Cosmetics companies made a fortune in anti-aging skin care products by promising a fairer and wrinkle-free ________.

化妝品公司藉由承諾更白皙、無皺紋的膚質，用抗老化保養品賺了很多錢。

A. modification　　B. complexion　　C. operation　　D. transformation

詳解　　　　答案：B

fair 形容皮膚時，表示「白皙」的意思。wrinkle-free（沒有皺紋的）也是形容皮膚的詞，所以表示「膚色、氣色」的 B. complexion 是正確答案。

補充說明

complex 當名詞的時候，有「情結」的意思。
superiority complex「優越情結」（優越感，自大心理）
inferiority complex「劣等情結」（自卑感）

|單字片語| **make a fortune** 賺很多錢 / **anti-aging** [ˌæntɪ`edʒɪŋ] adj. 抗老化的 / **fair** [fɛr] adj. 公正的；還可以的；白皙的 / **complexion** [kəm`plɛkʃən] n. 膚色，氣色 / **transformation** [ˌtrænsfɚ`meʃən] n. 變化，轉變

第二部分 段落填空

Questions 11-15

Parents of the 21st century are faced with a dilemma: is home learning more effective and efficient than traditional schools? (11) Generally speaking, homeschooling is beneficial for children as long as parents play an active role in coaching and monitoring. In fact, virtually all the available data show that (12) the performance of homeschooled children is above average. In addition, studies found that the academic performance of homeschoolers is (13) on par with that of children in prestigious private schools. On the other hand, one major concern is whether homeschooling helps or hampers a child's social development. Children (14) engaged in homeschooling spend less time with same-aged children and miss out on social interaction in school settings. In spite of this "flaw" in home learning, many parents are still willing to give it a try as they can counter this problem by taking their children to church, (15) where they can develop friendship with other children of similar age.

二十一世紀的父母面臨了兩難：在家學習比傳統學校更有效果和效率嗎？大致上來說，只要父母在指導以及監督方面扮演主動的角色，在家教育對小孩是有益的。事實上，幾乎所有可得的資料都顯示，在家教育的小孩，表現高於平均水準。而且，研究發現在家教育的小孩學業表現相當於就讀有名私校的小孩。另一方面，一個主要令人擔心的地方是在家教育會幫助還是阻礙小孩的社會發展。在家教育的小孩和同年齡的小孩在一起的時間比較少，也會失去在學校情境中社交互動的機會。雖然在家學習有這個「缺點」，但很多父母還是願意試試看，因為他們可以藉由帶小孩上教堂來對抗這個問題，而小孩在教堂可以和其他年齡相近的小孩發展友誼。

|單字片語| **be faced with** 面臨… / **dilemma** [dəˋlɛmə] n. 兩難的困境 / **homeschool** [ˋhomskul] v. 在家教育 / **virtually** [ˋvɝtʃʊəlɪ] adv. 實際上，幾乎 / **on par with** 與…同等 / **prestigious** [prɛsˋtɪdʒɪəs] adj. 有名望的，聲望很高的 / **private school** 私立學校 / **hamper** [ˋhæmpɚ] v. 阻礙 / **be engaged in** 忙於…，參加…，從事… / **miss out on** 失去…的機會 / **interaction** [ˌɪntəˋrækʃən] n. 互動；相互作用 / **setting** [ˋsɛtɪŋ] n. 環境 / **counter** [ˋkaʊntɚ] v. 反擊；抵銷

Q11

A. Generally speaking
B. On speaking terms
C. Speaking of
D. So to speak

詳解

答案：A

空格後面的句子很肯定地說 homeschooling is beneficial for children（在家教育對小孩有益），但前面填入 A. Generally speaking 之後，表示「一般而言」是如此，但可能也有例外。像這樣表示某個事實並非 100% 正確，可以增加文章的合理性和說服力。

補充說明

其他選項的使用方式示範如下：

We disagreed over something, and we are not on speaking terms anymore. 我們為了某件事意見不合，所以我們不再友好〔不再說話〕了。

Speaking of skiing, Canada is an ideal place. 談到滑雪，加拿大是個理想的地方。

Canada is like a paradise, so to speak. 可以說，加拿大像是天堂。

Q12

A. homeschooling helps children develop their social skills
在家教育幫助孩子發展他們的社交技能

B. the performance of homeschooled children is above average
在家教育的小孩，表現高於平均水準

C. homeschooling can have negative effects on children's performance
在家教育可能會對孩子的表現產生負面影響

D. homeschooled children report high levels of satisfaction with their lives
在家教育的小孩表示對自己生活的滿意程度很高

詳解

答案：B

空格所在句子的上一句說在家教育對小孩是有益的，而後面的句子又用 In addition（另外）開頭，進一步說明在家教育對於學業表現的效果。為了和前後的內容連貫，空格中的內容應該是在家教育對學業表現的正面效果，所以 B 是正確答案。除非空格所在的句子用表示語氣轉折的連接副詞（例如 However、Nonetheless 等等）和上一句銜接，否則負面敘述 C 的語氣和上一句會是不連貫的。

|單字片語| **social skills** 社交技能

A. on par with　　B. no way near　　C. inferior to　　D. unlike

詳解　　　**答案：A**

選項都是表示比較的用語。空格前後分別是 the academic performance of homeschoolers（在家教育的小孩的學業表現）和 that of children in prestigious private schools（就讀有名私立學校小孩的〔表現〕）。雖然文法上四個選項都沒錯，但要注意的是空格所在的句子以 In addition（除此之外）開頭，所以這個句子是針對上一句所作的進一步敘述。上一句說在家教育的小孩表現高於平均，所以這一句應該也是對於在家教育的正面評價，表示「與…同等」的 A. on par with 是正確答案。

|單字片語| **be no way near** 差…很遠 / **be inferior to** 比…差

Q14

A. compelled to　　B. engaged in
C. refrained from　　D. paralyzed by

詳解　　　**答案：B**

空格接在主詞 Children 後面，但這個句子已經有主要動詞 spend 了，所以選項裡面呈現的並不是過去式，而是在名詞後面做修飾的過去分詞；如果把這個句子看成 Children who are p.p. ...，結構就更清楚了。因為文章中討論的都是接受在家教育的小孩，所以表示 (be) engaged in something（從事某事）的 B 是正確答案。

〈補充說明〉

以下示範其他選項中出現的動詞用法。

Children who felt compelled to study usually lack motivation. 被迫讀書的孩子通常缺乏動力。

Children should refrain from shouting during class. 孩子在上課時應該不要喊叫。

Children who are paralyzed by a sense of failure tend to give up. 被挫折感癱瘓的孩子傾向於放棄。

|單字片語| **be compelled to do** 被迫做…（to 後面接動詞原形，而不是名詞）/ **refrain from** 忍住…，抑制…（表示自己進行抑制的自發行為，通常當不及物動詞使用）/ **paralyze** [ˋpærə͵laɪz] 使癱瘓

A. yet　　B. where　　C. because　　D. as if

詳解　　答案：B

空格要填入連接前後內容的詞彙，但選項中的連接詞 yet（但）、because（因為）、as if（彷彿）都不能將前後句的語意做適當的連接。關係副詞 B. where 同時具有連接兩個子句的作用，而且它引導的子句能為前面的地點 church（教堂）做補充說明，是正確答案。

Questions 16-20

Steven Paul Jobs, the co-founder, two-time CEO, and chairman of Apple Inc., passed away on October 5, 2011 after a courageous yet unsuccessful battle with cancer. He was only 56, and Apple fanatics around the world (16) lamented the loss of such a genius. The achievement in Jobs' career is phenomenal. He literally saved the music industry from collapsing by launching the iTunes Store. (17) Despite his accomplishment, the genius himself has once been shown the door as a result of office politics. Undaunted, he (18) diverted his endless energy into driving the then pretty much unknown Pixar Animation Studios from obscurity to prominence. *Toy Story* was a global success (19) owing to Steve Jobs' charisma, drive, and extraordinary vision. With his multiple inventions that shaped the future, the great man will surely go down in history (20) along with the likes of Thomas Edison, Isaac Newton, and even Albert Einstein.

蘋果公司的共同創辦人、兩度就任的執行長及董事長史蒂芬・保羅・賈伯斯，在勇敢抗癌但失敗之後，於 2011 年 10 月 5 日過世。他過世時年僅 56 歲，而全世界的蘋果迷都哀悼失去了這麼一位天才。賈伯斯生涯中的成就非常傑出。藉由開設 iTunes 商店，他簡直可以說解救了音樂產業，讓它免於瓦解。但儘管有所成就，這位天才也曾經因為辦公室鬥爭而被掃地出門。他沒有因而畏縮，而是將他無窮的精力轉向，驅使當時還不太為人所知的皮克斯影業從沒沒無聞走向傑出。由於賈伯斯的魅力、幹勁與超常的願景，《玩具總動員》獲得了全球性的成功。靠著他塑造了未來的多種發明，這個偉大的人物一定能和愛迪生、牛頓、甚至愛因斯坦這樣的人物一起在歷史上流傳下去。

|單字片語| **co-founder** [ko`faʊndɚ] n. 共同創辦人 / **chairman** [`tʃɛrmən] n. 主席，董事長 / **courageous** [kə`redʒəs] adj. 勇敢的 / **fanatic** [fə`nætɪk] n. 狂熱分子 / **lament** [lə`mɛnt] v. 哀悼 / **phenomenal** [fə`nɑmən]] adj. 非凡的，傑出的 / **literally** [`lɪtərəlɪ] adv. 照字面意義；簡直 / **show someone the door** 把某人趕出門 / **undaunted** [ʌn`dɔntɪd] adj. 無畏的，不屈不撓的 / **divert** [daɪ`vɝt] v. 使轉向，轉移 / **obscurity** [əb`skjʊrətɪ] n. 晦澀；沒沒無聞 / **prominence** [`prɑmənəns] n. 突出，顯著，顯赫 / **charisma** [kə`rɪzmə] n. 個人魅力 / **drive** [draɪv] n. 魄力，幹勁 / **vision** [`vɪʒən] n. 願景

Q16

A. lamented　　B. coveted　　C. relieved　　D. oppressed

詳解　　答案：A

空格是動詞，表示前面的主詞 Apple fanatics 的反應。fanatic 是「狂熱分子」的意思，也就是我們常說的「fan」，表示「非常喜愛什麼的人」。對於失去了賈伯斯這位 genius（天才），他們最有可能的反應是 A. lamented（哀悼）。

|單字片語| **covet** [`kʌvɪt] v. 貪圖，渴望 / **relieve** [rɪ`liv] n. 緩和，減輕 / **oppress** [ə`prɛs] 壓迫

Q17

A. As a consequence　結果
B. On a personal level　在個人層面上
C. Despite his accomplishment　儘管有所成就
D. Being committed to his vision　投入於他的願景

詳解　　答案：C

選項都是可以修飾句子的副詞性成分，但解題的重點在於選出意義上能夠自然連接上下文的答案。上一句說的是賈伯斯的成功事跡，但空格後面提到他曾經因為辦公室政治而被趕出門（has ... been shown the door），前後內容形成反差，所以表示「儘管有前面提到的成就…」的 C 是正確答案。選項 B 的意思是「在私生活或個人思考、感情方面」，但被公司趕出門並不屬於個人私生活的領域，所以 B 不適合用來修飾這個句子。分詞構句只能表示時間、理由、條件等等，而不能表示讓步（「雖然」、「儘管」的意思），所以 D 也不正確。

Q18

A. compensated　　B. diverted　　C. salvaged　　D. evacuated

詳解　　答案：B

前面提到賈伯斯被蘋果公司掃地出門，但這句開頭又說他是 Undaunted

（無畏的），並且把精力投入其他事情。所以，表示把精力「轉向」的 B. diverted 是正確答案。

|單字片語| **compensate** [ˋkɑmpən͵set] **v.** 補償 / **salvage** [ˋsælvɪdʒ] **v.** 打撈（沉船），挽救 / **evacuate** [ɪˋvækjʊ͵et] **v.** 撤離

A. owing to　　B. resulting in　　C. based on　　D. deprived of

詳解

答案：A

空格前面說《玩具總動員》是個 global success（全球性的成功），而空格後面接賈伯斯的 charisma, drive, and extraordinary vision（魅力、幹勁與超常的願景）等優點，所以答案是表示原因的介系詞 A. owing to（由於…）。be based on 表示「以…為基礎，根據…」，通常表示「決定／判斷是以什麼為基礎」、「作品是根據什麼而編寫」的意思，所以用在這裡並不恰當。

|單字片語| **result in** 導致… / **be based on** 以…為基礎，根據… / **be deprived of** 被剝奪了…，失去…

A. prior to　　B. along with　　C. in place of　　D. as well as

詳解

答案：B

句子的意思是「和愛迪生、牛頓、愛因斯坦一樣在歷史上流傳下去」，所以表示「和…一起」的 B 是正確答案。as well as 是連結緊接在前後、詞性相同的成分，用在這裡會錯誤連結成「除了愛迪生、牛頓、愛因斯坦之類的人，還有歷史」的意思。

Questions 21-22

Questions 21 and 22 are based on the information provided in the following chart.

Product Profitability Analysis
產品獲利能力分析

Product 產品	Revenue 收入	Production Cost 生產成本	Net Profit/ Loss 淨利／淨損	% of Total Profit 佔總利潤百分比
A	$852,000	$720,000	$132,000	32
B	$647,000	$550,000	$97,000	22
C	$439,000	$250,000	$189,000	46
D	$245,000	$250,000	-$5,000	N/A

|單字片語| **profitability** [ˌprɑfɪtəˋbɪlətɪ] n. 收益性，利潤率 / **revenue** [ˋrɛvəˌnju] n. 收入 / **net** [nɛt] adj. 淨值的

Based on the chart, which of the following statements is true?

根據這張表格，以下敘述何者正確？

A. All products are in the black.
所有產品都是黑字（獲利的）。

B. Product A is the most profitable.
產品 A 是最有獲利的。

C. Product B generates the highest turnover in sales.
產品 B 產生最高的銷售額。

D. About 80 percent of the total profits come from two products.
大約百分之 80 的總獲利來自兩項產品。

詳解

答案：D

根據表格內容，一一對照各選項是否正確。選項 A：in the black 表示「黑字的（獲利的）」，相反的說法是 in the red（赤字的）；因為產品 D 出現了 -$5,000 的虧損，所以這個選項不對。選項 B：產品 A 的 revenue（收入）、production cost（生產成本）都最高，但收入扣除生產成本之後，它的 net profit（淨利）其實不如產品 C，所以這個選項不對。選項 C：這裡必須要知道 turnover 是「營業額」的意思，也就是扣除成本費用之前的收入數字，在這張表格裡相當於 revenue 的部分，而在這一欄最高的是產品 A，所以這個選項不對。選項 D：產品 A 和產品 C 佔總利潤的百分比總和是 78%，接近 80%，所以這是正確答案。

|單字片語| **in the black** 黑字的，獲利的（⟷ in the red）/ **profitable** [ˋprɑfɪtəbl̩] adj. 獲利的 / **turnover** [ˋtɝn͵ovɚ] n. 營業額

What action should be taken according to the information provided in this chart?

根據表格中的資訊，應該採取什麼行動？

A. The company should scrap product A.
這家公司應該捨棄（停產）產品 A。

B. The company should invest the most marketing resources on product B.
這家公司應該在產品 B 上投資最多的行銷資源。

C. The company should focus more on product C.
這家公司應該更著重於產品 C。

D. The company should produce more of product D.
這家公司應該生產更多產品 D。

詳解

答案：C

判斷公司應該採取什麼行動的題目，看起來複雜，但只要先掌握表格中最重要的資訊即可：產品 C 的獲利最高，產品 B 的獲利最低，而四種產品中只有產品 D 是虧損的。所以，選項 C 說應該 focus more on product C（更著重於產品 C），是正確答案。

|單字片語| **scrap** [skræp] v. 廢棄 / **marketing** [ˋmɑrkɪtɪŋ] n. 行銷

Questions 23-25

There is no doubt that global warming is responsible for radical weather conditions experienced in the past decade. The polar bear's home – the Arctic – is experiencing the effects of global warming more than any other place. Temperatures in the Arctic are rising at almost twice the rate of the rest of the world, placing not only the polar bears but the entire Arctic ecosystem in jeopardy. Based on data provided by *National Geographic*, the amount of summer ice has declined by about 30 percent since 1979. The amount of sea ice is significant because apart from providing a hunting ground for polar bears, it is also a shelter for seals, walruses, arctic foxes, and the Inuit people.

Arctic sea ice also has a cooling effect on climate by reflecting light away from Earth's surface. With less sea ice than before, global warming advances even more quickly, and it in turn triggers a chain reaction which could negatively impact the environment around the world. Viewed from this perspective, saving polar bears' home is equivalent to saving ourselves from extinction.

全球暖化無疑是過去十年我們遭遇到的極端天氣情況的原因。北極熊的家，也就是北極地區，正在經歷比其他任何地方都要強烈的全球暖化影響。北極地區的溫度幾乎以地球其他地區兩倍的速率上升，使得不止是北極熊，也讓整個北極生態系統陷入危機中。依據《國家地理雜誌》提供的資料，夏季冰量自從 1979 年來減少了約百分之 30。海冰的量很重要，因為它不但為北極熊提供獵食的地方，也是海豹、海象、北極狐和因紐特人的住所。

藉由將光從地球表面反射出去，北極海冰也有冷卻氣候的效果。由於海冰比以前少，全球暖化進行得更快，進而引發可能對全球環境造成負面影響的連鎖反應。從這個觀點來看，拯救北極熊的家就是挽救我們自己免於滅絕。

|單字片語| **global warming** 全球暖化 / **radical** [ˋrædɪkl̩] adj. 極端的 / **decade** [ˋdɛked] n. 十年 / **polar bear** 北極熊 / **arctic** [ˋɑrktɪk] adj. 北極的 n. 北極地區（the Arctic） / **ecosystem** [ˋɛkoˏsɪstəm] n. 生態系統 / **jeopardy** [ˋdʒɛpɚdɪ] n. 危險（的情況） / **shelter** [ˋʃɛltɚ] n. 庇護所；住所 / **seal** [sil] n. 海豹 / **walrus** [ˋwɔlrəs] n. 海象 / **perspective** [pɚˋspɛktɪv] n. 觀點 / **extinction** [ɪkˋstɪŋkʃən] n. 滅絕

What is true about conditions in the Arctic according to the article?

根據這篇文章，關於北極的情況，以下何者正確？

A. Temperatures are within normal range.
溫度在正常範圍內。

B. The population of polar bears has doubled.
北極熊的數量倍增了。

C. Ice area has shrunk by close to one-third.
有冰的區域減少了將近三分之一。

D. Polar bears can threaten the life of the Inuit people.
北極熊會威脅因紐特人的生活。

詳解

答案：C

文中提到 the amount of summer ice has declined by about 30 percent（夏季冰量減少了約百分之 30），所以選項 C 是正確答案；文中的 about 30 percent 在選項中用 close to one-third 重新表達。其他選項在文中沒有提到。

|單字片語| **population** [ˌpɑpjəˋleʃən] n. 人口；某地區某種動物的總數

Q24

How does global warming affect animals and people in the Arctic?

全球暖化如何影響北極的動物和人？

A. It takes away their natural habitat. 使他們的天然棲息地所消失。
B. It allows them to migrate. 使他們能夠遷徙。
C. It provides more food for the local. 提供更多食物給當地人。
D. It forces animals to rise up against humans. 迫使動物起而對抗人類。

詳解

答案：A

因為全球暖化的影響，the amount of summer ice has declined（夏季冰量減少了）；文中也提到 sea ice... is also a shelter for seals, walruses, arctic foxes, and the Inuit people（海冰也是海豹、海象、北極狐和因紐特人的住所），可見全球暖化會使得某些動物、人類居住的冰區減少，所以 A 是正確答案；文中的 shelter（庇護所，住所）在選項中用 habitat（棲息地）重新表達。其他選項在文章中沒有提到。

|單字片語| **habitat** [ˋhæbəˌtæt] n. 棲息地 / **migrate** [ˋmaɪˌgret] v. 遷徙

Why would saving the polar bears be the same as saving the human race?

為什麼拯救北極熊就等於拯救人類？

A. Polar bears are at the top of the Arctic food chain.
北極熊在北極食物鍊的頂端。

B. The Arctic provides oxygen that cools down the Earth.
北極提供能冷卻地球的氧氣。

C. Lack of rain and water in the Arctic can cut down food supply.
北極缺少雨和水，可能造成食物供應減少。

D. A further reduction in ice mass in the Arctic could lead to global destruction.
北極冰量的進一步減少，可能導致全球性的破壞。

詳解　　答案：D

對應題目的部分是最後一句話：Viewed from this perspective, saving polar bears' home is equivalent to saving ourselves from extinction.（從這個觀點來看，拯救北極熊的家就是挽救我們自己免於滅絕）。所以，前面提到的某個 perspective 就是理由。上一句話說，With less sea ice than before, global warming advances even more quickly（由於海冰比以前少，全球暖化進行得更快），因此會造成 a chain reaction which could negatively impact the environment around the world（可能對全球環境造成負面影響的連鎖反應）。所以，選項 D 是正確答案。

|單字片語| **food chain** 食物鏈

Questions 26-29

Drunk driving is among the top causes of automobile accidents. Each year, drunk drivers cause tragedy and grief in thousands of car accidents. Drinkers will never admit that drinking affects their ability to drive, but the fact remains that the consumption of alcohol can temporarily impair vision and hearing and thus result in decreased muscle coordination and slower reaction. Ironically, after drunk-driving accidents, sometimes those who drive under the influence (DUI) of alcohol survive, while those who follow the rules are killed. This **paradox** can only be solved by stricter laws, better enforcement, and random checkpoints. The goal is to arrest more people who drive drunk to get them off the road. Without getting caught, drunk drivers might take their chances, thinking that a drink or two will not affect their judgment. Some US states even require repeated DUI offenders to install a key-ignition lock on their car that has an attached breathalyzer.

In all fifty states in America, the legal limit for driving under the influence of alcohol is a blood alcohol concentration (BAC) level of .08 or higher. BAC level is the percentage of alcohol in a person's blood, and it is related to one's drunkenness and sobriety. While a high BAC level makes it illegal to drive, a BAC level lower than .08 can still impair a person's senses somewhat, causing a higher risk than driving sober. As a precaution, all drivers should refrain from alcohol intake, no matter how small the amount is.

Although the enforcement of the laws can reduce drinking and driving to a certain extent, the easiest way is to educate people to make better decisions. For instance, something as simple as a designated driver can save people from car accidents. By putting a sober person behind the wheel, everyone can feel free to have a good time at the bar without putting anyone's life at risk on the road.

酒後駕駛是汽車車禍最主要的原因之一。每一年，酒後開車的人在數千場車禍中造成了悲劇與傷痛。喝酒的人永遠不會承認喝酒影響他們的開車能力，但事實上，飲酒還是會暫時減弱視力和聽力，而造成肌肉協調性降低以及反應變慢。諷刺的是，在酒後駕駛造成的車禍之後，有時候是酒後駕駛的人活下來，而遵守規則的人死了。這個矛盾只能藉由更嚴格的法律、更好的執法和隨機的檢查哨解決。這樣做的目標是逮捕更多酒後駕駛的人，把他們從路上去除。如果沒被抓到的話，酒後駕駛的人可能會心存僥倖，覺得喝一兩杯不會影響他們的判斷。美國有些州甚至要求酒後駕車的累犯在車上安裝連結酒測器的鑰匙發動鎖。

在美國的五十州，酒後駕駛的法律限制是血中酒精濃度（BAC） .08 以上。BAC 是一個人血液中的酒精百分比，和酒醉與清醒程度相關。雖然 BAC 很高時開車不合法，但低於 .08 的 BAC 還是可能稍微減弱一個人的感官，造成比清醒時開車更高的風險。為了預防危險，所有駕駛人都應該避免酒精攝取，不管量有多麼少。

雖然執行法律可以在一定程度上減少酒後駕車，但最簡單的方法是教育人們做出更好的選擇。例如，像指定駕駛這樣簡單的事情，就能讓人們免於車禍。藉由讓清醒的人開車，每個人在酒吧都可以任意享受美好時光，而不會在路上讓任何人的生命處於危險之中。

|單字片語|

（第一段）

drunk driving 酒後駕車（= driving under the influence） / **consumption** [kən`sʌmpʃən] n. 消耗，消費；飲用，食用 / **impair** [ɪm`pɛr] v. 減弱，損害（人體機能） / **coordination** [ko`ɔrdn̩ˌeʃən] n. 協調 / **ironically** [aɪ`rɑnɪkl̩ɪ] adv. 諷刺地 / **paradox** [`pærəˌdɑks] n. 矛盾 / **enforcement** [ɪn`forsmənt] n. （法令等的）執行 / **random** [`rændəm] adj. 隨機的 / **checkpoint** [`tʃɛkˌpɔɪnt] n. 檢查站，關卡 / **take one's chance** 碰運氣，冒險 / **offender** [ə`fɛndɚ] n. 違法者 / **ignition** [ɪg`nɪʃən] n. 點火，（汽車）發動 / **breathalyzer** [`brɛθəˌlaɪzɚ] n. 呼氣酒測器

（第二段）

concentration [ˌkɑnsɛn`treʃən] n. 集中；濃縮；濃度 / **drunkenness** [`drʌŋkənnɪs] n. 酒醉 / **sobriety** [sə`braɪətɪ] n. 清醒 / **sober** [`sobɚ] adj. 沒喝醉的，清醒的 / **precaution** [prɪ`kɔʃən] n. 預防措施 / **refrain from** 抑制…，戒絕…

（第三段）

designate [`dɛzɪgˌnet] v. 指定，指派 / **behind the wheel** 開著車

Q26

What is the main subject for this article?

這篇文章的主題是什麼？

A. New technology that deters drunk drivers from driving
阻止喝酒的人開車的新科技

B. Different methods to test alcohol levels of drivers
測試駕駛人酒精濃度的不同方法

C. The importance of prohibiting drinking during social events
在社交活動中禁止喝酒的重要性

D. Consequences of drunk driving and corrective measures
酒後開車的後果和導正措施

詳解　　答案：D

第一段說酒駕容易造成車禍：Each year, drunk drivers cause tragedy and grief in thousands of car accidents.（每一年，酒後開車的人在數千場車禍中造成了悲劇與傷痛），第二段討論 the legal limit for driving under the influence of alcohol（酒後駕駛的法律限制），第三段討論 reduce drinking and driving（減少酒駕）的方法。所以，提到 consequences（後果）和 corrective measures（導正措施）的 D 是正確答案。雖然 A 和第一段最後提到車內安裝 breathalyzer（酒測器）的部分有關，但這只是文章中一小部分的內容，所以不是最適當的答案。

|單字片語| **deter** [dɪ`tɝ] v. 嚇阻，防止 / **corrective** [kə`rɛktɪv] n. 改正的，矯正的

Which word has the closest meaning to the word <u>paradox</u>?

哪個字的意思和「paradox」最接近？

A. Joke　笑話
B. Irony　諷刺
C. Symptom　症狀
D. Metaphor　隱喻

詳解

答案：B

This paradox 是指上一句提到的事情：酒駕的人活下來，但遵守規則的人死了，paradox 在這裡表示原本用意是保障生命安全的交通規則，卻無法讓遵守規則的人免於不幸的矛盾狀態，選項中意思最相關的單字是 B. Irony（諷刺）。其實，上一句修飾整個句子的副詞就是 ironically（諷刺地），從這裡也可以看出答案。

Q28

Why is it important to catch drunk-drivers in the act?

為什麼逮捕酒駕現行犯很重要？

A. Otherwise they might turn themselves in.
不然他們可能自首。
B. Otherwise they might commit suicide.
不然他們可能自殺。
C. Otherwise they might be tempted to do it again.
不然他們可能想要再犯。
D. Otherwise they might be judged innocent.
不然他們可能被判無罪。

詳解

答案：C

第一段的後半部提到，stricter laws, better enforcement, and random checkpoints（更嚴格的法律、更好的執法和隨機的檢查哨）是為了 arrest more people who drive drunk（逮捕更多酒後駕駛的人），而且 Without getting caught, drunk drivers might take their chances（如果沒被抓到的話，酒後駕駛的人可能會碰運氣／冒險）。這裡的 take their chances 是指「雖然喝了酒，卻賭運氣上路，希望不會被逮到」，也就是沒被抓到就會想再犯的意思，所以 C 是正確答案。

|單字片語| **catch someone in the act (of doing something)** 當場逮到某人（做壞事）/ **turn oneself in** 自首 / **commit suicide** 自殺 / **tempted** [ˋtɛmptɪd] adj. 被引誘的；想要做什麼的

Q29

According to this article, what is true about accidents involving drunk drivers?

根據這篇文章，關於酒後開車者牽涉的車禍，何者正確？

A. They can sometimes escape death.　他們有時可以逃過死亡。
B. They often hurt their loved ones.　他們常常傷害自己所愛的人。
C. They are usually killed on the spot.　他們通常當場死亡。
D. They are often caught red-handed.　他們經常被當場逮到。

詳解　　答案：A

第一段中間提到，發生酒駕事故後，sometimes those who drive under the influence (DUI) of alcohol survive（有時候是酒後駕駛的人活下來），所以用 escape death（逃過死亡）重新表達 survive 的 A 是正確答案。

|單字片語| **on the spot** 當場，立即 / **red-handed** [ˋrɛdˋhændɪd] adj. 現行犯的，正在作案的

第1回 第2回 第3回 第4回 第5回 第6回

Questions 30-34

Questions 30-34 are based on the information provided in the following advertisement and email.

Fantastic Asia Tours
Discover different faces of Japan!

Japan is a country of incredible contrast. You can experience the most modern and the most traditional in this one country. From the dazzling neon lights of its futuristic cities, to ancient temples in the mountains, this country makes you feel like traveling through time in the cultural sense. It's truly like nowhere else on earth! Please consider our tour packages and let our guides help you discover the past and future of Japan.

Our Popular Tours

Best of Tokyo Tour Perfect for those who want to visit the most popular sites in Tokyo	Tokyo	5 days	NT$ 30,000 per person
Anime Flavor Tour Visit some of the popular anime spots while learning about Japan's subculture	Tokyo	5 days	NT$ 40,000 per person
Essence of Japan Tour In-depth travel with focus on traditional culture	Tokyo & Osaka	10 days	NT$ 60,000 per person
Luxury Japan Tour Travel luxuriously while enjoying top tier accommodations	Tokyo & Osaka	8 days	NT$ 80,000 per person

*Discounts available for groups of 10 or above

All prices include flights, accommodations, breakfasts, entrance fees, and local transportation.
For more detail, please contact service@fantasticasiatours.com.

美妙亞洲旅行社
發現日本的不同面貌！

日本是具有驚人對比的國家。您可以在這一個國家體驗到最現代和最傳統的事物。從未來感城市的眩目霓虹燈，到山間的古老寺廟，這個國家讓您感覺像是在文化方面進行時間旅行。它真的不像地球上其他任何地方！請考慮我們的旅遊套裝方案，並且讓我們的導遊幫助您發現日本的過去和未來。

我們受歡迎的旅遊

東京精選之旅 非常適合想拜訪東京最受歡迎景點的人	東京	5 天	每人 30,000 元
動畫風味之旅 參觀一些受歡迎的動畫景點，同時了解日本的次文化	東京	5 天	每人 40,000 元

日本精髓之旅 聚焦於傳統文化的深度旅遊	東京與大阪	10 天	每人 60,000 元
豪華日本之旅 進行豪華的旅行，同時享受最高級的住宿	東京與大阪	8 天	每人 80,000 元

*10 人以上團體享有折扣

所有價格包含機票、住宿、早餐、入場費用及當地交通。
欲知詳情，請聯絡 service@fantasticasiatours.com。

|單字片語|

dazzling [ˋdæzl̩ɪŋ] adj. 眩目的 / **neon light** 霓虹燈 / **subculture** [ˋsʌbˏkʌltʃɚ] n. 次文化 / **essence** [ˋɛsn̩s] n. 本質，精髓

From: Weimin Zhang <weimin88@lownet.net>
To: Tom Smith <tsmith@yabaimail.com>
Subject: Plan of visiting Japan
Attachment: FantasticAsia_Japan.pdf

Dear Tom,

After the pandemic years, we can finally travel to Japan without quarantine! I guess you must be as eager as me to revisit the places we've been to, so I'm planning to book a tour for us and our families.

I have attached a file, in which you can see some packages provided by Fantastic Asia Tours. I've heard that their cheaper tours are not bad, and the Anime Flavor Tour is popular among anime and comic fans because it includes attending subculture events in Akihabara. However, even though we both like Japan's animations, it seems to me that we should increase our budget and go for a better package. We're already familiar with Tokyo with our many travel experiences, but we rarely went to Osaka, so I think it will be great to explore the city this time. I'd like to stay in Japan as long as possible, and I also want to know more about the past of Japan, which we don't know much about yet.

Please let me know what you think. By the way, my parents, my wife and two sons are going with me, so if you bring your family with you, we'll be eligible for the discount.

Sincerely,
Weimin

寄件者：張偉民 <weimin88@lownet.net>
收件者：湯姆．史密斯 <tsmith@yabaimail.com>
主旨：拜訪日本的計畫
附件：FantasticAsia_Japan.pdf

親愛的湯姆：

在疫情的那些年之後，我們終於可以去日本旅行而不用隔離了！我猜你一定和我一樣很想再次拜訪我們去過的地方，所以我正打算為我們和我們的家人預訂旅行。

我附上了一個檔案，你可以在裡面看到美妙亞洲旅行社提供的一些套裝方案。我聽說他們比較便宜的旅行不差，而動畫風味之旅很受動漫迷歡迎，因為它包括在秋葉原參加次文化活動。不過，儘管我們都喜歡日本的動畫，我感覺我們應該增加預算，選擇比較好的套裝方案。我們有很多次旅遊經驗，已經很熟悉東京了，但我們很少去大阪，所以我認為這次探索這個城市會很好。我想在日本待越久越好，我也想要更了解日本的過去，這是我們還不太了解的。

請讓我知道你的想法。對了，我的爸媽、我的老婆和兩個兒子會跟我一起去，所以如果你帶你的家人一起去，我們就有資格得到折扣。

誠摯地
偉民

|單字片語|

pandemic [pænˋdɛmɪk] n. 疾病的大流行 / **quarantine** [ˋkwɔrən͵tin] n. 檢疫隔離 / **animation** [͵ænəˋmeʃən] n. 動畫

How does the advertisement make customers interested in Japan?

這則廣告如何讓顧客對日本有興趣？

A. By introducing its history　介紹日本的歷史
B. By emphasizing its peacefulness　強調日本的平靜
C. By demonstrating its economic development　說明日本的經濟發展
D. By focusing on its contrast of different aspects　聚焦於日本不同方面的對比

詳解

答案：D

廣告（第一篇文章）的開頭部分，說 Japan is a country of incredible contrast（日本是具有驚人對比的國家），然後說明日本傳統與現代、過去與未來的對比，所以 D 是正確答案。這段文字只是說明日本傳統與現代的面貌有何不同，而沒有介紹歷史，所以不能選 A。

What is true about Weimin and Tom?

關於偉民和湯姆，何者正確？

A. They frequently attend subculture events.　他們經常參加次文化活動。
B. They know Japan's history well.　他們很了解日本的歷史。
C. They have been to Tokyo many times.　他們曾經去過東京許多次。
D. They have never been to Osaka.　他們從來沒有去過大阪。

詳解

答案：C

在偉民所寫的電子郵件（第二篇文章）中，提到 We're already familiar with Tokyo with our many travel experiences（我們有很多次旅遊經驗，已經很熟悉東京了），顯示偉民和收件人湯姆曾經去過東京許多次，所以 C 是正確答案。A. 在文章中沒有提到。B. 文章中的 the past of Japan, which we don't know much about yet（我們不太了解的日本的過去）顯示兩人不太了解日本的歷史，和選項敘述相反。D. 文章中的 we rarely went to Osaka（我們很少去大阪）是去的次數很少，而不是從來沒去過的意思。

Q32

Which feature of the tours is NOT indicated in the advertisement?

廣告中沒有提到各種旅行的哪一項特徵？

A. The date of each tour　每種旅行的日期
B. The cost of each tour　每種旅行的費用
C. The destination of each tour　每種旅行的目的地
D. The duration of each tour　每種旅行的長度

詳解

答案：A

廣告（第一篇文章）上列出旅遊行程的表格中，依序提供了目的地、天數和價格等資訊，分別對應選項 C、D、B，所以沒有提供的 A 是正確答案。

Which tour does Weimin prefer to book?

偉民比較想要預訂哪個旅遊行程？

A. Best of Tokyo Tour　東京精選之旅
B. Anime Flavor Tour　動畫風味之旅
C. Essence of Japan Tour　日本精髓之旅
D. Luxury Japan Tour　豪華日本之旅

詳解

答案：C

這一題必須對照廣告（第一篇文章）中的旅遊行程介紹和電子郵件（第二篇文章）提到的偏好來解題。電子郵件先是特別提到動畫風味之旅，然後又說 However... it seems to me that we should increase our budget and go for a better package（不過，我感覺我們應該增加預算，選擇比較好的套裝方案），所以偉民希望選擇價格比動畫風味之旅更高的方案。之後他提到 I'd like to stay in Japan as long as possible, and I also want to know more about the past of Japan（我想在日本待越久越好，我也想要更了解日本的過去）。對照廣告的內容，天數最長，而且 with focus on traditional culture（聚焦於傳統文化）的是日本精髓之旅，所以 C 是正確答案。

At least how many people are there in Tom's family?

湯姆家裡至少有幾個人？

A. Two people　兩人
B. Three people　三人
C. Four people　四人
D. Five people　五人

詳解

答案：C

關於人數，廣告（第一篇文章）中的表格備註提到 Discounts available for groups of 10 or above（10 人以上團體享有折扣），而電子郵件中提到 my parents, my wife and two sons are going with me, so if you bring your family with you, we'll be eligible for the discount（我的爸媽、我的老婆和兩個兒子會跟我一起去，所以如果你帶你的家人一起去，我們就有資格得到折扣）。偉民家總共有六個人會去，所以湯姆家至少有四個人，C 是正確答案。

Questions 35-40

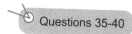

"Whatever the mind of man can conceive and believe, it can achieve." These are the famous words of a revolutionary thinker, Napoleon Hill. As a human race, we are inferior to most animals in terms of physical prowess. Yet incredibly, we can fly in airplanes faster than the speed of sound without wings on our backs. We conquered the moon and, more recently, sent a spacecraft into the orbit of Jupiter, the largest planet in the solar system. According to Napoleon Hill's Law of Attraction, intense desire combined with faith and strong emotions triggers an invincible mechanism within our subconscious mind. Once activated, a thought continues to gather strength until it manifests into physical being.

Since our brain cells communicate with each other by electrical impulses, thoughts are actually energy. The more committed we are to our cause, the stronger our beliefs, the faster our thoughts, ideas, and inspirations will materialize. Many of the world's most successful individuals remember the "Aha" moment that defined their breakthroughs. With your heart full of desire and your mind open to suggestions, a plan will gradually form. Once it takes shape, your path will become crystal-clear. Having said that, it doesn't necessarily mean a bed of roses ahead of you. Obstacles are thrown into the way to test your resolve and make you stronger. Oftentimes, you cannot see beyond the next step, and that's when you take a leap of faith, in the literal sense. Once you conquer your fears, be ready to witness miraculous events taking place before your eyes. Your success will exceed your wildest imagination.

Alas! Achieving is not so much a challenge as the believing part, where most people failed. Imagine an elephant that has been tied with a rope to a tree since it was young. Even though it grows up to possess the strength to uproot the tree, it will still believe that it cannot break free. Such is the power of negative thinking. People who are pessimistic tend to lack self-esteem and self-confidence. They often make excuses for themselves and drag their feet when confronted with problems. Their motto in life is "I won't fail as long as I put things off." In essence, this is a loser's mentality. In rare circumstances where they did try and failed, they simply shrug their shoulders rather than find out the reasons that lead to their failure.

「只要是腦中能夠想像，並且相信的，就能夠實現。」這是革命性的思想家拿破侖．希爾的名言。身為人類，我們在身體能力方面比大部分的動物來得差。但令人難以相信的是，我們背上沒有翅膀，也能在飛機上超越音速飛行。我們征服了月球，而且最近把太空船送到了太陽系最大行星——木星的軌道。根據拿破侖．希爾的「吸引力法則」，強烈的欲望結合了信念和強烈的情感，就會引發我們潛意識心靈所向無敵的機制。一旦想法被啟動了，它會持續累積力量，直到表現在實質的存在上。

因為我們的腦細胞會以電流的脈衝彼此溝通，所以思想其實是能量。我們對自己的目標越堅定，我們的信念就越強烈，而我們的想法、概念和靈感也會越快實現。世界上許多最成功的人都記得決定了自身突破的「啊哈」（頓悟）時刻。當你的心充滿欲望，而你的頭腦對建議保持開放，計畫就會逐漸形成。一旦它成形，你的道路就會非常清楚。話雖如此，這並不一定意味著未來就會萬事如意。路途中會有障礙測試你的決心，並且使你更堅強。你常常無法看到下一步以後的情況，而那就是你如同字面意義般做出「信心的跳躍」的時候。一旦你征服了恐懼，就準備見證奇蹟發生在你眼前吧。你的成功將會超越你最狂野的想像。

哎！達成的挑戰，還不如相信的挑戰來得大，而相信就是大部分的人失敗的地方。想像一隻從小就被繩子跟樹綁在一起的大象。即使牠長大後擁有把樹連根拔起的力量，牠還是會相信自己沒辦法掙脫。這就是負面思考的力量。悲觀的人傾向於缺少自尊和自信。他們經常為自己找藉口，面臨問題的時候也經常拖拖拉拉。他們生活的座右銘是「只要我拖延事情就不會失敗」。本質上，這就是輸家的心態。即使他們難得嘗試並且失敗了，他們也只是聳聳肩，而不是找出導致失敗的原因。

|單字片語|

（第一段）

conceive [kən`siv] v. 構想出，想像 / **revolutionary** [ˌrɛvə`luʃənˌɛrɪ] adj. 革命（性）的 / **prowess** [`praʊɪs] n. 技藝，才能 / **spacecraft** [`spesˌkræft] n. 太空船 / **orbit** [`ɔrbɪt] n. 天體繞行的軌道 / **solar system** 太陽系 / **trigger** [`trɪgɚ] v. 觸發 / **invincible** [ɪn`vɪnsəbḷ] adj. 無敵的，不能動搖的 / **mechanism** [`mɛkəˌnɪzəm] n. 機械裝置，機制 / **subconscious** [sʌb`kɑnʃəs] adj. 潛意識的 / **activate** [`æktəˌvet] v. 啟動，使活化 / **manifest** [`mænəˌfɛst] v. 表明；顯現

（第二段）

impulse [`ɪmpʌls] n. 衝動；脈衝 / **committed** [kə`mɪtɪd] adj. 忠誠的，堅定的 / **cause** [kɔz] n. 原因，理由；目標，志業 / **inspiration** [ˌɪnspə`reʃən] n. 靈感 / **materialize** [mə`tɪrɪəlˌaɪz] v. 具體化，實現 / **breakthrough** [`brekˌθru] n. 突破，突破性發展 / **take shape** 成形，形成 / **crystal-clear** [`krɪstḷ`klɪr] adj. 像水晶一樣透明的，非常清楚的 / **bed of roses** 稱心如意的境遇 / **resolve** [rɪ`zɑlv] v. 解決；下決心 n. 決心 / **oftentimes** [`ɔfṇˌtaɪmz] adv. 往往，常常 / **leap of faith** 「信

心的跳躍」（對於未知、冒險的事情，充滿信心投身其中） / **literal** [ˋlɪtərəl] adj. 字面上的，照字面意義的 / **miraculous** [mɪˋrækjələs] adj. 奇蹟般的

（第三段）
alas 哎（表示遺憾、憐憫、哀傷等等） / **uproot** [ʌpˋrut] v. 把…連根拔起 / **pessimistic** [ˌpɛsəˋmɪstɪk] a. 悲觀的 / **self-esteem** [ˌsɛlfəsˋtim] n. 自尊 / **drag one's feet** 拖拖拉拉 / **be confronted with** （非自願地）面臨… / **motto** [ˋmɑto] n. 座右銘，格言 / **in essence** 本質上 / **mentality** [mɛnˋtælətɪ] n. 心理狀態 / **shrug** [ʃrʌg] v. 聳肩

Q35

Which of the following statements is in line with Napoleon Hill's saying?

以下敘述，何者符合拿破侖．希爾的名言？

A. The sky is the limit.　沒有限制，一切都有可能。
B. Laughter is the best medicine.　笑是最好的藥方。
C. Time and tide wait for no man.　歲月不待人。
D. Never bite off more than what you can chew.　不要貪多嚼不爛。

詳解　　**答案：A**

這題考的是英文慣用的俗語。Napoleon Hill 說的 Whatever the mind of man can conceive and believe, it can achieve.（只要是腦中能夠想像，並且相信的，就能夠實現），是表示不管什麼事情都有可能實現。意思最接近的 A 是正確答案，雖然字面上是「天空就是極限」，但因為天空其實是無邊無際、常人無法到達的地方，所以「天空為限」就是幾乎沒有限制的意思。

Q36

What does the article imply about humans and animals?

關於人和動物，這篇文章暗示什麼？

A. Humans have superior physical strength.
人的身體能力比較優越。
B. Animals are conscious about their weaknesses.
動物知道自己的弱點。
C. Humans and animals are similar in many areas.
人和動物在許多領域相像。
D. Animals have better physical attributes compared to humans.
動物比起人類有更好的身體特質。

詳解

提到 humans and animals 的地方，在第一段的第二句話：As a human race, we are inferior to most animals in terms of physical prowess.（身為人類，我們在身體的能力方面比大部分的動物來得差），反過來說就是動物在身體能力方面比人優秀，所以 D 是正確答案。

|單字片語| **attribute** [`ætrə͵bjut] n. 屬性；特性，特質

What can be assumed about the Law of Attraction?

關於「吸引力法則」，我們可以推測什麼？

A. It was discovered by a prominent physicist.
它是卓越的物理學家發現的。

B. It involves the development of a single idea.
它需要對單一想法的發展。

C. It makes patients with mental disorder violent.
它使得有精神疾病的人變得暴力。

D. It only works on rare occasions.
它只在很罕見的情況下有效。

詳解

答案：B

介紹 Law of Attraction 的地方，在第一段後半，這裡說 intense desire... triggers an invincible mechanism（強烈的欲望引發無敵的機制），而且 Once activated, a thought continues to gather strength until it manifests into physical being.（一旦想法被啟動了，它會持續累積力量，直到表現在實質的存在上）。所以，根據吸引力法則，一開始是先有想法，累積了力量之後，就會實現在物質層面，用 idea 表達 thought 的選項 B 是正確答案。

|單字片語| **prominent** [`prɑmənənt] adj. 顯著的，卓越的 / **mental** [`mɛntl̩] adj. 精神層面的，精神健康的 / **disorder** [dɪs`ɔrdɚ] n. 失調

How can we put the Law of Attraction into motion?

我們可以怎樣讓吸引力法則運作？

A. By studying and passing an exam　讀書並且通過測驗
B. By undergoing a brain surgery　接受腦部手術
C. By committing ourselves to our goals　全心全意投入自己的目標
D. By venting our frustrations on others　向別人發洩自己的挫折感

詳解 **答案：C**

除了上一題的解析中提到的吸引力法則介紹以外，第二段的第二句話還說 The more committed we are to our cause, the stronger our beliefs, the faster our thoughts, ideas, and inspirations will materialize.（我們對自己的目標越堅定，我們的信念就越強烈，而我們的想法、概念和靈感也會越快實現）。being committed to our cause 就是 committing ourselves to our goals 的意思，所以 C 是正確答案。

|單字片語| **vent** [vɛnt] v. 發洩（感情）/ **frustration** [ˌfrʌsˋtreʃən] n. 挫折，挫折感

Q39

What is likely to happen once you formulate a plan?

當你構想出一個計畫，有可能發生什麼事？

A. Everything will be smooth sailing.　一切都會很順利。
B. Rewards will come very soon.　會很快得到回報。
C. Barriers will start to show up.　阻礙會開始出現。
D. People will pledge their support to you.　人們會承諾幫助你。

詳解 **答案：C**

第二段中間提到了 a plan will gradually form（計畫會逐漸形成），但後面也說 it doesn't necessarily mean a bed of roses ahead of you. Obstacles are thrown into the way...（不一定意味著未來就會萬事如意。路途中會有障礙…），所以用 barrier（障礙物）表達 obstacle 的選項 C 是正確答案。

|單字片語| **formulate** [ˋfɔrmjəˌlet] v. 構想，制定 / **be smooth sailing** 進行得很順利 / **barrier** [ˋbærɪr] n. 障礙物 / **pledge** [plɛdʒ] v. 承諾給予…

Q40

What is NOT true about people who have a negative mindset?

關於有負面心理的人，何者不正確？

A. They often find reasons for not trying.
他們經常為自己不去嘗試找理由。
B. They are accustomed to self-denial.
他們習慣了自我否定。
C. They hold on to their faith in the face of failure.
他們在面對失敗時維持信念。
D. They lack the initiative to look for solutions.
他們缺乏尋找解決方法的主動性。

詳解

答案：C

第三段中間開始提到了 negative thinking（負面思考），接下來說 People who are pessimistic（悲觀的人）有怎樣的傾向。often make excuses 對應選項 A，tend to lack self-esteem and self-confidence 對應選項 B，they simply shrug their shoulders rather than find out the reasons 對應選項 D。選項 C 和內容不符合，所以是正確答案。

全民英語能力分級檢定測驗
GENERAL ENGLISH PROFICIENCY TEST

中高級聽力測驗　第三回
HIGH-INTERMEDIATE LISTENING COMPREHENSION TEST

This listening comprehension test will test your ability to understand spoken English. In this test, each conversation, short talk and question will be spoken JUST ONE TIME. They will not be written out for you. There are three parts to this test. Special instructions will be given to you at the beginning of each part.

Part I: Answering Questions

In Part I, you will hear ten questions. After you hear a question, read the four choices in your test booklet and decide which one is the best answer to the question you have heard.

Example:

You will hear: Why did you slam the door?

You will read:
A. I just can't open it.
B. I didn't. I guess it's the wind.
C. Because someone is at the door.
D. Because the door knob is missing.

The best answer to the question "Why did you slam the door?" is B: "I didn't. I guess it's the wind." Therefore, you should choose answer B.

1. A. Sorry. I'm supposed to be on top.
   B. Sorry. I'm sure it belongs to me.
   C. Sorry. I'm not going to buy it.
   D. Sorry. I got them mixed up.

2. A. I will leave in five minutes.
   B. That would be unnecessary.
   C. It depends on quite a few factors.
   D. The typhoon is expected to leave tomorrow.

3. A. That's out of the question.
   B. I do it for a living.
   C. It's a matter of principle.
   D. There's an easy way out.

4. A. There's nothing to worry about.
   B. We are attending a funeral.
   C. Your brother is having an operation today.
   D. It's our wedding anniversary.

5. A. It's a gift for our supervisor.
   B. Do you have any suggestion?
   C. We'll review our staff welfare policies.
   D. Set the table for the luncheon.

6. A. Do I look like a coward?
   B. Can I teach another subject?
   C. Should I notify the authorities?
   D. Would I be kept in the dark?

7. A. I'm ready to proceed with stage two.
   B. I'm having cold feet now.
   C. It won't be delivered so soon.
   D. No, I haven't finished the report.

8. A. The giant rock blocked the road.
   B. Mr. Hamilton will lead by example.
   C. We all have a role to play.
   D. A promising stage actor.

9. A. Yes, I can make a profit.
   B. It's a perfect fit. I'll take it.
   C. I won't stay up all night.
   D. I don't take chances.

10. A. Exports may fall below expectations.
    B. I have an unobstructed view.
    C. The quarterback is very talented.
    D. We shouldn't judge someone by appearance.

Part II: Conversation

In part II, you will hear several conversations between a man and a woman. After each conversation, you will hear a question about the conversation. After you hear the question, read the four choices in your test booklet and choose the best answer to the question you have heard.

Example:

You will hear:	(Man)	Did you happen to see my earphones? I remember leaving them in the drawer. Someone must have taken it.
	(Woman)	It's more likely that you misplaced them. Did you search your briefcase?
	(Man)	I did, but they are not there. Wait a second. Oh. They are right here in my pocket.
	Question:	Who took the man's earphones?
You will read:	A. The woman. B. Someone else. C. No one. D. Another man.	

The best answer to the question "Who took the man's earphones?" is C: "No one." Therefore, you should choose answer C.

Please turn to the next page.

11. A. The number of vouchers he is entitled to.
    B. The insincere service provided by the clerk.
    C. The terms regarding the usage of coupons.
    D. The lack of channel for voicing his opinions.

12. A. A sportsman.
    B. A coach.
    C. A physician.
    D. A merchant.

13. A. He went to the clinic.
    B. He was infected by a virus.
    C. He is a novelist.
    D. He skipped school again.

14. A. In a restaurant.
    B. In a museum.
    C. In a university.
    D. In a theater.

15. A. He was hit by a truck.
    B. He was bitten by a snake.
    C. He was stung by a jellyfish.
    D. He was attacked by a bear.

16. A. It is a discounted item.
    B. It is made of real silk.
    C. It is the last piece left.
    D. It makes her look more slender.

17. A. To Italy and back by plane.
    B. To Italy and back by train.
    C. To Italy by plane and return by train.
    D. To Italy by train and return by plane.

18. A. Road safety.
    B. Multitasking.
    C. Driving tests.
    D. Plastic surgery.

19. A. She is trying to make a sale.
    B. She is trying to purchase something.
    C. She is trying to fight for equality.
    D. She is trying to care for her skin.

20. A. He is introducing himself to a journalist.
    B. He is talking with a career consultant.
    C. He is being interviewed for a job.
    D. He is doing a university interview.

21. A. He graduated at the age of 27.
    B. He has been an architect.
    C. He knew about civil engineering when he was young.
    D. He participated in the project of Taipei 102.

22. A. Tell Chris' family that she is his girlfriend.
    B. Introduce herself to Chris' friends.
    C. Talk to Chris about marriage.
    D. Try to finish her PhD first.

23. A. He and Anna have been together for seven years.
    B. He has not introduced Anna to his friends.
    C. He is attending graduate school.
    D. He does not want to start a family now.

24.

Classmate Info		
Name	Nationality	Address
Elizabeth Praat	American	351 Newton St., Boston
Julia Anderson	American	76 Casey Rd., Cambridge
Maria Rodriguez	Spanish	28 Delta St., Boston
Ana Rosa Santos Silva	Portuguese	183 Orchard St., Cambridge

A. Elizabeth Praat.
B. Julia Anderson.
C. Maria Rodriguez.
D. Ana Rosa Santos Silva.

25.

City	Average Air Pollution Index	Average Winter Temperature
Seattle	52	3.0°C
Los Angeles	107	9.6°C
Miami	60	17.2°C
Cleveland	92	-4.0°C

A. To Seattle.
B. To Los Angeles.
C. To Miami.
D. To Cleveland.

Please turn to the next page.

Part III: Short Talks

In part III, you will hear several short talks. After each talk, you will hear two to three questions about the talk. After you hear each question, read the four choices in your test booklet and choose the best answer to the question you have heard.

Example:

You will hear: Hello, thank you everyone for coming together to share this special day with Chris and I. We have been waiting for this moment forever, and after five years of dating, I can happily say that I am ready. Chris is caring and charming, and I appreciate my good fortune in marrying such a warm-hearted man. When he proposed to me, I realized that he had already become a part of my life. Even though I'm not a perfect cook or housekeeper, I know for sure that I will be a wonderful partner for Chris.

Question number 1: On what occasion is this talk most probably being given?

You will read:
A. A funeral.
B. A wedding.
C. A housewarming.
D. A farewell party.

The best answer to the question "On what occasion is this talk most probably being given?" is B: "A wedding." Therefore, you should choose answer B.

Now listen to another question based on the same talk.

You will hear: Question number 2: According to this talk, what does the woman like about Chris?

You will read: A. His perseverance.
B. His abundant wealth.
C. His cooking skill.
D. His amiable personality.

The best answer to the question "According to this talk, what does the woman like about Chris?" is D: "His amiable personality." Therefore, you should choose answer D.

Please turn to the next page. Now let us begin Part III with question number 26.

26. A. There are various types of membership.
    B. You can enjoy free service for a month.
    C. Children are not allowed on the premises.
    D. The center specializes in health food.

27. A. Employees are well-trained.
    B. Low calorie food is provided for members.
    C. The facilities and equipment are modern.
    D. There is an unconditional refund guarantee.

28. A. He was promoted.
    B. He has passed away.
    C. He ran away from home.
    D. He is under a lot of stress.

29. A. He had an affair with another woman.
    B. He neglected his children due to work.
    C. He was committed and faithful to his family.
    D. He didn't spend enough time with his family.

30. A. They found him very demanding.
    B. They talked behind his back.
    C. They admire his management style.
    D. They made him feel intimidated.

31. A. To remind James to update his Facebook.
    B. To remind James to hand out an award.
    C. To remind James of a change in plan.
    D. To remind James of an upcoming event.

32. A. The meeting was canceled due to terrorism.
    B. Mountain climbing is part of the training.
    C. Daniel will be responsible for any accident.
    D. The award's winner is still unknown.

33. A. It is a new practice.
    B. It is a crucial mistake.
    C. It is a popular feature.
    D. It is a company policy.

34. A. They are too frequent.
    B. They take a long time to download.
    C. They are different from previous versions.
    D. They corrupt files and emails.

35-37.

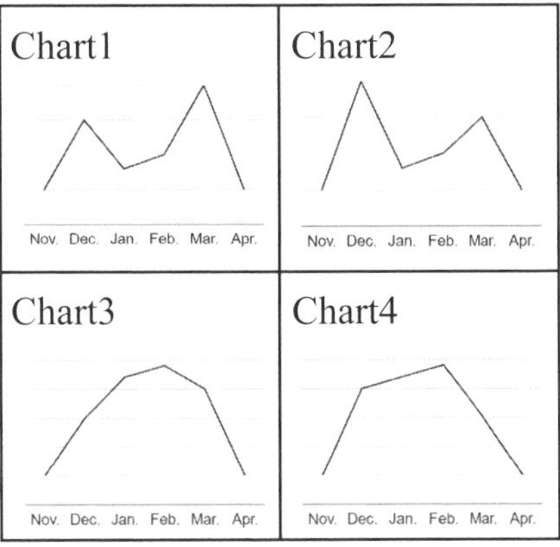

35. A. A travel agent.
    B. A manager of the ski resort.
    C. An analyst of the ski resort industry.
    D. An official in charge of administering ski resorts.

36. A. Chart 1.
    B. Chart 2.
    C. Chart 3.
    D. Chart 4.

37. A. Most of them have their own cabins.
    B. They prefer to go there by themselves.
    C. They like cold weather better.
    D. They usually ski there for more than one day.

Please turn to the next page.

38-40.

Crime Rates: number of persons / 100,000 persons

City	Vehicle Theft	Illegal Drug Use	?
Taipei	11	35	4
Hsinchu	38	20	6
Taichung	24	17	1
Kaohsiung	30	22	1

38. A. It has a high population density.
    B. There are not enough police officers.
    C. Many people commute with their own vehicles.
    D. The city is famous for being unsafe.

39. A. Burglary.
    B. Homicide.
    C. Stalking.
    D. Domestic violence.

40. A. Taipei.
    B. Hsinchu.
    C. Taichung.
    D. Kaohsiung.

READING COMPREHESION TEST

This is a three-part test with forty multiple-choice questions. Each question has four choices. Special instructions will be provided for each part. You will have fifty minutes to complete this test.

Part I: Sentence Completion

In this part of the test, there are ten incomplete sentences. Beneath each sentence you will see four words or phrases, marked A, B, C and D. You are to choose the word or phrase that best completes the sentence. Then on your answer sheet, find the number of the question and mark your answer.

1. We wonder why he did not follow the standard operation ________ written in the manual.

A. perspectives　　B. perceptions
C. procedures　　D. parameters

2. Gold prices plunged by nearly 20 percent before ________ its ascent to new record levels.

A. resuming　　B. condemning
C. hindering　　D. transmitting

3. Advertisements of all kinds that constantly pop up on your Internet browser can be quite a ________.

A. nuisance　　B. hazard
C. scandal　　D. plague

4. ________ the late night shift which only requires male employees, female staff will be assigned to the day or evening shift.

A. Except　　B. Besides
C. Despite　　D. Including

Please turn to the next page.

5. The nostalgic atmosphere of the restaurant is ________ the days when things were stable and simple.
   A. accountable for
   B. compassionate toward
   C. reminiscent of
   D. superstitious about

6. The domestic helper from the Philippines ________ my grandfather and nursed him back to good health.
   A. called on
   B. took on
   C. waited on
   D. rested on

7. Neither party was willing to make a compromise, and as a result, the deal ________.
   A. fell out
   B. fell down
   C. fell off
   D. fell through

8. Never in my life have I been so ________! The clerk searched me as if I was a thief.
   A. alienated
   B. fabricated
   C. humiliated
   D. insulated

9. The minister of health offered ________ answers when bombarded with questions by reporters concerning recent food safety issues.
   A. ambiguous
   B. anonymous
   C. autonomous
   D. ambitious

10. A handmade watch contains more than a hundred different ________, which are all assembled by masters with skillful hands.
   A. guidelines
   B. refreshments
   C. components
   D. organisms

Part Two: Cloze

In this part of the test, you will read two passages. Each passage contains five missing words or phrases. Beneath each passage, you will see five items, each with four choices, marked A, B, C and D. You are to choose the best answer for each missing word or phrase in the two passages. Then, on your answer sheet, find the number of the question and mark your answer.

Questions 11-15

Obesity results from the excessive ___(11)___ of body fat, which is usually caused by consuming too many calories. Therefore, ___(12)___. If we often overeat, we will gain weight; if we gain too much weight, we may become obese. Obesity is considered ___(13)___ disease that can affect us for a long time, like high blood pressure or diabetes. Obesity is also like an epidemic in developed countries, particularly the United States. More than two-thirds of Americans are overweight, including at least one in five children. Obesity rates are ___(14)___ in our society because food is abundant, and most of us are employed in positions that require little to no physical activity. Each year, Americans spend billions of dollars on dieting, diet foods, diet books, diet pills, and the like. Another $75 billion is spent on treating the diseases ___(15)___ obesity. In other words, a lot of medical resources can be reallocated if we keep our bodies in shape.

11. A. accumulation
    B. accommodation
    C. acceleration
    D. acclamation

12. A. we should eat to our hearts' content
    B. food is an indispensable part of our life
    C. we all need to lose weight to stay healthy
    D. whether we get overweight depends on our diet

13. A. an acute
B. a terminal
C. a chronic
D. a fatal

14. A. to be raised
B. on the rise
C. used to rising
D. rising in number

15. A. associated with
B. regardless of
C. instead of
D. especially with

Questions 16-20

Encompassing 15,950 square miles (41,290 square kilometers), Switzerland is a ___(16)___ point between northern and southern Europe. Its physical environment is ___(17)___ by a chain of mountains (the Jura), a densely urbanized plateau, and the Alps range, which forms a natural barrier to the south. ___(18)___ strategic area was of great military importance, and several ancient fortresses dating back to the Roman Empire are still intact – ___(19)___ advanced Roman engineering. Politically, Switzerland is a federation of twenty-six states called "cantons". There are four linguistic regions: German, French, Italian, and Romansh, respectively. One of the cultural differences between these regions is the more frequent use of a kiss ___(20)___ a handshake as a way of greeting in the French-speaking region. In addition to those European languages, English is also spoken and understood. Important announcements on trains will be given in English as well, so there is nothing to worry about.

16. A. transaction
B. transition
C. transformation
D. transfusion

17. A. delineated
B. saturated
C. characterized
D. featured

18. A. As such
B. Such a
C. So much a
D. Such that

19. A. a strong base of
B. a living testimony of
C. in sharp contrast to
D. in better position than

20. A. in spite of
B. rather than
C. let alone
D. contrary to

Part III: Reading Comprehension

In this part of the test, you will find several tasks. Each task contains one or two passages or charts, which are followed by two to six questions. You are to choose the best answer, A, B, C, or D, to each question on the basis of the information provided or implied in the passage or chart. Then, on your answer sheet, find the number of the question and mark your answer.

Questions 21-22

Accommodation in Venice

As one of the most popular cities in Europe, Venice is a must-visit place for tourists, who usually come in full force in summer. Therefore, there are a few things to be aware of when it comes to accommodation in Venice:

1. Space is limited in the city.
2. Accommodation in Venice can cost a lot.
3. Many visitors only come for a day trip.

The fact that Venice is often no more than a day trip destination does not help to mitigate the high prices of accommodation. Venice can't be truly appreciated unless one stays overnight, but it is a tough call as one ponders whether to break the bank.

Venice is full of hotels, but there aren't many hostels – the city just isn't known for cheap places to spend the night, unfortunately. Staying at youth hostels in Venice might be a great way to save money, but there is a condition: You have to be below 25 years of age to be considered a youth.

21. Which factor is NOT accountable for the high cost of lodging in Venice?
    A. Land constraint
    B. Worldwide fame
    C. High number of visitors
    D. Popularity of day tours

22. What dilemma does the writer mention in the article?
    A. To splurge on accommodation in order to experience more or to save money by going on a day trip
    B. To stay at a hotel and enjoy its service or to stay at a hostel that offers no service at all
    C. To decide if one should travel on land or by sea to reach Venice
    D. To weigh the advantages and disadvantages of visiting Venice compared to other cities in Europe

Questions 23-25

To Madam Shu-fen, Wang

This is a response to your inquiry regarding the safety of our toys. First and foremost, there are warnings on the box and the plastic bags reminding that these toys are only for children aged five and above. The components contained in the toy set are meant for assembly, not for consumption. The fact that our products are made of non-toxic materials does not imply that they are safe to eat. Children aged five years and above should not have trouble telling the difference between food and plastic. Nevertheless, we regret that your child choked on the components. We are pleased to offer you a new set of the toy you purchased instead of only replacing the missing parts. A hand-written card signed by the chief executive officer of XYZ Toys Co. was also delivered to your mailing address. We do wish your child a speedy recovery, though your claim for medical compensation was denied. We also wish to express our sympathies as it must have been a traumatic experience for your child.

Andrea Juan
Public Relations Officer

23. What is Madam Wang's chief complaint?
   A. Her child swallowed some parts of the toy.
   B. Her child ate something poisonous.
   C. Her child felt dizzy after playing with plastic toys.
   D. Her child was not sent to the hospital in time.

24. According to this letter, what is XYZ Toy's stance toward the complaint?
   A. It is not responsible for the unfortunate accident.
   B. It is willing to offer payment to settle the case.
   C. It admits that there is a flaw in the products it makes.
   D. It provides medical insurance for users who are hurt.

25. Which of the following shows a friendly gesture adopted by XYZ Toys?
   A. The chief executive officer visited the hospital.
   B. The public relations officer apologized in public.
   C. The customer is entitled to a full refund.
   D. The customer will receive a new set of toy.

Please turn to the next page.

Questions 26-29

One may conclude that a paralyzed elderly man who is confined to a wheelchair has nothing to contribute to society. Our perceptions will change once we hear the story of the late Stephen Hawking (1942-2018). In 1963, this exceptionally gifted individual developed a rare disease that caused muscle atrophy, which made him lose control of his limbs. What's worse, he gradually lost his speech ability. He was told he only had two years to live, but unbelievably, he beat death and defied all predictions of modern medical science. To compensate for his loss of speech, he used a custom-made speech-generating device, which is activated by tensing his cheek muscle.

Besides living well beyond the time his doctor decreed, he went on to Cambridge and became a brilliant researcher. From 1979 to 2009, he held the post of Lucasian Professor at Cambridge, the chair which has been held by Isaac Newton. Therefore, he is regarded as one of the most brilliant theoretical physicists since Einstein.

Stephen Hawking is also the author of *A Brief History of Time*, an international bestseller. This modern classic helps non-scientists know about fundamental questions of physics and our existence, particularly about the beginning and possible ending of our universe, with a minimum of technical jargon. Encompassing topics such as gravity, black holes, the Big Bang, the nature of time, the births and deaths of stars, etc., this book proves to be overwhelming for most readers, and it seems beyond imagination that Hawking successfully integrated all these difficult subjects into a theoretical system. By reading this book, we may understand the universe and get a glimpse of "the mind of God", in Hawking's terms.

26. What can be inferred about Stephen Hawking's physical condition?
   A. He was able to move freely with artificial limbs.
   B. He was able to type using his eyeball movements.
   C. He was able to communicate using special equipment.
   D. He was able to write with his left hand.

27. What can be considered a miracle in Stephen Hawking's life?
   A. He became a doctor.
   B. He defied death.
   C. He wrote a great book.
   D. He taught at universities.

28. Compared to other books on science, what made *A Brief History of Time* relatively readable for laymen?
   A. It provides very basic explanations of various subjects.
   B. It explained the creation of the Earth.
   C. It combined science and religion.
   D. It minimized the use of scientific terminology.

29. What topic is **NOT** covered in the book *A Brief History of Time*?
   A. An explanation of how the universe is formed
   B. A spiritual insight of the mind and will of God
   C. A hypothesis of how stars eventually disintegrate
   D. An in-depth discussion on overcoming physical handicaps

Please turn to the next page.

Questions 30-34 are based on the information provided in the following announcement and letter.

Sylvester University

Below are the minimum requirements for admissions into our university. Please note that meeting the minimum requirements does not guarantee a spot in our program. For students from countries where English is not the dominant language, an official English proficiency test score is required.

Academic

For admissions into one of our undergraduate programs, students must provide

- High school diploma or certificate of high school equivalency by the start of the program
- Official transcripts (must be provided directly from the awarding institution no more than 30 days after the start of the program)
- 3 reference letters in academic or personal background
- A personal statement outlining the reason for choosing Sylvester University

Financial

All International students are required by the U.S. government to submit a Certification of Finances, which is evidence that a student has sufficient funds to pay for tuition and living expenses for the first year. The estimated first year budget is $50,000 on average.

Research

Students are expected to conduct novel research in their field to successfully graduate from our institution.

If you have any questions, please contact us at admissions@sylvester.edu.

Dear admissions officer,

My name is Alicia Hernández. I am from Mexico. I would like to apply to your biomedical program for the year 2024. There are some reasons why I choose to study medicine.

First, my father is a surgeon. He has worked for many years for Doctors Without Borders and has helped kids in various countries combat malaria. My mother is also in the medical field. She is a nurse. I look up to them both in so many ways, and I aspire to do good for the world just as they do. When I decided that I was going to follow in their footsteps, I looked at the top list of biomedical engineering programs in your country. I am applying to Sylvester University because of its amazing reputation, small class sizes, and the fact that it is one of the leaders in the biomedical field.

While undergoing my high school studies, I participated in a multitude of activities that help benefit society. I volunteered for the blood drive, and I also organized several events on nutrition.

Enclosed are my high school diploma and reference letters. I hope to take my enthusiasm into your university and contribute to your vision of providing students that are willing to serve the community. Thank you for your consideration, and I hope to hear from you soon.

Sincerely,
Alicia Hernández

Please turn to the next page.

30. What is true about the requirements for applying to Sylvester University?
   A. The applicant must come from an English-speaking country.
   B. The applicant must be a high school graduate.
   C. The applicant must be recommended by other people.
   D. One who meets all the requirements listed will be accepted.

31. What do we learn about Alicia?
   A. She aspires to be a pharmacist.
   B. Her father has been to many countries.
   C. Her parents both did some medical studies.
   D. She leads a physically active lifestyle.

32. What is the reason that Alicia chooses to apply to Sylvester University?
   A. It is where her parents graduated from.
   B. It is the most well-known university in the U.S.
   C. There are not too many courses there to choose from.
   D. It is prestigious for its biomedical studies.

33. What document does Alicia still need to provide before the start of the program?
   A. Her English proficiency test score
   B. Her high school diploma
   C. Her official transcripts
   D. Her reference letters

34. What do students of Sylvester University need to do before they graduate?
   A. Do an internship in the last year of a program
   B. Provide their transcripts at the university
   C. Pay $50,000 to the university every year
   D. Do a study related to what they learn

Questions 35-40

I can't help but observe that visitors traveling in groups are behaving more and more like "zombies". The main selling proposition of package deal trips is to cover as much ground as possible in a minimum number of days. As a result, tourists fight against time just to take as many pictures as possible before rushing off to the next "cannot-be-missed" sight. Take a Europe tour for example: a seven-day trip can sometimes stretch over five different national capitals. Therefore, a large part of vacation time is spent on the road. One may argue that we can also take in the views while traveling along picturesque landscapes. Truth be told, visitors tend to find themselves dozing off on the coaches. No matter how breathtaking the scenery is, staring at the same expanse of land for hours can have a numbing effect. Upon reaching a new destination, these "zombies" come alive as they pose in front of landmarks and hunt for souvenirs which serve as "evidence" that they have been to a particular city. Once back on the bus, they return to a state of coma, oblivious to the rattling of the tour guide.

The "see-and-go" travel culture is a result of price competition among travel agencies. To attract business, travel agencies resort to underpricing, a new term that refers to offering ridiculously low prices that are beyond business sense. How can companies be profitable when costs and overheads exceed the price they charge? As a matter of fact, there is more than meets the eye. Cheap package deal trips are offset by shopping trips, in which travel agencies derive a handsome commission. At a souvenir store your guide takes you to, the same item can be marked up by 1,000%, and part of the overcharge will go to the guide and travel agency. Such practice is frowned upon by relevant authorities. However, a lot has been said, while little has been done.

As economical packaged tours become infamous for their hectic itineraries and unnecessary shopping trips, in-depth guided travel is gaining popularity. In recent years, tourists are no longer satisfied with running after the guide and squeezing more countries into their itineraries. Instead, they now prefer "deep" travel focused on getting under the skin of a place. It is about seeking out real-life experiences rather than fake culture packaged up for tourists. It means allocating more time to each destination and putting in an effort to understand the history, architecture, and daily lives of common

Please turn to the next page.

folks. In this way, tourists will be able to appreciate local idiosyncrasies and the details that make a place unique.

35. What is the main purpose of this article?
    A. To shed some light on what an ideal tour should be
    B. To explain how to travel to as many places as possible
    C. To argue that exotic scenery is the highlight of a trip
    D. To expose the unethical schemes of travel agencies

36. What does the writer suggest about package deal trips?
    A. Visitors get good value in return for money.
    B. Visitors can buy souvenirs at a lower price.
    C. Visitors are able to experience local culture.
    D. Visitors may end up paying more than they intend.

37. According to the writer, which word can best describe an economical packaged tour?
    A. Superficial B. Enlightening C. Marvelous D. Tragic

38. Why are visits to souvenir stores included in package deal trips?
    A. They are popular destinations among tourists.
    B. They enable travel agencies to make a killing.
    C. They help tourists understand the geography of a place.
    D. They allow visitors to bargain collectively.

39. What new trend did the author observe recently?
    A. Tourists prefer to travel to exotic places.
    B. Tourists prefer to experience life like a native.
    C. Tourists prefer to explore the deep sea.
    D. Tourists prefer to go on shopping sprees.

40. What is a possible drawback of an "in-depth" tour?
    A. Traveling to fewer countries or cities in a single trip
    B. Spending more on transportation and food
    C. Having less time to take pictures
    D. Difficulty in interacting with locals

第三回

初試 聽力測驗 解析

第一部分 回答問題

Q1

You have to arrange the books in alphabetical order using the authors' last names. This one is supposed to be on the top shelf.

你要把書依照作者的姓氏用字母排序。這一本應該放在書架最上層。

A. Sorry. I'm supposed to be on top.
B. Sorry. I'm sure it belongs to me.
C. Sorry. I'm not going to buy it.
D. Sorry. I got them mixed up.

A. 抱歉。我應該要在上面。
B. 抱歉。我確定這是我的東西。
C. 抱歉。我不會買這本書。
D. 抱歉。我把它們搞混了。

詳解

答案：D

說話者要求對方 You have to arrange the books in alphabetical order（你必須依照字母順序排列書），還有 This one is supposed to be...（這本應該在…），顯示這可能是圖書館或書店員工之間的對話。答案都是以 Sorry 開頭，所以表示弄錯書本排列方式的 D 是正確答案。

|單字片語| **alphabetical** [ˌælfə`bɛtɪkl] adj. 字母的，照字母順序的

Q2

May I know how soon can you confirm whether our loan application is approved?

我可以知道你多快可以確認我們的貸款申請有沒有核准嗎？

A. I will leave in five minutes.
B. That would be unnecessary.
C. It depends on quite a few factors.
D. The typhoon is expected to leave tomorrow.

A. 我會在五分鐘後離開。
B. 那是不必要的。
C. 取決於很多因素。
D. 颱風預料明天會離開。

詳解

答案：C

若只聽到 how soon 可能會以為答案是 A，但說話者問的是 how soon can you confirm...（你多快可以確認），所以 A 不對。正確答案 C 並沒有回答可以多快確認，而是說確認核准的速度取決於很多因素，暗示確認的速度會隨著情況而有所不同，所以現在不能給一個確切的答案。

補充說明

請分清楚這些形態相近的單字。

factor [`fæktɚ] 因素 / faction [`fækʃən]（組織的）派系 / fraction [`frækʃən] 一點點，（數學）分數

Q3

Why do you always have to make things difficult for yourself by contradicting your supervisor?
你為什麼總是要反駁上司，把情況弄得很困難呢？

A. That's out of the question.
B. I do it for a living.
C. It's a matter of principle.
D. There's an easy way out.

A. 那是不可能的。
B. 我做那件事維生。
C. 那是原則的問題。
D. 有簡單的解決方法。

詳解

答案：C

說話者問對方為什麼要 contradict your supervisor（反駁你的上司），所以要回答理由。C 回答「那是原則的問題」，暗示上司的某些作為違反了他的原則，使他反駁上司，是正確答案。

補充說明

請分清楚這兩個形態相近，而且發音相同的單字。

principle [`prɪnsəpl̩] n. 原則，原理 / principal [`prɪnsəpl̩] adj. 主要的 n. 校長

Q4

Whoa! What a spread! My mouth is watering. What's the special occasion today?

哇！真是豐盛！我在流口水了。今天是什麼特別的場合？

A. There's nothing to worry about. A. 沒什麼好擔心的。
B. We are attending a funeral. B. 我們要參加喪禮。
C. Your brother is having an operation today. C. 你哥哥今天要動手術。
D. It's our wedding anniversary. D. 是我們的結婚週年紀念。

詳解 答案：D

我們知道 spread 是攤開、展開的意思，但它當名詞的時候，在口語裡可以表示「盛宴」的意思。即使不知道這個意思，也可以從 My mouth is watering（我在流口水）和 special occasion（特別的場合）推測是因為看到特別豪華的食物才這麼說。說話者問是什麼場合，最有可能的答案是為了慶祝什麼，所以 D 是最適當的選項。

|單字片語| **spread** [sprɛd] v. 展開，攤開 n. 傳播，擴散；（口語）盛宴，豐盛的飯菜 / **operation** [ˌɑpəˋreʃən] n. 操作；營運；手術

Q5

Let's see if we can wrap things up before lunchtime. What is the first item on the agenda?

我們看看可不可以在午餐時間之前把事情完成。第一項議題是什麼？

A. It's a gift for our supervisor. A. 這是給我們主管的禮物。
B. Do you have any suggestion? B. 你有任何建議嗎？
C. We'll review our staff welfare policies. C. 我們會審視我們的員工福利政策。
D. Set the table for the luncheon. D. 為午餐會擺放桌上的餐具。

詳解 答案：C

必須知道 agenda 是「會議議程」的意思，才能得知兩人正在開會。說話者問議程的第一個 item（事項）是什麼，所以說明討論議題的 C 是正確答案。會議的議程應該是事先擬定好的，所以 B 不是適當的答案。D 是要做的事情，而不是討論的題目，所以也不對。

|單字片語| **wrap up** （口語）把…完成 / **agenda** [əˋdʒɛndə] n. （待議事項的）議程 / **set the table** 擺放好桌上的餐具 / **luncheon** [ˋlʌntʃən] n. （正式的）午餐會

Q6

Despite the risks involved, are you still keen to be a part of this science expedition?

即使其中有風險，你還是想要參加這次科學考察嗎？

A. Do I look like a coward?	A. 我看起像個懦夫嗎？
B. Can I teach another subject?	B. 我可以教其他科目嗎？
C. Should I notify the authorities?	C. 我應該通知相關當局嗎？
D. Would I be kept in the dark?	D. 我會被蒙在鼓裡嗎？

詳解 **答案：A**

說話者提到了 risks（風險），然後問對方 are you still keen to be a part of this science expedition?（你還是想要參加這次科學考察嗎），希望對方表明考量了風險之後，是否決定要參加。四個選項都沒有直接回答參加與否，但 A 反問「我看起來像個懦夫（coward）嗎」，暗示自己不是懦夫，所以不會害怕危險、會參加，是正確答案。

|單字片語| **expedition** [ˌɛkspɪˋdɪʃən] n. 遠征，探險，考察 / **coward** [ˋkaʊɚd] n. 懦夫 / **keep someone in the dark** 把某人蒙在鼓裡

Q7

Are you mentally prepared to go on stage and deliver the farewell speech?

你心理準備好要上台發表告別演說了嗎？

A. I'm ready to proceed with stage two.	A. 我準備好繼續進行第二階段了。
B. I'm having cold feet now.	B. 我現在臨陣退縮了。
C. It won't be delivered so soon.	C. 它不會那麼快被發表。
D. No, I haven't finished the report.	D. 沒有，我還沒完成報告。

詳解 **答案：B**

說話者問對方是否 mentally prepared（心理上準備好的），後面說出對方是要發表 farewell speech（告別演說）。選項中能表達心理狀態的是 B，have cold feet 表示「臨陣退縮」的意思。A 的 stage two（第二階段）不知道是指什麼，C 回答沒那麼快發表也答非所問。

|單字片語| **mentally** [ˋmɛntḷɪ] adv. 心理上 / **deliver** [dɪˋlɪvɚ] v. 遞送；發表（演說等） / **farewell** [ˋfɛrˋwɛl] n. 告別 / **proceed with** 繼續進行，接著進行…/ **have cold feet** 臨陣退縮

Q8

This looks like a potential blockbuster, but who will play the lead role?

這看起來可能成為一部票房非常好的電影，但誰會演主角呢？

A. The giant rock blocked the road.
B. Mr. Hamilton will lead by example.
C. We all have a role to play.
D. A promising stage actor.

A. 那塊巨大的岩石把路堵住了。
B. Hamilton 先生會帶頭以身作則。
C. 我們所有人都有自己的角色要扮演。
D. 一位前途有望的舞台劇演員。

詳解

答案：D

題目是問「誰」會演主角（who will play the lead role），可以先刪去沒有回答人物的 A。選項中，回答了「舞台劇演員」的 D 是正確答案。B 雖然回答了人名，但後面說的是他會 lead by example（以身作則），與題意不符。

|單字片語| **blockbuster** [ˋblɑkˏbʌstɚ] n. 很賣座的電影 / **lead role** 主角 / **lead by example** 以身作則 / **promising** [ˋprɑmɪsɪŋ] adj. 前途有望的

Q9

I heard that a man became a billionaire overnight. Do you want to try your luck at the casino this weekend?

我聽說有個男人一夜成為億萬富翁。你這週末想要在賭場試試運氣嗎？

A. Yes, I can make a profit.
B. It's a perfect fit. I'll take it.
C. I won't stay up all night.
D. I don't take chances.

A. 要，我會賺到利益。
B. 這完全合身。我要買下來。
C. 我不會整晚熬夜。
D. 我不冒險。

詳解

答案：D

說話者問 Do you want to try your luck at the casino（你想要在賭場試試運氣嗎），所以應該回答是否會去。A 雖然回答了 Yes，但 make a profit 是指經營或投資而賺到利益，不能用在賭博賺到錢的情況，所以不對。B 的 perfect fit 表示什麼東西很合身或者很搭，與題意不符。C 沒有回答問題。D 用 I don't take chances（我不冒險）表示自己不從事賭博之類的投機性活動，是適當的答案。

|單字片語| **billionaire** [ˌbɪljəˋnɛr] n. 億萬富翁 / **overnight** [ˋovɚˋnaɪt] adv. 整晚；一夜之間 / **try one's luck** 碰運氣 / **make a profit** 賺得利益 / **fit** [fɪt] n. 適合；合身 / **take chances** 冒險

Q10

What is your view on the economic outlook for the coming quarter?

你對於下一季經濟前景的看法是什麼？

A. Exports may fall below expectations.	A. 出口可能低於預期。
B. I have an unobstructed view.	B. 我有不受阻擋的風景。
C. The quarterback is very talented.	C. 那個四分衛很有天分。
D. We shouldn't judge someone by appearance.	D. 我們不應該以貌取人。

詳解

答案：A

說話者詢問對於 economic outlook（經濟前景）的 view（看法），所以提到和經濟相關的 Exports（出口）的 A 是正確答案。B、C、D 分別是利用題目中出現的 view、quarter、outlook（和表示「外表」的 look 相近）而製造的混淆選項。

|單字片語| **outlook** [ˋaʊtˌlʊk] n. 展望，前景 / **quarter** [ˋkwɔrtɚ] n. 四分之一；季度 / **expectation** [ˌɛkspɛkˋteʃən] n. 期望，預期 / **unobstructed** [ˌʌnəbˋstrʌktɪd] adj. 沒有阻礙的 / **quarterback** [ˋkwɔrtɚˌbæk] n. （美式足球）四分衛 / **talented** [ˋtæləntɪd] adj. 有天分的

第二部分 對話

Q11

W: With every purchase above NT$500, you are entitled to a 50-dollar voucher. 每次購物台幣 500 元以上，您可以獲得 50 元的折價券。

M: Can I use it now and get a 50-dollar rebate?
我可以現在就用，並且現折 50 元嗎？

W: I'm sorry, Sir. You can use it on your next purchase. Please be reminded that only one voucher is allowed to be used for every five hundred dollars you spend. 很抱歉，先生。您可以在下次購物時使用。提醒您，每消費 500 元只能使用一張折價券。

M: This is a very insincere way of giving out discounts. Don't you have a suggestion box? 這樣提供折扣是很不誠懇的。你們沒有意見箱嗎？

W: Yes, we do have a customer feedback form. Please fill it out, and I will pass it to my manager in person.
有的，我們有顧客回饋意見表。請填好表格，我會當面轉交我的主管。

Q: What is the man unhappy about?
男子對於什麼不滿意？

A. The number of vouchers he is entitled to.	A. 他可以得到的折價券數量。
B. The insincere service provided by the clerk.	B. 店員提供的服務不誠懇。
C. The terms regarding the usage of coupons.	C. 關於使用折價券的條款。
D. The lack of channel for voicing his opinions.	D. 表達意見管道的缺乏。

詳解 **答案：C**

女子提到 50-dollar voucher（50 元的折價券），男子問 Can I use it now（我可以現在用嗎），女子回答 You can use it on the next purchase（你可以在下次購物時使用）。對於女子的說明，男子表示 This is a very insincere way of giving out discounts.（這樣提供折扣是很不誠懇的）。題目問男子不滿意 unhappy about 的事項，所以答案是 C。如果只注意到對話中出現的 insincere（不誠懇的）這個字，有可能會誤選 B，但男子的抱怨是針對使用折價券的條件，而不是針對店員，所以這不是正確答案。

〈補充說明〉

rebate 是指在消費時立即給予消費者的現金退款。

|單字片語| **voucher** [ˋvaʊtʃɚ] n. 優惠券，兌換券 / **rebate** [ˋribet] n. 貼現（折扣的一種）/ **insincere** [ˌɪnsɪnˋsɪr] adj. 不誠懇的 / **be entitled to** 有資格得到⋯ / **terms** [tɝmz] n.（契約等的）條件，條款 / **voice** [vɔɪs] 說出⋯

Q12

M: I want you to visualize yourself standing up there, holding the gold medal in your hand. Can you see the flag of your country being raised? 我要你想像自己站在那裡，手中握著金牌。你能看到自己的國旗升起嗎？

W: Yes, I can see it in my mind. I can feel the intensity of emotions.
是的，我可以在腦中看到。我可以感受到情緒的強度。

M: Remember this feeling whenever you have any doubts about yourself. You are a world champion, and you will do your best to realize your dreams. 每當你懷疑自己的時候，就回想這個感覺。你是世界冠軍，你會盡全力實現你的夢想。

W: Is this the way all Olympic participants are being taught? It's like positive brainwashing.
這是教導所有奧運選手的方法嗎？這好像是正向的洗腦。

M: Julia, it is called neuro-linguistic programming.
Julia，這叫「神經語言規畫」。

W: Whatever. I hope it works. 隨便啦。我希望有用。

M: It only does if you believe in it. 你相信才會有用。

Q: What is the man's career likely to be?
男子的職業可能是什麼？

A. A sportsman.	A. 運動員。
B. A coach.	B. 教練。
C. A physician.	C. 內科醫師。
D. A merchant.	D. 商人。

詳解　　答案：B

從 gold medal（金牌）、world champion（世界冠軍）和 Olympic（奧運的）這些關鍵字，可推斷女子是運動員，而男子正在用某種方法鼓勵他，所以男子最有可能的職業是教練，B 是正確答案。A 是女子的職業才對，如果聽錯題目就有可能誤選。雖然對話中出現 neuro-linguistic programming 這種感覺像是醫學名詞的名稱，但男子所做的言語激勵並不是一般內科醫師會做的事情，所以不能選 C。

|單字片語| **visualize** [ˋvɪʒʊəˏlaɪz] v.（用畫面）想像 / **medal** [ˋmɛdl̩] n. 獎牌 / **intensity** [ɪnˋtɛnsətɪ] n. 強烈，強度 / **brainwashing** [ˋbrenˏwɑʃɪŋ] n. 洗腦 / **neuro-linguistic programming** 神經語言規畫（一種號稱可以用言語改變身心狀態的方法）/ **merchant** [ˋmɝtʃənt] n. 商人

Q13

W: Where is Andy? I haven't seen him around the whole morning. Don't tell me he played truant again.
Andy 在哪裡？我整個上午都沒看到他。別跟我說他又曠課了。

M: Wait till Professor Jefferson finds out. Let's see what kind of excuse Andy can make up this time.
等 Jefferson 教授查清楚吧。我們看看 Andy 這次可以編出哪種藉口。

W: The last time he said his pet was sick, and he had to take it to the veterinarian. 他上次說自己的寵物生病了，必須把牠帶到獸醫那邊。

M: I don't think Professor Jefferson is going to buy that sort of story again. 我覺得 Jefferson 教授不會再相信那種故事了。

W: When it comes to lying, Andy can be pretty creative and convincing.
說到撒謊，Andy 可以很有創意又讓人信服。

M: Oh, yes. And he can do it with such an innocent look.
噢，是啊。而且他可以用很無辜的樣子說謊。

W: I always fall for that. 我總是因為這樣上當。

Q: What is true about Andy?
關於 Andy，以下何者正確？

A. He went to the clinic. A. 他去了診所。
B. He was infected by a virus. B. 他被病毒感染了。
C. He is a novelist. C. 他是個小說家。
D. He skipped school again. D. 他又沒上學了。

詳解　　答案：D

談話中提到了 Professor Jefferson，可以判斷他們是學生；對話中最關鍵的部分是女子說的 Don't tell me he played truant again.（別跟我說他又曠課了）。Don't tell me... 並不是字面上「不要告訴我」的意思，而是表示不敢相信某件事又發生了的意思，所以 Andy 不在課堂上是事實，D 是正確答案。play truant（不上學）和 skip school 的意思相近，只是沒有那麼常聽到，有些人可能會對

這個用語覺得陌生。

|單字片語| **play truant** 不上學 / **make up** 編造… / **veterinarian** [ˌvɛtərəˋnɛrɪən] n. 獸醫（= vet）/ **buy** [baɪ] v. （口語）接受，相信 / **convincing** [kənˋvɪnsɪŋ] adj. 有說服力的 / **fall for** 上（謊言等等）的當

Q14

M: Look! It's not even noon yet, and the place is already crowded.
你看！都還沒到中午，這裡就已經很擠了。

W: This place looks like an imperial palace. Are they wearing ancient costumes from the Qing dynasty? I feel like a noble already.
這個地方看起來像是皇宮一樣。他們穿的是清朝的古裝嗎？我已經覺得自己像貴族一樣了。

M: Even the utensils are of the same design the emperors used. See this dragon here with claws? It's exquisite, isn't it? 就連餐具也和皇帝用的是一樣的設計。你看到這隻有爪子的龍嗎？很精緻，不是嗎？

W: What about the cuisine? 那料理怎麼樣呢？

M: A sumptuous feast of local flavor with more than a hundred main courses to choose from. 是本地風味的盛宴，有一百多種主菜可以選擇。

W: I can't wait to try them. 我等不及要吃吃看了。

Q: Where is this conversation probably taking place?
這段對話可能是在哪裡進行的？

A. In a restaurant. A. 在餐廳。
B. In a museum. B. 在博物館。
C. In a university. C. 在大學。
D. In a theater. D. 在劇場。

詳解

答案：A

從選項可以猜測，這可能是問對話場所的問題，所以要注意和場所相關的關鍵字。從對話後半段的 utensils（餐具）、cuisine（料理）、sumptuous feast（豪華的筵席）可知這裡是用餐的地方，A 是正確答案。

|單字片語| **imperial** [ɪmˋpɪrɪəl] adj. 帝國的，皇帝的 / **palace** [ˋpælɪs] n. 宮殿 / **utensil** [juˋtɛnsḷ] n. 廚房用具或餐具 / **emperor** [ˋɛmpərɚ] n. 皇帝 / **exquisite** [ˋɛkskwɪzɪt] adj. 精緻的 / **cuisine** [kwɪˋzin] n. 菜餚，料理 / **sumptuous** [ˋsʌmptʃʊəs] adj. 奢侈的，豪華的 /

Q15

W: Let me take a closer look at the wound. When did this happen?
讓我把傷口看仔細一點。什麼時候發生的？

M: About an hour ago. My friends sent me here as fast as they could. The whole area feels numb. I don't even feel any pain when I poked it. 大概一小時前。我朋友盡可能趕快把我送到這裡了。整個區域都覺得麻痺了。我戳它的時候甚至不會有任何痛的感覺。

W: You said you didn't see what bit you. What about your fellow hikers? Did anyone see anything? 你說你沒看到是什麼咬了你。那和你一起登山健行的同伴呢？有人看到什麼嗎？

M: One of my friends said it must be a reptile. He saw something brown and black disappear into some bushes. 有一個朋友說那一定是爬行動物。他看到有褐色和黑色的東西消失在灌木叢裡。

W: I'll give you a shot for now, but we have to monitor your condition and see what we can do.
我現在暫時給你打一針，但我們必須監測你的情況，看看我們能做什麼。

Q: What might have happened to the man?
男子可能發生了什麼事？

A. He was hit by a truck.	A. 他被卡車撞了。
B. He was bitten by a snake.	B. 他被蛇咬了。
C. He was stung by a jellyfish.	C. 他被水母螫了。
D. He was attacked by a bear.	D. 他被熊攻擊了。

詳解 **答案：B**

從選項都是 He 開頭來看，可以猜測題目會問男子發生的事，所以要注意關於他的情況的描述。一開始，女子說 Let me take a closer look at the wound. When did this happen?（讓我把傷口看仔細一點。什麼時候發生的？），可知男子受了傷；女子後來又說 You said you didn't see what bit you.（你說你沒看到是什麼咬了你），但男子補充說 One of my friends said it must be a reptile.（有一個朋友說那一定是爬行動物）。reptile 是指蜥蜴、蛇之類的動物，所以 B 是最合適的答案。

|單字片語| **poke** [pok] v. 戳 / **fellow** [ˋfɛlo] n. 伙伴 adj. 同伴的 / **reptile** [ˋrɛptaɪl] n. 爬行動物

Q16

M: We are having a special promotion now. All items are 15% off.
我們現在有特別促銷活動。所有商品都折扣 15%（打 85 折）。

W: The store next door is having a clearance sale at half-price.
隔壁的店正在半價清倉拍賣。

M: This blouse you are holding is made of authentic silk. The perfect material for summer.
您拿著的這件上衣是真絲製的。這是很適合夏天的材質。

W: It does feel comfortable, but the stripes make me feel like a zebra.
是感覺很舒服，但條紋讓我覺得像斑馬。

M: Pardon me for saying this, but stripes can create a visual effect that makes us look slimmer. Turn around and look at yourself in the mirror. 很抱歉這樣說，但條紋可以創造一種視覺效果，讓我們看起來比較苗條。請轉身看看您在鏡子裡的樣子。

W: I see what you mean. All right. I'll take it.
我明白你的意思了。好吧。我要買這件。

M: A good choice. This is the last piece we have.
選得好。這是我們最後一件了。

Q: Why is the woman convinced to buy the blouse?
女子為什麼被說服買這件上衣？

A. It is a discounted item. A. 這是折扣商品。
B. It is made of real silk. B. 這是真絲製的。
C. It is the last piece left. C. 這是剩下的最後一件。
D. It makes her look more slender. D. 這讓她看起來比較苗條。

詳解 **答案：D**

四個選項在對話中都有提到，而且都是事實，所以把問題聽清楚才能選出正確答案。題目問的是 Why is the woman convinced（女子為什麼被說服了），在整段對話裡面，女子對於這件衣服保持猶豫的態度，最後終於說 I see what you mean... I'll take it.（我明白你的意思了…我要買這件），所以在這之前男子所提的理由就是原因：stripes can create a visual effect that makes us look slimmer（條紋可以創造一種視覺效果，讓我們看起來比較苗條），D 是正確答案。

|單字片語| **clearance sale** 清倉拍賣 / **blouse** [blaʊz] n. 女性穿著的上衣 / **authentic** [ɔˋθɛntɪk] adj. 真正的 / **stripe** [straɪp] n. 條紋 / **slim** [slɪm] adj. 苗條的 / **slender** [ˋslɛndɚ] adj. 苗條的

Q17

W: Should we travel to Italy via train or plane? Both options are just as expensive, I guess cost is not a major factor to consider.
我們應該搭火車還是飛機到義大利旅行呢？兩個選擇一樣貴，我想費用大概不是主要的考慮因素。

M: We are not in a hurry to get there. If we travel by land, we can experience the wonders of nature first hand as we cross the Alps.
我們不急著到那裡。如果我們走陸路，我們就能在越過阿爾卑斯山時直接體驗自然的奇觀。

W: That's true, but I might get motion sickness with all the winding tracks round the mountains. Traveling by air is much faster, isn't it?
是啊，但是在山間繞行的軌道，可能會讓我暈車。搭飛機快得多，不是嗎？

M: Why don't we have the cake and eat it? We can have it both ways.
我們何不兩者兼得呢？我們可以兩種都選擇。

W: You mean a single trip by air and a return trip through the mountains? 你的意思是搭單程飛機，回程走山路？

M: That's right. 沒錯。

Q: How will the speakers travel to Italy and back?
說話者會怎樣往返義大利？

A. To Italy and back by plane. A. 往返都搭飛機。
B. To Italy and back by train. B. 往返都搭火車。
C. To Italy by plane and return by train. C. 去程搭飛機，回程搭火車。
D. To Italy by train and return by plane. D. 去程搭火車，回程搭飛機。

詳解 答案：C

選項列出去義大利和回程搭飛機或火車的可能組合，所以要注意對話中關於去程、回程交通方式的敘述。開頭女子就問 Should we travel to Italy via train or plane?（我們應該搭火車還是飛機到義大利旅行），兩人敘述搭火車和飛機的優缺點之後，男子說 Why don't we have the cake and eat it?（我們何不兩者兼得呢），表示兩種方法都使用，最後女子確認是 a single trip by air and a return trip through the mountains（搭單程飛機，回程走山路），所以答案是 C。

|單字片語| **wonder** [ˋwʌndɚ] n. 奇觀 / **motion sickness** 動暈症（暈車、暈船等等）/ **winding** [ˋwaɪndɪŋ] adj. 迂迴曲折的 / **have the cake and eat it** 「擁有蛋糕又吃它」→兩者兼得（經常用 can't... 的方式表達，表示不能兩者兼得）/ **have it both ways** 達成兩個互不相容的目標（也常用 can't... 的方式表達）/ **return trip** 回程

Q18

M: Could you stop doing that? 你可以不要那樣了嗎？

W: Stop doing what? 不要什麼？

M: Keep your eyes on the road and stop putting on your makeup!
注意看路，不要再化妝了！

W: Relax. I'm used to multitasking. Besides, we are caught in a jam, aren't we?
放輕鬆。我習慣同時做幾件事情。而且，我們塞在車陣裡，不是嗎？

M: Once I get my driver's license, I'll do the driving, and you can do whatever you like with your face.
我一拿到駕照，就要負責開車，那你隨便在臉上幹嘛都可以。

W: Frankly speaking, I don't mind at all. 老實說，我一點也不介意。

M: Please move forward, but take it easy on the accelerator.
請往前進，但是要輕輕踩油門。

Q: What is the man's concern?
男子擔心什麼？

A. Road safety.	A. 道路安全。
B. Multitasking.	B. 同時做幾件事情。
C. Driving tests.	C. 駕駛測驗。
D. Plastic surgery.	D. 整型手術。

詳解 答案：A

男子要求女子 Keep your eyes on the road and stop putting on your makeup（注意看路，不要再化妝），最後又說 Please move forward, but take it easy on the accelerator（請往前進，但是要輕輕踩油門），可知女子正在開車，而男子提醒她不要同時做別的事情，還有在該前進的時候踩油門，所以 A 是正確答案。雖然對話中提到了 multitasking（同時做幾件事情），但如果選 B 的話，意思是「男子擔心能不能同時做好幾件事情」，並不是最適當的答案。

|單字片語| **multitasking** [ˌmʌltɪˋtaskɪŋ] n. 同時做好幾件事，（電腦）多工處理 / **accelerator** [ækˋsɛləˌretɚ] n. 加速裝置→汽車的油門

Q19

W: Excuse me, Sir. Do you have sleeping problems?
不好意思，先生。您有睡眠問題嗎？

M: No. Why would you ask me that? Do I look exhausted?
沒有。你怎麼會問這個？我看起來很疲勞嗎？

W: Not really. I just can't help but notice the dark circles under your eyes. There is a latest product from Miracle Skin that can help you get rid of those dark circles and the fine lines around your eyes.
不是。我只是忍不住注意到您眼睛下面的黑眼圈。Miracle Skin 有一項最新產品，可以幫您去除黑眼圈和眼周細紋。

M: Isn't this stuff for women? 這東西不是女人用的嗎？

W: Sir, gender equality has taken on a whole new meaning. It's no longer women's privilege to care for their skin. Miracle Skin has a wide range of products specially designed for men.
先生，性別平等現在有了全新的意義。保養皮膚不再是女人的特權了。Miracle Skin 有專為男性設計的多樣產品。

Q: What is the woman trying to do?
女子試圖做什麼？

A. She is trying to make a sale. A. 她試圖賣出東西。
B. She is trying to purchase something. B. 她試圖購買某物。
C. She is trying to fight for equality. C. 她努力為平等奮鬥。
D. She is trying to care for her skin. D. 她努力保養皮膚。

詳解 **答案：A**

選項都是以 She is trying to 開頭，可以猜測題目會問女子想要做到什麼，所以要注意她說的話。女子說 I just can't help but notice the dark circles under your eyes. There is a latest product...（我只是忍不住注意到您眼睛下面的黑眼圈。有一項最新產品…），先指出男子的問題，然後介紹一項產品的功能，可知她在向男子推銷產品，所以 A 是正確答案。

|單字片語| **dark circle** 黑眼圈 / **gender equality** 性別平等 / **take on** 承接…，具有… / **privilege** [ˋprɪvəlɪdʒ] n. 特權 / **make a sale** （推銷員等）賣出東西

Questions 20-21

Questions number 20 and 21 are based on the following conversation.

W: Hello sir, thank you for joining me today. Can you start by telling me why you think you're a good fit for the position?
哈囉，先生，謝謝您今天跟我進行面試。可以先告訴我您認為自己適合這個職位的原因嗎？

M: Hi, my name is Diego Garcia. I'm 27 years old, and I've worked as a civil engineer for 4 years. I have a postgraduate degree in architecture. I'm a good fit for the position because I'm very adaptable and professional. 嗨，我的名字是迪亞哥・加西亞。我 27 歲，曾經擔任土木工程師 4 年。我有建築學的學士後教育學位。我很適合這個職位，因為我非常有適應力並且專業。

W: Why did you decide to be a civil engineer?
您為什麼決定當土木工程師呢？

M: My grandfather was one, so I had the chance from a young age to be exposed to the field.
我的祖父就是，所以我有機會從年少的時候就接觸到這個領域。

W: Is your grandfather the famous Cristóbal Garcia who built Taipei 102? 您的祖父是蓋了台北一〇二的那位有名的克里斯多福・加西亞嗎？

M: Yes, he is. 是的，就是他。

W: That's impressive! Well, I can tell that you're a good candidate. Expect to hear from us within a week or so about the result.
真令人印象深刻！嗯，我可以察覺到你是很好的人選。您可以預期在大約一週之內接到我們關於結果的通知。

|單字片語| **be a good fit for** 適合… / **civil engineer** 土木工程師 / **postgraduate** [post`grædʒuɪt] adj. 大學畢業後的，研究生的 / **adaptable** [ə`dæptəbl̩] adj. 有適應力的

Q20

What is the man doing?
男子在做什麼？

A. He is introducing himself to a journalist. A. 他在向記者介紹自己。
B. He is talking with a career consultant. B. 他在和職涯顧問談話。
C. He is being interviewed for a job. C. 他在接受工作面試。
D. He is doing a university interview. D. 他在進行大學面試。

詳解 **答案：C**

女子詢問 why you think you're a good fit for the position（你認為自己適合這個職位的原因），其中的 position（職位）是很重要的單字，聽到這裡就可以確定答案是 C 了。

|單字片語| **career consultant** 職涯顧問

Q21

What is true about the man?
關於男子，何者正確？

A. He graduated at the age of 27.
B. He has been an architect.
C. He knew about civil engineering when he was young.
D. He participated in the project of Taipei 102.

A. 他在 27 歲時畢業。
B. 他當過建築師。
C. 他在年輕的時候知道關於土木工程的事情。
D. 他參與了台北一〇二的案子。

詳解 **答案：C**

A. 對話中雖然提到男子 27 歲，但沒有提到畢業時是幾歲。B. 男子說自己當過的是 civil engineer（土木工程師）。建築師負責建築物大方向的設計，土木工程師則負責建築結構的細部規劃與施工，兩者是不同的職業。C. 男子說 I had the chance from a young age to be exposed to the field（我有機會從年少的時候就接觸到這個領域〔土木工程〕，符合選項敘述，所以 C 是正確答案。D. 參與台北一〇二建設案的是男子的祖父。

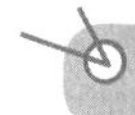

Questions 22-23

Questions number 22 and 23 are based on the following conversation.

W: I really like Chris, but I'm not sure if he would like to marry me.
我真的很喜歡克里斯，但我不確定他是不是想要跟我結婚。

M: Look, Anna, if he loves you, he will. Have you met his family? What do they think of you? 嗯，安娜，如果他愛你的話就會的。你跟他的家人見過面了嗎？他們對你有什麼想法？

W: Actually, no. It's been seven years, and he has not introduced me to anyone other than his friends. I honestly don't know what he's thinking about our future. 其實沒有。已經七年了，他還是沒把我介紹給朋友以外的人。我實在不知道他對於我們的未來在想什麼。

M: Did you talk to him about it? You should! Maybe something else is going on.
你跟他談過這件事了嗎？你應該談的！或許有什麼其他的原因。

W: Well, he told me that he wants to finish his PhD before he wants to start a family, but does that mean we won't get married before then? 嗯，他跟我說他想要先完成他的博士學位，然後才想要成家，但那意思是說我們在那之前不會結婚嗎？

M: It's reasonable for him to say that, but I still think you should try to meet his family and let them know your relationship.
他那樣說很合理，但我還是認為你應該試著跟他的家人見面，並且讓他們知道你們的關係。

|單字片語| **PhD** 博士學位

Q22

What does the man suggest the woman do next?
男子建議女子接下來做什麼？

A. Tell Chris' family that she is his girlfriend. A. 跟克里斯的家人說她是他的女朋友。
B. Introduce herself to Chris' friends. B. 向克里斯的朋友介紹自己。
C. Talk to Chris about marriage. C. 跟克里斯談結婚的事。
D. Try to finish her PhD first. D. 先努力完成她的博士學位。

詳解

答案：A

題目問男子建議女子接下來做的事，所以男子說的最後一句話應該是答案的關鍵。他說 you should try to meet his family and let them know your relationship（你應該試著跟他的家人見面，並且讓他們知道你們的關係），所以 A 是正確答案。

Q23

What is NOT true about Chris?
關於克里斯，何者不正確？

A. He and Anna have been together for seven years. A. 他和安娜在一起七年了。
B. He has not introduced Anna to his friends. B. 他沒有向朋友介紹安娜。
C. He is attending graduate school. C. 他正在上研究所。
D. He does not want to start a family now. D. 他現在不想要成家。

詳解　　答案：B

A. 女子（Anna）說 It's been seven years，表示已經交往七年，符合選項敘述。B. 女子說 he has not introduced me to anyone other than his friends，表示 Chris 沒有向其他人介紹她，只有向朋友介紹，不符合選項敘述，所以 B 是正確答案。C. D. 女子說 he wants to finish his PhD before he wants to start a family，表示現在 Chris 想要先完成博士學位，而不想成家，符合選項敘述。

For question number 24, please look at the contact information.

W: David, guess what I found. I was cleaning Josh's room, and I happened to see his diary.
大衛，猜猜我發現什麼。我在清理喬許的房間，偶然看到了他的日記。

M: Oh, my goodness. I don't think it's OK to invade our son's privacy.
噢，我的天啊。我覺得侵犯我們兒子的隱私並不好。

W: I didn't mean to. It just fell open at the page about a classmate he fell in love with. He wrote that he's afraid I won't accept her as his wife. 我不是故意的。就只是日記掉了下來，打開在關於他愛上的同學那一頁。他寫著，他怕我不會接受她當老婆。

M: Maybe I know who she is. I've seen him dating a girl. But why won't you accept her? 或許我知道她是誰。我看過他跟一個女孩子約會。但為什麼你不會接受她呢？

W: He wrote that she's a foreigner who came to America to study. Well, I really don't mind! By the way, where did you see her? 他寫著，她是來美國讀書的外國人。嗯，我真的不介意！對了，你是在哪裡看到她的？

M: Here in Boston. Does she live here? 在波士頓這裡。她住這裡嗎？

W: Well, it seems she lives in Cambridge, where the university is.
嗯，看起來她住在劍橋，就是大學所在的地方。

Classmate Info 同學資料		
Name 姓名	Nationality 國籍	Address 地址
Elizabeth Praat	American 美國人	351 Newton St., Boston
Julia Anderson	American 美國人	76 Casey Rd., Cambridge
Maria Rodriguez	Spanish 西班牙人	28 Delta St., Boston
Ana Rosa Santos Silva	Portuguese 葡萄牙人	183 Orchard St., Cambridge

Q: According to the conversation, who is most likely Josh's girlfriend?
根據這段對話，誰最有可能是喬許的女朋友？

A. Elizabeth Praat.
B. Julia Anderson.
C. Maria Rodriguez.
D. Ana Rosa Santos Silva.

詳解

答案：D

從女子一開始提到的 I was cleaning Josh's room（我在清理喬許的房間），可以確認接下來要談論關於他的事，而男子接著提到 our son's privacy（我們兒子的隱私），所以 Josh 是兩人的兒子。關於 Josh 的女朋友，女子先是提到 she's a foreigner who came to America to study（她是來美國讀書的外國人），所以可以排除兩位美國人。然後談到這位女性居住的地方，女子說 it seems she lives in Cambridge（看起來她住在劍橋），所以地址在劍橋的 D 是正確答案。

Q25

For question number 25, please look at the table.

M: Jane, do you have any idea where we'll retire?
珍，你對於我們退休後要去哪裡有任何想法嗎？

W: I have several cities in mind, and I've done some research. Here are some notes I've made.
我心裡想著幾個城市，也做了一些研究。這裡是我做的一些筆記。

M: Cool, but why did you include the information about air pollution?
很棒，但你為什麼包括了空氣污染的資訊呢？

W: You know I have asthma, so I have to avoid the triggers, including polluted air.
你知道我有氣喘，所以我必須避免誘發氣喘的因素，包括污染的空氣。

M: Oh, I see. So, what about Seattle? It's not far from where we live now, and it has the lowest air pollution level.
噢，我明白了。所以，西雅圖怎麼樣？那裡離我們現在住的地方不遠，而且那裡的空氣污染程度最低。

W: But I don't think I can stand the cold weather there. Days below 5 degrees Celsius are just too cold for me. I prefer the city in the South. Its air pollution level is just slightly higher, and it's not cold there in winter. 但我不覺得自己受得了那裡的冷天氣。低於攝氏 5 度的日子對我而言太冷了。我比較喜歡南部的那個城市。它的空氣污染程度只是稍微高一點，而且那裡冬天不冷。

|單字片語| **asthma** [ˋæzmə] n. 氣喘 / **trigger** [ˋtrɪgɚ] n. 誘發因素

City 城市	Average Air Pollution Index 平均空氣污染指數	Average Winter Temperature 平均冬季溫度
Seattle 西雅圖	52	3.0℃
Los Angeles 洛杉磯	107	9.6℃
Miami 邁阿密	60	17.2℃
Cleveland 克里夫蘭	92	-4.0℃

Q: Look at the table. Where will the woman most likely choose to retire?
請看表格。女子最有可能選擇退休到哪裡？

A. To Seattle. A. 西雅圖。
B. To Los Angeles. B. 洛杉磯。
C. To Miami. C. 邁阿密。
D. To Cleveland. D. 克里夫蘭。

詳解 答案：C

對於退休後要居住的地方，男子提議到西雅圖，因為它有 the lowest air pollution level（最低的空氣污染程度），由此可知表格中的數字越低，空氣污染程度也越低。女子則回應 Days below 5 degrees Celsius are just too cold for me（低於攝氏 5 度的日子對我而言太冷了），並且說自己比較喜歡南部的城市，因為 Its air pollution level is just slightly higher, and it's not cold there in winter（它的空氣污染程度只是稍微高一點，而且那裡冬天不冷）。在表格中，空氣污染程度只比西雅圖高一點，而且冬季平均溫度達到攝氏 17.2 度的邁阿密符合女子的敘述，所以 C 是正確答案。

第三部分 / 短篇獨白

Questions 26-27

Questions number 26 to 27 are based on the following radio commercial.

Here at Ever-Green Health Center, every member is a VIP. Whether you opt for the monthly, annual, or pay-as-you-visit membership plan, you will find our fees affordable and reasonable. On top of our state-of-the-art gym facilities, the center is also equipped with individual saunas and a recreation room for your kids, at no extra cost. Our staff have undergone extensive training so that they can provide you with high-quality service. You will be assigned with both a personal trainer and a diet adviser, who will assist you in your calorie intake. Call us now to book an appointment and take advantage of our one-week free trial. If you are not satisfied with our service in any way, you can have your money back with no strings attached.

在 Ever-Green 健康中心，每位會員都是 VIP（非常重要的人）。不管您選擇每月、每年或每次來訪付費的會員方案，您都會發現我們的費用是很便宜而且合理的。除了我們最先進的健身設施以外，本中心還配備個人三溫暖和供您的孩子使用的娛樂室，不用額外的費用。我們的員工接受過廣泛的訓練，這樣他們就能提供您高品質的服務。您會被分配到一位個人教練和一位飲食指導員，而飲食指導員會在卡路里攝取方面協助您。現在就打電話向我們預約，並且利用我們的一週免費體驗。如果您對我們的服務有任何不滿意，您可以獲得退費，而且沒有任何附帶條件。

|單字片語| **VIP (= very important person)** 重要人物 / **opt for** 選擇… / **affordable** [ə`fɔrdəbl] adj. 負擔得起的 / **on top of** 除了…以外還有 / **state-of-the-art** [`stetəvði`ɑrt] adj. 最先進的 / **be equipped with** 配備有… / **sauna** [`saʊnə] n. 蒸氣浴，三溫暖（室） / **recreation** [ˌrɛkrɪ`eʃən] n. 娛樂，消遣 / **undergo** [ˌʌndɚ`go] v. 經歷，接受 / **extensive** [ɪk`stɛnsɪv] adj. 廣泛的，大範圍的 / **so that** 為了…，以便… / **intake** [`ɪnˌtek] n. 攝取 / **take advantage of** 利用… / **trial** [`traɪəl] n. 試用，試驗 / **strings** [strɪŋz]（合約等的）附帶條件

Q26

What can you learn from the radio commercial?
從這則廣播廣告，你可以得知什麼？

A. There are various types of membership.
B. You can enjoy free service for a month.
C. Children are not allowed on the premises.
D. The center specializes in health food.

A. 提供多種會員類型。
B. 你可以享有一個月的免費服務。
C. 孩童不能進入。
D. 這家中心專門販賣健康食品。

詳解　　答案：A

廣告中的 monthly, annual, or pay-as-you-visit membership plan（每月、每年或每次來訪付費的會員方案），顯示有多種會員類型，所以 A 是正確答案。選項 B 和廣告中的 one-week free trial（一週的免費試用）不符。a recreation room for your kids（供您的孩子使用的娛樂室）顯示兒童可以進入設施，與選項 C 不符合。D 在廣告中沒有提到。

|單字片語| **premises** n. [ˋprɛmɪsɪz] 建築物及附屬場地 / **specialize in** 專門從事…，專營… / **health food** 健康食品

Q27

What is NOT mentioned in the radio commercial regarding Ever-Green Health Center?
關於 Ever-Green 健康中心，這則廣播廣告沒有提到什麼？

A. Employees are well-trained.
B. Low calorie food is provided for members.
C. The facilities and equipment are modern.
D. There is an unconditional refund guarantee.

A. 員工受到良好的訓練。
B. 提供低卡路里食物給會員。
C. 設施和設備很現代。
D. 有無條件退款保證。

詳解

廣告中的 Our staff have undergone extensive training（我們的員工接受過廣泛的訓練）對應選項 A，state-of-the-art gym facilities（最先進的健身房設施）對應選項 C，money back with no strings attached（沒有附帶條件的退費）對應選項 D。a diet adviser, who will assist you in your calorie intake（會在卡路里攝取方面協助您的飲食指導員）表示有人協助管理卡路里攝取，而不是會提供低卡食物，所以 B 是正確答案。

|單字片語| **unconditional** [ˌʌnkənˋdɪʃənl̩] adj. 無條件的 / **guarantee** [ˌgærənˋti] n. 保證 v. 保證

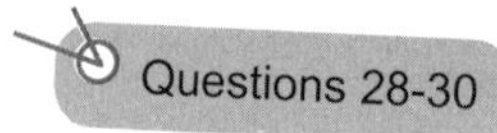

Questions 28-30

Questions number 28 to 30 are based on the following speech.

To all who are gathered here today, sorrow fills our hearts at this sad moment. Our beloved family, friend, and colleague, Arnold Smith, has silently departed from us. As we bid farewell to him, let us not forget the legacy that he has left behind. He was a man of passion and dedication. He was a visionary who was brilliant, innovative, and creative. He generously gave us his knowledge, expertise, and skills. He was living proof of how fine a person can be. He was a good boss to the people in his charge, a loving husband to his wife, and a devoted father to his children. He was also a good friend to many of us. His character might be summed up in a few words: Arnold Smith was sincere, earnest, and loyal. We will hold him dear in our memory.

對於今天聚集在這裡的所有人，哀痛在這個悲傷的時刻填滿了我們的心。我們親愛的家人、朋友、同事 Arnold Smith 靜靜地離開了我們。在我們向他告別的時候，我們不要忘記他遺留的東西。他是個有熱情和奉獻精神的人。他是個有遠見的人，出色、創新又有創意。他慷慨地給予我們他的知識、專業和技術。他是展現一個人可以多麼美好的活生生的證據。他對他所負責（管理）的人是個好上司，對太太是深情的丈夫，對孩子是個有奉獻精神的父親。他也是我們許多人的好朋友。他的人格可以用幾個字總結：Arnold Smith 既誠懇、認真又忠心。我們會在記憶中珍惜他。

|單字片語| **sorrow** [ˋsɑro] n. 哀傷 / **beloved** [bɪˋlʌvɪd] adj. 被喜愛的，鍾愛的 / **bid farewell to** 向…告別 / **legacy** [ˋlɛgəsɪ] n. 遺產，遺留的東西 / **dedication** [ˌdɛdəˋkeʃən] n. 奉獻，專心致力 / **innovative** [ˋɪnoˌvetɪv] adj. 革新的，創新的 / **generously** [ˋdʒɛnərəslɪ] adv. 慷慨地 / **expertise** [ˌɛkspɚˋtiz] n. 專門知識，專門技術 / **devoted** [dɪˋvotɪd] adj. 獻身的，專心致志的 / **sum up** 總

結… / **sincere** [sɪn`sɪr] adj. 真誠的 / **earnest** [`ɝnɪst] adj. 認真的 / **loyal** [`lɔɪəl] adj. 忠心的 / **hold dear** 珍視…

第1回 第2回 第3回 第4回 第5回 第6回

Q28

What happened to Arnold Smith?

Arnold Smith 發生了什麼事？

A. He was promoted. A. 他獲得升職。
B. He has passed away. B. 他過世了。
C. He ran away from home. C. 他離家出走。
D. He is under a lot of stress. D. 他壓力很大。

詳解 答案：B

說話者開頭說 sorrow fills our hearts... Arnold Smith, has silently departed from us（哀痛填滿我們的心⋯ Arnold Smith 靜靜地離開了我們），暗示 Arnold Smith 已經過世了，所以 B 是正確答案。

|單字片語| **promote** [prə`mot] v. 使升職 / **pass away** 過世

Q29

According to the speech, what is true about Arnold Smith's family life?

根據這段演說，關於 Arnold Smith 的家庭生活，何者正確？

A. He had an affair with another woman. A. 他和另一個女人發生了關係。
B. He neglected his children due to work. B. 他因為工作而忽略了小孩。
C. He was committed and faithful to his family. C. 他對家庭盡責而且忠誠。
D. He didn't spend enough time with his family. D. 他陪伴家人的時間不夠。

詳解 答案：C

提到 Arnold Smith 家庭生活的部分是倒數第三句：He was... a loving husband to his wife, and a devoted father to his children（他對太太是深情的丈夫，對孩子是個有奉獻精神的父親），所以 C 是正確答案。committed、faithful 的意思和 devoted 相近。

|單字片語| **have an affair with** 和某人有非婚姻的情愛關係 / **committed** [kə`mɪtɪd] adj. 盡心盡責的，忠誠的 / **faithful** [`feθfəl] adj. 忠誠的，忠實的

Q30

How was Arnold Smith's relationship with his colleagues?

Arnold Smith 和他同事的關係如何？

A. They found him very demanding.
B. They talked behind his back.
C. They admire his management style.
D. They made him feel intimidated.

A. 他們覺得他非常苛求。
B. 他們在他背後議論他。
C. 他們欣賞他的管理風格。
D. 他們讓他覺得膽怯。

詳解

和職場相關的敘述在倒數第三句：He was a good boss to the people in his charge（他對他所負責（管理）的人是個好上司），可知他的下屬欣賞他身為上司的作為，C 是正確答案。

|單字片語| **demanding** [dɪ`mændɪŋ] adj. 苛求的，使人吃力的 / **talk behind one's back** 在背後議論某人 / **admire** [əd`maɪr] v. 欣賞 / **intimidated** [ɪn`tɪmə͵detɪd] adj. 感到膽怯的

Questions 31-32

Questions number 31 to 32 are based on the following voice message.

Hi, James, this is Daniel. I sent you two private messages on Facebook, both still unread at the time of this call. The annual sales managers meeting, which was supposed to be held in the King's Hotel, has been canceled due to unfavorable weather conditions. Asking people to travel to a mountain resort during a hurricane isn't such a bright idea after all. I don't want to put my life at risk, and I don't think the organizer is keen about taking responsibility should anything unexpected happen. You must be disappointed because you are the most likely winner for the best salesman award. I guess you will just have to keep your fingers crossed for another month. By the way, what's with your Facebook account? You have not posted any updates for a week, which is really unusual for a Facebook maniac like you.

嗨，James，我是 Daniel。我在 Facebook 傳給你兩則私訊，打這通電話的時候都還未讀。預定在 King's 飯店舉辦的年度業務經理會議，因為天氣惡劣的關係，已經被取消了。要人在颱風期間到山上的度假村，終究不是很好的主意。我不希望冒生命危險，我也覺得主辦單位不想在萬一有意外發生的時候負責。你一定很失望，因為你是最有可能獲得最佳業務員獎的人。我想你只能再等一個月並祈禱你能得獎。對了，你的 Facebook 帳戶怎麼回事？你一個禮拜沒發表任何更新了，對於你這種 Facebook 狂熱使用者來說實在很不尋常。

|單字片語| **unfavorable** [ʌn`fevrəbl̩] adj. 不利的，不適宜的 / **resort** [rɪ`zɔrt] n. 度假村 / **keep one's fingers crossed** 祈求好運 / **maniac** [`menɪˌæk] n. 狂熱分子

Q31

What is the main purpose of this voice message?

這段語音訊息的主要目的是什麼？

A. To remind James to update his Facebook.	A. 提醒 James 更新 Facebook。
B. To remind James to hand out an award.	B. 提醒 James 頒獎。
C. To remind James of a change in plan.	C. 提醒 James 計畫的改變。
D. To remind James of an upcoming event.	D. 提醒 James 接下來的活動。

詳解

答案：C

留言的前面說到 The annual sales managers meeting... has been canceled（年度業務經理會議已經被取消了），後面又說 you will just have to keep your fingers crossed for another month（你只能再等一個月並祈禱你能獲得最佳業務員獎項），顯示頒發獎項的會議被取消，頒獎可能會延後一個月，所以提到 a change in plan 的 C 是正確答案。留言的最後雖然提到接收留言者 James 沒有更新 Facebook，但只是附帶提到，而不是留言的主要目的，所以不能選 A。

Q32

What is true about the voice message?
關於這段語音訊息，何者正確？

A. The meeting was canceled due to terrorism. A. 會議因為恐怖主義行動而被取消。
B. Mountain climbing is part of the training. B. 爬山是訓練的一部分。
C. Daniel will be responsible for any accident. C. Daniel 會需要對任何意外負責。
D. The award's winner is still unknown. D. 還不知道得獎人是誰。

詳解 答案：D

留言中提到 you are the most likely winner for the best salesman award... you will just have to keep your fingers crossed for another month（你是最有可能獲得最佳業務員獎的人…你只能再等一個月並祈禱你能得獎），表示雖然 James 很有可能得獎，但他還是需要等待並祈求好運，所以現在並不知道誰會得獎，D 是正確答案。其他選項在留言中沒有提到。

|單字片語| **terrorism** [ˋtɛrə͵rɪzəm] n. 恐怖主義，恐怖行動

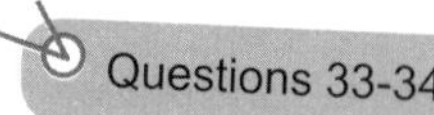
Questions 33-34

Questions number 33 to 34 are based on the following talk.

Based on the feedback given by our clients, I listed two areas that require our immediate action. First, clients complained about a lag in response via email. We promised to reply within 12 hours, but we made a critical error. Besides checking the mails in the morning, which is our current practice, we should also check them at 4 p.m. and offer a response by 5 p.m. before we leave the office. In this way, we will not exceed our self-imposed 12-hour deadline. The other area has to do with regular updates on our software. Some clients pointed out that they prefer some features in older versions, which are no longer available after the updates. In view of this, we will restore these popular features and also carry out a survey of client preference before installing the next update. Any questions?

根據我們客戶的回饋意見，我列出了兩個需要我們立即採取行動的領域。首先，客戶抱怨電子郵件回覆時間緩慢。我們承諾在 12 小時以內回覆，但我們犯了重大錯誤。我們現在的做法是在早上查看郵件，但除此之外，我們也應該在下午 4 點查看，並且在我們下班前的 5 點前回覆。這樣，我們就不會超過自己規定的 12 小時期限。另一個領域和我們的軟體定期更新有關。有些客戶指出，他們偏好舊版本的一些特別功能，而這些特別功能在更新之後就沒了。考慮到這一點，我們會恢復這些受歡迎的特別功能，並且在安裝下次更新之前進行客戶偏好的意見調查。有任何問題嗎？

|單字片語| **feedback** [ˋfid͵bæk] n. 回饋意見 / **critical** [ˋkrɪtɪk!] adj. 關鍵性的 / **self-imposed** [͵sɛlfɪmˋpozd] adj. （責任等）自己加在身上的 / **feature** [fitʃɚ] n. 特徵，特色，（特別的）功能 / **in view of** 考慮到… / **restore** [rɪˋstor] v. 恢復 / **survey** [ˋsɝve] n. 調查，意見調查

Q33

What can be said about the 12-hour response time mentioned in the talk?

關於談話中提到的 12 小時回覆，我們可以說什麼？

A. It is a new practice.	A. 這是新的措施。
B. It is a crucial mistake.	B. 這是重大的錯誤。
C. It is a popular feature.	C. 這是受歡迎的功能。
D. It is a company policy.	D. 這是公司政策。

詳解 答案：D

談話中關於 12 小時回覆的部分是 We promised to reply within 12 hours（我們承諾在 12 小時以內回覆）和 our self-imposed 12-hour deadline（我們加在自己身上的 12 小時期限），所以 12 小時回覆是他們自己願意執行的政策，D 是正確答案。

Q34

What is the problem with software updates?
軟體更新有什麼問題？

A. They are too frequent.
B. They take a long time to download.
C. They are different from previous versions.
D. They corrupt files and emails.

A. 太頻繁了。
B. 花很多時間下載。
C. 和之前的版本不一樣。
D. 會把檔案和電子郵件弄壞。

詳解

答案：C

談話中和 software updates 相關的部分，是從 The other area has to do with regular updates on our software.（另一個領域和我們的軟體定期更新有關）這句話開始的，下一句話就是問題所在：Some clients pointed out that they prefer some features in older versions, which are no longer available after the updates.（有些客戶指出，他們偏好舊版本的一些特別功能，而這些特別功能在更新之後沒有了）。選項中，最符合談話敘述的 C 是正確答案。

|單字片語| **corrupt** [kəˋrʌpt] v. 使腐壞，使（電腦檔案等）出錯

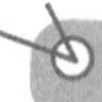
Questions 35-37

For questions number 35 to 37, please look at the charts.

Every year we have a lot of people at our ski resort. Our busiest month is December because it's Christmas time. Many holiday makers come with their family to enjoy the time. Even though there is more snowfall in January and February, making the months the best time to ski, casual skiers tend to avoid this time since it's quite cold. March is the second most popular month because students have spring break. Warmer temperatures and sunnier days also make it more enjoyable to ski.

Besides lift tickets, accommodation is also an important source of our income. Most of our visitors stay the night in our cabins, while others leave our premises and come back the next day. It's rumored that some of them own their cabins in the woods, but I'm not sure about that.

我們的滑雪度假村每年都有許多人。我們最忙碌的月份是 12 月，因為那是聖誕節的時候。許多度假者會和家人一起來享受這段時間。儘管 1 月和 2 月有比較多的降雪，使得這兩個月成為滑雪的最佳時期，但休閒滑雪客傾向於避開這個時間，因為天氣很冷。3 月是第二受歡迎的月份，因為學生有春假。比較溫暖的氣溫和比較晴朗的日子，也讓滑雪比較愉快。

除了纜車票以外，住宿也是我們收入的重要來源。我們大部分的訪客晚上會在我們的小屋住宿，其他人則會離開我們的場地，隔天再回來。有傳聞說其中一些人擁有森林裡的小屋，但我不確定。

|單字片語| **holiday maker** 度假者 / **snowfall** [`sno͵fɔl] n. 降雪 / **skier** [`skiɚ] n. 滑雪者 / **lift** [lɪft] n. 滑雪場載人到高處的纜車（通常為簡單的吊椅形式） / **cabin** [`kæbɪn] n. 小屋 / **premises** [`prɛmɪsɪz] n. 建築物與其腹地

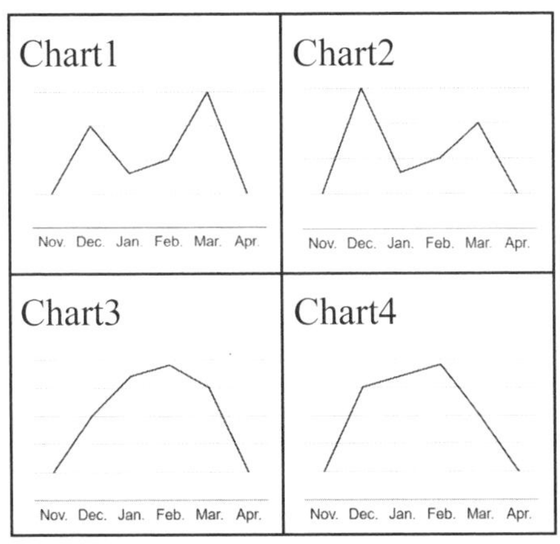

Q35

Who is most likely the speaker?
說話者最有可能是誰？

A. A travel agent. A. 旅行社員工。
B. A manager of the ski resort. B. 滑雪度假村的經理。
C. An analyst of the ski resort industry. C. 滑雪度假村產業的分析師。
D. An official in charge of administering ski resorts. D. 負責管理滑雪度假村的官員。

詳解 答案：B

說話者提到 we have a lot of people at our ski resort（我們的滑雪度假村有許

多人）、Most of our visitors（我們大部分的訪客），是以度假村的立場來說明來客的行為，所以 B 是正確答案。

Q36

Which chart best represents the number of skiers of each month?

哪張圖表最能表示每個月的滑雪者人數？

A. Chart 1.
B. Chart 2.
C. Chart 3.
D. Chart 4.

A. 圖表 1。
B. 圖表 2。
C. 圖表 3。
D. 圖表 4。

詳解

答案：B

說話者提到 Our busiest month is December（我們最忙碌的月份是 12 月）、March is the second most popular month（3 月是第二受歡迎的月份），所以人數最多的是 12 月，第二高的是 3 月。另外，關於 1 月和 2 月，說話者說 casual skiers tend to avoid this time（休閒滑雪客傾向於避開這個時間），表示這兩個月人數並不是特別多。綜合這些資訊，可知 B 是正確答案。

Q37

What is true about the visitors of the ski resort?

關於這座滑雪度假村的訪客，何者正確？

A. Most of them have their own cabins.
B. They prefer to go there by themselves.
C. They like cold weather better.
D. They usually ski there for more than one day.

A. 他們大部分擁有自己的小屋。
B. 他們偏好自己去。
C. 他們比較喜歡寒冷的天氣。
D. 他們通常在那裡滑雪超過一天。

詳解

答案：D

關於滑雪度假村的訪客，說話者提到 Most of our visitors stay the night in our cabins, while others leave our premises and come back the next day（我們大部分的訪客晚上會在我們的小屋住宿，其他人則會離開我們的場地，隔天再回來），兩種人都是在滑雪度假村活動超過一天，所以 D 是正確答案。

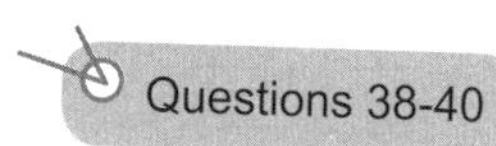

For questions number 38 to 40, please look at the table.

Generally speaking, the most common crime in Taiwan is vehicle theft. However, despite its high population density, Taipei has a relatively low rate of vehicle theft. The reason might be that it has the most convenient mass transportation systems, and many commuters don't have their own vehicles. Hsinchu, on the other hand, doesn't have an MRT yet, and it has the highest rate of motorcycle theft in Taiwan. And then, the second most common crime in Taiwan is drug use. Many people are worried their houses could be broken into, and their valuables could be stolen, but as we can see in the table, such a crime is quite rare now.

By the way, we might be under the impression that there is a lot of crime in Taichung and Kaohsiung, but their crime rates are not high. One of them has the least drug use cases, thanks to its frequent inspections of night clubs these years.

大致上來說，台灣最常見的犯罪是車輛竊盜。不過，儘管人口密度很高，台北的車輛竊盜率卻相對較低。原因可能是它有最便利的大眾交通系統，而許多通勤者沒有自己的車輛。另一方面，新竹還沒有捷運，而它的機車竊盜率是台灣最高的。然後，台灣第二常見的犯罪是使用毒品。許多人擔心他們的房子可能被闖入，而他們的貴重物品可能會被偷走，但如同我們可以從表格中看到的，這樣的犯罪現在相當少見。

對了，我們可能有台中和高雄常有犯罪活動的印象，但它們的犯罪率並不高。其中一個城市的使用毒品案件最少，要歸功於那裡近年來對夜店經常進行稽查。

|單字片語| **density** [ˋdɛnsətɪ] n. 密度 / **mass transportation system** 大眾運輸系統 / **commuter** [kəˋmjutɚ] n. 通勤者 / **break into** 闖入 / **valuables** [ˋvæljuəbl̩z] n. 貴重物品 / **inspection** [ɪnˋspɛkʃən] n. 視察

Crime Rates: number of persons / 100,000 persons

犯罪率：人數／100,000 人

City 城市	Vehicle Theft 車輛竊盜	Illegal Drug Use 違法使用藥物	?
Taipei 台北	11	35	4
Hsinchu 新竹	38	20	6
Taichung 台中	24	17	1
Kaohsiung 高雄	30	22	1

Q38

According to the speaker, what might be the reason that Hsinchu has a high rate of vehicle theft?

根據說話者，新竹車輛竊盜率高的原因可能是什麼？

A. It has a high population density. A. 它的人口密度很高。

B. There are not enough police officers. B. 警察不夠。

C. Many people commute with their own vehicles. C. 許多人用自己的車輛通勤。

D. The city is famous for being unsafe. D. 這座城市以不安全聞名。

詳解

關於車輛竊盜，說話者說台北發生率低的原因可能是 it has the most convenient mass transportation systems, and many commuters don't have their own vehicles（它有最便利的大眾交通系統，而許多通勤者沒有自己的車輛），而新竹則是 doesn't have an MRT yet（還沒有捷運），所以說話者想表達的是，用自己的車輛通勤的比率和車輛竊盜率高有關，所以 C 是正確答案。

Q39

Based on the talk, what should be written in the shaded area?
根據這段談話，灰底部分應該填入什麼？

A. Burglary. A. 入室盜竊。
B. Homicide. B. 殺人。
C. Stalking. C. 跟蹤騷擾。
D. Domestic violence. D. 家暴。

詳解 答案：A

關於表格中的灰底部分，說話者提到 Many people are worried their houses could be broken into, and their valuables could be stolen, but as we can see in the table, such a crime is quite rare now（許多人擔心他們的房子可能被闖入，而他們的貴重物品可能會被偷走，但如同我們可以從表格中看到的，這樣的犯罪現在相當少見）。在選項中，能表達侵入別人的房屋行竊的是 burglary，所以 A 是正確答案。

Q40

According to the speaker, which of the cities conduct frequent inspections of night clubs?
根據說話者，哪個城市對夜店進行頻繁的稽查？

A. Taipei. A. 台北。
B. Hsinchu. B. 新竹。
C. Taichung. C. 台中。
D. Kaohsiung. D. 高雄。

詳解 答案：C

在談話的最後，說話者提到台中和高雄的犯罪率不高，然後說 One of them has the least drug use cases, thanks to its frequent inspections of night clubs these years.（其中一個城市的使用毒品案件最少，要歸功於那裡近年來對夜店經常進行稽查）。表格中，毒品案件最少的是台中，所以 C 是正確答案。

第一部分 句子填空

Q1

We wonder why he did not follow the standard operation ________ written in the manual.

我們想知道他為什麼沒有遵守手冊中記載的標準操作程序。

A. perspectives　　B. perceptions
C. procedures　　D. parameters

詳解　　**答案：C**

選項都是名詞，而且是要被 follow（遵守）、會被寫在 manual（手冊）裡面的事物。所以，表示「程序」的 C. procedures 是正確答案。

|單字片語| **perspective** [pə`spɛktɪv] n. 觀點 / **perception** [pə`sɛpʃən] n. 感知（不可數名詞），看法 / **parameter** [pə`ræmətə] n. （數學）參數

Q2

Gold prices plunged by nearly 20 percent before ________ its ascent to new record levels.

金價在繼續上升到新紀錄之前，暴跌了將近 20%。

A. resuming　　B. condemning
C. hindering　　D. transmitting

詳解　　**答案：A**

空格後面接受詞 ascent（上升），而在空格表示的動作發生之前，Gold prices plunged（金價暴跌）。金價下跌之後又上升，所以表示「恢復，重新開始」（上升的趨勢）的 A. resuming 是正確答案。

|單字片語| **plunge** [plʌndʒ] v. 急降 / **ascent** [ə`sɛnt] n. 上升 / **resume** [rɪ`zjum] v. 恢復，重新開始 / **condemn** [kən`dɛm] v. 責難，責備 / **hinder** [`hɪndə] v. 妨礙，阻礙 / **transmit** [træns`mɪt] v. 傳送

Q3

Advertisements of all kinds that constantly pop up on your Internet browser can be quite a ________.

持續在你的網路瀏覽器上跳出的各種廣告，可能是很討厭的事情。

A. nuisance　　B. hazard　　C. scandal　　D. plague

詳解　　　　答案：A

空格是代表一直跳出的 advertisements（廣告）的名詞補語，選項中最適當的是 A. nuisance，表示「討厭的人事物」。

|單字片語| **pop up** 彈出，跳出 / **nuisance** [`njusṇs] n. 討厭的人事物 / **hazard** [`hæzɚd] n. 危險，造成危害的東西 / **scandal** [`skændḷ] 醜聞 / **plague** [pleg] n. 瘟疫，災禍

________ the late night shift which only requires male employees, female staff will be assigned to the day or evening shift.

只需要男性員工的大夜班除外，女性員工會被分配到日班或夜班。

A. Except　　B. Besides　　C. Despite　　D. Including

詳解　　　　答案：A

逗號前面提到「只需要男性的大夜班」，後面則是句子的主要部分「女性員工分配到日班或夜班」，所以空格填入的介系詞要能表示「大夜班除外」的意思，A. Except（除了…例外）是正確答案。besides 表示「除了…還有」，所以不能用在這裡。如果只看「除了」的部分，就很容易搞混這兩個詞的用法，所以請記住這裡提供的解釋。其他選項也是介系詞，despite 表示「儘管（有）…」，including 表示「包含…」

補充說明

請看以下的句子，區分 except 和 besides 的差別。

Except the weekends, I have to work every day.
除了週末例外，我每天都必須工作。（週一到週五工作）
Besides the weekends, I have to work every day.
除了週末以外，還有每天我都必須工作。（一週的每一天都工作）

Q5

The nostalgic atmosphere of the restaurant is ________ the days when things were stable and simple.

這家餐廳懷舊的氣氛讓人回憶起過去穩定又簡單的日子。

A. accountable for
B. compassionate toward
C. reminiscent of
D. superstitious about

詳解

答案：C

句子的開頭提到懷舊的氣氛，空格後面又提到過去的日子，所以表示「讓人回憶起…」的 C 是正確答案。

|單字片語| **nostalgic** [nɑs`tældʒɪk] **adj.** 懷舊的 / **be accountable for** 是能夠解釋…的原因 / **be compassionate toward** 同情… / **be reminiscent of** 讓人回憶起… / **be superstitious about** 對…心存迷信

Q6

The domestic helper from the Philippines ________ my grandfather and nursed him back to good health.

從菲律賓來的家庭幫傭服侍我的祖父，並且照顧他恢復健康。

A. called on
B. took on
C. waited on
D. rested on

詳解

答案：C

雖然選項裡出現的單字都很簡單，但搭配 on 之後，就變成意義相差頗大的動詞片語，所以這種動詞片語也需要像是個別的單字一樣記憶。domestic helper 字面上的意思是「家裡幫忙的人」，也就是「幫傭」，所以 C. waited on（服侍…）是最合理的答案。

|單字片語| **domestic helper** 幫傭 / **call on** 拜訪…；號召… / **take on** 承擔…，接受… / **wait on** 服侍… / **rest on** 依靠…

Q7

Neither party was willing to make a compromise, and as a result, the deal ________.

雙方都不願意妥協，結果協議告吹了。

A. fell out
B. fell down
C. fell off
D. fell through

詳解 答案：D

和上一題類似，這也是選擇動詞片語的題目。Neither party 表示「雙方都不」；沒有人願意 make a compromise（妥協），所以表示協議「無法實現，落空」的 D. fell through 是正確答案。

|單字片語| **compromise** [ˋkɑmprə͵maɪz] v. 妥協 n. 妥協 / **fall out** 脫落；鬧翻 / **fall down** 摔倒 / **fall off** 落下 / **fall through** 無法實現，落空

Never in my life have I been so ________! The clerk searched me as if I was a thief. **我這輩子從來沒有這麼被羞辱過！那個店員搜我的身，就好像我是小偷一樣。**

A. alienated　B. fabricated　C. humiliated　D. insulated

詳解 答案：C

選項中適合表達「像小偷一樣被搜身」的答案是 C. humiliated（被羞辱的）。第二個句子裡的 searched 是及物動詞的用法，表示「對…進行搜查」，和 search for（尋找…）的意義不同。另外，也請注意不要把選項 D 錯看成拼字類似的 insulted（被侮辱的）。

|單字片語| **alienate** [ˋeljən͵et] v. 使疏遠 / **fabricate** [ˋfæbrɪ͵ket] v. 捏造，虛構 / **humiliate** [hjuˋmɪlɪ͵et] v. 羞辱 / **insulate** [ˋɪnsə͵let] v. 隔熱，隔音，絕緣

The minister of health offered ________ answers when bombarded with questions by reporters concerning recent food safety issues.

被記者接二連三詢問近來的食安議題時，衛生部長提供了模稜兩可的答案。

A. ambiguous　B. anonymous　C. autonomous　D. ambitious

詳解 答案：A

這裡的 when bombarded with questions 其實就是 when asked questions（當被問到問題時）的意思，但 bombard with 表示「用…轟炸」，可以更生動地表現接二連三詢問，讓人招架不住的樣子。空格修飾 answers，選項中意思最合適的是 A. ambiguous（模稜兩可的）。因為已經知道回答的人是衛生部長，所以他的答案不會是 anonymous（匿名的）。

|單字片語| **minister** [ˋmɪnɪstɚ] n. （政府的）部長 / **bombard** [bɑmˋbɑrd] v. 轟炸，不斷攻擊 /

ambiguous [æm`bɪgjʊəs] adj. 模稜兩可的 / **anonymous** [ə`nɑnəməs] adj. 匿名的 / **autonomous** [ɔ`tɑnəməs] 自治的，自主的 / **ambitious** [æm`bɪʃəs] adj. 有野心的

Q10

A handmade watch contains more than a hundred different _______, which are all assembled by masters with skillful hands.

手工製造的手錶有一百多個不同的零件，全部由師傅以熟練的手組裝。

A. guidelines　B. refreshments　C. components　D. organisms

詳解　答案：C

空格是 watch（手錶）contains（包含）的東西，所以 C. components（零件）是正確答案。

補充說明

component 和動詞 compose 的字根相同。動詞 compose 表示「構成」（be composed of：由…組成），所以 component 是「構成的部分→零件」。

用動詞 compose 改寫題目裡的句子，可以這樣表達：

A handmade watch is composed of more than a hundred different components.

手工製造的手錶由一百多個不同的零件構成。

|單字片語| **guideline** [`gaɪd͵laɪn] n. 指導方針 / **refreshments** [rɪ`frɛʃmənts] n. 茶點 / **component** [kəm`ponənt] n. 構成要素，零件 / **organism** [`ɔrgən͵ɪzəm] n. 有機體，生物

第二部分 / 段落填空

Questions 11-15

Obesity results from the excessive (11) accumulation of body fat, which is usually caused by consuming too many calories. Therefore, (12) whether we get overweight depends on our diet. If we often overeat, we will gain weight; if we gain too much weight, we may become obese. Obesity is considered (13) a chronic disease that can affect us for a long time, like high blood pressure or diabetes. Obesity is also like an epidemic in developed countries, particularly the United States. More than two-thirds of Americans are overweight, including at least one in five children. Obesity rates are (14) on the rise in our society because food is abundant, and most of us are employed in positions that require little to no physical activity. Each year, Americans spend billions of dollars on dieting, diet foods, diet books, diet pills, and the like. Another $75 billion is spent on treating the diseases (15) associated with obesity. In other words, a lot of medical resources can be reallocated if we keep our bodies in shape.

肥胖是體脂肪過度堆積的結果，而這通常是攝取太多卡路里造成的。所以，我們是否會過重，取決於我們的飲食。如果我們經常吃得太多，我們的體重就會增加；如果我們增加的體重太多，我們就有可能變得肥胖。肥胖被認為是一種會長期影響我們的慢性疾病，就像高血壓或糖尿病一樣。肥胖在已開發國家，特別是美國，也像是流行病一樣。有超過三分之二的美國人過重，包括兒童之中的至少五分之一。我們社會的肥胖率正在上升中，因為食物很充足，而我們大部分的人都受雇於需要很少甚至沒有身體活動的職位。每一年，美國人花費數十、數百億美元在節食、減肥食物、減肥書、減肥藥之類的東西上。還有 750 億美元花在治療肥胖相關疾病。換句話說，如果我們保持身體健康的話，就可以把很多醫療資源分配到其他地方。

|單字片語| **obesity** [o`bisətɪ] n. 肥胖 / **excessive** [ɪk`sɛsɪv] adj. 過度的 / **accumulation** [əˏkjumjə`leʃən] n. 累積，積聚 / **consume** [kən`sjum] v. 消耗，吃，喝 / **overweight** [`ovəˏwet] adj. 過重的 / **overeat** [`ovə`it] v. 吃得太多 / **obese** [o`bis] adj. 肥胖的 / **chronic** [`kranɪk] adj.（疾病）慢性的 / **diabetes** [ˏdaɪə`bitiz] n. 糖尿病 / **epidemic** [ˏɛpɪ`dɛmɪk] n. 流行病，傳染病 / **on the rise** 上升中 / **abundant** [ə`bʌndənt] adj. 充足的，大量的 / **reallocate** [ˏrɪ`æləket] v. 重新分配 / **in shape** （身體）健康的

A. accumulation
B. accommodation
C. acceleration
D. acclamation

詳解

答案：A

這純粹是測試能否分辨類似單字的考題，只要知道單字的意思就不難回答。身體上 excess fat（過多脂肪）會怎樣造成 obesity（肥胖），唯一合理的選項是 A. accumulation（累積）。

|單字片語| **accommodation** [əˌkɑmə`deʃən] n. 住處 / **acceleration** [ækˌsɛlə`reʃən] n. 加速 / **acclamation** [ˌæklə`meʃən] n. 喝采

Q12

A. we should eat to our hearts' content
我們應該盡情地吃
B. food is an indispensable part of our life
食物是我們生活中不可或缺的一部分
C. we all need to lose weight to stay healthy
我們全都需要減重來保持健康
D. whether we get overweight depends on our diet
我們是否會過重，取決於我們的飲食

詳解

答案：D

空格前面有 Therefore（所以），表示上一句是空格內容的理由。上一句提到攝取太多卡路里會造成體脂肪過度堆積，下一句又提到吃太多會過重、肥胖，所以空格內容應該還是和飲食有關。在選項中，能呼應上一句，並且進一步說明飲食與過重關係的 D 是正確答案。在空格前後的部分還沒有談到肥胖對健康的影響，而且實際上也不是所有人都需要減重，所以 C 不是最適當的答案。

|單字片語| **to one's heart's content** 盡情地 / **indispensable** [ˌɪndɪs`pɛnsəbl] 不可或缺的

Q13

A. an acute　B. a terminal　C. a chronic　D. a fatal

詳解

答案：C

選項都是可以用來修飾 disease（疾病）的形容詞。因為後面的關係子句說明它可以 affect us for a long time（長時間影響我們），所以意義符合的 C. a chronic（慢性的）是正確答案。

〈補充說明〉

chronological [ˌkrɑnə`lɑdʒɪkḷ] adj. 依時間序記載的；按年代排序的
chronicle [`krɑnɪkḷ] n. 編年史

|單字片語| **acute** [ə`kjut] adj. （疾病）急性的 / **terminal** [`tɝmənḷ] adj. （疾病）末期的 / **fatal** [`fetḷ] adj. 致命的

Q14

A. to be raised　　B. on the rise
C. used to rising　　D. rising in number

詳解　　答案：B

前面的句子提到美國很多人肥胖的情況，這一句則解釋是因為某些原因，使得 obesity rates（肥胖率）怎麼了。雖然四個選項都提到「上升」，但能夠單純表示「（現在）上升中」的是把 rise 當成名詞的 B。選項 A 表示「將要被提高」，選項 C 表示「（人或動物）習慣於上升」，都不是適當的答案。另外，請注意選項 D 的意思是「數量增加」，也就是「變得有數量更多的肥胖率」，而不是指肥胖率顯示的數字增加。

Q15

A. associated with　　B. regardless of
C. instead of　　D. especially with

詳解　　答案：A

因為整段文章都在談肥胖，所以空格前面的 the diseases 應該也是和肥胖有關的疾病；選項 A 是用過去分詞 associated 搭配介系詞 with，表示「和…有關的」的意思，是適當的答案。associated with 也可以用 related to 表達。

|單字片語| **regardless of** 不管…，不顧… / **instead of** 代替…，而不是…

Questions 16-20

Encompassing 15,950 square miles (41,290 square kilometers), Switzerland is a (16) transition point between northern and southern Europe. Its physical environment is (17) characterized by a chain of mountains (the Jura), a densely urbanized plateau, and the Alps range, which forms a natural barrier to the south. (18) Such a strategic area was of great military importance, and several ancient fortresses dating back to the Roman Empire are still intact – (19) a living testimony of advanced Roman engineering. Politically, Switzerland is a federation of twenty-six states called "cantons". There are four linguistic regions: German, French, Italian, and Romansh, respectively. One of the cultural differences between these regions is the more frequent use of a kiss (20) rather than a handshake as a way of greeting in the French-speaking region. In addition to those European languages, English is also spoken and understood. Important announcements on trains will be given in English as well, so there is nothing to worry about.

範圍包含 15,950 平方英里（41,290 平方公里）的瑞士，是北歐和南歐之間的過渡點。這裡實體環境的特色是有一串山脈（侏羅山）、密集都市化的高原，和形成南部天然屏障的阿爾卑斯山脈。如此有戰略性的區域，以往有很大的軍事重要性，有幾座遠至羅馬帝國時代的古代堡壘仍然完好無損，是進步的羅馬工程技術的活證據。政治上，瑞士是由 26 個稱為「canton」的州所組成的聯邦。瑞士有四個語言區域：分別是德語、法語、義大利語和羅曼什語。這些區域之間的文化差異之一，是在法語區比較常用親吻而不是握手作為打招呼的方式。除了那些歐洲語言以外，瑞士人也說英語並且懂得英語。列車上的重要公告也會用英語播報，所以沒有什麼好擔心的。

|單字片語| **encompass** [ɪn`kʌmpəs] v. 包含；圍繞 / **transition** [træn`zɪʃən] n. 過渡，轉變 / **be characterized by** 以…為特徵 / **urbanize** [`ɝbən͵aɪz] v. 使都市化 / **plateau** [plæ`to] n. 高原 / **range** [rendʒ] n. 範圍；山脈 / **military** [`mɪlə͵tɛrɪ] adj. 軍事的，軍隊的 n. 軍隊 / **fortress** [`fɔrtrɪs] n. 要塞，堡壘 / **date back to** 起源於，追溯到（年代等） / **intact** [ɪn`tækt] adj. 完整無缺的，未受損傷的 / **testimony** [`tɛstə͵monɪ] n. 證詞，證據；見證 / **federation** [͵fɛdə`reʃən] n. 聯邦 / **linguistic** [lɪŋ`gwɪstɪk] adj. 語言的，語言學的 / **respectively** [rɪ`spɛktɪvlɪ] adv. 分別，各自

A. transaction　　B. transition　　C. transformation　　D. transfusion

詳解　　　答案：B

句意為瑞士是 northern and southern Europe（北歐和南歐）之間的什麼點，所以能和 point 結合為複合名詞的 B. transition 是正確答案；transition point 表示從一種狀態逐漸變成另一種狀態的「過渡點」或「轉變點」。

|單字片語| **transaction** [træn`zækʃən] n. 交易 / **transformation** [͵trænsfɚ`meʃən] n. 變化，改變（表示變得完全不一樣，非常戲劇性的變化） / **transfusion** [træns`fjuʒən] n. 輸血，輸液

Q17

A. delineated　B. saturated　C. characterized　D. featured

詳解　答案：C

空格所在的句子說，瑞士的 environment（環境）有 a chain of mountains（一串山脈）、plateau（高原）、Alps range（阿爾卑斯山脈），所以能和前後的 is... by 搭配，形成 is characterized by（以…為特徵）的 C 是正確答案。feature 雖然也可以表示「以…為特徵」，但不是用被動態，而是以主動態表達：Its physical environment features a chain of mountains...。

|單字片語| **delineate** [dɪˋlɪnɪˌet] v. 描繪輪廓，劃分…的界線 / **saturate** [ˋsætʃəˌret] v. 使飽和

Q18

A. As such　B. Such a　C. So much a　D. Such that

詳解　答案：B

選項看起來很難，但答案 B. Such a（這麼一個…）其實是很簡單的文法。such 是形容詞，代表前面提過的某種性質、特色，在這裡就是指前面所提的在南北歐交界、有山脈作為天然屏障。such 修飾可數名詞單數的時候，不定冠詞 a 放在 such 和名詞的中間。

補充說明

such 也用在感嘆句中。感嘆句的主要形式有以下三種：
How beautiful (this place is)!
What a beautiful place (this is)!
(This is) such a beautiful place!

|單字片語| **as such** 就其本身而言

Q19

A. a strong base of　…的堅實基礎
B. a living testimony of　…的活證據
C. in sharp contrast to　和…形成強烈對比
D. in better position than　處在比…要好的情況

詳解　答案：B

破折號後面的部分是對於前面句子的補充說明。前面提到有幾座羅馬帝國時代的古代堡壘還完好無損，而空格的後面又提到「進步的羅馬工程技術」，所以表示「古代堡壘還完好無損，證明了羅馬的工程技術」的 B 是正確答案。

A. in spite of　　B. rather than　　C. let alone　　D. contrary to

詳解

答案：B

空格所在的部分是 the use of a kiss _____ a handshake，後面接 as a way of greeting（作為打招呼的方式）。空格前後接的是「親吻」和「握手」兩種打招呼的方式，所以空格應該要填入有連接詞功能的詞語。正確答案是 B. rather than（…而不是…），可以連接名詞和名詞、動詞和動詞、形容詞和形容詞，表示「是前者而不是後者」。let alone 雖然也是連接詞，但會用在否定句，表示「（連…也不，）更別說…」的意思。

|單字片語| **in spite of** 儘管（有）… / **contrary to** 和…相反

第三部分 / 閱讀理解

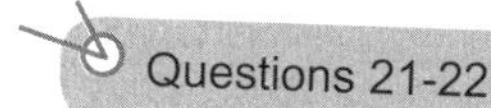

Accommodation in Venice

As one of the most popular cities in Europe, Venice is a must-visit place for tourists, who usually come in full force in summer. Therefore, there are a few things to be aware of when it comes to accommodation in Venice:

1. Space is limited in the city.
2. Accommodation in Venice can cost a lot.
3. Many visitors only come for a day trip.

The fact that Venice is often no more than a day trip destination does not help to mitigate the high prices of accommodation. Venice can't be truly appreciated unless one stays overnight, but it is a tough call as one ponders whether to break the bank.

Venice is full of hotels, but there aren't many hostels – the city just isn't known for cheap places to spend the night, unfortunately. Staying at youth hostels in Venice might be a great way to save money, but there is a condition: You have to be below 25 years of age to be considered a youth.

威尼斯的住宿

身為歐洲最受歡迎的城市之一，威尼斯是遊客必定到訪的地方，他們通常在夏天全軍出動。所以，說到威尼斯的住宿，有幾件事要知道：

1. 市內的（住宿）空間有限
2. 威尼斯的住宿有可能花很多錢
3. 很多參觀的人只在這裡進行一日遊

威尼斯通常不過是進行一日遊的地方，這件事實無助於緩和住宿的高價位。如果不住宿過夜，就無法真正欣賞威尼斯，但思考要不要花大筆金錢（住宿），是個很困難的決定。

威尼斯有很多飯店，但青年旅舍不多——很遺憾，這個城市並不是以便宜的過夜處而聞名。住在威尼斯的青年旅舍可能是省錢的好方法，但有條件：你必須要在 25 歲以下才會被認為是青年（而可以住宿）。

|單字片語| **accommodation** [ə͵kɑmə`deʃən] n. 住宿處 / **in full force** 全員出動 / **day trip** （當天來回的）一日遊 / **mitigate** [`mɪtə͵get] v. 緩和，減輕 / **tough call** 困難的決定 / **break the bank** 傾家蕩產，花太多錢 / **hostel** 旅舍（通常是 youth hostel = 青年旅舍）

Q21

Which factor is NOT accountable for the high cost of lodging in Venice?

哪個因素不能解釋威尼斯的高住宿費用？

A. Land constraint　土地限制
B. Worldwide fame　世界知名度
C. High number of visitors　很高的參觀人數
D. Popularity of day tours　一日遊的盛行

詳解

答案：D

第二段的第一句話 The fact that Venice is often no more than a day trip destination does not help to mitigate the high prices of accommodation.（威尼斯通常不過是進行一日遊的地方的事實，無助於緩和住宿的高價位），表示大部分的人通常在威尼斯只是一日遊，原本應該是降低住宿費用的因素〔一日遊是當天來回〕，但被其他助長住宿費的因素抵銷了。因為一日遊盛行不會是推高住宿費的原因，所以 D 是正確答案。

Q22

What dilemma does the writer mention in the article?

作者在文章中提到什麼兩難？

A. To splurge on accommodation in order to experience more or to save money by going on a day trip
揮霍金錢以體驗更多，還是要用一日遊省錢
B. To stay at a hotel and enjoy its service or to stay at a hostel that offers no service at all
要住在旅館並享受服務，還是住在根本不提供服務的旅舍
C. To decide if one should travel on land or by sea to reach Venice
決定應該走陸路還是海路抵達威尼斯
D. To weigh the advantages and disadvantages of visiting Venice compared to other cities in Europe
衡量去威尼斯和歐洲其他國家的優缺點

詳解

答案：A

第二段的後面提到，Venice can't be truly appreciated unless one stays overnight, but it is a tough call as one ponders whether to break the bank.（如果不住宿過夜，就無法真正欣賞威尼斯，但思考要不要花大筆金錢（住宿），是個很困難的決定），所以這裡說的兩難是要花大錢住宿以獲得深入的體驗，還是犧牲行程、用一日遊的方式省錢，正確答案是 A。選項 B 雖然和第三段的內容有關，但文章中並沒有談到住宿處的服務，所以這不是最好的答案。

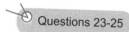

Questions 23-25

To Madam Shu-fen, Wang

This is a response to your inquiry regarding the safety of our toys. First and foremost, there are warnings on the box and the plastic bags reminding that these toys are only for children aged five and above. The components contained in the toy set are meant for assembly, not for consumption. The fact that our products are made of non-toxic materials does not imply that they are safe to eat. Children aged five years and above should not have trouble telling the difference between food and plastic. Nevertheless, we regret that your child choked on the components. We are pleased to offer you a new set of the toy you purchased instead of only replacing the missing parts. A hand-written card signed by the chief executive officer of XYZ Toys Co. was also delivered to your mailing address. We do wish your child a speedy recovery, though your claim for medical compensation was denied. We also wish to express our sympathies as it must have been a traumatic experience for your child.

Andrea Juan
Public Relations Officer

給王淑芬女士：

這是回覆您對我們玩具安全性的詢問。首先，盒子和塑膠袋上有警告，提醒這些玩具只供五歲以上的兒童使用。玩具組裡的零件是供組裝而不是食用。我們的產品由無毒材料製成，並不表示可以安全食用。五歲以上的兒童應該可以分辨食物和塑膠之間的差異。不過，我們對於您的孩子被零件噎住感到很抱歉。我們很樂意為您購買的玩具組提供一套新的，而不是只替換遺失的零件。由 XYZ 玩具公司執行長簽名的手寫卡片也送到了您的郵寄地址。雖然您對於醫藥費賠償的要求被拒絕了，我們還是希望您的孩子迅速康復。我們也希望表達我們的同情，因為這對於您的孩子一定是個創傷經驗。

Andrea Juan
公共關係主任

|單字片語| **foremost** [`for,most] adj. 最前面的；最重要的 / **component** [kəm`ponənt] n. 構成要素；零件 / **consumption** [kən`sʌmpʃən] n. 消耗；飲用，食用 / **toxic** [`tɑksɪk] adj. 有毒的 / **choke on** 被…噎住，被…嗆到 / **compensation** [,kɑmpən`seʃən] n. 彌補；賠償 / **traumatic** [trɔ`mætɪk] adj. 創傷的；精神創傷的

Q23

What is Madam Wang's chief complaint?
王女士的主要投訴是什麼？

A. Her child swallowed some parts of the toy.
她的小孩吞下了玩具的一些零件。
B. Her child ate something poisonous.
她的小孩吃了有毒的東西。
C. Her child felt dizzy after playing with plastic toys.
她的小孩玩了塑膠玩具以後覺得頭暈。
D. Her child was not sent to the hospital in time.
她的小孩沒有及時被送到醫院。

詳解

答案：A

王女士是這封信的收件人，所以題目問的是在這封信之前，王女士向 Andrea Juan 所屬的公司（XYZ Toys Co.）提出的投訴。信的開頭說 This is a response to your inquiry regarding the safety of our toys.（這是回覆您對我們玩具安全性的詢問），中間提到 we regret that your child choked on the components（我們對於您的孩子被零件噎住感到很抱歉），可知王女士反應了小孩子吞下玩具零件的問題，所以 A 是正確答案。信中說 our products are made of non-toxic materials（我們的產品由無毒材料製成），所以 B 不對。

補充說明

文中出現的 consumption 這個字，源自動詞 consume，而 consume 有「消耗，消費」和「吃，喝」的意思。所以，consumer（消費者，〔糧食等等的〕消耗者）、consupmtion（消耗；飲用，食用）都有這兩個層面的意義，要依照使用的情境判斷是哪一種。

|單字片語| **swallow** [`swɑlo] v. 吞嚥 / **poisonous** [`pɔɪznəs] adj. 有毒的 / **dizzy** [`dɪzɪ] adj. 頭暈目眩的

According to this letter, what is XYZ Toy's stance toward the complaint?

根據這封信，XYZ 玩具對於這件投訴的立場是什麼？

A. It is not responsible for the unfortunate accident.
 它對於這件不幸的意外沒有責任。
B. It is willing to offer payment to settle the case.
 它願意付錢解決這件事。
C. It admits that there is a flaw in the products it makes.
 它承認它製造的產品有瑕疵。
D. It provides medical insurance for users who are hurt.
 它提供醫療保險給受傷的使用者。

詳解 **答案：A**

信中強調玩具包裝上有 warnings（警告），說這個玩具是 only for children aged five and above（只供五歲以上的兒童使用），而且五歲以上的兒童 should not have trouble telling the difference between food and plastic（應該可以分辨食物和塑膠之間的差異）。也就是說，如果注意警告、不讓五歲以下的小孩玩的話，應該不會發生誤食的情況。關於王女士的小孩，信中說 We do wish your child a speedy recovery, though your claim for medical compensation was denied.（我們希望您的孩子迅速康復，雖然您對於醫藥費賠償的要求被拒絕了），表示他們並沒有賠償的打算。所以玩具公司認為自己對於意外沒有責任，答案是 A。

|單字片語| **stance** [stæns] n. 立場

Which of the following shows a friendly gesture adopted by XYZ Toys?

以下何者顯示出 XYZ 玩具的友善姿態？

A. The chief executive officer visited the hospital.
 執行長去了醫院。
B. The public relations officer apologized in public.
 公共關係主任公開道歉了。
C. The customer is entitled to a full refund.
 顧客可以得到全額退款。
D. The customer will receive a new set of toy.
 顧客會收到一套新的玩具。

第1回 第2回 第3回 第4回 第5回 第6回

詳解 **答案：D**

選項中唯一符合實際情況的是 D，對應信中的 We are pleased to offer you a new set of the toy you purchased（我們很樂意為您購買的玩具組提供一套新的）。其他選項在信中沒有提到。

|單字片語| **gesture** [ˋdʒɛstʃɚ] n. 姿勢；姿態 / **be entitled to** 有資格得到…

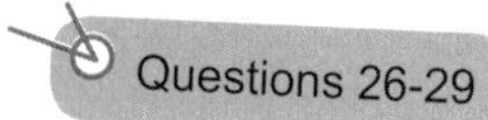

One may conclude that a paralyzed elderly man who is confined to a wheelchair has nothing to contribute to society. Our perceptions will change once we hear the story of the late Stephen Hawking (1942-2018). In 1963, this exceptionally gifted individual developed a rare disease that caused muscle atrophy, which made him lose control of his limbs. What's worse, he gradually lost his speech ability. He was told he only had two years to live, but unbelievably, he beat death and defied all predictions of modern medical science. To compensate for his loss of speech, he used a custom-made speech-generating device, which is activated by tensing his cheek muscle.

Besides living well beyond the time his doctor decreed, he went on to Cambridge and became a brilliant researcher. From 1979 to 2009, he held the post of Lucasian Professor at Cambridge, the chair which has been held by Isaac Newton. Therefore, he is regarded as one of the most brilliant theoretical physicists since Einstein.

Stephen Hawking is also the author of *A Brief History of Time*, an international bestseller. This modern classic helps non-scientists know about fundamental questions of physics and our existence, particularly about the beginning and possible ending of our universe, with a minimum of technical jargon. Encompassing topics such as gravity, black holes, the Big Bang, the nature of time, the births and deaths of stars, etc., this book proves to be overwhelming for most readers, and it seems beyond imagination that Hawking successfully integrated all these difficult subjects into a theoretical system. By reading this book, we may understand the universe and get a glimpse of "the mind of God", in Hawking's terms.

人們可能會斷定，被輪椅限制住的癱瘓老人沒有什麼可以貢獻社會的。聽到已故的史蒂芬・霍金（1942-2018）的故事，我們的看法就會改變。1963 年，這位非常有天分的人患上一種造成肌肉萎縮的罕見疾病，造成他無法控制自己的四肢。更糟的是，他逐漸失去了他的說話能力。他被告知只有兩年可活，但令人難以相信地，他擊敗了死亡，並且推翻了所有現代醫藥科學的預測。為了彌補他失去的說話能力，他使用訂製的語音生成設備，藉由緊縮他的臉頰肌肉來啟動。

除了活得遠遠超過醫生判定的時間以外，他也繼續在劍橋大學，成為出色的研究者。從 1979 年到 2009 年，他擔任劍橋大學的盧卡斯教授，這是艾薩克・牛頓曾經擔任過的職位。因此，他被認為是愛因斯坦以來最傑出的理論物理學家之一。

史蒂芬・霍金也是世界暢銷書《時間簡史》的作者。這部現代經典用最少的術語，幫助不是科學家的人了解關於物理學和我們存在的根本問題，尤其是關於我們宇宙的開始和可能的結束。這本書涵蓋引力、黑洞、大霹靂、時間的本質、恆星的誕生和死亡等等主題，實際上對於大部分讀者的確感覺來勢洶洶，而霍金能夠將這些困難的主題成功整合為一個理論體系，似乎也超越了想像。藉由閱讀這本書，用霍金的話來說，我們有可能了解宇宙，並且瞥見「神的心思」。

|單字片語|

（第一段）

paralyzed [ˋpærəˏlaɪzd] adj. 癱瘓的 / **confined** [kənˋfaɪnd] adj. 受限制的 / **perception** [pɚˋsɛpʃən] n. 感知，感覺；看法 / **gifted** [ˋgɪftɪd] adj. 有天賦的 / **atrophy** [ˋætrəfɪ] n. （醫學）萎縮 / **limb** [lɪm] n. 肢（手臂或腿） / **unbelievably** [ˏʌnbɪˋlivəblɪ] adv. 難以置信地 / **defy** [dɪˋfaɪ] v. 反抗；使…起不了作用 / **custom-made** [ˋkʌstəmˏmed] adj. 訂製的 / **activate** [ˋæktəˏvet] v. 使活化；啟動

（第二段）

decree [dɪˋkri] v. 頒布；命令（在本文是當成一種誇張的說法使用） / **theoretical** [ˏθiəˋrɛtɪkl] adj. 理論的

（第三段）

bestseller [ˏbɛstˋsɛlɚ] n. 暢銷書 / **jargon** [ˋdʒɑrgən] n. 行話；專門術語 / **encompass** [ɪnˋkʌmpəs] v. 圍繞；包含 / **prove to be** 結果證明是… / **overwhelming** [ˏovɚˋhwɛlmɪŋ] adj. 壓倒性的，讓人難以招架的 / **glimpse** [glɪmps] n. 瞥見，一瞥

What can be inferred about Stephen Hawking's physical condition?

關於史蒂芬·霍金的身體狀況，可以推斷什麼？

A. He was able to move freely with artificial limbs.
他能用義肢自由活動。

B. He was able to type using his eyeball movements.
他能用眼球運動打字。

C. He was able to communicate using special equipment.
他能用特殊的設備溝通。

D. He was able to write with his left hand.
他能用左手寫字。

詳解

答案：C

第一段的最後一句話說，To compensate for his loss of speech, he uses a custom-made computer device（為了彌補他失去的說話能力，他使用訂製的電腦設備），所以 C 是正確答案，選項中的 equipment（設備）表示文中提到的 device。其他選項在文章中沒有提到。

|單字片語| **artificial limb** 義肢 / **eyeball** [ˋaɪˏbɔl] n. 眼球

What can be considered a miracle in Stephen Hawking's life?　在史蒂芬·霍金的生命中，什麼可以被認為是一項奇蹟？

A. He became a doctor.　他成為了醫生。

B. He defied death.　他戰勝了死亡。

C. He wrote a great book.　他寫了一本很好的書。

D. He taught at universities.　他在大學教書。

詳解

答案：B

第一段提到 He was told he only had two years to live, but unbelievably, he beat death and defied all predictions of modern medical science.（他被告知只有兩年可活，但令人難以相信地，他擊敗了死亡，並且推翻了所有現代醫藥科學的預測）。因為他 unbelievably 活了下來，而且打破了 all predictions of modern medical science，所以能夠視為奇蹟，答案是 B。

補充說明

defy 後面會接 death、gravity 這種「不可抗力的事物」，表示就連這種事物都無法產生影響、非常神奇的感覺。defy death 可以解釋成「戰勝死神」，而 defy gravity 則是指人或事物好像不受地心引力影響，能夠自在飛翔或跳躍，或者建築物看似重心不穩卻不會倒下來的樣子。

Q28

Compared to other books on science, what made *A Brief History of Time* relatively readable for laymen?　相較於其他科學書籍，什麼使得《時間簡史》這本書讓外行人比較能夠閱讀？

A. It provides very basic explanations of various subjects.
　它為多種主題提供非常基本的解釋。

B. It explained the creation of the Earth.
　它解釋了地球的創造。

C. It combined science and religion.
　它結合了科學與宗教。

D. It minimized the use of scientific terminology.
　它把科學術語的使用減到最少。

詳解　　答案：D

介紹這本書的部分是文章的第三段。laymen 是指「外行人」，所以文中提到的 a minimum of technical jargon（最少的術語）可以幫助他們比較容易閱讀，選項 D 是正確答案，其中的 terminology（術語）相當於文中的 jargon。A 雖然也是能讓書容易閱讀的特色，但文中並沒有說書裡的解釋很基本，所以不對。

|單字片語| **layman** [ˋlemən] n. 外行人 / **terminology** [ˌtɝməˋnɑlədʒɪ] n. （總稱）術語，專門用語

What topic is NOT covered in the book *A Brief History of Time*?

哪一個主題不包含在《時間簡史》這本書裡？

A. An explanation of how the universe is formed
　關於宇宙如何形成的解釋

B. A spiritual insight of the mind and will of God
　對於上帝心思的精神性洞見

C. A hypothesis of how stars eventually disintegrate
　關於恆星最終如何瓦解的假設

D. An in-depth discussion on overcoming physical handicaps
　對於克服身體殘疾的深入討論

詳解

第三段提到的書中內容，the beginning... of our universe（我們宇宙的開始）對應選項 A，a glimpse of "the mind of God"（瞥見「神的心思」）對應選項 B，deaths of stars（恆星的死亡）對應選項 C。沒有提到的選項 D 是正確答案。

|單字片語| **spiritual** [ˋspɪrɪtʃʊəl] adj. 精神的，心靈的 / **hypothesis** [haɪˋpɑθəsɪs] n. 假說，假設 / **disintegrate** [dɪsˋɪntəgret] v. 瓦解，使瓦解 / **in-depth** [ˋɪnˋdɛpθ] adj. 深入的

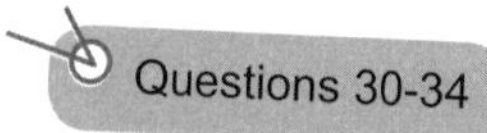

Questions 30-34

Questions 30-34 are based on the information provided in the following announcement and letter.

Sylvester University

Below are the minimum requirements for admissions into our university. Please note that meeting the minimum requirements does not guarantee a spot in our program. For students from countries where English is not the dominant language, an official English proficiency test score is required.

Academic

For admissions into one of our undergraduate programs, students must provide

- High school diploma or certificate of high school equivalency by the start of the program
- Official transcripts (must be provided directly from the awarding institution no more than 30 days after the start of the program)
- 3 reference letters in academic or personal background
- A personal statement outlining the reason for choosing Sylvester University

Financial

All International students are required by the U.S. government to submit a Certification of Finances, which is evidence that a student has sufficient funds to pay for tuition and living expenses for the first year. The estimated first year budget is $50,000 on average.

Research

Students are expected to conduct novel research in their field to successfully graduate from our institution.

If you have any questions, please contact us at admissions@sylvester.edu.

西爾維斯特大學

以下是進入本大學的最低要求條件。請注意，符合最低要求條件並不保證取得我們學程的名額。對於來自英語非主要語言國家的學生，必須有正式英語能力測驗的分數。

學術

要進入我們的大學學程，學生必須提供

- 於學程開始前提供高中畢業證書或高中同等學力證書
- 正式成績單（必須於學程開始後 30 天內由發行機構直接提供）
- 學術或個人背景的 3 封推薦信
- 概述選擇西爾維斯特大學原因的個人敘述

財務

美國政府要求所有國際學生提交財力證明，這是表示學生有充足資金支付第一年學費與生活費的證明。預估的第一年預算是平均 50,000 美元。

研究

學生被期望在自己的領域中進行新研究，才能從本校成功畢業。

如果您有任何問題，請寄信到 admissions@sylvester.edu 聯絡我們。

|單字片語| **undergraduate** [ˌʌndɚ`grædʒʊɪt] adj. 大學的 / **equivalency** [ɪ`kwɪvələnsɪ] n. 相等 / **transcript** [`trænˏskrɪpt] n. 成績報告單 / **reference letter** 推薦信 / **tuition** [tju`ɪʃən] n. 學費

Dear admissions officer,

My name is Alicia Hernández. I am from Mexico. I would like to apply to your biomedical program for the year 2024. There are some reasons why I choose to study medicine.

First, my father is a surgeon. He has worked for many years for Doctors Without Borders and has helped kids in various countries combat malaria. My mother is also in the medical field. She is a nurse. I look up to them both in so many ways, and I aspire to do good for the world just as they do. When I decided that I was going to follow in their footsteps, I looked at the top list of biomedical engineering programs in your country. I am applying to Sylvester University because of its amazing reputation, small class sizes, and the fact that it is one of the leaders in the biomedical field.

While undergoing my high school studies, I participated in a multitude of activities that help benefit society. I volunteered for the blood drive, and I also organized several events on nutrition.

Enclosed are my high school diploma and reference letters. I hope to take my enthusiasm into your university and contribute to your vision of providing students that are willing to serve the community. Thank you for your consideration, and I hope to hear from you soon.

Sincerely,
Alicia Hernández

親愛的招生負責人：

我的名字是艾莉西亞・赫南迪茲。我來自墨西哥。我想申請貴校 2024 年的生物醫學學程。我選擇學習醫學有一些原因。

首先，我的父親是外科醫師。他曾經為無國界醫生組織工作多年，並且幫助許多國家的兒童對抗瘧疾。我的母親也在醫學領域。她是護士。我在許多方面尊敬他們兩人，我也渴望像他們一樣對世界有所貢獻。當我決定要追隨他們的腳步時，我看了貴國生物醫學工程頂尖學程的列表。我申請進入西爾維斯特大學是因為它驚人的名聲、較少的班級人數，以及它是生物醫學領域領導者之一的事實。

在高中學習時，我參與了多種對社會有助益的活動。我當了鼓勵捐血活動的義工，也舉辦了幾場關於營養學的活動。

附件是我的高中畢業證書和推薦信。我希望將我的熱情帶到貴校，並且對於你們提供願意服務社會的學生的願景做出貢獻。感謝你們的考慮，我希望很快收到你們的回覆。

誠摯地
艾莉西亞・赫南迪茲

|單字片語| **biomedical** [ˌbaɪəˋmɛdɪkḷ] adj. 生物醫學的 / **combat** [ˋkɑmbæt] v. 戰鬥，對抗 / **malaria** [məˋlɛrɪə] n. 瘧疾 / **aspire to do** 渴望做…（表示未來的志向）/ **follow in someone's footsteps** 追隨某人的腳步（追隨長輩的人生選擇） / **multitude** [ˋmʌltəˌtjud] n. 許多 / **blood drive** 鼓勵人們捐血的活動

What is true about the requirements for applying to Sylvester University?

關於申請進入西爾維斯特大學的要求條件，何者正確？

A. The applicant must come from an English-speaking country.
申請者必須來自說英語的國家。

B. The applicant must be a high school graduate.
申請者必須是高中畢業生。

C. The applicant must be recommended by other people.
申請者必須受到其他人的推薦。

D. One who meets all the requirements listed will be accepted.
符合所有列出的要求條件的人會被接受。

詳解

答案：C

關於進入西爾維斯特大學的要求條件，公告（第一篇文章）提到必須要有 3 reference letters（3 封推薦信），reference letter 是認識的人推薦自己的信，所以 C 是正確答案。A. 文章中沒有提到。B. 文章中提到要提供 High school diploma or certificate of high school equivalency（高中畢業證書或高中同等學力證書），表示即使不是高中畢業，也可以用同等學力證明（例如參加正式測驗）來取代。D. 文章中提到 meeting the minimum requirements does not guarantee a spot in our program（符合最低要求條件並不保證取得我們學程的名額），不符合選項敘述。

What do we learn about Alicia?

關於艾莉西亞，我們知道什麼？

A. She aspires to be a pharmacist.　她渴望成為藥劑師。

B. Her father has been to many countries.　她的爸爸去過許多國家。

C. Her parents both did some medical studies.
她的父母都做了一些醫學研究。

D. She leads a physically active lifestyle.　她過著經常運動的生活。

詳解

答案：B

在艾莉西亞所寫的信（第二篇文章）中，提到她的爸爸 has helped kids in various countries combat malaria（曾經幫助許多國家的兒童對抗瘧疾），由此可知她的爸爸去過許多國家，所以 B 是正確答案。A. C. 文章中沒有提到。D. physically active 表示「身體方面很活躍」，也就是經常運動的意思，和文章中提到的經常參與活動無關。

Q32

What is the reason that Alicia chooses to apply to Sylvester University?

艾莉西亞選擇申請進入西爾維斯特大學的原因是什麼？

A. It is where her parents graduated from. 那是她父母畢業的大學。
B. It is the most well-known university in the U.S.
它是美國最知名的大學。
C. There are not too many courses there to choose from.
那裡沒有太多課程可以選擇。
D. It is prestigious for its biomedical studies.
它因為生物醫學的研究而很有聲望。

詳解 **答案：D**

關於申請進入西爾維斯特大學的原因，艾莉西亞所寫的信（第二篇文章）提到 I am applying to Sylvester University because of... the fact that it is one of the leaders in the biomedical field（我申請進入西爾維斯特大學是因為…它是生物醫學領域領導者之一的事實），所以 D 是正確答案。

Q33

What document does Alicia still need to provide before the start of the program?

艾莉西亞在學程開始前還需要提供什麼？

A. Her English proficiency test score 英語能力測驗分數
B. Her high school diploma 高中畢業證書
C. Her official transcripts 正式成績單
D. Her reference letters 推薦信

詳解 **答案：A**

這一題必須對照公告（第一篇文章）中的要求事項和信件（第二篇文章）的內容來解題。在信件中，艾莉西亞提到 Enclosed are my high school diploma and reference letters（附件是我的高中畢業證書和推薦信），所以可以先刪除選項 B 和 D。在公告中，提到 For students from countries where English is not the dominant language, an official English proficiency test score is required（對於來自英語非主要語言國家的學生，必須有正式英語能力測驗的分數），而艾莉西亞說 I am from Mexico（我來自墨西哥），卻沒有附英語能力測驗的分數，所以 A 是正確答案。另外，雖然公告中提到要有 Official transcripts（正式成績單），但提供的期限是 no more than 30 days after the start of the program（學程開始後 30 天內），不一定要在學程開始前提供，所以 C 不對。

What do students of Sylvester University need to do before they graduate?

西爾維斯特大學的學生在畢業前需要做什麼？

A. Do an internship in the last year of a program　在學程最後一年實習
B. Provide their transcripts at the university　提供大學的成績單
C. Pay $50,000 to the university every year　每年付 50,000 美元給大學
D. Do a study related to what they learn　進行和他們所學相關的研究

詳解

答案：D

關於大學畢業的要求條件，公告（第二篇文章）提到 Students are expected to conduct novel research in their field to successfully graduate from our institution（學生被期望在自己的領域中進行新研究，才能從本校成功畢業），所以 D 是正確答案。另外，公告中提到的 50,000 美元，是包括 tuition and living expenses（學費與生活費），而不是付給學校的金額。

|單字片語| **internship** [ˋɪntɝn͵ʃɪp] n. 實習

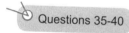

Questions 35-40

I can't help but observe that visitors traveling in groups are behaving more and more like "zombies". The main selling proposition of package deal trips is to cover as much ground as possible in a minimum number of days. As a result, tourists fight against time just to take as many pictures as possible before rushing off to the next "cannot-be-missed" sight. Take a Europe tour for example: a seven-day trip can sometimes stretch over five different national capitals. Therefore, a large part of vacation time is spent on the road. One may argue that we can also take in the views while traveling along picturesque landscapes. Truth be told, visitors tend to find themselves dozing off on the coaches. No matter how breathtaking the scenery is, staring at the same expanse of land for hours can have a numbing effect. Upon reaching a new destination, these "zombies" come alive as they pose in front of landmarks and hunt for souvenirs which serve as "evidence" that they have been to a particular city. Once back on the bus, they return to a state of coma, oblivious to the rattling of the tour guide.

The "see-and-go" travel culture is a result of price competition among travel agencies. To attract business, travel agencies resort to underpricing, a new term that refers to offering ridiculously low prices that are beyond business sense. How can companies be profitable when costs and overheads exceed the price they charge? As a matter of fact, there is more than meets the eye. Cheap package deal trips are offset by shopping trips, in which travel agencies derive a handsome commission. At a souvenir store your guide takes you to, the same item can be marked up by 1,000%, and part of the overcharge will go to the guide and travel agency. Such practice is frowned upon by relevant authorities. However, a lot has been said, while little has been done.

As economical packaged tours become infamous for their hectic itineraries and unnecessary shopping trips, in-depth guided travel is gaining popularity. In recent years, tourists are no longer satisfied with running after the guide and squeezing more countries into their itineraries. Instead, they now prefer “deep” travel focused on getting under the skin of a place. It is about seeking out real-life experiences rather than fake culture packaged up for tourists. It means allocating more time to each destination and putting in an effort to understand the history, architecture, and daily lives of common folks. In this way, tourists will be able to appreciate local idiosyncrasies and the details that make a place unique.

我不得不觀察到，團體旅行的觀光客表現得越來越像「僵屍」。套裝旅行的主要銷售訴求，是在最少的天數中涵蓋盡可能多的地方。結果，觀光客和時間對抗，就只為了在趕到下一個「不能錯過」的景點之前盡量多拍照片。舉歐洲旅遊為例：七天的旅行有時候會遍及五個不同國家的首都。所以，有大部分的度假時間花在（交通）路途上。有人可能會主張，我們在沿著如畫的風景旅行時，也可以觀賞景色。說實話，觀光客通常會發現自己在長途巴士上睡著。不管景色有多麼壯觀，好幾個小時盯著同一片土地還是會有麻痺的效果。到了新地點的時候，這些「僵屍」就會復活，在地標前面擺姿勢，並且尋找紀念品，當作到過特定城市的「證據」。一回到巴士上，他們又會回到昏迷狀態，對導遊的喋喋不休渾然不覺。

「看了就走」的旅行文化，是旅行社之間價格競爭的結果。為了吸引生意，旅行社訴諸於壓低價格，這個新的用語是指提供超乎業界常識的荒謬低價。當成本和經常費用超過他們的收費，公司怎麼能獲利呢？事實上，情況不是表面看起來那麼簡單。便宜的套裝旅行是用購物行程彌補的，旅行社可以從中得到可觀的佣金。在導遊帶你去的紀念品店，同樣物品的定價有可能被標高 1,000%，而超過的價錢有一部分會進導遊和旅行社的口袋。相關當局不贊成這種行為。不過，說得多，但做得少。

隨著經濟套裝旅遊因為匆忙的行程規畫和不必要的購物行程而惡名昭彰，深度導遊旅行變得越來越受歡迎。近年來，觀光客不再滿足於追著導遊、把多一點國家塞進行程裡。取而代之的是，他們現在偏好著重於深入一個地方的表層之下的「深度」旅遊。這種旅遊的要點在於尋找真實生活的體驗，而不是為觀光客打包好的虛假文化。它的用意是多分配時間給每個目的地，並且努力了解歷史、建築和一般人的日常生活。這樣一來，觀光客將能夠欣賞當地的特質，還有使一個地方獨特的細節。

|單字片語|

（第一段）

zombie [ˋzɑmbɪ] n. 殭屍 / **proposition** [ˏprɑpəˋzɪʃən] n. 主張 / **rush off** 匆匆離開 / **national capital** 國家首都 / **picturesque** [ˏpɪktʃəˋrɛsk] adj. 如畫一般的 / **doze off** 打瞌睡 / **breathtaking** [ˋbrɛθˏtekɪŋ] adj. （風景等）令人屏息的，壯觀的 / **expanse** [ɪkˋspæns] n. 廣闊的區域 / **numbing** [ˋnʌmɪŋ] adj. 使麻木的 / **coma** [ˋkomə] n. 昏迷狀態 / **oblivious** [əˋblɪvɪəs] adj. 忘卻的 / **rattle** [ˋrætḷ] v. 喋喋不休

（第二段）

overhead [ˋovɚˋhɛd] n. 經常費用，經常開支 / **there is more than meets the eye** 情況沒有看起來那麼簡單，另有隱情 / **offset** [ˋɔfˏsɛt] v. 抵銷，補償 / **commission** [kəˋmɪʃən] n. 佣金 / **mark up** 提高…的價格 / **frown upon** 「對…皺眉」→不贊成…

（第三段）

infamous [ˋɪnfəməs] adj. 惡名昭彰的 / **hectic** [ˋhɛktɪk] adj. 忙亂的 / **itinerary** [aɪˋtɪnəˏrɛrɪ] n. 旅行行程 / **in-depth** [ˋɪnˋdɛpθ] adj. 深入的 / **allocate** [ˋæləˏket] v. 分配 / **idiosyncrasy** [ˏɪdɪəˋsɪŋkrəsɪ] n. （獨自的）氣質，風格

Q35

What is the main purpose of this article?

這篇文章的主要目的是什麼？

A. To shed some light on what an ideal tour should be
說明理想的旅遊應該是什麼樣子

B. To explain how to travel to as many places as possible
說明如何旅行到盡可能多的地方

C. To argue that exotic scenery is the highlight of a trip
主張異國景色是旅行的重點

D. To expose the unethical schemes of travel agencies
揭露旅行社不道德的詭計

詳解

答案：A

第一段說 visitors traveling in groups are behaving more and more like "zombies"（團體旅行的觀光客表現得越來越像「僵屍」），並闡述匆忙的團體旅行有什麼缺點；第二段說明旅行社利用 shopping trips（購物行程）抽取 commission（佣金）的行為；第三段則說 in-depth guided travel（深度導遊旅行）越來越受歡迎，因為它讓旅行者能深入體驗一個地方。所以，作者是希望藉由以上的討論，呈現出旅遊的理想型態，答案是 A。雖然選項 D 在第二段談到了，但不是文章整體的主題。

|單字片語| **shed light on** 「照亮…」→闡明，解釋… / **exotic** [ɛg`zɑtɪk] adj. 異國風情的 / **highlight** [`haɪˌlaɪt] n. 最突出的部分，最重要的部分 / **unethical** [ʌn`ɛθɪkl̩] adj. 不道德的 / **scheme** [skim] n. 計畫；詭計

What does the writer suggest about package deal trips?
關於套裝旅行，作者暗示什麼？

A. Visitors get good value in return for money.
觀光客的錢換來很好的價值。
B. Visitors can buy souvenirs at a lower price.
觀光客可以用比較低的價格購買紀念品。
C. Visitors are able to experience local culture.
觀光客能夠體驗當地文化。
D. Visitors may end up paying more than they intend.
觀光客最後可能會付出比預期中還要多的錢。

詳解

答案：D

關於 package deal trips（套裝旅行），第二段的中間提到 Cheap package deal trips are offset by shopping trips（便宜的套裝旅行是用購物行程彌補的）、At a souvenir store your guide takes you to, the same item can be marked up by 1,000%, and part of the overcharge will go to the guide and travel agency.（在導遊帶你去的紀念品店，同樣物品的定價有可能被標高 1,000%，而超過的價錢有一部分會進導遊和旅行社的口袋）。所以，雖然行程本身便宜，但旅行者可能在購物行程中多花錢，正確答案是 D。

Q37

According to the writer, which word can best describe an economical packaged tour?

根據作者的說法，哪個單字最能描述經濟套裝旅遊？

A. Superficial　表面的
B. Enlightening　有啟發性的
C. Marvelous　驚奇的
D. Tragic　悲劇的

詳解　　答案：A

在第一段，作者把參加團體旅行的人稱為 zombies（殭屍），因為行程很匆忙，在觀光地點也只是 pose in front of landmarks and hunt for souvenirs（在地標前面擺姿勢，並且尋找紀念品）。第三段則說，相對於 economical packaged tours（經濟套裝旅遊），in-depth guided travel（深度導遊旅行）越來越受歡迎，因為旅行者變得比較喜歡 “deep” travel focused on getting under the skin of a place（著重於深入一個地方的表層之下的「深度」旅遊）。所以相較之下，economical packaged tour 是比較膚淺的旅遊，正確答案是 A。

Why are visits to souvenir stores included in package deal trips?　為什麼套裝旅行會包括紀念品店的行程？

A. They are popular destinations among tourists.
它們是很受觀光客歡迎的目的地。
B. They enable travel agencies to make a killing.
它們能讓旅行社大賺一筆。
C. They help tourists understand the geography of a place.
它們幫助觀光客了解一個地方的地理。
D. They allow visitors to bargain collectively.
它們讓觀光客能夠集體殺價。

詳解　　答案：B

第二段後半提到，旅行社可以 derive a handsome commission（得到可觀的佣金），因為 At a souvenir store your guide takes you to, the same item can be marked up by 1,000%, and part of the overcharge will go to the guide and travel agency（在導遊帶你去的紀念品店，同樣物品的定價有可能被標高 1,000%，而超過的價錢有一部分會進導遊和旅行社的口袋）。所以，用 make a killing（大賺一筆）重新表達 derive a handsome commission 的選項 B 是正確答案。

What new trend did the author observe recently?

作者最近觀察到什麼新趨勢？

A. Tourists prefer to travel to exotic places.
觀光客偏好到有異國風情的地點旅行。

B. Tourists prefer to experience life like a native.
觀光客偏好像當地人一樣體驗生活。

C. Tourists prefer to explore the deep sea.
觀光客偏好探索深海。

D. Tourists prefer to go on shopping sprees.
觀光客偏好瘋狂購物。

詳解

答案：B

提到旅遊新趨勢的部分是第三段。作者說旅行者 now prefer "deep" travel（現在偏好「深度」旅遊），而這種旅行的重點包括 seeking out real-life experiencese（尋找真實生活的體驗）、putting in an effort to understand the... daily lives of common folks（努力了解一般人們的日常生活），所以 B 是正確答案。

|單字片語| **shopping spree** 瘋狂購物的行為

What is a possible drawback of an "in-depth" tour?

「深度」旅行可能的缺點是什麼？

A. Traveling to fewer countries or cities in a single trip
在一次旅行中去比較少的國家或城市

B. Spending more on transportation and food
花比較多錢在交通和食物上

C. Having less time to take pictures
拍照的時間比較少

D. Difficulty in interacting with locals
很難和當地人互動

詳解

答案：A

關於 in-depth tour 的部分在第三段。深入旅遊的特色是 allocating more time to each destination（多分配時間給每個目的地），所以能去的國家、城市會比較少，正確答案是 A。

全民英語能力分級檢定測驗
GENERAL ENGLISH PROFICIENCY TEST

中高級聽力測驗　第四回
HIGH-INTERMEDIATE LISTENING COMPREHENSION TEST

This listening comprehension test will test your ability to understand spoken English. In this test, each conversation, short talk and question will be spoken JUST ONE TIME. They will not be written out for you. There are three parts to this test. Special instructions will be given to you at the beginning of each part.

Part I: Answering Questions

In Part I, you will hear ten questions. After you hear a question, read the four choices in your test booklet and decide which one is the best answer to the question you have heard.

Example:

You will hear: Why did you slam the door?

You will read:
A. I just can't open it.
B. I didn't. I guess it's the wind.
C. Because someone is at the door.
D. Because the door knob is missing.

The best answer to the question "Why did you slam the door?" is B: "I didn't. I guess it's the wind." Therefore, you should choose answer B.

1. A. Let's find some shade.
   B. Let me check the price.
   C. Let's put on some makeup.
   D. Let's get some cold medicine.

2. A. I'm afraid you have already missed it.
   B. It will be dead by this weekend.
   C. Whenever you are ready.
   D. It will expire in about a month.

3. A. I think the outer case is solid.
   B. I keep my passport and cash in it.
   C. I'll empty them right away.
   D. Thanks, but I can handle it myself.

4. A. Shouldn't we use the main entrance?
   B. Why don't we join the rest?
   C. What do you recommend?
   D. How could you cancel the course?

5. A. I've been practicing for almost a year.
   B. I've done it many times in the past.
   C. The swelling started about a week ago.
   D. The symphony ended long before you came.

6. A. I have bought enough local products already.
   B. Matters are a little complicated at the moment.
   C. The former is great, but the latter is impersonal.
   D. Whoever serves the ball has the advantage.

7. A. My classmates are fun to hang out with.
   B. Just go straight and then take a left.
   C. I have a slight cough and a sore back.
   D. They just mind their own business.

8. A. What's done cannot be undone.
   B. Your wish is my command.
   C. Nothing will ever remain the same.
   D. I am allergic to seafood.

9. A. Here you are. Could I have a receipt?
   B. Buckle up. I'm going to step on it.
   C. Oh, I left the parking token in the car.
   D. I didn't know that I couldn't park here.

10. A. Are you worried about the crowd?
    B. Are you sure that's a good idea?
    C. Are you always so indecisive?
    D. Are you keen on reaching the top?

Please turn to the next page.

Part II: Conversation

In part II, you will hear several conversations between a man and a woman. After each conversation, you will hear a question about the conversation. After you hear the question, read the four choices in your test booklet and choose the best answer to the question you have heard.

Example:

You will hear:	(Man)	Did you happen to see my earphones? I remember leaving them in the drawer. Someone must have taken it.
	(Woman)	It's more likely that you misplaced them. Did you search your briefcase?
	(Man)	I did, but they are not there. Wait a second. Oh. They are right here in my pocket.
	Question:	Who took the man's earphones?

You will read:

A. The woman.
B. Someone else.
C. No one.
D. Another man.

The best answer to the question "Who took the man's earphones?" is C: "No one." Therefore, you should choose answer C.

11. A. He can explore ancient ruins.
    B. He can pretend to be a teacher.
    C. He can read and write poems.
    D. He can imagine living in a story.

12. A. Get better grades in school.
    B. Avoid having a relationship with a girl.
    C. Take doing housework seriously.
    D. Develop an interest in fashion design.

13. A. Supportive.
    B. Considerate.
    C. Detached.
    D. Skeptical.

14. A. Certain staff abused the system.
    B. Staff welfare is not beneficial.
    C. A security camera was installed.
    D. Money has been missing.

15. A. Soccer coaches.
    B. Referees.
    C. Spectators.
    D. Commentators.

16. A. Exactly NT$100.
    B. At least NT$100.
    C. She needs to pay for the parts.
    D. She doesn't have to pay.

17. A. Subjects and personalities.
    B. Mathematicians and physicists.
    C. Sociology and sociability.
    D. Words and numbers.

18. A. Wash her face regularly.
    B. Monitor her diet.
    C. Take a kind of medicine.
    D. Apply oil on her skin.

19. A. She is at the wrong place.
    B. She is inappropriately dressed.
    C. She is worried about her safety.
    D. She is not photogenic.

Please turn to the next page. ⇨

20. A. He was cheating on his wife.
    B. He was preparing a surprise for his wife.
    C. He was planning a birthday party.
    D. He was trying to find a job.

21. A. The man has lost interest in his wife.
    B. The woman has faith in her husband.
    C. They got married not long ago.
    D. They will have a party tomorrow.

22. A. A babysitter.
    B. A career woman.
    C. A first-time mother.
    D. A single mother.

23. A. His daughter looks like him.
    B. His mother lives in the neighborhood.
    C. He has a light workload.
    D. He sometimes helps with the baby.

24.

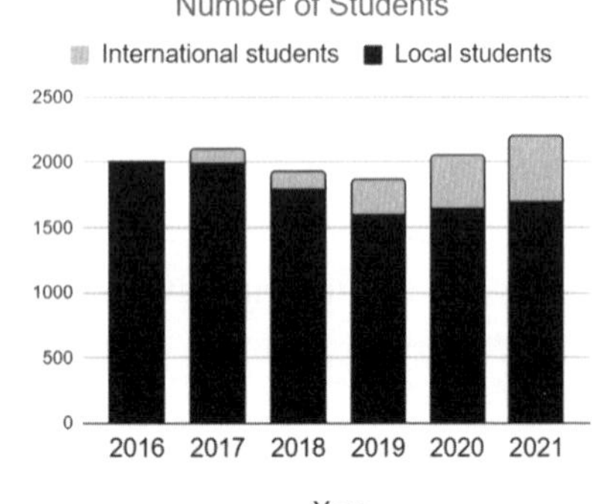

A. In 2017.
B. In 2018.
C. In 2019.
D. In 2020.

25.

Asia	
Bali 7 days NT$ 85,000/person	Maldives 5 days NT$ 72,000/person
Europe	
Malta 7 days NT$ 140,000/person	Cyprus 5 days NT$ 120,000/person

A. In Bali.
B. In Maldives.
C. In Malta.
D. In Cyprus.

Part III: Short Talks

In part III, you will hear several short talks. After each talk, you will hear two to three questions about the talk. After you hear each question, read the four choices in your test booklet and choose the best answer to the question you have heard.

Example:

You will hear: Hello, thank you everyone for coming together to share this special day with Chris and I. We have been waiting for this moment forever, and after five years of dating, I can happily say that I am ready. Chris is caring and charming, and I appreciate my good fortune in marrying such a warm-hearted man. When he proposed to me, I realized that he had already become a part of my life. Even though I'm not a perfect cook or housekeeper, I know for sure that I will be a wonderful partner for Chris.

Question number 1: On what occasion is this talk most probably being given?

You will read: A. A funeral.
B. A wedding.
C. A housewarming.
D. A farewell party.

The best answer to the question "On what occasion is this talk most probably being given?" is B: "A wedding." Therefore, you should choose answer B.

Now listen to another question based on the same talk.

Please turn to the next page.

You will hear: Question number 2: According to this talk, what does the woman like about Chris?

You will read: A. His perseverance.
B. His abundant wealth.
C. His cooking skill.
D. His amiable personality.

The best answer to the question "According to this talk, what does the woman like about Chris?" is D: "His amiable personality." Therefore, you should choose answer D.

Please turn to the next page. Now let us begin Part III with question number 26.

26. A. Pick up luggage immediately.
    B. Leave the train station.
    C. Remain on the platforms.
    D. Hide in the bomb shelter.

27. A. It is a routine fire drill.
    B. There was an explosion.
    C. Many children were injured.
    D. Passengers may need to use other modes of transportation.

28. A. Emily was told that she was fired.
    B. Simon didn't agree with Emily's proposal.
    C. Richard managed to persuade Simon.
    D. Everyone felt intimidated by Emily.

29. A. It is feasible.
    B. It lacks imagination.
    C. It needs some adjustment.
    D. It will be implemented.

30. A. The top three causes have nothing to do with weather.
    B. Fatal accidents are not as frequent as many people expect.
    C. There were more accidents on rainy days in the mountains.
    D. More accidents happen after dark than in daytime.

31. A. Drivers suffer from poor vision.
    B. Drivers lose control of their cars.
    C. Drivers are thrilled by the ride.
    D. Drivers have less time to react.

32. A. Drunk driving accidents tend to be in the headlines.
    B. Drunk driving leads to more deadly accidents than any other causes.
    C. Drunk drivers are unable to follow GPS instructions.
    D. Drunk drivers tend to drive faster and take more risks.

Please turn to the next page.

33. A. They expect war to break out soon.
    B. They have enough problems of their own.
    C. They believe refugees are mostly terrorists.
    D. They need financial aid from Western countries.

34. A. Jobs are scarce.
    B. Employers are biased.
    C. The pay is unreasonable.
    D. Their expertise is redundant.

35-37.

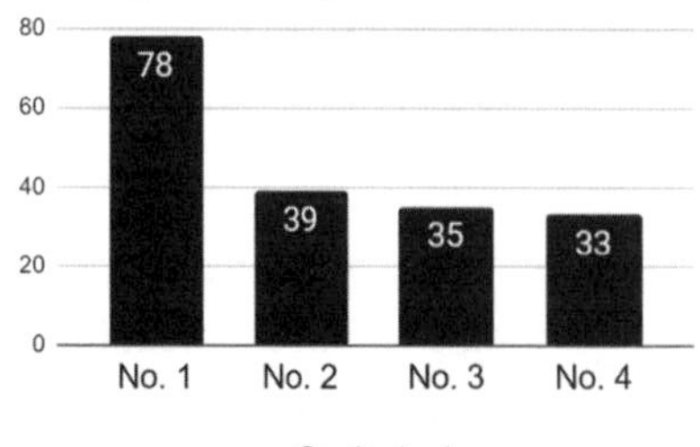

35. A. He has been a world record keeper.
    B. He has a total of 17 wins now.
    C. He won every year in the past 16 years.
    D. He narrowly won this year.

36. A. No. 1.
    B. No. 2.
    C. No. 3.
    D. No. 4.

37. A. Only men can enter the contest.
    B. It has been held for 50 times.
    C. It was canceled last year.
    D. It has the largest audience this year.

38-40.

	Pros	Cons
Online Learning	Less chance of virus exposure No transportation issues	Less ? Harder to focus
In-Person Learning	Easier to make new friends Reduce the burden of working parents	Risk of virus exposure More stressful for some kids

38.
A. Effective tests.
B. Social interaction.
C. Reference resources.
D. Motivation for learning.

39. A. A student.
    B. A teacher.
    C. A mother.
    D. A researcher.

40. A. It is behind the times.
    B. It needs to be transformed.
    C. It is always superior to online learning.
    D. It is essential for education.

Please turn to the next page.

READING COMPREHESION TEST

This is a three-part test with forty multiple-choice questions. Each question has four choices. Special instructions will be provided for each part. You will have fifty minutes to complete this test.

Part I: Sentence Completion

In this part of the test, there are ten incomplete sentences. Beneath each sentence you will see four words or phrases, marked A, B, C and D. You are to choose the word or phrase that best completes the sentence. Then on your answer sheet, find the number of the question and mark your answer.

1. Peace-keeping troops stationed in war-torn countries ensure that refugees are treated in a ________ manner according to international protocol.

   A. human　　B. humorous
   C. humiliating　　D. humanitarian

2. The likely ________ and side effects brought about by chemotherapy should be explained to the patient before treatment.

   A. anticipations　　B. evaluations
   C. implications　　D. precautions

3. Since young, the talented musician knew that he was unlike his peers in that he was ________ for great things.

   A. tempted　　B. pursued
   C. destined　　D. doomed

4. Those who ________ illegal drugs, as stated in the customs declaration form, could face the death penalty.

   A. assemble　　B. crumble
   C. mingle　　D. smuggle

5. This tropical rainforest in South Asia serves as a ________ where animals can live their natural lives in peace.
   A. boundary　　B. cemetery
   C. documentary　　D. sanctuary

6. Those who drag their feet while walking find their shoes ________ faster due to repeated friction.
   A. turn out　　B. put out
   C. sell out　　D. wear out

7. The senior executive was taken into custody after admitting that he ________ better-than-expected sales figures in an attempt to push up share prices.
   A. monopolized　　B. fabricated
   C. obscured　　D. undermined

8. At higher ________, there is a significant annual variation in the length of the day—much longer in summer and much shorter in winter.
   A. altitudes　　B. aptitudes
   C. latitudes　　D. longitudes

9. When it comes to architectural design, safety, rather than cost or appearance, should be given top ________.
   A. collaboration　　B. hierarchy
   C. transparency　　D. priority

10. Northern lights, the colorful lights seen in high-latitude regions, are a natural ________ caused by energized particles leaving the sun and colliding with particles in the earth's atmosphere.
   A. phenomenon　　B. symptom
   C. omen　　D. reminder

Please turn to the next page. ⇨

Part Two: Cloze

In this part of the test, you will read two passages. Each passage contains five missing words or phrases. Beneath each passage, you will see five items, each with four choices, marked A, B, C and D. You are to choose the best answer for each missing word or phrase in the two passages. Then, on your answer sheet, find the number of the question and mark your answer.

Questions 11-15

The most brutal form of punishment for theft in some Islamic states is to chop off the hands of the criminal, ___(11)___ gender. This extreme measure to discourage people from stealing is ___(12)___ by authorities based on a verse in the Quran, which is the Muslim equivalent of the Bible. Nevertheless, further reading of the Quran indicates that Allah, the God of Muslims, preaches forgiveness. As a matter of fact, there are many verses that tell us to forgive ___(13)___ the evil-doer repents. Forgiveness implies that no punishment is given. It is ___(14)___ to ask people to turn over a new leaf after chopping off their hands. Thus, it is obvious that the verse used to support such bloody punishment is taken out of context. While some may argue that the presence of such a barbaric law in modern society ___(15)___, others are of the opinion that it is way out of proportion. Law-breakers should be given a chance to regret their actions and make amends.

11. A. in principle
    B. not to mention
    C. regardless of
    D. save for

12. A. clarified
    B. mystified
    C. identified
    D. justified

13. A. as if
    B. in case
    C. so long as
    D. so as to

14. A. absurd
    B. ecstatic
    C. naïve
    D. sentimental

15. A. should be abolished for good
    B. proves that conservatism still exists
    C. does not reduce violent crime
    D. acts as a deterrent against crime

Questions 16-20

Singapore is among the most vibrant, robust, and competitive markets in the world. From 2007 to 2016, the World Bank kept ranking Singapore as the easiest place in the world to do business. While strongly ___(16)___ free-market policies and practices, which attract foreign investment, the Singapore government ___(17)___ its authoritative style of intervention in certain areas. This innovative and highly successful economic system is known as "the Singapore Model". ___(18)___, and thus has to open its economy to external markets in order for the economy to thrive. However, the heavy reliance on external markets has also compelled the government to ___(19)___ economic policies that would safeguard the country from perturbations in the global market. Apart from these policies, the government has also actively encouraged new industries to develop in Singapore ___(20)___ respond to the needs of the global market.

16. A. advocating
    B. indicating
    C. contemplating
    D. permeating

17. A. is in the know about
    B. also knows well about
    C. should also have known
    D. is also well-known for

18. A. Singapore has flourishing local businesses
    B. Singapore is famous for its strict regulations
    C. Singapore has a relatively small domestic market
    D. Singapore is trying to protect domestic industries

19. A. deprive
    B. nurture
    C. formulate
    D. tackle

20. A. so that
    B. such that
    C. so as to
    D. as such

Part III: Reading Comprehension

In this part of the test, you will find several tasks. Each task contains one or two passages or charts, which are followed by two to six questions. You are to choose the best answer, A, B, C, or D, to each question on the basis of the information provided or implied in the passage or chart. Then, on your answer sheet, find the number of the question and mark your answer.

Questions 21-22

Commencement of Works between Huddleston Street and St. Albert Avenue

Please note that work on the laying of replacement sewage pipes between Huddleston Street and St. Albert Avenue will commence on the 22nd of November. The replacement will ensure security of water supply to the southeastern Huddleston district. Work will be undertaken using trenchless construction method to minimize noise pollution, but the flow of traffic is expected to be affected.

However, traffic will be controlled in certain sections with a temporary traffic light system in operation. Work is scheduled to take place from 09:30 to 16:30, 7 days a week. There will be no further disruption to traffic after working hours. This work is scheduled to be completed by the end of December. Any inconvenience caused is regretted. We seek your cooperation by choosing an alternative route or avoiding roadwork hours.

21. What information can be derived from the notice?
    - A. A pipe burst caused disruption of traffic.
    - B. Traffic jams during lunchtime are expected.
    - C. Workers will go on strike as a result of long working hours.
    - D. Construction work will last for at least half a year.

22. What is **NOT** mentioned in the notice?
    - A. Traffic will be directed during construction hours.
    - B. Work will be carried out around the clock.
    - C. The construction crew will manage to reduce noise.
    - D. Problems can be avoided by taking other roads.

Questions 23-25

Among African leaders, Nelson Mandela is one of the few who have gained respect from around the world and across the political spectrum. His role in fighting apartheid (racial segregation in South Africa) and his ability to lead South Africa through its transformation process earned him the international reputation of being a successful negotiator and peacemaker.

Because of his opposition to apartheid, Mandela had been imprisoned for 27 years. When he finally won his freedom in 1990, instead of showing resentment or trying to revenge, he dedicated himself to the reconciliation of South Africa's conflicting ethnic groups, aiming at building a nation where cooperative governance is possible. By uniting the warring parties, Mandela saved South Africa from the verge of civil war and built up its people's confidence. He was elected as the President of South Africa in 1993, and the number of attending state leaders at his inauguration surpassed that at the funeral of former US President John Kennedy. Although very likely to win a second term if he wanted, Mandela did not hesitate to step down in 1999. He died from a lung infection on December 5th, 2013 at the age of 95.

Mandela's success did not come by chance. It is his outstanding negotiating skills, moral integrity, and sense of fairness that convinced disparate parties to compromise for the sake of peace. In today's world, we still see endless conflicts among ethnic and religious groups, but what Mandela had done shows us that with positive intention and perseverance, no conflict is unresolvable.

23. Which of the following statements is **NOT** true?
    A. Mandela preached forgiveness and unity.
    B. Mandela held the view that different races should not be separated.
    C. Mandela prevented a possible political upheaval from happening.
    D. Mandela held on to power for fear of imprisonment.

24. What trait in Mandela won him international respect?
    A. His generosity in sharing power and credit
    B. His commitment to harmony and tolerance
    C. His ambition for worldwide glory and fame
    D. His resourcefulness in negotiation and trade

25. What fact shows that Mandela was a globally prominent figure?
    A. He showed love and dedication to his homeland.
    B. His fight against apartheid took 27 years of his life.
    C. He refused to hold on to power even when he could.
    D. His inauguration was attended by important people from all over the world.

Questions 26-29

Most people feel stressed about job interviews because they are unsure what kind of behavior is expected. Indeed, every interview is unique, for the skills and personalities required for every position are different. Thankfully, there are some general principles you can follow. Below are some tips that can increase your chances of success.

- **Rehearse before the interview.** Try to imagine yourself as the interviewer. What kind of questions would you ask? List as many questions as you can think of. Recalling what you have been asked before in similar interviews will also help. You will definitely have to be prepared for some frequently asked questions (FAQs), which usually include job experience, education background, personal aspirations, strengths, and weaknesses. You may feel strange to talk to yourself in this way, but such practice can ease your nerves.
- **Dress appropriately.** Ideally, you should wear just the way employees in the company do. If you are not sure, it is always safer to look formal than casual. Some people feel uneasy in business attire because they are not used to it. In that case, it is advisable to wear the clothes several times before the interview.
- **Be confident.** A frightened look or unsure attitude can immediately spoil an interview. You should maintain eye contact with your interviewer and speak calmly, not hesitantly. Sit up straight and avoid scratching your head or playing with your hair. Such unnecessary hand movements are often considered as signs of lacking self-control.
- **Do research on the company.** With some basic knowledge about the company you want to work at, you can talk as if you are ready to hit the ground running on your first day of employment. The interviewer will know that you are serious about the job you apply for and be impressed by your effort.

Please turn to the next page.

26. What is the best title for this article?
    A. Relaxation techniques for handling job interviews
    B. General guidelines for typical job interviews
    C. Preparing for peculiar types of job interviews
    D. Ideal dress code required for all job interviews

27. Which of the following may **NOT** be a preparation method for an interview that the author would recommend?
    A. Obtain insider information about the interviewer's preferences
    B. Try to wear formally more often
    C. Rehearse answers to questions most likely to be asked
    D. Carry out background research on the prospective company

28. According to this article, what kind of strategy can we adopt to leave a good impression on interviewers?
    A. Scratching our heads to look humble
    B. Stammering so that we speak slower
    C. Keeping our composure to look reliable
    D. Inflating our strengths so that we appear superior

29. According to this article, why is body language important for job applicants during interviews?
    A. It is a criterion that interviewers may judge them with.
    B. It is the only thing that counts during an interview.
    C. It allows them to read other people's mind.
    D. It protects us from physical injury.

Questions 30-34 are based on the information provided in the following article and email.

The PLAT Diet: It Really Works!

Are you tired of diets that do not work? Then you should try the PLAT diet, which originated in Japan in 2005. Many women have sworn by its results. Although the diet has not been backed up by scientific research, multiple testimonials proved that it is effective for almost everyone, and its effect can last several months. Even though there are side effects such as having difficulty swallowing or breathing, the results are miraculous. Some participants lost 50 lbs in two weeks. There are even stars, such as Biancé, who have started to follow this trend.

The PLAT diet is simple: for two weeks straight, eat nothing but apples, lettuce leaves and rice, and drink one gallon of water every day. Also note that you should avoid eating things after 3 P.M. After you finish a cycle, remember to stop and return to your normal diet for at least a week. After you lose weight successfully with this method, please email your testimonial to weightlossmagazine@losethefat.com.

From: Felicia Patricia <feliciap@eurekamail.com>
To: <weightlossmagazine@losethefat.com>
Subject: On your article about PLAT diet

Dear Weight Loss Magazine,

My name is Felicia Patricia, and I'm writing to voice my concern over the PLAT diet introduced in your March issue. My sister, who has used the diet, is still hospitalized for its serious side effects.

She has battled with her weight for the past ten years. Every month, she reads every single page of your magazine. Finally, she came across the PLAT diet. She immediately decided to try it, and she saw some results. However, she also showed signs of malnutrition, such as tiredness and depression. I begged her to stop, but she just kept eating apples, lettuce, and rice and not having dinner. She also kept going to the bathroom because of drinking a lot of water.

After dieting non-stop for several months, one day she fainted in the bathroom with the most uncomfortable stomach ache and diarrhea. I sent her to a hospital and was told that her kidneys were starting to fail. This email is to let you know that there are people out there suffering from the side effects of the risky diet, and I ask you to only publish articles that are supported by scientific evidence.

Regards,
Felicia Patricia

30. What is true about the PLAT diet?
    A. It was invented in Japan.
    B. Its effects have been scientifically proven.
    C. It poses no risks for health.
    D. Biancé started the trend of using it.

31. What does Felicia want to tell the magazine in her email?
    A. The PLAT diet does not work.
    B. The method of the PLAT diet needs to be improved.
    C. The magazine should compensate her sister.
    D. It was irresponsible to publish the article on the PLAT diet.

32. According to Felicia, what did **NOT** happen to her sister?
    A. She felt down.
    B. She had an upset stomach.
    C. She vomited.
    D. She had kidney failure.

33. In the things that Felicia's sister did, what is different from the PLAT diet introduced in the article?
    A. Eating apples, lettuce, and rice
    B. Not having dinner
    C. Drinking a lot of water
    D. Dieting continuously for several months

34. What do we learn about *Weight Loss Magazine*?
    A. It tries to invent weight loss methods.
    B. Some of its articles are written by its readers.
    C. It is a monthly magazine.
    D. Its articles are reviewed by scientists.

Please turn to the next page.

Questions 35-40

With new breakthroughs in stem cell technology, the life span of human beings are expected to exceed a century and beyond. Stem cells can be divided into two categories: embryonic stem cells and adult stem cells. The former can come from human eggs fertilized in vitro in a laboratory, while the latter are found in fully developed human body. Unlike embryonic stem cells, adult stem cells only have the ability to transform into the same type of cells as in the tissue or organ from which it came. Bone marrow, for instance, can only regenerate bone marrow. On the other hand, embryonic stem cells can, theoretically, be cultivated into ANY type of cell found in the body. By manipulating embryonic stem cells, it is possible to make "custom-made" spare organs that will not incur any risk of rejection while transplanting.

In spite of the optimism of future medical breakthroughs in stem cell technology, many legal, ethical, and religious issues need to be tackled before this technology can be unleashed to reach its full potential. For example, some argue that killing lab-grown embryos to get stem cells is nothing different from abortion. The fact that fertilized human eggs are used for experimental and research purposes is considered unethical and even contrary to many religious beliefs. Scientists in favor of stem-cell technology have reiterated that an embryo is not a fetus (unborn baby) and obtaining embryonic cells is not equivalent to abortion. The problem lies in that it is hard to pinpoint exactly where life starts.

Some leading experts in stem cell technology have urged the public to separate science from religion. Researchers believe that technologies developed from their work will eventually be able to treat a wide variety of illnesses such as cancer, diabetes, and heart diseases. "We are entering a new era of science known as regenerative medicine," a scientist claimed.

There is a vision of a promising distant future among the most optimistic supporters, who believe that organ transplantation will be as common as changing spare parts for cars and machines. As a result, life expectancy is likely to increase dramatically. The elixir of life that eluded emperors and kings of the past could finally be found in our lifetime.

35. What is true about embryonic stem cells?
   A. They are not as useful as adult stem cells.
   B. They are of significant medical value.
   C. They can be extracted from young adults.
   D. They can be cultivated in young women

36. What is the main difference between adult and embryonic stem cells?
   A. Adult stem cells do not raise religious and ethical concerns.
   B. Adult stem cells can be cultivated into embryonic stem cells.
   C. Adult stem cells are riskier, while embryonic stem cells are safer.
   D. Adult stem cells are not as flexible as embryonic stem cells.

37. Which of the following patients is most likely to benefit from stem cell technology?
   A. Someone who is infected with a deadly virus
   B. Someone who suffers from kidney failure
   C. Someone who is paralyzed after a major car accident
   D. Someone who suffers from memory loss due to dementia

38. What accounts for a high success rate of treatment via stem cells developed from the patient?
   A. These cells are cultivated using state-of-the-art technology.
   B. These cells are able to transform into any organ the body needs.
   C. These cells are accepted by the immune system as part of the body.
   D. These cells can also be used to treat other patients with similar conditions.

39. In the opinion of some optimists, what does the future hold for stem cell technology?
   A. Stem cell technology will be a highly lucrative venture.
   B. Patients will be able to sell their body parts to hospitals.
   C. Human life span will be prolonged due to replaceable organs.
   D. Businesses will engage in sales of organs and organ transplantation.

Please turn to the next page.

40. What is the primary controversy regarding the use of embryonic stem cells?
    A. Embryonic stem cells are not 100% reliable.
    B. Embryonic stem cells are affecting our fertility.
    C. Embryonic stem cells are seen as potential babies.
    D. Embryonic stem cells are only available for the rich.

第四回 初試 聽力測驗解析

第一部分 回答問題

Q1

I have a skin rash all over my body on warm days like today. Or perhaps it is because of the material of my clothes. 在像今天一樣熱的日子，我全身皮膚就會起疹子。又或者是因為我衣服的材質。

A. Let's find some shade. A. 我們找個遮蔭的地方吧。
B. Let me check the price. B. 讓我看看價錢。
C. Let's put on some makeup. C. 我們化點妝吧。
D. Let's get some cold medicine. D. 我們買些感冒藥吧。

詳解 答案：A

這一題如果聽出關鍵詞 skin rash（皮膚的疹子）會比較容易答對。說話者說自己在 warm days like today（在像今天一樣熱的日子）會起疹子，或者是因為 the material of my clothes（我衣服的材質）才會這樣（起疹子）。選項中和題目比較相關的是 A，shade 表示陰涼的地方，也就是建議去不那麼熱的地方，是適當的回應。題目裡的 warm 雖然通常是「溫暖」的意思，但有時也表示「有點熱」的意思。

|單字片語| **rash** [ræʃ] n. 疹子 / **shade** [ʃed] 遮蔭處，陰涼處

Q2

Hi. I was told to come here to get a scholarship application form. By the way, when is the deadline?
嗨。我被告知要來這裡拿獎學金申請表。對了，截止期限是什麼時候？

A. I'm afraid you have already missed it. A. 恐怕你已經錯過了。
B. It will be dead by this weekend. B. 它會在這週結束之前死掉。
C. Whenever you are ready. C. 只要你準備好的時候。
D. It will expire in about a month. D. 會在大約一個月之後到期。

詳解

答案：A

說話者說自己來 get a scholarship application form（拿獎學金申請表），然後問 when is the deadline?（截止期限是什麼時候），所以必須回答關於截止期限的資訊。A 回答「恐怕你已經錯過了」，表示截止期限過了，是正確答案。B 雖然回答了時間，但我們不會用 It will be dead（它會死掉）來表示期限到了。C 應該是對於 When can I apply? 之類問題的回答，但說話者問的是 deadline 的時間，和「你準備好與否」沒有關係，所以這個選項不對。選項 D 用了動詞 expire（期滿，到期），主詞會是合約或食物等等，用在這裡並不恰當。

|單字片語| **application form** 申請表 / **expire** [ɪk`spaɪr] v. 期滿，到期

Q3

Please remove any liquids in your carry-on luggage, or they will be confiscated.

請移除您隨身行李中的任何液體，否則會被沒收。

A. I think the outer case is solid. A. 我想外殼很堅固。

B. I keep my passport and cash in it. B. 我把我的護照和現金放在裡面。

C. I'll empty them right away. C. 我會馬上清空。

D. Thanks, but I can handle it myself. D. 謝謝，但我可以自己處理。

詳解

答案：C

說話者要求 Please remove any liquids（請移除任何液體），並且說不這樣做的話 they will be confiscated（它們會被沒收），所以必須對這個要求作出反應。A、B 和題目無關。C 用動詞 empty（清空）表示會把容器清空、排除液體，是正確答案。empty 雖然常當成形容詞「空的」使用，但也可以當成動詞，表示「清空」。D 應該是對於 May I help you? 之類問題的回應，但這裡的說話者是提出要求，而不是想要幫忙，所以這不是適當的答案。

|單字片語| **carry-on luggage** 帶上飛機的隨身行李 / **confiscate** [`kɑnfɪs͵ket] v. 沒收

Q4

You have made an excellent choice. Would you like some wine to go along with the main course?

您選得很好。您想要來點酒搭配主菜嗎？

A. Shouldn't we use the main entrance? A. 我們不是應該用主要入口嗎？

B. Why don't we join the rest? B. 我們何不加入其他人呢？

C. What do you recommend? C. 你推薦什麼？

D. How could you cancel the course? D. 你怎麼可以取消課程呢？

詳解

答案：C

說話者問 Would you like some wine（你想要一點酒嗎），所以必須回答是否想要喝酒；後面的 main course（主菜）顯示這裡應該是餐廳。C 反問對方推薦什麼，暗示自己是想要喝酒的，希望對方建議酒的種類，是正確答案。其他選項都沒有回答到問題，而 A 和 D 是藉由題目中出現的 main、course 製造的混淆選項。請注意 course 有「一道菜」或「課程」的意思。

|單字片語| **course** [kors] n. 課程；一道菜

Q5

It doesn't look serious, but we should be cautious. How long has it been since you discovered such symptoms?

看起來不嚴重，但我們應該謹慎。你發現這些症狀多久了？

A. I've been practicing for almost a year. A. 我練習了將近一年。
B. I've done it many times in the past. B. 我以前做過很多次。
C. The swelling started about a week ago. C. 腫脹大約是一個禮拜之前開始的。
D. The symphony ended long before you came. D. 交響樂在你來的很久之前就結束了。

詳解

答案：C

說話者問 How long has it been（有多久了），而且後面提到關鍵字 symptom（症狀），應該回答症狀的持續期間。所以，雖然選項 A、C、D 都提到了持續期間或時間，但只有 C 說到症狀 swelling（腫脹），所以 C 是正確答案，而其他答案和問題無關。選項 D 利用 symptom 和 symphony 相近的發音製造混淆，要注意。

|單字片語| **symptom** [ˋsɪmptəm] n. 症狀 / **swelling** [ˋswɛlɪŋ] n. 腫脹 / **symphony** [ˋsɪmfənɪ] n. 交響樂

Q6

Could you tell us if you are satisfied with our product and the service we provide?

可否告訴我們你是否對我們的產品和提供的服務感到滿意？

A. I have bought enough local products already.
B. Matters are a little complicated at the moment.
C. The former is great, but the latter is impersonal.
D. Whoever serves the ball has the advantage.

A. 我已經買了足夠的本地產品。
B. 事情目前有點複雜。
C. 前者很好，但後者冷淡。
D. 只要是發球的人就會有優勢。

詳解

答案：C

說話者用 Could you tell us... 詢問對方的意見，問題是 if you are satisfied with our product and the service we provide（你是否滿意我們的產品和我們提供的服務），需要針對這兩者表達自己的意見。B 比較適合用來表達感情、局勢等等情況複雜的狀態，但題目是詢問對於事物滿意度的主觀感受，所以不適合用這個選項回答。C 以 the former... the latter...（前者＝產品，後者＝服務）的句型分別表達對兩者的意見，是正確答案。

|單字片語| **impersonal** [ɪm`pɝsn̩l] adj. 沒有人情味的 / **serve** [sɝv] v. 服務；供應；發（球）

Q7

Remember what I told you about establishing good relations with your new colleagues? How's it going?

你記得我告訴你關於和新同事建立良好關係的事嗎？進展得如何？

A. My classmates are fun to hang out with.
B. Just go straight and then take a left.
C. I have a slight cough and a sore back.
D. They just mind their own business.

A. 我的同學相處起來很有趣。
B. 只要直走然後左轉。
C. 我有輕微的咳嗽和背痛。
D. 他們只管自己的事情。

詳解

答案：D

題目最後的 How's it going? 是問別人「最近過得怎樣？」的說法，但還需要注意前面提到 establishing good relations with your new colleagues（和新同事建

立良好關係），所以回答要和職場人際關係相關。選項 A 回答 My classmates...，和題目詢問的事情不符合。選項 B 是對於 How should I go there? 之類問題的回答。選項 C 回答健康狀況，也不符合題目。選項 D 用 They 代稱 my new colleagues，說他們 just mind their own business（只管自己的事情），暗示他們不太和自己往來，關係並不好，是適當的答案。

|單字片語| **hang out** 消磨時間 / **mind one's own business** 管自己的事

Q8

Can you put everything back on the shelves after you finish labeling them?

你把東西都貼好標籤以後，可以全部放回架上嗎？

A. What's done cannot be undone. A. 已經做了的事就無法收回了。
B. Your wish is my command. B. 你的願望我都會實現。
C. Nothing will ever remain the same. C. 沒有什麼會保持相同。
D. I am allergic to seafood. D. 我對海鮮過敏。

詳解 答案：B

說話者用 Can you put everything back（你可以把東西都放回去嗎）提出要求，所以必須回答自己是否會照做。選項 B 表示「你的願望就是給我的命令」，表示對方想要的自己都會照做，是正確答案。這句話有點「古老」，會在古裝戲裡聽到，但現代人其實也可以用這句話，而且通常是男性對女性說。請注意不要把 shelves 聽成 shell（貝殼）而誤選 D。

|單字片語| **label** [ˋlebḷ] n. 標籤 v. 貼標籤 / **command** [kəˋmænd] n. 命令 v. 命令 / **allergic** [əˋlɝdʒɪk] adj. 過敏的

Q9

It says that we have to pay the parking fee using the automated machine.

這上面說我們必須用自動機器付停車費。

A. Here you are. Could I have a receipt? A. 拿去。我可以拿張收據嗎？
B. Buckle up. I'm going to step on it. B. 繫好安全帶。我要加速了。
C. Oh, I left the parking token in the car. C. 噢，我把停車代幣留在車子裡了。
D. I didn't know that I couldn't park here. D. 我不知道我不能在這裡停車。

詳解

答案：C

說話者可能在敘述某個標示上的文字（It says...），說必須用自動機器（automated machine）付停車費（parking fee），要選擇相關的回答。選項 B 和 D 分別提到開車和停車的事情，但和付停車費無關。選項 A 是在付帳或者交錢給收費員時會說的話。選項 C 說自己把 parking token（停車代幣）留在車子裡了，暗示需要先去拿停車代幣，才能用機器繳費，是正確答案。

|單字片語| **automated** [ˋɔtometɪd] adj. 自動化的 / **buckle up** 繫好安全帶 / **step on it** 加速，趕快 / **token** [ˋtokən] n. 代幣 /

Q10

It's hard to find accommodation during the peak season. Why don't you put up at my aunt's place?

旺季很難找到住宿處。你何不住在我阿姨家呢？

A. Are you worried about the crowd? A. 你擔心人潮嗎？
B. Are you sure that's a good idea? B. 你確定這是個好主意嗎？
C. Are you always so indecisive? C. 你總是這麼猶豫不決嗎？
D. Are you keen on reaching the top? D. 你很渴望登上巔峰嗎？

詳解

答案：B

說話者說 It's hard to find accommodation（很難找到住宿處），提議 put up at my aunt's place（暫住在我阿姨家）。四個選項都以問句回覆，其中 B 反問「這是個好主意嗎」，表示不確定是否應該這樣做，是適當的答案。選項 A、D 和題目無關，而 D 是利用 peak 和 top 的意義相似性製造的混淆選項。選項 C 說對方猶豫不決，但情況應該是回答者要為自己做決定才對。

|單字片語| **accommodation** [əˏkɑməˋdeʃən] n. 住處 / **peak season** 旺季 / **put up** 暫住，過夜 / **indecisive** [ˏɪndɪˋsaɪsɪv] adj. 猶豫不決的 / **be keen on** 熱衷於⋯

Q11

M: You should enroll for Mr. Jones's literature class. He is really innovative, and he makes the characters in the classics come alive. 你應該報名 Jones 老師的文學課。他真的很創新，讓經典作品裡的角色都活起來了。

W: What's so special about the way he teaches? 他教學的方法有什麼特別？

M: Last semester, he assigned roles to each of us. We pretended to be the characters in the story and then wrote a paper based on how we felt. 上學期，他分配角色給我們每個人。我們假裝是故事裡的人物，然後寫出關於我們感覺如何的報告。

W: Sounds kind of interesting. 聽起來有點趣味。

M: The best part is discussing what we would do if we could travel back in time and become the characters we were playing as. 最好的部分是討論我們如果能回到過去，並且成為自己扮演的角色的話，我們會怎麼做。

W: I must say I am tempted. 我必須說我心動了。

M: What are you waiting for, then? 那你還在等什麼呢？

Q: Why does the man like Mr. Jones's literature class?
男子為什麼喜歡 Jones 老師的文學課？

A. He can explore ancient ruins. A. 他可以探索古老的廢墟。
B. He can pretend to be a teacher. B. 他可以裝作老師。
C. He can read and write poems. C. 他可以讀詩、寫詩。
D. He can imagine living in a story. D. 他可以想像活在故事裡。

詳解 **答案：D**

男子開頭建議女子報名 Mr. Jones's literature class（Jones 老師的文學課），女子問他 What's so special（是什麼這麼特別），所以男子說明課堂上的活動：he assigned roles to each of us（他分配角色給我們每個人）、We pretended to be the characters in the story（我們假裝是故事裡的人物），又說 The best part（最好的部分）是 discussing what we would do if we could... become the characters（討論如果能成為角色的話會怎麼做）。符合這些敘述的 D 是正確答案。

|單字片語| **enroll for** 報名參加… / **innovative** [ˋɪno͵vetɪv] adj. 創新的 / **classic** [ˋklæsɪk] adj. 經典的 n. 經典作品 / **tempted** [ˋtɛmptɪd] adj. 有興趣的，被吸引的 / **ruins** [ˋruɪnz] n. 廢墟，遺跡

Q12

W: Johnny, how many times do I need to remind you to separate the white garments from the rest?
Johnny，我要提醒你多少次把白色衣服和其他衣服分開呢？

M: I'm sorry, Mom. May I ask why we need to do that?
對不起，媽。我可以問為什麼需要這樣做嗎？

W: Because I use bleach to clean the white shirts, and if you throw in any colored shirts, they will be ruined. 因為我用漂白劑清潔白襯衫，如果你丟進任何有顏色的襯衫，它們就會被毀掉。

M: Oh. No wonder my blue jacket turned purple.
噢。難怪我的藍色外套變成紫色了。

W: Doing household chores isn't as easy as you think, son. It requires a certain amount of knowledge. I hope they will teach you that in home economics. 兒子，做家事沒有你想的那麼簡單。做家事需要一定程度的知識。我希望他們在家政課會教你。

M: I used to think that was a girl's subject. 我一直覺得那是女生的科目。

W: Cooking also sounds like what a woman should do, right? Prepare your own breakfast then.
煮菜聽起來也像是女人應該做的事，是嗎？那你就做自己的早餐。

Q: What does the mother expect her son to do?
媽媽希望她的兒子做什麼？

A. Get better grades in school.	A. 在學校得到更好的成績。
B. Avoid having a relationship with a girl.	B. 避免和女孩子發展關係。
C. Take doing housework seriously.	C. 認真看待做家事這件事。
D. Develop an interest in fashion design.	D. 對時尚設計產生興趣。

詳解 **答案：C**

女子稱呼男子為 Johnny, son，男子稱女子為 Mom，可以確認他們的母子關係。媽媽要求 separate the white garments from the rest（把白色衣服和其他衣服分開），Johnny 問 why do we need to do that?（為什麼需要這樣做），於是媽媽解釋了原因，之後又說 Doing household chores isn't as easy as you think（做家事沒有你想的那麼簡單），所以 C 是正確答案，這裡用 housework 來表示對話中所說的 household chores。

|單字片語| **garment** [ˋgɑrmənt] n. 衣服，服裝 / **bleach** [blitʃ] n. 漂白劑 v. 漂白 / **ruin** [ˋruɪn] v. 毀壞 / **chores** [tʃorz] n. 家庭雜務 / **home economics** 家政學

Q13

M: Could you pass me the sports section? Thanks. What are you reading? 你可以把體育版拿給我嗎？謝謝。你在讀什麼？

W: I'm checking my horoscope. My lucky number for today is five, and my lucky color is violet. I do have a purple dress.
我在看我的星座運勢。我今天的幸運號碼是 5，幸運色是紫羅蘭色。我是有一件紫色的洋裝。

M: Do you really believe in that kind of thing? I never care about stars and signs. 你真的相信那種東西？我從來不在乎星星和星座。

W: I'd better get going because it says I may meet someone important on my way to work.
我最好出發了，因為它說我上班途中可能遇到重要的人。

M: Maybe you will get booked by a police officer for speeding. That would be someone important.
或許你會被警察登記超速駕駛。那就是重要的人了。

W: Thank you for being sarcastic. 謝謝你這麼諷刺。

Q: How is the man's attitude?
男子的態度是什麼？

A. Supportive.	A. 支持的。
B. Considerate.	B. 體貼的。
C. Detached.	C. 超然的。
D. Skeptical.	D. 懷疑的。

詳解　　答案：D

女子說 I'm checking my horoscope（我在看我的星座運勢），並且描述其中的內容。男子則反問 Do you really believe in that kind of thing?（你真的相信那種東西嗎）；女子說運勢提到她會遇見 someone important，男子又說 Maybe you will get booked by a police officer... That would be someone important（或許你會被警察登記在案⋯那就是重要的人了）來諷刺她，所以最能表示男子態度的選項是 D。

|單字片語| **section** [ˋsɛkʃən] n. 部分 / **horoscope** [ˋhɔrəˌskop] n. 占星術，星座運勢預測 / **sign** [saɪn] 符號；黃道十二宮的其中一宮 / **get going** 出發，動身 / **book** [bʊk] v. （警察）把某人登記在案 / **speeding** [ˋspidɪŋ] n. 超速行車 / **sarcastic** [sɑrˋkæstɪk] adj. 諷刺的

Q14

W: Did you read the notice on the bulletin board?
你讀過佈告欄上的通知了嗎？

M: Yes, I just did. I can't believe the company's cost-cutting measures include staff welfare. I mean, how much can beverage and snacks cost? 有，我剛讀了。我不敢相信公司削減成本的措施包括員工福利。我的意思是，飲料和零食能花多少錢呢？

W: The concern is not about money. Someone has been taking tea bags and coffee powder home instead of consuming them in the office. Even sugar and napkins are missing. 讓人擔心的不是錢。有人一直把茶包和咖啡粉拿回家，而不是在辦公室使用。就連糖和紙巾都不見了。

M: What? Then they should find those to blame instead of punishing everybody. 什麼？那他們應該找出要負責的人，不是處罰每個人。

W: Maybe they should install a security camera in the pantry.
或許他們應該在食品儲藏室裡安裝監視攝影機。

M: Any suspects in mind? 你有想到什麼嫌疑犯嗎？

W: I would rather keep my mouth shut. 我寧可保持沉默。

Q: How come beverage and snacks are no longer provided?　為什麼不再提供飲料和零食了？

A. Certain staff abused the system.　A. 有些員工濫用制度。
B. Staff welfare is not beneficial.　B. 員工福利沒有助益。
C. A security camera was installed.　C. 安裝了監視攝影機。
D. Money has been missing.　D. 錢一直不見。

詳解　　**答案：A**

對話中提到飲料和零食的地方是男子說的 how much can beverage and snacks cost?（飲料和零食能花多少錢呢）。他之所以說到這件事，是為了補充上一句說的 the company's cost-cutting measures include staff welfare（公司削減成本的措施包括員工福利），可知飲料和零食曾經是公司的福利，但被削減了。對於男子所說的話，女子回應 Someone has been taking tea bags and coffee powder home instead of consuming them in the office.（有人一直把茶包和咖啡粉拿回家，而不是在辦公室使用），可見這應該是福利被取消的原因。選項 A 用 abuse the system（濫用制度）表達這種不當使用員工福利的行為，是正確答案。

|單字片語| **bulletin board** 佈告欄 / **welfare** [\`wɛl͵fɛr] n. 福利 / **beverage** [\`bɛvərɪdʒ] n. 飲料 / **napkin** [\`næpkɪn] n. 餐巾，餐巾紙 / **pantry** [\`pæntrɪ] n. 食品儲藏室 / **keep one's mouth shut** 保持沉默 / **abuse** [ə\`bjus] v. 濫用 / **beneficial** [͵bɛnə\`fɪʃəl] adj. 有益的

M: Did you see that? 你看到了嗎？

W: See what? 看到什麼？

M: That was a clear foul, but the referee waved "play on". I suspect that he favors the visiting team.
那是很明顯的犯規，但是裁判揮手表示「繼續」。我懷疑他偏袒客隊。

W: Don't jump to conclusions based on a single incident. Referees are humans, too. They make mistakes just like everybody else. 不要根據單一事件就直接下結論。裁判也是人。他們就像其他所有人一樣會犯錯。

M: Look! He missed another foul by the visiting team player again.
你看！他又放過了客隊球員的另一次犯規。

W: Just sit down. You are blocking the people behind us.
先坐下來。你擋住了我們後面的人。

M: The home team coach is furious, and he is protesting. At least he shares my feelings.
主隊教練很生氣，他正在抗議。至少他的感覺和我一樣。

Q: Who might the speakers be?
說話者可能是誰？

A. Soccer coaches.	A. 足球教練。
B. Referees.	B. 裁判。
C. Spectators.	C. 觀眾。
D. Commentators.	D. 實況播報員。

詳解

答案：C

兩人的對話中提到 foul（犯規）、referee（裁判）、visiting team（客隊）和 home team（主隊），可知他們正在看運動比賽。決定答案的關鍵是女子在對話後半說的 You are blocking the people behind us（你擋住了我們後面的人），表示後面還有人在觀看比賽，所以他們最有可能是觀眾，答案是 C。

|單字片語| **foul** [faʊl] n. 犯規 / **referee** [ˌrɛfə`ri] n. 裁判 / **wave** [wev] v. 揮手示意 / **visiting team** （相對於主場隊伍的）客隊 / **jump to conclusions** 匆匆作出結論 / **home team** 主場隊伍，主隊 / **furious** [`fjʊrɪəs] adj. 非常憤怒的 / **protest** [prə`tɛst] v. 抗議 / **spectator** [spɛk`tetɚ] n. （比賽的）觀眾 / **commentator** [`kɑmənˌtetɚ] n. 實況播報員

Q16

W: What's wrong with the vacuum cleaner? I have only used it a couple of times, but it is not working now.
這台吸塵器怎麼搞的？我才用了幾次，但它現在不動了。

M: I'm sorry about it, Miss. Let me take a quick look and see where the problem lies. 我很抱歉，小姐。讓我很快看一下，看看問題在哪裡。

W: Here's the warranty card. See the date? I bought it just a month ago.
這是保證書。看到日期了嗎？我一個月前才剛買的。

M: I think you blew a fuse. No worries. I can replace it immediately.
我想是保險絲燒壞了。別擔心。我可以馬上替換。

W: Do I have to pay for anything? This card says there will be a minimum service charge of a hundred NT dollars.
我需要付錢嗎？這張卡片說會有台幣 100 元的最低服務費。

M: Since the product is under warranty, all related costs will be handled by the company.
因為產品還在保固期，所以所有相關費用都會由公司負擔。

Q: How much does the woman need to pay?
女子需要付多少錢？

A. Exactly NT$100. A. 台幣 100 元整。
B. At least NT$100. B. 至少台幣 100 元。
C. She needs to pay for the parts. C. 她需要付零件費用。
D. She doesn't have to pay. D. 她不用付錢。

詳解

答案：D

四個選項都和付款金額有關，所以要注意對話中關於金額的敘述。女子問 Do I have to pay?（我需要付錢嗎），又說 This card says there will be a minimum service charge of a hundred NT dollars.（這張卡片說會有台幣 100 元的最低服務費），但男子回答因為產品 is under warranty（在保固期內），所以 all related costs will be handled by the company（所有相關費用都會由公司處理），也就是說費用公司負擔，女子不用處理，正確答案是 D。

|單字片語| **vacuum cleaner** 真空吸塵器 / **warranty** [ˋwɔrəntɪ] n. 產品保固，保固期 / **blow** [blo] v. 吹；燒斷（保險絲）〔過去式是 blew [blu]〕 / **fuse** [fjuz] n. 保險絲 / **minimum** [ˋmɪnəməm] adj. 最小的，最少的

M: Students who major in humanities should be more creative and better at expressing themselves. Don't you think so? 主修人文科目的學生，應該更有創意，而且更擅長表達自己。你不覺得嗎？

W: Not really. I have a roommate who majors in sociology, but she isn't sociable at all. We have tried to bring her out of her shell to no avail. 不盡然。我有個主修社會學的室友，但她完全不擅長交際。我們試過讓她走出自己的殼，但完全沒有用。

M: It's a misconception, then. I guess that means not all physicists and mathematicians are nerds. 那這就是誤解了。我猜這意味著不是所有物理學家和數學家都是書呆子。

W: I'm not so sure. I haven't met any mathematician with a sense of humor. They talk with numbers instead of words, if you know what I mean. 我不是很確定。我沒遇過有幽默感的數學家。他們都用數字而不是文字講話，如果你知道我是什麼意思的話。

M: I do. Most of them are not good at communication. 我知道。他們大部分都不擅長溝通。

Q: What are the speakers discussing?
說話者在討論什麼？

A. Subjects and personalities.	A. 科目和個性。
B. Mathematicians and physicists.	B. 數學家和物理學家。
C. Sociology and sociability.	C. 社會學和社交能力。
D. Words and numbers.	D. 文字和數字。

詳解 **答案：A**

女子提到 I have a roommate who majors in sociology, but she isn't sociable at all（我有個主修社會學的室友，但她完全不擅長交際），男子則回應 I guess that means not all physicists and mathematicians are nerds（我猜這意味著不是所有物理學家和數學家都是書呆子），而女子接著又說 I haven't met any mathematician with a sense of humor.（我沒遇過有幽默感的數學家）。他們討論的內容都和各個學術領域的人個性如何有關，所以 A 是正確答案。B 和 C 都只能涵蓋對話中談到的部分內容。

|單字片語| **humanities** [hju`mænətɪz] n. 人文學科 / **major in** 主修… / **sociology** [ˌsoʃɪ`ɑlədʒɪ] n. 社會學 / **sociable** [`soʃəbl̩] adj. 喜歡交際的，善於交際的 / **to no avail** 完全沒用 / **misconception** [ˌmɪskən`sɛpʃən] n. 錯誤的想法，誤解 / **physicist** [`fɪzɪsɪst] n. 物理學家 / **mathematician** [ˌmæθəmə`tɪʃən] n. 數學家 / **nerd** [nɝd] n. 沉溺於科學、科技等領域而不善交際的人 / **sense of humor** 幽默感 / **sociability** [ˌsoʃə`bɪlətɪ] n. 社交性，社交能力

Q18

W: Why am I still getting pimples? I have long passed the puberty stage.
為什麼我還是會長青春痘？我都已經過了青春期很久了。

M: Age is not the only factor. Pimples and acne problems are caused by the amount of oil our skin produces.
年齡不是唯一的因素。面皰問題是我們皮膚產生的油脂量造成的。

W: I wash my face three times a day. I am careful with my diet, too. How can I get rid of this problem?
我每天洗臉三次。我也很注意自己的飲食。我要怎樣擺脱這個問題呢？

M: It's not about the surface of your skin or what you eat. There's a medication that controls the oil level beneath your skin. I tried it, and it solved my acne problem once and for all.
不是處理你的皮膚表層或你吃的東西。有一種藥物可以控制你皮膚底層的油脂量。我試過了，它也一勞永逸地解決了我的面皰問題。

W: You're right. I haven't seen any pimple on your face for a long time.
你説的對。我很長一段時間沒看到你臉上有痘子了。

Q: What does the man suggest the woman do?
男子建議女子做什麼？

A. Wash her face regularly.	A. 定時洗臉。
B. Monitor her diet.	B. 注意飲食。
C. Take a kind of medicine.	C. 吃一種藥。
D. Apply oil on her skin.	D. 在皮膚上擦油。

詳解　　答案：C

女子一開始就提到自己的困擾：Why am I still getting pimples?（為什麼我還是會長青春痘），也說明自己因為想解決問題而 wash my face three times a day（每天洗臉三次）、am careful with my diet（注意自己的飲食）。但是，對於女子的努力，男子反駁說 It's not about the surface of your skin or what you eat（不是關於你的皮膚表層或你吃的東西），並且介紹說 There's a medication... it solved my acne problem（有一種藥解決了我的粉刺問題）。題目問的是男子的建議，所以 C 是正確答案。

單字片語 **pimple** [ˋpɪmpl] n. 粉刺，青春痘（指單一的痘子） / **puberty** [ˋpjubətɪ] n. 青春期 / **acne** [ˋæknɪ] n. 痤瘡，面皰（持續長出許多粉刺／青春痘的皮膚狀況） / **medication** [ˌmɛdɪˋkeʃən] n. 藥物治療，藥物 / **once and for all** 以做一次就處理好的心態，一勞永逸地

Q19

M: Don't you think you look a little out of place? Everybody else is wearing heavy coats and hiking boots. It's going to be cold up there. 你不覺得你看起來有點突兀嗎？其他每個人都穿著厚重的外套和登山靴。山上會很冷。

W: But you say you will be taking some pictures. I want to look great. 但你說你會拍一些照片。我希望自己看起來很棒。

M: That doesn't mean you should wear a gown with high heels. 那不代表你應該穿禮服配高跟鞋。

W: I don't care. Looking great in pictures is a top priority for women. Come on. It's summer, and I don't think it will get as cold as you said. 我不在乎。看起來上相是女人第一優先。拜託。現在是夏天，我覺得不會像你說的那麼冷。

M: I'm more worried about your safety. The snow up there is hard and slippery. 我比較擔心你的安全。山上的雪又硬又滑。

W: I can take care of myself. 我可以照顧自己。

M: If you say so. 既然你都這麼說了。

Q: What is the woman's problem?
女子的問題是什麼？

A. She is at the wrong place.	A. 她在錯誤的地方。
B. She is inappropriately dressed.	B. 她穿著不適當。
C. She is worried about her safety.	C. 她擔心自己的安全。
D. She is not photogenic.	D. 她不上相。

詳解 **答案：B**

選項都以 She 開頭，可以猜測要選出符合女子情況的答案，所以要注意關於她的敘述。男子先說 you look a little out of place（你看起來有點突兀），因為 Everybody else is wearing heavy coats and hiking boots.（其他每個人都穿著厚重的外套和登山靴），後面又說 That doesn't mean you should wear a gown with high heels.（那不代表你應該穿禮服配高跟鞋），可知女子穿了和別人不一樣的衣服，而男子認為她不應該這樣穿，從這幾句話就可以判斷答案是 B。

|單字片語| **out of place** 不在適當的位置，顯得不適合周遭情況的 / **gown** [gaʊn] n. 女性禮服 / **high heels** 高跟鞋 / **top priority** 最優先的事情 / **slippery** [ˋslɪpərɪ] adj. 滑的，容易滑的 / **inappropriately** [ˌɪnəˋproprɪɪtlɪ] adv. 不適當地 / **dressed** [drɛst] adj. 穿好衣服的 / **photogenic** [ˌfotəˋdʒɛnɪk] adj. （外貌方面）上鏡頭的，上相的

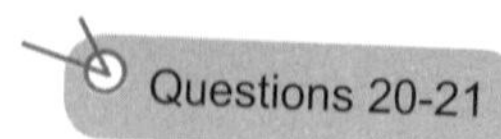

Questions 20-21

Questions number 20 and 21 are based on the following conversation.

M: Why are you being so difficult today? I don't understand why you're mad. 你今天怎麼這麼難搞？我不懂你為什麼生氣。

W: I'm mad because you were speaking to another woman, and you didn't want to tell me. Who is she?
我生氣是因為你跟其他女人講話，又不想告訴我。她是誰？

M: You don't need to know who she is. You just need to trust that I'm not doing anything wrong.
你不必知道她是誰。你只需要相信我不是在做不對的事。

W: Then why are you acting like you're hiding something?
那你怎麼表現得好像在隱藏什麼？

M: It's not what you think. You know what day tomorrow is? It's our wedding anniversary. I'm just trying not to ruin the surprise I've prepared for you. 不是你想的那樣。你知道明天是什麼日子嗎？是我們的結婚週年紀念日。我只是努力不要破壞我為你準備的驚喜。

W: Don't play games with me. Just be straight with me.
別跟我玩花樣。你只需要對我老實。

M: Alright. The woman you thought I was having a relationship with is actually the event coordinator for our special party.
好吧。你以為我在交往的女人其實是我們特別派對的活動企劃。

|單字片語| play games with 跟…玩花樣 / be straight with 對…老實 / event coordinator 活動企劃者

Q20

What has the man been doing? **男子之前在做什麼？**

A. He was cheating on his wife.	A. 他瞞著妻子外遇。
B. He was preparing a surprise for his wife.	B. 他在為妻子準備驚喜。
C. He was planning a birthday party.	C. 他在計劃生日派對。
D. He was trying to find a job.	D. 他在試圖找工作。

詳解 **答案：B**

女子質問跟男子交談的另一位女性是誰，男子則在對話中途提到 I'm just trying not to ruin the surprise I've prepared for you（我只是努力不要破壞我為你準備的驚喜），最後才說那位女性是 the event coordinator for our special party（我們特別派對的活動企劃），所以 B 是正確答案。另外，他們要慶祝的是 wedding anniversary（結婚週年紀念日），所以 C 不正確。

Q21

What is true about the man and the woman?
關於男子和女子，何者正確？

A. The man has lost interest in his wife. A. 男子對他的妻子失去興趣了。
B. The woman has faith in her husband. B. 女子對他的丈夫有信心。
C. They got married not long ago. C. 他們是不久之前結婚的。
D. They will have a party tomorrow. D. 他們明天會開派對。

詳解 **答案：D**

A 和 B 在對話中沒有提到。男子提到明天是他們的 wedding anniversary（結婚週年紀念日），表示他們至少結婚一年了，所以 C 不正確。因為明天是結婚紀念日，而且男子找了 event coordinator（活動企劃）來準備 special party（特別派對），可知明天會開結婚紀念派對，所以 D 是正確答案。

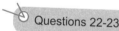

Questions number 22 and 23 are based on the following conversation.

M: Your baby is so cute! She really takes after you. She doesn't look like her father at all.
你的嬰兒真可愛！她真的很像你。她看起來完全不像她爸爸。

W: Thank you. I was kind of hoping that would be the case because Joe has a weird head. I don't want my daughter to grow up like that.
謝謝。我之前就有點希望會是這樣，因為喬的頭型很怪。我不想要我的女兒長成那樣。

M: You're so brutally honest! By the way, how old is she?
你真是太直白了！對了，她多大了？

W: About eight months now. She already began eating solid food, and she likes everything I make for her. 現在大約八個月。她已經開始吃固體食物了，而且她喜歡我為她做的每種食物。

M: That's great! I thought you'd have a hard time taking care of her since you have no experience before.
太好了！我以為你照顧她會很辛苦，因為你之前沒有經驗。

W: It's not easy, but fortunately, my mother-in-law lives nearby, so she can come whenever I need help. 這並不容易，但是幸好我婆婆住在附近，所以每當我需要幫忙的時候她都可以來。

M: What about your husband? 那你的丈夫呢？

W: He works overtime every day and says he's too exhausted to help. 他每天加班，而且說他太累了沒辦法幫忙。

|單字片語| **take after** 長得像（家族中的長輩） / **brutally** [ˋbrutḷɪ] adv. 殘忍地 / **mother-in-law** n. 婆婆或岳母

Q22

Who is the woman most likely to be?
女子最有可能是什麼人？

A. A babysitter. A. 保姆。
B. A career woman. B. 職業婦女。
C. A first-time mother. C. 新手媽媽。
D. A single mother. D. 單親媽媽。

詳解

答案：C

男子在對話開頭就提到 Your baby（你的嬰兒），表示女子是媽媽。在對話中途，男子又提到 you have no experience before（你之前沒有經驗），表示女子之前沒有照顧小孩的經驗，所以 C 是正確答案。

Q23

What is true about the woman's husband?
關於女子的丈夫，何者正確？

A. His daughter looks like him. A. 他的女兒長得像他。
B. His mother lives in the neighborhood. B. 他的母親住在附近。
C. He has a light workload. C. 他的工作量很少。
D. He sometimes helps with the baby. D. 他有時候幫忙照顧嬰兒。

詳解

答案：B

A. 男子說 She doesn't look like her father（她看起來不像她爸爸），表示女子的丈夫和女兒長得不像，不符合選項敘述。B. 女子說 my mother-in-law lives nearby（我婆婆住在附近），而妻子的 mother-in-law 就是指丈夫的母親，nearby

和 in the neighborhood 意思相近，符合選項敘述，所以 B 是正確答案。C. D. 女子說 He works overtime every day and says he's too exhausted to help（他每天加班，而且說他太累了沒辦法幫忙），表示她的丈夫工作繁忙，而且沒有幫忙照顧嬰兒，不符合選項敘述。

|單字片語| **workload** [ˋwɝkˏlod] n. 工作量

For question number 24, please look at the graph.

M: Welcome to *Education Time*. I'm your host Gary Madison, and this is our guest Sherry Wang. 歡迎來到《教育時間》。我是你的主持人蓋瑞・麥迪森，這位是我們的來賓雪莉・王。

W: Hi, everyone. I'm the dean of computer science at Jian-Hua University. I'm here to talk about how our student population has grown in the past few years. At first, there were no international students at all.
大家好。我是建華大學的計算機科學院長。我來這裡是要談我們的學生人數在過去幾年是如何成長的。一開始完全沒有外籍生（國際學生）。

M: How has your university become popular for international students? 貴校是怎麼變得受到外籍生歡迎的呢？

W: In the year when I started, we began to have classes in English, and that's when we had our first batch of international students. 在我開始任職的那年，我們開始有用英語上的課，那時候我們有了第一批外籍生。

M: That's fascinating. I think your international marketing efforts also play an important role. Would you agree? 聽起來不錯。我認為你們國際行銷方面的努力也扮演重要角色。您同意嗎？

M: I think so. Our international students started to multiply in the year we began advertising abroad, and the increase covered the decrease of local students. 我認為是的。我們的外籍生在我們開始對國外宣傳的那年開始倍增，外籍生的增加彌補了本國學生的減少。

|單字片語| **dean** [din] n. 學院院長 / **batch** [bætʃ] n. 一批 / **marketing** [ˋmɑrkɪtɪŋ] n. 行銷

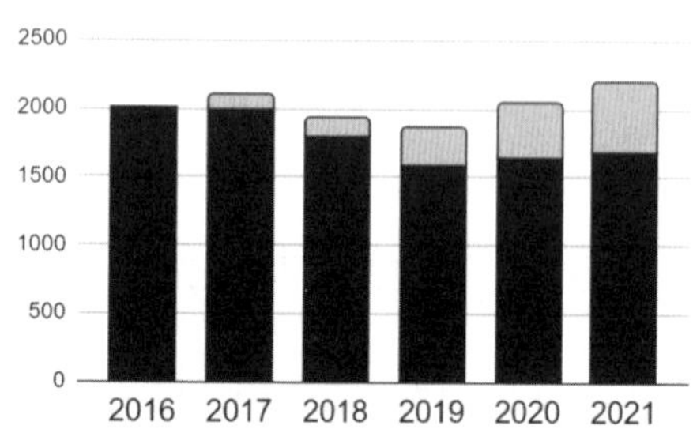

Q: Based on the woman's description, when did she start to be the dean of computer science at Jian-Hua University?

根據女子的敘述，她什麼時候開始成為建華大學的計算機科學院長？

A. In 2017.
B. In 2018.
C. In 2019.
D. In 2020.

A. 在 2017 年。
B. 在 2018 年。
C. 在 2019 年。
D. 在 2020 年。

詳解

答案：A

因為圖表中的資訊顯示答案和學生人數有關，所以要特別注意對話中談到這方面的部分。和題目有關的內容，是女子所說的 In the year when I started, we began to have classes in English, and that's when we had our first batch of international students.（在我開始任職的那年，我們開始有用英語上的課，那時候我們有了第一批外籍生），可知她開始任職的年份是外籍生開始出現的 2017 年，所以 A 是正確答案。

Q25

For question number 25, please look at the list of vacation packages.

M: I think it's time that we go out and travel to a new place. My company is giving us discounts on some vacation packages, and

here are the prices. What do you think?
我想是時候讓我們出門去新的地方旅遊了。我的公司正提供我們一些度假套裝方案的折扣，價錢在這裡。你覺得呢？

W: How about we choose from the islands in Europe? It would be even better if we could stay there for a whole week. 我們從歐洲的島嶼裡面選擇怎麼樣？如果我們能在那裡待一整個禮拜就更好了。

M: I wish I could go there, too, but I think the price is too high. It's more affordable for us to choose something under 100,000 dollars. 我也希望我可以去那裡，但我認為價格太高了。選擇價格低於 100,000 元的，對我們而言比較負擔得起。

W: I guess you're right. We still have a big mortgage to pay. Let's go for something less expensive, but I insist that we have a week-long vacation. 我想你是對的。我們還有一大筆房貸要付。我們選比較不貴的吧，但我堅持我們要有一週的假期。

|單字片語| **affordable** [ə`fɔrdəbl̩] adj. 負擔得起的，買得起的 / **mortgage** [`mɔrgɪdʒ] n. （房屋的）抵押貸款

Asia 亞洲	
Bali 峇里島 7 days 七天 NT$ 85,000/person 每人 85,000 元	Maldives 馬爾地夫 5 days 五天 NT$ 72,000/person 每人 72,000 元
Europe 歐洲	
Malta 馬爾他 7 days 七天 NT$ 140,000/person 每人 140,000 元	Cyprus 賽浦勒斯 5 days 五天 NT$ 120,000/person 每人 120,000 元

Q: According to the conversation, where will the woman most likely choose to go on vacation?
根據這段對話，女子最有可能選擇去哪裡度假？

A. In Bali.
B. In Maldives.
C. In Malta.
D. In Cyprus

A. 峇里島。
B. 馬爾地夫。
C. 馬爾他。
D. 賽浦勒斯。

詳解

答案：A

雖然女子一開始提議 choose from the islands in Europe（從歐洲的島嶼裡面選擇），但男子說 It's more affordable for us to choose something under 100,000 dollars（選擇價格低於 100,000 元的，對我們而言比較負擔得起），表示歐洲的行程太貴了。對此，女子說 I guess you're right 表示同意，並且說 Let's go for something less expensive, but I insist that we have a week-long vacation（我們選比較不貴的吧，但我堅持我們要有一週的假期），列表中符合價格低於 100,000 元、時間長達一週（七天）等條件的是峇里島，所以 A 是正確答案。

第三部分／短篇獨白

Questions 26-27

Questions number 26 to 27 are based on the following announcement.

May I have your attention, please? Due to an unidentified piece of luggage found on the track, all trains will cease operation until further notice. As a safety precaution, all passengers and staff are to evacuate to the town square outside the train station. Please proceed in an orderly manner, giving priority to the elderly and those with children. There is no immediate threat, so there is no need to panic. I repeat. There is no need to panic. All emergency personnel are to make their way to platform three right now. This is not a drill. Gather your gear and report to the officer on duty.

請各位注意。由於軌道上發現來路不明的行李，所有列車將停止運行，直到進一步通知為止。作為安全預防措施，所有乘客及員工必須撤離至車站外的市鎮廣場。請遵守秩序，讓老年人以及有小孩的人優先。沒有立即的威脅性，所以不需要驚慌。我再說一次。不需要驚慌。所有緊急應對人員必須立刻前往第三月台。這不是演習。請準備好裝備，向值勤員警報到。

|單字片語| **unidentified** [ˌʌnaɪˋdɛntɪˌfaɪd] adj. 沒有辨認出來的，未知的 / **baggage** [ˋbægɪdʒ] n. 行李 / **track** [træk] 軌道 / **cease** [sis] v. 停止，終止 / **until further notice** 直到有進一步通知為止 / **precaution** [prɪˋkɔʃən] n. 預防措施 / **evacuate** [ɪˋvækjʊˌet] v. 撤離 / **proceed** [prəˋsid] v. 行進 / **orderly** [ˋɔrdəlɪ] adj. 守秩序的 / **threat** [θrɛt] n. 威脅，恐嚇 / **panic** [ˋpænɪk] n. 恐慌 v. 恐慌 / **make one's way** 前進 / **drill** [drɪl] n. 演習 / **on duty** 值勤的

Q26

According to the announcement, what should commuters do?

根據公告，通勤者應該做什麼？

A. Pick up luggage immediately.　A. 立即領取行李。
B. Leave the train station.　B. 離開車站。
C. Remain on the platforms.　C. 留在月台上。
D. Hide in the bomb shelter.　D. 躲到防空洞。

詳解

答案：B

題目中的 commuters（通勤者）就是指公告裡面的 passengers（乘客）。這段公告給予乘客的指示是 all passengers... are to evacuate to the town square outside the train station.（所有乘客必須撤離至車站外的市鎮廣場），所以答案是 B。即使不知道 evacuate（撤離）這個單字，也可以從 to the town square outside the train station 的部分判斷是要往站外移動。

|單字片語| **bomb shelter** （防止炸彈轟炸的）防空洞

Q27

What can be said about the announcement?
關於公告，我們可以推論什麼？

A. It is a routine fire drill.
B. There was an explosion.
C. Many children were injured.
D. Passengers may need to use other modes of transportation.

A. 這是定期的火災演習。
B. 發生了爆炸。
C. 許多小孩受傷了。
D. 乘客可能需要使用其他交通方式。

詳解

答案：D

結尾提到 This is not a drill.（這不是演習），所以 A 不對。B 和 C 在公告中沒有提到，而且中間說 There is no immediate threat.（沒有立即的威脅），表示還沒有發生嚴重的情況。公告開頭的 all trains will cease operation until further notice（所有列車將停止運行，直到進一步通知為止）表示暫時不能搭乘列車，所以 D 是正確答案。

|單字片語| **explosion** [ɪk`sploʒən] **n.** 爆炸 / **mode of transportation** 交通方式

Questions 28-29

Questions number 28 to 29 are based on the following telephone message.

Emily, this is Richard. I know you are not in the mood to talk. In that case, why not just listen to me? What happened during the meeting today was nothing personal. Everyone has the right to voice their opinions, whether they support your proposal or not. Simon is always prudent, and he meant no harm when he questioned your assumptions.

The fact that you could not convince him just shows that you had not done your research properly. We are not against you, but merely raising our concerns. You should not confuse constructive criticism with sarcasm. Your idea is bold and innovative. I have to give you credit for that. All you need to do is look into the doubts Simon pointed out. The next meeting is three days from now. I am sure you have adequate time to revise your plan.

Emily，我是 Richard。我知道你沒有心情說話，那樣的話，何不就聽我說呢？今天會議發生的事情完全不是針對（你）個人。每個人都有權利說出自己的意見，不管他們支不支持你的提案。Simon 總是很慎重，他質疑你的假設不是想要傷害你。你不能說服他的事實只是顯示你沒有做好研究。我們不是反對你，只是提出我們的擔憂。你不應該把建設性的批評和諷刺搞混。你的想法很大膽也很創新。我必須稱讚你這一點。你需要做的就是研究 Simon 指出的懷疑。下次會議是現在的三天之後。我相信你有足夠的時間修改你的計畫。

|單字片語| **be in the mood to do** 有心情做… / **personal** [ˋpɝsn̩l] adj. 個人的，針對個人的 / **voice** [vɔɪs] v. 說出 / **proposal** [prəˋpozl̩] n. 提案 / **prudent** [ˋprudn̩t] adj. 審慎的 / **assumption** [əˋsʌmpʃən] n. 假定 / **convince** [kənˋvɪns] v. 說服 / **concern** [kənˋsɝn] n. 擔心或關切的事 / **constructive** [kənˋstrʌktɪv] adj. 建設性的 / **sarcasm** [ˋsɑrkæzəm] n. 諷刺 / **give someone credit for** 因為…而稱讚某人

Q28

What might have happened during the meeting?

會議中可能發生了什麼？

A. Emily was told that she was fired.
B. Simon didn't agree with Emily's proposal.
C. Richard managed to persuade Simon.
D. Everyone felt intimidated by Emily.

A. Emily 被告知她被解雇了。
B. Simon 不同意 Emily 的提案。
C. Richard 設法說服了 Simon。
D. 每個人都對 Emily 感覺很害怕。

詳解

說話者提到 Everyone has the right to voice their opinions, whether they support your proposal or not.（每個人都有權利說出自己的意見，不管他們支不支持你的提案），可知留言對象 Emily 在會議上提出了提案；接下來馬上提到了 Simon，說 he questioned your assumptions（他質疑你的假設），然後又說到 The fact that you could not convince him（你不能說服他的事實）。這些內容顯示

Simon 並不同意 Emily 的提案，正確答案是 B。其他選項在留言中沒有提到。

|單字片語| **intimidated** [ɪnˋtɪmə͵detɪd] adj. 害怕的，受到恐嚇的

Q29

What is true about Emily's proposal?

關於 Emily 的提案，何者正確？

A. It is feasible.	A. 是有可能實行的。
B. It lacks imagination.	B. 缺乏想像力。
C. It needs some adjustment.	C. 需要一點調整。
D. It will be implemented.	D. 將會被實施。

詳解

答案：C

Emily 的 proposal 雖然在會議上受到質疑，但說話者認為Your idea is bold and innovative.（你的想法很大膽也很創新），並且建議 All you need to do is look into the doubts Simon pointed out.（你需要做的就是研究 Simon 指出的懷疑），而且 you have adequate time to revise your plan（你有足夠的時間修改你的計畫），所以答案是 C。

Questions 30-32

Questions number 30 to 32 are based on the following lecture.

The latest findings on traffic accidents resulting in fatal or serious injuries turned out to be rather astonishing. One would assume that weather conditions, including poor visibility and slippery road surfaces, to be among the top three causes. Nevertheless, the main factors for deadly accidents were all human-related. Speeding tops the list as the likelihood of fatal accidents increases with every extra 10 kilometers per hour. The higher the speed, the less time there is to respond, and the greater the impact is upon collision. Distractions during driving come in second. Drivers take their eyes off the road for a number of reasons. Most drivers get distracted while answering and making phone calls, and some find it hard to focus on the road when they are busy following instructions on the GPS screen. Despite being the center of attention of the media, drunk driving ranks third.

最近關於造成死亡或嚴重傷害的交通事故的研究結果相當驚人。我們可能假設天氣狀況，包括能見度不佳和路面很滑，會在事故原因的前三名。但是，致死事故的主要因素都是人為（和人有關）的。超速是第一名，因為時速每增加 10 公里，致死車禍的發生機率都會增加。速度越快，能反應的時間就越少，撞擊時的衝擊力就越大。開車時分心是第二名。駕駛人會因為許多理由而把視線從路上移開。大部分的駕駛人會在應答電話和打電話的時候分心，而有些人覺得忙著遵循 GPS 螢幕上的指示時很難專注在路況上。雖然是媒體關注的焦點，但酒後駕駛是第三。

|單字片語| **fatal** [`fetl] adj. 致命的 / **astonishing** [ə`stanɪʃɪŋ] adj. 令人很驚訝的 / **visibility** [ˌvɪzə`bɪlətɪ] n. 能見度 / **slippery** [`slɪpərɪ] adj. 滑的，容易滑的 / **speeding** [`spidɪŋ] n. 超速行車 / **collision** [kə`lɪʒən] n. 碰撞 / **distraction** [dɪ`strækʃən] n. 分散注意力的事物 / **drunk driving** 酒後駕車 / **rank** [ræŋk] n. 等級 v. 排行（如何）

Q30

What is surprising about the latest findings on traffic accidents?

關於最近對於交通事故的研究結果，什麼是令人意外的？

A. The top three causes have nothing to do with weather. A. 前三名的原因和天氣無關。
B. Fatal accidents are not as frequent as many people expect. B. 致命的事故並不像許多人預期的那麼頻繁。
C. There were more accidents on rainy days in the mountains. C. 山區雨天發生的事故比較多。
D. More accidents happen after dark than in daytime. D. 晚上發生的事故比白天多。

詳解 **答案：A**

題目的重點在於 What is surprising，對應第一句話最後的 astonishing（很驚人的）。接下來就是在解釋為什麼最近的研究結果很驚人：One would assume that weather conditions... to be among the top three causes. Nevertheless, the main factors... were all human-related.（一個人可能會假設天氣狀況會在事故原因的前三名，但主要因素都是人為的），所以答案是 A。

Q31

What is the main reason that speeding became the number one cause of fatal accidents?

超速成為致命事故頭號原因的主要理由是什麼？

A. Drivers suffer from poor vision.
B. Drivers lose control of their cars.
C. Drivers are thrilled by the ride.
D. Drivers have less time to react.

A. 駕駛人的視力不好。
B. 駕駛人失去對車輛的控制。
C. 駕駛人覺得開車很刺激。
D. 駕駛人能反應的時間比較少。

詳解

答案：D

說話者依序說明了致命車禍的前三名因素，第一個就是 speeding。The higher the speed, the less time there is to respond（速度越快，能反應的時間就越少）顯示超速會減少可以作出反應的時間限度，所以答案是 D。

|單字片語| **suffer from** 受…之苦 / **vision** [ˋvɪʒən] n. 視覺；視力 / **thrilled** [θrɪld] adj. 很興奮的 / **ride** [raɪd] n. 騎乘；開車兜風；（遊樂設施）乘坐

Q32

What is implied about drunk driving?

關於酒後駕駛，說話者暗示什麼？

A. Drunk driving accidents tend to be in the headlines.
B. Drunk driving leads to more deadly accidents than any other causes.
C. Drunk drivers are unable to follow GPS instructions.
D. Drunk drivers tend to drive faster and take more risks.

A. 酒後駕駛事故經常會成為頭條新聞。
B. 酒後駕駛比其他原因造成更多死亡事故。
C. 酒後駕駛的人無法遵循 GPS 的指示。
D. 酒後駕駛的人通常開車比較快，也會冒更多的風險。

詳解

答案：A

只有一句話提到酒後駕駛：Despite being the center of attention of the media, drunk driving ranks third.（雖然是媒體關注的焦點，但酒後駕駛是第三名〔的致命車禍因素〕）。center of attention of the media 表示媒體對於酒後駕駛的集中關注，所以選項 A「經常成為頭條新聞」是可能發生的現象，是正確答案。雖然 B、C、D 也符合我們對於酒駕的一般認知，但因為在談話中沒有提到，所以不能選。

|單字片語| **headline** [ˋhɛd͵laɪn] n. 頭條標題，頭條新聞 / **deadly** [ˋdɛdlɪ] 致命的，致死的

Questions 33-34

Questions number 33 to 34 are based on the following radio broadcast.

The fates of hundreds of thousands of Syrian refugees remain bleak. Several Eastern Europe nations declared that they had closed the borders. Despite economic incentives offered by richer Western European countries, Hungary and Romania refused to admit more refugees into their territories, citing social and political issues as the main concerns. With so many refugees to feed and house, the already impoverished social welfare system could go broke. Furthermore, more immigrants could lead to more crimes. Even refugees who were trained as engineers or technicians find it hard to secure a job due to the fact that unemployment rates in Eastern European countries remain high. As a result, there is still no solution to the refugee crisis.

數十萬敘利亞難民的命運仍然慘澹。幾個東歐國家宣布關閉了邊界。雖然比較富有的西歐國家提供經濟獎勵，但匈牙利和羅馬尼亞拒絕接受更多難民進入領土，舉出社會和政治問題是它們主要的擔憂。有這麼多難民要供應食物和住宅，已經貧窮的社會福利體系可能會破產。而且，更多移民可能會導致更多犯罪。就連有工程師或技術人員訓練的難民，也發現很難找到工作，因為東歐國家的失業率仍然很高。結果，難民危機仍然沒有解決的方法。

|單字片語| **fate** [fet] n. 命運 / **refugee** [͵rɛfjʊˋdʒi] n. 難民 / **bleak** [blik] adj. 荒涼的；悽慘的 / **border** [ˋbɔrdɚ] n. 邊界；國界 / **incentive** [ɪnˋsɛntɪv] n. 刺激；獎勵；動機 / **territory** [ˋtɛrə͵torɪ] n. 領土 / **cite** [saɪt] v. 引用；舉出 / **impoverished** [ɪmˋpɑvərɪʃt] adj. 貧窮的 / **social welfare** 社會福利 / **immigrant** [ˋɪməgrənt] n. 外來移民 / **engineer** [͵ɛndʒəˋnɪr] n. 工程師 / **technician** [tɛkˋnɪʃən] n. 技術人員，技師 / **unemployment rate** 失業率 / **crisis** [ˋkraɪsɪs] n. 危機

Q33

According to the speaker, why did Hungary and Romania close their borders?
根據說話者的說法，匈牙利和羅馬尼亞為什麼關閉了邊界？

A. They expect war to break out soon. A. 他們預期戰爭很快會爆發。
B. They have enough problems of their own. B. 他們自己的問題就夠多了。
C. They believe refugees are mostly terrorists. C. 他們相信難民大多是恐怖分子。
D. They need financial aid from Western countries. D. 他們需要來自西歐國家的財務援助。

詳解

答案：B

提到 Hungary and Romania 的句子是 Hungary and Romania refused to admit more refugees..., citing social and political issues as the main concerns.（匈牙利和羅馬尼亞拒絕接受更多難民，並舉出社會和政治問題是它們主要的擔憂），下一句又說到 the already impoverished social welfare system could go broke（已經貧窮的社會福利體系可能會破產），可見它們自己的社會福利體系已經出問題了，接受難民可能讓問題變嚴重，所以 B 是正確答案。

|單字片語| **break out** 突然發生，爆發 / **terrorist** [ˋtɛrərɪst] n. 恐怖主義分子

Q34

According to the speaker, why do skilled refugees have a hard time seeking employment?
根據說話者的說法，為什麼有技術的難民很難找到工作？

A. Jobs are scarce. A. 工作很少。
B. Employers are biased. B. 雇主有偏見。
C. The pay is unreasonable. C. 薪水不合理。
D. Their expertise is redundant. D. 他們的專長是多餘的。

詳解

答案：A

關鍵語 skilled refugees 對應談話中的 refugees who were trained as engineers or technicians（有工程師或技術人員訓練的難民），這句話說之所以連他們也很難找到工作，是 due to the fact that unemployment rates in Eastern European countries remain high（因為東歐國家的失業率仍然很高）。失業率高很有可能和工作減少相關，所以 A 是正確答案。B 雖然看起來是很可能的因素，但因為談話中沒有提到，所以不能選。

|單字片語| **scarce** [skɛrs] adj. 缺乏的，不足的 / **biased** [ˋbaɪəst] adj. 有偏見的 / **redundant** [rɪˋdʌndənt] adj. 多餘的

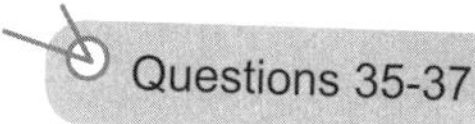

For questions number 35 to 37, please look at the chart.

In the men's division of this year's hot dog eating contest, John Cheshire won the competition for the 16th time by eating 78 hot dogs in 10 minutes, breaking his own world record of 75. He has won the contest in 15 of the past 16 years, and he's showing no signs of slowing down. Cheshire won by a wide margin this year, and only one of the other contestants, Ken Hayashi from Japan, managed to eat half of what Cheshire had eaten. The famous hot dog eating contest has been held almost every year since 50 years ago. Last year, due to the pandemic, it was held without an audience for the first time. Therefore, when people were again allowed to attend the contest this year, there was a larger audience than ever before.

在今年吃熱狗比賽的男子組，約翰・切希爾靠著在 10 分鐘內吃了 78 個熱狗堡而第 16 度贏得比賽，打破了他自己吃下 75 個的世界紀錄。他在過去 16 年有 15 年贏了比賽，而且沒有鬆懈的跡象。切希爾今年以大幅度的領先獲勝，其他參賽者只有一個人，來自日本的林健，勉強吃了切希爾的一半。這項知名的吃熱狗比賽從 50 年前以來幾乎每年舉辦。去年，由於疫情的關係，比賽首次在無觀眾的情況下舉辦。所以，當人們今年再度被允許觀賽時，觀眾比以往都還要多。

|單字片語| **contestant** [kənˋtɛstənt] n. 參賽者 / **pandemic** [pænˋdɛmɪk] n. 疾病的大範圍流行

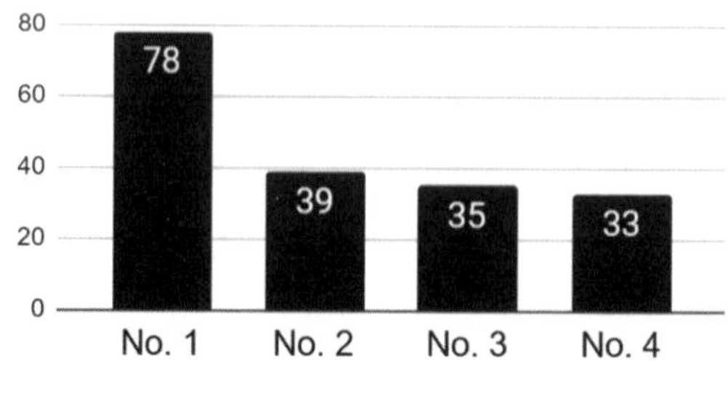

Q35

What is true about John Cheshire?

關於約翰·切希爾，何者正確？

A. He has been a world record keeper. A. 他是世界紀錄保持者。
B. He has a total of 17 wins now. B. 他現在已經贏了 17 次。
C. He won every year in the past 16 years. C. 他在過去 16 年每年都獲勝。
D. He narrowly won this year. D. 他今年是險勝。

詳解 **答案：A**

說話者提到 breaking his own world record（打破他自己的世界紀錄），表示約翰·切希爾之前是世界紀錄保持者，今年更創下新的紀錄，所以 A 是正確答案。B. 說話者提到 won the competition for the 16th time（第 16 度贏得比賽），不符合選項敘述。C. 說話者提到 He has won the contest in 15 of the past 16 years（他在過去 16 年有 15 年贏了比賽），不是每年都獲勝，不符合選項敘述。D. 說話者提到 Cheshire won by a wide margin（切希爾以大幅度的領先獲勝），並不是險勝，不符合選項敘述。

Q36

According to the report, which of the contestants in the chart is Ken Hayashi?
根據報導，圖表中的哪一位參賽者是林健？

A. No. 1.
B. No. 2.
C. No. 3.
D. No. 4.

詳解　　答案：B

說話者提到 John Cheshire won the competition... by eating 78 hot dogs（約翰．切希爾吃了 78 個熱狗堡而贏得比賽），所以 1 號參賽者是約翰．切希爾。至於林健，說話者說 only one of the other contestants, Ken Hayashi from Japan, managed to eat half of what Cheshire had eaten（其他參賽者只有一個人，來自日本的林健，勉強吃了切希爾的一半），所以在其他參賽者中吃的數量最多，而且剛好是切希爾的一半的 2 號參賽者是林健，B 是正確答案。

Q37

What is true about the hot dog eating contest?
關於吃熱狗比賽，何者正確？

A. Only men can enter the contest.　A. 只有男性能參加比賽。
B. It has been held for 50 times.　B. 被舉辦了 50 次。
C. It was canceled last year.　C. 去年被取消了。
D. It has the largest audience this year.　D. 今年的觀眾最多。

詳解　　答案：D

說話者最後提到 this year, there was a larger audience than ever before（今年觀眾比以往都還要多），表示今年的觀眾是最多的，所以 D 是正確答案。A. 說話者一開始提到 the men's division of this year's hot dog eating contest（今年吃熱狗比賽的男子組），顯示比賽應該還有女子組，不符合選項敘述。B. 說話者提到 The famous hot dog eating contest has been held almost every year since 50 years ago（這項知名的吃熱狗比賽從 50 年前以來幾乎每年舉辦），表示並不是每一年都舉辦，實際上的舉辦次數應該未滿 50 次，不符合選項敘述。C. 說話者提到 Last year, due to the pandemic, it was held without an audience（去年，由於疫情的關係，比賽在無觀眾的情況下舉辦），是無觀眾而不是沒有舉辦，不符合選項敘述。

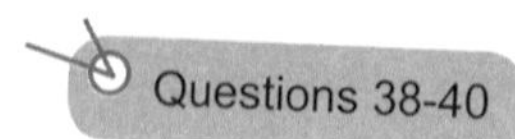

For questions number 38 to 40, please look at the table.

The pandemic forced schools to close their doors and move classes online. Many students find that online learning not only helps slow the spread of viruses but also leaves them with more free time because they don't need to travel to school. However, teachers are worried that students can easily be distracted at home. A bigger problem is that children may have less chance to communicate with their peers if they don't go to school, making it harder for them to fit in the society in the future. Personally, I'm against the idea of canceling in-person education permanently because I have a day job, and it's stressful thinking about what my child might be doing at home when I'm at work. Even though students may be exposed to viruses at school, and some of them find it difficult to adapt to the school setting, I still believe in-person learning is an indispensable part of education.

疫情迫使學校關門，並且將課程轉移到線上。許多學生覺得線上學習不但能幫助減緩病毒傳播，也讓他們有更多空閒時間，因為他們不需要移動到學校。不過，教師擔心學生在家可能很容易分心。更大的問題是如果不去學校的話，孩子可能比較少有機會和同儕溝通，使他們未來比較難融入社會。我個人反對永遠取消面對面學習，因為我有白天的工作（正職），在我工作時想著小孩可能在家做什麼是很有壓力的。儘管學生在學校可能會接觸到病毒，而且有些學生覺得很難適應學校的環境，但我仍然相信面對面學習是教育不可或缺的一部分。

|單字片語| **distract** [dɪˋstrækt] **v.** 使分心 / **indispensable** [ˌɪndɪsˋpɛnsəbḷ] **adj.** 不可或缺的

	Pros 優點	Cons 缺點
Online Learning 線上學習	Less chance of virus exposure 曝露於病毒的機率比較低 No transportation issues 沒有交通問題	Less ? 比較少的〔 ? 〕 Harder to focus 比較難專注

In-Person Learning 面對面學習	Easier to make new friends 比較容易交到新朋友 Reduce the burden of working parents 減少在職父母的負擔	Risk of virus exposure 曝露於病毒的風險 More stressful for some kids 對一些小孩比較有壓力

Q38

Based on the talk, what should be written in the shaded area?

根據這段談話，灰底部分應該填入什麼？

A. Effective tests.
B. Social interaction.
C. Reference resources.
D. Motivation for learning.

A. 有效的測驗。
B. 社會互動。
C. 參考資料來源。
D. 學習動機。

詳解

答案：B

關於線上學習的缺點，說話者提到 children may have less chance to communicate with their peers if they don't go to school（如果不去學校的話，孩子可能比較少有機會和同儕溝通），所以最能表達這一點的 B 是正確答案。

Q39

Who is the speaker?

說話者是什麼人？

A. A student.
B. A teacher.
C. A mother.
D. A researcher.

A. 學生。
B. 教師。
C. 母親。
D. 研究人員。

詳解

答案：C

關於自己的身分，說話者提到 it's stressful thinking about what my child might be doing at home when I'm at work（在我工作時想著小孩可能在家做什麼是很有壓力的），表示她是一位母親，所以 C 是正確答案。

Q40

What is the speaker's thought about in-person learning?

說話者對於面對面學習的想法是什麼？

A. It is behind the times. A. 它過時了。
B. It needs to be transformed. B. 它需要被改變。
C. It is always superior to online learning. C. 它總是比線上學習好。
D. It is essential for education. D. 它對於教育是不可或缺的。

詳解

答案：D

說話者在談話中分別提到了線上學習和面對面學習的優點和缺點，但最後還是下了這樣的結論：I still believe in-person learning is an indispensable part of education（我仍然相信面對面學習是教育不可或缺的一部分），所以意思最接近的 D 是正確答案。

第一部分 / 句子填空

Q1

Peace-keeping troops stationed in war-torn countries ensure that refugees are treated in a ________ manner according to international protocol. **駐守在被戰爭破壞的國家的和平部隊，確保依照國際協議讓難民獲得人道方式的對待。**

A. human　　B. humorous　　C. humiliating　　D. humanitarian

詳解　　答案：D

不定冠詞 a 和名詞 manner 中間，是形容詞的位置。human（人的，人本性的）雖然也能當形容詞用，但考慮到 refugees（難民）、according to international protocol（依照國際協議）等內容，D. humanitarian（人道主義的）是更適當的答案。

|單字片語| **peace-keeping** [ˋpisˏkipɪŋ] adj. 維護和平的 / **station** [ˋsteʃən] v. 派駐 / **refugee** [ˏrɛfjʊˋdʒi] n. 難民 / **protocol** [ˋprotəˏkɑl] n. 議定書，協議 / **human** [ˋhjumən] n. 人 adj. 人的，人本性的 / **humorous** [ˋhjumərəs] adj. 幽默的 / **humiliating** [hjuˋmɪlɪˏetɪŋ] adj. 羞辱人的 / **humanitarian** [hjuˏmænəˋtɛrɪən] adj. 人道主義的

Q2

The likely ________ and side effects brought about by chemotherapy should be explained to the patient before treatment.
化學治療可能帶來的結果和副作用，應該在治療之前向患者解釋。

A. anticipations　　B. evaluations　　C. implications　　D. precautions

詳解　　答案：C

空格和後面的 side effects（副作用）一樣，都是 chemotherapy（化學治療）

所帶來的結果，所以能表示結果的 C 是正確答案。

|單字片語| **side effect** 副作用 / **chemotherapy** [ˌkɛmoˋθɛrəpɪ] n. 化學療法（化療）/ **anticipation** [ænˌtɪsəˋpeʃən] n. 預期 / **evaluation** [ɪˌvæljʊˋeʃən] n. 評價 / **implication** [ˌɪmplɪˋkeʃən] n. 暗示；可能的結果 / **precaution** [prɪˋkɔʃən] n. 預防措施

Q3

Since young, the talented musician knew that he was unlike his peers in that he was ________ for great things.

從年輕的時候開始，這位有天分的音樂家就知道他和同儕不同，是註定要從事偉大的事情的。

A. tempted B. pursued C. destined D. doomed

詳解

答案：C

句中的 in that 是「基於…的理由」、「因為…」的意思。知道自己與眾不同，應該是因為天生可以做 great things，所以能和空格前後的 be 動詞、介系詞 for 搭配，形成 be destined for（註定有…的結果）的 C 是正確答案。

|單字片語| **tempted** [ˋtɛmptɪd] adj. 很想要做的（be tempted to do something）/ **pursue** [pɚˋsu] v. 追逐，追求 / **doomed** [dumd] adj. 註定不幸的

Q4

Those who ________ illegal drugs, as stated in the customs declaration form, could face the death penalty.

如海關申報表所述，走私違法藥物的人可能會面臨死刑。

A. assemble B. crumble C. mingle D. smuggle

詳解

答案：D

在選項中，能表示在機場（因為題目中提到海關）對於藥物所做的違法行為是 smuggle（走私），所以 D 是正確答案。另外，製造藥物是用 make 或 manufacture 來表達，而不會用 assemble（組裝，例如由各種零件組成的東西）來表達。

|單字片語| **customs declaration form** 海關申報表 / **death penalty** 死刑 / **crumble** [ˋkrʌmbḷ] v. 弄碎 / **mingle** [ˋmɪŋgḷ] v. 混合 / **smuggle** [ˋsmʌgḷ] v. 走私

This tropical rainforest in South Asia serves as a ________ where animals can live their natural lives in peace.
這座南亞的熱帶雨林是動物能平靜地度過自然生活的庇護之處。

A. boundary　B. cemetery　C. documentary　D. sanctuary

詳解　答案：D

空格被後面的關係子句修飾，表示這是動物能 live their natural lives in peace（平靜地度過自然生活）的地方，所以選項中能表示這種地方的 D 是正確答案。

|單字片語| **tropical** [ˋtrɑpɪkl] adj. 熱帶的 / **serve as** 有…的效果，作為… / **boundary** [ˋbaʊndrɪ] n. 邊界 / **cemetery** [ˋsɛmə͵tɛrɪ] n. 墓地 / **documentary** [͵dɑkjəˋmɛntərɪ] n. 紀錄片

Q6

Those who drag their feet while walking find their shoes ________ faster due to repeated friction.
拖著腳走路的人發現由於反覆磨擦的關係，自己的鞋子比較快磨壞。

A. turn out　B. put out　C. sell out　D. wear out

詳解　答案：D

雖然 wear 通常是「穿」的意思，但也有「磨損」的意思，而 wear out 就是磨壞到不堪使用的地步，也可以比喻耐心或精力被耗盡，例如 My patience is wearing thin.（我的耐心磨得越來越薄了）。名詞片語 wear and tear 則是指日常使用自然造成的磨損。

|單字片語| **friction** [ˋfrɪkʃən] n. 摩擦 / **turn out** 出現，出席；結果是… / **put out** 熄滅，撲滅（火） / **sell out** 賣完…

Q7

The senior executive was taken into custody after admitting that he ________ better-than-expected sales figures in an attempt to push up share prices. **承認捏造優於預期的銷售數字、試圖推升股價之後，那位資深主管被拘留了。**

A. monopolized　B. fabricated　C. obscured　D. undermined

詳解

答案：B

從 was taken into custody（被拘留）可知，資深主管做了非法的事。空格後面的受詞是 better-than-expected sales figures（優於預期的銷售數字），而且之所以做這件事是 in an attempt to push up share prices（試圖推升股價），所以 B. fabricated（偽造，杜撰）是最適當的答案。

|單字片語| **custody** [`kʌstədɪ] n. 拘留，拘禁 / **in an attempt to do** 試圖做… / **monopolize** [mə`nɑpḷ͵aɪz] v. 壟斷 / **fabricate** [`fæbrɪ͵ket] v. 偽造，杜撰 / **obscure** [əb`skjʊr] adj. 晦澀的，模糊的 v. 使…變得難以了解，混淆，掩蓋 / **undermine** [͵ʌndɚ`maɪn] v. 逐漸損害

Q8

At higher ________, there is a significant annual variation in the length of the day—much longer in summer and much shorter in winter.

在比較高緯度的地方，每年白天長度的變化很大——在夏天長得多，在冬天短得多。

A. altitudes B. aptitudes C. latitudes D. longitudes

詳解

答案：C

這是和地球科學知識有關的問題，日夜長度的季節變化會隨著緯度變高而更加明顯，所以 C 是正確答案。

|單字片語| **variation** [͵vɛrɪ`eʃən] n. 變化 / **altitude** [`æltə͵tjud] n. （海拔）高度 / **aptitude** [`æptə͵tjud] n. 天資 / **latitude** [`lætə͵tjud] n. 緯度 / **longitude** [`lɑndʒə`tjud] n. 經度

Q9

When it comes to architectural design, safety, rather than cost or appearance, should be given top ________.

說到建築設計，安全應該是第一優先，而不是費用或外觀。

A. collaboration B. hierarchy C. transparency D. priority

詳解

答案：D

句子後半的主要結構是 safety should be given top ______，中間插入了 rather than cost or appearance，表示和費用、外觀比起來，安全有優先的地位。表示什麼事情是第一優先，可以用 give top priority to something 來表達，所以 D 是正確答案。hierarchy 雖然意義相似，但這個字主要用來表示社會或組織中的「等級、地位」，所以不是最適當的答案。

|單字片語| **architectural** [ˌɑrkəˋtɛktʃərəl] adj. 建築的 / **collaboration** [kəˌlæbəˋreʃən] n. 合作，合力工作 / **hierarchy** [ˋhaɪəˌrɑrkɪ] n. （社會、組織等的）等級體系，等級制度 / **transparency** [trænsˋpɛrənsɪ] n. 透明 / **priority** [praɪˋɔrətɪ] n. 優先，優先權

Q10

Northern lights, the colorful lights seen in high-latitude regions, are a natural ________ caused by energized particles leaving the sun and colliding with particles in the earth's atmosphere. 高緯度可見色彩繽紛的北極光，是由離開太陽、帶有能量的粒子和地球大氣的粒子撞擊造成的自然現象。

A. phenomenon B. symptom C. omen D. reminder

詳解 答案：A

雖然句子後半對於 northern lights 的解釋比較不容易看懂，但至少可以知道這是 colorful lights seen in high-latitude regions（在高緯度地區看到的、色彩繽紛的光）。空格接在形容詞 natural 後面，最適當的答案是 A. phenomenon（現象）。

|單字片語| **energize** [ˋɛnɚˌdʒaɪz] v. 供給…能量 / **particle** [ˋpɑrtɪkḷ] n. 粒子 / **collide** [kəˋlaɪd] v. 碰撞 / **atmosphere** [ˋætməsˌfɪr] 大氣；氣氛

第二部分 / 段落填空

Questions 11-15

The most brutal form of punishment for theft in some Islamic states is to chop off the hands of the criminal, (11) regardless of gender. This extreme measure to discourage people from stealing is (12) justified by authorities based on a verse in the Quran, which is the Muslim equivalent of the Bible. Nevertheless, further reading of the Quran indicates that Allah, the God of Muslims, preaches forgiveness. As a matter of fact, there are many verses that tell us to forgive (13) so long as the evil-doer repents. Forgiveness implies that no punishment is given. It is (14) absurd to ask people to turn over a new leaf after chopping off their hands. Thus, it is obvious that the verse used to support such bloody punishment is taken out of context. While some may argue that the presence of such a barbaric law in modern society (15) acts as a deterrent against crime, others are of the opinion that it is way out of proportion. Law-breakers should be given a chance to regret their actions and make amends.

某些伊斯蘭國家對於竊盜最殘酷的懲罰形式，是把罪犯的手剁掉，不論性別。當局根據穆斯林的聖經——古蘭經裡的一節，為這種勸阻人們不去偷竊的極端手段的正當性辯護。儘管如此，對古蘭經更深入的閱讀顯示，穆斯林的神——阿拉宣揚寬恕。事實上，有許多節告訴我們，只要做壞事的人悔改，就要寬恕他們。寬恕意味著不給予懲罰。在把人的手剁掉以後要他們展開（人生）新的一頁是很不合理的。所以，顯然用來支持這種血腥懲罰的一節是被斷章取義（「被從原本的脈絡中拿出來」）。雖然有些人可能會主張現代社會中這種野蠻法律的存在可以嚇阻犯罪，但其他人的意見是，這種懲罰太不合比例了。犯法的人應該被給予悔過並且補償的機會。

|單字片語| **brutal** [ˋbrutḷ] adj. 殘忍的，野蠻的 / **chop off** 砍掉，剁掉 / **regardless of** 不管…，不顧… / **gender** [ˋdʒɛndɚ] n. 性別 / **justify** [ˋdʒʌstəˏfaɪ] v. 證明…為正當 / **preach** [pritʃ] v. 講道，宣揚；說教 / **forgiveness** [fɚˋgɪvnɪs] n. 原諒，寬恕 / **so long as** （表示條件）只要… / **repent** [rɪˋpɛnt] v. 懺悔 / **absurd** [əbˋsɝd] adj. 荒謬的 / **turn over a new leaf** 「展開新的一頁」→重新開始；改過自新 / **context** [ˋkɑntɛkst] n. 上下文，文章脈絡 / **barbaric** [bɑrˋbærɪk] adj. 野蠻的 / **deterrent** [dɪˋtɝrənt] n. 制止物 / **out of proportion** 不合比例 / **make amends** 賠罪，賠償

Q11

A. in principle　B. not to mention　C. regardless of　D. save for

詳解　答案：C

前面說 punishment for theft（偷竊的懲罰）是 chop off the hands of the criminal（把罪犯的手剁掉），而空格後面接的單字是 gender（性別）。gender 表示男性、女性的分別，regardless of gender 就表示「不管是男是女，一律如此」，所以 C. regardless of（不管…）是正確答案。

|單字片語| **in principle** 原則上 / **not to mention** 更別說… / **save for** 除了…以外

Q12

A. clarified　B. mystified　C. identified　D. justified

詳解　答案：D

將這個句子轉變為主動態的話，意思就是 The authorities ______ this extreme measure based on a verse in the Quran（當局根據古蘭經裡的一節，______這種極端的措施）。所以，表示「證明…的正當性」的 D. justified 是正確答案。

|單字片語| **clarify** [ˋklærəˌfaɪ] v. 澄清，闡明 / **mystify** [ˋmɪstəˌfaɪ] v. 將…神祕化；使困惑 / **identify** [aɪˋdɛntəˌfaɪ] v. 識別，認出；將…（和其他對象）視為同一事物

Q13

A. as if　B. in case　C. so long as　D. so as to

詳解　答案：C

空格後面接有主詞和動詞的完整子句，所以連接詞 A、B、C 是可能的答案。空格前面的部分說有很多經文告訴我們要寬恕（there are many verses that tell us to forgive），而空格後面是「做壞事的人悔改」（the evil-doer repents），所以表示條件的連接詞 C. so long as（只要…）是正確答案。as if 表示「彷彿…，好像…」，in case 表示「以防萬一…」。so as to 後面接動詞原形，表示「為了做…」的意思。

A. absurd　　B. ecstatic　　C. naïve　　D. sentimental

詳解

答案：A

空格所在的句子使用虛主詞 It，真正的主詞是從 to ask... 一直到句尾的部分，空格的形容詞表示這整件事的性質。turn over a new leaf（展開新的一頁）是一個比喻，表示「重新開始」的意思。不過，如果從字面上的意思看這個句子，也可以得到「剁了人家的手，就不可能要他們『翻開新的一頁』」這種解讀，顯示用這種懲罰要人重新開始是很荒謬的，所以答案是 A. absurd（荒謬的）。

|單字片語| **ecstatic** [ɛk`stætɪk] adj. 狂喜的 / **naïve** [nɑ`iv] adj. （缺乏經驗而）天真的 / **sentimental** [ˌsɛntə`mɛntl] adj. 多愁善感的

Q15

A. should be abolished for good
應該被永遠廢除

B. proves that conservatism still exists
證明保守主義仍然存在

C. does not reduce violent crime
不會減少暴力犯罪

D. acts as a deterrent against crime
能成為對犯罪的嚇阻

詳解

答案：D

整個句子的結構是 While some..., others...（雖然有些人…但其他人…），表示前後的內容是形成對比的意見。後半段說 it is way out of proportion（太不合比例了），是指懲罰遠遠大過犯行的嚴重程度，也就是對這種懲罰持負面看法，所以空格中應該是肯定這種懲罰方式的意見，D 是正確答案。

Questions 16-20

Singapore is among the most vibrant, robust, and competitive markets in the world. From 2007 to 2016, the World Bank kept ranking Singapore as the easiest place in the world to do business. While strongly (16) advocating free-market policies and practices, which attract foreign investment, the Singapore government (17) is also well-known for the authoritative style of intervention in certain areas. This innovative and highly successful economic system is known as "the Singapore Model". (18) Singapore has a relatively small domestic market, and thus has to open its economy to external markets in order for the economy to thrive. However, the heavy reliance on external markets has also compelled the government to (19) formulate economic policies that would safeguard the country from perturbations in the global market. Apart from these policies, the government has also actively encouraged new industries to develop in Singapore (20) so as to respond to the needs of the global market.

新加坡是世界上最有活力、最強盛、最有競爭力的市場之一。從 2007 年到 2016 年，世界銀行持續將新加坡評為世界最容易經商的國家。雖然新加坡政府強力提倡吸引國外投資的自由市場政策及實踐，但在某些領域專斷的干預方式也廣為人知。這個創新又非常成功的經濟體系，被稱為「新加坡模式」。新加坡的國內市場相對較小，所以必須將它的經濟對外部市場開放以求繁榮。但是，對於外部市場的重度依賴，也迫使新加坡政府制定能保護國家免於全球市場擾亂的經濟政策。除了這些政策以外，新加坡政府也積極鼓勵新產業在新加坡發展，以回應全球市場的需求。

|單字片語| **vibrant** [ˋvaɪbrənt] adj. 活潑的，充滿生機的 / **robust** [rəˋbʌst] adj. 強健的，健全的 / **rank** [ræŋk] v. 將…評級，排名；排名為… / **advocate** [ˋædvəˏket] v. 提倡 / **authoritative** [əˋθɔrəˏtetɪv] adj. 權威性的；專斷的 / **intervention** [ˏɪntɚˋvɛnʃən] n. 介入，干預 / **innovative** [ˋɪnoˏvetɪv] adj. 創新的 / **domestic** [dəˋmɛstɪk] adj. 家庭的；國內的 / **thrive** [θraɪv] v. 茁壯，繁榮，成功 / **reliance** [rɪˋlaɪəns] n. 依賴 / **compel** [kəmˋpɛl] v. 強迫，使不得不 / **formulate** [ˋfɔrmjəˏlet] v. 構想，制定 / **safeguard** [ˋsefˏgɑrd] v. 防衛，保護 / **perturbation** [ˏpɝtɚˋbeʃən] n. 擾亂

Q16

A. advocating　　B. indicating　　C. contemplating　　D. permeating

詳解　　**答案：A**

空格後面接的受詞是 free-market policies and practices（自由市場政策及實踐），選項中適合接「政策」當受詞，表示支持、鼓勵的只有 A. advocating（提倡）。

|單字片語| **indicate** [ˋɪndəˏket] v. 指示，指出 / **contemplate** [ˋkɑntɛmˏplet] v. 沉思；設想 / **permeate** [ˋpɝmɪˏet] v. 滲透，瀰漫

A. is in the know about　對…知情
B. also knows well about　也對…很了解
C. should also have known　應該也已經知道
D. is also well-known for　以…聞名

詳解　答案：D

空格後面的 its authoritative style（它專斷的風格）和前面的內容一樣，是關於新加坡治理方式的敘述，所以比起表示「知道」的選項 A、B、C，表示「因為…而為人所知」的 D 是比較恰當的答案。

Q18

A. Singapore has flourishing local businesses
新加坡有繁榮的國內商業
B. Singapore is famous for its strict regulations
新加坡以嚴格的管制聞名
C. Singapore has a relatively small domestic market
新加坡的國內市場相對較小
D. Singapore is trying to protect domestic industries
新加坡試圖保護國內產業

詳解　答案：C

空格後面是表示結果的 and thus has to open its economy to external markets in order for the economy to thrive（所以必須將它的經濟對外部市場開放以求繁榮），所以應該是因為國內市場的規模不夠而必須開放，C 是正確答案。

Q19

A. deprive　B. nurture　C. formulate　D. tackle

詳解　答案：C

空格要填入動詞，而它意義上的主詞是 government（政府），受詞則是 economic policies（經濟政策）。所以，能表示「制定」政策的 C. formulate 是正確答案。

|單字片語| **deprive** [dɪˋpraɪv] v. 剝奪，使喪失 / **nurture** [ˋnɝtʃɚ] v. 培育 / **tackle** [ˋtækl̩] v. 處理，應對

Q20

A. so that　　B. such that　　C. so as to　　D. as such

詳解　　答案：C

so that 和 so as to 都是「為了」、「以便」的意思，所以還需要從文法來判斷。so that 後面要接完整子句，so as to 後面則是接動詞原形，所以這裡的正確答案是 C. so as to。such that 表示「如此…以致於」，雖然也有「... is such that...」的說法，但 such 後面通常會接名詞片語。as such 表示「確切而言」或「完全（符合某個詞的定義）」的意思。

補充說明

請看以下的句子，比較 so that 和 so as to 的使用方式。

I study hard so that I can pass the test.
I study hard so as to pass the test.
（我為了通過測驗而努力讀書。）

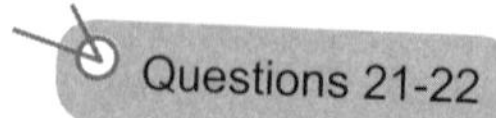

Commencement of Works between Huddleston Street and St. Albert Avenue

Please note that work on the laying of replacement sewage pipes between Huddleston Street and St. Albert Avenue will commence on the 22nd of November. The replacement will ensure security of water supply to the southeastern Huddleston district. Work will be undertaken using trenchless construction method to minimize noise pollution, but the flow of traffic is expected to be affected.

However, traffic will be controlled in certain sections with a temporary traffic light system in operation. Work is scheduled to take place from 09:30 to 16:30, 7 days a week. There will be no further disruption to traffic after working hours. This work is scheduled to be completed by the end of December. Any inconvenience caused is regretted. We seek your cooperation by choosing an alternative route or avoiding roadwork hours.

Huddleston 街與 St. Albert 大街之間開始施工

請注意，Huddleston 街與 St. Albert 大街之間鋪設替換污水管的工程將於 11 月 22 日開始。這次替換將確保 Huddleston 區東南部的供水安全。工程將以非開挖（無開挖溝渠）的方式進行，將噪音污染減到最小，但車流預期將受到影響。

不過，在特定區域將以臨時號誌系統控制交通。工程預定於週一至週日每天 9:30 至 16:30 進行。在施工時段過後，將不會對交通有更多擾亂。工程預定於 12 月底前完成。我們為造成的任何不便致歉。我們希望您能合作，選擇替代路線或者避開施工的時段。

|單字片語| **commencement** [kəˋmɛnsmənt] n. 開始 / **sewage** [ˋsjuɪdʒ] n. 汙水 / **commence** [kəˋmɛns] v. 開始 / **trenchless** [ˋtrɛntʃlɪs] adj. 不挖溝渠的（形容一種鋪設地下管線的工程方式）/ **disruption** [dɪsˋrʌpʃən] n. 中斷，擾亂

What information can be derived from the notice?
從這則通知可以推知什麼資訊？

A. A pipe burst caused disruption of traffic.
水管爆裂造成交通混亂。
B. Traffic jams during lunchtime are expected.
預期午餐時間將會塞車。
C. Workers will go on strike as a result of long working hours.
工人將會因為工時太長而罷工。
D. Construction work will last for at least half a year.
工程將會持續至少半年。

詳解 答案：B

一一核對各個選項的內容是否正確。A 和 C 沒有提到。和 B 相關的部分是第一段的 the flow of traffic is expected to be affected（車流預期將受到影響），還有第二段的 Work is scheduled to take place from 09:30 to 16:30（工程預定於 9:30 至 16:30 進行），所以午餐時間可能會塞車，B 是正確答案。和 D 相關的部分是第一段的 work... will commence on the 22nd of November（工程將於 11 月 22 日開始），還有第二段的 This work is scheduled to be completed by the end of December.（工程預定於 12 月底前完成），所以施工時期不到半年，選項與內文敘述不符。

|單字片語| **go on strike** 進行罷工運動

What is NOT mentioned in the notice?
通知中沒有提到什麼？

A. Traffic will be directed during construction hours.
工程時段交通將會受到指引。
B. Work will be carried out around the clock.
工程將會日以繼夜進行。
C. The construction crew will manage to reduce noise.
工程團隊將會設法減少噪音。
D. Problems can be avoided by taking other roads.
可以藉由走其他路避免問題。

詳解 答案：B

文章第二段的 traffic will be controlled 對應選項 A，第一段的 minimize noise pollution 對應選項 C，第二段的 cooperation by choosing an alternative route 對應選項 D。因為第二段明確提到工程會 take place from 09:30 to 16:30，所以不是 24 小時進行，選項 B 是正確答案。

|單字片語| around the clock 日以繼夜

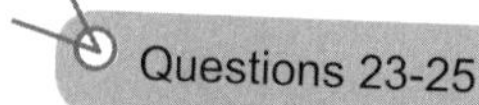

Among African leaders, Nelson Mandela is one of the few who have gained respect from around the world and across the political spectrum. His role in fighting apartheid (racial segregation in South Africa) and his ability to lead South Africa through its transformation process earned him the international reputation of being a successful negotiator and peacemaker.

Because of his opposition to apartheid, Mandela had been imprisoned for 27 years. When he finally won his freedom in 1990, instead of showing resentment or trying to revenge, he dedicated himself to the reconciliation of South Africa's conflicting ethnic groups, aiming at building a nation where cooperative governance is possible. By uniting the warring parties, Mandela saved South Africa from the verge of civil war and built up its people's confidence. He was elected as the President of South Africa in 1993, and the number of attending state leaders at his inauguration surpassed that at the funeral of former US President John Kennedy. Although very likely to win a second term if he wanted, Mandela did not hesitate to step down in 1999. He died from a lung infection on December 5th, 2013 at the age of 95.

Mandela's success did not come by chance. It is his outstanding negotiating skills, moral integrity, and sense of fairness that convinced disparate parties to compromise for the sake of peace. In today's world, we still see endless conflicts among ethnic and religious groups, but what Mandela had done shows us that with positive intention and perseverance, no conflict is unresolvable.

在非洲領導人之中，尼爾森・曼德拉是少數受到全世界和整個政治光譜（所有政治陣營）的尊敬的人。他在對抗南非種族隔離中扮演的角色，還有他在南非轉型過程中加以領導的能力，讓他在世界上獲得了成功的談判與調解者的名聲。

因為對於南非種族隔離的反對，曼德拉在監獄待了 27 年。當他 1990 年終於獲得自由時，他沒有表現出憤恨或者試圖復仇，而是致力於南非衝突的種族之間的和解，目標是建立一個讓合作治理成為可能的國家。藉由聯合交戰的各方，曼德拉把南非從逼近內戰的邊緣挽救回來，並且建立了人民的自信。他在 1993 年獲選為南非總統，而出席就職典禮的國家元首人數超過了美國前總統約翰·甘迺迪的葬禮。雖然如果想要的話，曼德拉很有可能贏得連任，但他在 1999 年毫不猶豫地退下了總統職位。他在 2013 年 12 月 5 日因為肺部感染而過世，享壽 95 歲。

曼德拉的成功並非偶然。是他優秀的談判技巧、道德節操和公正意識，說服了不同的各方為了和平而妥協。在今日的世界，我們還是看到民族與宗教團體之間永無止息的衝突，但曼德拉所做的讓我們看到，只要有正面的意圖和堅持不懈的精神，就沒有什麼衝突是不能解決的。

|單字片語|

（第一段）

spectrum [ˋspɛktrəm] n. 光譜；涵蓋兩極之間的全部範圍 / **apartheid** [əˋpɑrtˏhet] n. 南非曾經實行的種族隔離政策 / **segregation** [ˏsɛgrɪˋgeʃən] n. （種族）隔離 / **transformation** [ˏtrænsfɚˋmeʃən] n. 改變，轉變 / **negotiator** [nɪˋgoʃɪˏetɚ] n. 談判者 / **peacemaker** [ˋpisˏmekɚ] n. 調解者

（第二段）

resentment [rɪˋzɛntmənt] n. 憤恨 / **dedicate oneself to** 投身於…，致力於… / **reconciliation** [rɛkənˏsɪlɪˋeʃən] n. 和解，和好 / **ethnic** [ˋɛθnɪk] adj. 種族的 / **governance** [ˋgʌvɚnəns] n. 統治，治理 / **the verge of** 瀕臨…的邊緣 / **civil war** 內戰 / **inauguration** [ɪnˏɔgjəˋreʃən] n. 就職（典禮） / **surpass** [sɚˋpæs] v. 勝過，超越

（第三段）

by chance 偶然，意外地 / **integrity** [ɪnˋtɛgrətɪ] n. 正直，人格的健全 / **disparate** [ˋdɪspərɪt] adj. 迥然不同的 / **compromise** [ˋkɑmprəˏmaɪz] v. 妥協 / **perseverance** [ˏpɝsəˋvɪrəns] n. 堅持不懈

Q23

Which of the following statements is NOT true?

以下哪個敘述不正確？

A. Mandela preached forgiveness and unity.
曼德拉宣揚寬恕與團結。

B. Mandela held the view that different races should not be separated.
曼德拉認為不同種族不應該被分開。

C. Mandela prevented a possible political upheaval from happening.
曼德拉防止了可能的政治動亂發生。

D. Mandela held on to power for fear of imprisonment.
曼德拉因為懼怕受到監禁而緊抓權力不放。

詳解

答案：D

選項 A 對應第二段的 he dedicated himself to the reconciliation..., aiming at building a nation where cooperative governance is possible，選項 B 對應第一段的 His role in fighting apartheid (racial segregation in South Africa)，選項 C 對應第二段的 Mandela saved South Africa from the verge of civil war。和選項 D 相關的句子是 Although very likely to win a second term if he wanted, Mandela did not hesitate to step down in 1999.（雖然如果想要的話，曼德拉很有可能贏得連任，但他在 1999 年毫不猶豫地退下了總統職位），從這句話可知他並不眷戀權力，所以 D 不符合文章內容，是正確答案。

|單字片語| **preach** [pritʃ] v. 講道；說教；宣揚 / **forgiveness** [fɚˋgɪvnɪs] n. 寬恕 / **upheaval** [ʌpˋhivl̩] n. 動亂，動盪 / **hold on to** 緊抓…不放 / **for fear of** 因為害怕…

Q24

What trait in Mandela won him international respect?

曼德拉的什麼特質為他贏得了國際上的尊敬？

A. His generosity in sharing power and credit
他慷慨分享權力與榮譽

B. His commitment to harmony and tolerance
他為和諧與容忍奉獻

C. His ambition for worldwide glory and fame
他想得到全世界的榮耀與名氣的野心

D. His resourcefulness in negotiation and trade
他在談判與貿易方面的機智

詳解

答案：B

和題目關鍵語 international respect 相關的部分，是文章開頭的 Nelson Mandela is one of the few who have gained respect from around the world，下一個句子則說 His role in fighting apartheid... and his ability to lead South Africa... earned him the international reputation。從這裡可能還看不出答案，但從第二段的 he dedicated himself to the reconciliation of South Africa's conflicting ethnic groups（他致力於南非衝突的種族之間的和解）、第三段的 convinced disparate parties to compromise for the sake of peace（說服了不同的各方為了和平而妥協）等敘述，可以看出他對抗種族隔離是為了促進族群之間的和諧，所以 B 是正確答案。

|單字片語| **credit** [ˋkrɛdɪt] n. 信用；榮譽 / **resourcefulness** [rɪˋsorsfəlnɪs] n. 足智多謀

What fact shows that Mandela was a globally prominent figure?

什麼事實顯示曼德拉是一位擁有國際名望的人物？

A. He showed love and dedication to his homeland.
他展現對於祖國的愛和奉獻。

B. His fight against apartheid took 27 years of his life.
他對抗種族隔離政策花掉了 27 年的歲月。

C. He refused to hold on to power even when he could.
即使是可以緊握權力的時候，他也拒絕了。

D. His inauguration was attended by important people from all over the world.
他的就職典禮有來自世界各地的重要人物參加。

詳解　　答案：D

雖然四個選項的內容都是事實，但題目問的是 What fact shows...（什麼事實顯示…），所以要選擇能夠直接證明他是 globally prominent（在國際上重要的）的答案。第二段提到，the number of attending state leaders at his inauguration surpassed that at the funeral of former US President John Kennedy（出席他的就職典禮的國家元首人數超過了美國前總統約翰・甘迺迪的葬禮），可見他當時和美國總統有同等的重要性，所以 D 是正確答案。

Questions 26-29

Most people feel stressed about job interviews because they are unsure what kind of behavior is expected. Indeed, every interview is unique, for the skills and personalities required for every position are different. Thankfully, there are some general principles you can follow. Below are some tips that can increase your chances of success.

- **Rehearse before the interview.** Try to imagine yourself as the interviewer. What kind of questions would you ask? List as many questions as you can think of. Recalling what you have been asked before in similar interviews will also help. You will definitely have to be prepared for some frequently asked questions (FAQs), which usually include job experience, education background, personal aspirations, strengths, and weaknesses. You may feel strange to talk to yourself in this way, but such practice can ease your nerves.

- **Dress appropriately.** Ideally, you should wear just the way employees in the company do. If you are not sure, it is always safer to look formal than casual. Some people feel uneasy in business attire because they are not used to it. In that case, it is advisable to wear the clothes several times before the interview.
- **Be confident.** A frightened look or unsure attitude can immediately spoil an interview. You should maintain eye contact with your interviewer and speak calmly, not hesitantly. Sit up straight and avoid scratching your head or playing with your hair. Such unnecessary hand movements are often considered as signs of lacking self-control.
- **Do research on the company.** With some basic knowledge about the company you want to work at, you can talk as if you are ready to hit the ground running on your first day of employment. The interviewer will know that you are serious about the job you apply for and be impressed by your effort.

大部分的人都對於工作面試感覺有壓力，因為他們不確定對方預期看到怎樣的態度。的確，每次面試都是獨特的，因為每個職位要求的技能和性格都不同。幸好，有一些普遍原則是你可以遵守的。以下是一些可以增加你成功機率的建議。

- **在面試之前做演練。**試著想像你自己是面試官。你會問什麼樣的問題？盡量多列出你想得到的問題。回憶你自己在類似的面試中被問過的問題也有幫助。你一定要為常問的問題做好準備，通常包括工作經驗、教育背景、個人志向、優點和缺點。像這樣和自己講話，你可能會覺得奇怪，但這種練習可以減緩你的緊張。
- **穿著適當。**理想上，你應該穿得就像那間公司的員工一樣。如果你不確定的話，看起來正式總是比休閒來得安全。有些人穿商務服裝覺得不自在，因為他們不習慣。那樣的話，建議在面試之前把衣服穿個幾次。
- **有自信。**看起來害怕的樣子或者不確定的態度，有可能馬上搞砸一場面試。你應該和面試官保持眼神接觸，並且冷靜地說話，而不是很遲疑地說。坐直，並且避免抓頭或者玩頭髮。這種不必要的手部動作經常被認為是缺乏自制力的跡象。
- **研究公司。**對於你想要工作的公司有些基本的知識，你說起話來就能夠像是準備好在上班第一天迅速展開行動一樣。面試官會知道你對於自己應徵的工作是認真的，也會對你的努力感到印象深刻。

|單字片語| **thankfully** [ˋθæŋkfəlɪ] adv. 感謝地；幸好 / **rehearse** [rɪˋhɝs] v. 排演；演練 / **aspiration** [ˌæspəˋreʃən] n. 志向，抱負 / **ease one's nerves** 減緩某人的緊張 / **attire** [əˋtaɪr] n. 服裝，衣著 / **advisable** [ədˋvaɪzəbl] adj. 可取的，明智的 / **hesitantly** [ˋhɛzətəntlɪ] adj. 猶豫地 / **hit the ground running** 一從事新的活動就馬上展開行動

Q26

What is the best title for this article?

這篇文章最好的標題是什麼？

A. Relaxation techniques for handling job interviews
處理工作面試的放鬆技巧

B. General guidelines for typical job interviews
典型工作面試的一般守則

C. Preparing for peculiar types of job interviews
準備特定類型的工作面試

D. Ideal dress code required for all job interviews
所有工作面試需要的理想服裝規則

詳解 答案：B

開頭就提到了關鍵詞 job interviews 工作面試，接下來說到 there are some general principles you can follow. Below are some tips（有一些普遍原則是你可以遵守的。下面是一些建議）。所以，用 general guidelines 重新表達 general principles、tips 的選項 B 是正確答案。放鬆方法、服裝雖然也有提到，但都只是一部分的內容而已。

|單字片語| **dress code** 穿著的標準；服裝規定；派對規定的服裝主題

Q27

Which of the following may NOT be a preparation method for an interview that the author would recommend?

以下何者可能不是作者會建議的面試準備方法？

A. Obtain insider information about the interviewer's preferences
獲得關於面試官喜好的內幕消息

B. Try to wear formally more often 試著更常穿著正式服裝

C. Rehearse answers to questions most likely to be asked
演練最有可能被問到的問題的答案

D. Carry out background research on the prospective company
對於未來的公司進行背景研究

詳解

選項 B 對應第二項建議的 wear the clothes（指前面提到的 business attire）several times before the interview，選項 C 對應第一項建議的 be prepared for some frequently asked questions (FAQs)，選項 D 對應第四項建議 Do research on the company。選項 A 的 insider information 表示只有內部人士知道的資訊，這在文章中沒有提到，所以 A 是正確答案。

|單字片語| **insider** [ˋɪnˋsaɪdɚ] n. 內部人士，知情人士 / **prospective** [prəˋspɛktɪv] adj. 預期的，未來的

Q28

According to this article, what kind of strategy can we adopt to leave a good impression on interviewers?

根據這篇文章，我們可以採取什麼策略，在面試官心中留下好的印象？

A. Scratching our heads to look humble
抓頭，讓自己看起來謙虛

B. Stammering so that we speak slower
說話結巴，讓講話速度比較慢

C. Keeping our composure to look reliable
保持鎮靜，讓自己看起來可靠

D. Inflating our strengths so that we appear superior
誇大優點，讓我們看起來比較優秀

詳解

第三個建議是 Be confident（有自信），其中提到應該 maintain eye contact with your interviewer and speak calmly（和面試官保持眼神接觸，並且冷靜地說話）。選項 C 的 keep one's composure 就是「保持鎮靜」的意思，所以 C 是正確答案。A 和 B 都是文中提到不好的行為，而 D 在文章中沒有提到。

|單字片語| **humble** [ˋhʌmbl] adj. 謙遜的 / **stammer** [ˋstæmɚ] v. 結結巴巴地說話 / **composure** [kəmˋpoʒɚ] n. 鎮靜，沉著 / **inflate** [ɪnˋflet] v. 使膨脹；誇大

Q29

According to this article, why is body language important for job applicants during interviews?

根據這篇文章，對於面試中的應徵者而言，為什麼肢體語言很重要？

A. It is a criterion that interviewers may judge them with.
這是面試官可能用來評斷他們的一項基準。

B. It is the only thing that counts during an interview.
這是面試時唯一重要的事。
C. It allows them to read other people's mind.
它能讓他們看出別人的心思。
D. It protects us from physical injury.
它能保護我們不受肉體上的傷害。

詳解 **答案：A**

關於 body language，在第三個建議裡提到，要避免抓頭或者玩頭髮，因為 Such unnecessary hand movements are often considered as signs of lacking self-control.（這種不必要的手部動作經常被認為是缺乏自制力的跡象）。所以，不經意的動作可能會影響別人的判斷，認為自己具有某種特質，正確答案是 A。選項 C 的 read other people's mind 表示「看出別人在想什麼」，但文章裡並沒有說到可以從動作看出一個人的想法。

|單字片語| **criterion** [kraɪˋtɪrɪən] n. 標準，準則

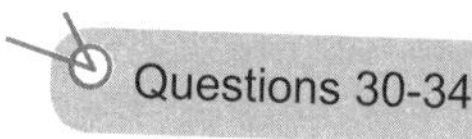

Questions 30-34 are based on the information provided in the following article and email.

The PLAT Diet: It Really Works!

Are you tired of diets that do not work? Then you should try the PLAT diet, which originated in Japan in 2005. Many women have sworn by its results. Although the diet has not been backed up by scientific research, multiple testimonials proved that it is effective for almost everyone, and its effect can last several months. Even though there are side effects such as having difficulty swallowing or breathing, the results are miraculous. Some participants lost 50 lbs in two weeks. There are even stars, such as Biancé, who have started to follow this trend.

The PLAT diet is simple: for two weeks straight, eat nothing but apples, lettuce leaves and rice, and drink one gallon of water every day. Also note that you should avoid eating things after 3 P.M. After you finish a cycle, remember to stop and return to your normal diet for at least a week. After you lose weight successfully with this method, please email your testimonial to weightlossmagazine@losethefat.com.

PLAT 飲食法：真的有效！

您厭倦了沒用的飲食法嗎？那麼您應該試試 2005 年源自日本的 PLAT 飲食法。許多女性非常相信它的效果。雖然這種飲食沒有科學研究的支持，但許多證言證明了它幾乎對每個人都有效，而且它的效果可以持續幾個月。儘管有像是吞嚥或呼吸困難的副作用，結果還是很神奇。一些參與者在兩週內瘦了 50 磅。甚至還有明星，例如碧安絲，已經開始追隨這股潮流。

PLAT 飲食很簡單：連續兩個星期只吃蘋果、萵苣葉和米飯，並且每天喝一加侖的水。也要注意應該避免在下午 3 點後吃東西。完成一輪之後，記得要停止並恢復正常飲食至少一週。用這個方法成功減重後，請將您的證言用電子郵件寄到 weightlossmagazine@losethefat.com。

|單字片語| **originate** [ə`rɪdʒə͵net] v. 發源，來自 / **swear by** 非常相信…的效果 / **testimonial** [͵tɛstə`monɪəl] n. （例如使用者證明效果的）證言 / **miraculous** [mɪ`rækjələs] adj. 神奇的

From: Felicia Patricia <feliciap@eurekamail.com>
To: <weightlossmagazine@losethefat.com>
Subject: On your article about PLAT diet

Dear Weight Loss Magazine,

My name is Felicia Patricia, and I'm writing to voice my concern over the PLAT diet introduced in your March issue. My sister, who has used the diet, is still hospitalized for its serious side effects.
She has battled with her weight for the past ten years. Every month, she reads every single page of your magazine. Finally, she came across the PLAT diet. She immediately decided to try it, and she saw some results. However, she also showed signs of malnutrition, such as tiredness and depression. I begged her to stop, but she just kept eating apples, lettuce, and rice and not having dinner. She also kept going to the bathroom because of drinking a lot of water.
After dieting non-stop for several months, one day she fainted in the bathroom with the most uncomfortable stomach ache and diarrhea. I sent her to a hospital and was told that her kidneys were starting to fail. This email is to let you know that there are people out there suffering from the side effects of the risky diet, and I ask you to only publish articles that are supported by scientific evidence.

Regards,
Felicia Patricia

寄件者：菲莉西亞．派翠西亞 <feliciap@eurekamail.com>
收件者：<weightlossmagazine@losethefat.com>
主旨：關於你們介紹 PLAT 飲食法的文章

親愛的《減重雜誌》：

我的名字是菲莉西亞．派翠西亞，我寫這封信是要對於你們三月號介紹的 PLAT 飲食法表達擔憂。我曾經使用這個飲食法的姊姊，現在還因為它嚴重的副作用而住院中。
過去十年她一直在對抗她的體重。她每個月都讀你們雜誌的每一頁。最後，她發現了 PLAT 飲食法。她馬上決定嘗試，而且看到了一點效果。不過，她也顯現出營養不良的跡象，例如倦怠和憂鬱。我求她停止，但她還是繼續吃蘋果、萵苣和米飯，而且不吃晚餐。她也因為喝許多水而一直上廁所。
連續節食幾個月而沒有停止之後，有一天她昏倒在廁所，胃痛得非常不舒服，而且腹瀉。我把她送到醫院，並且被告知她的腎臟開始有衰竭的情況。這封電子郵件是要讓你們知道，有人正因為這種危險飲食法的副作用而受苦，我也要求你們只發表有科學證據支持的文章。

致上問候
菲莉西亞．派翠西亞

|單字片語| **hospitalize** [ˋhɑspɪtḷˏaɪz] v. 使住院 / **malnutrition** [ˏmælnjuˋtrɪʃən] n. 營養不良 / **diarrhea** [ˏdaɪəˋriə] n. 腹瀉 / **risky** [ˋrɪskɪ] adj. 危險的

What is true about the PLAT diet?
關於 PLAT 飲食法，何者正確？

A. It was invented in Japan.　是在日本被發明的。
B. Its effects have been scientifically proven.　效果經過科學證明。
C. It poses no risks for health.　對健康沒有風險。
D. Biancé started the trend of using it.　碧安絲開始了使用它的潮流。

詳解　　**答案：A**

介紹 PLAT 飲食法的文章（第一篇文章）提到 the PLAT diet, which originated in Japan in 2005（2005 年源自日本的 PLAT 飲食法），表示它是在日本被發明的，所以 A 是正確答案。B. 文章中提到 the diet has not been backed up by scientific research（這種飲食沒有科學研究的支持），和選項敘述相反。C. 文

章中提到 there are side effects（有一些副作用），和選項敘述相反。D. 文章中的 There are even stars, such as Biancé, who have started to follow this trend（甚至還有明星，例如碧安絲，已經開始追隨這股潮流），是表示明星開始追隨風潮，而不是帶頭發起風潮的意思。

Q31

What does Felicia want to tell the magazine in her email?

菲莉西亞在電子郵件中想要告訴這家雜誌社什麼事？

A. The PLAT diet does not work.
PLAT 飲食法沒有用。

B. The method of the PLAT diet needs to be improved.
PLAT 飲食法的方式需要改善。

C. The magazine should compensate her sister.
雜誌社應該賠償她的姊姊。

D. It was irresponsible to publish the article on the PLAT diet.
發表那篇關於 PLAT 飲食法的文章是不負責任的。

詳解

答案：D

在菲莉西亞的電子郵件（第二篇文章）中，她提到姊姊因為使用雜誌介紹的飲食法而傷害了健康，而最後提到 This email is to let you know that there are people out there suffering... and I ask you to only publish articles that are supported by scientific evidence.（這封電子郵件是要讓你們知道，有人正在受苦…我也要求你們只發表有科學證據支持的文章），表示雜誌社不應發表那篇沒有科學證據的 PLAT 飲食法介紹，所以 D 是正確答案。

Q32

According to Felicia, what did NOT happen to her sister?

根據菲莉西亞，她的姊姊沒有發生什麼事？

A. She felt down. 她覺得憂鬱。

B. She had an upset stomach. 她的胃不舒服。

C. She vomited. 她吐了。

D. She had kidney failure. 她有腎衰竭。

詳解

答案：C

電子郵件（第二篇文章）提到了菲莉西亞的姊姊發生的一些症狀，其中 depression（憂鬱）對應 A，uncomfortable stomach（胃不舒服）對應 B，her kidneys were starting to fail（她的腎臟開始有衰竭的情況）對應 D，所以沒提到的 C 是正確答案。

Q33

In the things that Felicia's sister did, what is different from the PLAT diet introduced in the article?

在菲莉西亞的姊姊所做的事情中，哪件事和文章中介紹的 PLAT 飲食法不同？

A. Eating apples, lettuce, and rice　吃蘋果、萵苣和米飯
B. Not having dinner　不吃晚餐
C. Drinking a lot of water　喝許多水
D. Dieting continuously for several months　持續節食幾個月

詳解　　答案：D

這一題必須對照文章（第一篇文章）中對於 PLAT 飲食法的介紹和電子郵件（第二篇文章）提到菲莉西亞的姊姊所做的事來解題。文章中提到 for two weeks straight（連續兩週）和 After you finish a cycle, remember to stop and return to your normal diet for at least a week（完成一輪之後，記得要停止並恢復正常飲食至少一週），表示這個方法不能連續進行超過兩週，而電子郵件則提到 dieting non-stop for several months（連續節食幾個月而沒有停止），表示菲莉西亞的姊姊沒有遵守時間長度上的限制，所以 D 是正確答案。

What do we learn about *Weight Loss Magazine*?

關於《減重雜誌》，我們知道什麼？

A. It tries to invent weight loss methods.
　它試圖發明減重的方法。
B. Some of its articles are written by its readers.
　它的一些文章是讀者寫的。
C. It is a monthly magazine.
　它是月刊。
D. Its articles are reviewed by scientists.
　它的文章經過科學家審閱。

詳解　　答案：C

關於這份雜誌，電子郵件（第二篇文章）提到 your March issue（你們的三月號）和 Every month, she reads every single page of your magazine（她每個月都讀你們雜誌的每一頁），由此可知它是月刊，所以 C 是正確答案。

Questions 35-40

With new breakthroughs in stem cell technology, the life span of human beings are expected to exceed a century and beyond. Stem cells can be divided into two categories: embryonic stem cells and adult stem cells. The former can come from human eggs fertilized in vitro in a laboratory, while the latter are found in fully developed human body. Unlike embryonic stem cells, adult stem cells only have the ability to transform into the same type of cells as in the tissue or organ from which it came. Bone marrow, for instance, can only regenerate bone marrow. On the other hand, embryonic stem cells can, theoretically, be cultivated into ANY type of cell found in the body. By manipulating embryonic stem cells, it is possible to make "custom-made" spare organs that will not incur any risk of rejection while transplanting.

In spite of the optimism of future medical breakthroughs in stem cell technology, many legal, ethical, and religious issues need to be tackled before this technology can be unleashed to reach its full potential. For example, some argue that killing lab-grown embryos to get stem cells is nothing different from abortion. The fact that fertilized human eggs are used for experimental and research purposes is considered unethical and even contrary to many religious beliefs. Scientists in favor of stem-cell technology have reiterated that an embryo is not a fetus (unborn baby) and obtaining embryonic cells is not equivalent to abortion. The problem lies in that it is hard to pinpoint exactly where life starts.

Some leading experts in stem cell technology have urged the public to separate science from religion. Researchers believe that technologies developed from their work will eventually be able to treat a wide variety of illnesses such as cancer, diabetes, and heart diseases. "We are entering a new era of science known as regenerative medicine," a scientist claimed.

There is a vision of a promising distant future among the most optimistic supporters, who believe that organ transplantation will be as common as changing spare parts for cars and machines. As a result, life expectancy is likely to increase dramatically. The elixir of life that eluded emperors and kings of the past could finally be found in our lifetime.

隨著幹細胞技術新的突破，人類的壽命長度預期將超過一個世紀。幹細胞可以分為兩類：胚胎幹細胞和成體幹細胞。前者可以來自實驗室中在培養皿（體外）受精的人類卵子，而後者存在於完全發育的人體中。不像胚胎幹細胞，成體幹細胞只有轉變成和來源組織或器官相同類型細胞的能力。例如骨髓（細胞），就只能再生骨髓。另一方面，胚胎幹細胞理論上可以被培養成身體裡任何種類的細胞。藉由操縱胚胎幹細胞，有可能製造「訂做的」備用器官，而不會在移植時引起任何排斥的風險。

雖然對於未來幹細胞科技的醫學突破有樂觀的看法，但在這項科技被解放並且發揮所有潛力之前，有很多法律、道德和宗教議題需要處理。例如，有些人主張殺死實驗室培養的胚胎並取得幹細胞，和墮胎沒什麼兩樣。人類受精卵被用於實驗與研究目的的事實，被認為不道德，甚至違背許多宗教信仰。支持幹細胞科技的科學家重申，胚胎不是胎兒，而取得胚胎細胞並不等於墮胎。問題在於，很難精確指出生命究竟是從哪裡開始的。

領導幹細胞科技的一些專家勸大眾把科學和宗教分開。研究者相信，從他們所做的研究中開發的科技，最終將能夠治療種類廣泛的疾病，例如癌症、糖尿病和心臟疾病。一位科學家主張：「我們正進入所謂再生醫學的科學新時代。」

最樂觀的支持者對於前途看好的遙遠未來有所展望，他們相信器官移植將會和替換汽車和機器的備用零件一樣平常。結果，（人的）預期壽命很可能會急劇增加。過去的帝王得不到的長生不老藥，可能終於會在我們這一生被找到。

|單字片語|

（第一段）

breakthrough [`brek͵θru] n. 突破，突破性進展 / **stem cell** 幹細胞 / **life span** 壽命（長度） / **exceed** [ɪk`sid] v. 超過 / **category** [`kætə͵gorɪ] n. 種類，類型 / **embryonic** [͵ɛmbrɪ`ɑnɪk] adj. 胚胎的 / **fertilize** [`fɝtl̩͵aɪz] v. 施肥；使受精 / **in vitro** 在（實驗室的）玻璃容器內，在生物體外 / **tissue** [`tɪʃʊ] n. （生物的）組織 / **marrow** [`mæro] n. （骨）髓 / **regenerate** [rɪ`dʒɛnərɪt] v. 再生 / **theoretically** [͵θiə`rɛtɪkl̩ɪ] adv. 理論上 / **manipulate** [mə`nɪpjə͵let] v. 操縱 / **custom-made** [`kʌstəm͵med] adj. 訂做的 / **rejection** [rɪ`dʒɛkʃən] n. （醫學）排斥 / **transplant** [træns`plænt] v. 移植

（第二段）

optimism [`ɑptəmɪzəm] n. 樂觀 / **ethical** [`ɛθɪkl̩] adj. 倫理的，道德的 / **tackle** [`tækl̩] v. 處理，應對 / **unleash** [ʌn`liʃ] v. 解開…的束縛 / **embryo** [`ɛmbrɪ͵o] n. 胚胎 / **abortion** [ə`bɔrʃən] n. 墮胎 / **in favor of** 支持…，贊成… / **reiterate** [ri`ɪtə͵ret] v. 重申，反覆說 / **fetus** [`fitəs] n. 胎兒 / **pinpoint** [`pɪn͵pɔɪnt] v. 準確地確定

（第三段）

diabetes [͵daɪə`bitiz] n. 糖尿病 / **regenerative** [rɪ`dʒɛnə͵retɪv] adj. （生物）再生的

（第四段）

life expectancy 平均餘命（群體的預期壽命） / **elixir** [ɪ`lɪksɚ] n. 靈丹妙藥，不老長壽藥

What is true about embryonic stem cells?

關於胚胎幹細胞，何者正確？

A. They are not as useful as adult stem cells.
它們不像成體幹細胞那麼有用。

B. They are of significant medical value.
它們有很重要的醫學價值。

C. They can be extracted from young adults.
它們可以從年輕人身上取出。

D. They can be cultivated in young women
它們可以在年輕女人身上培養。

詳解

答案：B

第一段的後面提到 embryonic stem cells can, theoretically, be cultivated into ANY type of cell（胚胎幹細胞理論上可以被培養成任何種類的細胞），而且 it is possible to make "custom-made" spare organs that will not incur any risk of rejection（有可能製造「訂做的」備用器官，而不會引起任何排斥的風險），所以 B 是正確答案。

|單字片語| **extract** [ɪk`strækt] v. 取出，提取

Q36

What is the main difference between adult and embryonic stem cells?

成體和胚胎幹細胞的主要差異是什麼？

A. Adult stem cells do not raise religious and ethical concerns.
成體幹細胞不會引起宗教和道德顧慮。

B. Adult stem cells can be cultivated into embryonic stem cells.
成體幹細胞可以培養成胚胎幹細胞。

C. Adult stem cells are riskier, while embryonic stem cells are safer.
成體幹細胞比較危險，而胚胎幹細胞比較安全。

D. Adult stem cells are not as flexible as embryonic stem cells.
成體幹細胞不像胚胎幹細胞那麼有可塑性。

詳解

答案：D

比較這兩種幹細胞的部分是第一段。第一段提到，Unlike embryonic stem cells, adult stem cells only have the ability to transform into the same type of cells as in the tissue or organ from which it came.（不像胚胎幹細胞，成體幹細胞只有轉變

成和來源組織或器官相同類型細胞的能力），所以這兩種幹細胞的差異在於發展成不同細胞的可能性，而 adult stem cells 沒有那麼 flexible，所以 D 是正確答案。

Q37

Which of the following patients is most likely to benefit from stem cell technology?

以下哪個患者最有可能受益於幹細胞科技？

A. Someone who is infected with a deadly virus
感染致命病毒的人

B. Someone who suffers from kidney failure
患有腎臟衰竭的人

C. Someone who is paralyzed after a major car accident
在重大車禍後癱瘓的人

D. Someone who suffers from memory loss due to dementia
因為痴呆而有記憶損失的人

詳解　　答案：B

第一段提到，By manipulating embryonic stem cells, it is possible to make “custom-made” spare organs（藉由操縱胚胎幹細胞，有可能製造「訂做的」備用器官），所以有腎臟疾病的人將有可能利用幹細胞科技製造新的腎臟來替換，正確答案是 B。

Q38

What accounts for a high success rate of treatment via stem cells developed from the patient?

什麼可以解釋用病患身上培養出來的幹細胞進行治療的高成功率？

A. These cells are cultivated using state-of-the-art technology.
這些細胞是用最先進的科技培養的。

B. These cells are able to transform into any organ the body needs.
這些細胞能夠轉變成身體需要的任何器官。

C. These cells are accepted by the immune system as part of the body.
這些細胞被免疫系統當成身體的一部分來接受。

D. These cells can also be used to treat other patients with similar conditions.
這些細胞也能用來治療其他有類似症狀的病患。

詳解

答案：C

同樣在第一段的最後，文章中說用幹細胞科技製作的器官 will not incur any risk of rejection while transplanting（不會在移植時引起任何排斥的風險），也就是選項 C 說的 are accepted by the immune system，所以 C 是正確答案。

|單字片語| **state-of-the-art** [ˋstetəvðiˋɑrt] adj. 最先進的 / **immune** [ɪˋmjun] adj. 免疫的

Q39

In the opinion of some optimists, what does the future hold for stem cell technology?

根據某些樂觀主義者的意見，幹細胞科技的未來怎麼樣？

A. Stem cell technology will be a highly lucrative venture.
幹細胞科技會是非常高利潤的風險投資。

B. Patients will be able to sell their body parts to hospitals.
患者將能夠把身體部位販賣給醫院。

C. Human life span will be prolonged due to replaceable organs.
人類的壽命長度將會因為可替換的器官而被延長。

D. Businesses will engage in sales of organs and organ transplantation.
業者將會投入器官販賣和器官移植。

詳解

答案：C

最後一段提到，There is a vision of a promising distant future among the most optimistic supporters（最樂觀的支持者對於前途看好的未來有所展望），他們認為由於器官移植的普及，As a result, life expectancy is likely to increase dramatically.（結果，預期壽命很可能會急劇增加）。所以，正確答案是 C。其他選項在文章中沒有提到。

|單字片語| **lucrative** [ˋlukrətɪv] adj. 賺錢的，有利可圖的 / **venture** [ˋvɛntʃɚ] n. 風險投資

Q40

What is the primary controversy regarding the use of embryonic stem cells?

關於胚胎幹細胞使用的主要爭議是什麼？

A. Embryonic stem cells are not 100% reliable.
胚胎幹細胞不是百分之百可靠。

B. Embryonic stem cells are affecting our fertility.
胚胎幹細胞正在影響我們的生育能力。

C. Embryonic stem cells are seen as potential babies.
胚胎幹細胞被視為可能的嬰兒。

D. Embryonic stem cells are only available for the rich.
胚胎幹細胞只有富人能夠得到。

詳解 **答案：C**

關於 controversy 的部分是第二段。第二段提到，some argue that killing lab-grown embryos to get stem cells is nothing different from abortion（有些人主張殺死實驗室培養的胚胎並取得幹細胞，和墮胎沒什麼兩樣），而支持幹細胞科技的科學家則主張 an embryo is not a fetus (unborn baby)（胚胎不是胎兒）。所以，使用胚胎幹細胞的一項爭議是胚胎究竟是不是嬰兒，正確答案是 C。

|單字片語| **fertility** [fɝˋtɪlətɪ] n. 生育能力；（土壤的）肥沃

全民英語能力分級檢定測驗
GENERAL ENGLISH PROFICIENCY TEST

中高級聽力測驗　第五回
HIGH-INTERMEDIATE LISTENING COMPREHENSION TEST

This listening comprehension test will test your ability to understand spoken English. In this test, each conversation, short talk and question will be spoken JUST ONE TIME. They will not be written out for you. There are three parts to this test. Special instructions will be given to you at the beginning of each part.

Part I: Answering Questions

In Part I, you will hear ten questions. After you hear a question, read the four choices in your test booklet and decide which one is the best answer to the question you have heard.

Example:

You will hear: Why did you slam the door?

You will read:
A. I just can't open it.
B. I didn't. I guess it's the wind.
C. Because someone is at the door.
D. Because the door knob is missing.

The best answer to the question "Why did you slam the door?" is B: "I didn't. I guess it's the wind." Therefore, you should choose answer B.

1. A. As soon as the council makes a decision.
   B. Not until the monsoon season is over.
   C. The surgeon said it will be fine.
   D. Global warming might change things around.

2. A. I'm having cold feet.
   B. They are getting out of hand.
   C. Let's keep our fingers crossed.
   D. Two heads are better than one.

3. A. Please turn on the air-conditioning.
   B. Please count to three before you start.
   C. Please leave a message after the beep.
   D. Please connect me to extension 428.

4. A. Spend at least $100 at the store.
   B. Offer some sacrifices in a temple.
   C. Present your résumé and qualifications.
   D. Submit your still life paintings.

5. A. Right. Phone scams are truly concerning.
   B. The new intern has the best potential.
   C. Really? I don't know it's so effective.
   D. Honestly, temporary loss of vision is possible.

6. A. I found it using the online map.
   B. He's not my type of guy.
   C. It's a thriller that keeps you awake.
   D. What matters is the fertility of the soil.

7. A. I don't have any, not to mention a few.
   B. I'm not sure why they turned off the lights.
   C. I promise such a thing will not happen again.
   D. I happen to own one, but I can't lend it to you.

8. A. Low interest rates made buying homes easier.
   B. We've been waiting for this historic moment.
   C. It will cost a bomb to repair a house.
   D. It's achieved with very sophisticated technology.

Please turn to the next page. ⇨

9. A. Let's organize the match on the field instead.
   B. Let's review the manuscript before we send it.
   C. Let's compromise and opt for a settlement.
   D. Let's get a lawyer and sue them for slander.

10. A. Ten miles at most.
    B. I will do everything it takes.
    C. It depends on the car engine.
    D. Some say it's really worth it.

Part II: Conversation

In part II, you will hear several conversations between a man and a woman. After each conversation, you will hear a question about the conversation. After you hear the question, read the four choices in your test booklet and choose the best answer to the question you have heard.

Example:

You will hear:	(Man)	Did you happen to see my earphones? I remember leaving them in the drawer. Someone must have taken it.
	(Woman)	It's more likely that you misplaced them. Did you search your briefcase?
	(Man)	I did, but they are not there. Wait a second. Oh. They are right here in my pocket.
	Question:	Who took the man's earphones?

You will read:

A. The woman.
B. Someone else.
C. No one.
D. Another man.

The best answer to the question "Who took the man's earphones?" is C: "No one." Therefore, you should choose answer C.

11. A. Publicity department.
    B. Accounting department.
    C. Sales department.
    D. Maintenance department.

12. A. He thinks mathematics is too difficult.
    B. He doesn't enjoy his cooking lesson.
    C. He is on the edge of bankruptcy.
    D. He is hiding something from the woman.

13. A. It should be sold at a garage sale.
    B. It should be discarded.
    C. It should be used to heat pizzas.
    D. They should buy a new model.

14. A. He has a better ranking.
    B. He has more experience.
    C. He has better stamina.
    D. He has a slight limp.

15. A. Take care of the man's dental problem.
    B. Give the man a body massage.
    C. Perform physical therapy on the man.
    D. Write a speech for the man.

16. A. She will lose them all.
    B. She will have them developed.
    C. She will store them on i-Cloud.
    D. She will transfer them to D drive.

17. A. A travel plan.
    B. A church wedding.
    C. A conference schedule.
    D. A traveling exhibition.

18. A. On an airplane.
    B. In a cinema.
    C. In an auditorium.
    D. In a holiday resort.

19. A. Behaving intimately in front of others.
    B. Understanding a foreign culture.
    C. Finding food that suits her taste.
    D. Coping with the high cost of living.

20. A. Philosophy.
    B. Economics.
    C. Accounting.
    D. Business administration.

21. A. The stock market was soaring before it.
    B. There was a positive atmosphere then.
    C. It has nothing to do with foreign countries.
    D. Most people were in debt for their businesses.

22. A. The ATM is out of order.
    B. She has not activated her card.
    C. She has a bad credit history.
    D. Her card has expired.

23. A. Ask for a new card in person.
    B. Make an application on the phone.
    C. Extend the expiry date online.
    D. Send the card to one of the branches.

24.

Nishiba 65U8000 (65-inch)	Pansonic 55JX750 (55-inch)
- Internet connectivity - Surround sound - Color accuracy technology - NT$ 39,000	- Internet connectivity - Color accuracy technology - NT$ 23,900
Chime 55R-500 (55-inch)	**Heron 65JCH (65-inch)**
- Internet connectivity - Surround sound - NT$ 18,900	- Surround sound - NT$ 15,900

A. Nishiba 65U8000.
B. Pansonic 55JX750.
C. Chime 55R-500.
D. Heron 65JCH.

Please turn to the next page.

25.

Country	Cost of Living	Demand for Foreign Professionals
Australia	High	High
Malaysia	Average	Average
Japan	High	Average
Taiwan	Average	High

A. Australia.
B. Malaysia.
C. Japan.
D. Taiwan.

Part III: Short Talks

In part III, you will hear several short talks. After each talk, you will hear two to three questions about the talk. After you hear each question, read the four choices in your test booklet and choose the best answer to the question you have heard.

Example:

You will hear: Hello, thank you everyone for coming together to share this special day with Chris and I. We have been waiting for this moment forever, and after five years of dating, I can happily say that I am ready. Chris is caring and charming, and I appreciate my good fortune in marrying such a warm-hearted man. When he proposed to me, I realized that he had already become a part of my life. Even though I'm not a perfect cook or housekeeper, I know for sure that I will be a wonderful partner for Chris.

Question number 1: On what occasion is this talk most probably being given?

You will read:
A. A funeral.
B. A wedding.
C. A housewarming.
D. A farewell party.

The best answer to the question "On what occasion is this talk most probably being given?" is B: "A wedding." Therefore, you should choose answer B.

Now listen to another question based on the same talk.

Please turn to the next page.

You will hear: Question number 2: According to this talk, what does the woman like about Chris?

You will read: A. His perseverance.
B. His abundant wealth.
C. His cooking skill.
D. His amiable personality.

The best answer to the question "According to this talk, what does the woman like about Chris?" is D: "His amiable personality." Therefore, you should choose answer D.

Please turn to the next page. Now let us begin Part III with question number 26.

26. A. Provide details about the set of keys.
    B. Tell the clerk where they were stolen.
    C. Proceed to the supermarket immediately.
    D. Write a letter to explain what happened.

27. A. The department store will be closing soon.
    B. The discount is only for a limited time.
    C. All items in the supermarket are on sale.
    D. Only cardholders are entitled to the offer.

28. A. Rich and poor people's different habits.
    B. What the rich and poor have in common.
    C. Why the poor envy people who are rich.
    D. How come rich people are so busy.

29. A. They struggle to complete tasks in time.
    B. They spend too much time worrying.
    C. They work for wrong organizations.
    D. They waste time complaining about their bosses.

30. A. Scheduling things that need to be done.
    B. Seeking advice from the management.
    C. Asking for a deadline extension.
    D. Developing a sense of pride.

31. A. A spray that prevents insect bites.
    B. A wearable item that wards off bugs.
    C. A magnet that keeps mosquitoes away.
    D. A device that terminates pests.

32. A. Where to purchase the product.
    B. How to use the product.
    C. How to receive a special discount.
    D. How to prolong its effects.

33. A. A firefighter was killed during the fire.
    B. A gas leak led to the accident.
    C. Three lives were lost due to the explosion.
    D. A man killed his children before suiciding.

Please turn to the next page.

34. A. He wanted a divorce.
B. He survived the fire.
C. He was emotionally unstable.
D. He made a killing in the stock market.

35-37.

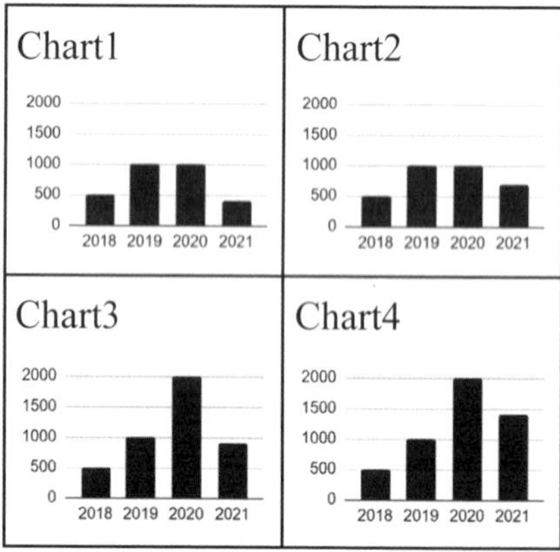

35. A. The president of the university.
B. A director of the university.
C. A teacher of the university.
D. A student of the university.

36. A. Chart 1.
B. Chart 2.
C. Chart 3.
D. Chart 4.

37. A. The new president is incompetent.
B. The younger population is getting smaller.
C. The university's reputation is bad.
D. The university spent less money on advertising.

38-40.

Destination	Votes	Activities
Yilan	9	Cold spring, factory tour
Chiayi	5	?, watching the sunrise
Pingtung	16	Snorkeling, night market

38. A. Hiking.
B. Camping.
C. Jogging.
D. Safari.

39. A. They like water sports.
B. They want to visit night markets.
C. They will attend a music festival.
D. Many youngsters think it is an awesome place.

40. A. Yilan.
B. Chiayi.
C. Pingtung.
D. He does not have a preference.

READING COMPREHEHESION TEST

This is a three-part test with forty multiple-choice questions. Each question has four choices. Special instructions will be provided for each part. You will have fifty minutes to complete this test.

Part I: Sentence Completion

In this part of the test, there are ten incomplete sentences. Beneath each sentence you will see four words or phrases, marked A, B, C and D. You are to choose the word or phrase that best completes the sentence. Then on your answer sheet, find the number of the question and mark your answer.

1. There was a heated debate over whether leadership is an intrinsic trait or a skill that can be learned and ________.

   A. bolstered　　B. probed
   C. nurtured　　D. trimmed

2. The soccer match turned out to be a ________ after several sections of the stadium collapsed, killing at least eight hundred spectators.

   A. catastrophe　　B. tournament
   C. paralysis　　D. humiliation

3. The burglar ________ gloves, for there is not a single fingerprint to be found.

   A. ought to put on　　B. was to put on
   C. must have put on　　D. should have put on

4. It has been thirty years since he entered the teaching profession. ________, he has no regrets dedicating his youth coaching teenagers.

   A. In turn　　B. In contrast
   C. In particular　　D. In retrospect

Please turn to the next page.

5. Work on the Gothic-style cathedral, which ________ over a period of fifteen years, was finally completed last month.
   A. spanned B. persisted
   C. sustained D. postponed

6. I have lost contact with my former colleague Jane for many years, but last week she sent me a letter ________.
   A. on the spot B. off the record
   C. out of the blue D. once in a while

7. One common trait among successful people is that they seem to ______ a sense of satisfaction from their work.
   A. derive B. magnify
   C. reconcile D. seduce

8. To solve manpower shortage problems, workers are offered double their usual pay as an ________ for working during holidays.
   A. accessory B. incentive
   C. obligation D. evaluation

9. Among teachers who were interviewed, a majority believed that punishment helps to correct undesirable behavior to a certain ________.
   A. expanse B. expense
   C. extent D. extend

10. White materials can reflect light and heat effectively. ________, black materials absorb light and heat, which is why you feel warmer when you are dressed in black.
   A. Ultimately B. Conversely
   C. Inevitably D. Accordingly

Part Two: Cloze

In this part of the test, you will read two passages. Each passage contains five missing words or phrases. Beneath each passage, you will see five items, each with four choices, marked A, B, C and D. You are to choose the best answer for each missing word or phrase in the two passages. Then, on your answer sheet, find the number of the question and mark your answer.

Questions 11-15

For both children and adults alike, a visit to the dentist can be a terrifying experience. For one, having someone ___(11)___ inside your mouth with sharp metallic instruments is not pleasant at all. For another, the frightening drilling noise does make your heart beat faster. Actually, I also have had some unpleasant experiences with dentists myself. I remember when I went to a dentist as a child, I dared not move my tongue ___(12)___ it gets pierced by the drill. As I grew up, however, ___(13)___. I use a psychological technique ___(14)___ the appointment with my dentist. I keep telling myself it is going to hurt a lot. After a while, I kind of resign myself to my fate. Even if the treatment turns out to be really painful, the ___(15)___ is rarely beyond my imagination.

11. A. caress
    B. maneuver
    C. probe
    D. torture

12. A. for now
    B. for that
    C. in case
    D. in order that

13. A. the trauma is still haunting me
    B. I learned how to overcome my fear
    C. I do not need to see a dentist that often
    D. visiting a dentist has not become any easier

Please turn to the next page.

14. A. prior to
B. in addition to
C. out of
D. in front of

15. A. agony
B. irony
C. vanity
D. diversity

Questions 16-20

A novelist who penned a story about a failed bank robbery ___(16)___ by carrying out a crime identical to the one he wrote about. Like the character in his book, the writer found himself struggling to ___(17)___, so he decided to hold up a bank. However, just like in his book, things didn't go ___(18)___ the plan. On August 14 this year, he entered a bank wearing a mask. ___(19)___ with a pistol, he threatened staff and ordered a teller to open the safe, which was protected by a time delay system. After 25 minutes on the premises, he fled with $32,000, a tiny fraction of the millions of dollars the character in the novel made away with. In his book, the villain flees on a bike and changes clothes behind an oak tree. In real life, the robber novelist also had a bike. Eventually, the character in the book was caught after two hours, while the novelist himself was ___(20)___ and arrested by the police two minutes after leaving the bank. The same factor as in his book led to his failure: the silent alarm system installed in all banks.

16. A. stuck to his word
B. turned fiction into reality
C. fully realized his potential
D. performed well above expectations

18. A. according to
B. regardless of
C. in addition to
D. as a result of

17. A. learn the ropes
B. make ends meet
C. pay lip service
D. steal the limelight

19. A. Arm
B. Armed
C. Arming
D. To arm

20. A. ambushed
B. collaborated
C. irritated
D. recruited

Please turn to the next page.

Part III: Reading Comprehension

In this part of the test, you will find several tasks. Each task contains one or two passages or charts, which are followed by two to six questions. You are to choose the best answer, A, B, C, or D, to each question on the basis of the information provided or implied in the passage or chart. Then, on your answer sheet, find the number of the question and mark your answer.

Questions 21-22 are based on the information provided in the following chart.

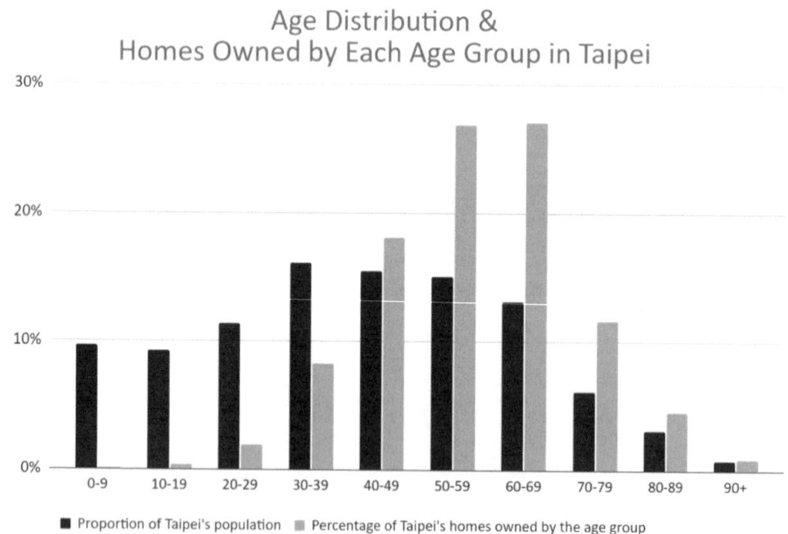

21. Based on the chart, which of the following statements is true?
    A. Every person in Taipei begins to have a home in his or her 40s.
    B. Over half of the homes in Taipei are owned by people aged 50-69.
    C. In Taipei, about one in two persons aged 30-39 has his or her own home.
    D. People aged under 30 and over 89 both have low home-ownership rates.

22. To help more people in Taipei own their own homes, which of the following strategies will be the most effective?
   A. Building more homes that are affordable for people under 40
   B. Offering lower home loan interest rates for the elderly
   C. Encouraging retired people to invest in real estate
   D. Offering more real estate jobs for young people

Questions 23-25

According to Greek mythology, Prometheus stole fire from Zeus and handed it over to man because he felt that man was superior to all other animals. The mastery of fire allowed mankind to defend themselves from wild creatures, but it angered the gods, Zeus in particular. Zeus, the king of all Greek gods and goddesses, viewed the use of fire as an unfair advantage to mankind.

Legend has it that Zeus created a woman named Pandora, which means “all-gifted”. To punish mankind, Zeus ordered the other gods to gift Pandora with their unique powers to rival man. Pandora was given some traits from the different gods: Hephaestus molded her out of clay and gave her form; Zeus made her idle, mischievous, and foolish; Aphrodite gave her beauty; Hera gave her curiosity; Hermes, along with giving her cunning, boldness, and charm, also gave Pandora a box.

Pandora was then given to Epimetheus, the brother of Prometheus. Adhering to his brother’s advice, Epimetheus told Pandora never to open the box she had received. One day, however, Pandora’s curiosity got the better of her, and she opened the box, releasing all the misfortunes of mankind: sickness, sorrow, poverty, crime, etc. It was said that all human sufferings began from the day Pandora’s box was opened. Fortunately, there was a twist to the story in the end. Pandora shut the box in time to keep one thing in the box: *hope*. In spite of all challenges and misery that befall upon mankind, there is always hope.

Please turn to the next page.

23. Why was Zeus furious that mankind obtained the ability of using fire?
    A. Humans might use the power of fire to rebel against the gods.
    B. Humans and animals should fight on an even playing field.
    C. Humans could abuse this gift and bring about their own destruction.
    D. Humans should discover the secret only after working hard for it.

24. What is true about the gifts Pandora received from the gods?
    A. Hephaestus created her from his own body.
    B. Zeus made her diligent so she can help man.
    C. Hera's gift caused her to disobey Epimetheus.
    D. Hermes taught her how to be meek and humble.

25. What message does the thing kept inside Pandora's box implies?
    A. Never despair in the face of hardships.
    B. Wisdom is more precious than wealth.
    C. Always respect the gods and never risk their wrath.
    D. Beware of women with great beauty.

Questions 26-29

Are you envious of the lifestyles of the rich and famous? Have you ever wondered how the world's elites managed to make so much money? The secret lies in diversification, meaning they have multiple streams of income. Apart from their primary jobs, which may be acting, news anchoring, singing, or playing sports, these celebrities also make money by investing in financial markets and/or running their own businesses. In addition, their image and reputation can also earn them some easy money once in a while.

Product endorsements are where they make the big bucks. With shrewd marketing strategies, companies are able to sell more products with the aid of these superstars. The seemingly outrageous fees, ranging from hundreds of thousands to millions in dollars, are but a small percentage of the net profits turned in by multinational corporations. A more recent trend sees celebrities putting their names and money behind restaurants or hotels to bring in more revenue, both for the businesses and for themselves. Creating their own brands is also a way that celebrities can make a killing. Guess how much revenue Kim Kardashian's beauty brand brings in per year: a staggering $100 million! That's an astronomical sum for those of us who aspire to be millionaires.

While celebrities make a killing and live a luxurious life through various sources of income, ordinary people may find it unfair that their own salaries are only enough to feed themselves. According to Pareto's 80/20 Principle, 20 percent of the people possess 80 percent of the wealth. This universal law has been proven again and again in every society and nation. Communist countries may be exceptions, but when their economy is liberated, even to a limited extent, the "invisible hand" seems to work in favor of the top-20-percent elites. While the top 20 percent enjoy the abundance of 80 percent of wealth in a given society, 80 percent of the population struggle and fight for the scraps in the remaining 20 percent of wealth. This is indeed a concerning situation.

Please turn to the next page.

26. According to the article, what is the secret to an extraordinarily high level of income?
    A. Maintaining a young appearance
    B. Attaining above-average intelligence
    C. Purchasing products at a low price
    D. Generating revenue from various sources

27. Which of the following is **NOT** a way celebrities make money as mentioned in the article?
    A. Investing in the hospitality industry
    B. Buying and selling stocks
    C. Teaching people how to build their reputation
    D. Appearing in the media to promote products

28. What is true about a celebrity's additional sources of income?
    A. They may have nothing to do with his or her main job.
    B. They are usually for the sake of charity.
    C. They are not controllable.
    D. They are only available before retirement.

29. Why are some companies willing to pay a large sum of money to have celebrities endorse their products?
    A. They think that having a good image is more important than earning more.
    B. The prospective growth of profits can exceed the cost of product endorsement.
    C. It will be easier to convince the celebrities to invest in their businesses.
    D. The celebrities themselves will become loyal users and keep buying.

Questions 30-34 are based on the information provided in the following advertisement and email.

Room for Rent

23 Latue Road (near the subway)
1 bedroom / 1 bath
0918 887 0918 Rll@rentthemall.com

Big, bright, and sunny apartment awaits you in Downtown Boston. This is a one-bedroom, one-bath apartment. It features not only all-new appliances but also a trash chute, so you do not have to take out garbage by yourself. This newly renovated apartment could be available for you for $5,000 a month. The apartment comes with: washing and drying machines, oven, microwave, lighting fixtures, bed, mattress, sofa, etc. All you need to do is bring your things and move in. Even though there is only one bedroom, it is quite large, so the apartment is suitable for couples who do not have kids. The apartment does not accept dogs, but cats are okay. If you are interested in renting this apartment, please send us an email with your name, phone number, and a description of yourself so that we may pass it on to the owner. Feel free to contact us for more information about this apartment or other rental properties in the Northeast.

Please turn to the next page.

From: Rasmina Modi <RModi@polliemail.com>
To: <Rll@rentthemall.com>
Subject: The Latue Road Apartment

Greetings,

My name is Rasmina Modi. I'm from India, and I have a PhD in neurophysics from Yale. I'm interested in renting the Latue Road apartment listed on your website because I've decided to move to the neighborhood with my husband. I'll be working as a lecturer at the university there, and the apartment is just across the street from it, so the location is ideal for me. However, I was wondering if it would be possible for the owner to lower the rent to $4,000 a month if we bring our own furniture. Also, we don't need the kitchen appliances since we have just bought new ones.

We have a tabby cat, which is rather quiet and well-behaved, so I believe it won't cause any problems. We have no kids, but we're planning to have one. If the apartment is still available, please do not hesitate to contact me at 123-456-7798.

Best Regards,
Rasmina Modi

30. What is **NOT** true about the apartment?
   A. It is close to public transportation.
   B. Trash will be taken out by someone else.
   C. It is in a newly constructed building.
   D. It comes with some furniture.

31. Who may be the writer of the advertisement?
   A. The owner of the apartment
   B. The manager of the apartment building
   C. A university housing officer
   D. A real estate agent

32. What may be a problem for someone who lives in this apartment?
   A. Having a cat
   B. Having a child
   C. Having a spouse
   D. Having a day job

33. What do we learn about Rasmina?
   A. She is a teacher at Yale University.
   B. She will work in Boston.
   C. She got married recently.
   D. She is a working mother.

34. What fact may discourage Rasmina from renting this apartment?
   A. The rent is high for her.
   B. It does not allow pets.
   C. It does not have kitchen appliances.
   D. She has to walk from there to work.

Please turn to the next page. ⇨

Questions 35-40

The environmental impact of meat consumption has long been cited by advocates of vegetarianism to promote a vegetable-based, meat-free lifestyle. Some in-depth research on this issue, however, shows that vegetarianism does not necessarily help reduce energy use and greenhouse gas emissions. The findings of a new study by US scientists indicate that decreasing meat consumption and increasing vegetable intake could actually be **detrimental** to the environment. The reason is that compared to meat, vegetables are far less effective sources of calories, which means that you have to eat a lot more vegetables to gain the same amount of calories as by eating meat. The scientists calculated the amount of greenhouse gas emissions per calorie for each kind of food, and they found that eating lettuce is three-time more environmentally unfriendly than eating bacon. Eggplant, celery, and cucumbers are also significantly worse than pork and chicken under such calculation.

While it is still true that meat production is a major source of pollution and greenhouse gases, this new study offers a different way to see the whole situation. It takes into consideration the effectiveness of foods to human bodies, which is generally neglected in pro-vegetarianism studies. Just imagine that you have to eat broccoli instead of beef to maintain your energy intake. If you used to eat a kilogram of beef per day, that will be 6.7 kilograms of broccoli. As you can see, it is unreasonable not to adopt a human-centered point of view in such studies.

The new study introduces a new dimension for us to reconsider how environmentally friendly our diet is. Also, we should note that eating healthily is not equal to eating in an eco-friendly way, and vice versa. Besides, there are actually many other factors that affect our food choices, such as our tastes, religious beliefs, and food prices, just to name a few. Therefore, it is in fact unhuman to believe that everyone should think about carbon footprint before they eat. All in all, it is best for us to strike a balance and not be over-reliant on any particular food source.

35. The word “detrimental” in the first paragraph is closest in meaning to
   A. irrelevant
   B. suitable
   C. harmful
   D. beneficial

36. Which of the following argument against eating meat is challenged in this article?
   A. Eating meat is against religious beliefs in many cultures.
   B. Meat production leads to greater pollution than vegetable farming.
   C. Current farming methods are cruel to animals.
   D. Meat consumption negatively affects our well-being.

37. What is the most important finding of the new scientific study?
   A. What we eat has nothing to do with our health.
   B. Meat is essential as our bodies need it to function well.
   C. Certain vegetables are low in nutritious values.
   D. Vegetarian diets may cause more harm to the environment.

38. In what way is the new scientific study innovative?
   A. It proves that meat production is actually environmentally friendly.
   B. It recommends a completely new diet that helps us to eat a lot less.
   C. Its findings suggest that eating meat can make us healthier than eating vegetables.
   D. It analyzes the data with a method that most scientists haven’t thought of.

39. What kind of eating habit does the author consider to be appropriate?
   A. Consuming various types of food every day
   B. Eating meat instead of vegetables if possible
   C. Choosing eco-friendly food all the time
   D. Avoiding vegetables that are low in calories

40. Which of the following is the most appropriate title for this article?
   A. Eco-friendly food is not the best for your health
   B. New study breaks the myth that vegetarian diet can save the earth
   C. Guidelines for making healthy and responsible food choices
   D. How a biased perspective can distort the results of a scientific study

第五回

初試 聽力測驗解析

第一部分 回答問題

Q1

I can't stand the rain. When can we expect the weather conditions to change for the better?

我受不了下雨了。我們什麼時候可以期待天氣狀況好轉呢？

A. As soon as the council makes a decision. A. 只要議會做出決定。
B. Not until the monsoon season is over. B. 在雨季結束之前都不會。
C. The surgeon said it will be fine. C. 外科醫師說會變好的。
D. Global warming might change things around. D. 全球暖化可能會把一切逆轉。

詳解 答案：B

說話者說他 can't stand the rain（受不了下雨），問 When... the weather conditions to change for the better（什麼時候天氣狀況會好轉）。A 和 B 使用了表示時間點的連接詞 as soon as（一…就）和 not until（直到…都不），但只有 B 的 the monsoon season is over（雨季結束）和下雨有關，是正確答案。

|單字片語| **council** [ˋkaʊnsḷ] n. 會議；議會 / **monsoon** [mɑnˋsun] n. 季風；雨季 / **surgeon** [ˋsɝdʒən] n. 外科醫師 / **global warming** 全球暖化 / **around** [əˋraʊnd] adv. 朝相反方向

Q2

What's taking them so long to announce the champion? Do you think we stand a chance?

是什麼讓他們花這麼多時間去宣布冠軍？你覺得我們有機會嗎？

A. I'm having cold feet. A. 我退縮了。
B. They are getting out of hand. B. 他們要失控了。
C. Let's keep our fingers crossed. C. 我們祈求會有好運吧。
D. Two heads are better than one. D. 兩個人的智慧勝過一個人。

詳解 答案：C

說話者說的 What's taking them so long to announce the champion? 表示花了很久的時間還沒宣布冠軍，所以應該是某種競賽結束了，正在等待結果發表。說話者又問 Do you think we stand a chance?，顯示兩人參與了比賽，要問對方是否認為彼此有機會奪冠。所以，應該回答關於結果發表或得名機會的內容。選項 C 的 keep one's fingers crossed 代表交叉手指、祈求有好運的動作，表示雖然不知道結果怎樣，但希望結果是好的，是最適當的答案。A 是表示參加活動之前臨陣退縮的感覺。D 是表示兩個人一起想辦法會比單打獨鬥來得好。

|單字片語| **champion** [ˋtʃæmpɪən] n. 優勝者，冠軍 / **stand a chance** 有機會，有希望（成功等等）/ **have cold feet** 臨陣退縮 / **get out of hand** 失去控制 / **keep one's fingers crossed** 祈求好運 / **two heads are better than one** 兩個人的智慧勝過一個人

Q3

A very warm good afternoon to you. This is Orange Tree Consultancy. How may I be of assistance?

向您致上溫暖的午安問候。這裡是 Orange Tree 顧問公司。有什麼我可以幫忙的嗎？

A. Please turn on the air-conditioning. A. 請把空調打開。
B. Please count to three before you start. B. 請在開始之前數到三。
C. Please leave a message after the beep. C. 請在嗶聲之後留言。
D. Please connect me to extension 428. D. 請幫我轉接分機 428。

詳解 答案：D

說話者並不是說下午很溫暖，而是要向對方致上很溫暖的「good afternoon」。說話者用 This is... 說出公司名稱，並且問 How may I be of assistance?（有什麼我可以幫忙的嗎），可以得知這個人剛接起電話，而且可能是公司的總機。所以，要求轉接到某個分機號碼的 D 是正確答案。

|單字片語| **be of assistance** 幫上忙 / **air-conditioning** [ˋɛrkən͵dɪʃənɪŋ] n. 空調 / **beep** [bip] n. 嗶聲 / **extension** [ɪkˋstɛnʃən] n. 電話分機

Q4

Look at that! The first prize is a BMW convertible. How can I enter the prize draw?

你看那個！頭獎是一台 BMW 敞篷車。我要怎樣才能參加抽獎呢？

A. Spend at least $100 at the store.
B. Offer some sacrifices in a temple.
C. Present your résumé and qualifications.
D. Submit your still life paintings.

A. 在這家店消費至少 100 美元。
B. 提供一些供品給廟方。
C. 提出你的履歷和資格證明。
D. 提交你的靜物畫。

詳解

答案：A

說話者問 How can I enter the prize draw?（我要怎樣才能參加抽獎呢？），所以要回答參加 prize draw 的方法。prize draw 通常是商店的促銷抽獎活動，所以回答消費滿額的 A 是最合理的答案。

|單字片語| **convertible** [kən`vɝtəbl̩] n. 敞篷車 / **prize draw** 抽獎 / **sacrifice** [`sækrə͵faɪs] n. 祭品 / **qualification** [͵kwɑləfə`keʃən] 資格，資格證書 / **still life** 靜物畫

Q5

I'm considering laser eye surgery, but I'm also concerned if there are potential side effects.

我正在考慮眼睛雷射手術，但我也擔心是否有可能的副作用。

A. Right. Phone scams are truly concerning.
B. The new intern has the best potential.
C. Really? I don't know it's so effective.
D. Honestly, temporary loss of vision is possible.

A. 沒錯。電話詐騙真的很令人擔憂。
B. 新來的實習生有最好的潛力。
C. 真的嗎？我不知道它這麼有效。
D. 老實說，暫時性的視力損失是有可能的。

詳解

答案：D

說話者在考慮眼睛雷射手術（laser eye surgery），但也擔心是否有可能的副作用（potential side effects）。之所以這麼說，是希望對方能提供一些關於副作用的資訊，作為考慮是否動手術的參考。所以，提到副作用 loss of vision（視力損失）的 D 是正確答案。

|單字片語| **laser** [\`lezɚ] n. 雷射 / **concerned** [kən\`sɝnd] adj. 擔心的 / **potential** [pə\`tɛnʃəl] adj. 潛在的，可能的 n. 潛力，可能性 / **side effects** 副作用 / **scam** [\`skæm] n. 騙局，詐騙 / **concerning** [kən\`sɝnɪŋ] adj. 令人擔心的 / **intern** [ɪn\`tɝn] n. 實習生

Q6

Besides the characters, how do you find the plot in Stephen King's latest novel?

除了人物以外，你覺得史蒂芬・金最新的小說情節怎麼樣？

A. I found it using the online map. A. 我用線上地圖找到了。
B. He's not my type of guy. B. 他不是我喜歡的那種男人。
C. It's a thriller that keeps you awake. C. 那是一部讓你睡不著的驚悚小說。
D. What matters is the fertility of the soil. D. 重要的是土壤的肥沃度。

詳解 答案：C

說話者問的是 how do you find the plot in... novel（你覺得小說情節怎樣），find 在這裡表示「發覺、覺得」的意思，所以要回答和小說情節相關的敘述。C 回答那是一部 thriller（驚悚作品），而且 keeps you awake（讓你保持警醒→睡不著），表示小說情節讓人覺得緊張、不敢鬆懈，是正確答案。thriller 也可以表示「驚悚電影」，意思和 horror film 相近。

|單字片語| **thriller** [\`θrɪlɚ] n. 驚悚小說、電影等等 / **fertility** [fɝ\`tɪlətɪ] n. 肥沃（度）

Q7

You are a half hour late, young lady. You are aware that the dormitory has a curfew, aren't you?

年輕的小姐，你晚了半小時了。你知道宿舍有宵禁吧？

A. I don't have any, not to mention a few. A. 我一個都沒有，更別說有幾個了。
B. I'm not sure why they turned off the lights. B. 我不確定他們為什麼把燈關掉了。
C. I promise such a thing will not happen again. C. 我保證這種事不會再發生。
D. I happen to own one, but I can't lend it to you. D. 我剛好有一個，但我不能借你。

詳解

答案：C

說話者對一位女性（young lady）說 You are a half hour late（你晚了半小時），並且提醒對方應該知道宿舍有 curfew（宵禁），表示對方違反了宵禁規定。因為做錯了事，所以像 C 一樣保證自己不會再犯，是合理的回答。curfew 這個字比較難，但在這一題如果知道這個字的意思會比較容易作答。

|單字片語| **dormitory** [ˋdɔrmə͵torɪ] n. 宿舍 / **curfew** [ˋkɝfju] n. 宵禁 / **happen to do** 碰巧…

Q8

I just don't get it. Why are home prices going through the roof and breaking new records?

我就是不懂。為什麼房價急升，破了新紀錄呢？

A. Low interest rates made buying homes easier.
B. We've been waiting for this historic moment.
C. It will cost a bomb to repair a house.
D. It's achieved with very sophisticated technology.

A. 低利率讓買房子變得比較容易。
B. 我們一直在等待這歷史性的一刻。
C. 修理房子要花很多錢。
D. 這是靠著非常精密的科技達成的。

詳解

答案：A

說話者問為什麼（Why）房價 going through the roof（衝破屋頂，比喻「飆升」）並且 breaking new records（打破新紀錄），所以要回答房價上升的理由。A 回答低（貸款）利率讓買房子變得容易（因為買的人多，房價就容易上漲），是正確答案。

|單字片語| **interest rate** 利率 / **historic** [hɪsˋtɔrɪk] adj. 有歷史意義的 / **cost a bomb** （口語）花很多錢 / **achieve** [əˋtʃiv] v. 達成 / **sophisticated** [səˋfɪstɪ͵ketɪd] adj. 精密的

Q9

Let's think win-win. Is there any way we can resolve the issue without going to court?
我們思考雙贏的方法吧。有我們能夠解決問題而不用上法院的方法嗎？

A. Let's organize the match on the field instead.　A. 我們改在那片場地辦比賽吧。
B. Let's review the manuscript before we send it.　B. 我們在送出手稿之前先檢查吧。
C. Let's compromise and opt for a settlement.　C. 我們妥協並且選擇和解吧。
D. Let's get a lawyer and sue them for slander.　D. 我們找律師並且控告他們誹謗吧。

詳解　答案：C

think win-win 是指「以雙贏的思維思考」。說話者詢問有什麼辦法可以 resolve the issue without going to court（解決問題而不用上法院），所以要回答避免訴訟的方法。C 回答要 compromise（妥協），並且選擇 settlement（和解）；settlement 就是用訴訟以外的方式協調並解決爭議，所以這是正確答案。

|單字片語| **manuscript** [ˋmænjəˏskrɪpt] n. 手稿，原稿 / **compromise** [ˋkɑmprəˏmaɪz] v. 妥協 / **settlement** [ˋsɛtḷmənt] n. 和解 / **sue** [su] v. 控告 / **slander** [ˋslændɚ] n. 誹謗

Q10

Some people sell their souls to the devil. How far will you go to pursue fame and glory?　**有些人出賣自己的靈魂給惡魔。你會為了追求名聲和榮耀做到什麼地步？**

A. Ten miles at most.　A. 最多十英里。
B. I will do everything it takes.　B. 我會做任何需要做的事。
C. It depends on the car engine.　C. 取決於汽車引擎。
D. Some say it's really worth it.　D. 有些人說真的很值得。

詳解　答案：B

how far will you go 表示「你會為了某件事做到什麼地步」的意思。所以，說話者是在問對方為了 pursue fame and glory（追求名聲和榮耀）願意付出多少。B 表示會不計代價，是正確答案。D 雖然看起來也像是可能的答案，但因為是問自己的態度，所以回答「有些人」是不恰當的。

第二部分 對話

Q11

W: What about "diamonds are forever"? It's an old slogan, but from a woman's point of view, the truth is never outdated. 「鑽石是永恆的」怎樣？這是很老的標語，但從女人的角度來看，這個事實永遠不會過時。

M: My superior wants something original, subtle yet effective.
我的上司想要有原創性、微妙但又有效的東西。

W: I'm glad I'm not in your department. It's far easier to deal with figures and keep the books.
我很高興自己不在你的部門。處理數字、記帳簡單多了。

M: There is another brainstorming session tomorrow morning. I need to come up with something.
明天早上還有另一場腦力激盪會議。我需要想出東西。

W: Sorry I wasn't much help. 抱歉我沒幫上什麼忙。

M: It's all right. 沒關係。

W: Good luck. 祝你好運。

Q: Which department does the woman probably work in? **女子可能在哪個部門工作？**

A. Publicity department. A. 宣傳部門。
B. Accounting department. B. 會計部門。
C. Sales department. C. 業務部門。
D. Maintenance department. D. 維護部門。

詳解 **答案：B**

選項都是公司裡的部門，所以要特別注意提到部門或部門工作內容的敘述。女子一開始建議了一句話，說 It's an old slogan, but...（這是很老的標語，但…），可以推測她正在構思廣告標語。男子則說 My superior wants something...（我的上司想要的是…的東西），可知是男子的上司要求想出一個標語。女子接下來說的話是關鍵：I'm glad I'm not in your department. It's far easier to deal with figures and keep the books.（我很高興自己不在你的部門。處理數字、記帳簡單多了）。所以，男子應該在宣傳部門，而女子其實不是宣傳部，而是會計部的員工，構想標語只是為了幫忙。題目問的是女子的部門，所以答案是 B。一定要聽清楚題目問的是 man 還是 woman，否則就會答錯。

|單字片語| **slogan** [ˋslogən] n. 口號，標語 / **outdated** [ˌaʊtˋdetɪd] adj. 過時的 / **superior** [səˋpɪrɪɚ] n. 上司 / **subtle** [ˋsʌtl̩] adj. 微妙的 / **figure** [ˋfɪgjɚ] n. 數字 / **keep books** 簿記，記帳 / **brainstorming** [ˋbrenˌstɔrmɪŋ] n. 腦力激盪 / **come up with** 想出…

M: This advanced arithmetic concept is so abstract. It is beyond my understanding. I'm sure I will flunk the final exams. 這個進階的算術概念很抽象。它超過了我的理解範圍。我很確定自己期末考會不及格。

W: Basically, both sides of the equation have to be equal. Whatever you add or subtract on one side, the same must be done on the other side. Is that clear so far? 基本上，等式的兩邊必須相等。你在一邊不管是加還是減，在另一邊都必須做同樣的事。到目前為止清楚嗎？

M: That part is OK, but I find it hard to apply the formulas.
這部分 OK，但我覺得套用公式很難。

W: It's like following a recipe. Just do it step by step.
這就好像照著食譜一樣。只要一步一步做就好。

M: Frankly speaking, I don't understand these questions at all.
老實說，我完全不懂這些問題。

W: Before we move on to these challenging problems, let's understand the principles and work out the easy questions first. 在我們繼續進行這些有挑戰性的問題之前，讓我們先了解原則，並且先處理簡單的問題。

M: OK. I'll try question number one again. OK。我會再試試看第一題。

Q: What seems to be the man's problem?
男子的問題似乎是什麼？

A. He thinks mathematics is too difficult.	A. 他認為數學太難。
B. He doesn't enjoy his cooking lesson.	B. 他不喜歡烹飪課。
C. He is on the edge of bankruptcy.	C. 他瀕臨破產。
D. He is hiding something from the woman.	D. 他正在對女子隱瞞什麼。

詳解 **答案：A**

選項都以 He 開頭，所以要注意男子的感想。他覺得某個 arithmetic concept（算術的概念）很 abstract（抽象的），但 arithmetic 這個字有點難，光從這裡並不容易判斷答案。不過，之後女子的解釋提到了 equation（等式）、add or subtract（加或減），男子又提到了 apply the formulas（運用公式），這些關鍵字都和數學有關，可以推測男子有數學方面的問題，所以 A 是正確答案。在聽力題目中，即使有某些字聽不懂，也不要放棄，應該用其他聽得懂的單字來幫助判斷答案。

|單字片語| **arithmetic** [ə`rɪθmətɪk] n. 算術 adj. 算術的 / **flunk** [flʌŋk] v. 在（考試）不及格 / **equation** [ɪ`kweʃən] n. 相等；等式 / **subtract** [səb`trækt] v. 減，減去 / **formula** [`fɔrmjələ] n. 公式；配方 / **work out** 計算，解決 / **bankruptcy** [`bæŋkrəptsɪ] n. 破產

第1回 第2回 第3回 第4回 第5回 第6回

W: We have to get rid of the microwave oven. 我們必須把微波爐丟了。

M: Yeah. It's about time we get ourselves a new one. This one has been with us for six years. 是啊。是時候買台新的了。這台跟著我們六年了。

W: Haven't you seen the news? Microwave reduces the amount of nutrients in food. I want a ban on microwave usage from now on. 你沒看到新聞嗎？微波會減少食物中營養素的含量。我希望從現在開始禁止微波爐的使用。

M: What am I supposed to do with all the frozen pizza I bought? 那我該拿我買的那些冷凍披薩怎麼辦？

W: From now on, we will only eat freshly baked pizzas. 從現在開始，我們只會吃剛烤好的披薩。

M: You can't be serious. I have a dozen in the fridge. 你不是認真的吧。我在冰箱裡放了十二塊。

W: Feed them to the dogs if you wish. 你想要的話就餵狗吧。

Q: What does the woman imply about the microwave oven? **關於微波爐，女子暗示什麼？**

A. It should be sold at a garage sale. A. 應該在車庫拍賣賣掉。
B. It should be discarded. B. 應該被丟掉。
C. It should be used to heat pizzas. C. 應該用來熱披薩。
D. They should buy a new model. D. 他們應該買新的型號。

詳解 **答案：B**

女子開頭說要 get rid of the microwave oven（丟掉微波爐），男子以為是要換新的，但女子說微波會減少食物的營養，所以 I want a ban on microwave usage（我希望禁止微波爐的使用），選項中最符合女子意見的是 B。A 雖然也是處理不用的東西的方法，但對話中並沒有提到要用什麼方法處理，所以這不是最適當的答案。D 是男子的意見。

|單字片語| **get rid of** 擺脫…，丟掉… / **microwave oven** 微波爐 / **microwave** [ˋmaɪkroˏwev] n. 微波；微波爐 / **nutrient** [ˋnjutrɪənt] n. 營養物質 / **garage sale** 車庫拍賣 / **discard** [dɪsˋkɑrd] v. 拋棄，丟棄 / **model** [ˋmɑdḷ] n. 型號，款式

M: Who do you think is going to win? 你覺得誰會贏？

W: I'll put my bet on the Austrian player. 我賭那個奧地利選手會贏。

M: Are you kidding? The French guy is ranked fifth, and this Austrian rookie is not even a seeded player. 你開玩笑嗎？那個法國人排名第五，而這個奧地利菜鳥連種子選手都不是。

W: It seems that both players are evenly matched. They have been playing for three hours, and the player from France is showing signs of fatigue. Can't you see that he is limping a little?
看起來這兩名選手不相上下。他們打了三個小時，而法國來的選手露出了疲勞的跡象。你沒看到他的腿有點跛嗎？

M: I don't agree. He is much older than his opponent, but I believe he can count on his experience to prevail.
我不同意。他比他的對手老得多，但我相信他可以依靠經驗讓自己獲勝。

Q: Why does the woman believe the Austrian player will win? **為什麼女子相信奧地利選手會贏？**

A. He has a better ranking.	A. 他的排名比較好。
B. He has more experience.	B. 他經驗比較多。
C. He has better stamina.	C. 他的耐力比較好。
D. He has a slight limp.	D. 他的腿有一點跛。

詳解 **答案：C**

兩人在討論來自奧地利和法國的選手誰會贏。女子認為奧地利選手會贏，男子則說法國選手有排名優勢（The French guy is ranked fifth），但女子反駁 They have been playing for three hours, and the player from France is showing signs of fatigue.（他們打了三個小時，而法國來的選手露出了疲勞的跡象），可見相對於法國選手，奧地利選手比較有耐力。選項 C 用 stamina 表達「耐力」，是正確答案。這一題也要注意題目問的是男子或女子的意見，以及是關於哪個選手的意見，否則就有可能誤選男子提到的 A 和 B。D 雖然也是女子提到的理由，但腿跛的是法國選手，而這裡的 He 是指奧地利選手，所以不對。

|單字片語| **put bet on** 把賭注下在…（賭…會贏）/ **rank** [ræŋk] v. 排名（如何）/ **rookie** [ˋrʊkɪ] n. 菜鳥 / **seeded player** 種子選手 / **fatigue** [fəˋtig] n. 疲勞 / **limp** [lɪmp] n. 腿跛 v. 腿跛 / **count on** 依靠…，依賴… / **prevail** [prɪˋvel] v. 佔優勢，戰勝 / **stamina** [ˋstæmənə] n. 耐力

Q15

W: Although I have given you local anesthesia, a certain degree of pain is to be expected. Please bear with it.
雖然我幫你做了局部麻醉，但還是可能會有一定程度的疼痛。請你忍耐。

M: Okay. My gums feel numb. OK。我的牙齦覺得麻。

W: I will proceed with the root canal treatment now. Do not attempt to speak or move your tongue.
我現在要接著進行根管治療。不要嘗試講話或移動你的舌頭。

M: What if the pain is unbearable? 如果疼痛受不了呢？

W: Raise your hand and I will stop immediately.
舉起你的手，我就會馬上停止。

M: Oh my gosh. Make it quick. 噢，我的天啊。快點弄完。

W: Try your best to relax. 盡量放鬆。

Q: What will the woman probably do next?
女子接下來可能會做什麼？

A. Take care of the man's dental problem. A. 處理男子的牙齒問題。
B. Give the man a body massage. B. 為男子進行身體按摩。
C. Perform physical therapy on the man. C. 對男子進行物理治療。
D. Write a speech for the man. D. 為男子寫演講稿。

詳解 **答案：A**

女子明確表示接下來要做的事，是在中間的 I will proceed with the root canal treatment now.（我現在要接著進行根管治療）這句話，但也很有可能因為聽不懂而錯過。所以，也可以從 local anesthesia（局部麻醉）、My gums feel numb（我的牙齦覺得麻）、Do not attempt to speak or move your tongue（不要嘗試講話或移動你的舌頭）這些句子判斷女子要為男子進行牙科治療，所以 A 是正確答案。雖然是問「do next」的題目，但從最後幾句無法判斷正確答案，所以從頭到尾都集中注意力聆聽，並且掌握整體的對話內容，是很重要的。

|單字片語| **local** [`lokḷ] adj. 本地的，地方性的；局部的 / **anesthesia** [ˌænəs`θiʒə] n. 麻醉 / **gums** [gʌmz] n. 牙齦 / **root canal** 牙齒的根管 / **unbearable** [ʌn`bɛrəbḷ] adj. 不能忍受的 / **dental** [`dɛntḷ] adj. 牙齒的，牙科的 / **physical therapy** （為了身體復健等的）物理治療 /

Q16

M: I'm afraid a Trojan Horse malware has infected your operating system. I have to reformat the hard disk. 恐怕特洛依木馬惡意軟體已經感染了你的作業系統。我必須把硬碟重新格式化。

W: What about my files and all my pictures? Can you retrieve them? 那我的檔案和所有照片怎麼辦呢？你可以救回來嗎？

M: If you have them on the D drive, I can make a copy for you, but if they are on the C drive, you have to prepare for the worst. 如果你把它們放在 D 槽的話，我可以幫你複製一份，但如果是在 C 槽的話，你就要有最壞的打算了。

W: I have no idea where my picture folder is. 我不知道我照片資料夾在哪。

M: All pictures are saved in the C drive by default. 所有照片都預設存在 C 槽。

W: What? So... 什麼？所以…

M: So once I reformat it, all files will be erased. 所以我一重新格式化，所有檔案就會被消除。

W: Is there a better way? 有更好的方法嗎？

M: Look, you can't access them anyway since the computer is already corrupted. You can save your future pictures on i-Cloud. 聽我說，不管怎樣你都不能存取照片了，因為電腦已經被破壞了。你可以把未來的照片存在 i-Cloud。

Q: What will happen to the woman's pictures?
女子的照片會發生什麼事？

A. She will lose them all. A. 她會失去所有照片。
B. She will have them developed. B. 她會把它們拿去沖印。
C. She will store them on i-Cloud. C. 她會把它們存在 i-Cloud。
D. She will transfer them to D drive. D. 她會把它們轉移到 D 槽。

詳解 答案：A

男子開頭說 I have to reformat the hard disk.（我必須把硬碟重新格式化），於是女子問 What about my files and all my pictures?（那我的檔案和所有照片怎麼辦）。之後男子和女子談論照片是放在 C 槽還是 D 槽，女子不知道放在哪裡，所以男子判斷 once I reformat it, all files will be erased.（我一重新格式化，所有檔案就會被消除）。所以，用 lose them all 表達 files will be erased 這件事情的選項 A 是正確答案。

|單字片語| **Trojan Horse** 特洛依木馬（也指一種夾帶在其他程式或文件中的惡意軟體）/ **malware** [ˋmælˏwɛr] n. 惡意軟體 / **infect** [ɪnˋfɛkt] v. 感染 / **reformat** [riˋfɔrmæt] v. 重新格式化 / **hard disk** 硬碟（= hard drive）/ **retrieve** [rɪˋtriv] v. 取回；存取（電腦檔案）/ **by default** 預設，在預設情況 / **erase** [ɪˋres] v. 擦掉，抹去，消除 / **access** [ˋæksɛs] v. 接近，存取 / **corrupt** [kəˋrʌpt] v. 使腐壞；使出錯 / **develop** [dɪˋvɛləp] v. 培養；使（底片）顯像

Q17

W: I just received the itinerary. Would you like to take a look?
我剛收到旅遊行程。你想看一下嗎？

M: Of course. The Vatican city. Interesting. But why do we have to spend a whole day there?
當然。梵諦岡。有趣。但我們為什麼要在那裡花一整天呢？

W: According to what I read on the Internet, even a whole day might not be enough. The museum alone might take us at least four hours. We would probably spend another three hours in Saint Peter's Basilica. 根據我在網路上讀到的，一整天可能也不夠。單單博物館就可能花我們至少四個小時。我們在聖彼得大教堂可能會再花三個小時。

M: I guess the highlight is the paintings on the ceilings in Sistine Chapel. Look, we will be spending three days in Rome and another in Florence. 我猜亮點是西斯汀教堂天花板的繪畫。你看，我們會花三天在羅馬，另一天在佛羅倫斯。

W: What about Venice? Is it in the itinerary? 威尼斯呢？在旅遊行程上嗎？

M: I'm afraid not. 恐怕沒有。

Q: What are the speakers mainly discussing?
說話者主要在討論什麼？

A. A travel plan.	A. 旅行計畫。
B. A church wedding.	B. 教堂婚禮。
C. A conference schedule.	C. 會議時間表。
D. A traveling exhibition.	D. 巡迴展覽。

詳解 **答案：A**

其實只要聽到第一句話的 itinerary（旅行行程），就可以知道這段話在討論旅行的事情，後面提到要去的 museum（博物館）、three days in Rome and another in Florence（三天在羅馬，另一天在佛羅倫斯）也是旅行的計畫，所以 A 是正確答案。要注意選項 D 指的並不是旅遊展，而是「巡迴（移動）的展覽」。旅遊展稱為 travel fair。

|單字片語| **itinerary** [aɪˋtɪnə͵rɛrɪ] n. 旅行行程 / **highlight** [ˋhaɪ͵laɪt] n. 最突出的部分，最精彩的部分 / **traveling** [ˋtrævḷɪŋ] adj. 移動的，巡迴的

Q18

M: The conductor is making some final checks on the orchestra. Did you turn your cell phone off? It will be embarrassing if it rings or beeps. 指揮正在對管絃樂團進行最後的檢查。你把手機關了嗎？如果鈴聲響或者發出嗶嗶聲會讓人很尷尬。

W: Don't worry. I set it to vibration mode. 別擔心。我設定成震動模式了。

M: It would still make annoying noise. Turn it off completely. 那還是會發出惱人的噪音。把它完全關掉。

W: All right. I'll switch it to silent mode. 好吧。我會切換到靜音模式。

M: Okay. Let's sit back and enjoy ourselves. OK。我們靠椅背坐著，度過愉快的時光吧。

W: Here. Care to have some snacks? 給你。你要吃零食嗎？

M: Julia! What's wrong with you? We're not watching a movie! Put it back in your handbag before someone sees it. I can't believe this. Julia！你有什麼問題啊？我們不是在看電影！在別人看到之前把它放回你的手提包。我真不敢相信。

Q: Where is this conversation probably taking place?
這段對話可能發生在哪裡？

A. On an airplane. A. 在飛機上。
B. In a cinema. B. 在電影院。
C. In an auditorium. C. 在禮堂。
D. In a holiday resort. D. 在度假村。

詳解 答案：C

選項都是場所，所以要注意和兩人所在場所有關的內容。第一句話提到 conductor（指揮者）、orchestra（管絃樂團），而且男子要求女子 turn your cell phone off（把你的手機關掉），顯示這個地方將會進行古典音樂演出，所以選項中最合理的場所是 C。之後的內容只提到關掉手機、不要吃東西、We are not watching a movie（我們不是在看電影），雖然也可以用刪去法判斷答案，但還是不如聽懂第一句話並且直接判斷答案來得有效率。

|單字片語| **conductor** [kənˋdʌktɚ] n. 指揮者 / **orchestra** [ˋɔrkɪstrə] n. 管絃樂團 / **embarrassing** [ɪmˋbærəsɪŋ] adj. 令人尷尬的 / **vibration** [vaɪˋbreʃən] n. 震動 / **annoying** [əˋnɔɪɪŋ] adj. 惱人的 / **switch** [swɪtʃ] v. 切換 / **sit back** 靠著椅背坐 / **enjoy oneself** 過得愉快 / **handbag** [ˋhænd͵bæg] n. （女用）手提包 / **auditorium** [͵ɔdəˋtorɪəm] n. 禮堂

Q19

W: I got culture shock during the first few months in Paris. Couples behave intimately in public places. 我在巴黎一開始的幾個月受到了文化衝擊。情侶在公共場所表現得很親密。

M: That's why a wet kiss is known as a French kiss. It's supposed to be a romantic city. You should've gotten used to it by now. 那就是為什麼深吻被稱為法式吻。它被認為是個浪漫的城市。你現在應該習慣了吧。

W: Yeah. Kind of. But I just can't adapt my taste buds to French cuisine. A friend gave me a treat at a high-class restaurant, and I had to pretend that I actually enjoyed eating a plate of snails.
是啊。有點。但我就是沒辦法讓味蕾習慣法國料理。有個朋友請我在高級餐廳吃飯，我必須裝作我真的很享受吃一盤蝸牛。

M: Sounds like you are a little homesick. Did you manage to find that Chinese restaurant I told you about?
聽起來你有點想家了。你找到我告訴你的中式餐廳了嗎？

W: Yes. I tried it once, but I don't think I'm going back. It wasn't like anything I had back home, and the price is outrageous. 有。我試過一次，但我覺得我不會再去。它不像我在家吃的任何東西，價錢也很離譜。

Q: What does the woman have difficulty with?
女子對於什麼有困難？

A. Behaving intimately in front of others.	A. 在別人面前表現親密。
B. Understanding a foreign culture.	B. 了解外國文化。
C. Finding food that suits her taste.	C. 找到適合她的口味的食物。
D. Coping with the high cost of living.	D. 處理很高的生活費用。

詳解 **答案：C**

一開始，女子說自己受到了 culture shock（文化衝擊），因為 Couples behave intimately in public places.（情侶在公共場所表現得很親密）。男子說 You should've gotten used to it by now.（你現在應該習慣了吧），女子回答 Kind of. But I just can't adapt my taste buds to French cuisine.（有點。但我就是沒辦法讓味蕾習慣法國料理）。Kind of. 表示雖然不完全，但有一點的意思；後面的句子則是很明確的否定，表示自己不習慣法國料理是很確定的事情。後面又說到雖然找了中式餐廳，但不像家鄉口味，所以最符合談話內容的答案是 C。這一題要注意的地方在於，雖然 A 和 B 看起來也像是對的，但因為中間出現了 Kind of (used to it)，所以並不是女子最主要的問題。

|單字片語| **culture shock** 文化衝擊 / **intimately** [ˋɪntəmɪtlɪ] adv. 親密地 / **romantic** [rəˋmæntɪk] adj. 浪漫的 / **taste bud** 味蕾 / **cuisine** [kwɪˋzin] n. 烹飪，料理 / **give someone a treat** 向某

人請客 / **homesick** [ˋhomˏsɪk] adj. 想家的，想念故鄉的 / **manage to do** 設法做到… / **outrageous** [aʊtˋredʒəs] adj. 無法無天的，離譜的 / **cope with** 處理…

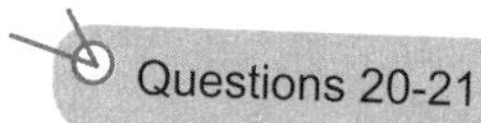

Questions number 20 and 21 are based on the following conversation.

W: Good afternoon, class. So today we're going to be reading about the Great Depression. Who here knows about it? 下午好，同學們。今天我們要讀關於大蕭條的事。這裡有誰知道大蕭條？

M: I do, Miss! It was a time in the 1920s when the United States was going through a really bad recession. 老師，我知道！那是 1920 年代的一個時期，當時美國正經歷很糟糕的衰退。

W: Very good, Tommy, and what do you think was the main reason that happened? 非常好，湯米，那麼你認為它發生的主要原因是什麼？

M: Well, I think it's because too many people used their loans to invest in the ever-rising stock market. When the bubble bursted, they could not but sell their stocks to pay their debt, so the stock market kept going down. The result was that consumer spending and business investment drastically declined, and many people lost their jobs. 嗯，我認為是因為太多人用他們的貸款投資持續上漲的股市。當泡沫破滅時，他們不得不賣出股票來償還債務，所以股市持續下滑。結果是消費者支出和商業投資急劇減少，許多人失去了工作。

W: Yeah, you're right, but that's just part of the story. In today's class, I'll also talk about the reduction of global trade at that time and the international factors at play. 是啊，你說的對，但那只是故事的一部分。在今天的課堂上，我也會談到當時全球貿易的減少，以及在其中起作用的國際因素。

|單字片語| **depression** [dɪˋprɛʃən] n. 蕭條，不景氣 / **recession** [rɪˋsɛʃən] n. （經濟的）衰退 / **consumer spending** 消費者支出 / **drastically** [ˋdræstɪkl̩ɪ] adv. 急劇地 / **at play** 起作用

Q20

What might be the subject of the class?

這堂課的主題可能是什麼？

A. Philosophy. A. 哲學。
B. Economics. B. 經濟學。
C. Accounting. C. 會計學。
D. Business administration. D. 企業管理。

詳解 答案：B

如果知道 Great Depression（大蕭條）是指經濟大衰退的時期，就能知道答案是 B。就算不知道，從對話中的 recession（衰退）、consumer spending（消費者支出）、business investment（企業投資）、global trade（全球貿易）等內容，也可以判斷答案。

Q21

What is true about the Great Depression?

關於大蕭條，何者正確？

A. The stock market was soaring before it. A. 股市在那之前大漲。
B. There was a positive atmosphere then. B. 當時有一股正面的氣氛。
C. It has nothing to do with foreign countries. C. 和外國沒有關係。
D. Most people were in debt for their businesses. D. 大部分的人因為他們的事業而負債。

詳解 答案：A

A. 男子提到 ever-rising stock market（持續上漲的股市），表示在大蕭條之前股市一直上漲，符合選項敘述，所以 A 是正確答案。B. 在對話中沒有提到。C. 女子最後提到 international factors（國際因素），表示大蕭條和其他國家也有關係，不符合選項敘述。D. 在對話中沒有提到，而且男子提到 too many people used their loans to invest in the... stock market，表示很多人是借錢投資股市而非創業。

|單字片語| **soar** [sor] v. 大漲

Questions 22-23

Questions number 22 and 23 are based on the following conversation.

M: Welcome to First Bank customer service. My name is Andrew. How may I help you?
歡迎您致電第一銀行客服。我的名字是安德魯。有什麼我能幫您的呢？

W: Hi, the ATM is not accepting my card. Can you help me with this?
嗨，ATM 不接受我的卡片。你可以幫我處理這件事嗎？

M: Sure. Have you activated your card? 當然。您開卡了嗎？

W: Yes, I've already activated it, and I've been using it without any problem for three years. Besides, my credit history is good. What might be the problem, then? 是的，我已經開卡了，而且我用了三年都沒有任何問題。而且，我的信用紀錄很好。那麼，會是什麼問題呢？

M: I'm afraid your card may have expired. Please check the "valid dates" on the front of your card. What is the set of numbers on the right? 您的卡片恐怕已經到期了。請看您卡片正面的「有效日期」。右邊的那組數字是什麼？

W: It's 08/21. 是 08/21。

M: Well, that's exactly the problem, Ma'am. The card is not valid anymore. 嗯，那就是問題所在，女士。這張卡片已經不再有效了。

W: Really? What am I supposed to do? 真的嗎？我該怎麼辦？

M: Please visit one of our branches so we can reissue one for you.
請到我們的其中一家分行，好讓我們能為您重行發行卡片。

|單字片語| **activate** [ˋæktəˏvet] v. 啟動，啟用 / **credit history** 信用紀錄 / **expire** [ɪkˋspaɪr] v. 到期 / **valid** [ˋvælɪd] adj. 有效的 / **branch** [bræntʃ] n. （銀行的）分行 / **reissue** [riˋɪʃjʊ] v. 重新發行

Q22

What is the reason for the woman's problem?
女子問題的原因是什麼？

A. The ATM is out of order. A. ATM 故障了。
B. She has not activated her card. B. 她沒有開卡。
C. She has a bad credit history. C. 她的信用紀錄不好。
D. Her card has expired. D. 她的卡片到期了。

詳解

答案：D

女子說 I've already activated it（我已經開卡了）、my credit history is good（我的信用紀錄很好），所以 B 和 C 都不是造成問題的原因。男子懷疑可能是卡片到期，詢問卡片上寫的日期數字之後，說 The card is not valid anymore.（卡片已經不再有效了），所以卡片到期就是問題的原因，D 是正確答案。

Q23

How can the woman solve the problem?

女子可以怎樣解決問題？

A. Ask for a new card in person. A. 當面要求新卡片。
B. Make an application on the phone. B. 在電話上申請。
C. Extend the expiry date online. C. 在網路上延長到期日。
D. Send the card to one of the branches. D. 把卡片寄到一家分行。

詳解

答案：A

在對話的最後，女子詢問卡片到期問題的解決方法，男子回答 Please visit one of our branches so we can reissue one for you（請到我們的其中一家分行，好讓我們能為您重行發行卡片），也就是到銀行分行申請新卡片的意思，所以 A 是正確答案。要小心陷阱選項 D，雖然提到了 one of the braches，但方法（send the card）是錯誤的。

補充說明

對話中女子的卡片應該是 debit card，在台灣稱為「簽帳金融卡」。debit card 和銀行帳戶連結，「刷卡」時直接從帳戶扣款。除此之外，debit card 也可以當成提款卡，直接從 ATM 提領現金。

Q24

For question number 24, please look at the list of television models.

W: Hello, how may I help you today? 哈囉，今天有什麼我能幫您的呢？

M: I'd like to buy a TV for my grandma, so I think the bigger, the better.
我想為我的祖母買一台電視，所以我想越大越好。

W: Let's see. We have two 65-inch models, and I highly recommend the one from Nishiba. It has powerful surround sound and very realistic colors. 我們來看看。我們有兩個 65 吋的型號，我非常推薦 Nishiba 的那台。它有強力的環繞音響和非常真實的色彩。

M: Sounds great, but it's not so affordable for me. The other model has a reasonable price, but it's a shame it can't connect to the Internet. 聽起來很棒，但對我來說不太負擔得起。另一個型號有合理的價格，但很可惜它不能連上網路。

W: How about the smaller ones, then? They both have internet connectivity, but their features are slightly different. 那比較小的呢？它們都有連上網路的能力，但它們的特色稍微不同。

M: Well, the other features really don't matter to me. I just want something within my budget of 20,000 dollars. 嗯，其他特色對我來說真的不重要。我只想要在我 20,000 元預算以內的。

|單字片語| **affordable** [ə`fɔrdəbl] adj. 可負擔的，買得起的 / **connectivity** [kə`nɛktɪvə͵tɪ] n. 連接能力

Nishiba 65U8000 (65-inch)	Pansonic 55JX750 (55-inch)
- Internet connectivity 可連網路 - Surround sound 環繞音效 - Color accuracy technology 顏色正確技術 - NT$ 39,000	- Internet connectivity 可連網路 - Color accuracy technology 顏色正確技術 - NT$ 23,900
Chime 55R-500 (55-inch) - Internet connectivity 可連網路 - Surround sound 環繞音效 - NT$ 18,900	Heron 65JCH (65-inch) - Surround sound 環繞音效 - NT$ 15,900

Q: According to the conversation, which model will the man most likely buy?
根據對話，男子最有可能買哪個型號？

A. Nishiba 65U8000.
B. Pansonic 55JX750.
C. Chime 55R-500.
D. Heron 65JCH.

詳解 **答案：C**

看各款電視的簡介時，要注意尺寸、網路連線、音效、顏色、價格等資

訊。一開始店員介紹 65 吋的型號，但男子說 Nishiba 的 not so affordable（不太負擔得起），另一款則是 can't connect to the Internet（不能連上網路）。於是店員介紹比較小（55 吋）、同樣具有網路連線能力的兩款，而男子回答自己不在意（網路連線以外的）其他功能，只希望 within my budget of 20,000 dollars（在我 20,000 元預算以內），所以符合他需求的是能夠連上網路、價格低於 20,000 元的 Chime 55R-500，正確答案是 C。

For question number 25, please look at the table.

W: Can you give me some advice? I'm looking to move to a new country to pursue my Master's degree, but I haven't decided which country yet. 你可以給我一點建議嗎？我在考慮搬到另一個國家攻讀碩士學位，但我還沒決定是哪個國家。

M: What's the reason you want to study abroad?
你想要在海外留學的理由是什麼？

W: Actually, I'm thinking about the long-term. I'd like to live and work in that country after I graduate.
事實上，我在考慮長期的事。畢業後我想在那個國家生活、工作。

M: Then you should consider the countries where there are more job opportunities for foreign professionals.
那你應該考慮提供比較多工作機會給外國專業人士的國家。

W: That's a good point. What else do you think I should take into consideration? 那是很好的觀點。你認為我還應該考慮什麼？

M: I'd say cost of living. You'll have a hard time if it costs a lot just to feed yourself. 我會說是生活費用。如果光是餵飽你自己就要花很多錢，你會過得很辛苦。

Country 國家	Cost of Living 生活費用	Demand for Foreign Professionals 對外國專業人士的需求
Australia 澳洲	High 高	High 高
Malaysia 馬來西亞	Average 平均	Average 平均
Japan 日本	High 高	Average 平均
Taiwan 台灣	Average 平均	High 高

Q: According to the man, which country is the most ideal for the woman to study in?

根據男子所說的，哪個國家最適合女子留學？

A. Australia. A. 澳洲。
B. Malaysia. B. 馬來西亞。
C. Japan. C. 日本。
D. Taiwan. D. 台灣。

詳解 **答案：D**

女子向男子尋求選擇留學國家的建議，男子的建議是 you should consider the countries where there are more job opportunities for foreign professionals（你應該考慮提供比較多工作機會給外國專業人士的國家）和 You'll have a hard time if it costs a lot just to feed yourself（如果光是餵飽你自己就要花很多錢，你會過得很辛苦），對外國專業人士需求高、生活費不算高的台灣是比較理想的，D 是正確答案。

第三部分／短篇獨白

Questions 26-27

Questions number 26 to 27 are based on the following announcement.

Attention, all shoppers. A set of keys was found in the women's room on the fourth floor. To ensure that the keys are returned to the rightful owner, we shall not disclose any details. Please describe the leather pouch that contained the keys and the total number of keys when you collect them from the lost and found counter, which is located in basement two, next to the supermarket. By the way, all organic vegetables and fruits in the supermarket are now on sale. You can enjoy 10% to 20% off, but the offer is only until 6 p.m., so hurry while stocks last.

各位購物客請注意。4 樓女廁拾獲一串鑰匙。為了確保鑰匙歸還給正當的主人，我們不應該公開任何細節。在位於地下二樓超市旁邊的失物招領櫃台領取時，請描述裝著鑰匙的皮革包，還有鑰匙的總數。另外，超市所有有機蔬菜水果現在都在特賣中。您可以享有 10% 到 20% 的折扣，但優惠只到下午 6 點為止。存貨有限、售完為止（在還有存貨的時候趕快選購）。

|單字片語| **rightful** [ˋraɪtfəl] adj. 正當的，合法的 / **disclose** [dɪsˋkloz] v. 透露 / **leather** [ˋlɛðɚ] n. 皮革 / **pouch** [paʊtʃ] n. 小袋子，錢包 / **lost and found** 失物招領處 / **basement** [ˋbesmənt] n. 地下室 / **organic** [ɔrˋgænɪk] adj. 有機的 / **stock** [stɑk] n. 存貨

Q26

What should the owner of the keys do?

鑰匙的主人應該做什麼？

A. Provide details about the set of keys. A. 提供那串鑰匙的細節。
B. Tell the clerk where they were stolen. B. 告訴店員鑰匙在哪裡被偷的。
C. Proceed to the supermarket immediately. C. 馬上前往超市。
D. Write a letter to explain what happened. D. 寫一封信解釋發生了什麼事情。

詳解 **答案：A**

在聽這段公告的時候，應該注意到前後談到的內容不同；前面說的是關於 keys 的事情，而在 By the way 之後就轉換話題，宣布關於 supermarket 的事情。這一題問的是 keys 的主人應該做什麼，所以答案在前半：Please describe the leather pouch that contained the keys and the total number of keys when you collect them（在領取時，請描述裝著鑰匙的皮革袋，還有鑰匙的總數），表示必須描述鑰匙的特徵才能領取，所以用 provide details 來表達的選項 A 是正確答案。

Q27

What was mentioned at the end of the announcement?

公告的最後提到了什麼？

A. The department store will be closing soon. A. 百貨公司即將打烊。
B. The discount is only for a limited time. B. 折扣只限特定時段。
C. All items in the supermarket are on sale. C. 超市所有商品都在特賣。
D. Only cardholders are entitled to the offer. D. 只有持有卡片的人能夠得到優惠。

詳解 **答案：B**

公告的後半提到 You can enjoy 10% to 20% off, but the offer is only until 6 p.m.（您可以享有 10% 到 20% 的折扣，但優惠只到下午 6 點為止），所以說 discount is only for a limited time 的選項 B 是正確答案。要注意不能誤選 C，因為公告說的特賣商品是 all organic vegetables and fruits（所有有機蔬菜水果），但超市販賣的商品並不只有這些而已，所以不能說 all items 都在特賣。

Questions 28-30

Questions number 28 to 30 are based on the following lecture.

What do the rich and poor have in common? Time. No matter how rich or poor you are, you have 24 hours a day. The main difference between the rich and the poor is what they do with their time. Generally speaking, affluent people are better at managing their time. They are busy, yet they have more leisure time. How? Efficiency and multi-tasking are the answer. On the other hand, for people who are stuck in poverty, time seems to slip through their hands like sand. They are always rushing to meet deadlines, and they tend to complain about not having enough time. The true reason is not time itself, but time management. Poor people are more likely to waste their time due to a lack of planning, organization, and a sense of urgency. In conclusion, what you do with your free time will determine how wealthy you become in the long run.

富人和窮人都擁有的是什麼？時間。不管你多富有、多貧窮，你每天都有 24 小時。富人和窮人主要的差別是利用時間的方式。大致上來說，富足的人比較擅長管理時間。他們很忙碌，但他們有比較多的休閒時間。怎麼做到的？效率和同時處理許多工作就是答案。另一方面，對於困在貧窮之中的人而言，時間似乎就像沙子一樣從他們手中溜過。他們總是匆忙趕上期限，而他們容易抱怨沒有足夠的時間。真正的理由不是時間本身，而是時間管理。窮人比較有可能因為缺乏計畫、組織和急迫感而浪費時間。總結來說，你運用自己空閒時間的方式會決定你長期而言會變得多富有。

|單字片語| **in common** 共同 / **affluent** [ˋæfluənt] adj. 富裕的 / **leisure** [ˋliʒɚ] n. 閒暇 adj. 休閒的 / **efficiency** [ɪˋfɪʃənsɪ] n. 效率 / **multi-tasking** [ˋmʌltɪˏtæskɪŋ] n. 同時做幾件事，（電腦）多工處理 / **poverty** [ˋpɑvɚtɪ] n. 貧窮 / **deadline** [ˋdɛdˏlaɪn] n. 截止期限 / **management** [ˋmænɪdʒmənt] n. 管理；經營 / **urgency** [ˋɝdʒənsɪ] n. 緊急，急迫 / **determine** [dɪˋtɝmɪn] v. 決定 / **wealthy** [ˋwɛlθɪ] 富裕的 / **in the long run** 長期來看

Q28

Which is an appropriate title for the lecture?
何者是這段演說適合的標題？

A. Rich and poor people's different habits. A. 富有和貧窮者的不同習慣。
B. What the rich and poor have in common. B. 富有和貧窮者的共同點。
C. Why the poor envy people who are rich. C. 為什麼窮人嫉妒富有的人。
D. How come rich people are so busy. D. 富人為什麼這麼忙。

詳解 答案：A

雖然談話開頭提到，富人和窮人 have in common（同樣擁有）的東西是 time（時間），但後面就說 The main difference between the rich and the poor is what they do with their time.（富人和窮人主要的差別是利用時間的方式），並且開始闡述兩者運用時間、管理時間的方式有什麼不同，所以 A 是適當的答案。

Q29

What is a common problem among people who are poor? 貧窮的人常見的問題是什麼？

A. They struggle to complete tasks in time. A. 他們很難及時完成工作。
B. They spend too much time worrying. B. 他們花太多時間擔心。
C. They work for wrong organizations. C. 他們為錯誤的機構工作。
D. They waste time complaining about their bosses. D. 他們浪費時間抱怨老闆。

詳解 答案：A

關於窮人的描述在後半段，其中提到 They are always rushing to meet deadlines, and they tend to complain about not having enough time.（他們總是匆忙趕上期限，而他們容易抱怨沒有足夠的時間）。選項 A 用 struggle to complete tasks in time（很難及時完成工作）表達 are always rushing to meet deadlines 的意思，是正確答案。選項 B 在談話中沒有提到。選項 C 的 organization 是「組織，團體」的意思，但談話中提到的 lack of... organization 是「欠缺組織→沒有條理」的意思。選項 D 提到抱怨老闆，但談話中說的是抱怨時間不夠。

Q30

According to the speaker, doing what can prevent wasting time?
根據說話者的說法，做什麼可以避免浪費時間？

A. Scheduling things that need to be done. A. 對需要做的事情做進度規畫。
B. Seeking advice from the management. B. 向經營團隊尋求建議。
C. Asking for a deadline extension. C. 要求期限延長。
D. Developing a sense of pride. D. 培養自豪感。

詳解 答案：A

提到 wasting time 的部分是這個句子：Poor people are more likely to waste their time due to a lack of planning, organization, and a sense of urgency.（窮人比較有可能因為缺乏計畫、組織和急迫感而浪費時間）。其中的 planning 可以理解為 scheduling things 的意思，所以 A 是正確答案。選項 B 的 management 雖然是「管理」的意思，但在公司裡面，尤其是以 the management 的形式使用的時候，經常表示「經營團隊」的意思。

Questions 31-32

Questions number 31 to 32 are based on the following commercial.

It's summer again, a great time for outdoor activities, despite the fact that this is also the season when mosquitoes are out in full force. If you find spray-on insect repellent sticky and uncomfortable, Nature Shield wristband is the perfect solution. Made of purely natural ingredients, Nature Shield has a pleasant scent that keeps mosquitoes and other bugs away at the same time. There are no chemicals used, so you and your kids can use it with peace of mind. After breaking the seal, simply wear it on your wrist, and it can provide up to 12 hours of effective protection. Call us now for a free sample.

又到夏天了，這是戶外活動的好時節，雖然事實上這也是蚊子全員出動的季節。如果你覺得噴灑式的驅蟲劑（防蚊液）又黏又不舒服，Nature Shield 手環就是完美的解決方法。由純天然成分製成，Nature Shield 有令人愉快的氣味，同時又能讓蚊子和其他蟲子遠離。沒有使用化學物質，所以你和你的孩子可以安心使用。弄破封條後，只要戴在手腕上，就能提供最多 12 小時的有效保護。現在就打電話給我們，索取免費試用品。

|單字片語| **mosquito** [məs`kito] n. 蚊子 / **in full force** （團體等）全員出動 / **repellent** [rɪ`pɛlənt] n. 驅除劑 / **wristband** [`rɪst͵bænd] 腕帶，手環 / **scent** [sɛnt] n. 香味，氣味 / **chemical** [`kɛmɪkl] adj. 化學的 n. 化學物質 / **with peace of mind** 心靈平靜地 / **seal** [sil] n. 封條 / **sample** [`sæmpl] n. 樣品，試用品

Q31

What product is being advertised?
廣告宣傳的是什麼產品？

A. A spray that prevents insect bites.	A. 一種預防昆蟲叮咬的噴霧。
B. A wearable item that wards off bugs.	B. 一種防止蟲子的可穿戴產品。
C. A magnet that keeps mosquitoes away.	C. 一種讓蚊子遠離的磁鐵。
D. A device that terminates pests.	D. 一種終結害蟲的設備。

詳解

四個選項的內容很接近，所以必須完全理解這是什麼型態的產品，又是用什麼方式來驅除害蟲，才能選對答案。第二句話 If you find spray-on insect repellent sticky and uncomfortable, Nature Shield wristband is the perfect solution. 表示 Nature Shield 不是 spray-on repellent（噴灑式的驅蟲劑），而是一種 wristband（手環）；第三句話提到它 has a pleasant scent that keeps mosquitoes and other bugs away（有令人愉快的氣味，能讓蚊子和其他蟲子遠離）。所以，用 wearable item（可穿戴產品）代替 wristband、用 ward off bugs（防止蟲子）代替 keep mosquitoes and other bugs away 的選項 B 是正確答案。請注意選項 D 的 terminate（終結）在這裡表示「殺死」或「消滅」的意思，但廣告中並沒有說這項產品可以殺蟲。

|單字片語| **wearable** [ˋwɛrəbl̩] adj. 可穿戴的 / **magnet** [ˋmægnɪt] n. 磁鐵 / **terminate** [ˋtɝməˏnet] v. 終結 / **pest** [pɛst] n. 害蟲

Q32

What information is given about the product?
關於這個產品，提供了什麼資訊？

A. Where to purchase the product. A. 在哪裡購買產品。
B. How to use the product. B. 如何使用產品。
C. How to receive a special discount. C. 如何獲得特別折扣。
D. How to prolong its effects. D. 如何延長它的效果。

詳解 **答案：B**

介紹了這項產品的特色之後，說話者說 After breaking the seal, simply wear it on your wrist, and it can provide up to 12 hours of effective protection.（弄破封條後，只要戴在手腕上，就能提供最多 12 小時的有效保護）。這部分描述的是產品的使用方法，所以 B 是正確答案。雖然也提到了有效時間，但說的是最長可以維持多久，而不是說應該怎麼延長效果，所以不能選 D。A 和 C 在廣告中沒有提到。

Questions 33-34

Questions number 33 to 34 are based on the following news report.

A family tragedy was reported in the Wanhua District, Taipei City earlier today. A man turned on the gas and lit a cigarette, causing an explosion that killed him on the spot. The fire that erupted devoured the apartment building within minutes. Two other bodies, believed to be the man's children, were found by firefighters after the fire was put out. Neighbors interviewed said that the man used to be a taxi driver, but he lost a lot of money in the stock market and had to sell his car. He was heavily in debt, though he managed to find a job. The man's wife was hysterical when she heard the news. She admitted that her husband was suffering from depression, but she never expected him to commit suicide.

今天稍早，台北市萬華區傳出一樁家庭悲劇。一名男子打開瓦斯並點燃香菸，造成了爆炸，男子當場死亡。爆發的火勢在幾分鐘內吞噬了公寓大樓。另外兩具據信是男子小孩的屍體，在火災撲滅後被消防人員發現。受訪鄰居表示男子以前是計程車司機，但他在股市中賠了許多錢，不得不賣掉他的車。雖然他設法找到了工作，但他負債累累。這名男子的妻子聽到消息時情緒失控（歇斯底里）。她承認自己的丈夫有憂鬱症，但她從來沒想到他會自殺。

|單字片語| **explosion** [ɪk`sploʒən] n. 爆炸 / **on the spot** 當場，立刻 / **erupt** [ɪ`rʌpt] v. 噴出，爆發 / **devour** [dɪ`vaʊr] v. 吞沒，吞噬 / **put out** 撲滅（火） / **stock market** 股市 / **in debt** 負債的 / **manage to** 設法做到… / **hysterical** [hɪs`tɛrɪkḷ] adj. 歇斯底里的，情緒非常激動的 / **depression** [dɪ`prɛʃən] 沮喪，憂鬱症 / **commit suicide** 自殺

Q33

What is true about the news report?

關於這則新聞報導，何者正確？

A. A firefighter was killed during the fire. A. 一名消防員在火災中身亡。

B. A gas leak led to the accident. B. 瓦斯漏氣導致了意外。

C. Three lives were lost due to the explosion. C. 由於爆炸而失去了三條性命。

D. A man killed his children before suiciding. D. 一名男子殺了自己的小孩之後自殺。

詳解 答案：C

這一題難度比較高，因為不能從單一的句子直接得知答案。一開始說到 A man turned on the gas and lit a cigarette, causing an explosion that killed him on the spot.（一名男子打開瓦斯並點燃香菸，造成了爆炸，男子當場死亡），之後又說 Two other bodies... were found by firefighters（消防人員找到另外兩具屍體），所以選項 C 提到 Three lives were lost（失去了三條性命）和 explosion（爆炸），是正確答案。因為男子是自己把瓦斯打開的，所以 B 用 gas leak（瓦斯漏氣）表達不正確。選項 D 提到男子先殺了小孩，但從報導內容無法得知。

Q34

What can be inferred about the man?
關於男子，可以推斷什麼？

A. He wanted a divorce. A. 他想要離婚。
B. He survived the fire. B. 他從火災中生還了。
C. He was emotionally unstable. C. 他情緒不穩定。
D. He made a killing in the stock market. D. 他在股市大賺。

詳解 答案：C

報導的最後提到 The man's wife... admitted that her husband was suffering from depression, but she never expected him to commit suicide.（男子的妻子承認自己的丈夫有憂鬱症，但她從來沒想到他會自殺），所以用 emotionally unstable（情緒不穩定）表達 depression 的選項 C 是正確答案。

|單字片語| **divorce** [də`vors] n. 離婚 v. 離婚 / **survive** [sɚ`vaɪv] v. 經歷…而倖存 / **emotionally** [ɪ`moʃənl̩ɪ] adv. 情緒上 / **unstable** [ʌn`stebl̩] adj. 不穩定的 / **make a killing** 大賺一筆

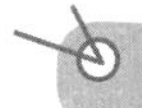
Questions 35-37

For questions number 35 to 37, please look at the charts.

Our number of new students over the past four years has shifted a lot. When we started our university in 2018, we had about 500 students. That was a lot for us at that time, especially because we had to get people to trust us. Things went smoothly in the succeeding two years: the number of new students doubled in 2019, and then again in 2020. However, things changed after our new president took office. The number of new students decreased more than half. It's true that the younger population is getting smaller and smaller, but it seems to me that there are more important factors. We still have a high reputation among educators, yet only a few young people know about us, especially after we cut our expenses on advertising.

我們的新生人數在過去四年有很大的變動。當我們在 2018 年開辦我們的大學時，我們有大約 500 名學生。當時那對我們而言是很多的，尤其是因為我們必須讓人們相信我們。情況在接下來的兩年很順利：新生人數在 2019 年變成兩倍，2020 年再度加倍。不過，我們的新校長任職後情況就改變了。新生人數減少了超過一半。比較年輕的人口越來越少是事實，但在我看來，似乎有更重要的因素。我們在教育者之間還是有很高的評價，但只有少數年輕人知道我們，尤其在我們減少廣告費用之後。

|單字片語| **succeeding** [sək`sidɪŋ] adj. 後續的 / **take office** 就任

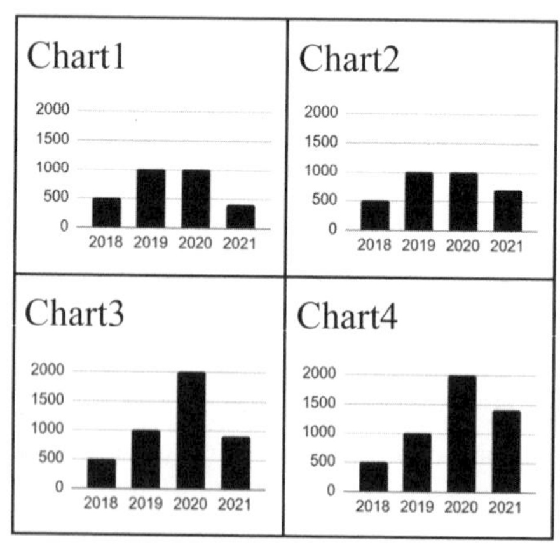

Q35

Who is most likely the speaker?

說話者最有可能是誰？

A. The president of the university.
B. A director of the university.
C. A teacher of the university.
D. A student of the university.

A. 這所大學的校長。
B. 這所大學的董事。
C. 這所大學的老師。
D. 這所大學的學生。

詳解 **答案：B**

說話者在討論學校新生人數的變化，以及後來人數減少的可能原因，所以說話者應該屬於學校的經營團隊。另外，說話者也提到 things changed after our new president took office（我們的新校長任職後情況改變了），顯示說話者並不是校長，所以 B 是正確答案。

Q36

Which chart best represents the number of new students every year?

哪張圖表最能表示每年的新生人數？

A. Chart 1.	A. 圖表 1。
B. Chart 2.	B. 圖表 2。
C. Chart 3.	C. 圖表 3。
D. Chart 4.	D. 圖表 4。

詳解 **答案：C**

關於新生人數，說話者提到 in 2018, we had about 500 students（在 2018 年，我們有大約 500 名學生）、the number of new students doubled in 2019, and then again in 2020（新生人數在 2019 年變成兩倍，2020 再度加倍）、after our new president took office... The number of new students decreased more than half（我們的新校長任職後，新生人數減少了超過一半）。所以，顯示 2019 年大約有 1,000 人、2020 年約 2,000 人、2021 年減到低於 1,000 人的圖表 3 最符合敘述，C 是正確答案。

Q37

In the speaker's opinion, what is the main reason that the number of new students decreased?

依照說話者的意見，新生人數減少的主要原因是什麼？

A. The new president is incompetent.	A. 新校長不適任。
B. The younger population is getting smaller.	B. 比較年輕的人口越來越少。
C. The university's reputation is bad.	C. 這所大學的名聲不好。
D. The university spent less money on advertising.	D. 這所大學花了比較少的錢在廣告上。

詳解　　答案：D

雖然說話者提到新校長、年輕人口減少，但他說 it seems to me that there are more important factors（在我看來，似乎有更重要的因素），也就是後面提到的 only a few young people know about us, especially after we cut our expenses on advertising（只有少數年輕人知道我們，尤其在我們減少廣告費用之後），所以 D 是正確答案。另外，說話者提到 We still have a high reputation（我們還是有很高的評價），和選項 C 的敘述正好相反。

|單字片語| **incompetent** [ɪn`kɑmpətənt] adj. 沒有能力的，不勝任的

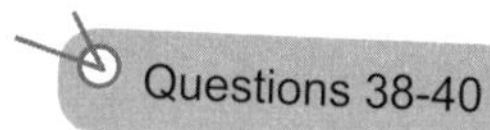

For questions number 38 to 40, please look at the table.

Let's talk about our graduation trip. We took a vote on where we're going, and here is the result. The least favored destination is Chiayi. Some of us think that it'll be a breathtaking experience to watch the sunrise, but there are more people who say they're night owls and have problems getting up early. Besides, most of us think it's strenuous to go up and down the mountain. The most popular destination, on the other hand, is Pingtung. More than half of the class voted for it, and they look forward to trying water sports and visiting night markets. According to them, however, the most important reason is that they think it's a cool place for young people like us, especially Kenting, which is famous for its music festivals and dance parties. Personally, I prefer to enjoy a leisurely trip to Yilan, but majority rules. We'll go to Pingtung for the graduation trip.

我們來談談我們的畢業旅行。我們進行了目的地的投票，這裡是結果。最不受到喜愛的目的地是嘉義。我們有些人認為看日出會是讓人嘆為觀止的經驗，但有更多人說他們是夜貓子，而且很難早起。此外，我們大部分的人認為上山下山很累。另一方面，最受歡迎的目的地是屏東。班上超過一半的人投票給它，他們很期待嘗試水上運動和拜訪夜市。不過，根據他們的意見，最重要的原因是，他們認為那對於像我們一樣的年輕人是很酷的地方，尤其是以音樂節和跳舞派對聞名的墾丁。我個人偏好到宜蘭享受悠閒的旅行，但少數服從多數。我們會去屏東進行畢業旅行。

|單字片語| **breathtaking** [`brɛθ͵tekɪŋ] adj. 驚人的，令人屏息的 / **night owl** 夜貓子（晚睡的人） / **strenuous** [`strɛnjʊəs] adj. 費力的 / **leisurely** [`liʒəlɪ] adj. 悠閒的

Destination 目的地	Votes 票數	Activities 活動
Yilan 宜蘭	9	Cold spring, factory tour 冷泉、工廠參觀
Chiayi 嘉義	5	?, watching the sunrise 〔？〕、看日出
Pingtung 屏東	16	Snorkeling, night market 浮潛、夜市

Q38

Based on the talk, what should be written in the shaded area?

根據這段談話，灰底部分應該填入什麼？

A. Hiking. A. 健行。
B. Camping. B. 露營。
C. Jogging. C. 慢跑。
D. Safari. D.（尤其是在非洲的）尋找野生動物之旅。

詳解 答案：A

關於在嘉義的旅遊活動，說話者提到 most of us think it's strenuous to go up and down the mountain（我們大部分的人認為上山下山很累），所以能表示上山、下山所做的行為的 A 是正確答案。

Q39

What is the main reason that most of the class chose Pingtung?

班上大部分的人選擇屏東的主要原因是什麼？

A. They like water sports. A. 他們喜歡水上運動。
B. They want to visit night markets. B. 他們想要去夜市。
C. They will attend a music festival. C. 他們會參加一場音樂節。
D. Many youngsters think it is an awesome place. D. 許多年輕人認為那是很酷的地方。

詳解

答案：D

選擇屏東的人，雖然也表示很期待水上運動和夜市，但說話者補充說，the most important reason is that they think it's a cool place for young people like us（最重要的原因是，他們認為那對於像我們一樣的年輕人是很酷的地方），所以 D 是正確答案。後面雖然提到墾丁有音樂節，但那只是他們認為很酷的理由，而不是說他們會去音樂節。

Q40

Which destination does the speaker like more?

說話者比較喜歡哪個目的地？

A. Yilan.
B. Chiayi.
C. Pingtung.
D. He does not have a preference.

A. 宜蘭。
B. 嘉義。
C. 屏東。
D. 他沒有偏好的地方。

詳解

答案：A

關於自己的偏好，說話者說 I prefer to enjoy a leisurely trip to Yilan（我偏好到宜蘭享受悠閒的旅行），所以 A 是正確答案。雖然最後他說要去屏東，但那是因為大部分的人選擇了屏東，而不是因為他個人的偏好。

第五回 初試 閱讀測驗解析

第一部分 句子填空

Q1

There was a heated debate over whether leadership is an intrinsic trait or a skill that can be learned and ________.
關於領導力是個人本身的特質，還是能夠學習並且培育的技能，有激烈的辯論。

A. bolstered B. probed C. nurtured D. trimmed

詳解 答案：C

首先要注意到這裡使用了 whether... or... 的句型，用來連接互相對立的內容。一種看法認為領導力是 an intrinsic trait（本身的特質），而另一種看法認為領導力是 a skill that can be learned and _____（能夠學習並且_____的技能）。所以，意思和「天生賦予」、「本身具有」相反的 C. nurtured（培育）是正確答案。

|單字片語| **heated** [ˋhitɪd] adj.（討論等）激烈的 / **intrinsic** [ɪnˋtrɪnsɪk] adj. 本身的，本質的 / **trait** [tret] n. 特點，特性 / **nurture** [ˋnɝtʃɚ] v. 養育，培育 / **bolster** [ˋbolstɚ] v. 支撐，增強 / **probe** [prob] v. 探查，探測 / **trim** [trɪm] v. 修剪

Q2

The soccer match turned out to be a ________ after several sections of the stadium collapsed, killing at least eight hundred spectators. **這場足球比賽在體育場的幾個部分倒塌、奪走至少 800 名觀眾的性命之後，成為一場大災難。**

A. catastrophe B. tournament C. paralysis D. humiliation

詳解 答案：A

turn out to be 是「結果變成…」的意思。雖然前面提到 soccer match（足球比賽），後面卻說 several sections of the stadium collapsed（體育場的幾個部分倒

塌），造成觀眾死亡，所以能夠代表這種情況的 A. catastrophe（大災難）是正確答案。

|單字片語| **catastrophe** [kəˋtæstrəfɪ] n. 大災難 / **tournament** [ˋtɝnəmənt] n. 錦標賽 / **paralysis** [pəˋræləsɪs] n. 麻痺，癱瘓 / **humiliation** [hjuˏmɪlɪˋeʃən] n. 羞辱

The burglar ________ gloves, for there is not a single fingerprint to be found.
竊賊一定是戴了手套，因為一個指紋都找不到。

A. ought to put on　　B. was to put on
C. must have put on　　D. should have put on

詳解　　**答案：C**

there is not a single fingerprint to be found（一個指紋都找不到）這句話表示正在找指紋，所以竊盜的犯行已經發生了，「竊賊戴了手套」是過去的事情。選項 A 和 B 都表示「當時應該要戴」的意思，選項 D 表示「以前應該要戴好」，這三個選項都會表現出「應該戴手套，才不會留下指紋被發現」的態度，但說話者並不是站在竊賊的立場說話，所以不能這樣說。選項 C 用 must 表示非常確定的推測，後面接「have + p.p.」表示是過去的事情，是最適當的答案。

|單字片語| **fingerprint** [ˋfɪŋgɚˏprɪnt] n. 指紋 / **ought to do**（表示義務、建議等）應該做… / **be to do**（表示預定的計畫、義務等）應該做…

Q4

It has been thirty years since he entered the teaching profession. ________, he has no regrets dedicating his youth coaching teenagers. **他從事教職已經三十年了。回想起來，他不後悔奉獻他的青春指導年輕人。**

A. In turn　　B. In contrast
C. In particular　　D. In retrospect

詳解　　**答案：D**

空格要填入副詞性的片語，修飾後面的整個句子。前面的句子提到他從事教職三十年，而後面的句子說 he has no regrets（他不後悔），所以後面的句子是前面的延續。選項 D. In retrospect 表示「回顧過去」的意思，符合這裡「回顧過去三十年」的情況，是正確答案。in turn 表示「轉而，反過來（方向或立場倒轉）」，in contrast 表示「相比之下（對比）」，in particular 表示「尤其…（特別舉出某個例子）」，都不太符合兩個句子之間的關係。

Q5

Work on the Gothic-style cathedral, which ________ over a period of fifteen years, was finally completed last month.

那間哥德式大教堂跨越十五年期間的工程，終於在上個月完成了。

A. spanned B. persisted C. sustained D. postponed

詳解

答案：A

兩個逗號之間的部分，是修飾先行詞 Work on... cathedral 的關係子句，說明工程進行的時間長度，屬於非限定（補述）用法。在選項中，能表示期間長度的動詞 A. spanned 是正確答案。span over 表示「跨越（範圍或期間）」。persist 雖然也有「持續」的意思，但應該用在症狀／惡劣天氣持續的情況。sustain 和 postpone 是及物動詞，後面應該接受詞。

|單字片語| **cathedral** [kəˋθidrəl] n. 大教堂（教區的總教堂） / **persist** [pɚˋsɪst] v. 堅持，持續 / **sustain** [səˋsten] 維持，承受 / **postpone** [postˋpon] 使延期

Q6

I have lost contact with my former colleague Jane for many years, but last week she sent me a letter ________.

我和前同事珍失去聯繫已經很多年了，但上禮拜她突然寄給我一封信。

A. on the spot B. off the record
C. out of the blue D. once in a while

詳解

答案：C

空格要填入修飾 sent me a letter 的片語。因為是多年沒聯絡之後寄信，所以表示「突然」的 C. out of the blue 是最適合的答案。off the record 是表示「私底下」說話或發表意見，而不希望其他人知道，但寄信本來就是私人之間的事情，所以不適合用 off the record 修飾。

|單字片語| **on the spot** 當場，在現場 / **off the record** 私底下 / **out of the blue** 突然，出乎意料 / **once in a while** 偶爾

Q7

One common trait among successful people is that they seem to ________ a sense of satisfaction from their work.

成功人士一個常見的特點是，他們似乎會從自己的工作中得到滿足感。

A. derive　　B. magnify　　C. reconcile　　D. seduce

詳解

答案：A

這裡要注意的是句子最後的介系詞片語 from their work，表示 a sense of satisfaction（滿足感）來自於工作。選項中適合和介系詞 from 搭配使用，表示「從…得到」的 A. derive 是正確答案。magnify（放大）的意義似乎也合理，但因為不適合和後面的 from their work 搭配，所以不是正確答案。

|單字片語| **derive** [dɪˋraɪv] v. 取得，得到 / **magnify** [ˋmægnə͵faɪ] v. 放大 / **reconcile** [ˋrɛkənsaɪl] v. 調停，使和解 / **seduce** [sɪˋdjus] v. 誘惑，引誘

Q8

To solve manpower shortage problems, workers are offered double their usual pay as an ________ for working during holidays.

為了解決人力短缺的問題，所以提供員工平常薪水的兩倍，作為在假日工作的獎勵。

A. accessory　　B. incentive　　C. obligation　　D. evaluation

詳解

答案：B

空格前面的介系詞 as「作為…」，表示前面的 double their usual pay（平常薪水的兩倍）被當作什麼。所以，選項中表示「獎勵」的 B. incentive 是正確答案。

|單字片語| **manpower** [ˋmæn͵paʊɚ] n. 人力，勞動力 / **incentive** [ɪnˋsɛntɪv] n. 刺激；獎勵 / **accessory** [ækˋsɛsərɪ] n. 配件；飾品 / **obligation** [͵ɑbləˋgeʃən] n. 義務，責任 / **evaluation** [ɪ͵væljʊˋeʃən] n. 評估；評價

Q9

Among teachers who were interviewed, a majority believed that punishment helps to correct undesirable behavior to a certain ________.

在受訪的教師中，大部分的人認為處罰在一定程度上有助於矯正不受歡迎的行為。

A. expanse　B. expense　C. extent　D. extend

詳解　答案：C

to a certain extent 表示「到一定程度，某種程度上」，也就是雖然並非 100% 如此，但句中的說法有一定程度的正確性，或者某件事有一定的影響力、效果等等。所以，C 是正確答案。extent 是名詞，請不要和動詞 extend 搞混。

|單字片語| **undesirable** [ˌʌndɪˋzaɪrəbl̩] adj. 不受歡迎的，令人不快的 / **expanse** [ɪkˋspæns] n. 廣闊的區域 / **expense** [ɪkˋspɛns] n. 費用，支出 / **extent** [ɪkˋstɛnt] n. 程度 / **extend** [ɪkˋstɛnd] v. 延長，延伸；伸出，提供

Q10

White materials can reflect light and heat effectively. ________, black materials absorb light and heat, which is why you feel warmer when you are dressed in black.

白色的物質可以有效反射光和熱。相反地，黑色物質會吸收光和熱，所以你穿黑色的時候會覺得比較熱。

A. Ultimately　B. Conversely　C. Inevitably　D. Accordingly

詳解　答案：B

前面的句子說白色的東西 reflect light and heat，後面則說黑色的東西 absorb light and heat，前後是相反的內容，所以 B. Conversely（相反地）是正確答案。

|單字片語| **conversely** [kənˋvɝslɪ] adv. 相反地 / **ultimately** [ˋʌltəmɪtlɪ] adv. 最終，最後 / **inevitably** [ɪnˋɛvətəblɪ] adv. 不可避免地 / **accordingly** [əˋkɔrdɪŋlɪ] adv. 相應地，照著；因此

第二部分 / 段落填空

Questions 11-15

For both children and adults alike, a visit to the dentist can be a terrifying experience. For one, having someone (11) probe inside your mouth with sharp metallic instruments is not pleasant at all. For another, the frightening drilling noise does make your heart beat faster. Actually, I also have had some unpleasant experiences with dentists myself. I remember when I went to a dentist as a child, I dared not move my tongue (12) in case it gets pierced by the drill. As I grew up, however, (13) I learned how to overcome my fear. I use a psychological technique (14) prior to the appointment with my dentist. I keep telling myself it is going to hurt a lot. After a while, I kind of resign myself to my fate. Even if the treatment turns out to be really painful, the (15) agony is rarely beyond my imagination.

對於小孩和大人，去看牙醫可能同樣是個可怕的經驗。首先，讓人用尖銳的金屬器具探測你的嘴巴完全不令人愉快。還有，嚇人的鑽孔聲的確會讓你的心跳加速。事實上，我自己也有過一些不愉快的看牙醫經驗。我記得小時候看牙醫時，我不敢動我的舌頭，以防它被鑽子刺穿。不過，隨著我長大，我學會了如何克服我的恐懼。在看牙醫之前，我使用一種心理技巧。我持續告訴自己會很痛。過了一會兒以後，我就有點聽天由命了。即使治療真的很痛，痛苦也很少超出我的想像。

|單字片語| **alike** [əˋlaɪk] adj. 相同的 adv. 同樣地 / **terrifying** [ˋtɛrəˏfaɪɪŋ] adj. 可怕的 / **probe** [prob] v. 探查，探測 / **metallic** [məˋtælɪk] adj. 金屬的 / **unpleasant** [ʌnˋplɛznt] adj. 令人不愉快的 / **in case** 以防萬一 / **pierce** [pɪrs] v. 刺穿 / **resign** [rɪˋzaɪn] v. 放棄；（**resign oneself to**）聽任，順從 / **agony** [ˋægənɪ] n. 極度痛苦

A. caress　B. maneuver　C. probe　D. torture

詳解　　**答案：C**

空格表示牙醫 inside your mouth（在你的嘴裡）的動作，而且是 with sharp metallic instruments（用尖銳的金屬器具），所以表示「探查、探測」的 C. probe 是正確答案。caress 和 torture 都是必須接受詞的及物動詞，但這裡的動詞沒有受詞，所以不適用。

|單字片語| **caress** [kəˋrɛs] v. 撫摸，愛撫 / **maneuver** [məˋnuvɚ] v. 進行演習；操縱⋯ / **torture** [ˋtɔrtʃɚ] v. 折磨

Q12

A. for now B. for that C. in case D. in order that

詳解 答案：C

空格前面說「不敢移動舌頭」，後面說「被鑽子刺穿」，所以空格應該要表達「為了避免⋯」的意思，C. in case（以防萬一）是正確答案。for now 表示「現在，暫時」，不能用來引導後面的子句。如果填入 for that（因為⋯）的話，因為後面接的是現在簡單式，所以表示常態發生的現象：「因為舌頭是會被鑽子刺穿的」，但其實很少有牙醫把病人的舌頭刺穿，所以這個表達方式不恰當。如果填入 in order that（為了⋯）的話，就會產生「為了讓舌頭被刺穿而不敢動舌頭」這種不合邏輯的意義。

Q13

A. the trauma is still haunting me
創傷還是糾纏著我
B. I learned how to overcome my fear
我學會了如何克服我的恐懼
C. I do not need to see a dentist that often
我不需要那麼常看牙醫了
D. visiting a dentist has not become any easier
去看牙醫一點也沒有變得比較輕鬆

詳解 答案：B

前面的內容提到作者小時候看牙醫的不愉快經驗，但空格前面出現了 As I grew up, however，表示要敘述長大之後有所不同的情況。再加上空格之後的部分是說明作者克服心理障礙的方法，所以能提示接下來要說明如何克服恐懼的 B. 是正確答案。

|單字片語| **trauma** [ˋtrɔmə] n. （肉體或精神上的）創傷 / **haunt** [hɔnt] v. （經歷、感受等）糾纏，揮之不去

Q14

A. prior to　　B. in addition to　　C. out of　　D. in front of

詳解　　答案：A

空格所在的句子說到，作者為了看牙醫而 use a psychological technique（使用一種心理技巧）。空格後面接的名詞片語是 the appointment with my dentist（和牙醫的會面→看診），所以空格要填入的可能是表示時間、期間的介系詞。選項中，A. Prior to（在…之前）可以表示「看牙醫之前」，是正確答案。in addition to 表示「除了…還有」（同類事物的列舉），out of 表示「在…之外」或「從某種材料製作」，in front of 表示「物理位置在…前面」。

Q15

A. agony　　B. irony　　C. vanity　　D. diversity

詳解　　答案：A

空格前面說到「即使治療真的很痛」，所以空格應該是表示「治療」或「痛苦」的名詞。所以，選項中和文意相關的 A. agony（極度痛苦）是正確答案。

|單字片語| **irony** [`aɪrənɪ] n. 諷刺 / **vanity** [`vænətɪ] n. 虛榮 / **diversity** [daɪ`vɝsətɪ] n. 多樣性，差異性

Questions 16-20

A novelist who penned a story about a failed bank robbery (16) turned fiction into reality by carrying out a crime identical to the one he wrote about. Like the character in his book, the writer found himself struggling to (17) make ends meet, so he decided to hold up a bank. However, just like in his book, things didn't go (18) according to the plan. On August 14 this year, he entered a bank wearing a mask. (19) Armed with a pistol, he threatened staff and ordered a teller to open the safe, which was protected by a time delay system. After 25 minutes on the premises, he fled with $32,000, a tiny fraction of the millions of dollars the character in the novel made away with. In his book, the villain flees on a bike and changes clothes behind an oak tree. In real life, the robber novelist also had a bike. Eventually, the character in the book was caught after two hours, while the novelist himself was (20) ambushed and arrested by the police two minutes after leaving the bank. The same factor as in his book led to his failure: the silent alarm system installed in all banks.

一名寫過銀行搶劫失敗故事的小說家，把虛構變成了現實，也就是實際犯下了和他所寫的故事相同的罪行。就像他書裡的角色一樣，這名作家發現自己很難收支平衡，所以他決定搶銀行。但是，就像在他的書裡一樣，事情並沒有依照計畫進行。在今年 8 月 14 日，他戴著面具進入銀行。他帶了手槍當武器，威脅員工並且命令出納員打開以延時系統保護的保險箱。在銀行待了 25 分鐘之後，他帶著 32,000 美元逃走，是小說中的人物帶走的好幾百萬元的一小部分。在他的書裡，這個壞人騎單車逃走，並且在橡樹後面換衣服。在現實生活中，這個搶劫小說家也有單車。最後，書裡的角色在兩個小時後被抓到，而小說家本身在離開銀行兩分鐘之後被警方伏擊並逮捕。和書中故事相同的因素導致了他的失敗：所有銀行都有安裝的無聲警報系統。

|單字片語| **pen** [pɛn] v. 寫，寫作 / **make ends meet** 使收支平衡 / **hold up** 支撐；舉起；延誤；搶劫 / **armed** [ɑrmd] adj. 武裝的，有武器的 / **pistol** [ˋpɪstḷ] n. 手槍 / **teller** [ˋtɛlɚ] n. 銀行出納員 / **premises** [ˋprɛmɪsɪz] n. 建築物及附屬場地 / **fraction** [ˋfrækʃən] n. 小部分 / **make away with** 帶著…逃走 / **villain** [ˋvɪlən] n. 壞人，歹徒；反派角色 / **ambush** [ˋæmbʊʃ] v. 埋伏攻擊

Q16

A. stuck to his word　信守諾言
B. turned fiction into reality　把虛構變成了現實
C. fully realized his potential　完全實現了他的潛能
D. performed well above expectations　表現遠高於期待

詳解　　**答案：B**

整段文章都在說這位小說家是如何犯下了和他小說內容類似的罪行，所以 B. 是最適當的答案。因為文章描述的是犯罪行為，所以不能選擇其他帶有正面意味的選項。

Q17

A. learn the ropes　　B. make ends meet
C. pay lip service　　D. steal the limelight

詳解　　**答案：B**

struggle to do... 表示「做…很困難」，所以很難做到空格中的事情，是他決

定搶銀行的理由，正確答案是 B. make ends meet（使收支平衡）。

|單字片語| **learn the ropes** 掌握要領 / **pay lip service** 說說而已，光說不練 / **steal the limelight** 搶盡鋒頭

Q18

A. according to　　B. regardless of
C. in addition to　　D. as a result of

詳解　　答案：A

空格後面接的是 the plan（計畫），所以在這裡能表示「依照」計畫進行的 A. according to 是正確答案。things go... 表示「情況／事情進行得怎樣」，例如 things go well 就表示「很順利」。regardless of 表示「不管，不顧」，in addition to 表示「除了…還有」，as a result of 表示「由於…」。

Q19

A. Arm　　B. Armed　　C. Arming　　D. To arm

詳解　　答案：B

這是分詞構句的句型。當兩個句子主詞相同時，除了使用連接詞以外，也可以將其中一句改用分詞片語呈現。例如本文中的句子，要表達的意思是 He was armed with a pistol when he threatened staff...，所以分詞構句是 Armed with a pistol, he...，正確答案是 B. Armed。arm 當動詞時，表示「使配備武器」的意思，所以「有了武器」是用表示被動的過去分詞 armed 來表現。

補充說明

也可以用 arm oneself（為自己配備武器）來表達同樣的意思。
He armed himself with a pistol. 他為自己配備了手槍→他帶了手槍。

Q20

A. ambushed　　B. collaborated　　C. irritated　　D. recruited

詳解　　答案：A

空格表示 the police 對 the novelist 做的事情，而且是在 arrested（逮捕）之前。所以，能和 ... and arrested 搭配，表示「伏擊並且逮捕」的 A. ambushed（埋伏攻擊）是正確答案。

|單字片語| **collaborate** [kəˋlæbəˏret] v. 共同工作，合作 / **irritate** [ˋɪrəˏtet] v. 激怒 / **recruit** [rɪˋkrut] v. 招募

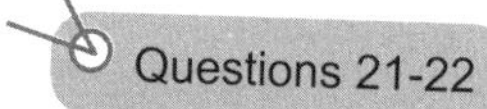

Questions 21-22 are based on the information provided in the following chart.

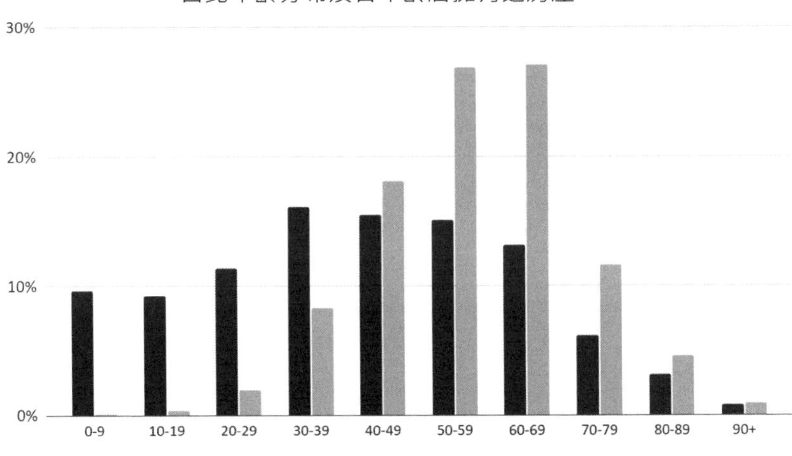

Based on the chart, which of the following statements is true? **根據圖表內容，以下敘述何者正確？**

A. Every person in Taipei begins to have a home in his or her 40s.
台北的每個人在 40 幾歲的時候都開始擁有房屋。

B. Over half of the homes in Taipei are owned by people aged 50-69.
台北有超過一半的房屋是 50-69 歲的人擁有的。

C. In Taipei, about one in two persons aged 30-39 has his or her own home.
在台北，30-39 歲每兩人中約有一人擁有自己的房屋。

D. People aged under 30 and over 89 both have low home-ownership rates.
未滿 30 歲和超過 89 歲的人，住宅自有率都很低。

詳解 **答案：B**

首先要注意長條圖顯示的是「佔人口的比例」和「擁有的房屋佔百分之幾」，數字都是相對於總數的百分比。因為人口總數和房屋總數不同，而且不清楚確切的數目是多少，所以絕對不能把兩項數據的長條直接拿來比較。當同一個年齡層顯示的百分比相近時（例如 40-49 歲），並不代表這個年齡層的人數和房屋數差不多。所以，A 和 C 無法從圖表判斷是否正確。B. 因為 50-59 和 60-69 歲的擁有房屋佔比都超過 25%，兩者相加超過一半，所以 B 是正確答案。D. home-ownership rate 是指居住在自己擁有的房屋的比率，其實和圖表顯示的數據只是間接相關；另外，雖然圖表中顯示未滿 30 歲擁有的房屋相對於人口佔比而言很少，但 90 歲以上的情況是房屋和人口佔比差不多，所以兩者的情況不能相提並論。

|單字片語| **home-ownership rate** 住房自有率（居住在自己擁有的房屋的比率）

To help more people in Taipei own their own homes, which of the following strategies will be the most effective?
為了幫助台北的更多人擁有自己的房子，以下哪個策略最有效？

A. Building more homes that are affordable for people under 40
建造更多對於未滿 40 歲的人而言可負擔的房屋
B. Offering lower home loan interest rates for the elderly
為老年人提供較低的房貸利率
C. Encouraging retired people to invest in real estate
鼓勵退休人士投資不動產
D. Offering more real estate jobs for young people
為年輕人提供更多不動產工作

詳解 **答案：A**

從圖表內容可以得知，台北大部分的房屋集中在高年齡層手中，而青壯年族群擁有的房屋較少，所以這個族群擁有房屋的人應該也比較少。因此，能夠幫助未滿 40 歲族群的 A 是最能提高擁有住宅人數的方法。選項 D 雖然也提到年輕人，但提供不動產工作和幫助擁有房屋是兩回事。

|單字片語| **affordable** [ə`fɔrdəbl] **adj.** 可負擔的 / **home loan** 房屋貸款 / **real estate** 不動產

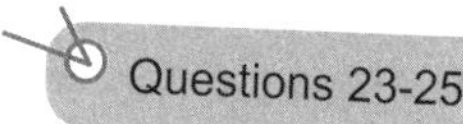

Questions 23-25

According to Greek mythology, Prometheus stole fire from Zeus and handed it over to man because he felt that man was superior to all other animals. The mastery of fire allowed mankind to defend themselves from wild creatures, but it angered the gods, Zeus in particular. Zeus, the king of all Greek gods and goddesses, viewed the use of fire as an unfair advantage to mankind.

Legend has it that Zeus created a woman named Pandora, which means "all-gifted". To punish mankind, Zeus ordered the other gods to gift Pandora with their unique powers to rival man. Pandora was given some traits from the different gods: Hephaestus molded her out of clay and gave her form; Zeus made her idle, mischievous, and foolish; Aphrodite gave her beauty; Hera gave her curiosity; Hermes, along with giving her cunning, boldness, and charm, also gave Pandora a box.

Pandora was then given to Epimetheus, the brother of Prometheus. Adhering to his brother's advice, Epimetheus told Pandora never to open the box she had received. One day, however, Pandora's curiosity got the better of her, and she opened the box, releasing all the misfortunes of mankind: sickness, sorrow, poverty, crime, etc. It was said that all human sufferings began from the day Pandora's box was opened. Fortunately, there was a twist to the story in the end. Pandora shut the box in time to keep one thing in the box: *hope.* In spite of all challenges and misery that befall upon mankind, there is always hope.

根據希臘神話，普羅米修斯從宙斯那邊偷走了火，並且交給了人類，因為他覺得人比其他所有動物都要優秀。對於火的掌握，使人類能夠抵禦野生動物，但這使眾神很生氣，尤其是宙斯。希臘所有男神女神之王宙斯，將火的使用視為人類不公平的優勢。

傳說宙斯創造了名為潘朵拉的女人，意思是「被賦予所有的」。為了處罰人類，宙斯命令其他的神把他們獨特的力量賦予潘朵拉，和人類對抗。潘朵拉從不同的神得到了一些特質：赫菲斯托斯用泥土塑造了她，並且給了她形體；宙斯使她懶惰、淘氣、愚笨；阿芙蘿黛蒂給了她美貌；希拉給了她好奇心；赫密斯除了給予狡猾、大膽和魅力以外，也給了潘朵拉一個盒子。

潘朵拉於是被交給了普羅米修斯的弟弟伊比米修斯。伊比米修斯遵守他哥哥的忠告，告訴潘朵拉絕對不要打開她得到的盒子。但有一天，潘朵拉的好奇心戰勝了她，她打開了盒子，釋放出人類的所有不幸：疾病、悲傷、貧窮、犯罪等等。據說人類所有的苦難就從潘朵拉的盒子被打開的那一天開始。幸好，故事在最後有了轉折。潘朵拉及時關上了盒子，把一樣東西留在盒子裡：希望。雖然有各種挑戰和不幸降臨在人類身上，但總是有希望。

|單字片語|

（第一段）
mythology [mɪˋθɑlədʒɪ] n. 神話 / **mastery** [ˋmæstərɪ] n. 熟練；精通；掌握

（第二段）
rival [ˋraɪvl̩] n. 競爭者 v. 與…競爭 / **trait** [tret] n. 特徵，特點 / **mold** [mold] v. 塑造 / **mischievous** [ˋmɪstʃɪvəs] adj. 調皮的，淘氣的 / **curiosity** [ˌkjʊrɪˋɑsətɪ] n. 好奇心 / **cunning** [ˋkʌnɪŋ] adj. 狡猾的 n. 狡猾 / **boldness** [ˋboldnɪs] n. 勇敢；冒失

（第三段）
adhere [ədˋhɪr] v. 遵守 / **get the better of** 勝過…，戰勝… / **twist** [twɪst] n. （故事的）意外轉折 / **befall** [bɪˋfɔl] v. （不幸）降臨

Why was Zeus furious that mankind obtained the ability of using fire?

為什麼宙斯對於人類得到了使用火的能力而憤怒？

A. Humans might use the power of fire to rebel against the gods.
人類可能用火的力量反抗神。

B. Humans and animals should fight on an even playing field.
人和動物應該在平等的立場上競爭。

C. Humans could abuse this gift and bring about their own destruction.
人類可能濫用這個禮物，並且造成自身的毀滅。

D. Humans should discover the secret only after working hard for it.
人類應該只能在努力之後才發現這個祕密。

詳解 **答案：B**

第一段提到，The mastery of fire... angered the gods, Zeus in particular（對於火的掌握…使眾神很生氣，尤其是宙斯），然後說 Zeus... viewed the use of fire as an unfair advantage to mankind.（宙斯將火的使用視為人類不公平的優勢）。這裡是指 Zeus 認為人不應該有相對於其他物種的 advantage，所以 B 是正確答案。even playing field 表示「公平的比賽場地」，所以 fight on an even playing field 是比喻「公平競爭」。

|單字片語| **furious** [ˋfjʊərɪəs] n. 狂怒的 / **rebel** [rɪˋbɛl] v. 反抗

What is true about the gifts Pandora received from the gods?

關於潘朵拉從眾神得到的禮物（天賦），何者正確？

A. Hephaestus created her from his own body.
赫菲斯托斯從自己的身體創造了她。

B. Zeus made her diligent so she can help man.
宙斯使她很勤奮，讓她能夠幫助人類。

C. Hera's gift caused her to disobey Epimetheus.
希拉的禮物使她不服從伊比米修斯。

D. Hermes taught her how to be meek and humble.
赫密斯教她如何溫順、謙遜。

詳解　　答案：C

雖然關於潘朵拉獲得的天賦的部分是第二段，但這一題還需要參考其他段落才能作答。第三段提到，Epimetheus told Pandora never to open the box（伊比米修斯告訴潘朵拉絕對不要打開盒子）、Pandora's curiosity got the better of her, and she opened the box（潘朵拉的好奇心戰勝了她，而她打開了盒子），而從第二段可知 curiosity 是 Hera 給她的。綜合這些內容，可知 C 是正確答案。

|單字片語| **disobey** [ˌdɪsəˋbe] v. 不服從 / **meek** [mik] adj. 溫順的

What message does the thing kept inside Pandora's box implies?

潘朵拉的盒子裡面的東西，暗示什麼訊息？

A. Never despair in the face of hardships.
面臨困難的時候永遠不要絕望。

B. Wisdom is more precious than wealth.
智慧比財富更可貴。

C. Always respect the gods and never risk their wrath.
總是尊敬神，絕對不要冒惹神憤怒的風險。

D. Beware of women with great beauty.
小心非常美麗的女人。

詳解　　答案：A

關於 Pandora's box 裡面的東西，第三段的最後提到 Pandora shut the box in time to keep one thing in the box: hope.（潘朵拉及時關上了盒子，把一樣東西留

在盒子裡：希望），並且說 In spite of all challenges and misery that befall upon mankind, there is always hope.（雖然有各種挑戰和不幸降臨在人類身上，但總是有希望）。所以，提到 Never despair（永遠不要絕望）的 A 是正確答案。

|單字片語| **in the face of** 面對… / **wrath** [ræθ] n. 狂怒 / **beware (of)** [bɪˋwɛr] v. 當心，小心

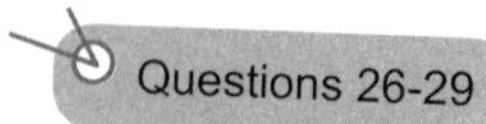

Are you envious of the lifestyles of the rich and famous? Have you ever wondered how the world's elites managed to make so much money? The secret lies in diversification, meaning they have multiple streams of income. Apart from their primary jobs, which may be acting, news anchoring, singing, or playing sports, these celebrities also make money by investing in financial markets and/or running their own businesses. In addition, their image and reputation can also earn them some easy money once in a while.

Product endorsements are where they make the big bucks. With shrewd marketing strategies, companies are able to sell more products with the aid of these superstars. The seemingly outrageous fees, ranging from hundreds of thousands to millions in dollars, are but a small percentage of the net profits turned in by multinational corporations. A more recent trend sees celebrities putting their names and money behind restaurants or hotels to bring in more revenue, both for the businesses and for themselves. Creating their own brands is also a way that celebrities can make a killing. Guess how much revenue Kim Kardashian's beauty brand brings in per year: a staggering $100 million! That's an astronomical sum for those of us who aspire to be millionaires.

While celebrities make a killing and live a luxurious life through various sources of income, ordinary people may find it unfair that their own salaries are only enough to feed themselves. According to Pareto's 80/20 Principle, 20 percent of the people possess 80 percent of the wealth. This universal law has been proven again and again in every society and nation. Communist countries may be exceptions, but when their economy is liberated, even to a limited extent, the "invisible hand" seems to work in favor of the top-20-percent elites. While the top 20 percent enjoy the abundance of 80 percent of wealth in a given society, 80 percent of the population struggle and fight for the scraps in the remaining 20 percent of wealth. This is indeed a concerning situation.

你羨慕有錢又有名的人的生活方式嗎？你曾經好奇世界上的菁英如何設法賺到這麼多錢嗎？祕密在於多樣化，意思是他們有多種收入流。除了他們主要的工作——可能是演戲、播報新聞、唱歌，或者從事體育活動——這些名人也靠著投資金融市場和／或經營自己的事業來賺錢。除此之外，他們的形象和名聲偶爾也能讓他們賺到一些容易得到的錢。

產品代言是他們賺大錢的地方。靠著精明的行銷策略，公司可以靠著這些超級明星的幫助賣出更多產品。看似誇張的費用，從數十萬到數百萬美元，只是跨國企業賺進的淨利的一小部分。比較近期的趨勢是，名人把自己的名聲和金錢投入餐廳或飯店，為這些事業和他們自己帶來更多收入。創造自己的品牌也是名人能大賺一筆的方法。猜猜看金·卡達夏的美妝品牌每年賺進多少營收：驚人的一億美元！對我們想要成為百萬富翁的人來說，這是個天文數字。

當名人透過多種收入來源賺大錢、過著奢華生活的時候，普通人可能覺得不公平，因為薪水只夠餵飽自己。根據帕雷托的 80/20 法則，20% 的人擁有 80% 的財富。這個通用的法則在每個社會和國家一再獲得證明。共產國家可能是例外，但當它們的經濟被自由化，即使程度有限，「看不見的手」似乎就會以有利於上層 20% 菁英的方式運作。當社會上層 20% 的人享受 80% 財富的充足時，人口中的 80% 為了剩下 20% 財富中的一點點而掙扎奮鬥。這的確是令人擔心的情況。

|單字片語|

（第一段）

elite [e`lit] n. 菁英 / **manage to do** 設法做到… / **diversification** [daɪˏvɝsəfə`keʃən] n. 多樣化，多樣化經營 / **anchor** [`æŋkɚ] n. 新聞主播 v. （擔任主播）播報新聞

（第二段）

endorsement [ɪn`dɔrsmənt] n. 背書，（產品）代言 / **big bucks** 很多的錢 / **shrewd** [ʃrud] adj. 精明的 / **marketing** [`mɑrkɪtiŋ] n. 市場行銷 / **outrageous** [aʊt`redʒəs] adj. 無法無天的，非常離譜的 / **multinational** [`mʌltɪ`næʃənl̩] adj. 跨國的，多國的 / **avenue** [`ævəˏnju] n. 大街；途徑，方法 / **staggering** [`stægərɪŋ] adj. 驚人的，巨大的 / **astronomical** [ˏæstrə`nɑmɪkl̩] adj. 天文學的；天文數字般的 / **aspire** [ə`spaɪr] v. 渴望，嚮往

（第三段）

make a killing 賺大錢 / **universal** [ˏjunə`vɝsl̩] adj. 普遍的，通用的 / **communist** [`kɑmjʊˏnɪst] adj. 共產主義的 n. 共產主義者 / **liberate** [`lɪbəˏret] v. 解放；使自由 / **in favor of** 對…有利 / **abundance** [ə`bʌndəns] n. 豐富，充足 / **scrap** [skræp] n. 碎片；少量

According to the article, what is the secret to an extraordinarily high level of income?

根據這篇文章，非常高的收入的祕密是什麼？

A. Maintaining a young appearance
維持年輕的外貌

B. Attaining above-average intelligence
得到超過平均的智慧

C. Purchasing products at a low price
用低價購買產品

D. Generating revenue from various sources
從多種來源產生收入

詳解　　答案：D

文章開頭就問讀者是否好奇為什麼名人能賺這麼多錢，然後說 The secret lies in diversification, meaning they have multiple streams of income.（祕密在於多樣化，意思是他們有多種收入流），所以用 revenue 表示 income、用 various sources 表示 multiple streams 的 D 是正確答案。

Q27

Which of the following is NOT a way celebrities make money as mentioned in the article?

以下何者不是文章中提到的名人賺錢方法？

A. Investing in the hospitality industry
投資服務業

B. Buying and selling stocks
買賣股票

C. Teaching people how to build their reputation
教導別人如何建立自己的名聲

D. Appearing in the media to promote products
出現在媒體裡宣傳產品

詳解　　答案：C

文章的前兩段介紹了名人賺錢的方法。第二段的 putting their names and money behind restaurants or hotels（把自己的名聲和金錢投入餐廳或飯店）對應選項 A，第一段的 investing in financial markets（投資金融市場）對應選項 B，第二段的 Product endorsements（產品代言）對應選項 D。文章中沒有提到的選項 C 是正確答案。

|單字片語| **hospitality industry** 服務業

What is true about a celebrity's additional sources of income?

關於名人的額外收入來源，何者正確？

A. They may have nothing to do with his or her main job.
可能和他的主要工作無關。
B. They are usually for the sake of charity.
通常是為了慈善。
C. They are not controllable.
它們是無法控制的。
D. They are only available before retirement.
只有在退休之前才能得到。

詳解 答案：A

第一段提到，Apart from their primary jobs, which may be acting, news anchoring, singing, or playing sports, these celebrities also make money by investing in financial markets and/or running their own businesses.（除了他們主要的工作——可能是演戲、播報新聞、唱歌，或者從事體育活動——這些名人也靠著投資金融市場和／或經營自己的事業來賺錢）。演藝活動和金融投資、事業經營沒有必然的關係，所以用 have nothing to do with（和…無關）來表達的 A 是正確答案。

Why are some companies willing to pay a large sum of money to have celebrities endorse their products?

為什麼有些公司願意付很多錢讓名人代言產品？

A. They think that having a good image is more important than earning more.
他們認為擁有好的形象比賺更多來得重要。
B. The prospective growth of profits can exceed the cost of product endorsement.
預期的利潤成長可能超過產品代言的費用。
C. It will be easier to convince the celebrities to invest in their businesses.

會比較容易說服這些名人投資他們的事業。

D. The celebrities themselves will become loyal users and keep buying.
這些名人會成為忠實使用者並且持續購買。

詳解 答案：B

關於產品代言的部分是第二段前半。這裡提到 companies are able to sell more products with the aid of these superstars（公司可以靠著這些超級明星的幫助賣出更多產品）、The seemingly outrageous fees... are but a small percentage of the net profits turned in by multinational corporations（看似誇張的費用，只是跨國企業賺進的淨利的一小部分）。所以，有些公司並不覺得名人代言很貴，而且名人代言可以促進產品銷售，所以 B 是正確答案。

|單字片語| **endorse** [ɪn`dɔrs] v. 背書；代言（產品）/ **prospective** [prə`spɛktɪv] adj. 預期的

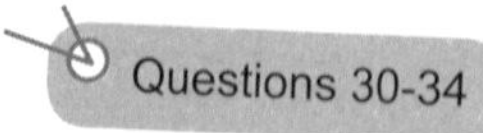

Questions 30-34 are based on the information provided in the following advertisement and email.

Room for Rent
23 Latue Road (near the subway)
1 bedroom / 1 bath
0918 887 0918 Rll@rentthemall.com

Big, bright, and sunny apartment awaits you in Downtown Boston. This is a one-bedroom, one-bath apartment. It features not only all-new appliances but also a trash chute, so you do not have to take out garbage by yourself. This newly renovated apartment could be available for you for $5,000 a month. The apartment comes with: washing and drying machines, oven, microwave, lighting fixtures, bed, mattress, sofa, etc. All you need to do is bring your things and move in. Even though there is only one bedroom, it is quite large, so the apartment is suitable for couples who do not have kids. The apartment does not accept dogs, but cats are okay. If you are interested in renting this apartment, please send us an email with your name, phone number, and a description of yourself so that we may pass it on to the owner. Feel free to contact us for more information about this apartment or other rental properties in the Northeast.

房屋出租

Latue 路 23 號（近地鐵）
一房／一衛浴
0918 887 0918　Rll@rentthemall.com

又大又晴朗明亮的公寓在波士頓市中心等著您。這是一房一衛浴的公寓。它不但有全新的家電，還有垃圾滑槽，所以您不必自己把垃圾拿出門。這間新整修的公寓可以用每月 5,000 美元的價格租給您。公寓附有：洗衣機和烘衣機、烤箱、微波爐、燈具、床、床墊、沙發等等。您需要做的就只是帶著您的東西搬進去。儘管只有一間臥室，但它很大，所以這間公寓適合沒有小孩的伴侶。這間公寓不接受狗，但貓可以。如果您有興趣租這間公寓，請寄電子郵件給我們，附上您的姓名、電話號碼以及自我介紹，讓我們能向屋主轉達。請隨時聯絡我們，取得更多關於這間公寓或其他東北地區出租物件的資訊。

|單字片語| **trash chute** 垃圾滑槽（建築物中收集垃圾的通道） / **renovate** [ˋrɛnəˏvet] **v.** 翻新 / **lighting fixture** 固定式的燈具 / **mattress** [ˋmætrɪs] **n.** 床墊

From: Rasmina Modi <RModi@polliemail.com>
To: <Rll@rentthemall.com>
Subject: The Latue Road Apartment

Greetings,

My name is Rasmina Modi. I'm from India, and I have a PhD in neurophysics from Yale. I'm interested in renting the Latue Road apartment listed on your website because I've decided to move to the neighborhood with my husband. I'll be working as a lecturer at the university there, and the apartment is just across the street from it, so the location is ideal for me. However, I was wondering if it would be possible for the owner to lower the rent to $4,000 a month if we bring our own furniture. Also, we don't need the kitchen appliances since we have just bought new ones.
We have a tabby cat, which is rather quiet and well-behaved, so I believe it won't cause any problems. We have no kids, but we're planning to have one. If the apartment is still available, please do not hesitate to contact me at 123-456-7798.

Best Regards,
Rasmina Modi

寄件者：拉斯米娜・莫迪 <RModi@polliemail.com>
收件者：<Rll@rentthemall.com>
主旨：Latue 路的公寓

您好：

我的名字是拉斯米娜・莫迪。我來自印度，我有耶魯大學的神經物理學博士學位。我想要租你們的網站上刊登的 Latue 路公寓，因為我已經決定和丈夫搬到那一帶。我會在那裡的大學擔任講師，那間公寓就在大學的對街，所以地點對我而言很理想。不過，我想知道如果我們帶自己的家具，屋主有沒有可能把租金降到每月 4,000 美元。我們也不需要廚房家電，因為我們剛買了新的。

我們有一隻虎斑貓，牠很安靜也很乖，所以我相信牠不會造成任何問題。我們沒有小孩，但我們正打算要有一個。如果這間公寓還能租的話，請隨時撥打 123-456-7798 聯絡我。

致上問候
拉斯米娜・莫迪

|單字片語| **neurophysics** [ˌnjʊrəˋfɪzɪks] n. 神經物理學 / **tabby cat** 虎斑貓

What is NOT true about the apartment?
關於這間公寓，何者不正確？

A. It is close to public transportation.　它接近大眾運輸。
B. Trash will be taken out by someone else.　垃圾會有別人丟出去。
C. It is in a newly constructed building.　它在新落成的大樓裡面。
D. It comes with some furniture.　它附有一些家具。

詳解　　**答案：C**

在介紹公寓的廣告（第一篇文章）中，near the subway（近地鐵）對應 A，It features... a trash chute, so you do not have to take out garbage by yourself（它有垃圾滑槽，所以您不必自己把垃圾拿出門）對應 B，bed（床）、sofa（沙發）對應 D，所以沒提到的 C 是正確答案。

Q31

Who may be the writer of the advertisement?

這則廣告的作者可能是誰？

A. The owner of the apartment　公寓的屋主
B. The manager of the apartment building　公寓大樓的管理員
C. A university housing officer　大學住宿組人員
D. A real estate agent　不動產仲介

詳解　　答案：D

關於廣告（第一篇文章）作者的身分，文章的最後提到 we may pass it on to the owner（我們可以向屋主轉達），所以作者不是屋主。下一句 Feel free to contact us for more information about this apartment or other rental properties in the Northeast（請隨時聯絡我們，取得更多關於這間公寓或其他東北地區出租物件的資訊）是歡迎讀者洽詢，並且提到也可以提供美國東北地區其他出租物件的資訊，所以作者最有可能是不動產仲介，D 是正確答案。

Q32

What may be a problem for someone who lives in this apartment?

對於住在這間公寓的人，什麼可能會是問題？

A. Having a cat　有貓
B. Having a child　有小孩
C. Having a spouse　有配偶
D. Having a day job　有日間的（正職）工作

詳解　　答案：B

廣告（第一篇文章）中提到 there is only one bedroom（只有一間臥室）、the apartment is suitable for couples who do not have kids（這間公寓適合沒有小孩的伴侶），暗示著如果有小孩的話，沒有另一間臥室可以住，可能會造成問題，所以 B 是正確答案。

What do we learn about Rasmina?

關於拉斯米娜，我們知道什麼？

A. She is a teacher at Yale University. 她是耶魯大學的老師。
B. She will work in Boston. 她會在波士頓工作。
C. She got married recently. 她最近結婚了。
D. She is a working mother. 她是在職的母親。

詳解

答案：B

雖然關於拉斯米娜的資訊似乎只會出現在她所寫的電子郵件（第二篇文章）裡，但這題卻要同時參考廣告（第一篇文章）才能得知正確答案。電子郵件中提到 I'll be working as a lecturer at the university there, and the apartment is just across the street from it（我會在那裡的大學擔任講師，那間公寓就在大學的對街），而廣告提到這間公寓在 Downtown Boston（波士頓市中心），由此可知拉斯米娜將會在波士頓的大學工作，所以 B 是正確答案。

Q34

What fact may discourage Rasmina from renting this apartment?

什麼事實可能讓拉斯米娜打消租這間公寓的念頭？

A. The rent is high for her. 租金對她而言很高。
B. It does not allow pets. 那裡不允許寵物。
C. It does not have kitchen appliances. 那裡沒有廚房家電。
D. She has to walk from there to work. 她必須從那裡走路上班。

詳解

答案：A

在電子郵件（第二篇文章）中，拉斯米娜先是說公寓的地點很好，之後則說 I was wondering if it would be possible for the owner to lower the rent to $4,000 a month（我想知道屋主有沒有可能把租金降到每月 4,000 美元），表示她認為原本 5,000 美元的租金很貴，所以 A 是正確答案。

Questions 35-40

The environmental impact of meat consumption has long been cited by advocates of vegetarianism to promote a vegetable-based, meat-free lifestyle. Some in-depth research on this issue, however, shows that vegetarianism does not necessarily help reduce energy use and greenhouse gas emissions. The findings of a new study by US scientists indicate that decreasing meat consumption and increasing vegetable intake could actually be **detrimental** to the environment. The reason is that compared to meat, vegetables are far less effective sources of calories, which means that you have to eat a lot more vegetables to gain the same amount of calories as by eating meat. The scientists calculated the amount of greenhouse gas emissions per calorie for each kind of food, and they found that eating lettuce is three-time more environmentally unfriendly than eating bacon. Eggplant, celery, and cucumbers are also significantly worse than pork and chicken under such calculation.

While it is still true that meat production is a major source of pollution and greenhouse gases, this new study offers a different way to see the whole situation. It takes into consideration the effectiveness of foods to human bodies, which is generally neglected in pro-vegetarianism studies. Just imagine that you have to eat broccoli instead of beef to maintain your energy intake. If you used to eat a kilogram of beef per day, that will be 6.7 kilograms of broccoli. As you can see, it is unreasonable not to adopt a human-centered point of view in such studies.

The new study introduces a new dimension for us to reconsider how environmentally friendly our diet is. Also, we should note that eating healthily is not equal to eating in an eco-friendly way, and vice versa. Besides, there are actually many other factors that affect our food choices, such as our tastes, religious beliefs, and food prices, just to name a few. Therefore, it is in fact unhuman to believe that everyone should think about carbon footprint before they eat. All in all, it is best for us to strike a balance and not be over-reliant on any particular food source.

長久以來，吃肉造成的環境影響一直被提倡素食主義的人提到，藉以推廣蔬菜為主、無肉的生活型態。然而，對於這個議題的某些深入研究顯示，素食不一定有助於減少能源的使用及溫室氣體的排放。美國科學家一項新研究的結果指出，減少吃肉並增加蔬菜的攝取，實際上可能對環境造成傷害。原因在於，和肉比起來，蔬菜是效率低得多的熱量來源，意思是你必須吃多上許多的蔬菜來獲得和吃肉一樣的熱量。這些科學家計算每種食物、每一卡路里的溫室氣體排放，他們發現吃萵苣比吃培根來得三倍不環保。在這樣的計算之下，茄子、芹菜、小黃瓜也比豬肉、雞肉差得多。

雖然肉類生產是污染和溫室氣體主要來源的這一點仍然是事實，但這個新研究提供了一個看待整體情況的新方法。它考慮到食物對於人體的效率，這一點在支持素食的研究大致上都被忽略。只要想像看看你必須吃青花菜取代牛肉來維持能量攝取。如果以前你習慣每天吃一公斤的牛肉，那就是 6.7 公斤的青花菜。你可以看到，在這種研究中不採用以人類為中心的觀點是不合理的。

這項新的研究帶進新的層面，讓我們重新考慮自己的飲食有多環保。而且，我們也應該注意，吃得健康並不等於吃得環保，反之亦然。除此之外，還有很多其他因素影響我們的食物選擇，像是我們的口味、宗教信仰和食物價格，這裡只是列出幾個而已。所以，認為每個人在吃東西之前都要考慮碳足跡其實是沒有人性的。總而言之，我們最好維持平衡，並且不要太過依賴任何特定的食物來源。

|單字片語|

（第一段）

consumption [kən`sʌmpʃən] n. 消耗，消費 / **advocate** [`ædvəkɪt] n. 提倡者，擁護者 / **vegetarianism** [ˏvɛdʒə`tɛrɪənɪzəm] n. 素食主義 / **in-depth** [`ɪn`dɛpθ] adj. 深入的 / **greenhouse gas** 促進溫室效應的氣體 / **emission** [ɪ`mɪʃən] n. 排放 / **intake** [`ɪnˏtek] n. 攝取 / **detrimental** [dɛtrə`mɛntl] adj. 有害的 / **celery** [`sɛlərɪ] n. 芹菜

（第二段）

broccoli [`brɑkəlɪ] n. 青花菜（綠色花椰菜） / **-centered** 以…為中心的

（第三段）

dimension [dɪ`mɛnʃən] n. 方面（= aspect） / **just to name a few** 以上只是列出幾個 / **unhuman** [ʌn`hjumən] adj. 沒有人情味的 / **carbon footprint** 碳足跡（生產某種產品或進行某種活動牽涉的碳排放總量） / **strike a balance** 維持平衡

The word “detrimental” in the first paragraph is closest in meaning to

第一段的「detrimental」，意思最接近

A. irrelevant　不相關的
B. suitable　適合的
C. harmful　有害的
D. beneficial　有益的

詳解

答案：C

前面的句子提到，vegetarianism does not necessarily help reduce energy use and greenhouse gas emissions（素食不一定有助於減少能源的使用及溫室氣體的排放），而 detrimental 所在的句子說 increasing vegetable intake could actually be detrimental to the environment。因為這應該是在延續上一句的話題，也就是素食可能也對環境有害，所以 C 是正確答案。

Q36

Which of the following argument against eating meat is challenged in this article?

以下哪個反對吃肉的論點在這篇文章裡遭到挑戰？

A. Eating meat is against religious beliefs in many cultures.
吃肉在許多文化中違反宗教信仰。

B. Meat production leads to greater pollution than vegetable farming.
肉的生產會導致比種植蔬菜更嚴重的污染。

C. Current farming methods are cruel to animals.
目前的養殖方式對動物很殘酷。

D. Meat consumption negatively affects our well-being.
吃肉對於我們的健康有負面影響。

詳解

答案：B

第一段開頭就說 The environmental impact of meat consumption has long been cited by advocates of vegetarianism（長久以來，吃肉造成的環境影響一直被提倡素食主義的人提到），但中間又說 The findings of a new study... indicate that decreasing meat consumption and increasing vegetable intake could actually be detrimental to the environment（一項新研究的結果指出，減少吃肉並增加蔬菜的攝取，實際上可能對環境造成傷害）。接下來的部分則說明為什麼純蔬食可能產生更多溫室氣體排放。所以，在文章中遭到挑戰的論點是 B。

What is the most important finding of the new scientific study?

新的科學研究最重要的發現是什麼？

A. What we eat has nothing to do with our health.
我們吃的東西和自己的健康無關。

B. Meat is essential as our bodies need it to function well.
肉是必要的，因為我們的身體需要它才能運作良好。

C. Certain vegetables are low in nutritious values.
某些蔬菜的營養價值很低。

D. Vegetarian diets may cause more harm to the environment.
素食飲食可能會對環境造成更多傷害。

詳解

答案：D

如同上一題的解析所指出的，新的研究認為增加蔬菜攝取可能對環境造成更大的傷害。第一段後半詳細說明了這個研究的論據：vegetables are far less effective sources of calories（蔬菜是效率低得多的熱量來源）、The scientists calculated the amount of greenhouse gas emissions per calorie for each kind of food, and they found that eating lettuce is three-time more environmentally unfriendly than eating bacon.（這些科學家計算每種食物、每個卡路里的溫室氣體排放，他們發現吃萵苣比吃培根來得三倍不環保）。所以，D 是正確答案。C 雖然有提到，但那只是證明的過程中提到的事實，而不是研究中「最重要的發現」。

Q38

In what way is the new scientific study innovative?
這個新的科學研究為什麼是很創新的？

A. It proves that meat production is actually environmentally friendly.
它證明肉類生產事實上是環保的。

B. It recommends a completely new diet that helps us to eat a lot less.
它建議一種全新的飲食方式，讓我們吃東西的量能少很多。

C. Its findings suggest that eating meat can make us healthier than eating vegetables.
它的研究結果暗示吃肉能讓我們比吃蔬菜更健康。

D. It analyzes the data with a method that most scientists haven't thought of.
它用大部分科學家不曾想到的方法來分析數據。

詳解

答案：D

第二段提到，this new study offers a different way to see the whole situation（這個新研究提供了一個看待整體情況的新方法），因為 It takes into consideration the effectiveness of foods to human bodies, which is generally neglected in pro-vegetarianism studies.（它考慮到食物對於人體的效率，這一點在支持素食的研究大致上都被忽略）。所以，這個研究分析資料的方式是很創新的，也就是以熱量而非食物本身的重量計算溫室氣體排放量，所以答案是 D。

Q39

What kind of eating habit does the author consider to be appropriate?

作者認為什麼樣的飲食習慣是適當的？

A. Consuming various types of food every day
每天吃多樣的食物
B. Eating meat instead of vegetables if possible
如果可能的話吃肉來代替蔬菜
C. Choosing eco-friendly food all the time
總是選擇環保的食物
D. Avoiding vegetables that are low in calories
避免熱量低的蔬菜

詳解　答案：A

在文章的最後一句話，作者下的結論是 it is best for us to strike a balance and not be over-reliant on any particular food source（我們最好維持平衡，並且不要太過依賴任何特定的食物來源），所以他認為應該攝取多種食物，正確答案是A。

Which of the following is the most appropriate title for this article?

以下何者是這篇文章最適當的標題？

A. Eco-friendly food is not the best for your health
環保的食物對於你的健康不是最好的
B. New study breaks the myth that vegetarian diet can save the earth
新研究打破素食飲食能拯救地球的迷思
C. Guidelines for making healthy and responsible food choices
幫助做出健康而且負責任的食物選擇的指南
D. How a biased perspective can distort the results of a scientific study
偏頗的觀點如何扭曲科學研究的結果

詳解　答案：B

這篇文章的三段都和 new study 相關。第一段說這個新研究 indicate that increasing vegetable intake could actually be detrimental to the environment（增加蔬菜的攝取，實際上可能對環境造成傷害），而一、二段都在說明之所以得到這個結論的理由；第三段則說這個研究讓我們 reconsider how environmentally friendly our diet is（重新考慮自己的飲食有多麼環保）。所以，B 是最適合整篇文章的標題。

|單字片語| **myth** [mɪθ] n. 神話；沒有事實根據的觀點 / **biased** [`baɪəst] adj. 有偏見的 / **distort** [dɪs`tɔrt] v. 扭曲

全民英語能力分級檢定測驗

GENERAL ENGLISH PROFICIENCY TEST

中高級聽力測驗　第六回

HIGH-INTERMEDIATE LISTENING COMPREHESION TEST

This listening comprehension test will test your ability to understand spoken English. In this test, each conversation, short talk and question will be spoken JUST ONE TIME. They will not be written out for you. There are three parts to this test. Special instructions will be given to you at the beginning of each part.

Part I: Answering Questions

In Part I, you will hear ten questions. After you hear a question, read the four choices in your test booklet and decide which one is the best answer to the question you have heard.

Example:

You will hear: Why did you slam the door?

You will read:
A. I just can't open it.
B. I didn't. I guess it's the wind.
C. Because someone is at the door.
D. Because the door knob is missing.

The best answer to the question "Why did you slam the door?" is B: "I didn't. I guess it's the wind." Therefore, you should choose answer B.

1. A. I must have misplaced them somewhere.
   B. I only turn them on when necessary.
   C. I know, but it's tough to change a habit.
   D. You're right. That firm is competitive.

2. A. Yes, but conditions apply.
   B. Yes, there is a special discount.
   C. No, batteries are not included.
   D. No, you won't get a commission.

3. A. Does that mean I have to report to him?
   B. Who would expect him to be promoted?
   C. When will you be back on track?
   D. Shall we hold a farewell party?

4. A. I believe we can achieve our goals.
   B. I suggest we adjust the figures a little.
   C. I guess I had better watch my diet.
   D. I'm sure I can eat as much as I want.

5. A. Just show them the way to go.
   B. You should set a limit and stick to it.
   C. It isn't always easy to express your feelings.
   D. I think it's fine to spend a day together.

6. A. Will it take long before I am seated?
   B. May I reserve a table for four?
   C. Can I exchange this for something else?
   D. Have you upgraded your server?

7. A. I agree with and support your decision.
   B. I have the experience and expertise required.
   C. I enjoy working out in my leisure time.
   D. I am glad to be given the opportunity.

8. A. Let's work harder next time.
   B. Let's check if anything is missing.
   C. Let's reset the time on the clock.
   D. Let's see if we have a spare key.

9. A. No wonder we can't find it anywhere.
   B. I had better fill up my fuel tank soon.
   C. The frozen food will turn bad without electricity.
   D. That's why I rarely turn on the air-conditioner.

10. A. No one can predict the weather.
    B. We can never afford it.
    C. That's what coupons are for.
    D. Maybe we should buy a home elsewhere.

Please turn to the next page.

Part II: Conversation

In part II, you will hear several conversations between a man and a woman. After each conversation, you will hear a question about the conversation. After you hear the question, read the four choices in your test booklet and choose the best answer to the question you have heard.

Example:

You will hear:	(Man)	Did you happen to see my earphones? I remember leaving them in the drawer. Someone must have taken it.
	(Woman)	It's more likely that you misplaced them. Did you search your briefcase?
	(Man)	I did, but they are not there. Wait a second. Oh. They are right here in my pocket.
	Question:	Who took the man's earphones?

You will read:

A. The woman.
B. Someone else.
C. No one.
D. Another man.

The best answer to the question "Who took the man's earphones?" is C: "No one." Therefore, you should choose answer C.

11. A. It is not very safe during this period.
    B. It is advisable to visit fewer countries.
    C. It is more affordable if they travel by train.
    D. It is possible to go anywhere they want.

12. A. She wanted to lose weight.
    B. She hurt the man accidentally.
    C. She refused to take her medication.
    D. She just underwent an operation.

13. A. In an investment firm.
    B. In a funeral home.
    C. In an attorney's office.
    D. In a charitable foundation.

14. A. The passing away of an animal.
    B. Adopting a new pet.
    C. Medical aid for the elderly.
    D. Financial planning for old age.

15. A. Harry is not a trustworthy person.
    B. Harry is passionate about imported cars.
    C. Harry has a lot of money in the bank.
    D. Harry has fallen in love with the woman.

16. A. Her son committed a crime.
    B. Her son broke the rules she laid down.
    C. Her son is a victim of bullying in school.
    D. Her son is addicted to an electronic product.

17. A. The price is attractive.
    B. The service is awesome.
    C. The dessert is tasty.
    D. The water is free.

18. A. The weather phenomenon is abnormal.
    B. Christmas celebrations were canceled.
    C. It's very hot in the mountains in summer.
    D. Flash floods happen when it starts snowing.

19. A. He discriminates against women.
    B. He mixes personal affairs with office work.
    C. He only gives promotions to women.
    D. He hardly blames the man when he makes an error.

Please turn to the next page.

20. A. At a clinic.
    B. At a market.
    C. At a drugstore.
    D. At a medical school.

21. A. Only face masks.
    B. Hand sanitizer and alcohol spray.
    C. Face masks, hand sanitizer, and alcohol spray.
    D. Face masks, hand sanitizer, alcohol spray, and painkillers.

22. A. The food of a restaurant.
    B. The popularity of a restaurant.
    C. The dress sense of the woman.
    D. The availability of the woman.

23. A. She will not be able to dress up.
    B. She does not have nice clothes.
    C. She will have to work overtime.
    D. The restaurant's food tastes bad.

24.

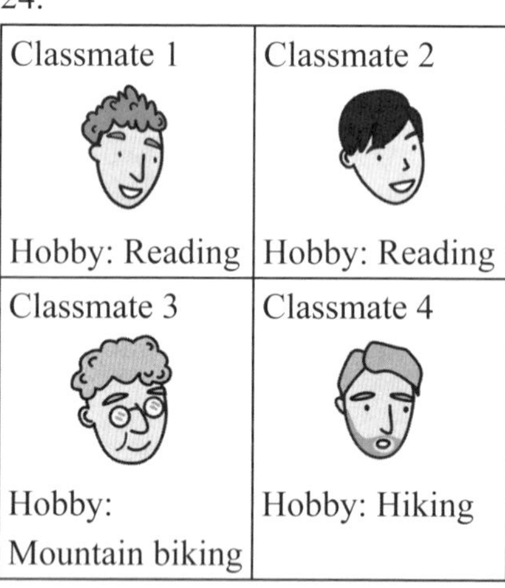

Classmate 1	Classmate 2
Hobby: Reading	Hobby: Reading
Classmate 3	Classmate 4
Hobby: Mountain biking	Hobby: Hiking

    A. Classmate 1.
    B. Classmate 2.
    C. Classmate 3.
    D. Classmate 4.

25.

Apartments for rent	
11 Xinmin Rd., Banqiao - Washing machine, refrigerator - Pets allowed NT$ 15,000/month	26 Meizhu St., Banqiao - Balcony - Washing machine - Pets allowed NT$ 14,000/month
67 Xinguang St., Tucheng - Balcony - Washing machine NT$ 13,000/month	100 Jianguo Rd., Tucheng - Washing machine, refrigerator - Pets allowed NT$ 12,000/month

A. The one at 11 Xinmin Rd., Banqiao.
B. The one at 26 Meizhu St., Banqiao.
C. The one at 67 Xinguang St., Tucheng.
D. The one at 100 Jianguo Rd., Tucheng.

Please turn to the next page.

Part III: Short Talks

In part III, you will hear several short talks. After each talk, you will hear two to three questions about the talk. After you hear each question, read the four choices in your test booklet and choose the best answer to the question you have heard.

Example:

You will hear: Hello, thank you everyone for coming together to share this special day with Chris and I. We have been waiting for this moment forever, and after five years of dating, I can happily say that I am ready. Chris is caring and charming, and I appreciate my good fortune in marrying such a warm-hearted man. When he proposed to me, I realized that he had already become a part of my life. Even though I'm not a perfect cook or housekeeper, I know for sure that I will be a wonderful partner for Chris.

Question number 1: On what occasion is this talk most probably being given?

You will read:
A. A funeral.
B. A wedding.
C. A housewarming.
D. A farewell party.

The best answer to the question "On what occasion is this talk most probably being given?" is B: "A wedding." Therefore, you should choose answer B.

Now listen to another question based on the same talk.

You will hear:	Question number 2: According to this talk, what does the woman like about Chris?
You will read:	A. His perseverance. B. His abundant wealth. C. His cooking skill. D. His amiable personality.

The best answer to the question "According to this talk, what does the woman like about Chris?" is D: "His amiable personality." Therefore, you should choose answer D.

Please turn to the next page. Now let us begin Part III with question number 26.

Please turn to the next page.

26. A. Press one.
B. Press two.
C. Press three.
D. Press nine.

27. A. All conversations will be recorded.
B. There are job vacancies for customer service representatives.
C. Existing customers have a privilege.
D. All phone calls are handled by machines.

28. A. A host.
B. A musician.
C. A commentator.
D. A newscaster.

29. A. There will be five award winners.
B. The winner is a Russian actor.
C. The video taught the audience how to pronounce.
D. The ceremony can be watched online.

30. A. The winner will give a short speech.
B. The speaker will take a Russian class.
C. The audience will ask a few questions.
D. A play will be performed.

31. A. The planting process of high-quality grapes.
B. The switch from selling wine to selling grapes.
C. The popularity of imported red wine.
D. The breakthrough in grape growing.

32. A. They are building more wine distilleries.
B. They are promoting alcoholic fruit drinks.
C. They are making a handsome profit.
D. They are setting up branches globally.

33. A. People who have a quick temper.
B. People who wish to start their businesses.
C. People who have an interest in performance arts.
D. People who are forgetful and absent-minded.

34. A. Never bring work back home.
B. Watch movies as a way to release tension.
C. Learn to give and get advice.
D. Understand why others feel the way they do.

35-37.

Dish	% of Respondents	Note
No. 1	60%	Easy to make
No. 2	22%	?
No. 3	11%	Suggested by a customer
No. 4	7%	Authentic flavor

35. A. It did a survey of its customers.
    B. It is a Singaporean restaurant.
    C. Its chef is Italian.
    D. It has French fries on its menu.

36. A. No. 1.
    B. No. 2.
    C. No. 3.
    D. No. 4.

37. A. Inexpensive ingredients.
    B. Favored by customers.
    C. Most popular among the staff.
    D. Similar to an existing dish.

38-40.

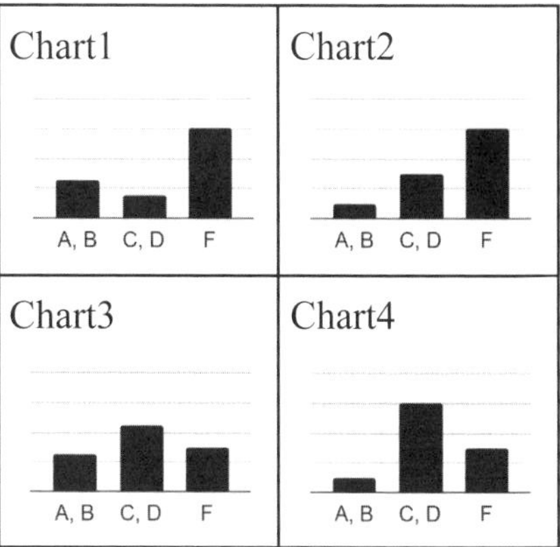

38. A. A teacher.
    B. A principal.
    C. A parent.
    D. A class leader.

39. A. Chart 1.
    B. Chart 2.
    C. Chart 3.
    D. Chart 4.

40. A. Most students never skip class.
    B. There were essay questions on the midterm exam.
    C. The midterm and final exams have the same difficulty.
    D. Every student has to take this course.

Please turn to the next page.

READING COMPREHEHESION TEST

This is a three-part test with forty multiple-choice questions. Each question has four choices. Special instructions will be provided for each part. You will have fifty minutes to complete this test.

Part I: Sentence Completion

In this part of the test, there are ten incomplete sentences. Beneath each sentence you will see four words or phrases, marked A, B, C and D. You are to choose the word or phrase that best completes the sentence. Then on your answer sheet, find the number of the question and mark your answer.

1. Chinese parents tend to value academic achievements highly, so they might ________ their children for not getting perfect grades.
   A. reproach B. supervise
   C. unleash D. victimize

2. The United States declared that the economic ________ on Iran will be lifted as long as it allows nuclear plants to be inspected.
   A. integration B. liability
   C. embargo D. trade-off

3. The civil war, which started out with both sides evenly matched, quickly turned ________ the rebel forces after the government forces made a big mistake.
   A. in spite of B. in favor of
   C. at the end of D. at the risk of

4. Having goals and plans does not ________ bring success. Many people failed to carry out their plans, and even more give up when things do not go according to plan.
   A. intermittently B. occasionally
   C. particularly D. necessarily

5. The young man was so ________ fame that he lost sight of things which are far more valuable, including his health and family.
   A. satisfied with
   B. obsessed with
   C. suppressed by
   D. overwhelmed by

6. Performing the same mundane chores day after day can be ________ and dull. That's why products that help to simplify housework are popular.
   A. tedious
   B. perilous
   C. continuous
   D. mischievous

7. According to the latest data, there are ________ 26 million refugees worldwide, and many of them are children under the age of 18.
   A. mostly
   B. partially
   C. roughly
   D. solely

8. The old man is full of ________ and won't stop talking about his past achievements.
   A. concept
   B. conceit
   C. conception
   D. concession

9. Traffic was brought to an ________ halt when two trucks collided at the crossroads.
   A. abrupt B. eccentric C. optimum D. integral

10. Selling ivory was and still is ________, and the enormous potential profit lures many into killing elephants.
   A. beneficial
   B. economical
   C. invaluable
   D. lucrative

Please turn to the next page.

Part Two: Cloze

In this part of the test, you will read two passages. Each passage contains five missing words or phrases. Beneath each passage, you will see five items, each with four choices, marked A, B, C and D. You are to choose the best answer for each missing word or phrase in the two passages. Then, on your answer sheet, find the number of the question and mark your answer.

Questions 11-15

Getting people trained in horseback archery is the mission of the Mounted Archers Association. We regret that there is a prerequisite for membership. Most of our fresh ___(11)___ have some experience with archery or horse riding. If you have never drawn a bow or ridden a horse before, you might want to get started on ___(12)___ before joining us. ___(13)___, you can achieve what you could not by yourself. Besides training, we also hold annual horseback archery competitions, which take place in our specially-designed ___(14)___ made of natural materials. During our events, members are advised to bring their own horses if possible, but we also have horses ___(15)___ on a daily basis.

11. A. bachelors
    B. instructors
    C. employees
    D. recruits

12. A. another one
    B. the other one
    C. either one
    D. neither one

13. A. By making the most of your ability
    B. With the new equipment in our facility
    C. If you are well-prepared for the challenge
    D. With our experience and training techniques

14. A. arena
    B. gym
    C. rink
    D. studio

15. A. for sale
    B. for lease
    C. by insurance
    D. by installments

Questions 16-20

It might seem bizarre that a boring three-mile running race would be all the rage, but the national trend shows that running ___(16)___ are indeed on the rise. According to the "State of the Sport" report from Running USA, mini-marathon, which literally means a much shorter version of a regular marathon, is the fastest growing running event in the U.S., the 5K (five-kilometer) run in particular. ___(17)___, the longer the race, the more logistical challenges there are to staging an event, which explains the high number of 5Ks being organized. Also, 5K runs ___(18)___. It is a common sight to see families and friends taking part in a mini-marathon ___(19)___ it is not as physically demanding as a full-length marathon. Such events are usually hosted on main streets ___(20)___ to attract more spectators and the interest of the media.

16. A. extremists
    B. activists
    C. enthusiasts
    D. fundamentalists

17. A. Generally speaking
    B. In retrospect
    C. On the contrary
    D. Above all

18. A. have been held in all kinds of places
    B. are suitable for all ages and skill levels
    C. have been proved to improve our health
    D. can serve as a tool to promote physical activity

19. A. while
    B. yet
    C. therefore
    D. since

20. A. as a last resort
    B. in a bid
    C. by no means
    D. with respect

Part III: Reading Comprehension

In this part of the test, you will find several tasks. Each task contains one or two passages or charts, which are followed by two to six questions. You are to choose the best answer, A, B, C, or D, to each question on the basis of the information provided or implied in the passage or chart. Then, on your answer sheet, find the number of the question and mark your answer.

Please turn to the next page.

Questions 21-22

Rose Bank Rewards Credit Card

Earn points everywhere!

Simply shop in your own way and accumulate reward points every day. With a Rose Bank Rewards Credit Card, you can get more out of every purchase you make at more than 500 partnering businesses, including:

- **Online shopping sites:** Amazon, Zappos, Etsy…
- **Hypermarkets:** Walmart, Kroger, Costco…
- **Department stores:** Sears, Macy's, Bloomingdale's…
- **Bookstores:** Barnes & Noble, Books-A-Million…

The points you have earned will not expire, as long as your card is valid. You can exchange reward points for gifts, or use them to offset any outstanding payments due. Apply now, and your annual fee will be waived for the first two years. Terms and conditions apply.
Note: Interest rates for late payment range from 12% to 24%, depending on your credit score.

21. What kind of person is most likely to apply for this credit card?
    A. One who eats out frequently
    B. One who runs a used-book store
    C. One who travels a lot on business
    D. One who buys groceries regularly
22. Based on the advertisement, which of the following statements is **NOT** true?
    A. Bonus points can be brought forward to the next year.
    B. Card holders can use reward points as payment.
    C. There is a discount on the annual fee for the first two years.
    D. You will be charged more if you don't pay bills on time.

Questions 23-25

No matter you travel for business or for leisure, a good hotel can make the experience much more enjoyable. To get a quick impression of a hotel, check its website. You can expect to see its facilities and room rates, which usually vary depending on the date. Generally speaking, the sooner you book, the cheaper a room costs. If you arrive at a hotel without a reservation, be prepared to be "**extorted**". In case you need to cancel your booking, you should also read the fine print regarding cancel policy. You can usually get a full refund if you cancel 48 hours in advance.

You may also want to check photos and reviews by guests on booking sites. By doing so, you can find out more details that only some people will notice. It is worth mentioning, however, that other people's opinions may differ from what you experience in person. That's not to say that some reviews are not genuine; it's just that people have different tastes and expectations, and what some find fabulous may leave others unimpressed. Also, the service quality of a hotel may not be the same all the time.

Besides the hotel itself, location is also an important factor to consider. Staying in the city center means less time wasted on traveling. You can enjoy the luxury of strolling around without worrying about the sky getting dark. On the other hand, staying in a hotel which is hard to reach can save you a few bucks, but it also means that for your safety, you should get back before dark, especially when you are not familiar with the place.

Some people prefer to stay in a hostel rather than a hotel, especially when the budget is tight. If you choose to stay in a hostel, the most important thing is to keep your personal belongings attended all the time because theft is a recurring problem. Leave your valuables in the lockers or carry them with you, even to the toilet. Finally, exercise wisdom and discretion when interacting with other roommates. Avoid arguments at all costs. Whatever hostile circumstances you find yourself in, swallow your pride and keep the peace.

Please turn to the next page. ⇨

23. What does it mean to be "**extorted**"?
    A. To get a good bargain
    B. To be rejected by others
    C. To be attacked without warning
    D. To pay way above the market rate

24. Why does the author recommend hotels in the downtown area?
    A. Hotels located in city centers are cheaper.
    B. Public transportation in the urban areas is more accessible.
    C. Returning to a hotel in a remote area at night can be risky.
    D. The crime rate in city centers is lower.

25. Which of the following is **NOT** part of the advice given by the author for those who stay in a hostel?
    A. Avoid confrontation and fights
    B. Keep an eye on your personal belongings
    C. Lock up important things
    D. Interact with roommates privately if possible

Questions 26-29

The Bermuda triangle is considered by many as a mysterious stretch of area. Some claim that there have been significantly more aircrafts and ships that disappeared for inexplicable reasons in the area between Florida, Puerto Rico, and Bermuda. According to the statistics, however, the frequency of accidents is actually lower than average in this area, and many flights and cruise ships regularly go through it. It is the popular culture's focus on some particularly bizarre events that strengthened the myth. Nevertheless, it may still arouse our curiosity to read some of the stories.

One of the most mysterious events happened to a ship called Mary Celeste. On December 4th, 1872, the ship was found stranded in the sea but without any crew member on it. Since the cargos and valuables were intact, it is unlikely that the ship had been attacked by pirates. Seaquakes and food poisoning have also been considered as possible reasons, but neither seems plausible. Moreover, the weather was fine, and it seems unreasonable for the crew to abandon the ship.

Another incident, which involved the most people missing, happened to one of the US Coast Guard's non-combat ships in March 1918. With 306 crew members and passengers on it, the ship was supposed to sail through the Bermuda Triangle, but was lost halfway. The area had been searched, but no remains or any of the passengers were found. The incident also happened when the weather was fine, thus the ship's disappearance is considered a mystery.

Some people who look at the so-called Bermuda triangle phenomenon with a rational perspective have found some reasonable explanations, such as the effects of magnetic declination and the Gulf Stream. As long as people are fascinated with supernatural forces, however, the mystery will live on.

Please turn to the next page. ⇨

26. What was puzzling about the Mary Celeste incident?
    A. A storm should have caused damage to the ship.
    B. The ones who attacked the ship were never found.
    C. It was not even in the vicinity of the Bermuda triangle.
    D. No one can explain what might have happened to the people on board.

27. Why is it unlikely that Mary Celeste ran into pirates?
    A. The weather was in good condition.
    B. The US coast guard patrols the region vigilantly.
    C. Precious goods on the ship were left untouched.
    D. The crewmen were armed with weapons.

28. What is true about the incident in 1918?
    A. It is among the most serious ones in the area.
    B. The ship was a military warship.
    C. It was revealed during a search.
    D. Most of the sailors were found dead.

29. What is the author's attitude toward the Bermuda triangle phenomenon?
    A. It is more of a popular belief than a truth.
    B. It is something to be concerned about.
    C. It is a supernatural phenomenon.
    D. It is an important subject of scientific research.

Questions 30-34 are based on the information provided in the following announcement and letter.

Taiwan Scholarship

Have you ever wanted to study in Taiwan? Here is your chance. The Ministry of Foreign Affairs is awarding scholarships to top applicants from countries that have diplomatic relations with Taiwan. These scholarships will pay full tuition at a university of your choice and a monthly stipend of 25,000 NTD as living expenses, and they include economy-class plane tickets for direct flights to and from Taiwan. Here are the eligibility requirements:

- You must be a national of a country that Taiwan has diplomatic relations with*
- You must have a high school graduation diploma
- You must be under the age of 30
- You must not have another scholarship awarded from the Taiwanese government
- You must have a passion for Taiwanese culture

*Those who are from other countries (except mainland China) are encouraged to apply for scholarships awarded by the Ministry of Education

Documents

Please attach the following information to your application:

- High school diploma
- Official academic transcripts
- Reference letters
- A study plan

Please submit your application along with the documents to the Taiwan embassy, consulate, or representative office in your country. For more information, please email to Amy Li, the scholarship program director, at amyli@taiwantopmail.com.

Emilia Mouse
534 Bloomfield Ave.
Atlanta, Georgia 30303
U.S.A.

March 14, 2025

Dear representative,

My name is Emilia Mouse. I am 19, and I just graduated from high school. It is with great pleasure that I am applying for Taiwan Scholarship.

Ever since I was a young girl, I have always dreamed of going to Taiwan. After watching a lot of Taiwanese dramas and listening to songs by Taiwanese artists such as Jolene Dai, I am determined to study in Taiwan. However, the problem is that my family is underprivileged. I have five siblings, and my parents both work two jobs to make our ends meet. My motivation to apply for your scholarship program stems from the fact that I want to help my family. After completing my degree in Taiwan, I plan to return to my home country and help my family prosper, and I dream of becoming a Chinese interpreter for the United Nations someday. Your scholarship would be a great help for me and my family.

I have enclosed the application and required documents along with this letter. I hope to hear from you soon.

Sincerely,
Emilia Mouse

30. What is **NOT** covered by the scholarship?
A. School fees
B. Living expenses
C. Air travels
D. Field trips

31. Why may the readers of the announcement send emails to Amy Li?
A. To apply for the scholarship
B. To inquire about the scholarship
C. To verify their documents
D. To consult about studying abroad

32. What do we learn about Emilia?
A. She has a passion for Taiwanese culture.
B. There are seven people in her family.
C. Her parents live a wealthy life.
D. She can speak Chinese fluently.

33. Why may Emilia's application be rejected?
A. She is from the United States.
B. She is under 20 years old.
C. She has not attended high school.
D. She has not prepared the necessary documents.

34. What can Emilia do if her application is rejected?
A. Submit her application again with sufficient documents
B. Send an email to Amy Li to ask for a second review of her documents
C. Talk with someone at the local representative office of Taiwan
D. Apply for another scholarship awarded from Taiwanese government

Please turn to the next page.

Questions 35-40

Smartphones enable us to share our daily life experiences anytime, anywhere, but just like a double-edged sword, they can also do harm to us if abused. As many social networking services and mobile games prompt their users to open the apps once in a while, usually with notifications, some users check their smartphones every few minutes or even more frequently. Smartphone addiction, or compulsive usage of smartphones, makes people stick to their phones when they are supposed to work or study, resulting in the decline in productivity and academic performance.

Smartphones have also become a distraction during social activities, decreasing our real-life interactions. While eating out, for example, it is possible that people would rather chat with their friends online than exchange ideas with those in front of them. Such kind of social gathering is supposed to strengthen relationships with family or friends, while the lack of conversation caused by smartphone usage can render it ineffective, or even make relationship issues worse. It is also concerning that some parents choose to indulge in their online world when they feel bothered by their kids. Young children need parents' attention most of the time, and those who are often neglected will feel insecure and develop low self-esteem. They will also think that using a smartphone is a good way to escape from the real world when they see their parents do so. Therefore, it is especially important that parents pay more attention to their kids than to their mobile devices.

In addition, statistics revealed that the use of hand-held electronic devices significantly increases the risk of traffic accidents. Taking one's eyes off the road for merely a few seconds could result in fatal collisions. Using smartphones while walking could also have serious consequences, such as bumping into a lamppost or ending up in a manhole. Even though everyone has been taught the golden rule of "Stop-Look-Listen", it just goes out of the window when one stares at a little screen. There has been a traffic accident in which a pedestrian was hit, and both the car driver and the pedestrian were using their smartphones. The driver was undoubtedly responsible for not stepping on the brakes in time, but the pedestrian could have avoided the car if he were more aware of his surroundings.

The emergence of "location-based" mobile games has made matters worse. The global hit called *Pokémon Go* requires players to search for monsters at real-world locations. To collect the monsters, players must leave their homes and walk around. Many find the game helps them get more exercise and interact with other players in person, but the game is also designed in such a way that players feel encouraged to walk while looking at the screen, even though they are reminded to "be alert at all times," as written on the game's loading screen. No matter how fascinating the virtual world is, we should never lose sight of the physical world around us.

35. What is a suitable title for this article?
    A. The pros and cons of technology
    B. How to make the most of your smartphone
    C. The risks of obsession with smartphones
    D. The safety issues of smartphone usage

36. Which of the following is **NOT** a result of indulgence in smartphones mentioned in the article?
    A. Negligence of road safety
    B. Lack of interaction among family members
    C. Child physical abuse
    D. Poor work quality

37. According to the article, what could happen when parents use smartphones for too long?
    A. Their kids might seek their attention more eagerly.
    B. Their kids might lack confidence in themselves.
    C. Their kids will tend to escape doing assignments.
    D. They will be asked by their kids to buy smartphones for them.

Please turn to the next page.

38. According to the article, what is a reason that we should not use smartphones while walking or driving?
    A. The number of traffic accidents has significantly increased.
    B. We will be held responsible if we are involved in an accident.
    C. We tend to go faster while using smartphones.
    D. We could overlook unseen hazards around us.

39. What aspect of *Pokémon Go* makes players look at their smartphone screens while walking?
    A. Fitness tracking function
    B. Interactive nature
    C. Style of gameplay
    D. Lack of warning

40. What is the author's attitude toward the use of smartphones?
    A. The use of smartphones should be banned at workplaces.
    B. Smartphones make us less willing to express ourselves.
    C. We should pay attention to our real life even with our smartphones.
    D. Children should be familiar with smartphones as soon as possible.

第六回

初試 聽力測驗 解析

第一部分 / 回答問題

Q1

If you keep putting things off, you will never complete your assignments on time.

如果你持續拖延事情，你就永遠不會準時完成你的作業。

A. I must have misplaced them somewhere.
B. I only turn them on when necessary.
C. I know, but it's tough to change a habit.
D. You're right. That firm is competitive.

A. 我一定是把它們忘在哪裡了。
B. 我只在必要的時候把它們打開。
C. 我知道，但是改變習慣很困難。
D. 你說的對。那家企業很有競爭力。

詳解 **答案：C**

題目用 If you keep doing... 的形式，說如果你一直拖延就不會準時完成作業，意思是希望對方不要繼續拖延下去，所以應該針對「一直拖延」這件事作出回應。選項 C 說 it's tough to change a habit（改變習慣很困難），就是表示改變拖延的 habit 很難，恐怕自己無法滿足對方的期待，是正確答案。

補充說明

「拖延」的行為也可以用不及物動詞 procrastinate 來表達。

|單字片語| **put off** 使…延後，拖延… / **assignment** [əˋsaɪnmənt] n. 分配的任務，作業 / **misplace** [mɪsˋples] v. 把…放錯地方，把…放在想不起來的地方 / **competitive** [kəmˋpɛtətɪv] adj. 競爭的，有競爭力的

Q2

I'm not exactly sure if this is the right tool for me. Does it come with a money-back guarantee?
我不完全確定這對我來說是不是對的工具。這有退款保證嗎？

A. Yes, but conditions apply.
B. Yes, there is a special discount.
C. No, batteries are not included.
D. No, you won't get a commission.

A. 有，但是有條件。
B. 有，有特別的折扣。
C. 沒有，不含電池。
D. 沒有，你不會得到佣金。

詳解

答案：A

說話者問某個東西是否有 money-back guarantee，所以要知道這是「讓購買者可以要求退款的保證」才能回答。A 回答 Yes，但也說 conditions apply，表示雖然有退款保證，但不是無條件退款，是正確答案。合約裡面會規定一些 conditions，說明合約適用的條件和例外的情況。其他選項的內容都和（因為發生問題等原因的）產品退款無關。

|單字片語| **money-back guarantee** （對購買的產品不滿意時的）退款保證 / **condition** [kən`dɪʃən] n. 條件 / **commission** [kə`mɪʃən] n. （銷售物品時抽取的）佣金

Q3

While I am away on business these few days, Eric will take over my duties.
我這些天出差的時候，Eric 會接管我的職責。

A. Does that mean I have to report to him?
B. Who would expect him to be promoted?
C. When will you be back on track?
D. Shall we hold a farewell party?

A. 這意思是我必須和他彙報（從屬於他）嗎？
B. 誰會料到他獲得升職呢？
C. 你什麼時候會重回正軌？
D. 我們要不要辦個告別派對呢？

詳解

答案：A

說話者說自己 away on business（出差不在）的時候，Eric 會 take over（接管）他的 duties（職責），表示 Eric 將會暫時代替他。A 問自己是不是要 report to him，這裡的 report to 是指「下屬從屬於上司」的意思，顯示對方是上司；這個句子是詢問對方不在的時候，是不是應該把 Eric 當成上司，是合理的答案。

題目的說話者是要出差，不是要離職，也不代表 Eric 獲得升職了，所以 B 和 D 不對。選項 C 的 back on track（重回正軌）是表示曾經出問題而耽誤正在進行的事情，或者情況沒有順利發展，但之後重新上了軌道的情況。

|單字片語| **on business** 為了公事（出差） / **take over** 接管… / **report to** 從屬於… / **promote** [prə`mot] v. 使升職 / **back on track** 重回正軌 / **farewell** [`fɛr`wɛl] n. 告別

Q4

Apart from your cholesterol level, which is on the high side, everything else is within normal range.
除了你的膽固醇偏高以外，其他都在正常範圍。

A. I believe we can achieve our goals. A. 我相信我們能達到我們的目標。
B. I suggest we adjust the figures a little. B. 我建議我們稍微調整數字。
C. I guess I had better watch my diet. C. 我猜我最好注意我的飲食。
D. I'm sure I can eat as much as I want. D. 我相信我可以吃想吃多少就吃多少。

詳解

答案：C

題目的重點在於 your cholesterol level... is on the high side（你的膽固醇水準偏高），可知說話者在談論對方的健康檢查結果，所以應該針對這方面作出回應。因為膽固醇偏高顯示健康不佳，所以 C 說 I had better watch my diet（我最好注意我的飲食），暗示將藉由調整飲食來控制膽固醇，是合理的答案。

|單字片語| **cholesterol** [kə`lɛstə͵rol] n. 膽固醇 / **level** [`lɛvl̩] n. 水平，水準 / **on the high side** 偏高 / **range** [rendʒ] n. 範圍 / **figure** [`fɪgjɚ] n. 數字 / **diet** [`daɪət] n. 飲食

Q5

It's hard to say no when my kids want new toys, though I know I shouldn't let them have their way.
小孩要新玩具的時候我很難說不，雖然我知道不該讓他們隨心所欲。

A. Just show them the way to go. A. 就告訴他們應該去哪裡。
B. You should set a limit and stick to it. B. 你應該設定限制並且堅守它。
C. It isn't always easy to express your feelings. C. 表達你的情感並不是隨時都很容易。
D. I think it's fine to spend a day together. D. 我覺得花一天的時間在一起沒有關係。

詳解

答案：B

說話者表達自己的問題，是小孩要新玩具時 It's hard to say no，暗示對方回答孩子要求買玩具時該怎麼解決。B 回答 set a limit（設定限制），就是明定買玩具的限制，並且 stick to（堅守）這個限制，是適當的答案。選項 C 說 express your feelings（表達你的情感）不容易，通常是表示比較感性的想法，而不是禁止小孩買玩具這種事情。選項 D 的 spend 是當成「花時間」而不是「花錢」的意思來使用，請注意。

|單字片語| **let someone have one's way** 讓某人隨心所欲 / **stick to** 堅持…，忠於…

Q6

We don't take reservations. First-come, first-served is the policy of our restaurant.

我們不接受預約。先到先服務是我們餐廳的政策。

A. Will it take long before I am seated?	A. 我需要等很久才能入座嗎？
B. May I reserve a table for four?	B. 我可以預約四人座嗎？
C. Can I exchange this for something else?	C. 我可以把這個換成別的嗎？
D. Have you upgraded your server?	D. 你們升級伺服器了嗎？

詳解

答案：A

題目的重點在於 First-come, first-served，這表示客人依照先來後到的次序，依序獲得服務。不過，即使不知道這個用語，聽到前面的 We don't take reservations. 也可以明確得知這家 restaurant 並不接受預約，所以要求預約的 B 不可能是正確答案。既然不接受預約，又要依照順序等候服務，所以 A 用 be seated 表示「被安排入座」，詢問在那之前會不會 take long（花很久的時間），是合理的回應。

|單字片語| **policy** [ˋpɑləsɪ] n. 政策 / **be seated** 就座 / **server** [ˋsɝvɚ] n. 上菜的人；伺服器

第1回 第2回 第3回 第4回 第5回 第6回

Q7

In your opinion, what makes you stand out from the rest of the applicants for this position?
就你的意見，對於這個職位，是什麼讓你能比其他應徵者突出？

A. I agree with and support your decision. A. 我同意並支持你的決定。
B. I have the experience and expertise required. B. 我有必要的經驗和專業能力。
C. I enjoy working out in my leisure time. C. 我很喜歡在休閒時間健身。
D. I am glad to be given the opportunity. D. 我很高興能得到這個機會。

詳解 答案：B

說話者問 what makes you stand out... for this position?（對於這個職位，是什麼讓你顯得突出），可知對方可能是申請 position（職位）的 applicants（應徵者）之一，而說話者是面試官。對於這種典型的面試問題，應徵者應該說明自己的能力優勢，所以表明自己有 experience and expertise（經驗和專業能力）的選項 B 是正確答案。請注意不要看到選項 C 的 working 就以為是工作的意思，因為 work out 表示做高強度的運動；in my leisure time（在我的休閒時間）也和工作沒有關係，所以這不是最適當的答案。

|單字片語| **stand out** 突出 / **position** [pə`zɪʃən] n. 位置；職位 / **expertise** [ˌɛkspɚ`tiz] 專業知識，專業能力 / **work out** 運動，健身 / **leisure** [`liʒɚ] n. 閒暇 adj. 空閒的

Q8

Why is the gate unlocked? Don't tell me the security alarm failed to work again.
為什麼門的鎖被打開了？別告訴我保全警鈴又沒起作用了。

A. Let's work harder next time. A. 我們下次再努力點吧。
B. Let's check if anything is missing. B. 我們檢查看看有沒有東西不見了。
C. Let's reset the time on the clock. C. 我們重新設定時鐘的時間吧。
D. Let's see if we have a spare key. D. 我們看看是不是有備用鑰匙。

詳解 答案：B

說話者提到門是 unlocked（鎖打開了）的狀態，並且說 Don't tell me the security alarm failed to work again.（別告訴我保全警鈴又沒起作用了），並不是真的叫對方「不要告訴我」，而是不希望又發生了保全失效的狀況。因為門在

兩人不在的時候打開了，有可能遭小偷，所以 B 建議 check if anything is missing（檢查看看有沒有東西不見了），是合理的回應。C 是利用 alarm（警鈴；鬧鐘）和 clock 在意義上的相關性而設計的陷阱選項。

|單字片語| **unlock** [ʌn`lɑk] v. 把…的鎖打開 / **spare** [spɛr] adj. 備用的

Q9

Have you heard the news? Due to a shortage of power, utility bills are going up again! **你聽到消息了嗎？因為電力短缺，公用事業的帳單（費用）又要漲價了！**

A. No wonder we can't find it anywhere. A. 難怪我們到處都找不到。
B. I had better fill up my fuel tank soon. B. 我最好趕快裝滿我的油箱。
C. The frozen food will turn bad without electricity. C. 冷凍食品沒有電會壞掉。
D. That's why I rarely turn on the air-conditioner. D. 那就是為什麼我很少開空調。

詳解 **答案：D**

utility bills 包含水費、電費、瓦斯費等等，不過說話者提到 shortage of power（電力短缺），所以他指的 bills 是電費帳單。選項 D 回答自己 rarely turn on the air-conditioner（很少開空調），作為應對電費調漲的方法，是合理的回應。選項 B 的 fuel tank 是指車輛的油箱，但從電費的話題直接跳到加油，已經離題了。選項 C 說 without electricity（沒有電）的話食物會壞掉，但電費上漲應該不至於造成停電的情況。

|單字片語| **shortage** [`ʃɔrtɪdʒ] n. 短缺 / **utility** [ju`tɪlətɪ] n. 公用事業（水、電、瓦斯等等） / **had better do** 最好做… / **fuel tank** 燃料槽，（車輛的）油箱

Q10

There's a reason why properties in this area are relatively cheap. It floods whenever there is heavy rain. **這區的房地產相對便宜是有原因的。只要下大雨就會淹水。**

A. No one can predict the weather.
B. We can never afford it.
C. That's what coupons are for.
D. Maybe we should buy a home elsewhere.

A. 沒有人能預測天氣。
B. 我們永遠買不起。
C. 這就是優惠券的用途。
D. 或許我們應該買其他地方的房子。

詳解 **答案：D**

說話者提到這個地區的 properties（房地產）便宜，因為下大雨的時候 it floods（淹水）。所以，對方應該針對該地區的房地產價格或環境作出回應。A 回答天氣無法預測，但並沒有針對這個地區作出評論，所以不是最好的答案。B 表示買不起，但當地的房子比較便宜，應該是比較買得起才對。C 和題目完全無關。D 說應該買其他地方的房子，表示因為淹水的問題，對當地的房子有顧慮，所以應該考慮其他地方，是適當的回應。

|單字片語| **property** [ˋprɑpɚtɪ] n. 財產，房地產 / **coupon** [ˋkupɑn] n. 優惠券

第二部分／對話

Q11

M: I don't think it is a good idea to squeeze so many destinations into our itinerary. 我不覺得把這麼多目的地擠進我們的旅遊行程是個好主意。

W: Why not? The air tickets to Europe alone cost us a bomb.
為什麼不是？光是到歐洲的機票就要花我們很多錢。

M: I agree. But visiting too many countries means we will spend a lot of time on the road.
我同意。但是拜訪太多國家就意味著我們會花很多時間在路途上。

W: We can enjoy the scenery along the way. 我們可以沿路欣賞風景。

M: That's beside the point. I would rather stay at the same place for one or two more days so we can truly experience local culture.
這跟那沒有關係。我寧願在同一個地方多留一兩天，讓我們可以真正體驗當地文化。

W: I already told my friends I will be going to France, Germany, Switzerland, Italy, and Spain.
我已經告訴我的朋友說我會去法國、德國、瑞士、義大利和西班牙了。

M: Do you realize how expensive it is to travel by train in Europe?
你注意到在歐洲搭火車旅行有多貴嗎？

Q: What does the man imply? 男子暗示什麼？

A. It is not very safe during this period. A. 這個時期不是非常安全。
B. It is advisable to visit fewer countries. B. 最好少拜訪一些國家。
C. It is more affordable if they travel by train. C. 如果他們搭火車旅行比較便宜。
D. It is possible to go anywhere they want. D. 去他們想去的任何地方是有可能的。

詳解 答案：B

男子一開始就說 I don't think it is a good idea to squeeze so many destinations（我不覺得擠進這麼多目的地是個好主意），之後又說 visiting too many countries means we will spend a lot of time on the road（拜訪太多國家意味著我們會在路途上花很多時間），所以他認為最好不要拜訪太多國家。選項 B 用 It is advisable to do（做…是明智的）的句型，表示男子的建議是 visit fewer countries（拜訪比較少的國家），是正確答案。選項 C 和男子最後說的 Do you realize how expensive it is to travel by train（你注意到搭火車旅行有多貴嗎）正好相反。

|單字片語| **squeeze** [skwiz] v. 擠，塞入 / **destination** [ˌdɛstəˋneʃən] n. 目的地 / **itinerary** [aɪˋtɪnəˌrɛrɪ] n. 旅遊行程 / **air ticket** 機票（= flight ticket）/ **cost a bomb** 花很多錢 / **beside the point** 離題 / **local** [ˋlokḷ] adj. 地方的，當地的，本地的 / **advisable** [ədˋvaɪzəbḷ] adj. 明智的，可取的 / **affordable** [əˋfɔrdəbḷ] adj. 負擔得起的

Q12

W: Just leave me alone. 讓我自己一個人。

M: Come on. You have to eat something to regain your strength.
拜託。你必須吃點東西恢復你的體力。

W: I have no appetite. Get me another painkiller, will you?
我沒有食慾。再給我一顆止痛藥，好嗎？

M: No way. I insist that you finish the porridge. I know it doesn't taste great, but I am following the doctor's advice.
不行。我堅持你要把粥吃完。我知道不好吃，但我是遵守醫生的建議。

W: It hurts when I move. My wound has barely healed.
我一動就會痛。我的傷口幾乎沒有好。

M: It will in time, if you eat and stay strong. Let me feed you. That's my girl. 終究會好的，如果你吃東西並且保持強健的話。讓我餵你。這才是我的好女孩。

Q: What might be wrong with the woman?
女子可能有什麼問題？

A. She wanted to lose weight.	A. 她想要減重。
B. She hurt the man accidentally.	B. 她不小心傷到了男子。
C. She refused to take her medication.	C. 她拒絕吃藥。
D. She just underwent an operation.	D. 她剛接受了手術。

詳解 **答案：D**

選項都是 She 開頭，可以推測題目可能問女子的情況，所以要注意關於她的情況的描述。女子說 I have no appetite. Get me another painkiller（我沒有食慾。再給我一顆止痛藥），以及 My wound has barely healed.（我的傷口幾乎沒有好），可知女子的傷口很痛，而且她吃不下東西。雖然女子也有可能是因為意外受傷，但選項裡沒有這個答案，所以有可能造成這種情況的 D. She just underwent an operation.（她剛接受了手術）是正確答案。A 和 B 在對話中沒有提到，而 C 不符合女子的情況，因為她會吃 painkiller（止痛藥）。

|單字片語| **regain** [rɪˋgen] v. 重新獲得，恢復 / **appetite** [ˋæpəˌtaɪt] n. 食慾，胃口 / **painkiller** [ˋpenˌkɪlɚ] n. 止痛藥 / **porridge** [ˋpɔrɪdʒ] n. 粥 / **wound** [wund] n. 傷口

Q13

M: Please take a seat, ma'am. This paperwork will take less than 5 minutes. In the event of your death, both your daughters will divide your estate equally. 女士請坐。這個書面作業會花不到五分鐘的時間。萬一發生您死亡的情況，您的兩個女兒將會平分您的財產。

W: Yes, but my savings and cash assets will be donated to charity. 是的，但我的存款和現金資產將會捐給慈善機構。

M: It is all written down in black and white, with your signature and that of a witness. 都用白紙黑字寫下來了，有您和見證人的簽名。

W: That ungrateful son of mine will not get a dime, right? 我那不知感謝的兒子不會得到一毛錢，是嗎？

M: Yes, according to this new will, he will receive nothing. 是的，根據這個新的遺囑，他不會得到任何東西。

Q: Where is this conversation probably taking place?
這段對話可能發生在哪裡？

A. In an investment firm. A. 在投資公司。
B. In a funeral home. B. 在殯儀館。
C. In an attorney's office. C. 在律師事務所。
D. In a charitable foundation. D. 在慈善基金會。

詳解 答案：C

一開始男子提到了 paperwork（書面作業），然後說 In the event of your death, both your daughters will divide your estate equally.（萬一發生您死亡的情況，您的兩個女兒將會平分您的財產），可知兩人應該是在處理女子的遺囑。男子最後說到 this new will（這個新的遺囑），更可以確定是在處理遺囑沒錯。遺囑通常會請律師幫忙處理，所以 C 是最合理的答案。

|單字片語| **paperwork** [ˋpepɚ͵wɝk] n. 文書作業，書面作業 / **in the event of** 假如發生… / **estate** [ɪsˋtet] n. 財產，地產 / **savings** [ˋsevɪŋz] n. 存款 / **asset** [ˋæsɛt] n. 資產 / **black and white** 白紙黑字（寫在紙上） / **witness** [ˋwɪtnɪs] n. 見證人；目擊者 / **ungrateful** [ʌnˋgretfəl] adj. 不知感謝的 / **will** [wɪl] n. 遺囑 / **funeral home** 殯儀館 / **attorney** [əˋtɝnɪ] n. 律師 / **charitable** [ˋtʃærətəbḷ] adj. 慈善的

Q14

W: I still can't get over it. Bobby had been my faithful companion for nearly twenty years.
我還是不能恢復過來。Bobby 有將近二十年都是我忠誠的同伴。

M: You did all you could. You took him to the veterinarian and gave him the best treatment available. For a golden retriever, he enjoyed an unusual long life. 你已經做了你能做的一切。你帶他去看獸醫，又給他最好的治療。對於黃金獵犬而言，他享有不尋常的長壽。

W: He was not just a pet. He was my friend, my most loyal friend. How am I going to live without him? 他不只是隻寵物。他是我的朋友，我最忠心的朋友。我沒有他要怎麼活下去？

M: Look what I have here. 你看我這裡有什麼。

W: A pup? He looks exactly like Bobby!
一隻小狗？他看起來就像 Bobby 一樣！

Q: What are the speakers mainly discussing?
說話者主要在討論什麼？

A. The passing away of an animal. A. 一隻動物的過世。
B. Adopting a new pet. B. 領養新的寵物。
C. Medical aid for the elderly. C. 老年人的醫療協助。
D. Financial planning for old age. D. 為了老年時期所做的財務規畫。

詳解 **答案：A**

女子開頭說 Bobby had been my faithful companion（Bobby 是我忠誠的同伴），但從對話中出現的 veterinarian（獸醫）、golden retriever（黃金獵犬）、pet（寵物）等單字，可知 Bobby 其實是一隻狗。男子說 You did all you could... gave him the best treatment（你做了你能做的一切…給他最好的治療），而女子說 How am I going to live without him?（我沒有他要怎麼活下去），暗示 Bobby 雖然接受了治療，但還是離開了女子（過世了），所以 A 是正確答案。最後女子雖然看到男子帶來像 Bobby 的小狗，但這並不是對話中最主要的部分，所以不能選 B。

|單字片語| **get over** 克服…，脫離痛苦的情況並且恢復 / **faithful** [`feθfəl] adj. 忠誠的 / **companion** [kəm`pænjən] n. 同伴 / **veterinarian** [ˌvɛtərə`nɛrɪən] n. 獸醫（= vet） / **golden retriever** 黃金獵犬 / **loyal** [`lɔɪəl] adj. 忠心的 / **pup** [pʌp] n. 小狗（= puppy）

Q15

M: What? Harry bought a new car? He took a loan from me six months ago. 什麼？Harry 買了一台新車？他六個月前跟我借了錢。

W: He offered to give me a ride home after work in his new BMW.
他提議下班以後要開他新的 BMW 載我回家。

M: I can't believe it! He changed the subject every time when I mentioned payment. He even gave me the impression that he was broke. I was wrong about him. I'm going to have a word with him right now! 我不敢相信！每次我提到付款他就改變話題。他甚至給我他破產的印象。我看錯他了。我現在要跟他談談！

W: Well, I bet he will say that he spent all his money on the car.
嗯，我打賭他會說他把錢都花在車上了。

M: I don't care what he does with his money. I just want mine back!
我不在乎他對他的錢做什麼。我只想要回我的錢！

Q: What does the man imply about Harry?
關於 Harry，男子暗示什麼？

A. Harry is not a trustworthy person. A. Harry 不是一個值得信賴的人。
B. Harry is passionate about imported cars. B. Harry 對於進口車很熱衷。
C. Harry has a lot of money in the bank. C. Harry 在銀行有很多錢。
D. Harry has fallen in love with the woman. D. Harry 愛上這名女子了。

詳解　　答案：A

關於 Harry，男子說 He took a loan from me（他跟我借了錢），但是他 changed the subject every time when I mentioned payment（每次我提到付款就改變話題），表示 Henry 故意不還錢，所以說 I was wrong about him.（我對他的看法錯了），最符合這些敘述的是 A。

|單字片語| **give someone the impression that** 給某人…的印象，使某人以為… / **have a word with** 和…談談 / **trustworthy** [ˋtrʌst͵wɝðɪ] adj. 值得信賴的 / **passionate** [ˋpæʃənɪt] adj. 熱情的

Q16

W: What's wrong with teenagers nowadays? My son would rather stare at his cell phone than speak with me.
現在的年輕人是怎麼了？我兒子寧願盯著他的手機也不要跟我講話。

M: Didn't you explain some basic rules and cell phone manners to him before you bought him the phone?
你買手機給他之前沒有解釋一些基本的規則和手機禮儀嗎？

W: I guess we overlooked that part. It was a reward for his performance in school. But ever since he got the phone, his grades have plunged.
我猜我們忽略了這個部分。這是作為他在學校表現的回報。但自從他得到了手機之後，他的成績就快速下降。

M: Maybe you should take away his phone. 或許你應該拿走他的手機。

W: I tried it once, but he got so mad that he refused to go to school.
我試過一次，但他生氣到拒絕上學。

M: In that case, I can only wish you good luck.
那樣的話，我只能祝你好運了。

Q: What problem did the woman encounter?
女子遇到了什麼問題？

A. Her son committed a crime.
B. Her son broke the rules she laid down.
C. Her son is a victim of bullying in school.
D. Her son is addicted to an electronic product.

A. 她的兒子犯了罪。
B. 她的兒子違反了她制定的規則。
C. 她的兒子是校園霸凌的受害者。
D. 她的兒子對電子產品上癮。

詳解 **答案：D**

女子開頭就說 My son would rather stare at his cell phone than speak with me.（我兒子寧願盯著他的手機也不要跟我講話），而且 his grades have plunged（他的成績快速下降），所以用 is addicted to an electronic product（對電子產品上癮）表示過度使用手機的 D 是正確答案。和選項 B 相關的部分，是男子說的 Didn't you explain some basic rules（你沒解釋一些基本的規則嗎），而女子回答 we overlooked that part（我們忽略了這個部分），所以女子沒有制定規則。

|單字片語| **overlook** [ˌovə`lʊk] v. 忽略，看漏 / **plunge** [plʌndʒ] v. 急降 / **commit** [kə`mɪt] v. 犯（罪） / **lay down** 把…放平，制定（規則） / **victim** [`vɪktɪm] n. 犧牲者，受害者 / **bullying** [`bʊlɪŋ] n. 霸凌行為 / **be addicted to** 對…上癮

Q17

M: How do you find Thai cuisine? I hope it is not too spicy for you.
你覺得泰式料理怎麼樣？我希望對你來說不會太辣。

W: I refilled my glass six times. What do you think? Why does every dish have to be hot? And I had to get the water myself because the waiter was nowhere to be seen.
我重裝了我的玻璃杯六次。你覺得怎樣？為什麼每道菜都要是辣的呢？我還要自己去拿水，因為到處都看不到服務生。

M: I saw him helping out in the kitchen. This is a family business. I believe the waiter is the son.
我看到他在廚房幫忙。這是家庭事業。我相信服務生是兒子。

W: At least this coconut pudding is to my liking. It's not too sweet, and it smells great. 至少這個椰香布丁合我的口味。不會太甜，而且很香。

M: I forgot to tell you that we are getting a good deal. Look at the bill. 我忘了告訴你，我們得到很划算的交易。你看看帳單。

Q: What is a positive aspect of the woman's dining experience? **女子用餐經驗中正面的方面是什麼？**

A. The price is attractive. A. 價格很吸引人。
B. The service is awesome. B. 服務很棒。
C. The dessert is tasty. C. 點心很好吃。
D. The water is free. D. 水是免費的。

詳解 **答案：C**

女子一開始嫌 Why does every dish have to be hot?（為什麼每道菜都要是辣的）、the waiter was nowhere to be seen（到處都看不到服務生），但後面稱讚 this coconut pudding is to my liking（這個椰香布丁合我的口味），所以 C 是正確答案，dessert（點心）代表女子所說的 pudding。雖然水應該是免費的，但女子沒有稱讚這一點，所以不能選 D。選項 A 是男子提到的：we are getting a good deal（我們得到很划算的交易）。

|單字片語| **cuisine** [kwɪˋzin] n. 菜餚，料理 / **to one's liking** 合某人的口味

Q18

W: They say seeing is believing, but I can't believe my eyes. Is that snow? 人家說眼見為憑，但我不能相信我的眼睛。那是雪嗎？

M: It is. I finally know what my Canadian friends mean when they say a white Christmas. Look at all these trees.
是啊。我終於知道我的加拿大朋友所說的白色聖誕了。你看這些樹。

W: Yes, we are three thousand feet above sea level, but it is June. This is not supposed to be happening. It's freezing cold. 是啊，我們在海拔三千英尺的地方，但現在是六月。這不應該發生的。冷得像要結凍一樣。

M: Thank goodness I kept our winter clothes in the trunk. What we lack are gloves.
謝天謝地我在汽車行李箱裡放了我們冬天的衣服。我們缺少的是手套。

W: There might be a flash flood when the snow melts.
雪融化的時候可能會有暴發的洪水。

M: We should be safe up here, right? 我們在這上面應該安全，對嗎？

W: Stay clear of rivers and streams. 遠離河流和溪流。

M: Yes, ma'am. 是的，女士。

Q: Based on the conversation, what is probably true?
根據這段對話，何者可能是正確的？

A. The weather phenomenon is abnormal. A. 天氣現象異常。
B. Christmas celebrations were canceled. B. 聖誕節的慶祝被取消了。
C. It's very hot in the mountains in summer. C. 夏天的時候山上非常熱。
D. Flash floods happen when it starts snowing. D. 暴洪會在開始下雪時發生。

詳解 **答案：A**

女子說 I can't believe my eyes（我不能相信我的眼睛），問 Is that snow?，又說 we are three thousand feet above sea level, but it is June. This is not supposed to be happening（我們在海拔三千英尺的地方，但現在是六月。這不應該發生），表示現在下雪是異常現象，所以 A 是正確答案。三千英尺相當於九百多公尺，和陽明山擎天崗的海拔高度差不多。

|單字片語| **seeing is believing** 眼見為憑 / **sea level** 海平面 / **trunk** [trʌŋk] n. 車尾行李箱 / **flash flood** 突然發生的短暫洪水

Q19

M: My boss treats female employees differently. He seldom raises his voice at them or reproaches them openly. When I make a mistake, you can hear him yelling from a mile away.
我的上司對待女性員工不一樣。他很少對她們大聲講話，也很少公然責備她們。當我犯錯的時候，你可以在一英里以外聽到他大叫。

W: Maybe that's because you are his most trusted right-hand man. You can't afford to make a blunder. You have heavy responsibilities. 或許是因為你是他最信賴的得力助手。你沒有犯大錯的本錢。你責任重大。

M: I think he has a soft spot for young women, especially those with good looks or a nice figure.
我想他會對年輕女子心軟，尤其是長得好看或者身材好的。

W: You make your boss sound so evil. Is he really that bad?
你讓你的上司聽起來好邪惡。他真的那麼壞嗎？

M: Do you need solid proof? I will give it to you. Once he invited a newcomer, a lady of course, to his private mansion. How do you justify that? 你需要強力的證據嗎？我就告訴你。有一次，他邀請一位新人，當然是女的，到他私人的豪華別墅。你要怎麼為這件事辯護呢？

Q: According to the man, what is correct about his boss?　根據男子的說法，關於他的上司何者正確？

A. He discriminates against women.　A. 他歧視女性。
B. He mixes personal affairs with office work.　B. 他把個人的事情和辦公室工作混在一起。
C. He only gives promotions to women.　C. 他只讓女人升職。
D. He hardly blames the man when he makes an error.　D. 男子犯錯的時候他很少責備他。

詳解　答案：B

男子說他的老闆 treats female employees differently（對待女性員工不一樣）、has a soft spot for young women（對年輕女子心軟），而且 invited a newcomer... to his private mansion（邀請新人到他的私人豪華別墅）。選項中符合這位上司的敘述是 B，因為邀請還未熟識的新人到私人住宅，已經超越了正常的工作互動，可以說是把公事和私事混在一起。A、C 在對話中沒有提到。D 和男子說的 When I make a mistake, you can hear him yelling from a mile away.（當我犯錯的時候，你可以在一英里以外聽到他大叫）正好相反。

|單字片語| **reproach** [rɪ`protʃ] v. 責備，斥責 / **right-hand man** 得力助手，左右手 / **afford to do** 有本錢做⋯ / **make a blunder** 犯大錯 / **have a soft spot for** 對⋯心軟 / **figure** [`fɪgjɚ] n. 體形，體態 / **solid** [`sɑlɪd] 固體的；結實的；可靠的 / **newcomer** [`nju`kʌmɚ] n. 新進成員 / **justify** [`dʒʌstəˌfaɪ] v. 證明⋯為正當

Questions 20-21

Questions number 20 and 21 are based on the following conversation.

W: Hello. Is there anything that I can help you with today?
哈囉，今天有什麼我能幫您的嗎？

M: Yes, I'm actually looking for some face masks. You know, the flu is going around, yet my daughter still has to go to school. In order to reduce the risk, I think it's better for her to keep the mask on.
是的，其實我在找一些口罩。你知道的，流行性感冒正在流行，但我的女兒還是必須上學。為了減少風險，我想她一直戴著口罩比較好。

W: Well, face masks are on aisle 2. However, it's equally important to prevent contact transmission. I recommend getting some hand sanitizer so your daughter can keep her hands clean. Alcohol spray is also useful, as you can use it to disinfect your desk and cell phone. 嗯，口罩在第 2 條走道。不過，預防接觸傳染同樣重要。我推薦買點乾洗手，好讓您的女兒能保持手部清潔。酒精噴霧也很有用，因為您可以用它來消毒桌子和手機。

M: OK, I'll get a bottle of both, besides face masks.
好，除了口罩以外，我兩種各買一瓶。

W: Would you also like some painkillers? 您也想要一些止痛藥嗎？

M: Uhm, I already have some at home. I think I'm good.
呃，我家裡已經有一些了。我想我不用了。

|單字片語| **aisle** [aɪl] n. 通道，走道 / **transmission** [træns`mɪʃən] n. 傳播，傳染 / **hand sanitizer** 乾洗手 / **disinfect** [ˌdɪsɪn`fɛkt] v. 消毒 / **painkiller** [`penˌkɪlɚ] 止痛藥

Q20

Where most likely is this conversation taking place? **這段對話最有可能是在哪裡進行的？**

A. At a clinic. A. 診所。
B. At a market. B. 市場。
C. At a drugstore. C. 藥局。
D. At a medical school. D. 醫學院。

詳解

答案：C

從女子說的 face masks are on aisle 2（口罩在第 2 條走道），可知兩人在某種賣場，而從對話中提到的乾洗手、酒精噴霧、止痛藥等物品，可知 C 是最合理的答案。

Q21

What will the man purchase? **男子會買什麼？**

A. Only face masks. A. 只有口罩。
B. Hand sanitizer and alcohol spray. B. 乾洗手和酒精噴霧。
C. Face masks, hand sanitizer, and alcohol spray. C. 口罩、乾洗手和酒精噴霧。
D. Face masks, hand sanitizer, alcohol spray, and painkillers. D. 口罩、乾洗手、酒精噴霧和止痛藥。

詳解

　女子建議男子買乾洗手和酒精噴霧，男子回答 I'll get a bottle of both, besides face masks，表示除了口罩以外，也要買乾洗手和酒精噴霧各一瓶。至於最後提到的止痛藥，男子說 I think I'm good 並不是想要買的意思，而是表示「不用了」，所以 C 是正確答案。

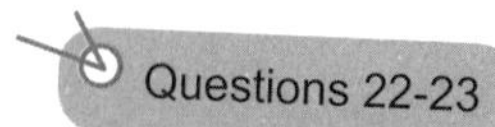

Questions number 22 and 23 are based on the following conversation.

M: Hey, babe, I want to take you to a really nice restaurant on Saturday. I've already made a reservation.
嘿，寶貝，星期六我想帶你去一間很好的餐廳。我已經預約了。

W: What time is the reservation? I'll be working on that day, you know.
預約是幾點？我那天會工作，你知道的。

M: It's 6 p.m. Will you be able to make it? 是下午 6 點。你能到嗎？

W: I don't think so. I won't work overtime and will get off work at 5 p.m., but that'll be too late for me to go home and get changed before going to the restaurant. You said it's really nice, so I don't want to be too casual. Can we pick another time like, maybe 8 p.m.?
我想不行。我不會加班，而且會在下午 5 點下班，但那會太晚了，我沒辦法在去餐廳之前回家換衣服。你說那間餐廳很好，所以我不想要太休閒。我們可不可以選其他時間，或許晚上 8 點？

M: That's going to be impossible, honey. That restaurant is booked solid for the next six months. Well, don't worry about your outfit. Just being together with you is enough to make me happy.
不可能，親愛的。那間餐廳接下來六個月都預約滿了。嗯，別擔心你的穿著了。只要跟你在一起就足夠讓我開心了。

W: But I don't want to look like I have a bad taste in clothes.
但我不想要看起來像是衣服品味很差。

|單字片語| **get off work** 下班 / **get changed** 換衣服 / **be booked solid** 被預約滿了 / **outfit** [ˋaʊtˌfɪt] 一套服裝

Q22

What are the speakers mainly talking about?
兩位說話者主要在談論什麼？

A. The food of a restaurant. A. 一家餐廳的食物。
B. The popularity of a restaurant. B. 一家餐廳受歡迎的程度。
C. The dress sense of the woman. C. 女子的穿著品味。
D. The availability of the woman. D. 女子是否有空。

詳解 答案：D

這段對話是男子邀請女子去餐廳吃飯，並且詢問女子是否能在他預約的時間到場，所以 D 是正確答案。A 在對話中完全沒提到。B 和 C 雖然稍微提到了，但不是整段對話的核心內容。

|單字片語| **dress sense** 穿著品味 / **availability** [əˌveləˋbɪlətɪ] n. 可得性，（人）能否出席

Q23

Why is the woman reluctant to go to the restaurant? **女子為什麼不想去餐廳？**

A. She will not be able to dress up. A. 她沒辦法盛裝打扮。
B. She does not have nice clothes. B. 她沒有很好的衣服。
C. She will have to work overtime. C. 她必須加班。
D. The restaurant's food tastes bad. D. 那家餐廳的食物不好吃。

詳解 答案：A

男子問 Will you be able to make it?（你能到嗎？），女子回答 I don't think so（我想不行）之後，說明了她可能無法去餐廳的理由，主要是因為下班的時間 too late for me to go home and get changed before going to the restaurant（太晚了，我沒辦法在去餐廳之前回家換衣服）。之所以需要換衣服，則是因為 it's really nice, so I don't want to be too casual（那間餐廳很好，所以我不想要太休閒）。綜合這些說明，可知女子不想去的原因是 A。B. 在對話中沒有提到。C. 和女子說的 I won't work overtime（我不會加班）不符合。D. 在對話中沒有提到，另外也請注意女子最後說的 bad taste in clothes 是指「不好的衣服品味」，而不是食物的味道。

Q24

For question number 24, please look at the pictures and descriptions.

M: Janice, why do you look so happy? 珍妮斯，為什麼你看起來這麼高興？

W: I think I fell in love with Eugene. He's one of my classmates.
我想我愛上尤金了。他是我的同學。

M: You mean the guy who came to our home last weekend? I remember he was wearing glasses.
你是說上週末來我們家那個男的嗎？我記得他戴眼鏡。

W: That's not him. Eugene is just a bit short-sighted, so he can do without glasses. Let me show you a picture of him. 那不是他。尤金只是有點近視，所以他可以不戴眼鏡。我讓你看他的照片。

M: Oh, so he has straight hair. I was so wrong to think you like that curly hair guy. I guess he must like reading novels, just like you. Am I right this time? 噢，所以他是直髮。我真是大錯特錯，以為你喜歡那個捲髮的男生。我猜他一定喜歡讀小說，就像你一樣。這次我對了嗎？

W: Well, actually, he's an outdoor guy. He likes to get in touch with nature on weekends.
嗯，事實上，他是熱愛戶外活動的人。他週末喜歡接觸大自然。

|單字片語| **short-sighted** [ˋʃɔrtˋsaɪtɪd] adj. 近視的 / **curly** [ˋkɝlɪ] adj. （頭髮）捲的

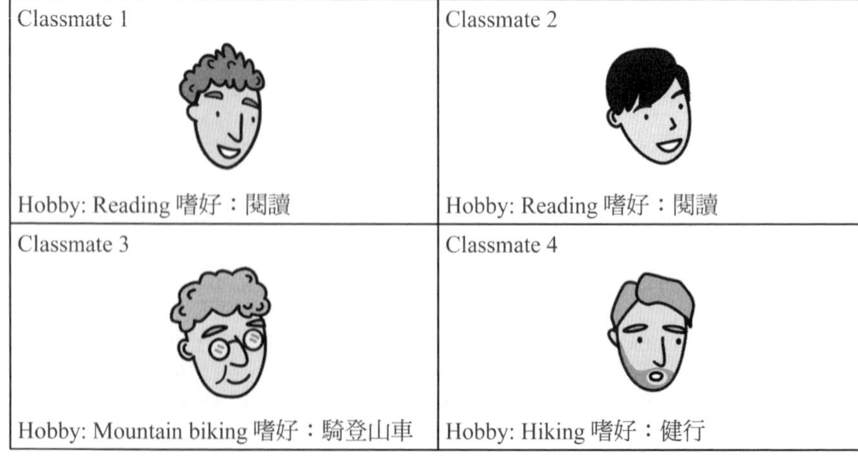

Classmate 1	Classmate 2
Hobby: Reading 嗜好：閱讀	Hobby: Reading 嗜好：閱讀
Classmate 3	Classmate 4
Hobby: Mountain biking 嗜好：騎登山車	Hobby: Hiking 嗜好：健行

Q: Based on the woman's description, who is Eugene?
根據女子的敘述，誰是尤金？

A. Classmate 1.　　A. 同學 1。
B. Classmate 2.　　B. 同學 2。
C. Classmate 3.　　C. 同學 3。
D. Classmate 4.　　D. 同學 4。

詳解　　**答案：D**

要小心對話中夾雜了一些關於別人的描述，必須清楚分辨他們說的是 Eugene 還是另一個人。關於 Eugene，女子說 he can do without glasses（他可以不戴眼鏡），因此可以先排除同學 3。然後女子讓男子看 Eugene 的照片，男子說 so he has straight hair（所以他是直髮），進一步把範圍縮小到同學 2 和 4。最後他們談到 Eugene 的嗜好，女子說 he's an outdoor guy（他是熱愛戶外活動的人），所以嗜好是健行的同學 4 就是 Eugene，D 是正確答案。

Q25

For question number 25, please look at the list of apartments for rent.

M: Hi, I'm looking for an apartment that allows cats.
嗨，我在找允許養貓的公寓。

W: No problem. Here are some choices for you. If you have a tight budget, I recommend the one in Tucheng. It's the cheapest we have.
沒問題。這裡是給您的一些選擇。如果您預算很緊的話，我推薦土城的這一間。這是我們最便宜的。

M: It looks fine, but it's a bit far from where I work, so it seems the ones in Banqiao are more suitable. Also, I'd like a balcony where I can hang out the laundry. 看起來不錯，但離我工作的地方有點遠，所以看起來位於板橋的比較適合。還有，我想要可以讓我晾衣服的陽台。

W: Got it, but don't you need a refrigerator? 明白了，但您不需要冰箱嗎？

M: I always eat out, so I think I can do without it.
我總是外食，所以我想我沒有冰箱也可以。

|單字片語| **hang out the laundry** 晾衣服

Apartments for rent 待租公寓	
11 Xinmin Rd., Banqiao 板橋新民路 11 號 - Washing machine, refrigerator 洗衣機、冰箱 - Pets allowed 寵物可 NT$ 15,000/month 每月 15,000 元	26 Meizhu St., Banqiao 板橋梅竹街 26 號 - Balcony 陽台 - Washing machine 洗衣機 - Pets allowed 寵物可 NT$ 14,000/month 每月 14,000 元
67 Xinguang St., Tucheng 土城新光街 67 號 - Balcony 陽台 - Washing machine 洗衣機 NT$ 13,000/month 每月 13,000 元	100 Jianguo Rd., Tucheng 土城建國路 100 號 - Washing machine, refrigerator 洗衣機、冰箱 - Pets allowed 寵物可 NT$ 12,000/month 每月 12,000 元

Q: Look at the list. Which apartment will the man most likely rent?

請看列表。男子最有可能租哪間公寓？

A. The one at 11 Xinmin Rd., Banqiao. A. 板橋新民路 11 號那間。
B. The one at 26 Meizhu St., Banqiao. B. 板橋梅竹街 26 號那間。
C. The one at 67 Xinguang St., Tucheng. C. 土城新光街 67 號那間。
D. The one at 100 Jianguo Rd., Tucheng. D. 土城建國路 100 號那間。

詳解 **答案：B**

關於男子希望的條件，他提到 allows cats（允許養貓）、the ones in Banqiao are more suitable（位於板橋的比較適合）、I'd like a balcony（我想要陽台），所以符合這些條件的 B 是正確答案。請注意，雖然女子提到價錢和冰箱，但這些並不是男子所考慮的條件。

第三部分／短篇獨白

Questions 26-27

Questions number 26 to 27 are based on the following telephone message.

Thank you for calling Rocket Telecom Service. This is an automated recording. For more information on our special promotion for new subscribers, please press one. For matters related to billing, charges, and late payments, please press two. For other questions, please enter three, followed by your mobile number, and you will be connected to one of our customer service representatives immediately. If you are not our customer yet, please press nine to speak to our customer service representatives. Due to a shortage of manpower, the estimated waiting time is two to five minutes. Your call is important to us. Have a nice day.

感謝您來電 Rocket 電信服務。這是自動的錄音。要獲得更多關於我們給新用戶的特別促銷資訊，請按 1。關於請款、收費與逾期付款事宜，請按 2。其他問題，請按 3，再按您的行動電話號碼，您就會立即接通到我們的客服人員。如果您還不是我們的顧客，請按 9 和我們的客服人員談。由於人力短缺，估計的等候時間是二到五分鐘。您的來電對我們很重要。祝您有美好的一天。

|單字片語| **automated** [`ɔtometɪd] adj. 自動化的 / **subscriber** [səb`skraɪbɚ] n. 訂閱者；定期付費使用服務的用戶 / **billing** [`bɪlɪŋ] n.（對收費的對象）請款 / **customer service representative** 客服專員 / **manpower** [`mæn,paʊɚ] n. 人力，勞動力

Q26

What should you do if there is an error in your monthly bill? **如果你的每月帳單有錯誤，你應該做什麼？**

A. Press one.	A. 按 1。
B. Press two.	B. 按 2。
C. Press three.	C. 按 3。
D. Press nine.	D. 按 9。

詳解 答案：B

從選項就可以推測這是詢問在自動語音系統中應該按什麼數字的題目，所

以要特別注意每個數字代表的意義。按 1 可以得知 special promotion（特別促銷），按 2 是詢問 billing, charges（請款與收費），按 3 是聯絡 customer service representatives（客服專員），而如果 you are not our customer yet（你還不是我們的顧客）就按 9。題目問的是 monthly bill（每月帳單），跟 billing（請款）有關，所以 B 是正確答案。

Q27

What is true about the telephone message?
關於這則電話訊息，何者正確？

A. All conversations will be recorded.	A. 所有對話都會被錄下來。
B. There are job vacancies for customer service representatives.	B. 有客服人員的職缺。
C. Existing customers have a privilege.	C. 現有的顧客有特權。
D. All phone calls are handled by machines.	D. 所有來電都以機器處理。

詳解　　答案：C

選項 A 和 B 沒有提到（雖然提到 shortage of manpower，但沒有提到有職缺可以應徵）。和選項 C 相關的部分，是按 3 和按 9 的差別：按 3 可以 immediately（立即）聯絡 customer service representatives（客服專員），但 If you are not our customer yet（如果你還不是我們的顧客），就要按 9 聯絡客服，而且 waiting time is two to five minutes（等候時間是二到五分鐘），所以可以說現有的顧客有特權，C 是正確答案。因為可以聯絡客服，表示不是完全以機器處理，所以 D 不對。

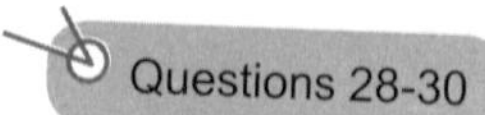

Questions number 28 to 30 are based on the following speech.

Good evening to all distinguished guests and audience watching this live broadcast. I am delighted to be here at the annual Golden Goose Award ceremony. As usual, there are five nominees for the best male and female lead respectively. Thank goodness for the introduction video because I was afraid I might pronounce their names wrong, especially those of our Russian friends. And now, the moment we have all been waiting for. The best male lead for 2016 goes to… Dmitry Kuznetsov! I just warned you about my poor pronunciation, apologies. Congratulations! Please say a few words.

所有貴賓與收看現場轉播的觀眾晚安。我很高興來到一年一度的金鵝獎頒獎典禮。如同往常，最佳男女主角分別有五位入圍者。很感謝有介紹影片，因為我怕我會把他們的名字念錯，尤其是我們俄羅斯朋友的名字。現在，我們都在等待的這個時刻。2016 年的最佳男主角是… Dmitry Kuznetsov！我警告過你們我的發音很差了，抱歉。恭喜！請說幾句話。

|單字片語| **distinguished** [dɪˋstɪŋgwɪʃt] adj. 著名的，顯赫的 / **broadcast** [ˋbrɔdˏkæst] v. （用廣播或電視）廣播，播送 n. 廣播的節目 / **nominee** [ˏnɑməˋni] n. 被提名人 / **lead** [lid] n. 主角（= leading actor, leading actress） / **respectively** [rɪˋspɛktɪvlɪ] adv. 各自，分別

Q28

Who might be giving this speech?
誰可能在發表這段談話？

A. A host. A. 主持人。
B. A musician. B. 音樂家。
C. A commentator. C. 實況播報員。
D. A newscaster. D. 新聞播報員。

詳解

答案：A

說話者說這是 award ceremony（頒獎典禮），並且宣布 best male lead（最佳男主角）是誰。雖然可以說他是 (award) presenter（頒獎人），但選項裡沒有這個答案，所以最有可能頒發獎項的 A 是正確答案。

Q29

What can we know from the speech?
從這段談話我們可以知道什麼？

A. There will be five award winners. A. 會有五名得獎者。
B. The winner is a Russian actor. B. 得獎者是俄國演員。
C. The video taught the audience how to pronounce. C. 影片教觀眾如何發音。
D. The ceremony can be watched online. D. 典禮可以在網路上觀看。

詳解

答案：B

說話者說 I might pronounce their names wrong, especially those of our Russian friends（我可能會把他們的名字念錯，尤其是我們俄羅斯朋友的名字），而宣布得獎者之後又說 I just warned you about my poor pronunciation（我警告過你們我的發音很差了），所以可以推測得獎者是俄國人，B 是正確答案。雖然說話者說這是 live broadcast（現場轉播節目），但沒有提到是否有網路轉播，所以不能選 D。

Q30

What will probably happen next?

接下來可能會發生什麼事？

A. The winner will give a short speech. A. 得獎者會發表簡短的演說。
B. The speaker will take a Russian class. B. 說話者會上俄語課。
C. The audience will ask a few questions. C. 觀眾會問一些問題。
D. A play will be performed. D. 將會表演一齣舞台劇。

詳解

說話者最後請得獎者 say a few words，就是請他 give a short speech 的意思，所以 A 是正確答案。

Questions 31-32

Questions number 31 to 32 are based on the following radio broadcast.

Directly imported from the finest vineyards in Italy, these grapes are perfect for making red wine. However, instead of waiting for years to turn them into vintage wine, Italian farmers have found a faster and more lucrative trade. How? Simply sell these high-quality grapes wholesale to supermarkets with a global reach. As a matter of fact, farmers make more money this way as they cut down on operation costs. Though selling at a premium price, these little purple, red, and green fruits are extremely popular among consumers. You don't need to be a drinker to enjoy these top-class grape varieties.

這些葡萄從義大利最好的葡萄園進口，非常適合製造紅酒。不過，與其等許多年讓葡萄變成年份酒，義大利的農夫找到了更快而且更有利的交易。怎麼做？只要把這些高品質葡萄批發賣給有全球市場的超級市場。事實上，農夫這樣可以賺更多錢，因為他們減少了經營成本。雖然以高級價格出售，但這些小小的紫色、紅色和綠色的果實，非常受到消費者歡迎。你不必是個喝酒的人才能享受這些頂級的葡萄品種。

|單字片語| **vineyard** [ˋvɪnjɚd] n. 葡萄園 / **vintage** [ˋvɪntɪdʒ] n. 釀酒年份 adj. 釀造年份好的 / **lucrative** [ˋlukrətɪv] adj. 有利可圖的，賺錢的 / **wholesale** [ˋhol͵sel] n. 批發 adj. 批發的 adv. 以批發方式 / **premium** [ˋprimɪəm] adj. 優質高價的 / **variety** [vəˋraɪətɪ] n. 品種

Q31

What is the main subject of this radio broadcast?
這段廣播的主題是什麼？

A. The planting process of high-quality grapes. A. 高品質葡萄的種植過程。
B. The switch from selling wine to selling grapes. B. 從賣酒到賣葡萄的轉換。
C. The popularity of imported red wine. C. 進口紅酒的流行度。
D. The breakthrough in grape growing. D. 葡萄種植的突破。

詳解 **答案：B**

說話者一開始說 these grapes are perfect for making red wine（這些葡萄對於製造紅酒很完美），但又說 instead of waiting for years to turn them into vintage wine, Italian farmers... sell these high-quality grapes（與其等許多年讓葡萄變成年份酒，義大利的農夫賣掉這些高品質葡萄），之後談到賣葡萄帶來的獲利和銷售情況。所以，B 是最適當的答案。

|單字片語| **breakthrough** [ˋbrek͵θru] n. 突破，突破性進展

Q32

What is implied regarding vineyard owners in Italy?
關於義大利葡萄園擁有者，這段話暗示什麼？

A. They are building more wine distilleries. A. 他們正在建造更多蒸餾酒廠。
B. They are promoting alcoholic fruit drinks. B. 他們正在宣傳水果酒精飲料。
C. They are making a handsome profit. C. 他們現在賺到相當多的利潤。
D. They are setting up branches globally. D. 他們正在全球設立分公司。

詳解 答案：C

說話者提到 Italian farmers... sell these high-quality grapes（義大利農夫賣掉這些高品質葡萄），可以 make more money（賺更多錢），而且這些以 premium price（高級價格）出售的葡萄非常 popular（受歡迎的）。所以用 handsome（可觀的，相當大的）形容利潤很多的 C 是正確答案。

|單字片語| **distillery** [dɪˋstɪlərɪ] n. 蒸餾酒廠

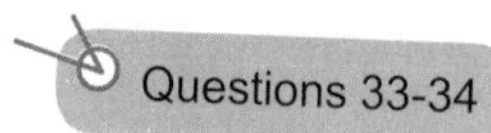

Questions 33-34

Questions number 33 to 34 are based on the following talk.

Here are three tips to better emotion management in the office. Tip one: never let the sun set on your anger. Whatever it is that drives you nuts, make sure you let go of your anger before sunset. Never bring your frustrations at work back home. Tip two: always put yourself into other people's shoes. Rather than getting annoyed, observe yourself from a third party's perspective. In other words, pretend that you are part of the audience and view your colleagues and yourself as characters in the movie. Tip three: learn to forgive and forget. Some people forgive, but they never forget. As a result, negative emotions build up over time, causing you to feel bitter and depressed. Follow these three simple tips and start enjoying life.

這裡有在辦公室做到更好的情緒管理的三個訣竅。訣竅一：永遠不要「讓太陽落在你的憤怒上」。不管是什麼讓你發瘋，一定要在日落之前釋放你的憤怒。永遠不要把你在工作上的挫折感帶回家。訣竅二：總是設身處地為別人著想。不要被激怒，而是要從第三方的角度來觀察自己。換句話說，假裝你是觀眾的一部分，並且把你的同事和你自己看成電影裡的角色。訣竅三：學習原諒並且遺忘。有些人會原諒，但永遠不會忘記。結果，負面情緒就會隨著時間增加，使得你感覺痛苦又沮喪。遵守這三個簡單的訣竅，並且開始享受生活。

|單字片語| **nuts** [nʌts] adj. 發瘋的（drive someone nuts = drive someone crazy）/ **let go of** 放開…，釋放… / **frustration** [ˌfrʌsˋtreʃən] n. 挫折，挫折感 / **put oneself in someone's shoes** 設身處地，從某人的角度著想 / **third party** 第三方 / **perspective** [pəˋspɛktɪv] n. 觀點 / **build up** 增加，加強

Q33

Who might be listening to this talk?
誰可能在聽這段談話？

A. People who have a quick temper.　A. 容易發脾氣的人。
B. People who wish to start their businesses.　B. 想要創業的人。
C. People who have an interest in performance arts.　C. 對於表演藝術有興趣的人。
D. People who are forgetful and absent-minded.　D. 健忘而且心不在焉的人。

詳解

答案：A

說話者說自己提供的是 emotion management（情緒管理）的訣竅，也提到了 let go of your anger（釋放你的憤怒）、Rather than getting annoyed...（不要被激怒），所以聽眾可能是容易覺得生氣的人，用 have a quick temper 表示「容易生氣」的 A 是正確答案。

|單字片語| **have a quick temper** 容易發脾氣 / **performance art** 表演藝術 / **forgetful** [fəˋgɛtfəl] adj. 健忘的 / **absent-minded** [ˋæbsntˋmaɪndɪd] adj. 心不在焉的

Q34

Which of the following is a suggestion mentioned in the talk? 以下哪個是談話中提到的建議？

A. Never bring work back home.
B. Watch movies as a way to release tension.
C. Learn to give and get advice.
D. Understand why others feel the way they do.

A. 永遠不要把工作帶回家。
B. 看電影作為釋放緊張的方法。
C. 學習給予並且獲得建議。
D. 了解別人為什麼會有那樣的感覺。

詳解　　答案：D

說話者建議的第二個訣竅 always put yourself into other people's shoes 是指「設身處地為別人著想」，就好像穿別人的鞋子、體會別人的感覺一樣，所以 D 是正確答案。請注意選項 A~C 和談話中的這些部分類似：Never bring your frustrations at work back home、view your colleagues and yourself as characters in the movie、learn to forgive and forget，需要仔細聆聽才能發現其中的差異，如果只是感覺好像聽到了和選項類似的文字，就很容易選錯。

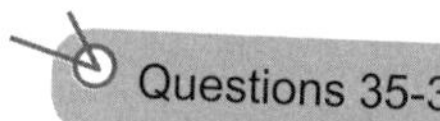

For questions number 35 to 37, please look at the table.

We did a survey on the dish we should add to our menu, and here is the result. Our chef proposed to make chicken rice because he's from Singapore, and he believes that the authentic Singaporean flavor will attract many new customers. However, it's the least popular choice among our staff. Most of us think it's weird to have such a dish in an Italian restaurant. The most popular choice, on the other hand, is hashed potato, for it's rather easy to make. In my opinion, though, it feels redundant because we're already making French fries. In the rest of the choices, I prefer baked salmon to lamb steak, not only because it's more favored by our staff, but also because it has a lower cost of ingredients.

我們做了關於應該加什麼菜色到我們菜單的調查，這裡是結果。我們的主廚提議做（海南）雞飯，因為他來自新加坡，也相信正統的新加坡口味會吸引許多新顧客。不過，這是最不受我們員工歡迎的選擇。我們大部分的人認為在義大利餐廳有這樣一道料理很怪。另一方面，最受歡迎的選擇是薯餅，因為做起來很簡單。但就我的意見而言，它感覺是多餘的，因為我們已經在做薯條了。在剩下的選擇中，我偏好烤鮭魚勝過羊排，不只是因為它比較受到我們員工的偏好，也是因為它的材料成本比較低。

|單字片語| **hashed potato** 薯餅 / **redundant** [rɪˋdʌndənt] adj. 多餘的

Dish 菜色	% of Respondents 回答者百分比	Note 註
No. 1	60%	Easy to make 容易製作
No. 2	22%	?
No. 3	11%	Suggested by a customer 一位顧客建議
No. 4	7%	Authentic flavor 正統風味

Q35

What do we learn about the restaurant?

關於這家餐廳，我們知道什麼？

A. It did a survey of its customers. A. 它進行了顧客調查。
B. It is a Singaporean restaurant. B. 它是新加坡式餐廳。
C. Its chef is Italian. C. 它的主廚是義大利人。
D. It has French fries on its menu. D. 它的菜單上有薯條。

詳解 **答案：D**

關於餐廳的敘述中，說話者提到 we're already making French fries（我們已經在做薯條了），表示菜單上有這一道料理，所以 D 是正確答案。A. 關於針對新料理所做的調查，說話者提到 least popular choice among our staff（最不受我們員工歡迎的選擇），表示這項調查是對員工進行的，而不是顧客，不符合選項敘述。B. C. 說話者提到 Our chef... he's from Singapore（我們的主廚來自新加坡）和 Italian restaurant（義大利餐廳），正好和選項的敘述相反。

Q36

Based on the talk, which item in the table is lamb steak?

根據這段談話，表格中的哪一項是羊排？

A. No. 1.
B. No. 2.
C. No. 3.
D. No. 4.

詳解　　答案：C

說話者說 chicken rice 是 the least popular choice（最不受歡迎的選擇），以及 The most popular choice... is hashed potato（最受歡迎的選擇是薯餅）。至於另外兩道料理，說話者說 I prefer baked salmon to lamb steak, not only because it's more favored by our staff（我偏好烤鮭魚勝過羊排，不只是因為它比較受到我們員工的偏好）。由此可知，受歡迎程度第二名的是烤鮭魚，第三名才是羊排，所以 C 是正確答案。

Q37

Based on the talk, what should be written in the shaded area?

根據這段談話，灰底部分應該填入什麼？

A. Inexpensive ingredients.　A. 不貴的材料。
B. Favored by customers.　B. 受到顧客的偏好。
C. Most popular among the staff.　C. 最受員工歡迎。
D. Similar to an existing dish.　D. 和現有的一道料理類似。

詳解　　答案：A

如同上一題所說明的，受歡迎程度第二名的是烤鮭魚，而說話者說 it has a lower cost of ingredients（它的材料成本比較低），所以意思相近的 A 是正確答案。

Questions 38-40

For questions number 38 to 40, please look at the charts.

The results of the midterm exam are disappointing. The questions weren't difficult, yet over half of you failed the exam. Even though a few of you managed to get an A or B, the overall performance is terrible. It may be hasty to say that, but I think it has something to do with our low attendance rates. You can say my lectures are boring, but it's impossible to learn well just by yourselves. In the final, there will be some essay questions, which were absent in the midterm. It means the final will be harder, so I hope you'll get well prepared, even if you hate this subject. It's required for all students, so you have to get a passing grade after all.

期中考的結果很令人失望。問題並不難，但你們有超過一半的人考試不及格。儘管有少數人得到了 A 或 B，但整體的表現很糟糕。這麼說可能很草率，但我認為這和我們很低的出席率有點關係。你們可以說我的講課無聊，但你們光靠自己是不可能學好的。在期末考會有一些申論題，在期中考是沒有的。這意味著期末考會比較難，所以我希望你們好好準備，就算你們討厭這個科目。這是所有學生的必修科目，所以你們終究得拿到及格的分數才行。

|單字片語| **attendance** [əˋtɛndəns] n. 出席

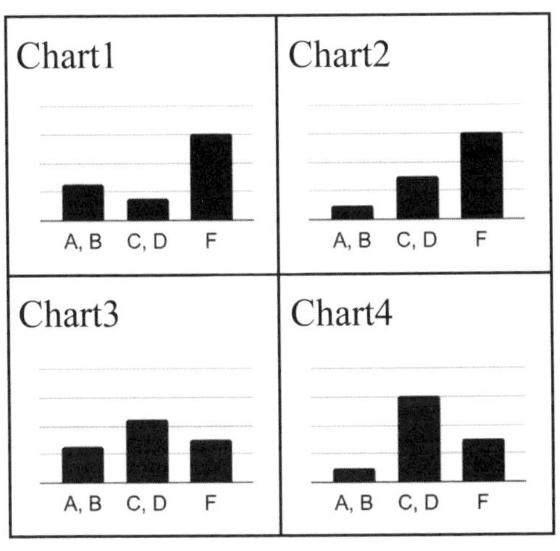

Q38

Who is the speaker?
說話者是什麼人？

A. A teacher.
B. A principal.
C. A parent.
D. A class leader.

A. 老師。
B. 校長。
C. 母親。
D. 班長。

詳解

答案：A

說話者提到許多和考試、上課有關的事，其中能判斷身分的關鍵是 my lectures（我的講課），從這裡可以確定 A 是正確答案。

Q39

Which chart best represents the distribution of grades on the midterm exam?
哪張圖表最能表示期中考的成績分布？

A. Chart 1.
B. Chart 2.
C. Chart 3.
D. Chart 4.

A. 圖表 1。
B. 圖表 2。
C. 圖表 3。
D. 圖表 4。

詳解

答案：B

關於期中考的成績，說話者提到 over half of you failed the exam（你們有超過一半的人考試不及格）、Even though a few of you managed to get an A or B, the overall performance is terrible（儘管有少數人得到了 A 或 B，但整體的表現很糟糕），圖表中顯示只有少數人得到 A 或 B、大部分的人得到 F 的是第 2 張，所以 B 是正確答案。

Q40

What do we learn about the course?
關於這門課，我們知道什麼？

A. Most students never skip class. A. 大部分的學生不蹺課。
B. There were essay questions on the midterm exam. B. 期中考有申論題。
C. The midterm and final exams have the same difficulty. C. 期中考和期末考難度相同。
D. Every student has to take this course. D. 每個學生都必須修這門課。

詳解

答案：D

關於這門課，說話者提到 It's required for all students（這是所有學生的必修科目），所以 D 是正確答案。A. 說話者提到 our low attendance rates（我們很低的出席率），不符合選項敘述。B. 說話者提到 In the final, there will be some essay questions, which were absent in the midterm（在期末考會有一些申論題，在期中考是沒有的），不符合選項敘述。C. 說話者提到 the final will be harder（期末考會比較難），不符合選項敘述。

第一部分 句子填空

Q1

Chinese parents tend to value academic achievements highly, so they might __________ their children for not getting perfect grades. **華人父母傾向於重視學業成就，所以他們可能會責備孩子沒有得到完美的成績。**

A. reproach　　B. supervise　　C. unleash　　D. victimize

詳解　　　　**答案：A**

句子最後的 for not getting... 是指小孩沒有得到完美的成績，是華人父母對小孩做某個行為的理由，選項中最合理的答案是 A.。supervise（監督）看起來似乎是可能的答案，但它沒有「動詞 + 受詞 + for + 表示受詞行為的動名詞」這樣的用法。victimize 同樣沒有這種用法，而且是表示不公平地對待或迫害。

|單字片語| **reproach** [rɪ`protʃ] v. 責備 / **supervise** [`supɚ,vaɪz] v. 監督 / **unleash** [ʌn`liʃ] v. 解除…的束縛 / **victimize** [`vɪktɪ,maɪz] 使受害，迫害

Q2

The United States declared that the economic __________ on Iran will be lifted as long as it allows nuclear plants to be inspected. **美國宣布對於伊朗的經濟制裁將會解除，只要伊朗允許讓核電廠接受檢查的話。**

A. integration　　B. liability　　C. embargo　　D. trade-off

詳解　　　　**答案：C**

句子後半用 as long as 表示條件，所以 it (Iran) allows nuclear plants to be inspected 是 the economic _____ on Iran will be lifted 的交換條件。選項中，適合被 economic 修飾，而且可以 be lifted（被解除）的是 C. embargo（貿易禁令），表示對於貿易往來的限制，是一種制裁其他國家的手法。

|單字片語| **lift** [lɪft] v. 解除，撤銷（封鎖等） / **nuclear plant** 核能發電廠 / **integration** [ˌɪntəˋgreʃən] n. 整合 / **liability** [ˌlaɪəˋbɪlətɪ] n. 責任；（會計）負債 / **embargo** [ɪmˋbɑrgo] n. 貿易禁令 / **trade-off** [ˋtredˌɔf] n. 交換，交易

Q3

The civil war, which started out with both sides evenly matched, quickly turned _________ the rebel forces after the government forces made a big mistake. **一開始雙方勢均力敵的內戰，在政府軍出了大差錯之後，很快就變得對叛軍有利。**

A. in spite of
B. in favor of
C. at the end of
D. at the risk of

詳解 **答案：B**

情況一開始是 both sides evenly matched（雙方勢均力敵），但 quickly turned（快速轉變）成為某種情況。因為是在 the government forces made a big mistake（政府軍出了大差錯）之後，所以情況應該是變得對另一方有利，所以 B. in favor of（對…有利）是正確答案。in spite of 表示「不管…」，at the end of 表示「在…的最後」，at the risk of 表示「冒著…的風險」。

|單字片語| **civil war** 內戰 / **rebel** [ˋrɛbḷ] adj. 反叛的 / **forces** [ˋforsɪz] n. 軍事力量，軍隊

Q4

Having goals and plans does not _________ bring success. Many people failed to carry out their plans, and even more give up when things do not go according to plan. **有目標和計畫並不一定帶來成功。很多人無法實行他們的計畫，而更多人在事情不照計畫進行的時候放棄。**

A. intermittently
B. occasionally
C. particularly
D. necessarily

詳解 **答案：D**

第二句話說「有些人不能實現計畫，而有更多人會放棄」。考慮到兩句話之間的連貫性，第一句話的 Having goals and plans，應該是「不一定」會 bring success。在英文裡，「不一定」可以用 not necessarily（不必然）表達，所以 D. necessarily（必然）是正確答案。intermittently 表示「間歇地」，occasionally 表示「偶爾」，particularly 表示「尤其」、「特別是…」。

|單字片語| **carry out** 實行 / **go according to plan** 依照計畫進行

The young man was so __________ fame that he lost sight of things which are far more valuable, including his health and family. **那個年輕人如此執迷於名利，以致於讓他看不到更有價值的東西，包括他的健康和家庭。**

A. satisfied with　　B. obsessed with
C. suppressed by　　D. overwhelmed by

詳解　　答案：B

這裡用的是「so... that + 子句」（如此…以致於…）的句型。that 的後面說 he lost sight of things which are far more valuable（他看不到〔忽視〕更有價值的東西），所以前面的部分應該是表達「他太過注重 fame」的意思，所以 B. obsessed with（為…著迷的）是正確答案。satisfied with 表示「滿足於…的」，suppressed by 表示「被…壓抑的」，overwhelmed by 表示「感覺被…壓倒／征服的」。

|單字片語| **lose sight of** 看不見…，忽略…

Performing the same mundane chores day after day can be __________ and dull. That's why products that help to simplify housework are popular.
日復一日進行同樣平凡的家事可能很冗長乏味而且無聊。這就是為什麼幫助簡化家事的產品很受歡迎。

A. tedious　B. perilous　C. continuous　D. mischievous

詳解　　答案：A

空格和另一個形容詞 dull（乏味的，單調的）連在一起，而且後面的句子說「這就是為什麼幫助簡化家事的產品很受歡迎」，所以空格應該也是表示麻煩、無聊的形容詞，正確答案是 A. tedious（冗長乏味的）。

|單字片語| **mundane** [ˋmʌnden] adj. 世俗的；平凡的 / **chores** [tʃorz] n. 家庭雜務 / **tedious** [ˋtidɪəs] adj. 冗長乏味的 / **perilous** [ˋpɛrələs] adj. 危險的 / **continuous** [kənˋtɪnjʊəs] adj. 連續的 / **mischievous** [ˋmɪstʃɪvəs] adj. 淘氣的

Q7

According to the latest data, there are ________ 26 million refugees worldwide, and many of them are children under the age of 18. 根據最新的數據，全世界有大約 2600 萬名難民，而其中有許多是未滿 18 歲的兒童。

A. mostly　B. partially　C. roughly　D. solely

詳解　答案：C

空格要填入修飾數量的副詞，選項中最適合的是 C. roughly（大約）。mostly 是指比例上「大多…」，partially 表示「一部分」或「不完全」的意思，solely 表示「僅僅」涉及某個人事物或某方面，而不涉及其他。

|單字片語| **partially** [ˋpɑrʃəlɪ] adv. 部分地 / **roughly** [ˋrʌflɪ] adv. 粗略地，大約 / **solely** [ˋsollɪ] adv. 僅僅，單獨地

Q8

The old man is full of ________ and won't stop talking about his past achievements.
那個老人非常自負，他會講自己過去的成就講個不停。

A. concept　B. conceit　C. conception　D. concession

詳解　答案：B

這個老人 won't stop talking about his past achievements（不會停止講自己過去的成就），可見他對自己的成就非常驕傲，選項中可以表達這種性格特質的是 B. conceit（自負，自大）。

|單字片語| **concept** [ˋkɑnsɛpt] n. 概念 / **conceit** [kənˋsit] n. 自負，自大 / **conception** [kənˋsɛpʃən] n. 概念，構想；受孕 / **concession** [kənˋsɛʃən] n. 讓步

Q9

Traffic was brought to an ________ halt when two trucks collided at the crossroads.
兩台卡車在十字路口衝撞時，交通突然停擺。

A. abrupt　B. eccentric　C. optimum　D. integral

詳解 答案：A

bring... to a halt 是「使…中止」的意思。這裡要填入修飾 halt（停止）的形容詞，因為是突然發生的交通事故，所以 A. abrupt（突然的）是最合適的答案。

|單字片語| **collide** [kə`laɪd] v. 碰撞 / **abrupt** [ə`brʌpt] adj. 突然的 / **eccentric** [ɪk`sɛntrɪk] adj. 古怪的，反常的 / **optimum** [`ɑptəməm] adj. 最理想的，最佳的 / **integral** [`ɪntəgrəl] adj. 完整的，整體的

Selling ivory was and still is __________, and the enormous potential profit lures many into killing elephants. 販售象牙從過去到現在都是有利可圖的，而巨大的潛在利益誘惑許多人獵殺大象。

A. beneficial　　B. economical　　C. invaluable　　D. lucrative

詳解 答案：D

句子前後用 and 連接，後面說 the enormous potential profit lures many（巨大的潛在利益誘惑許多人），所以 selling ivory 這件事應該是很賺錢的，答案是 D. lucrative（有利可圖的，賺錢的）。beneficial 表示「有益的」，比起金錢的利益，更常用來表示「對人、組織或環境有益」；賣象牙會造成生態的破壞，所以整體來說，不算是一件 beneficial 的事情。invaluable（無價的，非常寶貴的）雖然看起來也像是可能的答案，但它是表示一件事情本身很有價值，無法以金錢衡量；我們可以說 ivory is invaluable，但這裡的主詞是「selling ivory」（賣象牙），這個行為本身並不是一件「很寶貴」的事，所以不能用 invaluable 來形容。

|單字片語| **lucrative** [`lukrətɪv] adj. 有利可圖的，賺錢的 / **lure** [lʊr] v. 引誘 / **beneficial** [͵bɛnə`fɪʃəl] adj. 有益的 / **economical** [͵ikə`nɑmɪkl] adj. 節約的，經濟的 / **invaluable** [ɪn`væljəbl̩] 無價的，非常寶貴的

第二部分／段落填空

Questions 11-15

Getting people trained in horseback archery is the mission of the Mounted Archers Association. We regret that there is a prerequisite for membership. Most of our fresh (11) recruits have some experience with archery or horse riding. If you have never drawn a bow or ridden a horse before, you might want to get started on (12) either one before joining us. (13) With our experience and training techniques, you can achieve what you could not by yourself. Besides training, we also hold annual horseback archery competitions, which take place in our specially-designed (14) arena made of natural materials. During our events, members are advised to bring their own horses if possible, but we also have horses (15) for lease on a daily basis.

讓人們接受騎馬射箭的訓練，是騎射協會的任務。很抱歉我們有對於會員資格的必要條件。我們大部分的新進成員都有一些箭術或騎馬的經驗。如果你以前從來沒有拉過弓或騎過馬，你可能會想要在加入我們之前開始進行其中一項。靠著我們的經驗和訓練技巧，你可以達成以前你自己做不到的事。除了訓練以外，我們也舉辦年度騎馬射箭比賽，在我們特別設計、由天然建材建立而成的競技場舉行。在我們的活動中，建議會員如果可能的話帶自己的馬，但我們也提供按日出租的馬。

|單字片語| **horseback** [`hɔrs͵bæk] n. 馬背 / **archery** [`ɑrtʃərɪ] n. 箭術 / **mounted** [`maʊntɪd] adj. 騎馬的 / **archer** [`ɑrtʃɚ] n. 弓箭手 / **prerequisite** [͵pri`rɛkwəzɪt] n. 先決條件，必要條件 adj. 事先必需的 / **recruit** [rɪ`krut] n. 新成員 v. 招募（新成員） / **arena** [ə`rinə] n. 競技場 / **lease** [lis] n. 租賃

Q11

A. bachelors B. instructors C. employees D. recruits

詳解

答案：D

前面的句子提到，membership（會員身分）是有 prerequisite（必要條件）的，而空格所在的句子就說明大部分的 fresh _____ 都有射箭或騎馬的經驗。所以空格就是指 member，而 fresh 是表示「新的」，所以能表示「新成員」的 D. recruits 是正確答案。instructor 和 employee 都是員工，他們的身分不會用 membership 來表達。

|單字片語| **bachelor** [ˋbætʃələ] n. 單身男子；（大寫）學士

Q12

A. another one　B. the other one　C. either one　D. neither one

詳解　答案：C

上一句提到大部分的新成員都有 archery or horse riding（射箭或騎馬）的經驗，所以如果 you have never drawn a bow or ridden a horse before（你以前從來沒有拉過弓或騎過馬），應該先學會其中一項才行，表示「（射箭或騎馬）兩者之中任何一個」的 C. either one 是正確答案。neither one 表示「兩者都不」。

Q13

A. By making the most of your ability
藉由充分運用你的能力
B. With the new equipment in our facility
靠著我們設施的新設備
C. If you are well-prepared for the challenge
如果你對挑戰做了充分的準備
D. With our experience and training techniques
靠著我們的經驗和訓練技巧

詳解　答案：D

空格後面說「你可以達成以前你自己做不到的事」，下一句又提到「除了（提供）訓練之外…」，所以提到用訓練技巧來幫助會員達成目標的 D 是正確答案。因為空格後面提到「以前自己做不到」，所以空格的內容必然和他人的幫助有關，因此其他選項都不適合。

Q14

A. arena　B. gym　C. rink　D. studio

詳解　答案：A

因為是 horseback archery（騎馬射箭）的比賽，所以表示「競技場」的 A. arena 是正確答案。雖然 arena 通常會讓人想到球類運動等用途的競技場，但也有鋪上砂石、專門用來騎馬的 riding arena / horse arena。

|單字片語| **gym** [dʒɪm] n. 健身房；體育場 / **rink** [rɪŋk] n. 溜冰場（**ice rink** 或 **skating rink**）/ **studio** [ˋstjudɪˏo] n. 工作室；攝影棚；電影製片公司

A. for sale　　B. for lease　　C. by insurance　　D. by installments

詳解　　答案：B

句子前半說「建議帶自己的馬」，中間用 but 連接，所以後面應該是表達除了帶自己的馬以外還有什麼方式。這裡要注意的是空格後面的 on a daily basis（按日…），表示依照天數計算費用等等，所以能表示按照天數出租的 B. for lease（供租用的）是正確答案。for sale 表示「供出售的」，by insurance 表示「用保險」，by installments 表示「用分期付款的方式」。

|單字片語| **installment** [ɪn`stɔlmənt] n. 分期付款（每期的款項）

Questions 16-20

It might seem bizarre that a boring three-mile running race would be all the rage, but the national trend shows that running (16) enthusiasts are indeed on the rise. According to the "State of the Sport" report from Running USA, mini-marathon, which literally means a much shorter version of a regular marathon, is the fastest growing running event in the U.S., the 5K (five-kilometer) run in particular. (17) Generally speaking, the longer the race, the more logistical challenges there are to staging an event, which explains the high number of 5Ks being organized. Also, 5K runs (18) are suitable for all ages and skill levels. It is a common sight to see families and friends taking part in a mini-marathon (19) since it is not as physically demanding as a full-length marathon. Such events are usually hosted on main streets (20) in a bid to attract more spectators and the interest of the media.

無聊的 3 英里跑步比賽變得非常風行，可能顯得很奇怪，但這個全國的趨勢顯示熱愛跑步的人的確正在增加。根據 Running USA 的「運動現狀」報告，迷你馬拉松，字面上的意思就是普通馬拉松變短很多的版本，是美國成長最快的跑步活動，尤其是 5K（五公里）跑步。大致說來，賽跑長度越長，舉辦活動時在安排上的挑戰就更多，這也解釋了舉辦的 5K 活動為什麼這麼多。另外，5K 跑步適合所有年齡與技能水準。常常看到家庭和朋友參加迷你馬拉松，因為它不像全程馬拉松對身體那麼吃力。這種活動通常在主要街道上舉辦，以吸引更多觀眾，以及引起媒體的興趣。

|單字片語| **bizarre** [bɪˋzɑr] adj. 怪異的 / **all the rage** 非常風行 / **enthusiast** [ɪnˋθjuzɪˏæst] n. 熱衷者 / **literally** [ˋlɪtərəlɪ] adv. 照字面意義；簡直，確實 / **logistical** [ləˋdʒɪstɪkḷ] adj. 物流的；組織與安排方面的 / **stage** [stedʒ] v. 上演（戲劇）；組織（活動） / **in a bid to** 試圖…，為了…

Q16

A. extremists B. activists C. enthusiasts D. fundamentalists

詳解 **答案：C**

這裡說 running _____ 的確正在上升中（增加中），所以空格應該表示熱愛跑步的人。選項中，能表示「熱衷者」的 C. enthusiasts 是正確答案。extremist（極端分子）、activist（激進分子）通常表示在社會運動中非常激進的參與者。fundamentalist 是表示堅守宗教原本教義的「基本教義派」。

|單字片語| **extremist** [ɪkˋstrimɪst] n. 極端分子 / **activist** [ˋæktəvɪst] n. 激進分子 / **fundamentalist** [ˏfʌndəˋmɛntḷɪst] n. 原教旨主義者，基本教義派

Q17

A. Generally speaking B. In retrospect
C. On the contrary D. Above all

詳解 **答案：A**

空格後面的部分說，跑步長度越長，舉辦活動的挑戰就越多。這是普遍的常理，所以 A. Generally speaking（一般而言）是正確答案。in retrospect 表示「回顧過去，回想起來」，on the contrary 表示「相反地，正好相反」，above all 表示「最重要的是…，尤其」。

Q18

A. have been held in all kinds of places
已經在各種地方舉辦過
B. are suitable for all ages and skill levels
適合所有年齡與技能水準
C. have been proved to improve our health
已經被證明能增進我們的健康
D. can serve as a tool to promote physical activity
可以作為促進身體活動的工具

詳解

答案：B

前面說完 5K 跑步因為距離短而容易舉辦之後，這裡用 Also 帶出另一個論點。接下來的句子解釋說，因為迷你馬拉松不像全程馬拉松那麼吃力，所以常看到家庭和朋友參加，由此可以推斷空格的內容應該和任何人都能輕鬆參加有關。因此，B 是最適合的答案。

Q19

A. while　B. yet　C. therefore　D. since

詳解

答案：D

空格前後都是完整的子句。前面說「很常看到家庭和朋友參加迷你馬拉松」，後面說「它（迷你馬拉松）不像全程馬拉松對身體那麼吃力」，後者應該是前者的理由，所以表示理由的 D. since（因為…）是正確答案。while 表示「在…時」或「然而…」，yet 表示「但是…」，therefore 表示「所以…」。

Q20

A. as a last resort　B. in a bid　C. by no means　D. with respect

詳解

答案：B

main street 是指城鎮中最主要的商業街道，也是人潮容易聚集的地方，所以在 main street 辦馬拉松有助於吸引群眾觀看，表示目的的 B. in a bid (to do...)（試圖…，為了做…）是適當的答案。as a last resort to do 表示「作為做…的最後手段」。by no means 表示「絕不，一點也不」。with respect to 表示「就…而言」、「至於…」，但請注意它的 to 是介系詞，所以後面接名詞而不是動詞原形。

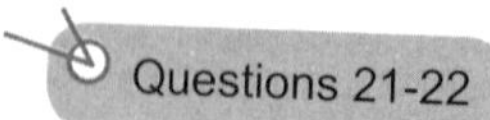

Questions 21-22

Rose Bank Rewards Credit Card
Earn points everywhere!

Simply shop in your own way and accumulate reward points every day. With a Rose Bank Rewards Credit Card, you can get more out of every purchase you make at more than 500 partnering businesses, including:

- **Online shopping sites:** Amazon, Zappos, Etsy...
- **Hypermarkets:** Walmart, Kroger, Costco...
- **Department stores:** Sears, Macy's, Bloomingdale's...
- **Bookstores:** Barnes & Noble, Books-A-Million...

The points you have earned will not expire, as long as your card is valid. You can exchange reward points for gifts, or use them to offset any outstanding payments due. Apply now, and your annual fee will be waived for the first two years. Terms and conditions apply.

Note: Interest rates for late payment range from 12% to 24%, depending on your credit score.

Rose 銀行回饋信用卡
到處賺取點數！

只要用你的方式購物，就能每天累積回饋點數。有了 Rose 銀行回饋信用卡，你可以在超過 500 家合作業者購物時得到更多，包括：

- 購物網站：Amazon、Zappos、Etsy...
- 大賣場：Walmart、Kroger、Costco...
- 百貨公司：Sears、Macy's、Bloomingdale's...
- 書店：Barnes & Noble、Books-A-Million...

只要你的卡片有效，你賺取的點數將不會過期。你可以將回饋點數換成禮物，或者用點數折抵任何應支付而尚未支付的款項。現在申請，前兩年免年費。以上受到（信用卡的）條件與條款約束。

註：遲繳帳單的利率從 12% 到 24%，取決於您的信用分數。

|單字片語| **accumulate** [əˋkjumjə͵let] v. 累積 / **partner** [ˋpɑrtnɚ] v. 搭檔，合作 / **hypermarket** [͵haɪpɚˋmɑrkɪt] n. 大型超市，大賣場 / **expire** [ɪkˋspaɪr] v. 到期，期滿 / **offset** [ˋɔf͵sɛt] v. 抵銷 / **outstanding** [ˋaʊtˋstændɪŋ] adj. 未償還的，未付的 / **waive** [wev] v. 免除

What kind of person is most likely to apply for this credit card? 哪一種人最有可能申請這張信用卡？

A. One who eats out frequently 常常外食的人
B. One who runs a used-book store 經營二手書店的人
C. One who travels a lot on business 很常出差的人
D. One who buys groceries regularly 定期購買食品雜貨的人

詳解

答案：D

廣告中間列出了一些 partnering businesses（合作業者），其中有一項是 hypermarkets（大型超市，大賣場），是可以 buy groceries（買食品雜貨）的地方。只要辦這張信用卡，就可以在購買食品雜貨時 accumulate reward points（累積回饋點數），所以選項 D 這種人可能會申辦。經營二手書店的人不一定會經常在書店買書，所以不能選 B。

Q22

Based on the advertisement, which of the following statements is NOT true?
根據這則廣告，以下哪個敘述不正確？

A. Bonus points can be brought forward to the next year.
點數可以延續到下一年。
B. Card holders can use reward points as payment.
持卡人可以使用回饋點數作為付款。
C. There is a discount on the annual fee for the first two years.
前兩年年費有折扣。
D. You will be charged more if you don't pay bills on time.
如果你不準時付帳單的話，會被要求付更多錢。

詳解

答案：C

廣告中，The points you have earned will not expire 對應選項 A，use them (reward points) to offset any outstanding payments due 對應選項 B，Interest rates for late payment 對應選項 D。和選項 C 相關的部分是 Apply now, and your annual fee will be waived for the first two years.（現在申請，前兩年免年費），waive 是

表示「不收取原本應該收的費用」，在這裡就是前兩年完全不收年費的意思，並不是打折，所以 C 是正確答案。

Questions 23-25

No matter you travel for business or for leisure, a good hotel can make the experience much more enjoyable. To get a quick impression of a hotel, check its website. You can expect to see its facilities and room rates, which usually vary depending on the date. Generally speaking, the sooner you book, the cheaper a room costs. If you arrive at a hotel without a reservation, be prepared to be "**extorted**". In case you need to cancel your booking, you should also read the fine print regarding cancel policy. You can usually get a full refund if you cancel 48 hours in advance.

You may also want to check photos and reviews by guests on booking sites. By doing so, you can find out more details that only some people will notice. It is worth mentioning, however, that other people's opinions may differ from what you experience in person. That's not to say that some reviews are not genuine; it's just that people have different tastes and expectations, and what some find fabulous may leave others unimpressed. Also, the service quality of a hotel may not be the same all the time.

Besides the hotel itself, location is also an important factor to consider. Staying in the city center means less time wasted on traveling. You can enjoy the luxury of strolling around without worrying about the sky getting dark. On the other hand, staying in a hotel which is hard to reach can save you a few bucks, but it also means that for your safety, you should get back before dark, especially when you are not familiar with the place.

Some people prefer to stay in a hostel rather than a hotel, especially when the budget is tight. If you choose to stay in a hostel, the most important thing is to keep your personal belongings attended all the time because theft is a recurring problem. Leave your valuables in the lockers or carry them with you, even to the toilet. Finally, exercise wisdom and discretion when interacting with other roommates. Avoid arguments at all costs. Whatever hostile circumstances you find yourself in, swallow your pride and keep the peace.

不管你是商務旅遊或休閒旅遊，一間好的旅館可以讓你的經驗愉快得多。要對一間旅館得到快速的印象，就看它的網站。你可以預期看到它的設施和房間價錢，通常會隨著日期而不同。大致來說，你越早訂房，房間就越便宜。如果你沒有預約就到旅館，那就準備好被「敲詐」。為了預防萬一你需要取消預約，你也應該閱讀關於取消政策的附加小字。如果你在 48 小時之前取消的話，通常可以得到全額退款。

你可能也會想要在訂房網站看看住宿客的照片和評論。這樣做的話，你可以發現更多只有某些人會注意到的細節。不過，值得一提的是，別人的意見可能會和你親身體驗的不同。這並不是說有些評論不是真的，只是人們有不同的喜好和期待，有些人覺得很棒的，或許其他人沒什麼感覺。而且，一間旅館的服務品質可能不會隨時都一樣。

除了旅館本身，地點也是要考慮的重要因素。住在市中心意味著比較少時間浪費在旅行（移動）上。你可以享受四處漫步的奢侈，而不用擔心天色變暗。相反的，住在不容易到達的旅館可以幫你省一點錢，但也意味著為了安全，你應該在天色變暗之前回去，尤其在你不熟悉那個地方的時候。

有些人偏好住在青年旅舍而不是旅館，尤其是在預算很緊的時候。如果你選擇住在青年旅舍，最重要的事情是隨時照顧好你的個人財物，因為竊盜是反覆發生的問題。把你的貴重物品留在置物櫃，或者隨身帶著，甚至帶進廁所。最後，和其他室友互動時要運用智慧和謹慎。要盡力避免爭吵。不管你發現自己處在怎樣不友善的情況，都要吞下你的自尊並且保持和平。

|單字片語| **extort** [ɪk`stɔrt] v. 敲詐，勒索 / **fine print** 附加的小字（例如廣告或合約的附帶條款說明）/ **fabulous** [`fæbjələs] adj. 非常好的 / **unimpressed** [ˌʌnɪm`prɛst] adj. （人）沒有感受到深刻印象的，覺得不怎麼樣的 / **stroll** [strol] v. 散步，閒逛 / **buck** [bʌk] n. （口語）錢，一塊錢 / **hostel** [`hastl] n. 旅舍，青年旅舍 / **personal belongings** 個人財物 / **recurring** [rɪ`kɝɪŋ] adj. 再發的，反覆發生的 / **discretion** [dɪ`skrɛʃən] n. 謹慎 / **at all costs** 不惜代價，無論如何 / **hostile** [`hastɪl] adj. 有敵意的，不友善的

Q23

What does it mean to be "extorted"? 被 extort 是什麼意思？

A. To get a good bargain 得到划算的交易
B. To be rejected by others 被別人拒絕
C. To be attacked without warning 無預警被攻擊
D. To pay way above the market rate 付出比市價高很多的錢

詳解

答案：D

在 extorted 這個字之前，作者說 the sooner you book, the cheaper a room costs（你越早訂房，房間就越便宜），所以 arrive at a hotel without a reservation（沒有預約就到旅館）能夠得到的價格優惠應該最少，可知 be extorted 應該是被收很多錢的意思，正確答案是 D。extort 其實是「勒索錢財」的意思，在這裡是一種比喻。

Q24

Why does the author recommend hotels in the downtown area? 作者為什麼建議市中心區的旅館？

A. Hotels located in city centers are cheaper.
位於市中心的旅館比較便宜。

B. Public transportation in the urban areas is more accessible.
都會區比較容易使用大眾運輸。

C. Returning to a hotel in a remote area at night can be risky.
晚上回到遙遠地區的飯店可能很危險。

D. The crime rate in city centers is lower.
市中心的犯罪率比較低。

詳解

答案：C

比較市中心和偏遠地區的部分是第三段。作者建議住在市中心的正面理由是 less time wasted on traveling（比較少時間浪費在移動上），另一方面又說 staying in a hotel which is hard to reach... means that for your safety, you should get back before dark（住在不容易到達的旅館意味著為了安全，你應該在天色變暗之前回去），表示在晚上回到偏遠的飯店很危險，所以 C 是正確答案。

Q25

Which of the following is NOT part of the advice given by the author for those who stay in a hostel? 對於住在青年旅舍的人，以下哪個不是作者所給的建議？

A. Avoid confrontation and fights　避免衝突和爭吵

B. Keep an eye on your personal belongings　注意你的個人財物

C. Lock up important things　把重要的東西鎖起來

D. Interact with roommates privately if possible
如果可能的話，和室友私底下互動

詳解

答案：D

關於 hostel 的部分是第四段。作者給的建議中，Avoid arguments 對應選項

A，keep your personal belongings attended 對應選項 B，Leave your valuables in the lockers 對應選項 C。關於 D 的部分是 exercise wisdom and discretion when interacting with other roommates（和其他室友互動時要運用智慧和謹慎），作者沒有建議和室友私底下互動，所以 D 是正確答案。

|單字片語| **confrontation** [ˌkɑnfrʌnˋteʃən] n. 對抗；衝突

Questions 26-29

The Bermuda triangle is considered by many as a mysterious stretch of area. Some claim that there have been significantly more aircrafts and ships that disappeared for inexplicable reasons in the area between Florida, Puerto Rico, and Bermuda. According to the statistics, however, the frequency of accidents is actually lower than average in this area, and many flights and cruise ships regularly go through it. It is the popular culture's focus on some particularly bizarre events that strengthened the myth. Nevertheless, it may still arouse our curiosity to read some of the stories.

One of the most mysterious events happened to a ship called Mary Celeste. On December 4th, 1872, the ship was found stranded in the sea but without any crew member on it. Since the cargos and valuables were intact, it is unlikely that the ship had been attacked by pirates. Seaquakes and food poisoning have also been considered as possible reasons, but neither seems plausible. Moreover, the weather was fine, and it seems unreasonable for the crew to abandon the ship.

Another incident, which involved the most people missing, happened to one of the US Coast Guard's non-combat ships in March 1918. With 306 crew members and passengers on it, the ship was supposed to sail through the Bermuda Triangle, but was lost halfway. The area had been searched, but no remains or any of the passengers were found. The incident also happened when the weather was fine, thus the ship's disappearance is considered a mystery.

Some people who look at the so-called Bermuda triangle phenomenon with a rational perspective have found some reasonable explanations, such as the effects of magnetic declination and the Gulf Stream. As long as people are fascinated with supernatural forces, however, the mystery will live on.

百慕達三角被許多人認為是個神祕的地帶。有些人聲稱在佛羅里達、波多黎各和百慕達之間的地帶，因為無法解釋的理由而消失的飛機和船顯著較多。不過，根據統計數字，這個地區的意外發生頻率其實低於平均，而且很多飛機航班和遊輪會定期經過這裡。是流行文化對於某些特別奇怪的事件的關注，強化了這個迷思。不過，閱讀某些故事，可能還是會激發我們的好奇心。

最神祕的事件之一，發生在稱為 Mary Celeste 的船上。在 1872 年 12 月 4 日，這艘船被發現孤立在海上，但船上沒有任何船員。由於貨物和貴重物品都完好，所以這艘船不太可能是被海盜攻擊。海上地震和食物中毒也曾經被認為是可能的理由，但兩者似乎都不可信。而且，當時天氣很好，船員棄船似乎不合理。

另一起造成了最多人失蹤的事件，1918 年 3 月發生在美國海岸防衛隊的一艘非戰鬥船上。船上有 306 名船員和乘客，這艘船應該要航行穿過百慕達三角，但在途中失蹤了。這個地區經過搜索，但沒有找到任何船的遺骸或乘客。這起事件也發生在天氣好的時候，所以這艘船的消失被認為是個神祕事件。

有些用理性觀點看待所謂百慕達三角現象的人，找到了一些合理的解釋，例如地磁偏角和墨西哥灣暖流的影響。不過，只要人們為超自然力量著迷，這個神祕傳說就會繼續下去。

|單字片語|

（第一段）

statistics [stə`tɪstɪks] n. 統計，統計資料 / **cruise ship** （巡航的）遊輪 / **bizarre** [bɪ`zɑr] adj. 怪異的 / **myth** [mɪθ] n. 沒有事實根據的觀點，「迷思」

（第二段）

stranded [`strændɪd] adj. 擱淺的；孤立無援的 / **cargo** [`kɑrgo] n. 貨物 / **intact** [ɪn`tækt] adj. 完好無損的 / **seaquake** [`si͵kwek] n. 海底地震 / **food poisoning** 食物中毒 / **plausible** [`plɔzəbl̩] adj. 似乎合理的

（第三段）

coast guard 海岸防衛隊 / **remains** [rɪ`menz] n. 遺跡，遺骸

（第四段）

magnetic declination 地磁偏角 / **Gulf Stream** 墨西哥灣暖流 / **supernatural** [͵supɚ`nætʃərəl] adj. 超自然的

What was puzzling about the Mary Celeste incident?

關於 Mary Celeste 事件，什麼令人困惑？

A. A storm should have caused damage to the ship.

風暴應該造成船的損傷。

B. The ones who attacked the ship were never found.
攻擊船的人從來沒有被找到。

C. It was not even in the vicinity of the Bermuda triangle.
它甚至沒有接近百慕達三角。

D. No one can explain what might have happened to the people on board. 沒有人能解釋船上的人可能發生了什麼。

詳解 答案：D

第二段提到 Mary Celeste 這艘船被發現 without any crew member on it（沒有任何船員在船上），雖然有人提出可能的解釋，但 neither seems plausible（兩者似乎都不可信），而且 it seems unreasonable for the crew to abandon the ship（船員棄船似乎不合理）。所以，符合這些內容的選項是 D。因為 cargos and valuables were intact（貨物和貴重物品都完好）、weather was fine（當時天氣很好），所以應該沒有選項 A、B 所說的「風暴」、「攻擊船的人」等問題。

|單字片語| **puzzling** [ˋpʌzlɪŋ] adj. 令人困惑的 / **vicinity** [vəˋsɪnətɪ] n. 鄰近地區 / **on board** 在船上，在飛機上

Q27

Why is it unlikely that Mary Celeste ran into pirates?

為什麼 Mary Celeste 不太可能是遇到了海盜？

A. The weather was in good condition.
天氣狀況很好。

B. The US coast guard patrols the region vigilantly.
美國海岸守衛會警覺地巡邏這個區域。

C. Precious goods on the ship were left untouched.
船上貴重的貨品毫髮無傷。

D. The crewmen were armed with weapons.
船員配有武器。

詳解 答案：C

第二段提到，Since the cargos and valuables were intact, it is unlikely that the ship had been attacked by pirates.（由於貨物和貴重物品都完好，所以這艘船不太可能是被海盜攻擊），所以用 precious goods 代替 cargos and valuables、用 untouched 代替 intact 的 C 是正確答案。

|單字片語| **patrol** [pəˋtrol] v. 巡邏 / **vigilantly** [ˋvɪdʒələntlɪ] adv. 警覺地 / **untouched** [ʌnˋtʌtʃt] adj. 未受損傷的 / **crewman** [ˋkrumən] n. 船員 / **armed** [ɑrmd] adj. 武裝的，有武器的

Q28

What is true about the incident in 1918?

關於 1918 年的事件，何者正確？

A. It is among the most serious ones in the area.
是這個地區最嚴重的事件之一。
B. The ship was a military warship.　船是軍方的戰艦。
C. It was revealed during a search.
這個事件是在一次搜索中被揭露的。
D. Most of the sailors were found dead.　大部分的船員被發現死了。

詳解　　答案：A

第三段開頭說 Another incident, which involved the most people missing, happened... in March 1918.（另一起造成了最多人失蹤的事件，發生在 1918 年 3 月）。因為最多人失蹤，所以可說是最嚴重的事件之一，正確答案是 A。one of the US Coast Guard's non-combat ships（美國海岸防衛隊的一艘非戰鬥船）顯示這不是戰艦，所以 B 不對；The area had been searched, but no remains or any of the passengers were found.（這個地區經過搜索，但沒有找到任何船的遺骸或乘客）顯示找不到船和乘客，而且應該是先發覺船隻失蹤才開始搜索，所以 C 和 D 不對。

|單字片語| **warship** [ˋwɔr͵ʃɪp] n. 軍艦，戰艦 / **search** [sɝtʃ] n. 搜查

Q29

What is the author's attitude toward the Bermuda triangle phenomenon?　作者對於百慕達三角現象的態度是什麼？

A. It is more of a popular belief than a truth.
與其說是事實，還不如說是一般人相信的事情。
B. It is something to be concerned about.　是需要擔心的事情。
C. It is a supernatural phenomenon.　是超自然現象。
D. It is an important subject of scientific research.　是重要的科學研究主題。

詳解　　答案：A

作者在第一段就舉出統計資料和定期航線經過等證據，證明百慕達三角並不是特別容易發生事故的地方，航空公司和遊輪公司也不會避開。中間雖然介紹了兩個神祕事件，但最後又說有人為所謂的百慕達現象找到解釋。最後一句話 As long as people are fascinated with supernatural forces, however, the mystery will live on. 並不表示作者真的認為這是個 mystery，而是大眾對於 supernatural forces 的著迷，讓他們持續相信 mystery 的存在。所以，正確答案是 A。

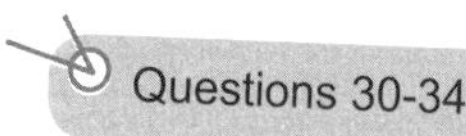

Questions 30-34 are based on the information provided in the following announcement and letter.

Taiwan Scholarship

Have you ever wanted to study in Taiwan? Here is your chance. The Ministry of Foreign Affairs is awarding scholarships to top applicants from countries that have diplomatic relations with Taiwan. These scholarships will pay full tuition at a university of your choice and a monthly stipend of 25,000 NTD as living expenses, and they include economy-class plane tickets for direct flights to and from Taiwan. Here are the eligibility requirements:

- You must be a national of a country that Taiwan has diplomatic relations with*
- You must have a high school graduation diploma
- You must be under the age of 30
- You must not have another scholarship awarded from the Taiwanese government
- You must have a passion for Taiwanese culture

*Those who are from other countries (except mainland China) are encouraged to apply for scholarships awarded by the Ministry of Education

Documents

Please attach the following information to your application:

- High school diploma
- Official academic transcripts
- Reference letters
- A study plan

Please submit your application along with the documents to the Taiwan embassy, consulate, or representative office in your country. For more information, please email to Amy Li, the scholarship program director, at amyli@taiwantopmail.com.

台灣獎學金

您想過要在台灣留學嗎？這是您的機會。外交部現正頒發獎學金給來自台灣邦交國的優秀申請者。獎學金將支付您選擇之大學的全額學費和作為生活費的每月 25,000 元津貼，也包含往返台灣的直飛班機經濟艙機票。以下是資格條件：

- 您必須是台灣邦交國的國民*
- 您必須擁有高中畢業證書
- 您必須未滿 30 歲
- 您不可擁有台灣政府頒發的其他獎學金
- 您必須對台灣文化有熱情

*來自其他國家（中國大陸除外）者，建議申請由教育部頒發的獎學金

文件

請為您的申請表附上以下資訊：

- 高中畢業證書
- 正式成績單
- 推薦信
- 學習計畫

請將您的申請表連同文件提交至貴國的台灣大使館、領事館或代表辦事處。欲知更多資訊，請寄電子郵件至 amyli@taiwantopmail.com 聯絡獎學金計畫主任李艾咪。

|單字片語| **Ministry of Foreign Affairs** 外交部 / **diplomatic relations** 邦交關係 / **stipend** [ˋstaɪpɛnd] n. 津貼 / **eligibility** [ˌɛlɪdʒəˋbɪlətɪ] 資格 / **Ministry of Education** 教育部 / **consulate** [ˋkɑnsḷɪt] n. 領事館

Emilia Mouse
534 Bloomfield Ave.
Atlanta, Georgia 30303
U.S.A.

March 14, 2025

Dear representative,

My name is Emilia Mouse. I am 19, and I just graduated from high school. It is with great pleasure that I am applying for Taiwan

Scholarship.

Ever since I was a young girl, I have always dreamed of going to Taiwan. After watching a lot of Taiwanese dramas and listening to songs by Taiwanese artists such as Jolene Dai, I am determined to study in Taiwan. However, the problem is that my family is underprivileged. I have five siblings, and my parents both work two jobs to make our ends meet. My motivation to apply for your scholarship program stems from the fact that I want to help my family. After completing my degree in Taiwan, I plan to return to my home country and help my family prosper, and I dream of becoming a Chinese interpreter for the United Nations someday. Your scholarship would be a great help for me and my family.

I have enclosed the application and required documents along with this letter. I hope to hear from you soon.

Sincerely,
Emilia Mouse

艾蜜莉亞・茅斯
Bloomfield 大街 534 號
亞特蘭大，喬治亞州 30303
美國

2025 年 3 月 14 日

親愛的代表人：

我的名字是艾蜜莉亞・茅斯。我 19 歲，剛從高中畢業。我很高興能申請台灣獎學金。

從我還是個小女孩的時候，我就一直夢想要去台灣。看了許多台灣戲劇，並且聽了戴依琳等台灣藝人的歌曲之後，我下定決心要在台灣留學。不過，問題是我的家庭很弱勢。我有五個兄弟姊妹，為了收支平衡，父母都有兩份工作。我申請你們獎學金計畫的動機，源自我想要幫助家人的事實。完成在台灣的學位之後，我打算回到母國並幫助我的家庭變得富有，我也夢想有一天能在聯合國擔任中文口譯員。你們的獎學金對於我和我的家人將會是很大的幫助。

我隨信附上了申請書和必要的文件。我希望能早日收到你們的回覆。

誠摯地

艾蜜莉亞・茅斯

|單字片語| **underprivileged** [ˌʌndɚˋprɪvəlɪdʒd] adj. 弱勢的 / **sibling** [ˋsɪblɪŋ] n. 兄弟姊妹 / **stem from** 起源於…

Q30

What is NOT covered by the scholarship?

獎學金不負擔什麼？

A. School fees　學校費用
B. Living expenses　生活費
C. Air travels　航空旅行
D. Field trips　校外旅行

詳解

答案：D

關於獎學金支付的費用，公告（第一篇文章）中提到的 tuition（學費）對應 A，living expenses（生活費）對應 B，plane tickets（機票）對應 C，所以沒提到的 D 是正確答案。

Q31

Why may the readers of the announcement send emails to Amy Li?

公告的讀者可能為了什麼寄電子郵件給李艾咪？

A. To apply for the scholarship　為了申請獎學金
B. To inquire about the scholarship　為了詢問關於獎學金的事
C. To verify their documents　為了核對文件
D. To consult about studying abroad　為了諮詢海外留學的事

詳解

答案：B

關於李艾咪，公告（第一篇文章）的最後提到 For more information, please email to Amy Li, the scholarship program director（欲知更多資訊，請寄電子郵件聯絡獎學金計畫主任李艾咪），所以 B 是正確答案。請注意上一句提到申請者必須把申請文件寄給自己國內的台灣大使館、領事館或代表辦事處，而不是寄給李艾咪，所以 A 不對。

What do we learn about Emilia?
關於艾蜜莉亞，我們知道什麼？

A. She has a passion for Taiwanese culture.　她對台灣文化有熱情。
B. There are seven people in her family.　她的家裡有七個人。
C. Her parents live a wealthy life.　她的父母過著富有的生活。
D. She can speak Chinese fluently.　她能說流利的中文。

詳解　　答案：A

艾蜜莉亞的信件（第二篇文章）提到，After watching a lot of Taiwanese dramas and listening to songs by Taiwanese artists such as Jolene Dai, I am determined to study in Taiwan（看了許多台灣戲劇，並且聽了戴依琳等台灣藝人的歌曲之後，我下定決心要在台灣留學），顯示她喜歡台灣的戲劇和音樂，所以 A 是正確答案。B. 信件中的 I have five siblings, and my parents 顯示有五個兄弟姊妹和爸爸、媽媽，再加上艾蜜莉亞自己，她的家應該是八個人才對。C. 信件中的 my family is underprivileged 顯示他們是弱勢家庭，和選項敘述相反。D. 在文章中沒有提到。

Why may Emilia's application be rejected?
艾蜜莉亞的申請為什麼可能被退回？

A. She is from the United States.　她來自美國。
B. She is under 20 years old.　她未滿 20 歲。
C. She has not attended high school.　她沒上高中。
D. She has not prepared the necessary documents.
　她沒有準備必要的文件。

詳解　　答案：A

這一題必須對照公告（第一篇文章）所說明的獎學金申請條件和信件（第二篇文章）中關於艾蜜莉亞的資訊來解題。在公告中，提到 You must be a national of a country that Taiwan has diplomatic relations with（您必須是台灣邦交國的國民），而艾蜜莉亞的信件地址顯示她來自 U.S.A.（美國），不符合申請條件，所以 A 是正確答案。

What can Emilia do if her application is rejected?
如果艾蜜莉亞的申請被退回了，她可以做什麼？

A. Submit her application again with sufficient documents
附上足夠的文件再次提交申請
B. Send an email to Amy Li to ask for a second review of her documents　寄電子郵件給李艾咪要求再次審閱她的文件
C. Talk with someone at the local representative office of Taiwan
和當地台灣代表辦事處的人談
D. Apply for another scholarship awarded from Taiwanese government　申請由台灣政府頒發的另一種獎學金

詳解　　答案：D

承上題，因為艾蜜莉亞的國籍不符合，所以不可能申請台灣外交部的獎學金。但在公告中有一項備註，寫著 Those who are from other countries... are encouraged to apply for scholarships awarded by the Ministry of Education（來自其他國家者，建議申請由教育部頒發的獎學金），表示非邦交國的人可以申請教育部獎學金，所以 D 是正確答案。

Questions 35-40

Smartphones enable us to share our daily life experiences anytime, anywhere, but just like a double-edged sword, they can also do harm to us if abused. As many social networking services and mobile games prompt their users to open the apps once in a while, usually with notifications, some users check their smartphones every few minutes or even more frequently. Smartphone addiction, or compulsive usage of smartphones, makes people stick to their phones when they are supposed to work or study, resulting in the decline in productivity and academic performance.

Smartphones have also become a distraction during social activities, decreasing our real-life interactions. While eating out, for example, it is possible that people would rather chat with their friends online than exchange ideas with those in front of them. Such kind of social gathering is supposed to strengthen relationships with family or friends, while the lack of conversation caused by smartphone usage can render it ineffective, or even make relationship issues worse. It is also concerning that some parents choose to indulge in their online world when they feel bothered by their kids. Young children need parents' attention most of the time, and those who are often neglected will feel insecure and develop low self-esteem. They will also think that using a smartphone is a good way to escape from the real world when they see their parents do so. Therefore, it is especially important that parents pay more attention to their kids than to their mobile devices.

In addition, statistics revealed that the use of hand-held electronic devices significantly increases the risk of traffic accidents. Taking one's eyes off the road for merely a few seconds could result in fatal collisions. Using smartphones while walking could also have serious consequences, such as bumping into a lamppost or ending up in a manhole. Even though everyone has been taught the golden rule of "Stop-Look-Listen", it just goes out of the window when one stares at a little screen. There has been a traffic accident in which a pedestrian was hit, and both the car driver and the pedestrian were using their smartphones. The driver was undoubtedly responsible for not stepping on the brakes in time, but the pedestrian could have avoided the car if he were more aware of his surroundings.

The emergence of "location-based" mobile games has made matters worse. The global hit called *Pokémon Go* requires players to search for monsters at real-world locations. To collect the monsters, players must leave their homes and walk around. Many find the game helps them get more exercise and interact with other players in person, but the game is also designed in such a way that players feel encouraged to walk while looking at the screen, even though they are reminded to "be alert at all times," as written on the game's loading screen. No matter how fascinating the virtual world is, we should never lose sight of the physical world around us.

智慧型手機讓我們能隨時隨地分享我們的日常生活經驗，但就像雙刃劍一樣，如果被濫用的話，它們也有可能傷害我們。由於許多社交網路服務和手機遊戲會偶爾提醒使用者打開 app，通常是以通知的方式，所以有些使用者每幾分鐘就查看他們的手機，甚至更頻繁。智慧型手機上癮，或者對於智慧型手機的強迫性使用，使得人們在應該工作或學習的時候黏著手機，造成生產力和學業表現的下降。

智慧型手機也成為社交活動中令人分心的東西，減少了我們實際生活中的互動。例如在外食的時候，人們可能寧願和他們網路上的朋友聊天，也不想和眼前的人交換想法。這種社交聚會原本應該能強化和家人或朋友的關係，而使用智慧型手機造成的缺少交談可能會讓它變得無效，甚至使關係的問題更糟糕。有些父母在感覺被小孩打擾時選擇沉浸在自己的網路世界，也很令人擔心。年幼的小孩大多數的時間需要父母的注意，而經常被忽略的小孩會覺得不安，而且缺乏自尊。他們也會在看到父母用手機的時候認為這是逃避現實世界的好方法。所以，父母把較多的注意力放在小孩而不是行動裝置上尤其重要。

此外，統計顯示使用手持電子裝置會顯著增加交通事故的風險。把眼睛從馬路移開僅僅幾秒，就可能造成致命的衝撞。走路時用智慧型手機也有可能造成嚴重的後果，例如撞到路燈柱或者掉進下水道孔。即使每個人都被教導過「停看聽」的金律，但當人盯著小小的螢幕時，這規則就被拋在腦後了。曾經有過行人被撞的車禍，而汽車駕駛和行人都在用手機。無疑地，駕駛要為他沒有及時踩煞車負責，但行人如果更注意他的周遭的話，就可能避開那部車。

「手機定位（以位置為基礎的）」遊戲的興起，使得情況更糟糕。稱為「Pokémon Go」的全球熱門遊戲，要玩家在真實世界的地點尋找怪獸。為了收集怪獸，玩家必須離開家裡並且四處行走。許多人發現這個遊戲幫助他們做更多運動，並且和其他玩家親身互動，但遊戲設計的方式也讓玩家覺得被鼓勵邊看螢幕邊走路，即使他們被提醒要「隨時保持警覺」，就像遊戲的載入畫面所寫的一樣。不管虛擬世界有多麼迷人，我們絕不能忽視在我們週遭的實體世界。

|單字片語|

（第一段）

double-edged sword 雙刃劍（同時有正面和反面效果的事物） / **social networking** 網路社交 / **prompt** [prɑmpt] v. 促使；提示 / **notification** [ˌnotəfəˋkeʃən] n. 通知 / **addiction** [əˋdɪkʃən] n. 癮 / **compulsive** [kəmˋpʌlsɪv] adj. 強迫性的 / **productivity** [ˌprodʌkˋtɪvətɪ] n. 生產力

（第二段）

distraction [dɪˋstrækʃən] n. 分散注意的事物 / **interaction** [ˌɪntəˋrækʃən] n. 互動 / **gathering** [ˋgæðərɪŋ] n. 聚會 / **render** [ˋrɛndɚ] v. 使…成為… / **ineffective** [ɪnəˋfɛktɪv] adj. 無效的 / **indulge** [ɪnˋdʌldʒ] v. 沉溺 / **insecure** [ˌɪnsɪˋkjʊr] adj. 不安全的，缺乏信心的 / **self-esteem** [ˌsɛlfəsˋtim] n. 自尊

（第三段）

collision [kəˋlɪʒən] n. 碰撞 / **lamppost** [ˋlæmpˌpost] n. 路燈柱 / **manhole** [ˋmænˌhol] n. 下水道孔，「人孔」 / **golden rule** 金科玉律 / **go out of the window** 被丟掉，不被理會 / **undoubtedly** [ʌnˋdaʊtɪdlɪ] adv. 無疑地

（第四段）

virtual [ˋvɝtʃʊəl] adj. 虛擬的 / **lose sight of** 看不見…，忽略…

What is a suitable title for this article?

這篇文章適合的標題是什麼？

A. The pros and cons of technology　科技的優缺點
B. How to make the most of your smartphone
如何把你的智慧型手機運用到極致
C. The risks of obsession with smartphones
沉迷於智慧型手機的風險
D. The safety issues of smartphone usage
使用智慧型手機的安全問題

詳解　答案：C

這篇文章的四段內容分別陳述智慧型手機對工作與學習的影響、對社交與親子關係的影響、對交通安全的影響，以及手機定位遊戲造成的新問題。所以，能夠概括這四段內容的標題是 C。A 的範圍太寬，D 只和文章的一部分有關。

|單字片語| **pros and cons** 優點與缺點；贊成與反對的理由 / **obsession** [əbˋsɛʃən] n. 著迷

Q36

Which of the following is NOT a result of indulgence in smartphones mentioned in the article?

以下哪一個不是文章中提到沉溺於智慧型手機的後果？

A. Negligence of road safety　忽視道路安全
B. Lack of interaction among family members　家庭成員之間缺少互動
C. Child physical abuse.　兒童身體虐待
D. Poor work quality　不好的工作品質

詳解　答案：C

第三段的 it (the golden rule of "Stop-Look-Listen") just goes out of the window when one stares at a little screen. 對應選項 A，第二段的 decreasing our real-life interactions 對應選項 B，第一段的 decline in productivity 對應選項 D。第二段雖然提到給予小孩的關注不足，但沒有提到身體虐待，所以 C 是正確答案。

|單字片語| **negligence** [ˋnɛglɪdʒəns] n. 疏忽

According to the article, what could happen when parents use smartphones for too long?

根據這篇文章，父母用智慧型手機太久可能會發生什麼事？

A. Their kids might seek their attention more eagerly.
小孩可能會更急切尋求關注。

B. Their kids might lack confidence in themselves.
小孩可能會對自己缺乏信心。

C. Their kids will tend to escape doing assignments.
小孩會傾向於逃避做功課。

D. They will be asked by their kids to buy smartphones for them.
他們會被小孩要求買智慧型手機給他們。

詳解　答案：B

關於父母用智慧型手機太久的部分，是從第二段的這句話開始：It is also concerning that some parents choose to indulge in their online world when they feel bothered by their kids.（有些父母選擇在感覺被小孩打擾時沉浸在自己的網路世界，也很令人擔心）。下一句提到的 those (children) who are often neglected will feel insecure and develop low self-esteem（經常被忽略的小孩會覺得不安，而且缺乏自尊），是因為過度使用手機而忽略小孩會造成的結果。所以，用 lack confidence in themselves 重新表達 develop low self-esteem 的選項 B 是正確答案。

Q38

According to the article, what is a reason that we should not use smartphones while walking or driving?

根據這篇文章，我們不應該在走路或開車時使用智慧型手機的理由是什麼？

A. The number of traffic accidents has significantly increased.
交通事故的件數顯著增加了。

B. We will be held responsible if we are involved in an accident.
我們牽涉到意外事故時會被認為應該負責。

C. We tend to go faster while using smartphones.
我們用智慧型手機的時候傾向於走得／開得比較快。

D. We could overlook unseen hazards around us.
我們可能會忽視周遭沒看到的危險。

詳解　答案：D

關於交通安全的部分是第三段。第三段提到 Taking one’s eyes off the road

for merely a few seconds could result in fatal collisions.（把眼睛從馬路移開僅僅幾秒，就可能造成致命的衝撞）、Using smartphones while walking could also have serious consequences, such as bumping into a lamppost or ending up in a manhole.（走路時用智慧型手機也有可能造成嚴重的後果，例如撞到路燈柱或者掉進下水道孔），這些都是忽視周遭情況造成的意外，所以 D 是正確答案。

|單字片語| **hazard** [ˋhæzɚd] n. 危險；危害物

What aspect of *Pokémon Go* makes players look at their smartphone screens while walking?

Pokémon Go 的哪個方面使得玩家在走路的時候看他們的智慧型手機螢幕？

A. Fitness tracking function　體能追蹤功能
B. Interactive nature　互動的性質
C. Style of gameplay　玩遊戲的方式
D. Lack of warning　缺乏警告

詳解　　答案：C

關於 Pokémon Go 的部分是第四段，這裡提到 the game is also designed in such a way that players feel encouraged to walk while looking at the screen（遊戲設計的方式也讓玩家覺得被鼓勵邊看螢幕邊走路），這是因為前面提到，這種 location-based（以位置為基礎的）遊戲需要玩家前往 real-world locations（真實世界的地點）。所以，表示「遊戲方法」的 C 是正確答案。

What is the author's attitude toward the use of smartphones?　作者對於使用智慧型手機的態度是什麼？

A. The use of smartphones should be banned at workplaces.
在工作場所應該禁止使用智慧型手機。
B. Smartphones make us less willing to express ourselves.
智慧型手機使得我們比較不願意表達自我。
C. We should pay attention to our real life even with our smartphones.
即使有了智慧型手機，我們也應該注意到真實生活。
D. Children should be familiar with smartphones as soon as possible.
小孩應該盡早熟悉智慧型手機。

詳解

文章最後一句話的結論是，No matter how fascinating the virtual world is, we should never lose sight of the physical world around us.（不管虛擬世界有多麼迷人，我們絕不能忽視在我們週遭的實體世界），所以用 real life 重新表達 physical world 的 C 是正確答案。其他選項在文章中沒有提到。

國際學村 全民英語能力分級檢定測驗 中高級初試答案紙（第一回）

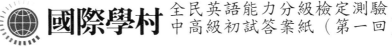

聽力、閱讀測驗答對題數與分數對照表

40	120	30	90	20	60	10	30
39	117	29	87	19	57	9	27
38	114	28	84	18	54	8	24
37	111	27	81	17	51	7	21
36	108	26	78	16	48	6	18
35	105	25	75	15	45	5	15
34	102	24	72	14	42	4	12
33	99	23	69	13	39	3	9
32	96	22	66	12	36	2	6
31	93	21	63	11	33	1	3

聽力測驗		閱讀測驗	
01 ⒶⒷⒸⒹ	26 ⒶⒷⒸⒹ	01 ⒶⒷⒸⒹ	26 ⒶⒷⒸⒹ
02 ⒶⒷⒸⒹ	27 ⒶⒷⒸⒹ	02 ⒶⒷⒸⒹ	27 ⒶⒷⒸⒹ
03 ⒶⒷⒸⒹ	28 ⒶⒷⒸⒹ	03 ⒶⒷⒸⒹ	28 ⒶⒷⒸⒹ
04 ⒶⒷⒸⒹ	29 ⒶⒷⒸⒹ	04 ⒶⒷⒸⒹ	29 ⒶⒷⒸⒹ
05 ⒶⒷⒸⒹ	30 ⒶⒷⒸⒹ	05 ⒶⒷⒸⒹ	30 ⒶⒷⒸⒹ
06 ⒶⒷⒸⒹ	31 ⒶⒷⒸⒹ	06 ⒶⒷⒸⒹ	31 ⒶⒷⒸⒹ
07 ⒶⒷⒸⒹ	32 ⒶⒷⒸⒹ	07 ⒶⒷⒸⒹ	32 ⒶⒷⒸⒹ
08 ⒶⒷⒸⒹ	33 ⒶⒷⒸⒹ	08 ⒶⒷⒸⒹ	33 ⒶⒷⒸⒹ
09 ⒶⒷⒸⒹ	34 ⒶⒷⒸⒹ	09 ⒶⒷⒸⒹ	34 ⒶⒷⒸⒹ
10 ⒶⒷⒸⒹ	35 ⒶⒷⒸⒹ	10 ⒶⒷⒸⒹ	35 ⒶⒷⒸⒹ
11 ⒶⒷⒸⒹ	36 ⒶⒷⒸⒹ	11 ⒶⒷⒸⒹ	36 ⒶⒷⒸⒹ
12 ⒶⒷⒸⒹ	37 ⒶⒷⒸⒹ	12 ⒶⒷⒸⒹ	37 ⒶⒷⒸⒹ
13 ⒶⒷⒸⒹ	38 ⒶⒷⒸⒹ	13 ⒶⒷⒸⒹ	38 ⒶⒷⒸⒹ
14 ⒶⒷⒸⒹ	39 ⒶⒷⒸⒹ	14 ⒶⒷⒸⒹ	39 ⒶⒷⒸⒹ
15 ⒶⒷⒸⒹ	40 ⒶⒷⒸⒹ	15 ⒶⒷⒸⒹ	40 ⒶⒷⒸⒹ
16 ⒶⒷⒸⒹ		16 ⒶⒷⒸⒹ	
17 ⒶⒷⒸⒹ		17 ⒶⒷⒸⒹ	
18 ⒶⒷⒸⒹ		18 ⒶⒷⒸⒹ	
19 ⒶⒷⒸⒹ		19 ⒶⒷⒸⒹ	
20 ⒶⒷⒸⒹ		20 ⒶⒷⒸⒹ	
21 ⒶⒷⒸⒹ		21 ⒶⒷⒸⒹ	
22 ⒶⒷⒸⒹ		22 ⒶⒷⒸⒹ	
23 ⒶⒷⒸⒹ		23 ⒶⒷⒸⒹ	
24 ⒶⒷⒸⒹ		24 ⒶⒷⒸⒹ	
25 ⒶⒷⒸⒹ		25 ⒶⒷⒸⒹ	

考生姓名：＿＿＿＿＿＿

注意事項：

1. 限用 2B 鉛筆作答，否則不予計分。
2. 劃記要黑、清晰、不可出格，擦拭要清潔，若劃記過輕或污損不清，不為機器所接受，考生自行負責。
3. 劃記範例：

正確 ●	錯誤 ○ ✔ ✖ ◉ ⊙ ○

國際學村 全民英語能力分級檢定測驗 中高級初試答案紙（第二回）

聽力、閱讀測驗答對題數與分數對照表							
40	120	30	90	20	60	10	30
39	117	29	87	19	57	9	27
38	114	28	84	18	54	8	24
37	111	27	81	17	51	7	21
36	108	26	78	16	48	6	18
35	105	25	75	15	45	5	15
34	102	24	72	14	42	4	12
33	99	23	69	13	39	3	9
32	96	22	66	12	36	2	6
31	93	21	63	11	33	1	3

考生姓名：＿＿＿＿＿＿

注意事項：

1. 限用 2B 鉛筆作答，否則不予計分。
2. 劃記要黑、清晰、不可出格，擦拭要清潔，若劃記過輕或污損不清，不為機器所接受，考生自行負責。
3. 劃記範例：

正確 ●	錯誤 ○ ✔ ✗ ◕ ⊙ ◯

聽力測驗		閱讀測驗	
01 ⒶⒷⒸⒹ	26 ⒶⒷⒸⒹ	01 ⒶⒷⒸⒹ	26 ⒶⒷⒸⒹ
02 ⒶⒷⒸⒹ	27 ⒶⒷⒸⒹ	02 ⒶⒷⒸⒹ	27 ⒶⒷⒸⒹ
03 ⒶⒷⒸⒹ	28 ⒶⒷⒸⒹ	03 ⒶⒷⒸⒹ	28 ⒶⒷⒸⒹ
04 ⒶⒷⒸⒹ	29 ⒶⒷⒸⒹ	04 ⒶⒷⒸⒹ	29 ⒶⒷⒸⒹ
05 ⒶⒷⒸⒹ	30 ⒶⒷⒸⒹ	05 ⒶⒷⒸⒹ	30 ⒶⒷⒸⒹ
06 ⒶⒷⒸⒹ	31 ⒶⒷⒸⒹ	06 ⒶⒷⒸⒹ	31 ⒶⒷⒸⒹ
07 ⒶⒷⒸⒹ	32 ⒶⒷⒸⒹ	07 ⒶⒷⒸⒹ	32 ⒶⒷⒸⒹ
08 ⒶⒷⒸⒹ	33 ⒶⒷⒸⒹ	08 ⒶⒷⒸⒹ	33 ⒶⒷⒸⒹ
09 ⒶⒷⒸⒹ	34 ⒶⒷⒸⒹ	09 ⒶⒷⒸⒹ	34 ⒶⒷⒸⒹ
10 ⒶⒷⒸⒹ	35 ⒶⒷⒸⒹ	10 ⒶⒷⒸⒹ	35 ⒶⒷⒸⒹ
11 ⒶⒷⒸⒹ	36 ⒶⒷⒸⒹ	11 ⒶⒷⒸⒹ	36 ⒶⒷⒸⒹ
12 ⒶⒷⒸⒹ	37 ⒶⒷⒸⒹ	12 ⒶⒷⒸⒹ	37 ⒶⒷⒸⒹ
13 ⒶⒷⒸⒹ	38 ⒶⒷⒸⒹ	13 ⒶⒷⒸⒹ	38 ⒶⒷⒸⒹ
14 ⒶⒷⒸⒹ	39 ⒶⒷⒸⒹ	14 ⒶⒷⒸⒹ	39 ⒶⒷⒸⒹ
15 ⒶⒷⒸⒹ	40 ⒶⒷⒸⒹ	15 ⒶⒷⒸⒹ	40 ⒶⒷⒸⒹ
16 ⒶⒷⒸⒹ		16 ⒶⒷⒸⒹ	
17 ⒶⒷⒸⒹ		17 ⒶⒷⒸⒹ	
18 ⒶⒷⒸⒹ		18 ⒶⒷⒸⒹ	
19 ⒶⒷⒸⒹ		19 ⒶⒷⒸⒹ	
20 ⒶⒷⒸⒹ		20 ⒶⒷⒸⒹ	
21 ⒶⒷⒸⒹ		21 ⒶⒷⒸⒹ	
22 ⒶⒷⒸⒹ		22 ⒶⒷⒸⒹ	
23 ⒶⒷⒸⒹ		23 ⒶⒷⒸⒹ	
24 ⒶⒷⒸⒹ		24 ⒶⒷⒸⒹ	
25 ⒶⒷⒸⒹ		25 ⒶⒷⒸⒹ	

國際學村 全民英語能力分級檢定測驗 中高級初試答案紙（第三回）

聽力、閱讀測驗答對題數與分數對照表							
40	120	30	90	20	60	10	30
39	117	29	87	19	57	9	27
38	114	28	84	18	54	8	24
37	111	27	81	17	51	7	21
36	108	26	78	16	48	6	18
35	105	25	75	15	45	5	15
34	102	24	72	14	42	4	12
33	99	23	69	13	39	3	9
32	96	22	66	12	36	2	6
31	93	21	63	11	33	1	3

考生姓名：＿＿＿＿＿＿

注意事項：

1. 限用 2B 鉛筆作答，否則不予計分。
2. 劃記要黑、清晰、不可出格，擦拭要清潔，若劃記過輕或污損不清，不為機器所接受，考生自行負責。
3. 劃記範例：

正確 ●	錯誤 ◯ ✔ ✖ ◐ ⊙ ○

聽力測驗		閱讀測驗	
01 Ⓐ Ⓑ Ⓒ Ⓓ	26 Ⓐ Ⓑ Ⓒ Ⓓ	01 Ⓐ Ⓑ Ⓒ Ⓓ	26 Ⓐ Ⓑ Ⓒ Ⓓ
02 Ⓐ Ⓑ Ⓒ Ⓓ	27 Ⓐ Ⓑ Ⓒ Ⓓ	02 Ⓐ Ⓑ Ⓒ Ⓓ	27 Ⓐ Ⓑ Ⓒ Ⓓ
03 Ⓐ Ⓑ Ⓒ Ⓓ	28 Ⓐ Ⓑ Ⓒ Ⓓ	03 Ⓐ Ⓑ Ⓒ Ⓓ	28 Ⓐ Ⓑ Ⓒ Ⓓ
04 Ⓐ Ⓑ Ⓒ Ⓓ	29 Ⓐ Ⓑ Ⓒ Ⓓ	04 Ⓐ Ⓑ Ⓒ Ⓓ	29 Ⓐ Ⓑ Ⓒ Ⓓ
05 Ⓐ Ⓑ Ⓒ Ⓓ	30 Ⓐ Ⓑ Ⓒ Ⓓ	05 Ⓐ Ⓑ Ⓒ Ⓓ	30 Ⓐ Ⓑ Ⓒ Ⓓ
06 Ⓐ Ⓑ Ⓒ Ⓓ	31 Ⓐ Ⓑ Ⓒ Ⓓ	06 Ⓐ Ⓑ Ⓒ Ⓓ	31 Ⓐ Ⓑ Ⓒ Ⓓ
07 Ⓐ Ⓑ Ⓒ Ⓓ	32 Ⓐ Ⓑ Ⓒ Ⓓ	07 Ⓐ Ⓑ Ⓒ Ⓓ	32 Ⓐ Ⓑ Ⓒ Ⓓ
08 Ⓐ Ⓑ Ⓒ Ⓓ	33 Ⓐ Ⓑ Ⓒ Ⓓ	08 Ⓐ Ⓑ Ⓒ Ⓓ	33 Ⓐ Ⓑ Ⓒ Ⓓ
09 Ⓐ Ⓑ Ⓒ Ⓓ	34 Ⓐ Ⓑ Ⓒ Ⓓ	09 Ⓐ Ⓑ Ⓒ Ⓓ	34 Ⓐ Ⓑ Ⓒ Ⓓ
10 Ⓐ Ⓑ Ⓒ Ⓓ	35 Ⓐ Ⓑ Ⓒ Ⓓ	10 Ⓐ Ⓑ Ⓒ Ⓓ	35 Ⓐ Ⓑ Ⓒ Ⓓ
11 Ⓐ Ⓑ Ⓒ Ⓓ	36 Ⓐ Ⓑ Ⓒ Ⓓ	11 Ⓐ Ⓑ Ⓒ Ⓓ	36 Ⓐ Ⓑ Ⓒ Ⓓ
12 Ⓐ Ⓑ Ⓒ Ⓓ	37 Ⓐ Ⓑ Ⓒ Ⓓ	12 Ⓐ Ⓑ Ⓒ Ⓓ	37 Ⓐ Ⓑ Ⓒ Ⓓ
13 Ⓐ Ⓑ Ⓒ Ⓓ	38 Ⓐ Ⓑ Ⓒ Ⓓ	13 Ⓐ Ⓑ Ⓒ Ⓓ	38 Ⓐ Ⓑ Ⓒ Ⓓ
14 Ⓐ Ⓑ Ⓒ Ⓓ	39 Ⓐ Ⓑ Ⓒ Ⓓ	14 Ⓐ Ⓑ Ⓒ Ⓓ	39 Ⓐ Ⓑ Ⓒ Ⓓ
15 Ⓐ Ⓑ Ⓒ Ⓓ	40 Ⓐ Ⓑ Ⓒ Ⓓ	15 Ⓐ Ⓑ Ⓒ Ⓓ	40 Ⓐ Ⓑ Ⓒ Ⓓ
16 Ⓐ Ⓑ Ⓒ Ⓓ		16 Ⓐ Ⓑ Ⓒ Ⓓ	
17 Ⓐ Ⓑ Ⓒ Ⓓ		17 Ⓐ Ⓑ Ⓒ Ⓓ	
18 Ⓐ Ⓑ Ⓒ Ⓓ		18 Ⓐ Ⓑ Ⓒ Ⓓ	
19 Ⓐ Ⓑ Ⓒ Ⓓ		19 Ⓐ Ⓑ Ⓒ Ⓓ	
20 Ⓐ Ⓑ Ⓒ Ⓓ		20 Ⓐ Ⓑ Ⓒ Ⓓ	
21 Ⓐ Ⓑ Ⓒ Ⓓ		21 Ⓐ Ⓑ Ⓒ Ⓓ	
22 Ⓐ Ⓑ Ⓒ Ⓓ		22 Ⓐ Ⓑ Ⓒ Ⓓ	
23 Ⓐ Ⓑ Ⓒ Ⓓ		23 Ⓐ Ⓑ Ⓒ Ⓓ	
24 Ⓐ Ⓑ Ⓒ Ⓓ		24 Ⓐ Ⓑ Ⓒ Ⓓ	
25 Ⓐ Ⓑ Ⓒ Ⓓ		25 Ⓐ Ⓑ Ⓒ Ⓓ	

國際學村 全民英語能力分級檢定測驗 中高級初試答案紙（第四回）

聽力、閱讀測驗答對題數與分數對照表							
40	120	30	90	20	60	10	30
39	117	29	87	19	57	9	27
38	114	28	84	18	54	8	24
37	111	27	81	17	51	7	21
36	108	26	78	16	48	6	18
35	105	25	75	15	45	5	15
34	102	24	72	14	42	4	12
33	99	23	69	13	39	3	9
32	96	22	66	12	36	2	6
31	93	21	63	11	33	1	3

考生姓名：＿＿＿＿＿＿

注意事項：

1. 限用 2B 鉛筆作答，否則不予計分。
2. 劃記要黑、清晰、不可出格，擦拭要清潔，若劃記過輕或污損不清，不為機器所接受，考生自行負責。
3. 劃記範例：

正確 ●	錯誤 ○ ✔ ✖ ◐ ⊙ O

聽力測驗		閱讀測驗	
01 Ⓐ Ⓑ Ⓒ Ⓓ	26 Ⓐ Ⓑ Ⓒ Ⓓ	01 Ⓐ Ⓑ Ⓒ Ⓓ	26 Ⓐ Ⓑ Ⓒ Ⓓ
02 Ⓐ Ⓑ Ⓒ Ⓓ	27 Ⓐ Ⓑ Ⓒ Ⓓ	02 Ⓐ Ⓑ Ⓒ Ⓓ	27 Ⓐ Ⓑ Ⓒ Ⓓ
03 Ⓐ Ⓑ Ⓒ Ⓓ	28 Ⓐ Ⓑ Ⓒ Ⓓ	03 Ⓐ Ⓑ Ⓒ Ⓓ	28 Ⓐ Ⓑ Ⓒ Ⓓ
04 Ⓐ Ⓑ Ⓒ Ⓓ	29 Ⓐ Ⓑ Ⓒ Ⓓ	04 Ⓐ Ⓑ Ⓒ Ⓓ	29 Ⓐ Ⓑ Ⓒ Ⓓ
05 Ⓐ Ⓑ Ⓒ Ⓓ	30 Ⓐ Ⓑ Ⓒ Ⓓ	05 Ⓐ Ⓑ Ⓒ Ⓓ	30 Ⓐ Ⓑ Ⓒ Ⓓ
06 Ⓐ Ⓑ Ⓒ Ⓓ	31 Ⓐ Ⓑ Ⓒ Ⓓ	06 Ⓐ Ⓑ Ⓒ Ⓓ	31 Ⓐ Ⓑ Ⓒ Ⓓ
07 Ⓐ Ⓑ Ⓒ Ⓓ	32 Ⓐ Ⓑ Ⓒ Ⓓ	07 Ⓐ Ⓑ Ⓒ Ⓓ	32 Ⓐ Ⓑ Ⓒ Ⓓ
08 Ⓐ Ⓑ Ⓒ Ⓓ	33 Ⓐ Ⓑ Ⓒ Ⓓ	08 Ⓐ Ⓑ Ⓒ Ⓓ	33 Ⓐ Ⓑ Ⓒ Ⓓ
09 Ⓐ Ⓑ Ⓒ Ⓓ	34 Ⓐ Ⓑ Ⓒ Ⓓ	09 Ⓐ Ⓑ Ⓒ Ⓓ	34 Ⓐ Ⓑ Ⓒ Ⓓ
10 Ⓐ Ⓑ Ⓒ Ⓓ	35 Ⓐ Ⓑ Ⓒ Ⓓ	10 Ⓐ Ⓑ Ⓒ Ⓓ	35 Ⓐ Ⓑ Ⓒ Ⓓ
11 Ⓐ Ⓑ Ⓒ Ⓓ	36 Ⓐ Ⓑ Ⓒ Ⓓ	11 Ⓐ Ⓑ Ⓒ Ⓓ	36 Ⓐ Ⓑ Ⓒ Ⓓ
12 Ⓐ Ⓑ Ⓒ Ⓓ	37 Ⓐ Ⓑ Ⓒ Ⓓ	12 Ⓐ Ⓑ Ⓒ Ⓓ	37 Ⓐ Ⓑ Ⓒ Ⓓ
13 Ⓐ Ⓑ Ⓒ Ⓓ	38 Ⓐ Ⓑ Ⓒ Ⓓ	13 Ⓐ Ⓑ Ⓒ Ⓓ	38 Ⓐ Ⓑ Ⓒ Ⓓ
14 Ⓐ Ⓑ Ⓒ Ⓓ	39 Ⓐ Ⓑ Ⓒ Ⓓ	14 Ⓐ Ⓑ Ⓒ Ⓓ	39 Ⓐ Ⓑ Ⓒ Ⓓ
15 Ⓐ Ⓑ Ⓒ Ⓓ	40 Ⓐ Ⓑ Ⓒ Ⓓ	15 Ⓐ Ⓑ Ⓒ Ⓓ	40 Ⓐ Ⓑ Ⓒ Ⓓ
16 Ⓐ Ⓑ Ⓒ Ⓓ		16 Ⓐ Ⓑ Ⓒ Ⓓ	
17 Ⓐ Ⓑ Ⓒ Ⓓ		17 Ⓐ Ⓑ Ⓒ Ⓓ	
18 Ⓐ Ⓑ Ⓒ Ⓓ		18 Ⓐ Ⓑ Ⓒ Ⓓ	
19 Ⓐ Ⓑ Ⓒ Ⓓ		19 Ⓐ Ⓑ Ⓒ Ⓓ	
20 Ⓐ Ⓑ Ⓒ Ⓓ		20 Ⓐ Ⓑ Ⓒ Ⓓ	
21 Ⓐ Ⓑ Ⓒ Ⓓ		21 Ⓐ Ⓑ Ⓒ Ⓓ	
22 Ⓐ Ⓑ Ⓒ Ⓓ		22 Ⓐ Ⓑ Ⓒ Ⓓ	
23 Ⓐ Ⓑ Ⓒ Ⓓ		23 Ⓐ Ⓑ Ⓒ Ⓓ	
24 Ⓐ Ⓑ Ⓒ Ⓓ		24 Ⓐ Ⓑ Ⓒ Ⓓ	
25 Ⓐ Ⓑ Ⓒ Ⓓ		25 Ⓐ Ⓑ Ⓒ Ⓓ	

全民英語能力分級檢定測驗 中高級初試答案紙（第五回）

聽力、閱讀測驗答對題數與分數對照表							
40	120	30	90	20	60	10	30
39	117	29	87	19	57	9	27
38	114	28	84	18	54	8	24
37	111	27	81	17	51	7	21
36	108	26	78	16	48	6	18
35	105	25	75	15	45	5	15
34	102	24	72	14	42	4	12
33	99	23	69	13	39	3	9
32	96	22	66	12	36	2	6
31	93	21	63	11	33	1	3

考生姓名：＿＿＿＿＿＿

注意事項：

1. 限用 2B 鉛筆作答，否則不予計分。
2. 劃記要黑、清晰、不可出格，擦拭要清潔，若劃記過輕或污損不清，不為機器所接受，考生自行負責。
3. 劃記範例：

正確 ●	錯誤 ○ ✔ ✖ ◐ ⊙ ○

聽力測驗		閱讀測驗	
01 Ⓐ Ⓑ Ⓒ Ⓓ	26 Ⓐ Ⓑ Ⓒ Ⓓ	01 Ⓐ Ⓑ Ⓒ Ⓓ	26 Ⓐ Ⓑ Ⓒ Ⓓ
02 Ⓐ Ⓑ Ⓒ Ⓓ	27 Ⓐ Ⓑ Ⓒ Ⓓ	02 Ⓐ Ⓑ Ⓒ Ⓓ	27 Ⓐ Ⓑ Ⓒ Ⓓ
03 Ⓐ Ⓑ Ⓒ Ⓓ	28 Ⓐ Ⓑ Ⓒ Ⓓ	03 Ⓐ Ⓑ Ⓒ Ⓓ	28 Ⓐ Ⓑ Ⓒ Ⓓ
04 Ⓐ Ⓑ Ⓒ Ⓓ	29 Ⓐ Ⓑ Ⓒ Ⓓ	04 Ⓐ Ⓑ Ⓒ Ⓓ	29 Ⓐ Ⓑ Ⓒ Ⓓ
05 Ⓐ Ⓑ Ⓒ Ⓓ	30 Ⓐ Ⓑ Ⓒ Ⓓ	05 Ⓐ Ⓑ Ⓒ Ⓓ	30 Ⓐ Ⓑ Ⓒ Ⓓ
06 Ⓐ Ⓑ Ⓒ Ⓓ	31 Ⓐ Ⓑ Ⓒ Ⓓ	06 Ⓐ Ⓑ Ⓒ Ⓓ	31 Ⓐ Ⓑ Ⓒ Ⓓ
07 Ⓐ Ⓑ Ⓒ Ⓓ	32 Ⓐ Ⓑ Ⓒ Ⓓ	07 Ⓐ Ⓑ Ⓒ Ⓓ	32 Ⓐ Ⓑ Ⓒ Ⓓ
08 Ⓐ Ⓑ Ⓒ Ⓓ	33 Ⓐ Ⓑ Ⓒ Ⓓ	08 Ⓐ Ⓑ Ⓒ Ⓓ	33 Ⓐ Ⓑ Ⓒ Ⓓ
09 Ⓐ Ⓑ Ⓒ Ⓓ	34 Ⓐ Ⓑ Ⓒ Ⓓ	09 Ⓐ Ⓑ Ⓒ Ⓓ	34 Ⓐ Ⓑ Ⓒ Ⓓ
10 Ⓐ Ⓑ Ⓒ Ⓓ	35 Ⓐ Ⓑ Ⓒ Ⓓ	10 Ⓐ Ⓑ Ⓒ Ⓓ	35 Ⓐ Ⓑ Ⓒ Ⓓ
11 Ⓐ Ⓑ Ⓒ Ⓓ	36 Ⓐ Ⓑ Ⓒ Ⓓ	11 Ⓐ Ⓑ Ⓒ Ⓓ	36 Ⓐ Ⓑ Ⓒ Ⓓ
12 Ⓐ Ⓑ Ⓒ Ⓓ	37 Ⓐ Ⓑ Ⓒ Ⓓ	12 Ⓐ Ⓑ Ⓒ Ⓓ	37 Ⓐ Ⓑ Ⓒ Ⓓ
13 Ⓐ Ⓑ Ⓒ Ⓓ	38 Ⓐ Ⓑ Ⓒ Ⓓ	13 Ⓐ Ⓑ Ⓒ Ⓓ	38 Ⓐ Ⓑ Ⓒ Ⓓ
14 Ⓐ Ⓑ Ⓒ Ⓓ	39 Ⓐ Ⓑ Ⓒ Ⓓ	14 Ⓐ Ⓑ Ⓒ Ⓓ	39 Ⓐ Ⓑ Ⓒ Ⓓ
15 Ⓐ Ⓑ Ⓒ Ⓓ	40 Ⓐ Ⓑ Ⓒ Ⓓ	15 Ⓐ Ⓑ Ⓒ Ⓓ	40 Ⓐ Ⓑ Ⓒ Ⓓ
16 Ⓐ Ⓑ Ⓒ Ⓓ		16 Ⓐ Ⓑ Ⓒ Ⓓ	
17 Ⓐ Ⓑ Ⓒ Ⓓ		17 Ⓐ Ⓑ Ⓒ Ⓓ	
18 Ⓐ Ⓑ Ⓒ Ⓓ		18 Ⓐ Ⓑ Ⓒ Ⓓ	
19 Ⓐ Ⓑ Ⓒ Ⓓ		19 Ⓐ Ⓑ Ⓒ Ⓓ	
20 Ⓐ Ⓑ Ⓒ Ⓓ		20 Ⓐ Ⓑ Ⓒ Ⓓ	
21 Ⓐ Ⓑ Ⓒ Ⓓ		21 Ⓐ Ⓑ Ⓒ Ⓓ	
22 Ⓐ Ⓑ Ⓒ Ⓓ		22 Ⓐ Ⓑ Ⓒ Ⓓ	
23 Ⓐ Ⓑ Ⓒ Ⓓ		23 Ⓐ Ⓑ Ⓒ Ⓓ	
24 Ⓐ Ⓑ Ⓒ Ⓓ		24 Ⓐ Ⓑ Ⓒ Ⓓ	
25 Ⓐ Ⓑ Ⓒ Ⓓ		25 Ⓐ Ⓑ Ⓒ Ⓓ	

國際學村 全民英語能力分級檢定測驗 中高級初試答案紙（第六回）

聽力、閱讀測驗答對題數與分數對照表							
40	120	30	90	20	60	10	30
39	117	29	87	19	57	9	27
38	114	28	84	18	54	8	24
37	111	27	81	17	51	7	21
36	108	26	78	16	48	6	18
35	105	25	75	15	45	5	15
34	102	24	72	14	42	4	12
33	99	23	69	13	39	3	9
32	96	22	66	12	36	2	6
31	93	21	63	11	33	1	3

考生姓名：________

注意事項：

1. 限用 2B 鉛筆作答，否則不予計分。
2. 劃記要黑、清晰、不可出格，擦拭要清潔，若劃記過輕或污損不清，不為機器所接受，考生自行負責。
3. 劃記範例：

正確 ●	錯誤 ○ ✔ ✘ ◉ ⊙ O

聽力測驗		閱讀測驗	
01 Ⓐ Ⓑ Ⓒ Ⓓ	26 Ⓐ Ⓑ Ⓒ Ⓓ	01 Ⓐ Ⓑ Ⓒ Ⓓ	26 Ⓐ Ⓑ Ⓒ Ⓓ
02 Ⓐ Ⓑ Ⓒ Ⓓ	27 Ⓐ Ⓑ Ⓒ Ⓓ	02 Ⓐ Ⓑ Ⓒ Ⓓ	27 Ⓐ Ⓑ Ⓒ Ⓓ
03 Ⓐ Ⓑ Ⓒ Ⓓ	28 Ⓐ Ⓑ Ⓒ Ⓓ	03 Ⓐ Ⓑ Ⓒ Ⓓ	28 Ⓐ Ⓑ Ⓒ Ⓓ
04 Ⓐ Ⓑ Ⓒ Ⓓ	29 Ⓐ Ⓑ Ⓒ Ⓓ	04 Ⓐ Ⓑ Ⓒ Ⓓ	29 Ⓐ Ⓑ Ⓒ Ⓓ
05 Ⓐ Ⓑ Ⓒ Ⓓ	30 Ⓐ Ⓑ Ⓒ Ⓓ	05 Ⓐ Ⓑ Ⓒ Ⓓ	30 Ⓐ Ⓑ Ⓒ Ⓓ
06 Ⓐ Ⓑ Ⓒ Ⓓ	31 Ⓐ Ⓑ Ⓒ Ⓓ	06 Ⓐ Ⓑ Ⓒ Ⓓ	31 Ⓐ Ⓑ Ⓒ Ⓓ
07 Ⓐ Ⓑ Ⓒ Ⓓ	32 Ⓐ Ⓑ Ⓒ Ⓓ	07 Ⓐ Ⓑ Ⓒ Ⓓ	32 Ⓐ Ⓑ Ⓒ Ⓓ
08 Ⓐ Ⓑ Ⓒ Ⓓ	33 Ⓐ Ⓑ Ⓒ Ⓓ	08 Ⓐ Ⓑ Ⓒ Ⓓ	33 Ⓐ Ⓑ Ⓒ Ⓓ
09 Ⓐ Ⓑ Ⓒ Ⓓ	34 Ⓐ Ⓑ Ⓒ Ⓓ	09 Ⓐ Ⓑ Ⓒ Ⓓ	34 Ⓐ Ⓑ Ⓒ Ⓓ
10 Ⓐ Ⓑ Ⓒ Ⓓ	35 Ⓐ Ⓑ Ⓒ Ⓓ	10 Ⓐ Ⓑ Ⓒ Ⓓ	35 Ⓐ Ⓑ Ⓒ Ⓓ
11 Ⓐ Ⓑ Ⓒ Ⓓ	36 Ⓐ Ⓑ Ⓒ Ⓓ	11 Ⓐ Ⓑ Ⓒ Ⓓ	36 Ⓐ Ⓑ Ⓒ Ⓓ
12 Ⓐ Ⓑ Ⓒ Ⓓ	37 Ⓐ Ⓑ Ⓒ Ⓓ	12 Ⓐ Ⓑ Ⓒ Ⓓ	37 Ⓐ Ⓑ Ⓒ Ⓓ
13 Ⓐ Ⓑ Ⓒ Ⓓ	38 Ⓐ Ⓑ Ⓒ Ⓓ	13 Ⓐ Ⓑ Ⓒ Ⓓ	38 Ⓐ Ⓑ Ⓒ Ⓓ
14 Ⓐ Ⓑ Ⓒ Ⓓ	39 Ⓐ Ⓑ Ⓒ Ⓓ	14 Ⓐ Ⓑ Ⓒ Ⓓ	39 Ⓐ Ⓑ Ⓒ Ⓓ
15 Ⓐ Ⓑ Ⓒ Ⓓ	40 Ⓐ Ⓑ Ⓒ Ⓓ	15 Ⓐ Ⓑ Ⓒ Ⓓ	40 Ⓐ Ⓑ Ⓒ Ⓓ
16 Ⓐ Ⓑ Ⓒ Ⓓ		16 Ⓐ Ⓑ Ⓒ Ⓓ	
17 Ⓐ Ⓑ Ⓒ Ⓓ		17 Ⓐ Ⓑ Ⓒ Ⓓ	
18 Ⓐ Ⓑ Ⓒ Ⓓ		18 Ⓐ Ⓑ Ⓒ Ⓓ	
19 Ⓐ Ⓑ Ⓒ Ⓓ		19 Ⓐ Ⓑ Ⓒ Ⓓ	
20 Ⓐ Ⓑ Ⓒ Ⓓ		20 Ⓐ Ⓑ Ⓒ Ⓓ	
21 Ⓐ Ⓑ Ⓒ Ⓓ		21 Ⓐ Ⓑ Ⓒ Ⓓ	
22 Ⓐ Ⓑ Ⓒ Ⓓ		22 Ⓐ Ⓑ Ⓒ Ⓓ	
23 Ⓐ Ⓑ Ⓒ Ⓓ		23 Ⓐ Ⓑ Ⓒ Ⓓ	
24 Ⓐ Ⓑ Ⓒ Ⓓ		24 Ⓐ Ⓑ Ⓒ Ⓓ	
25 Ⓐ Ⓑ Ⓒ Ⓓ		25 Ⓐ Ⓑ Ⓒ Ⓓ	

學習筆記欄

台灣廣廈 國際出版集團
Taiwan Mansion International Group

國家圖書館出版品預行編目（CIP）資料

NEW GEPT全新全民英檢中高級聽力＆閱讀題庫解析/國際語言中心委員會, 郭文興, Emie Lomba著.
-- 初版. -- 新北市 : 國際學村出版社, 2021.08
面； 公分
ISBN 978-986-454-173-7(平裝)

1.英語 2.讀本

805.1892 110011587

國際學村

NEW GEPT 全新全民英檢中高級聽力＆閱讀題庫解析【新制修訂版】

作　　者／國際語言中心委員會、郭文興、Emie Lomba
編輯中心編輯長／伍峻宏
編輯／賴敬宗
封面設計／林珈伃・**內頁排版**／菩薩蠻數位文化有限公司
製版・印刷・裝訂／皇甫・秉成

行企研發中心總監／陳冠蒨
媒體公關組／陳柔彣
綜合業務組／何欣穎

發 行 人／江媛珍
法律顧問／第一國際法律事務所 余淑杏律師・北辰著作權事務所 蕭雄淋律師
出　　版／國際學村
發　　行／台灣廣廈有聲圖書有限公司
地址：新北市235中和區中山路二段359巷7號2樓
電話：（886）2-2225-5777・傳真：（886）2-2225-8052

代理印務・全球總經銷／知遠文化事業有限公司
地址：新北市222深坑區北深路三段155巷25號5樓
電話：（886）2-2664-8800・傳真：（886）2-2664-8801
郵政劃撥／劃撥帳號：18836722
劃撥戶名：知遠文化事業有限公司（※單次購書金額未達1000元，請另付70元郵資。）

■出版日期：2021年8月
2023年8月7刷
ISBN：978-986-454-173-7